ABDALLA THE MOOR

AND THE

SPANISH KNIGHT.

A ROMANCE OF MEXICO.

BY DR BIRD

AUTHOR OF "THE HAWKS OF HAWK-HOLLOW," Etc., Etc.

Escucha, pues, un rato, y, diré cosas,
Estrañas y espantosas, poco á poco.
GARCILASO DE LA VEG .

LONDON:

PUBLISHED BY E. LLOYD, SALISBURY-SQUARE, FLEET-STREET.

No. 1.

ABDALLA THE MOOR.

CHAPTER I.

In the year of Grace fifteen hundred and twenty, upon a day in the month of May thereof, the sun rose over the islands of the new deep, and the mountains that divided it from an ocean yet unknown, and looked upon the havoc, which, in the name of God, a Christian people were working upon the loveliest of his regions. He had seen, in the revolution of a day, the strange transformations which a few years had brought upon all the climes and races of his love. The standard of Portugal waved from the minarets of the east; a Portuguese admiral swept the Persian Gulf, and bombarded the walls of Ormuz; a Portuguese viceroy held his court on the shores of the Indian ocean; the princes of the eastern continent had exchanged their bracelets of gold for the iron fetters of the invader; and among the odours of the Spice Islands, the fumes of frankincense ascended to the God of their new masters. He passed on his course: the breakers that dashed upon the sands of Africa were not whiter than the squadrons that rolled among them; the chapel was built on the shore, and under the shadow of the crucifix was fastened the first rivet in the slavery of her miserable children. Then rose he over the blue Atlantic: the new continent emerged from the dusky deep; the ships of discoverers were penetrating its estuaries and straits, from the Isles of Fire even to the frozen promontories of Labrador; and the roar of cannon went up to heaven, mingled with the groans and blood of naked savages. But peace had descended upon the islands of America; the gentle tribes of these paradises of ocean wept in subjection over the graves of more than half their race; hamlets and cities were springing up in their valleys and on their coasts; the culverin bellowed from the fortress, the bell pealed from the monastery; and the civilization and vices of Europe had supplanted the barbarism and innocence of the feeble native. Still, as he careered to the west, new spectacles were displayed before him; the followers of Balboa had built a proud city on the shores, and were launching their hasty barks on the surges of the New Ocean; the hunter of the Fountain of Youth was perishing under the arrows of the wild warriors of Florida, and the armed Spaniards were at last retreating before a Pagan multitude. One more sight of pomp and of grief awaited him: he rose on the mountains of Mexico; the trumpet of the Spaniards echoed among the peaks; he looked upon the bay of Ulua, and, as his beams stole tremblingly over the swelling current, they fell upon the black hulls and furled canvass of a great fleet riding tranquilly at its moorings. The fate of Mexico was in the scales of destiny; the second army of invaders had been poured upon her shores. In truth, it was a goodly sight to look upon the armed vessels that thronged this unfrequented bay; for peacefully and majestically they slept on the tide, and as the morning hymn of the mariners swelled faintly on the air, one would have thought they bore with them to the heathen the tidings of great joy, and the good will and grace of their divine faith, instead of the earthly passions which were to cover the land with lamentation and death.

With the morning sunbeam stole into the harbour one of those little caravels, wherein the men of those days dared the perils of unknown deeps, and sought out new paths to renown and fortune; and as she drew nigh to the reposing fleet, the hardy adventurers who thronged her deck gazed with new interest and admiration on the shores of that empire, the fame of whose wild grandeur and wealth had already driven from their minds the dreams of Golconda and the Moluccas. No fortress frowned on the low islands, no city glistened among the sand-hills on the shore: the surf rolled on the coast of an uninhabited waste: the tents of the armourer and other artisans, the palm-thatched sheds of the sick, and some heaps of military stores, covered with sails and glimmering in the sun, were the only evidences of life on a beach which was, in after times, to become the site of a rich and bustling port. But beyond the low desert margin of the sea, and over the rank and lovely belt of verdure, which succeeded the glittering sand-hills, rose a rampart of mountains green with an eternal vegetation, over which again peered chain after chain, and crag after crag, with still the majestic Perote and the colossal Orizabo frowning over all, until those who had dwelt among the Pyrenees, or looked upon the Alps, as some of that adventurous company had done, dreamed what wealth should be in a land, whose first disclosure was so full of grandeur.

Of the four score individuals who crowded the decks of the little caravel, there was not one whose countenance, at that spectacle, did not betray a touch of the enthusiasm—the mingled lust of glory and of lucre—which had already transformed so many ruffians into heroes. Among this motley throng might be seen all sorts of martial madmen, from the scarred veteran who had fought the Moors under the walls of Oran, to the runagate stripling who had hanselled his sword of lath on the curs of Seville; from the hidalgo who remembered the pride of his ancestors, in the cloak of his grandsire, to the boor who dreamed of the crown of a Pagan emperor, in a leather shirt and cork shoes. here was a brigand, who had cursed the Santa Herman dad of all Castile, and now rejoiced over a land where he could cut throats at his leisure; there a grey-haired extortioner, whom roguery had reduced to bankruptcy, but who hoped to repair his fortune by following the pack of man-hunters, and picking up the offals they despised, or cheating them of the prizes they had secured; here too was a holy secular, who came to exult over the confusion and destruction of all barbarians who should see nothing diviner in the crucifix than in their own idols. The greater number, however, was composed of debauched and decayed planters of the islands, who ceased to lament their narrow acres and decreasing bondmen, snatched away by the good fortune of some fellow-profligate, when they thought of territories for an estate, and whole tribes for a household. Indeed, in all the group, however elevated and ennobled, for the moment, by the excitement of the scene, and by the resolute impatience they displayed to rush upon adventures well known to be full of suffering and peril, there was but one whom a truly noble-hearted gentleman would have chosen to regard with respect or to approach with friendship.

This was a young cavalier, who, in propriety of habiliments, in excellence of person, and in nobleness of carriage, differed greatly from them all; and, to say the truth, he himself seemed highly conscious of the difference, since he regarded all his fellow-voyagers, saving only his own particular and armed attendants, with the disdain befitting so distinguished a personage. His frame, tall and moderately athletic, was arrayed in hose and doublet of a dusky brown cloth, slashed with purple: his cap and cloak were of black velvet, and in the band of one, and on the shoulder of the other, were symbols of his faith and his profession—the first being a plain crucifix of silver, and the second a cross of white cloth of eight points, inserted in the mantle. In addition to these badges of devotion, he wore a cross of gold, pointed like the former, and suspended to his neck by a chain of such length and massiveness, as to imbue his companions with high notions of his rank and affluence.

The only point in which he exhibited any feeling in common with his companions, was in admiration of the noble prospect that stretched before him, and which was every moment disclosing itself with newer and greater beauty, as the wind wafted his little vessel nearer to it. His cheek flushed, his eye kindled, and smiting his hands together in his ardour, he dropped so much of his dignity as to address many of his observations to the obsequious but not ungentle master.

"By St. John! senor capitan," he cried, with rapture, "this is a most noble land to be wasted upon savages."

"True, Senor Don Amador," replied the thrice-honoured master; "a noble land, a rich land, a most glorious land; and, I warrant me, man has never before looked on its equal."

"For my part," said the youth, proudly, "I have seen some lands that, in the estimation of those who know better, may be pronounced divine; among which I may mention the Greek islands, the keys of the Nile, the banks of the Hellespont, and the hills of Palestine—not to speak of Italy, and many divisions of our own country: yet, to be honest, I must allow I have never yet looked upon a land which, at the first sight, impressed me with such strange ideas of magnificence."

"What, then, will be your admiration, noble cavalier," said the captain, "when you have passed this sandy shore and yonder rugged hills, and find yourself among the golden valleys they encompass? for all those who have returned from the interior

thus speak of them, and declare upon the gospels and their honour, no man can conceive properly of paradise, until he has looked upon the valleys of Mexico."

"I long to be among them," said the youth; "and the sooner I am mounted on my good steed, Forgoso (whom God restore to his legs and spirit, for this cursed ship has cramped both), I say, the sooner I am mounted upon my good horse, and scattering this heathen sand from under his hoofs, the better will it be for myself, as well as for him. Harkee, good captain; I know not by what sort of miracle I shall surmount yonder tall and majestic pinnacles; but it will be some consolation, while stumbling among them, to be able at least to pronounce their names. What call you yon mountain to the north, with the huge coffer-like crag on its summit?"

"Your favour has even hit the name, in finding a similitude for the crag," said the captain. "The Indians call it by a name which signifies the Square Mountain; but poor mariners like myself, who can scarce pronounce their prayers, much less the uncouth and horrible articulations of these barbarians, are content to call it the Coffer Mountain. It lies hard by the route to the great city, and is said to be such a desolate fire-blasted spot as will sicken a man with horror."

"And yon kingly monster," continued the cavalier, "that raises his snowy cone up to heaven, and mixes his smoke with the morning clouds—that proudest of all—what call you him?"

"Spaniards have named him Orizaba," said the master; "but these godless pagans, who cover every human object with some diabolical superstition, call that peak the Starry Mountain; because the light of his conflagration, seen afar by night, shines like to a planet, and is thought by them to be one of their gods, descending to keep watch over their empire."

"A most heathenish and damning belief," said the youth, with a devout indignation; "and I do not marvel that heaven has given over to bondage and destruction a race stained with such beastly idolatry. But nevertheless, senor capitan, and notwithstanding that it is befouled with such impious heresies, I must say, that I have looked upon Mount Olympus, a mountain in Greece, whereon, they say, dwelt the accursed old heathen gods (whom Heaven confound), before the time that our blessed Saviour hurled them into the pit; and yet that Olympus is but a hang-dog Turk's head with a turban, compared to this most royal Orizaba, that raiseth up his front like an old patriarch, and smokes with the glory of his Maker."

"And yet they say," continued the captain, "that there is a mountain of fire even taller and nobler than this, and that hard by the great city. But your worship will see this for yourself, with many other wonders, when your worship fights the savages in the interior."

"If it please Heaven," said the cavalier, "I will see this mountain, and those other wonders, whereof you speak; but as to fighting the savages, I must give you to know, that I cannot perceive how a man who has used his sword upon raging Mussulmans, with a sultan at their head, can condescend to draw it upon poor, trembling barbarians, who fight with flints and fish-bones, and run away, a thousand of them together, from six not over-valiant Christians."

"Your favour," said the captain, "has heard of the miserable poltroonery of the island Indians, who, truth to say, are neither Turks nor Moors of

Barbary; but, Senor Don Amador de Leste, you will find these dogs of Mexico to be another sort of people, who live in stone cities instead of bowers of palm-leaves; have crowned emperors in place of feathered caciques; are marshalled into armies, with drums, banners, and generals, like Christian warriors; and, finally, go into battle with a most resolute and commendable good will. They will pierce a cuirass with their copper lances, crush an iron helmet with their hardened war-clubs, and, as has twice or thrice happened with the men of Hernan Cortes, they will, with their battle-axes of flint, smite through the neck of a horse, as one would pierce a yam with his dagger. Truly, Senor Caballero these Mexicans are a warlike people.'

"What you tell me," said Don Amador, "I have heard in the islands; as well as that these same mountain Indians roast their prisoners with pepper and green maize, and think the dish both savoury and wholesome; all which matters, excepting only the last, which is reasonable enough of such children of the devil, I do most firmly disbelieve: for how, were they not cowardly caitiffs, could this rebellious cavalier, the valiant Hernan Cortes, with six hundred mutineers, have forced his way even to the great city Tenochtitlan, and into the palace of the emperor? By my faith," and here the Senor Don Amador twisted his finger into his right mustachio with exceeding great complacency, "these same Mexicans may be brave enemies to the cavaliers of the plantations, who have studied the art of war among the tribes of Santo Domingo and Cuba; but to a soldier who, as I said before, has fought the Turks, and that too at the siege of Rhodes, they must be even such chicken-hearted slaves as it would be shame and disgrace to draw sword upon."

The master of the caravel regarded Don Amador with admiration for a moment, and then said, with much emphasis—"May I die the death of a mule, if I am not of your way of thinking, most noble Don Amador. To tell you the truth, these scurvy Mexicans, of whose ferocity and courage so much is said by those most interested to have them thought so, are even just such poor, spiritless, contemptible creatures as the Arrowauks of the isles, only that there are more of them; and, to be honest, I know nothing that should tempt a soldier and hidalgo to make war on them, except their gold, of which the worst that can be said is, first, that there is not much of it, and secondly, that there are too many hands to share it. There is neither honour nor wealth to be had in Tenochtitlan. But if a true soldier and a right noble gentleman, as the world esteems Don Amador de Leste, should seek a path worthy of himself, he has but to say the word, and there is one to be found from which he may return with more gold than has yet been gathered by any fortunate adventurer, and more renown than has been won by any other man in the new world: ay, by St. James, and diadems may be found there, provided one have the heart to contest for them with men who fight like the wolves of Catalonia, and die with their brows to the battle."

"Now, by St. John of Jerusalem!" said Amador, kindling with enthusiasm. "that is a path which, as I am a true Christian and Castilian, I should be rejoiced to tread. For the gold of which you speak, it might come if it would, for gold is a good thing, even to one who is neither needy nor covetous; but I should be an idle hand to gather it. As for the diadems, I have my doubts whether a man, not born by the grace of God to inherit them, has any right to wear them, unless, indeed, he should marry a king's daughter: but here the kings are all infidels, and, I vow to Heaven, I would sooner burn at a stake, along with a Christian beggar, than sell my soul to perdition in the arms of any infidel princess whatever. But for the renown of subduing a nation of such valiant Pagans as those you speak of, and of converting them to the true faith, that is even such a thought as makes my blood tingle within me; and were I in all particulars the master of my own actions, I should say to you—Right worthy and courageous captain (for truly those honourable scars on your front and temple, and from your way of thinking, I esteem you such a man), point me out that path, and, with the blessing of Heaven, I will see to what honour it may lead me."

"Your favour," said the captain, "has heard of the great island, Florida, and of the renowned Senor Don Ponce de Leon, its discoverer?"

"I have heard of such names, both of isle and of man, I think," said Don Amador; "but, to say truth, senor commandante, you have here, in this new world, such a multitude of wonderful territories, and of heroic men, that, were I to give a month's labour to the study, I think I should not muster the names of all of them. Truly, in Rhodes, where the poor knights of the Hospital stood at bay before Solymon *El Magnifico*, and did such deeds as the world had not heard of since the days of Leonidas and his brave knights of Sparta—I say, even in Rhodes, where all men thought of their honour and religion, and never a moment of their blood, we heard not of so many heroes as have risen up here in this corner of the earth, in a few years chasing of the wild Indians."

"The Senor Ponce de Leon," said the captain, without regarding the sneer of the proud soldier, "the Senor Ponce de Leon, Adelantado of Bimini and of Florida, in search of the miraculous Fountain of Youth, which, the Indians say, lies somewhere to the north, landed eight years ago, with the crews of three ships, all of them bigger and better than this little rotten Sangre de Cristro, whereof I myself commanded one. Of the extraordinary beauty and fertility of the land of Florida, thus discovered, I will say nothing. Your favour will delight more to hear me speak of its inhabitants. These were men of a noble stature, and full of such resolution, that we were no sooner ashore than they fell upon us; and I must say, we found we were now at variance with a people in nowise resembling those naked idiots of Cuba, or those cowardly hinds of Mexico. They cared not a jot for swordsman, arcubalister, or musketeer. To our rapiers they opposed their stone battle-axes, which gushed through the brain more like a thunderbolt than a Christian espada; no crossbowman could drive an arrow with more mortal aim and fury than could these wild archers with their horn bows (for know, senor, they have, in that country of Florida, some prodigious animal, which yields them abundant material for their weapons); and, what filled us with much surprise, and no little fear, instead of betaking themselves to their heels at the sound of our firelocks, as we looked for them to do, no sooner had they heard the roar of these arms, than they fetched many most loud and frightful yells, to express their contempt of our warlike din, and rushed upon us with such renewed and increasing violence, that, to be honest, as a Christian of my years should be, we were fain to betake ourselves to our ships with what speed and good fortune we could. And now, senor, you will be ashamed to hear that our courage was so much modified by this repulse and our fears of engaging further with such despera does so urgent and potent, that we straightway set sail, and, in the vain search for the enchanted fountain, quite forgot the nobler objects of the voyage."

"What you have said," quoth Don Amador, "convinces me that these savages of Florida are a warlike people, and worthy the wrath of a brave soldier; but you have said nothing of the ores and diadems, whereof, I think, you first spake, and which, heaven save the mark! by some strange mutation of mind, have made a deeper impression on my imagination than such trifles should."

"We learned of some wounded captives we carried to the ships," continued the master, "as well at least as we could understand by their signs, that there was a vast country to the north-west, where dwelt nations of fire-worshippers, governed by kings, very rich and powerful, on the banks of a great river; and from some things we gathered, it was thought by many that the miraculous fountain was in that land, and not in the island Bimini; and this think I myself, for, senor, I have seen a man who, with others, had slaked his thirst in every spring that gushes from that island, and, by my faith, he died of an apoplexy the day after his arrival in the Habana. Wherefore, it is clear, that marvellous fountain must be in the country of the fire-worshippers. But, notwithstanding all these things, senor, our commander, Don Ponce, would resolve upon nought but to return to the Bahamas, where our ships were divided, each in search of the island called Bimini. It was my fortune to be dispatched westward; and here, what with the aid of a tempest that blew from the east, and some little hankering of mine own appetite after that land of the fire-worshippers, I found myself many a league beyond where any Christian had ever navigated before, where a fresh and turbid current rolled through the deep, bearing the trunks of countless great trees, many of them scorched with fire; whereupon I knew that I was near to the object of my desires, which, however, the fears and the discontent of my crew prevented my reaching. I was even compelled to obey them, and conduct them to Cuba."

"Senor capitan," said Amador, who had listened to the master's narrative with great attention, "I give you praise for your bold and most commendable daring in having sailed so far, and I condole with you for your misfortune in being compelled to abide the government of a crew of such runagate and false companions, whom I marvel exceedingly you did not hang, every man of 'em, to some convenient corner of your ship, as was the due of such disloyal knaves; but yet, credit me, I see not what this turbid and fresh flood, and what these floating trees had to do with the gold and the diadems, of which you were speaking."

"Senor," said the captain, earnestly, "I have navigated the deep for, perhaps, more years than your favour has lived; and it was my fortune to be with the Admiral ——"

"With Colon," cried the youth.

"With his excellency, the admiral, Don Cristobal Colon, the discoverer of this new world," replied the master, proudly, "in his own good ship, when we sailed into the Serpent's Mouth, which, we knew not then, laved the shores of the great continent; and I remember that when the admiral had beheld the trees floating in the current, and had tasted of the fresh water of that boiling gulf, he told us that these came from a great river rolling through a mighty continent. And, in after times, the words of the admiral were proved to be just; for there his captain, the young Pinzon, found the great river Oronoko."

"There is no man," said Don Amador, who more reverences the memory of the admiral than I; and I feel the more regard for yourself, that you have sailed with him on his discoveries. Moreover, I beg your pardon, insomuch as I have been slow to unravel your meaning. But now, I perceive, you think you had reached that river of the infidel fire-worshippers, whom God confound with fire and flame! as doubtless he will. And hath no man again sought the mouth of that river? I marvel you did not yourself make a second attempt."

"I could not prevail upon any cavaliers, rich enough for the undertaking," said the master, "to league with me in it. Men like not the spirit of the northern savages; and, in truth, there were a thousand other lands where the barbarians could be subdued with less peril, and, as they thought, with a better hope of gain. And yet, by our lady, that river bore with it the evidences of the wealth on its banks; for what were those scorched trees but the relics of the fires with which the kings of the land were smelting their ores? and what quantity of gold must there not have been where such prodigious furnaces were kindled."

"By the mass!" said Amador, with ardour, "you speak the truth; it is even a most wonderful land; and if a few thousand pesoes would float an expedition, by my faith, I think I could find them."

"A few thousand pesoes, and the countenance of such a leader as Don Amador de Leste, a knight of the holy and valiant order San Juan—"

"A knight by right, but not by vow," said Don Amador, hastily: "I give you to understand, senor capitan, that I am not a sworn brother of that most ancient, honourable, and knightly order, but an humble volunteer, attached, for certain reasons of my own, to them, and privileged by the consent of his most eminent highness, the grand master, to wear these badges, wherein I am arrayed, in acknowledgment that I did some service not unworthy knighthood in the trenches of Rhodes."

"Your favour will not lead the less worthily for that," said the captain; "I know an hundred cavaliers who would throw their ducats, as well as their arms, into the adventure prescribed by the Senor Don Amador; and a thousand crossbows, with three or four score arquebusiers, would flock to the standard as soon as we had preached through the islands a crusade to the fire-worshippers, and a pilgrimage to the Waters of Life."

"And is it truly believed," said Amador, eagerly, "that such waters are to be found in these heathen lands?"

"Who can doubt it?" said the captain; "the Indians of the Bahamas have spoken of them for years; no Spaniard hath ever thought of questioning their existence; and at this moment, so great is the certainty of finding them, that my old leader, Don Ponce, is collecting round him men for a second expedition, with which he will depart I know not how soon. But I know Don Ponce; the draught of youth is not for him; he will seek the fountain on his great island of Florida, and find it not: it will bubble only to the lips of those who seek it near the great river of the great continent."

"By Heaven!" said Don Amador, what might not a man do, who could drink of this miraculous fountain. A draught of it would have carried the great Alejandro so far into the east, as to have left but small work for the knaves of Portugal. And then our friends! Dios mio! we could keep our friends by us for ever! But hold, senor capitan—a thought strikes me: have you ever heard the opinion of a holy clergyman on this subject? Is it lawful for a man to drink of such a fountain?"

"By my faith," replied the master, "I have never heard priest or layman advance an argument against its lawfulness; and I know not how it should be criminal, since Providence hath given us the privilege to drink of any well, whose waters are not to our misliking."

"For my part," said Amador, "I must say, I have my doubts whether Providence hath given us any such privilege; the exercise of which, in general, would greatly confound the world, by over-peopling it, and, in particular, would seem, in a measure, to put man in a condition to defy his Maker, and to defeat all the ends of divine goodness and justice: for how should a man be punished for his sins, who had in him the power of endless life? and how should a man keep from sinning, who had no fear of death and the devil? and, finally, how should we ever receive any of the benefits of the most holy atonement, after drinking such a life-preserving draught?—for it is my opinion, senor capitan, no man would wish to go to heaven who had the power of remaining on earth."

"By my soul," said the captain, earnestly, "this is a consideration which never occupied me before; and I shall take counsel upon it with the first holy man I meet."

"At all events," said the cavalier, "there is inducement enough to make search after this river, were it only to fight the fire-worshippers, convert them to the true faith, and see what may be the curiosities of their land. Yet I must give you warning, it will rest with another whom I am now seeking, whether I may league with you in this enterprise or not. Give me his consent and leading, and I will take leave of these poor rogues of Tenoch-titlan, as soon as I have looked a little upon their wonders: and then, with the blessing of God and St. John, have at the valiant fire-worshippers, with all my heart! But, how now, senor capitan? What means your pilot to cast anchor here among the fleet, and not carry us forthwith to the shore?"

"I dare not proceed farther," said the captain, "without the authority of the senor cavallero, admiral of this squadron, and governor of this harbour of San Juan de Ulua. It is necessary I should report myself to him for examination, on board the Capitana, and receive his instructions concerning my cargo and fellow-voyagers."

"His instructions concerning your fellow-voyagers!" said Don Amador, sternly. "I, for one, am a voyager, who will receive no instructions for the government of my actions, neither myself nor by proxy; and, with God's blessing, I will neither ask permission to disembark, nor allow it to be asked for myself, or for my grooms; and the senor cavallere, or any other senor, that thinks to stop me, had better grind both sides of his sword, by way of preparation for such folly."

"Your favour has no cause for anger," said the master, moderately. "This is the custom and the law, and it becomes the more necessary to enforce it, in the present situation of things. Your favour will receive no check, but rather assistance; and it is only necessary to assure the admiral you do not come as a league and helpmate of the mutineer, Cortes, to receive free license, a safe conduct, and perhaps even guides, to go whithersoever you list throughout this empire. This, senor, is only a form of courtesy, such as one cavalier should expect of another, and no more."

"Truly, then, if you assure me so," said Don

Amador, complacently, "I will not refuse to go myself in person to his excellency, the admiral; and the more readily that, I fancy, from the name, there is some sort of blood-relationship between his excellency and myself. But, by Heaven, I would rather, at present, be coursing Fogoso over yon glittering sand, than winding a bolero on my cousin's deck, though he were a king's admiral."

CHAPTER II.

Don Amador de Leste was interrupted in the agreeable duty (the last to be performed in the little caravel) of inquiring into the health and condition of his war-horse, Fogoso, by a summons, or, as it was more courteously expressed, an invitation, to attend the admiral on board his own vessel. Giving a thousand charges to his attendants, all of which were received with due deference and humility, he stepped into the boat, which, in a few moments, he exchanged for the decks of the Capitana—not, however, without some doubt as to the degree of loftiness he should assume during the interview with his excellency, the admiral, his kinsman. His pride had already twice, or thrice, since his appearance among the islands of the New World, been incensed by the arrogant assumption of their petty dignitaries to inquire into and control the independence of his movements: and he remembered with high displeasure, that the royal adelantado of Cuba, the renowned Velasquez, a man of whom, as he was pleased to say, he had never heard so much as the name until he found himself within his territories, had not only dared to disregard the privileges of his birth and decorations, but had well-nigh answered his ire and menaces, by giving him to chains and captivity. Nor when, at last, the pious exertions of the good friars of Santiago had allayed the growing storm, and appeased his own indignation, by urging the necessity their governor was under to examine into the character and objects of all persons, who, by declining to visit the new El Dorado under the authority of the commander, might reasonably be suspected of a desire to join his rebellious lieutenant —not even then could the proud Amador forget that, whatever might be the excuse, his independence had been questioned, and might be again, by any inflated official whom he should be so unlucky as to meet. His doubt, however, in this case, was immediately dispelled by the degree of state and ceremony with which he was received on board the Capitana, and conducted to his excellency; and the last shadow of hesitation departed from his brow, when he beheld the admiral prepared to welcome him with such courtesy and deference as were only accorded to the most noble and favoured.

"If I do not err," said the admiral, with a bow of great reverence, and a smile of prodigious suavity, "I behold, in the Senor Don Amador de Leste, a gentleman of Valencia, whom I make free, as I shall be proud, to welcome as my countryman and kinsman?"

"Senor Almirante," replied Amador, with equal amenity, "my mother was a Valencian, and of the house of Cavallero. Wherefore, I take it for granted, we are in some sort related; but in what degree I am not able to determine; nor do I think that a matter very important to be questioned into, since in these savage corners of the earth, the farthest degree of consanguinity should draw men together as firmly as the closest."

"You are right, senor cavalier and kinsman," said the admiral: "affinity of any degree should be a claim to the intimacy and affection of brotherhood; and although this is the first time I have enjoyed the felicity to behold my right worthy and much honoured cousin, I welcome him with good will to such hospitalities as my poor bark and this barbarous clime can afford; marvelling, however, amid all my satisfaction, what strange fortune has driven him to exchange the knightly combats of Christendom for the ignoble campaigns of this wild hemisphere."

"As to that, most noble and excellent cousin," said the cavalier, "I will not scruple to inform your excellency, together with all other matters wherein, as my kinsman, you are entitled to question; previous to which, however, I must demand of your goodness to know how far your interrogatories are to bear the stamp of office and authority, the satisfaction of my mind on which point will materially affect the character of my answers."

"Surely," said the admiral, courteously, and seemingly with great frankness, "I will only presume to question you as a friend and relative, and, as such, no farther than it may suit your pleasure to allow. My office I will only use so far as it may enable me to assist you in your objects, if, as I will make bold to believe, you may need such assistance in this land of Mexico."

"I thank your excellency,' said Amador, now receiving and pressing the hand of the commander with much cordiality, "both for your offers of assistance, which, if I may need it, I will freely accept, and for your assurance you do not mean to trouble me with your authority—a mark of extreme civility and good sense, which virtues, under your favour, I have not found so common among your fellow-commanders in these heathen lands as I was led to expect."

The admiral smiled pleasantly on his kinsman while replying—"I must beg your allowance for the presumption of my brothers in command, who, sooth to say, have had so much dealing with the wild Indians and rough reprobates of these regions, as somewhat to have forgot their manners, when treating with gentlemen and nobles. My superior and governor, the worthy and thrice-honoured Velasquez (whom God grant many and wiser counsellors!) is rather hot of head and unreasonable of temper; and has, doubtless, thrown some obstructions in the way of your visit to this disturbed land. But you should remember, that the junction of so brave a cavalier as Don Amador de Leste, with the mutinous bands of the Senor Cortes, is a thing to excite both dread and opposition."

"I remember," said Amador, "that some such excuse was made for him, and that my assurance that my business had no more to do with that valiant rebel than with his own crabbed excellency, was no more believed than the assertion of any common hind—a piece of incredulity I shall take great pleasure, at some more convenient period, of removing, at my sword's point, from his excellency's body."

"I am grieved you should have cause to complain of the governor," said the Senor Cavallero; "and verily I myself cannot pretend to justify his rash and tyrannical opposition, especially in the matter of yourself, who, I take it for granted, come hither as the kinsman of the Knight Calavar, to search out and remove that crack-brained cavalier from these scenes of tumult and danger."

"The knight Calavar," said the young soldier, sternly, "like other men, has his eccentricities and follies; but if God has smitten him with a sorer infirmity than others, he has left him so much strength of arm and resoluteness of heart, and withal has given him friends of so unhesitating a devotion, that it will always be wise to pronounce his name with the respect which his great worth and valiant deeds have proved to be his due."

"Surely," said the admiral, good-humouredly, "it is my boast that I can claim, through yourself, to be distantly related to this most renowned and unhappy gentleman; and, while I would sharply rebuke a stranger for mentioning him with discourtesy, I held myself at liberty to speak of him with freedom to yourself."

"I beg your pardon then," said Amador, "if I took offence at your utterance of a word, which seemed to me to savour more of the heartless ridicule with which the world is disposed to remark a mental calamity, than the respectful pity which, it is my opinion, in such cases should be always accorded. Your excellency did right to suppose my business in this hemisphere was to seek out the Knight Calavar; not, however, as you have hinted, to remove him from among savages (for I give you to understand, he is ever capable of being the guide and director of his own actions); but to render him the dutiful service of his kinsman and esquire, and to submit myself to his will and government, whether it be to fight these rogues of Mexico, or any other heathens whatever."

"I give you praise for your fidelity and affection," said the Senor Cavallero, "which, I think, will stand the knight in good stead, if it be his pleasure to remain longer in this wild country. But tell me, Don Amador:—as a cavallero of Valencia, I could not be ignorant of the misfortune of our very renowned cousin; yet was I never able to compass the cause of his melancholy. I remember that when he fleshed his boyish sword, for the first time, among the Moors of the Alpujarras, he was accounted not only of valour, but of discretion, far beyond his years. There was no patrimony in all Granada so rich and enviable as the lordship of Calavar; no nobleman of Spain was thought to have fairer and loftier prospects than the young Don Gines Gabriel de Calavar; none had greater reason to laugh and be merry, for before the beard had darkened on his lip, he had enjoyed the reputation of a brave soldier; yet, no sooner came he to man's estate, than, utterly disregarding the interests of his house, and the common impulses of youth, he flung himself into the arms of the knights of Rhodes, vowed himself to toil and sorrow, and has, ever since, been remembered by those who knew him in his boyhood, as the saddest and maddest of men."

"So much I have heard, and so much I know, of the good knight," said Amador, with a sigh; "little more can I add to the story, but that some calamity, the nature of which I never dared to inquire, suddenly wrought this change in him, even in the midst of his youth, and led him to devote his life to the cause of the faithful."

"Thou hast heard it suggested," said Cavallero, significantly, "that, in the matter of the Alpujarras, his heart was hotter, and his hand redder than became a Christian knight, even when striking on the hearth of the infidel?"

"Senor cousin and admiral," said Amador, decidedly, "in my soul, I believe you are uttering these suggestions only from a kinsman's concern for the honour and welfare of the party in question, and therefore do I make bold to tell you, the man who, in my hearing, asperses the Knight Calavar, charging his grief of mind to be the fruit of any criminal or dishonourable deed, shall abide the issue of the slander as ruefully as if it had been cast on the ashes of my mother!"

"So shall he win his deservings," said the commander. "Nevertheless doth Calavar himself give some cause for these foolish surmises, of which indiscreet persons have occasionally delivered themselves; for the evident misery of heart, and distraction of head, the austere and penitential self-denial of his life, nay, the very ostentation of grief and contrition, which is written in his deportment and blazoned on his armour, and which has gained him, in these lands, the appellation of the Penitent Knight, seem almost to warrant the suspicion of an unquiet and remorseful conscience, brooding over the memory of an unabsolved crime. But I say this not so much to justify, as, in part, to excuse those idle impertinents, who are so free with their inuendoes. I have ever pondered with wonder on the secret of the brave knight's unrest; yet, I must confess to thee, I was struck with no less astonishment, when, returning from Nombre de Dios to Santiago, I heard that a famous Knight Hospitaller, and he no other than Don Gines Gabriel de Calavar, had arrived among the islands, frenzied with the opportunity of slaying Pagans at his pleasure, and had already followed on the path of Cortes to Mexico. It gave me great pain, and caused me no little marvel, to find he had come and vanished with so little of the retinue of his rank, and of the attendance necessary to one in his condition, that two or three ignorant grooms were his only attendants."

"I have no doubt," said Amador, "I can allay your wonder as to these matters. Your excellency need not be told that the banner of the Turk now floats over the broken ramparts of Rhodes, and over the corses of those noble knights of San Juan, who defended them for more than two hundred years, and at last perished among their ruins. This is a catastrophe that has pealed over all Christendom like the roar of a funeral bell, and its sound has even pierced to these lands of twilight. No knight among all that band of warriors and martyrs, as I am myself a witness, did more brave and heroical actions throughout the black and bloody siege, than my lord and kinsman, Calavar. But the good and ever-gracious Saint, the patron of this most ancient and chivalric brotherhood, saved him, with a few other knights, out of the jaws of destruction, and restored him again to his own country. Rhodes was fallen; there was no longer a home for the destitute knights; they wandered over Europe, whithersoever their destinies listed, but particularly wheresoever there was an infidel to be slain. Our monarch of Spain contemplating a crusade among the Moors of Barbary, the descendants of that accursed—(why should I not say wretched, for they are exiles,)—that wretched race who had once o'ermastered our own beloved land; the Knight Calavar entered into this project with alacrity, and set himself to such preparations as should win him good vengeance for the blood of his brothers lost at Rhodes. I did myself, in obedience to his will, betake me to the business of seeing what honest Christians might be prevailed on to fight under his banner; and while thus engaged, at a distance from my beloved lord, with,

perhaps, as I should confess with shame, less energy and more sloth than were becoming in his follower, I suffered certain worldly allurements to step between me and my duty, and, for a time, almost forgot my renowned and unhappy kinsman. Now, senor," continued the youth, with some little hesitation, and a deep sigh, "it is not necessary I should trouble you with any very particular account of my forgetfulness and stupidity: it was soon known that the enthusiasm of our king was somewhat abated touching the matter of the African crusade—perhaps swallowed up in the interest wherewith he regarded the new world which God and the great Colon had given him; the enthusiasm of his subjects diminished in like manner: there was no more talk of Africa. This, senor, may perhaps in a measure excuse my own lethargy; but you may be assured I awoke out of it with shame and mortification, when I discovered that the good knight, left to himself, and deprived of that excitement of combat, or the hope of combat, so necessary to the well-being of his mind, had suddenly (doubtless in one of those paroxysms of eccentricity—or deliriums, as I may call it to you,) departed from the land, and was now cleaving the surges that divided us from the new hemisphere. There was nothing left for me but to follow him in the first ship that sailed on the same adventure. This I have done; I have tracked my leader from Palos to Cuba; from Cuba to this barren coast; and now, with your good leave and aidance, I will take the last step of the pursuit, and render myself up to his authority in the barbaric city, Tenochtitlan."

"I respect your motive, and praise your devotion, most worthy cousin," said the admiral, with much kindness; "and yet you must forgive me, if I dare to express to you some degree of pity. My long acquaintance with these countries, both of isle and main, has well instructed me what you have to expect among them; and I can truly conceive what sacrifices you have made for the good knight's sake. In any case, I beg leave to apprise you, you can command all my services, either to persist in seeking him, or to return to Spain. My advice is, that you leave this place forthwith, in a ship which I am to-morrow to dispatch to Andalusia; return to your native land; betake yourself to those allurements, and that lethargy, which I can well believe may bring you happiness; commend yourself to your honourable lady-love, and think no more of the wild Calavar. Here, if you lose not life, before you have looked on your kinsman, as there is much fear, you must resolve to pass your days in such suffering and misery, and withal in ignoble warfare with naked savages, supported by such mean and desperate companions as, I am sure, you were never born to."

"What you counsel me," said Amador, coolly "is doubtless both wisdom and friendship; nevertheless, if your excellency will be good enough to reconsider your advice, you will perceive it involves such selfishness, meanness, and dishonour, as cannot be listened to with any propriety by a kinsman of the knight of Calavar. I do not say I come hither to condescend to this ignoble warfare, though if it be worthy my good knight, I shall have no reason to scorn it. I bear with me, to my kinsman, the despatch of his most eminent highness, the Grand Master of the most illustrious order of San Juan, wherein, although it be recommended to him, if such warfare seem to him honourable and advantageous to the cause of Christ, to strike fast and well, it is, if such strife be otherwise, strongly urged on him to return without delay to Europe, and to the Isle of Malta, which, it is announced, our monarch of Spain will speedily give to the good knights. It is therefore," continued the cavalier, "from the nature of things and of mine own will, clearly impossible I should follow your advice; in default of which, I must beg such other counsel and assistance of your excellency as your excellency may think needful to bestow; only premising, that as I have many a weary league of sand and mountain to compass, the sooner you benefit me with these good things the better."

"Your journey will be neither so long nor so wearisome as you imagine," said Cavallero; "but, I fear me, will present more obstructions than you may be prepared to encounter. I take it for granted, the Governor Velasquez has furnished you with no commands to his general, Don Panfilo de Narvaez, since he gave you none to myself."

"This is even the fact," said Amador; "I entered the caravel which brought me here, as I thought, in defiance of his authority, and not without apprehensions of being obliged to cut off the ears of some dozen or two of his rogues, who might be ordered to detain me. Nevertheless, I left the island without a contest, and equally without aidance of any kind from this discourteous ruler."

"I must give thee some counsel then," said the admiral, "for I apprehend the governor did, very perfidiously as I esteem it, when he ceased his opposition, rest much hope on that of his general. Thou art acquainted with the character of Narvaez?"

"By my faith, I am so ignorant of all matters appertaining to these climates, that, saving thine own, and the Knight Calavar's, and one or two others which I acquired this morning, I am familiar only with those of two other persons—to wit, of Velasquez, whom I consider a very scurvy and ill bred personage, and of Cortes, a man whom I hold in much esteem, ever since I heard he burned his fleet to keep his followers from running away, and made prisoner the great Mexican emperor in his own capital. In addition to this, I know the aforesaid governor doth very hotly hate, and hath disgraced, with titles of rebel and outlaw, this same respectable and courageous Cortes; but for what reason, as I have been kept in somewhat too great a passion to inquire, I am yet altogether ignorant."

"For one who may soon share an important part in the events of this region, I think thou showest a most princely indifference to them," said the admiral, smiling. "I will not say the safety, but the facility with which thou mayest traverse these lands, will be greatly increased by knowing some little of their history; and that knowledge I will hasten to impart to thee, and with what brevity I can. If I should be led to speak with more freedom of certain persons than may seem fitting in an inferior and a colleague, I must beseech thee to remember I am doing so to a kinsman, and for his especial information and good. Know then, Senor Don Amador, the person whom it pleased our viceroy, the son of Colon, to set over us, and whom it has since pleased his most devout majesty, the emperor, to confirm in the government of Cuba, and even to that to add the further dignity of ruler of the kings of Mexico, is, as I hinted to thee before, afflicted with so irascible a temper and so jealous a fancy, that, were I not restrained by the office I hold under him, I should say he was, at the least, as mad as any other man in his dominion. The desire of immortalising himself by some great exploit would be commendable in him, were it not accompanied by the ambition to achieve it by the hands of another. Ever since the discovery of this fair empire of Montezuma by the Senor Cordova, he has thirsted for the glory of subduing it; and has taken all the steps necessary to such a purpose, except the single one of attempting it in person;—an omission not in itself important, since there are a hundred other cavaliers more capable of the task, only that, besides the other munitions with which he furnishes his lieutenant, he follows him ever with so plentiful a store of distrust, that it is utterly impossible his officer should have a chance to immortalise him. After much seeking of a man whose ambition should extend no further than to the glory of winning a crown for the purpose of seeing his excellency wear it, he fixed upon the worthy hidalgo, Hernan Cortes, a gentleman of Medellin in Estremadura, and dispatched him on the business of conquest. Now, no sooner was his general gone, than this jealous imagination whereof I spake, instantly presented to his mind the image of Cortes as a conqueror, suddenly laying claim, before the emperor and the world, to the sole merit of the conquest—a spectacle so infinitely intolerable, that without delay he set himself at work to hinder Cortes from making any conquest at all."

"Surely," said Amador, "this Governor Velasquez is a fool, as well as a knave!"

"Heaven have him in keeping! You should mention him with respect: but as you are speaking in the confidence of blood-relationship, I cannot take notice of your sarcasm," said the admiral. "The Senor Cortes, however," continued Cavallero, "was by no means disposed to second the disloyal frenzy of the governor: (disloyal I call it, since it threatened to deprive his majesty, the Emperor Charles, of the opportunity of adding a new empire to his diadem). On the other hand, Cortes was fully determined to do his duty, and thought the governor could do nothing better than to follow his example. But in the end, this same Cortes, though of as meek a temper as is desirable in the commander of an army, became greatly incensed at the sottish and grievous distrust of his governor; and calling his army together, and representing to them the foolish predicament in which his excellency had placed them, he threw down his truncheon with contempt, and told them that as Velasquez had left them without a leader, the wisest thing that remained for them was to find another as soon as possible: as for himself, he disdained to hold his commission longer under such a commander."

"By Heaven, a most proper-spirited and gallant gentleman!" cried Amador. "I honour him for the act, but chiefly for the contempt it argued of this jackfeather ruler."

"I must beg of your favour," said the admiral gravely, "to remember that his excellency is my chief and commander; though, in justice, I think you have some reason to censure him. What remained for the army of Cortes, now no longer having a general? They were loath to leave the fair empire that appeared almost in their grasp, and enraged at the governor, who seemed determined to rob them of it. There was only one way to secure the conquest for their royal master they absolved themselves of the allegiance to the governor, swore themselves the soldiers and subjects of the emperor alone, and erecting themselves into a colony, forthwith elected Cortes their governor and commander-in-chief; and dispatched advice of the same to Don Carlos, with a petition for permission to pursue and conclude the conquest of Tenochtitlan in his name."

"A very loyal, defensible, and, indeed, praiseworthy action," said Don Amador, with emphasis; "and I marvel your jealous governor did not stab himself forthwith out of pure chagrin, to be so sharply and justly outwitted."

"Instead of that," said the admiral, "boiling with vexation and rage, and devoting Cortes to the fiend who had first suggested him as a proper lieutenant, his excellency equipped a second army, more than twice as strong as that he had ordered Cortes to raise; and this, one would have thought, he would have commanded in person. But the old whim of conquering by lieutenants, and becoming famous by proxy, still beset the brain of his wisdom. He gave the command of an army of more than a thousand men to the Senor Panfilo de Narvaez, a Biscayan, of whom the best I can say is, that he swore eternal fidelity to Velasquez—resolving privately in his own mind that, as soon as he had subdued Cortes, he would follow his example, and throw off the authority of his distrustful commander."

"I should call this treachery," said Amador, "but that I think the absurdity of the chief a full excuse for the defection of the follower."

"The wisdom of the proceeding is now made manifest," continued the admiral. "Its scarce a month since it was my misfortune, as commander of the naval division of this expedition, to land the forces of Narvaez on this shore. Here I learned, with much admiration, that Cortes, notwithstanding the meagreness of his army, had absolutely, after certain bloody combats with savages on the wayside, marched into the great city, taken possession of the body of the barbarous emperor, and, through him, virtually, of all the lands which acknowledged his sway; and you may understand how much, as a true and reasonable subject of our Catholic monarch, I was afflicted to learn, in addition, that the sending of the new force by Velasquez only served the purpose of snatching the conquest out of our hands. For Cortes, under a delusion which may be pardoned him, on account of its loyalty, regarding himself, in obedience to the command of his followers, as the only true representative and general of our king, and ourselves, by consequence, as traitors and rebels, to his majesty, did forthwith resolve to drive us from the land; to do which, it was needful he should withdraw his forces from Tenochtitlan; and, therefore, Tenochtitlan is lost."

"Thou sayest the Senor Cortes hath an army not half so powerful as the Biscayan's?"

"Nay, 'tis much short of five hundred men, and weakened by a year's campaign, and still further diminished by the necessity of maintaining a garrison in his port of Vera Cruz, which he doth humorously denominate the Rich City, and leaving another of more than a hundred men, with one of his best captains, in the goodly city, out of a hope, which I myself reckon both vain and foolish, still to retain possession of it."

"And with this shattered and pitiful handful, which I think cannot exceed three hundred men," said Amador, "the brave Cortes is resolute to resist the Biscayan, and his thousand fresh combatants?"

"It is even so," replied Cavallero.

"I give him the praise of a most dauntless and heroic leader," cried Amador: "and I am eager to proffer him the hand of friendship."

"Not only resolute to resist," said the admiral, "but, from the most undeniable tokens, impatient to attack; as, indeed, are all his people. As an evidence of which I may tell thee, that Narvaez having quartered his host at an Indian city called Zempoala, within a few leagues of this aforsaid stockade and Rich City of the True Cross, he straightway dispatched certain officers, military, civil, and religious, to demand the surrender of the same at the hands of the very young and very simple-minded senor, Don Gonzalo de Sandoval, its commandant. What answer, thinkest thou, was made by this foolish captain, so many leagues separated from his commander, and so far from all assistance? Faith, he flings me the encelvoys into certain bags of network, as one would live quails, and tossing them upon the backs of lusty savages, in lieu of asses, dispatched them forthwith over the mountains to his general. And this is the only answer my colleague and most excellent friend, the General Narvaez, ever received to his summons for surrender of the Rich City of the True Cross."

"A spirited and ever-to-be-commended youth, this same bold Sandoval," said Amador, earnestly; "and I begin to bethink me, I shall not be loath to remain for a time in the company of a leader, who hath such worthy spirits for his companions. But tell me, senor cavalier and cousin, hath Cortes yet struck a blow for his honour and his right?"

"By our Lady, no!" said the admiral: "and upon reflection," continued he, "I must confess, that though he has not yet drawn a Christian sabre on the Biscayan, he has done him much hurt with a certain weapon of gold, the use of which he learned at Mexico, and whose blows, by the operation of a kind of magic, have the virtue to paralyse the wrath, without spilling the blood, of an adversary."

"This is a weapon of the devil!" said the young cavalier, indignantly, "which I marvel much should be used by so worthy a soldier. Nevertheless, as it does not shed blood, the use of it may be justifiable in a contest between brothers and countrymen, wherein humanity and mercy are always more Christian qualities than rage and bloodthirstiness of another warfare. But, notwithstanding all this, if such enchanted arms (if such indeed exist, as I cannot believe,) be in vogue among the followers of Cortes, I swear to God and Saint John, I will eschew them as I would the gifts of the fiend; and if compelled by the command of my good knight to fight in their company, it shall be with such sword and spear as I can use with a free conscience and an honest arm."

"I commend your honourable resolution," said the admiral, amused with the literal straight forwardness of his kinsman, but without thinking fit to undeceive him; "but how long the Cavalier Cortes will employ so bloodless a rapier is more than I can determine. He now lies within a few leagues of my colleague, the Biscayan; and although apparently more ripe for negociation than combat, I shall be much mistaken if he do not, at some convenient season, so fling his crew of desperadoes at the head of Narvaez, as shall make his excellency stare. Indeed, there is now little hope of pacification; for Narvaez has very grievously insulted Cortes, by proclaiming him a rebel and an outlaw, and setting a price on his head; and such is his hotheadedness, that it was but yesterday he compelled me to ship to Cuba the king's oidor, Vasques, whom he had arrested for daring to speak to him of amicable treaty. I look daily for intelligence of a battle."

"I vow to Heaven!" said Amador, his eyes sparkling with animation, "I vow to Heaven! I have no desire to mingle in a civil fray of any kind; but if these mad fellows must be e'en at it, I see no reason why I should not stand hard by, to be a witness of their bravery. Wherefore, most excellent cousin, I must entreat of your favour to dispatch me, without delay, with such guides, or instructions, as will enable me to reach the Senor Cortes before the combat begins."

"If it would suit thee as well to survey this spectacle from the camp of Narvaez," said Cavallero, "I could gratify thee without any difficulty. But I must apprise thee, that to reach Cortes, it will be necessary to pass the lines of Narvaez; and what obstructions he may choose to throw in thy way is more than I can very satisfactorily determine, though I may counsel thee how best to overcome them."

"Please Heaven," said Amador, proudly, "he shall make me no opposition which he shall not answer to the cost of his body. For I am here, a free hidalgo of Spain, knowing no authority but the king's will and my own; a neophyte (and, as I may add, a knight by right, though unsworn,) of the illustrious order of San Juan, bearing the instructions of his most eminent highness, the grand master, to a vowed knight, and therefore liable to the command of no other man, save only, as before excepted, the king; and he who thinks to hinder me in my passage, besides provoking the wrath of the aforesaid privileged order, must, as I said before, do it under the peril of my own sword."

"It would not become me to question your privileges, or the danger with which they might be invaded," said the admiral, "nor will I repeat to you in how little regard these matters may be had by a man who has presumed to arrest and imprison the representative of his majesty himself, and who, surrounded by an army, and separated from the sway of the laws, is beyond the present responsibility of any government but that of his own conscience. I can only remind you, that, as an emissary of the holy order, you are doubly bound to avoid a quarrel with a Christian and countryman; especially when, as will presently be your case, you are in the lands of the Infidel. I must beg to remind you, too, that the Biscayan, holding, as he believes, the authority of the king, and compelled to act as may seem to him necessary for the preservation of the king's interest, should be respected accordingly; and his humours, as well as his rightful commands, borne without anger or opposition."

"May his majesty live a thousand years!" said the cavalier. "It is no part of my principle to oppose his pleasure; wherefore, if contesting the authority of this Biscayan general be such disloyalty, I will refrain from it; that is, as long as I can. But, nevertheless, I will protest against any authority that may hinder my present journey."

"Moderation, and the exercise of patience," said Cavallero, "will doubtless secure you from restraint and insult. It is quite necessary you report the object of your travel to the commander Narvaez; and even to desire his permission (a courtesy that has in it nothing of degradation) to continue your journey."

"Doubtless," said Amador, sarcastically, "you will tell me, as did the Senor Gomez, the captain of the caravel, that this submission of myself to his commands will be nothing more than the rendering of a customary compliment to his dignity. If there be any way by which I may pass by the camp of Narvaez, I shall be much bound to your excellency to inform me of it; and I will pursue it, be it ever so rough and long, with much more satisfaction than I can ever make my entreaties to him."

"There is no other way," said the admiral. "The Indian city, Zempoala, where Narvaez has established his head-quarters, lies immediately on the path to the Villa Rica; and the scouts of Narvaez, occupying all the intermediate ground, render it impossible you should pass him without observation, or them without their leader's commands. I am now about to dispatch to Narvaez certain reinforcements, in whose company I recommend you to travel, and with whom I will send such representations to the general as, I think, will secure you his instant permission, and doubtless aid, to join your kinsman, the good knight, without delay. Only let me entreat of you, as your true friend and relation, not wantonly, by any overbearing pride, to exasperate the peevish temper of my colleague."

"I will take your advice," said the cavalier, complacently, "and treat the Biscayan with as much respect as he may seem to deserve. Only, as it may be a long day's journey to this Zempoala, I must entreat your excellency to give orders for the instant debarkation of my horses and attendants, and permit me to follow them as soon as possible."

"This shall be instantly done," said the admiral. "In the mean while I must beg to entertain you with the sight of one of those personages who will be your companions on the journey."

CHAPTER III.

At the signal of the admiral, an officer made his appearance, received certain commands, the most agreeable of which to the young cavalier were those in reference to his own liberation, and then immediately withdrew.

"Thou wilt not see, worthy cousin," said Cavallero, "a man whom, although a base Moor and Infidel, thou shouldst regard with some sort of admiration; since, from the reports of those who brought him hither, he is endowed with a spirit and pugnacity worthy even of a Christian."

While the admiral spoke, the door of the cabin was darkened by the bodies of several men, who, at his beck, advanced, and stood full in view of the neophyte. He perceived in these, besides two or three officers of the ship, nothing more, with a single exception, than the rough figures of ordinary sailors. This exception presented itself in the bronzed visage and wildly-attired person of the Moor; and Amador almost started, when the bright eyes of the Pagan rolled from the admiral to himself in a brief but most penetrating stare. In person, the Moor was somewhat above the ordinary stature, but his limbs, though hardy and active enough, were much attenuated. His face emaciated and bony, and the long black locks falling wildly over it, gave it an appearance exceedingly haggard—a character greatly augmented by the white eyeballs flashing like stars in its almost Nubian blackness. Something perhaps was to be allowed for the effect of his uncouth and savage attire, which was composed almost entirely of skins, seemingly of dogs or wolves, a portion of which encircled his loins as a tunic, while the remainder lay, like a cape or short cloak, about his shoulders. Under this latter garment, however, was a shirt of cotton, stained with bright colours; and a kerchief of similar material glittered, not so much like a turban as a fillet, round his head. Rude sandals, strapped as high as the midleg with shreds cut from his cloak, completed the primitive costume of the barbarian.

"This fellow," said the admiral, turning from him to one who seemed as chief of the seamen, "this fellow is then the commander of that Sallee pirate you took among the Canaries?"

"Commander or not, I cannot say," said the sailor, with a shrug; "but chief varlet at the gun, as I am free to maintain; and freer was he at that same ordnance than was like to be safe for the good snow, La Encarnacion, as her ribs may yet testify. But the knave speaks Spanish; and if your excellency chooses to ask him, can tell you his rank and condition."

"No commander—no pirate!" said the Moor, with a voice whose soft and harmonious accents contrasted strangely with his rude appearance. "No commander—no pirate!" he repeated, in good Castilian; "but a poor Morisco of Fez, voyaging in a harmless trader to the Gibbel-al-Tarik."

"The Gibbel-al-Tarik," said the admiral, drily, "would have been much beholden for the new visit of an infidel."

"No commander, no pirate, no infidel!" said the Moor, earnestly; "but a poor shepherd of Fez, brought to a knowledge of the true faith, and driven from the home of his fathers for the exercise of it, to the land of his fathers' enemies."

"Moor," said the admiral, composedly, "there are three reasons why I should not believe thee: first, because thou art a Moor, and therefore born to be a liar and deceiver; secondly, because, unless God should have worked a greater miracle for the good of a besotted heathen than he often vouchsafes to prayerful Christians, there is no possibility thou couldst be converted to the faith among the sands of Barbary; and thirdly, because the fact that thou art skilful in the management of ordnance, is sufficient proof thou canst not be an ignorant shepherd of Fez, whose hands are more commonly trained to the spear and arrow, than to quoin and linstock."

"He manages them," said the sailor, "as if he had been born with them in his hands; as I have made proof, sometimes, for my amusement, during the tedium of the voyage."

"If my lord will listen to me," said the Moor, eagerly, though humbly, "I will make it apparent that I speak nothing but the truth. My father drew his first breath among the Almogavars of the desert; his son opened his eyes among the hills of Granada."

"Ha!" cried the admiral; "thou art then one of the accursed tribe of mine own land!"

"A Morisco of the Alpujarras," said the Moor, submissively, "whom, in my very early youth, it pleased my father to have baptised in the holy faith, as was the command of his most faithful and ever-blessed majesty, the King Fernando, the conqueror of the kings of Granada. This will show, my lord, that I speak the words of a Christian. As an Almogavar, I was born to be a soldier, and so trained to all arms of an Almogavar, the knife and dart, the spear and axe, the cross-bow and musket, as well as other weapons of Christians. This will show my lord how it came that I was found so skilful at the cannon."

"Thou speakest like a cunning and most honest man," said the admiral, gravely; "but all this revelation does not show me how an Almogavar of Granada became a herdsman of the desert; and, after that, how the herdsman of the desert was transformed into the gunner of a Sallee corsair, or, as thou callest her, a harmless trader, on her innocent voyage to Gibraltar."

"May it please my lord," said the Almogavar, bending for a moment his troubled eyes on the admiral, as if to resolve himself whether or not these questions were put to him in mockery, and then casting them instantly on the floor, "may it please my lord to remember, that after the fall of Granada and the subjugation of the Alpujarras, many Moors, Christian as well as Pagan, preferring rather to lament their miseries at a distance than in their own enslaved country, choose to accept the merciful permission of the king, and withdrew from the land altogether. This did I, my lord's servant and slave. I fled to the country of my father; and although there I suffered many indignities and hardships, as well as constant peril, as being suspected to be an apostate to the faith of the land, I had been content to drag out a wearisome life, but for one grief that was sharper than others."

"I will shrive thee as patiently as thy confessor," said the admiral; "but while thou art speaking the sharpest of thy calamities, it will be much proof to me of the sincerity of thy religion, if thou usest language somewhat of the briefest."

"My son," said the Moor, hurriedly, "my son, that was the lamp of my eyesight, the perfume of my nostrils, the song and music of my soul, was in great danger to be led astray, and converted back to infidelity. To save him from the contagion of heathenism, I resolved to return to Granada, where, though he might grow up to bondage, he should be free from the thrall of darkness: it was better he should be a slave than an infidel. With these thoughts and these hopes in my heart, I embarked in the Sallee trader; when it was my hard fate to be arrested in my course by these men of the Canaries."

"Thy course," said the admiral, "was none of the straightest; and how thou couldst find thy way to Gibraltar by way of the Fortunate Isles, is much more than my nautical experience can teach me to understand."

"A great storm," said the Moor, with the deepest humility, "drove us from our course; and it was the will of God, when the tempest subsided, we should find ourselves beset by two strong ships, which nothing but the fears and desperation of our captain could have tempted him to think of resisting. We fought, and were subdued; the lives of my son and myself were preserved out of the horrors of that combat. The ships were traders of the Islands, bound to these new lands; they brought us hither; where there is nothing left us but to claim the privileges of our faith, acknowledge ourselves the thrall and bondmen of his majesty the king, and entreat of my lord to send us, when it may suit his good pleasure, to our homes and our altars in Granada."

The Moor concluded his speech with a degree of eagerness approaching almost to vehemence. The admiral indifferently rejoined—"Thy name is Abdalla—?"

"Abdoul al Sidi," said the Moor, hastily. "When my father gave me up to be baptized, he called me, in token of his true devotion and humility, Esclavo de la Cruz; but in my days of darkness I was known as Abdoul al Sidi, a poor Almogavar, but descended from the ancient lords of Fez."

"Sidi Abdalla, or Sir Slave of the Cross, whichever it may please you to be called," said the admiral, coolly, "in respect to your lordly descent and most dignified title, which I think no Christian has dared to assume since the days of the Cid Rodrigo, I will, before determining how far I can make your fate agreeable to your wishes, condescend to compare your story with that of the brave sailor, master of the Encarnacion, who captured you."

"If I am to say any thing," said the master, gruffly, it will be first to pronounce this same Abdalla, or Esclavo, as he calls himself, a hypocrite and knave not to be trusted. It is true there was a great storm, which might have driven his piratical galley into the neighbourhood of the Canaries; but that he showed any extraordinary ardour to escape, as long as my consort was out of sight, is a matter not to be believed. Trusting to his skill in the management of the great *mangonneau*, with which the galley was armed, and not doubting to cripple me with some lucky ball, before I could approach him, he fell to with right goodwill; and it was not until my consort joined in the *melee* that I was able to lay him aboard. Even then, when our crews were springing on his decks, and his fellow-pirates had fled in dismay below, I saw him, this very knave Abdalla, with mine own eyes, lay match to the last charge that thundered against us; immediately after which, with a most devilish spirit of desperation, he snatched up his boy, as one would a kitten, and springing to the opposite side, was in the act of dashing himself into the sea, when he was brought down by a pistol-shot."

"I thought they would have murdered my poor Jacinto," said the Almogavar, in a low voice: "and in my desperation, desired he should rather die the easy death of the deep, than be mangled by cruel daggers."

"There was much fear of that," said the master; "for my sailors had marked him at the linstock with no great love. In faith, there were some five or six cutlasses aimed at his prostrate body; but I could not bear they should slay the boy, who lay on his breast; and therefore I commanded them to hold."

"Thou art a right worthy and noble heart!" said Amador, ardently, interrupting him: "for there is no reason a brave soldier, even in the heat of blood, and with a pagan under his foot, should strike at the life of a boy: and hadst thou done otherwise, I swear to thee, I was so much moved by the relation, I should have gone nigh to slay thee for thy barbarity!"

"And besides, senor," said the master, complacently, "I was beset with the idea, that if I preserved his life, and brought him to this land of Mexico, I might sell him at a good price as an able cannonier; such a man, as I had good reason to know, being worth the value of a dozen bloodhounds. And besides," he continued, without regarding the expression of disgust and contempt which drove the look of benevolence from the visage of the cavalier, "I had greater reason to applaud my clemency, when I discovered that the boy Jacinto, besides being a comely and very dexterous stripling, was so great a master of the Moorish lute, singing withal in a most agreeable manner, that I was well assured some noble cavalier among the invaders would not scruple, at any price, to have him for a page."

"I am a Christian! the boy is a Christian!" cried the Moor, hurriedly; "and neither of us can be sold to bondage, except at the command of his most faithful and merciful majesty, the emperor and kin; to whose gracious will and pleasure I desire, with my boy, to be rendered."

"Good Cid," said the admiral, "that is a matter wherein, if his majesty's will were certainly known, thou shouldst not have to complain of our negligence: but, under present circumstances, we must make our own judgment the representative of the royal wisdom, and dispose of thee in such manner as we may think most conducive to his majesty's interest. We are resolute thou wilt serve him better by directing the thunders of his cannon against the heathen hordes of Mexico, than by cultivating his vines and fig-trees on the hills of Granada. We must send thee to the commander Narvaez, whom, if thou please, he will doubtless advance thee to the command of a falconet, wherewith thou mayest divert many of thy Almogavar propensities for battle and bloodshed. As for the boy, it not appearing to me that the strumming of his strings, or the uplifting of his voice in ballad and redondilla, are, in any wise, necessary to the conquest of this barbarous empire, I may be able, if thou insistest upon that, to send him to Spain."

"I take my lord at his word!" said Abdoul, trembling with eagerness and anxiety; let the boy be sent to Spain—to Granada—to either of the ports Algeciras, Malaga, or Almeria; and he will find some friends there to protect his youth and inexperience, while I submit to my harder fate in Mexico."

"To Almeria?" said Amador, quickly; "I have myself some acquaintance with that town; and it may perhaps advantage thee to make me thy confidant, if there be any secret friend there thou wouldst send the boy to, or take my counsel as to what Christians may be persuaded to show him kindness."

The Moor regarded Amador for an instant with a disturbed but piercing eye. His answer was, however, prevented, by the admiral saying—"Sir Slave of the Cross, (with the consent of my very noble kinsman,) to cut short all needless discussion on this subject, I may as well inform thee, first, that if the boy be sent to Spain, it will not be to any port of thy choosing, but to such a one as may seem most fit to other persons, and which will most probably be the port of Seville; wherefrom thou canst better imagine than myself how thy boy will be helped to Granada. In the second place, as I deem it but honesty to acquaint thee, if the youth be taken from this land, he will first be sent to the excellent senor, the honourable Don Diego Velasquez, governor of Cuba, to be disposed of by him as may seem most agreeable to his judgment; and I warn thee, if the lad be an adept at the lute, as is asserted, Don Diego will find him such employment in twangling to the ladies of our brave cavaliers, as will leave it uncertain how much sooner than doomsday he will bethink him to advance the poor youth on his voyage."

"It is enough!" said the Moor, with a gloomy countenance. "God is with us; and it may be better to have the boy among the perils of death than the seductions of pleasure. Let my boy stay with me, and I am content to follow my lord's bidding."

He bowed his head upon his breast, and, at the signal of the admiral, was led away.

"Senor captain," continued Cavallero, addressing the master, who still lingered in the cabin, "I will satisfy thee for the armament thou hast brought, by acknowledgments which thou must present to the governor. What more Moors hast thou brought with thee from the galley, capable of doing service in these exigencies?"

"The father and son are all," replied the master. "The others, as I told your excellency, had fled below from the fury of my sailors. To make all sure, while rummaging about their cabin, we had fastened down the hatches. We had not picked up many things of value, before there was a sudden cry that the pirate was sinking. Whether this happened from a shot she may have received, or because the accursed runagates below had knocked a hole in her bottom, was more than was ever determined. The alarm sent us scampering to our own vessel; and in our hurry, as was natural enough, we forgot the infidels in the hold; so that, when she went down, which she did as soon as we were well clear of her, her crew went along with her. But your excellency has not told me whether I am to receive pay for Sidi and the boy?"

"I swear to heaven," said the admiral, "thou hast no more heart than thine anchor! Thou shockest me with the detail of a catastrophe, which, though affecting the lives of nothing but heathen Moors, is nevertheless both dreadful and pitiable; and yet thou dost abruptly demand of me, ' Shall I have payment for the two lives I saved?' Thou wilt have payment, if it please the governor, and not otherwise. Betake thee to thy ship: I will send thee thy warranties, and the sooner thou leavest with them the better."

The master departed, and again Amador found himself alone with the admiral.

"Cousin," said Cavallero, "I am now able to comply with your wishes. I should have been rejoiced to keep you a prisoner on board the Capitana for a few days; but I will not invite you, when I perceive you are so impatient for freedom. Your horses are doubtless at this moment rolling on the beach; your grooms are with them, either combing the sand from their manes, or scraping the sea-spots from your armour. A company of artisans, with a military escort, is on the eve of marching to the camp of Narvaez. I have given such commands as will secure you the company and friendly aidance of that escort; in addition to which, I will immediately send after you a trusty officer with despatches concerning yourself, to the general, and recommendations to him to assist you in joining your kinsman, the Knight Calavar, without delay. You will easily reach Zempoala by nightfall. I beseech you to salute the general with courtesy; and to-morrow you will be in the arms of your leader."

"I am so overjoyed," said the cavalier, "at the thought of once more bestriding my poor Fogoso, and exchanging the stupid pitching of a ship for the bound of his gallop and curvet, that I know not how I can do otherwise than treat the Biscayan with urbanity."

"A barge is ready to conduct you to the shore," continued the admiral, leading the young soldier to the side of the vessel. I pray Heaven to give you a prosperous journey, and to carry you with as much safety as honour through the weapons of the heathen multitude. Make my devoirs to his noble valour, the good knight of Rhodes; and say to the Senor Cortes, that though fate has arrayed me against him as an enemy, I cannot forget the friendship of our past lives. Nay," continued Cavallero, with emphasis, "tell him, that though it does not become me, as an officer commissioned by Velasquez, to hold any communications with him excepting those of simple form and civility, I shall be well pleased when Heaven has removed the obstruction, and left me at liberty to meet him with full friendship and confidence. This salutation," said the admiral, significantly, "there is no reason thou shouldst impart to Narvaez; for he is distrustful and suspicious to that degree, that, I do not doubt, he would torture its harmlessness into a matured treason."

"I will do your bidding," said Amador, blithely, "both to the Biscayan and the cavalier of Medellin; and now, with a thousand acknowledgments for your favour and assistance, and as many wishes for your weal and comfort, I bid you the farewell of a kinsman and true friend."

And so saying, and heartily shaking the hand of his excellency, the young cavalier sprang into the boat, and was soon wafted to the beach.

CHAPTER IV.

The rapture with which Don Amador de Leste exchanged the confined decks of the caravel for the boundless sands of Ulua, and these again for the back of his impatient steed, was fully as great as he had promised himself. Profound was his joy to find the demon of ennui, which had beset the cribbed and confined charger as sorely as the cabined master, flying from his dilated nostrils, and giving place to the mettlesome ardour which had won him the title of the Fiery. The neigh that he sent forth was like the welcome of the battle; the fire that flashed in his eye was bright as the red reflection of a banner; and when he reared up under his rider, it was as if to paw down the opposition of crouching spearmen. A few snuffs of the morning breeze, a few bounds over the sandy hillocks, and the beast that had pined in stupefaction, in a narrow stall on the sea, was converted into an animal fit for the seat of a warrior.

The cavalier galloped about for a few moments, hile his attendants made their preparations for the journey. Then returning, like a thoughtful leader, to inquire into their welfare, he beheld them with great satisfaction, both horse and man, in good condition to commence their adventurous campaign.

The elder of his followers was a personage of years and gravity; a mass of grizzled locks fell from under his iron skull-cap, and a shaggy beard of the same reverend hue ornamented his cheeks and throat. He had seen long and sharp service, for besides the many scars that marked his swarthy visage, one of which, from its livid hue, seemed to have been won in recent combat, a sabre cut, extending over his left cheek and brow, had darkened the sinister eye for ever. But his frame, though somewhat short and squat, was robust and even gigantic in proportions; and the muscles springing under the narrow cuishes, which, together with a heavy breast-plate, made nearly the whole of his defensive armour, did not seem less of iron than their covering. He was truly a man-at-arms worthy to follow at the heels of a valiant cavalier.

The second attendant, though armed with little more care than the former, had contrived, by the judicious distribution of riband-knots and sashes about his person, to assume a more gallant appearance: and in addition, he had the smoother features and gayer looks of youth. Both were provided with horses, strong and not inactive; and both, as Amador returned, were busily engaged in disposing the mails and accoutrements of the cavalier about the bulky loins of their animals.

"Hearken, Lazaro, thou varlet, that flingest my mailed shirt over thy crupper, as if it were a vile horse-cloth," he cried, to the younger follower, "have more care what thou art doing. Give my helmet to Baltasar, and let him sling it, with my buckler, over his broad shoulders. I will not intrust thee with such matters; nor by'r lady, with my pistols neither."

"If I can make bold to speak," said Baltasar, bending his eye bluffly, and with a sort of rude affection, on his young lord, "I can advise a way to dispose of both casque and buckler, more agreeably and usefully than on the back of either Lazaro or myself."

"Thou meanest upon mine own, no doubt," said Amador: "I have ever found thee fonder of carrying the arms of a dead foeman than of a living master, though it were the Knight Calavar himself."

"That is very true," said the veteran, chuckling grimly at the compliment disguised in the sarcasm. "I am never loath to do such duty; because, then, my conscience tells me I am bearing arms which can no longer be of use to their owner."

"And thou desirest now to intimate, that, if I were arrayed in my harness, I might put it to some use?"

"*Quien sabe!* who knows," said Baltasar, looking around him with an earnest eye. "We are now in a strange land, possessed by barbarians, who are good at spear and bow, and fonder of fighting from an ambuscado than on an open field; and with no true companions that I can see, to look that they be not lurking among yonder woodlands, some of which, I take it for granted, we have to pass. I should grieve sorely to see an arrow, even in a boy's hand, aimed at your honour's present hauberk of cloth and velvet.'

"Well, thy wisdom will not perish for want of utterance," said Amador: "and in very truth, I must own, it has sometimes stood me in good stead. I will therefore relieve thee of thy burthen, and Lazaro shall hang it to my own shoulders."

He descended, and the linked surcoat soon invested his person.

"I will also presume to recommend your honour to have these snap-dragons hung to your saddle-bow," said Baltasar, extending the rude and ponderous pistols—weapons then scarcely creeping into notice, but within twenty years not uncommon in the hands of horsemen: "for if it should come to pass, that some cut-throat Pagan should discharge a missile at us from the bushes, it will doubtless afford your honour much satisfaction to shoot him dead on the spot—a punishment that would not be so certain with the weapons in my own hands, or in Lazaro's. And before I could bring my cross-bow from my back, it is possible the knave might have another opportunity to do us mischief."

"In this matter also," said Amador, good-humouredly, "I will follow thy instructions. But, I give thee warning, there is something in the feeling of my hauberk under this raging sun, that admonishes me how soon my brain would seeth, as in a stew-pan, under the cover of a steel helmet. Wherefore I will have thee carry in thine own hands, until from the change of atmosphere or the appearance of an enemy, I may see fit to alter my resolution."

"I have ever found," said Baltasar, with the pertinacity of age, and, perhaps, of a favourite, "that, under a broiling sun, a well-polished casque of metal is something cooler than a cloth cap; a fact, the reason for which I do not myself understand, and which I should esteem too marvellous for belief, had I not oft-times put it to the proof."

"There is even much truth in what thou art saying," quoth the cavalier, "and I have perhaps philosophy enough to explain the marvel to thee, but that I know philosophy is not much to thy liking. There must be a cold head, however, under the bright cap; otherwise, and with a brain as inflammable as my own, I am very well convinced that bright steel would be just as ignitible as dull iron." And so saying, he again bestrode the champing Fogoso.

"It must be as your honour says," muttered the man-at-arms. "But, as we are all as well prepared now to begin our journey as we will be to-morrow, I would fain know of your favour whither lies our path, or where lags the jackanapes that is to guide us? I heard some talk in the carevel of a great troop of horse and foot, that was to accompany us; but, unless it may have been the herd of vagabonds, who, a full hour since, took up their march along the sands, I know not where to look for them among these few tinkers and sailors that are strolling yonder among the huts of bamboo.'

"I have much reliance on the friendship and courtesy of my cousin, the admiral," said Amador, hastily; "but I must confess, that, saving the appearance of yonder bridled horse, (which may be in waiting for the officer he told me of,) it looks very much, now, as if he had left me to mine own guidance. Nay, I wrong the worthy senor," he cried, quickly, as, turning with some doubt and indignation towards the ship, he beheld a boat leave her, and approach the shore with all the speed of oars; "the guide he promised me is, without doubt in that barge; and the bridled horse, which, as I can perceive, even at this distance, is none of the bravest, is the beast whereon he will keep us company.'

As Amador conjectured, the boat contained his promised companion, who instantly sprang upon the beach, and on the caparisoned animal, and in a few moments was at the side of the cavalier. He was young and handsome, an adult in stature, but scarcely a man in deportment, for as he removed his cap to make the obeisance of an inferior, there was a strong tincture of confusion and trepidation in his countenance. This was perhaps owing, in part, to a consciousness of having merited a reprimand for over delay, and in part also to his suddenly finding himself confronted with so warlike a personage as the neophyte. Amador of the caravel was a different person from Amador armed and mounted: and, indeed, as he sat on his noble bay, mailed and sworded, and with two goodly armsmen at his back, he was such a martial figure as might have moved an older messenger to reverence.

"Senor Caballero," said the youth, with a stammering voice, "my master and patron, the admiral, has appointed me, his secretary, to be your guide to the Indian city, Zempoala; and I have to beg your pardon, if, waiting for the letters wherewith it was his excellency's will to charge me, and to make some needful preparation of my own, I have detained your favour somewhat longer than was agreeable."

"I am ever bound to thank his excellency," said Amador; "and, as I well suppose, your own preparations had some weighty relation to the business you have in charge, I will not take it upon me to express any dissatisfaction with your delay."

"In truth," said the secretary, ingenuously, "I was loath to depart without such armour about me as should beseem the attendant of a true cavalier; in the fitting of which I fell into some perplexity, as not finding a corselet that did not, in some manner, incommode my ribs; and besides, the sabres were all so unwieldy and rough about the hilts, I was in some despair I should never find one to my liking."

"Senor Secretario," said Amador, with a smile of good-humoured contempt, surveying the youth, and observing the cuirass chosen with no discretion, and donned without skill, "I am of opinion, that in the company of myself and my attendants, you will find no occasion for such troublesome apparel; and it is my advice, grounded on your admission of inexperience in such matters, that, should we, on our march, be beset by any enemies, you take post instantly behind my veteran, Baltasar, whose broad breast will stand you in greater stead than your ill-chosen cuirass, and whose arm will do you better service than the sabre in your own hands."

"Senor," said the youth, colouring, "I am no soldier nor cavalier; I have ever had my breast more bruised by the scribe's table than the weight of a breast-plate, and my fingers have heretofore known more of the goose-quill than the sword. Nevertheless I am both willing and desirous to be placed where the knowledge of weapons may be obtained, and to encounter such risks as are the helpers to knowledge. It was from no lack of beseeching on mine own part, that his excellency has heretofore denied me permission to try my fate among the cavaliers ashore; nor should I have hoped that pleasure so early, but that I found his excellency was bent to do you honour, by making a confidential servant your attendant, and was therefore easily persuaded to give me the opportunity I have so long coveted, of looking a little into the strange sights of this marvellous land."

"I am to understand, then," said Amador, gravely, "that his excellency, the admiral, has intrusted the charge of guiding me to Zempoala, to an individual who has never before put foot on the wilderness that divides us from it?"

"It is true, senor," said the secretary, "that I have never been to Zempoala. But I hope your favour will not doubt me for that reason, nor take offence at the admiral. I am enjoined to conduct you to the reinforcement that set out an hour ago. Its tracks are plain enough along the beach; and as it is composed principally of footmen, there is no doubt we will overtake it before another hour has elapsed. I am confident I can lead your favour without difficulty to the party, among which are guides well acquainted with the country.

"Let us set out then, in Heaven's name," said the cavalier: "the day is wasting apace; the sun climbs high in the vault, and the sooner we are sheltered from its fury among some of yonder distant forests, the better will it be for us. St. John be our guide, and the Holy Virgin favour us. —Amen! Let us depart."

CHAPTER V.

As the secretary anticipated, the tracts of the reinforcement were plainly discernible over the sandy downs and by the margins of the pestilent fens, which gave an air of desolation to this part of the Mexican coast, not much relieved by an occasional clump of palms, nor by the spectacle, here and there disclosed, of the broad ocean blackening among the low islets; though the hazy and verdant ramparts which stretched between these burning deserts and the imagined paradises of the interior, ever presented a field of refreshment and interest to the eyes of the travellers. The novelty of their situation, felt more or less intensely by all, was exciting: and many a dream of barbaric monarchs reposing on thrones of gold and emeralds, and canopied by flowers and feathers, of dusky armies deploying among green valleys and on the borders of fair lakes,—and perhaps of themselves doing the work of heroes among these mystic multitudes,—wandered through their over-troubled fancies.

Such visions flitted over the brain of Amador, but mingled with others, with which the past had more to do than the present; for, despite the eager longing with which he looked forward to a meeting with his good knight and kinsman, and notwithstanding his impatient ardour to gaze with his own eyes upon those scenes which were filling the minds of men with wonder, he looked back from a sandhill to the distant ships, and sighed, as in an instant of time his soul was borne from them, over the broad surges, to the pleasant hills of Spain.

But with the view of the squadron vanished his memory and his melancholy: the narrow belt of sand-hills along the coast had been exchanged for the first zone of vegetation; the mimosa afforded its shade; the breeze and the paroquet chattered together on its top; and when he came, at last, to journey among the shadows of a forest, rich in magnificent and unknown trees and plants, with here a lagoon fringed with stately ceibas (the cotton-wood trees of Mexico) and gigantic canes, and there a water-course murmuring among palms and other tropical trees, he gave himself up to a complacent rapture. He remarked with satisfaction the bright plumage of water-fowl,— the egret, the pelican, the heron, and sometimes the flamingo, sporting among the pools; gazed with wonder after the little picaflor, or humming bird, darting, like a sunbeam, from flower to flower; with still greater admiration listened to the song of the calandra and the cardinal, and to the magical *centzontli*,—the hundred-tongued,—as it caught and repeated, as if with a thousand voices, the thousand roundelays of other songsters scattered among the boughs; and it was not until the notes of a trumpet, swelling suddenly in the distance, invaded his reveries, that he roused from the voluptuous intoxication of such a scene.

"It is the trumpet of the soldiers, senor!" cried the secretary, joyously; "and it rejoices me much, for I know not how much longer I could have followed their obscure tracks through this forest. And besides, I find, as I must in honesty confess, I have in me so little of the skill of a leader, that I would gladly submit to be led myself, especially by your worship, though it were to follow you to battle as an humble esquire."

"I must commend your spirit, Senor Lorenzo Fabueno," (for so the secretary had called himself,) "though I must needs believe your inexperience in all matters of war might render such an attempt exceedingly difficult, if not altogether impossible."

"Senor," said the secretary, eagerly, "I have the wish, and doubtless the ability, in course of time, to learn all the duties, and to acquire some of the skill, of a soldier; and under so noble a leader as your favour, I am sure I should advance much faster than ever I did in the learning of a clerk. And, in addition to the little service I might render with my sword, I have such skill with the pen as might be of good use to your honour."

"I have no certain assurance," said Amador, "that I shall have any occasion to use my own sword; it is utterly beyond my imagination to discover to what use I could put the inkhorn of a secretary; and finally, I know not how the course of events in these deserts may require me to add

to the number of my associates. Nevertheless, Senor Lorenzo, if it be the wish of his excellency the admiral, that his secretary should be transformed into a soldier, I see not how I can refuse to give my assistance to the conversion."

"I know not why I should be dungeoned in a ship's cabin," said Lorenzo, with a sort of petulance, "when other youths are roaming at liberty among these brave hills; and gnawing a quill with disgust, when all my old schoolmates are carving out reputation with more manly implements. I am sure I was not born to slave for ever at the desk."

"This may be all true, as, in my opinion, it is both natural and reasonable," said Amador, with gravity; "for it seems to me, man was brought into the world for a nobler purpose than to scribble on paper. Yet you have not made it apparent that the admiral's wishes are in this matter consonant with your own."

"I know not that they are," replied the secretary, "but, as I now feel myself at liberty with both horse and sword, I cannot help feeling that they ought to be. How I can ever have the heart to return to my bondage again, is more than I can tell; and I am confident, if it were your favour's desire he should grant me permission to follow you through this land, he would make no opposition, the more particularly that your favour is his kinsman."

"I doubt whether the consent would not be wrung from his courtesy; and I cannot well agree to rob him of one who may be a valuable servant. Neither, under such circumstances, can I think of encouraging you in your ardour, or recommending you, at present, to change your pursuits, for which you are better fitted than for mine. Nay," said the cavalier, good-naturedly, observing the chagrin of the youth, "if you are resolutely bent on your purpose, it is my advice you make your petitions to his excellency; and when he has granted them, as doubtless he will, you can, with a free mind, seek the patronage of some cavalier engaged in these armies of invasion. Hark! the trumpet sounds louder and nearer, and, by my faith, I see on yonder rising ground the bodies of men and the glimmer of weapons! Spur thy horse a little (and, I pr'ythee, fling thy shoulders a jot backwards, sitting erect and at ease; for I promise thee, this manner of riding, as if thou wouldst presently be hugging at thy nag's neck, is neither becoming nor advantageous); spur me up a little, and we will join company with them.

The long and straggling train with which the travellers caught up, just as it issued from the forest upon an open tract of low sandy hills and plains, was composed of motley materials. A few mounted men, who, by their armour and bustling activity, seemed the leaders and commanders, were scattered among a horde of footmen, a portion of whom were armed and ranked as a company of military, but the greater part being the ordinary native labourers, who served the office of mules, and bore on their backs the burdens of the invaders. Some five or six score of these swarthy creatures, followed by a dozen Castilian crossbowmen and a single horseman, brought up the rear. They stalked in a line one after another, each bending to his burden; and in their uniformity of equipment, gait, muscular figures, and solemn visages, added not a little to the singularity of the spectacle. A narrow strip of some vegetable texture, so rude and coarse that it seemed rather a mat than a cloth, was wrapped round the loins of each, leaving their strong and tawny bodies otherwise naked. No sandal protected their soles from the heated soil ; and no covering, save only the long and matted locks swinging about their countenances, defended their heads from the scorching sun. A huge basket of cane, the *pella-calli*, or *pctaca* of the Spaniards, carelessly covered with matting, and evidently well charged with military stores and provisions, weighed upon the shoulders of each, while it was connected by a broad strap to the forehead. Thus burthened, however, and thus exposed to a temperature which, as the day advanced, seemed, in the open plains, nearly intolerable to their Christian companions, they strode on with a slow but vigorous step, each bearing a knot of gay flowers or of brilliant feathers, wherewith he defended his face from insects, and perhaps, occasionally, his eyes, from the dazzling reflection of the soil. These were *Tlamémé*, or carriers of Mexico.

The eye of Amador, though at first attracted by this singular train, dwelt with more surprise and curiosity on the crossbowmen, who were sweltering, in common with nearly every Christian of the party, under the thick and uncouth investment of the *escaupil*, a sort of armour which the invaders of Mexico had not disdained to borrow from their despised enemies. This consisted of nothing more than garments of woollen or cotton cloth, cut as much after the fashions of Spain as was possible, quilted so thickly with cotton as to be able to resist the arrowheads and lancepoints of the Indians ; which virtue, added to the facility with which it could be obtained and adapted to every part of the body, gave the escaupil a decided preference over the few pieces of iron mail which the poverty of the combatants denied them the power of extending to the whole frame. In truth, so common had become this armour, that there were few among the cavaliers of the conquest, except those leaders who despised so unknightly and so unsightly an ttire, who were provided with any other. Nevertheless many distinguished captains concealed garments of this material under their iron armour, and the common soldiers of Cortes, after long experience, had fallen upon the plan of quilting it in pieces imitative of morions and breast-plates, which were far from being uncouth or unwieldy. But its efficacy, though strongly explained and urged by the secretary Fabueno, could not blind Don Amador to its ungainliness, as seen in the fashions of raw recruits ; and even the solemn gravity of Baltasar was changed to a grin of ineffable derision, and the good-humoured vivacity of Lazaro to a laugh of contempt, when the secretary advised the cavalier to provide his followers with such coats of mail.

"What thinkest thou, Lazaro, rogue?" said Don Amador, merrily. "Thou wert but a bitter groaner over the only cut it was ever thy good hap to meet : and that was by a fair and courteous pistol-shot, which hath something of an oily way about it ; whereas these infidel flints and hard woods gash as painfully as an oyster-shell. What sayest thou ? Shall I give thee an escaupil, to save thee from new lamentation ?"

"May your honour live a thousand years !" said the serving-man. "The tortoise to his shell, the Turk to his turban · Heaven never thrust a hornet into the cocoon of a caterpillar, nor a lion into a sheep's skin. Wherefore I will keep my sting and my claws free from the cotton bags ; the only merit of which is, that when a man is wounded in them he has lint ever ready at his fingers."

"For my part," said Baltasar, "I am, in this matter, much of Lazaro's way of thinking. Howsoever, please your favour, when I see these lubberly lumps fight more courageously than myself in my iron trifles, I will straightway change my mind on the subject."

"Hold thy tongue, then," said the cavalier, "lest thou give offence to some of these worthy cotton-coats, who have, in no manner, furnished thee with cause for a quarrel."

The cavalier rode on, followed closely by his attendants, courteously returning the salutations which were every where rendered to his apparent rank and martial appearance by the Spanish portion of the train ; though not even the glitter of his mail, the proud tramp of his war-horse, nor the stout appearance of his followers, drew a glance from the Tlamémé. The dull apathy which the oppression of ages has flung over the spirits of Mexicans at the present epoch, had already been instilled into the hearts of this class of natives, which with some others, under the prevalence of the common feudalism of barbarians, were little better than bondmen. He rode slowly by them, admiring the sinewy bulk of their limbs, and the ease with which they moved under their heavy burdens.

The van of the train was formed by a score of footmen, all arrayed in the escaupil, and all, with the exception of some five or six, who bore firelocks, armed with sword and spear. A cavalier of goodly presence, and well mounted, rode at their head ; and Amador, thinking he perceived in him the tokens of gentle blood and manners, pressed forward to salute him. The ringing of Fogoso's heels arrested the attention of the leader, who, turning round and beholding the gallant array of the stranger, instantly returned upon his path, and met him with many courteous expressions. At the very moment of meeting, Amador's eye was attracted by a figure, which, in making way for the steed of the leader, had wellnigh been trodden under the hoofs of his own ; and in which, when removed from this peril, he instantly remarked the spare person and haggard countenance of the Moor. Holding fast the hand of the Almogavar, and indeed, for an instant while the danger lasted, wrapped anxiously in his arms, was a boy, whose youth and terror might have won a second notice, had not the salutation of the officer immediately occupied his attention.

"The Senor Amador de Leste," said he—"Thou varlet of an infidel, I will strike thee with my lance!' (This menacing objurgation was addressed to the Moor, at the moment when, most endangered, he wavered with his boy between the horses.) "The Senor Amador de Leste," he continued, as the Moor, recovering himself, cowered away, "will not be surprised to find his coming expected, and his presence welcomed, by the General Narvaez, or by his excellency's humble friend and captain, Juan Salvatierra."

"Senor Salvatierra, I give you good thanks," replied Amador ; "and although I know not what avant-courier has proclaimed the approach of so obscure an individual as myself, I will not, for that reason, receive your courtesy less gratefully."

"I have with me here," said Savatierra, with a stately condescension, "several of your fellow-voyagers of the caravel ; among whom it would have been strange indeed if any had forgotten the name of so honourable a companion."

"Those cavaliers of the caravel," said Amador, drily, "who condescend to claim me as a companion, do me thereby a greater honour than I am desirous to do myself. My companions are, as you may see, my two men-at-arms; to which we will at present add the young Senor Fabueno, whom, as the secretary of his excellency the Admiral Cavallero, I am not indisposed to acknowledge."

There was something in the tone of the haughty and even arrogant neophyte, that might have nettled his new friend; but its only effect, beside bringing a colour upon his rather pallid cheeks, was to rob his suavity of somewhat of its loftiness.

"It is for hidalgos and cavaliers of knightly orders," he said, "and not for ignoble adventurers, to aspire to the fellowship of a valiant knight of San Juan."

"I am no knight of San Juan," said Amador, "but a simple novice, who may one day claim admission to the illustrious order (by right of birth) or not, as it may please the destinies and mine own humour. Nevertheless, I have much pleasure to speak of the order and its valiant brothers, at every opportunity, and at the present moment I am moved to ask your favour, as relying much on your knowledge, what tidings have been last had of the good Knight Calavar, an eminent branch of that most lordly, though thunder-stricken, stock."

"Concerning the Knight of Calavar," said Salvatierra, blandly, "it is my grief to assure you that his madness—"

"Call it his melancholy, or his humour!" said Amador, sternly; "and let it be some mitigation to your surprise, if my correction sound like a rebuke, to know that I am his kinsman."

Again did the colour mount in the cheeks of the cavalier, and again did his courtesy, or his discretion, get the better of the impulse that raised it.

"The kinsman of that valiant and renowned gentleman," he said, politely, "shall command me to any epithet he chooses. The Senor De Leste will doubtless lament to hear that his kinsman, with an eccentricity scarce worthy his high birth and knightly dignity, still stoops to be the follower of an inferior and rebel, the outcast and proclaimed outlaw, Hernan Cortes."

"As far as my own judgment is concerned in this matter, Senor Caballero," said Amador, coolly, "I very much doubt whether I shall lament that circumstance at all. The Knight Calavar will not disparage his dignity or his profession, by choosing to serve where a little-minded man might covet to command. Such a condescension in him, besides being a new proof of magnanimity and fidelity to his vows, whereby he is sworn never to make peace with the infidel, is only an evidence to me that the Cavalier Cortes, whom you call a rebel and outlaw, must be a man worthy of much more respectful appellations; as indeed, methinks, your own reflections should show you must be the due of any associate of the Knight of Calavar."

The unaffected surprise, and even consternation, with which the follower of Narvaez heard the neophyte thus speak of his leader's enemy, might perhaps have urged Amador to the utterance of commendations still more unequivocal, had not his eye at that moment been caught by the shadow on the sand of a man striding nearer to the flanks of Fogoso than he had supposed any footman to be. His own position was near the side of the company of musketeers and spearmen mentioned before; his

followers, not being willing to obtrude upon the privacy of the cavaliers, had fallen a little back; and the Morisco, as he took it for granted, was lagging some distance behind. His surprise was therefore not a little excited, when looking round, he beheld the Almogavar so close at his side as to be able to overhear all that was said, and drinking his words with an expression of the intensest interest.

"Son of a dog!" cried Salvatierra, who beheld him at the same time, and who was not unwilling to vent some of the gall that Amador had raised in his bosom upon so legitimate an object,—"I will see if I cannot teach thee how to thrust thyself among soldiers and hidalgos!"

"Softly, Senor Caballero!" cried Amador, observing the captain raising his lance; "strike not Abdalla; for I have it in my power to inform you, that, although in some sense your prisoner, and to the eye of a stranger, a most helpless and wretched varlet, he has shown himself to be possessed of a spirit so worthy of respect, that you will do yourself foul shame to strike him."

The lance of the cavalier was turned away from the shrinking Moor.

"Don Amador de Leste shall command my weapon, whether it be to smite or to spare," said Salvatierra, smothering the rage which every word and action of the neophyte seemed fated to inspire, and advancing to the head of the train.

"Harkee, Sidi Abdalla," continued Amador, beckoning complacently to the retiring Morisco, "it is not in my nature to see indignity of any kind heaped upon a man who hath not the power of vengeance, and especially a man who hath in him the virtue of courage, without raising a hand in his defence."

"My lord speaks the truth," said Abdoul, with a subdued voice: "the Almogavar hath not the power of vengeance: the strong man may strike him, the proud may trample, and he cannot resist; the cavalier may wound with the lance, the soldier may smite with the unthonged bow—it is all one; his head is bare, his breast open, his hand empty—he can neither resist nor avenge."

"By St. John of Jerusalem," said the cavalier, warmly, moved to a stronger feeling for the friendless Morisco, "I remember, as was confessed by that beast of a Canary captain, that when thine enemies were on thy decks, and thy friends fled from thy side (for which they deserved to sink to the bottom, as they did), thou hadst the courage to discharge thy maugonneau into the victorious trader; for which reason chiefly, partly because thou hast avowed thyself a Christian proselyte, I will take it upon me, as far as it may be in my power, to be thy protector and champion."

"My lord is good," said the Moor, bending his head low on his breast; "and in the day of my death I will not forget his benevolence. The Almogavar was born to grief; trouble came to him at his first hour; his first breath was the sigh of Granada, his first cry was mingled with the groans of his enslaved people, his first look was on the tears of his father. Sorrow came in youth, anguish in manhood, and misery is in the footsteps of years. My lord is great and powerful; he protects me from the blow of a spear. He can save me from a grief that strikes deeper than a thousand spears!"

"As I am a true gentleman and Christian," said Amador, "I will hold to my word, to give thee protection and aid, as far as my power lies."

"The feeble boy that totters over these scorching sands" said the Moor, raising his eyes wistfully to the cavalier, and turning them for an instant with a look of unspeakable wildness to his son. The cavalier looked back, in that momentary pause, and beheld the young Morisco. He seemed a boy of not more than twelve years. The soldier judged only from his stature, for a garment of escaupil of unusual thickness completely invested and concealed his figure; while his face drooping, as if from weariness, on his breast, was hidden by a cap slouching in disorder, and by long ringlets that fell in childish profusion over his shoulders.

"The boy!" continued Abdalla, turning again to the neophyte, and raising his clasped hands as if in supplication. "Is it fit his tender years should be passed among the horrors of a camp? among the dangers of a wild war? among the vices and contaminations of a brutal soldiery? If it were possible,"—and here the voice of the Almogavar trembled with eagerness—"if it were possible that boy could be sent to Granada,—nay, to Barbary,—any where, where, for his father's sake, he should be granted a refuge and asylum, then might the curse be uttered, the blow struck, and Abdoul, receiving it as the payment of his debt, would not call upon his lord for vengeance."

"Thou heardest from the admiral," said Amador, "how impossible would be the gratification of such a wish; since even were he parted from this shore, it rests with another, who I can, upon mine own knowledge, assure thee, is not likely to help him on his way, whether he shall not waste his days among the planters of the islands, who, according to common report, are not a whit less wild and debauched than their friends here in Mexico."

"God is just!" cried the Moor, clasping his hands in despair.

"Nevertheless," continued Amador, "I will not fail to make thy petition, backed with my own respect, to the Senor Narvaez; and at the worst, it is not improbable some good cavalier may be found who will consent to receive him as a page, and treat him with kindness."

"God is just!" reiterated the Moor, with a gloomy sorrow; "and the arrow of the savage may save him from the wrong of the Christian."

"I tell thee again," said Amador, "I will not forget to do my best for his welfare, at the first opportunity. But tell me, Abdalla"—The Morisco was dropping behind: he returned—"I had forgotten to ask thee a question for which I first called thee. I was speaking to this hot-tempered captain of the Knight Calavar—By Heaven! it was thus I saw thine eyes sparkle before! Is there any magic in the name, that it should move thee to such emotion?"

"The Knight Calavar," said the Morisco, "was among the conquerors of the Alpujarras; and how can I hear his name, and not bethink me of the black day of my country? His name is in our Moorish ballads; and when the orphan sings them, he mourns over the fate of his father."

"That the Knight Calavar did good service among those rebellious mountaineers, I can well believe," said the cavalier, hastily; "but that he did not temper his valour with mercy, is an assertion which no man can make to me with perfect safety. As to those ballads of which you speak, I am not certain if they be not the invention of some devilish magician, opposed to honourable war and glory; since it is their sole purpose to keep one thinking of certain sorrowful particulars, that may be a consequence of victory and conquest, such as tearful widows and destitute orphans; and I must declare, for my own part, such is the mischievous tendency of these

madrigals, that sometimes, after hearing them, I have had my imagination so enchanted, as to look with disgust at war, and almost to lament that I ever had struck at the life of a human being. I shall like well to have thy boy to sing to me; but, as I will tell him beforehand, it must be of love-lorn knights and of knights going to battle and never about widows and orphans?"

CHAPTER VI.

At midday, the squadron, after having accomplished more than half the journey, halted for rest and refreshment on the banks of a little river, under the shade of pleasant trees. The Tlamémé threw down their bundles, and, apart from the rest, betook themselves to their frugal meal. A plaintain, a cake of maize, or a morsel of some of the nameless but delicious fruits of the clime, perhaps growing at their side, prepared them for the enjoyment of slumber; while the Spaniards, grouped among the trees, added to this simple repast the more substantial luxury of the *tasajo*, or jerked beef of the islands.

As for the Cavalier De Leste, not having bethought him to give orders for the preparation of such needful munitions, he was glad to accept the invitation of the Captain Salvatierra to share his meal; and this he did the more readily, that, having entered into farther conversation with the leader, after the affair of the lance, it was the good fortune of this gentleman to stumble upon no more offensive topics. In addition to this, he observed, with great satisfaction, that Salvatierra, preserving among his subalterns the stateliness which he had veiled to the neophyte, did not mean to trouble him with their society; and it was only at his express desire that the secretary Fabueno was admitted to partake of their repast. The excellent taste of the worthy commander, or perhaps the wisdom of his attendants, several of whom, both Christian and Pagan, being in constant waiting, gave him an appearance of great rank and importance, had provided a stock of food, which, in variety and quantity, might have satisfied the hunger of half the squadron. Here, besides the heavenly anana, the grateful manioc, and other fruits and roots with which the cavalier had become acquainted in the islands, he was introduced to the royal chirimoya, the zapote, and other fruits as new as they were delicious. But, above all these delights with which Providence has so bountifully enriched the lands of Mexico, did Don Amador admire the appearance of certain fowls, which, though neither reeking nor smoking with their savoury juices, but drawn cold from their covering of green leaves, were of so agreeable a character as to fill his mind with transport."

"Either this land is the very paradise of earth!" said he, "or, Senor Salvatierra, you have the most goodly purveyors among your household that ever loaded the table of man. I will be much beholden to your favour to know the name of this fowl I am eating, which, from its bulk, one might esteem a goose, but which, I am sure, is no such contemptible creature."

"That," said the leader, "is a sort of great pheasant, the name of which I have not yet schooled my organs to pronounce, but which, being taken among the hills and trained in the cottages of the Indians, becomes as familiar and loving as a dog; and is therefore always ready when its master is hungry.

"By my life, then," said Amador, "I am loath to eat it; for it seems to me, the creature that loves us is more worthy to be consecrated in the heart, than immolated to the cravings of the stomach. I will therefore desire to know something of that other featherless monster at your elbow, previous to determining upon its fitness for mastication."

"Your favour need entertain no scruples about this bird," said the captain; "for although domesticated, and kept by the Indians about their houses in great flocks, it hath too much affection for itself to trouble itself much about its master. It is a kind of peacock, and without possessing any of the resplendent beauty of that animal, it is endowed with all its vanity and pride; so that, when strutting about with its shaven head and long-gobbeted beard, its feathers ruffled in a majestic self-conceit, our soldiers have sometimes, for want of a better name, called it *el Turco*."

"A better name could not have been invented," said the neophyte; "for if it be true, as is sometimes asserted by those who know better than myself, that heretics and infidels are the food of the devil, I know no morsel should be more agreeable to his appetite than one of those same Pagans that give name to his foolish and savoury creature."

The thoughts of Amador, as he sat testing the merits of the noble fowl, which is one among the many blessings America, in after days, scattered over the whole world, wandered from Mexico to Rhodes, from the peaceful enjoyment of his dinner to the uproar and horror of a siege, from a dead fowl to the turbaned Turk; and then, by a similar vagary, jumped at once from the magnificent infidel to the poor Morisco, who had lately trod the desert at his side. As the image of Abdoul al Sidi entered his brain, he looked round and beheld the proselyte sitting with his boy in the shadow of a palm, remote from the rest; and a pang smote him, as he perceived that, among the scores who sat glutting their appetites around, not one had dropped a morsel of food into the hands of the Almogavar or his child.

"Harkee, Lazaro, thou gluttonous villain!" he cried, with a voice that instantly brought the follower, staring, to his side; "dost thou feed like a pelican, and yet refuse to share thy meal, as a pelican would, with a helpless fellow of thy race? Take me this lump of a Turk to Sidi Abdalla, and bid him feed his boy."

"I will suggest to your favour," said the Captain Salvatierra, with a grin, "that Lazaro be directed to bring the urchin hither with his lute, of which it is said he is no mean master; and before he eats he shall sing us a song, which, thus, he will doubtless execute with more perfection than after he has gorged himself into stupidity or the asthma."

"I agree to that with all my heart," said the neophyte. "The boy can sing while we are eating, provided the poor fellow be not too hungry."

Lazaro strode to the Moriscos; and in an instant, as they rose, Amador beheld the Sidi take the instrument from his own back where he had carried it, and put it into the hands of his offspring. The boy received it, and, as Amador thought, removed the gay covering with a faltering hand. Nevertheless, in a few moments, this preparation was accomplished, and, with Abdalla, the stripling stood trembling from weariness or timidity at the side of the group.

"Moor," said Salvatierra, before Amador had commenced his benevolent greeting, "the noble and valiant cavalier hath charitably commanded thou shouldst eat thy dinner at our feet; which, whilst thou art doing, we will expect thy lad to entertain us with such sample of his skill in luting and singing as may make our own repast more agreeable."

"That is, if the boy be not too hungry," said the good-natured neophyte. "I should blush to owe my pleasures to any torments of his own, however slight; and (as I know by some little famine wherewith we were afflicted at Rhodes), there is no more intolerable anguish with which one can be cursed, than this same unhumoured appetite."

"Jacinto will sing to my lord," said the Almogavar, submissively.

But Jacinto was seized with such a fit of trembling, as seemed for a time to leave him incapable; and when, at last, he had sufficiently subdued his terror, to begin tuning his instrument, he did it with so slow and so hesitating a hand, that Salvatierra lost patience, and reproved him harshly and violently.

It happened, unluckily for the young Moor, that, at that moment, the eye of Amador wandered to Fogoso, and beheld him wallowing with more of the spirit of a yeoman's hog than a warrior's charger, in a certain miry spot near to which he had been suffered to crop the green leaves. He called hastily and wrathfully to Lazaro, and, in his indignation, entirely lost sight of his dinner, his host, and the musician.

"Whelp of a heathen!" said Salvatierra to the shrinking lad; "hast thou no more skill or manners, but to make this accursed jangling, to which there seems no end? Bestir thyself, or I will teach thee activity."

The boy, frightened at the violence of the soldier, rose to his feet, and dropping his instrument in alarm, clung to Abdalla. The wrath of the hot-tempered Salvatierra exceeded the bounds of decorum and of humanity. He had a twig in his hand, and with this he raised his arm to strike the unfortunate urchin. But just then the neophyte turned round, and beheld the act of tyranny.

"Senor!" he cried, with a voice even more harsh and angry than his own, and seizing the uplifted hand with no ceremonious grasp—"senor! you will not so far forget your manhood as to do violence to the child? Know that I have taken him for this journey into my protection;—know also, thou canst not inflict a stripe upon his feeble body that will not degrade thee into the baseness of a hind, and that will not especially draw upon thee the inconvenience of my own displeasure!"

The heart of Salvatierra sunk before the flaming countenance of the cavalier; but observing that several of his nearest followers had taken note of the insult, and were grasping their arms, as if to avenge it, he said, with an air of firmness—"The Senor De Leste has twice or thrice taken occasion to requite my courtesies with such shame as is hard to be borne, and in particular by interfering with the just exercise of my authority; and I have to assure him that when the duties of my office shall release me from restraint, his injuries shall not be unremembered."

"If thou art an hidalgo," said the cavalier, sternly, "thou hast the right to command me; if of ignoble blood, as from thy deportment to this trembling child, I am constrained to believe, I have, nevertheless, eaten of thy bread and salt, and cannot refuse to meet thee with such weapons and in such way as thou mayest desire; and to this obligation do I hold myself bound and fettered."

Some half-dozen followers of the captain had crowded round their leader, and were lowering ominously and menacingly on the neophyte. Lazaro and Baltasar beheld the jeopardy of their master, and silently but resolutely placed themselves at his side; nay, even the youthful Fabueno, though seemingly bewildered, as if doubting on which side to array himself, had snatched up his bloodless sabre; and it seemed for an instant as if this unlucky rupture might end in blows. The Senor Salvatierra looked from his followers to the angry hidalgo; the flush faded from his cheek; and it was remarked by some of his soldiers, not a little to his dispraise, that when, as if conquering his passion, he motioned them to retire, it was with a hurried hand and tremulous lip.

"The Senor De Leste is right," he said, with a disturbed voice; "I should have done myself dishonour to harm the boy; and although the reproof was none of the most gentle and honeyed, I can still thank him that it preserved me from the shame of giving too much rein to my ill-temper. I therefore forget the injury, as one that was merited, discharge my anger as causeless, and desiring rather to devote my blood to the subjugation of Pagans than to squander it in contest with a fellow-Christian, offer the hand of reconciliation and of friendship to Don Amador De Leste."

There was an appearance of magnanimity in his confession of fault and offer of composition, that won upon the good opinion of the neophyte; and he frankly gave his hand to the captain. Then turning to the innocent cause of his trouble, who, during the time that there seemed danger of a conflict, had exhibited the greatest dismay, he found him sobbing bitterly in the arms of Abdalla.

"Poor child!" said the benevolent cavalier, "thou art fitter to touch thy lute in the bower of a lady, than to wake it among these wild and troubled deserts. It is enough, Abdalla: conduct thy son to some shade, where he may eat and sleep; and when we renew our march, I will think of some device to spare his tender feet the pain of trudging longer over the sands."

The Moor laid his hand on his heart, bowed with the deepest submission and gratitude, and led the boy away to a covert.

CHAPTER VII.

"Didst thou observe, brother henchman," said Lazaro, as, after having finished his meal, and taken good note of the tethers of the horses, he threw himself on the ground by the side of Baltasar, as if to imitate the other members of the party, who were making what preparations they could for the indulgence of the siesta—"didst thou observe, I say, old sinner, that this moment we were like to have made experience of the virtue of cotton corslets? By my faith, this gentle master of mine would not suffer our hands to be idle, so long as there be savages to curse

the faith, or hidalgos to cross his humours. I am ever bound to the magnanimous senor commander, that he thought fit to swallow his wrath, and send me those black-browed vagabonds back to their dinner; for otherwise, I assure thee, there was much fear of our supping in purgatory."

"For my part," said Baltasar, raising his head from the saddle, which served him for a pillow, and looking curiously round on the various groups, "I am of opinion, there was more discretion than dignity about that same captain, when he became so moderate of a sudden; for so sure as he was very foolish to get into a quarrel with the boy Amador, who, I am free to say, is no way unworthy to be a kinsman and esquire of my master the knight, so surely would the boy have dinged the feathers off his gilt casque with the first blow, and how much of his head might have followed the feathers, is more than I will take upon me to determine."

"Thou art so hungry after war," said Lazaro, 'thou canst not perceive the valour of foregoing an opportunity of battle now and then. Hast thou never seen a man turn pale from anger, as well as cowardice?"

"Of a truth I have," said the veteran: "and, provided there be a steady countenance along with it, this sickly hue is ever a sight to be dreaded more than the woman's blush, which some men fall into in their anger. But a coward's mouth is always playing him dog's tricks: I have sometimes seen the nether lip shake in a brave man; but when the trembling is all up in the corners, I have learned to know, after divers lessons, it is a sign the heart is in a flutter. There are, doubtless certain strings, whereby the heart is fastened to the mouth; and it is when the corners are writhing about in this cowardly, snaky manner, that the heart is drawn up further than is comfortable; a thing, I have no doubt, may have happened to yourself."

"If it have, may I become a Turk's slave!" said Lazaro, with great indignation; "and if it do, I hope it may be transferred, at that moment, from my own mouth to a dog's, to be made a dinner of!"

"Thou art an ass, to be in a passion, at any rate," said Baltasar, coolly, "and a very improbable idiot to deny, in thy vain glory, what has happened to braver men than thyself; and, which I am free to confess, has sometimes chanced to myself, especially in my youth, when I first went to fight the Moors; and, I very well remember, that besides perceiving there was a sort of emptiness under my ribs, on such occasions, I could feel my heart beating at the back of my throat as plainly as I ever felt the arrow-heads tapping about my buckler. But it always went to its place again, when we were come to close quarters."

"May I die of the bastinado, if I ever felt any such thing!" said Lazaro, proudly. "I was born without any such gaingiving; and the only uncomfortable feeling I have had, under such circumstances, was a sort of cold creeping about the stomach, as if it were raining inside of me."

"Or as if there was a cold air brewing in your gizzard!" said Baltasar, triumphantly. "That is the very same thing—the emptiness I was talking about; and if you never felt the beating in your throat, it was because your heart was in such a fit of fright as to have no power of beating left."

"Ay! that may be," said Lazaro, with a grin

"that beating is a business I keep for my arm, and when that is in service, my heart is ever wise enough to be quiet. But concerning the captain. Dost thou really esteem him a coward?"

"Who knows?" said the veteran. "A man may be once in fear, and strong-hearted ever after. Yet was there such a working about that cavalier's mouth, as made me think he longed to strike Don Amador, if he durst, and which still persuades me he has some bitter thoughts about the matter of the insult; for, as you may remember, Don Amador said he was more of a hind than an hidalgo, with other such loving remarks as might stir a man's choler. For this reason, I am of opinion, it will be good service of thee to thy master to keep thine eyes open while he is taking his siesta, lest, mayhap, some mischief might come to him sleeping."

"I am ever bound to your good-natured discretion," said Lazaro, with a laugh. "I have no doubt it would be more profitable to sit for an hour or two, watching the sunbeams stealing through the wood, than, for the same time, to slumber and snore, without any other amusement than an occasional buffeting of one's nose, to keep the flies off. I will, therefore, surrender this agreeable privilege to thyself, as being my senior and better; while I nap a little, and that so lightly, that if an emmet do but creep near my master, I shall hear the rustling of his footsteps. But harkee, Baltasar; there is much wit about thee, for an old man that has endured so many hard knocks; and ever, about once in a hundred times, I have found thy conjectures to be very reasonable. What is thy opinion concerning those infidel Moors under the bush yonder? and by what sort of magic dost thou suppose they have so wrought upon our commander, that he will neither suffer lance-shaft nor cane-twig to be laid upon them?"

"Ay, there they are!" said Baltasar, looking towards the father and son. "The boy lies with his head on Abdalla's knee, and Abdalla covers him with his skin mantle; and the mantle shakes, as if the boy were sobbing under it. It is my opinion, the lad has been used to milder treatment than he seems likely to meet in these parts, unless Don Amador should see fit to take him into his own keeping; and it is also my opinion, if he be so much affected at the sight of a green twig, he will go nigh to die with terror at the flash of a savage's sword."

"That is my opinion I have, in part, formed for myself," said the junior, coolly; "and one that I think is shared in common with every other person in this quilted company, that has looked in the manikin's face."

"It is as white," said Baltasar, "as that mountain top we saw from the caravel; whereas the children of common Moriscos are much the hue of my own weather-beaten boots."

"The boy was in a most pestilent fright," said Lazaro, "and therefore somewhat more snowy than was natural; nevertheless, I have seen darker skins among the damsels of La Mancha."

"And he is, in a manner, well figured and comely," said the veteran.

"If thou hadst said he was such a Ganymede as might hold the wine-cup and trencher to a princess, I should have thought better of thine eyesight. By cross and spear! he has such eyes as I shall be glad to find in any wench I may be predestined to marry."

"And his hand," said Baltasar, "is as small as an hidalgo's son's. He hath an amiable countenance, and such gravity in it, when not disturbed, as belongs to older years; and he ever keeps it bent to the earth, as if to shun observation."

"Ay—I see what thou art driving at," said Lazaro, significantly. "Thou thinkest Sidi Abdalla is some infidel prince of Granada—a Zegri or Abencerrage——"

"I think no such thing," said Baltasar, gruffly. "I have fought, myself, hand to hand with a Zegri, while my young lord Gabriel was cleaving the head of another; to which knightly and majestic infidels the wretch Sidi bears such resemblance as, in comparison, doth the hedgehog to a leopard."

"Thou art of opinion then, doubtless," said Lazaro, "that the boy Jacinto is some Christian nobleman's son, stolen in his infancy by Sidi, to be made a sacrifice to the devil?"

"I am no such ass," said Baltasar, "to entertain any such notion."

"A bird's flight by his feather, a beast's rage by his claw, and a man's thoughts by his tongue," said Lazaro; "but how I am to judge thee, is more than I know. What a-God's name, dost thou think then of these Christian heathens?"

"I think nothing at all," said Baltasar, drily: "I only wonder by what chance a Morisco boor came to have so tender and so handsome a boy."

"Well, Heaven be with thee, old oracle," said Lazaro, laying his head on his saddle: "if I should resolve thy wonder in my dreams, I will enlighten thee when I wake."

The veteran gave a look to the horses; to his master, who, by the attentions of the Captain Salvatierra, had been enabled to enjoy the luxury of a hammock, slung between two trees; to the Moor, who sat watching over his child, to the Tlaméme, who slumbered by their packs,—to the Spaniards, who slept, as they had eaten, in groups,—to the few sentinels, who stood nodding under the trees, —and then, dismissing all care, as if satisfied with the security of the motley encampment, he was not slow to follow the example of his companion.

CHAPTER VIII.

Two or three hours before sunset, the sleepers were roused to renew their march. Horses were saddled and armour buckled, and Don Amador de Leste mounted his steed with great satisfaction at the thought of still further diminishing the distance that separated him from his knight. As the train began to ford the rivulet, he turned round and beckoned to Abdoul, who, with Jacinto, had taken the station assigned them behind the musketeers.

"Sidi Abdalla," said he, "I have thought it a great shame that thy weary boy should trudge over these sands afoot, when such men as myself and my people are resting our lazy limbs on horseback. I have, therefore, given order to my soldier, Lazaro, to take the youth behind him; whereby much discomfort and suffering may be avoided."

"My lord will scorn the thanks of the poor Morisco," said Abdoul, humbly. "Sleep, and the food which it pleased my noble lord to give to the boy, have so refreshed his strength and his spirits, that now, in the pleasant evening air, he will journey without pain, as he has often, of yore, in the deserts of Barbary. And let not my lord be displeased to know, that Jacinto will be of better heart at the side of his father, than on the saddle of my lord's servant."

"If it be as thou sayest," said the cavalier, "I am content. Heaven forbid I should take him from thee, but for his good, which, doubtless, thou must know better how to compass than myself. Yet if he should at any time grow weary, make me acquainted with it, and Lazaro shall still be prepared to give him relief."

The Moor bent his head to the ground, and fell back; while Amador, followed by his attendants and the secretary, rode to the head of the train.

No occurrence of moment interrupted the monotony of the journey, until a thunder-storm, accompanied by rain, drove them for shelter into a forest, where their march was interrupted for a time. But with a capriciousness equal to the fury with which they had gathered, the clouds parted and vanished in the sunbeams; the earth was gladdened; the trees shook the liquid treasure from their leaves; a breeze came from the distant surges; and, resuming their path, the train and cavalcade went on their way rejoicing.

As they advanced, and as the day declined, the country assumed a more agreeable aspect, the woods were thicker and more luxuriant; the mountains approached nearer to the sea, and the streams gambolled among piles of rocks, instead of creeping sluggishly through the sands; the flowers were more abundant; and the birds, resuming their songs, prepared their vespers for the sinking luminary. At last he set: the curlew wheeled his last flight, the plover sent his last whistle from the air; and the stars, stealing out from the dusky air, shed their celestial light over the path of the travellers. With these lamps of heaven were also lit the torches of the cucujos —those phosphorescent beetles, with which Don Amador had been made acquainted in the islands. But he did not the less admire the splendour of the spectacle, when he saw these resplendent insects glistening among the trees, or flashing by him like little meteors. The moon rose from the sea, and as her mellow radiance streamed over the tree-tops, or sheeted itself on the sands, and as a thousand delicious scents came to the nostrils of the soldier, he thought he had never before, not even when watching the same planet in the calm bosom of the Levantine sea, looked upon a scene of more beautiful repose. The commander of the squadron had not, since the affair of the dinner, thought fit, frequently, to trouble Don Amador with his presence, but by the murmurs of satisfaction and curiosity which were breathed about him, the cavalier knew he was approaching the Indian city, Zempoala. The party issued from the wood upon what seemed a fair waving plain, dotted in certain places with clumps of trees, and doubtless, in other spots, enriched with plantations of maize and bananas. In the distance, from a dark and shadowy mass, which might have been a lofty grove or low hillock, and whose gloom was alike broken by the glare of insects and the flash of many flambeaux, arose three lofty towers, square and white, and glittering in the moonbeams as if covered over with plates of silver.

"Zempoala!" whispered an hundred voices, as these gleaming fabrics came fairly into view. The languid horseman raised himself on his saddle; the foot-soldier strode onwards with a firmer and quicker step; and at each moment, as the three towers reflected the moonbeams with increasing brilliancy, more torches flickered and more structures were seen shining among the trees; and it was evident to Don Amador that he was approaching a city or town of no little magnitude.

The secretary had pressed to his side, and overhearing his exclamations of surprise, took the liberty of addressing him.

"Senor!" he cried, "they say this Pagan city is bigger and lovelier than Seville. I have often before heard of the Silver Towers; for truly, when the men of Cortes first saw them, they thought they were built of blocks of plate, and rode forward to hack away some samples with their swords; whereupon, to their great shame and disappointment, they discovered the brilliance to be owing to a certain white and polished plaster, with which these barbarians have the art to beautify their temples."

"Are these then the sanctuaries of the fiend?" said the neophyte, raising himself, and surveying the structures with a frown of infinite hostility. "It drives me to little esteem, to know that the Senor Narvaez and his companions should rest in sight of these accursed places, without hurling them to the dust."

"They are no longer the houses of devils," said Lorenzo: "Cortes, the great rebel, tore the idols from their altars, and putting an image of our Blessed Lady in their place, consecrated them forthwith to the service of God."

"I hear nothing of Cortes, that does not convince me he is a truly noble and faithful cavalier," said Amador, with emphasis.

"There can be no doubt of that," said the secretary; "nevertheless, if I may presume to advise your favour, I would beseech you not to mention the name of Cortes among these men of Narvaez; or at least, not with the respect which you may think his due."

"Dost thou know," said Amador, addressing Fabueno so sternly as to cause him instantly to repent his presumption—"dost thou know, that what thou art saying is of so base and boorish a spirit, that, if it be the true prompting of thy heart, thou art utterly unworthy to take upon thee the arms, as thou art wholly incapable of winning the fame, of a soldier? Know thou, for it is good thou shouldst be told, that all hypocrisy is the offspring of cowardice, and is therefore impossible to be practised by a brave man: and know, in conclusion, that when thou art called upon for thy opinion, if thou givest not that which is in thy heart, thou art guilty of that hypocrisy which is cowardice, and that deceit which is perjury."

"I beg your worship's pardon," said Lorenzo, abashed and confounded, and somewhat bewildered by the chivalrous and fantastic system of honour disclosed in the reproof of the cavalier. "I meant only to let your favour know, that there could be no travelling beyond this Indian city, without the good will of Narvaez and his officers, which might not be gained by commending their enemy. And moreover, senor, if you will suffer me to justify myself—while I confess it would be both cowardly and impious, as your worship says, to conceal or alter a sentiment, when it is called for, yet was I thinking it could be in nowise dishonourable to retain in our own minds opinions not called for, particularly when they might be disagreeable to those upon whom they were thus, as I may say, forced.'

"By my faith, thou art, in a measure, very right," said Amador, "and I hereby recall any expressions which may have reflected on thy courage or thy religion; for I perceive thou wert only touching upon the obligation all men are under not to force their opinions upon others—an obligation of which I am myself so sensible, that, provided I am not called upon by the questions of these people, or the enforcements of mine own honour, I shall surely utter nothing to displease them. But canst thou tell me, Senor Secretario, how far from this town lies the commander, of whom we were speaking?"

"I have heard, only at the distance of two or three leagues," replied Fabueno; "but I should think, considering the wisdom of Cortes, he would be fain to increase that distance, as soon as he came to know the strength of Narvaez. Your favour may see, by the many torches glimmering through the streets, and the many voices that go chaunting up and down, that there is a goodly multitude with him."

"I see, by the same tokens," said Amador, "he has a set of riotous, disorderly vagabonds, who seem to think they are keeping carnival in Cristendom, rather than defending a camp among infidels: and, by St. John, I know not any very good reason, why the valiant Cortes might not, this instant, with his knot of brave men, steal upon the town, and snatch it out of the hands of the Biscayan. There is neither outpost in the field, nor sentinel in the suburbs."

There seemed some grounds for this notion of the cavalier. As he approached nearer to Zempoala, there was audible a concert of sounds, such as one would not have looked for in the camp of a good general. A great fire had been lit, as it appeared, among the Silver Towers, the ruddy reflection of which, mingled with the purer light of the moon, had given them so shiny an appearance, even at a distance. In this neighbourhood, as Amador judged by the direction and variety of cries, was the chief place of the revellers; though in divers quarters of the town might be heard the voices, and sometimes the musical instruments, of idle soldiers, struggling in rivalry with the ruder songs and harsher instruments of the natives. Besides the bonfires among the temples, there was another in the quarter of the town which the train was just entering, and apparently upon the very street which they were to pass. The cavalier had, however, under-rated the vigilance of the sentinels; for, just as he had concluded his denunciation, the trumpet with which Salvatierra announced his approach to his companions, was answered by a flourish from the fire; and there was straightway seen a group of armed men advancing to challenge the party. In fact, an outpost was stationed at the fire; the worthy warriors of which, in the absence of any important duties, had got together the means of amusement in the persons of certain Indian tumblers and merry-andrews, who were diverting them with feats of agility. Besides these

tawny sons of joyance, there were others of the same race, whose business it was to add to the pleasures of the entertainment the din of the musical instruments common to barbarians; only, as it seemed to Amador, that if there was nothing superior in the tone or management of these which he now heard, they had an advantage over those of the islanders, in being wrought with greater skill and ornamented with a more refined taste. Thus, of the little drums which were suspended to the necks of the musicians, and which were at least equal in sound to the tabours of Europe, some were carved and painted in a very gay manner; while the flutes of cane, though not less monotonous than the pipes of other savages, had about them an air of elegance, from being furnished with pendants of rich flowers, or beautiful feathers.

As Amador rode by, his attention was in a measure diverted from the tumblers by the agitation of Fogoso, who regarded neither the great fire nor the wild-looking artists with friendship; and when, having subdued his alarm, he turned to gratify his wonder, his eye was caught by the appearance of the Moor, who had stolen to his side, and now stood with a countenance even more disturbed than when shrinking from the blow of Salvatierra, and with hands upraised and clasped, as if to beseech his notice.

"My lord is benevolent to the friendless, and pitiful to the orphan," he cried, anxiously, as soon as he perceived that Amador regarded him; "he has been the champion of the father, and the protector of the son; and when the heart's blood of Abdoul can requite his benefactor, Abdoul will not deny it."

"Good Sidi," said Amador, "that I have protected both yourself and your son Jacinto, from unjust violence, is more than can be denied; but why it is needful to thank me so many times for the favour, is more than I can easily understand. I must therefore command you to find some more novel subject for conversation."

"My lord is a knight of Rhodes," said Abdalla, quickly, "and therefore by vow bound to charity, justice, pity, and all the other good virtues acknowledged as well by infidels as Christians?"

"I am no knight; a novice of the order I may be called," said Amador, "but no knight; though," he added, with a most dolorous sigh, "how soon I may take the vows after returning from the lands of Mexico, is more than I can pronounce. I have therefore not bound myself by oath to any of those virtues of which you spoke; but had you been born of nobler blood than I can account that of the Lord of Fez, you should have known, that, being a gentleman and a Christian, I cannot release myself from any of their natural obligations."

"For myself," said Abdalla, "though insult and danger will come to me among these riotous soldiers, who are the enemies of my race, and these barbarians, who are surely the enemies of all, I can submit to my griefs; but Jacinto needs the arm of power to protect him. If my lord will take him to be his servant, he will be merciful to misfortune; the prayers of gratitude will ascend to heaven; and the love of a faithful boy will watch ever at his side like the vigilance of an armed follower."

"Art thou content the boy should be parted from thee?" demanded Amador. "I know not low, among these strange lands and unknown wildernesses, I may be able to take that care of his tender years which should be the duty of a good master; nor, to tell thee the truth, do I know in what manner I can make use of his services."

"Let not my lord despise his skill," said the Almogavar, "because his fright and weariness palsied his hand, when he should have played before him. He hath good skill with the lute, and he has in his memory a thousand redondillas, with which he may divert the leisure of my lord. Besides this skill, he hath a fidelity which nothing can corrupt, and a loving heart, which, once gained by kindness, no temptation can lure from his master: and in these qualities will I vouch for him with my head. I know not in truth," continued Abdalla, faltering, "since he has never before served a master, if he have any other qualifications. But he is quick to acquire, and perhaps—perhaps he may soon learn to preserve the armour of my lord—yes, he will soon make himself useful to my lord."

"The cleaning of my armour," said Amador, in a very matter-of-fact manner, "is a duty which belongs particularly to Lazaro, whose fidelity, as well as that of Baltasar, is of so unquestionable a character, that it fully meets all the exigencies of my course of life. I would therefore receive thy son chiefly out of a hope to be comforted, at times, with his music, and partly out of pity for his forlornness. He will doubtless serve me as a page and cupbearer; in which capacity, promising to give him as much protection and kindness as may be in my power, I consent to receive him."

"And my lord will permit that I shall often see him?" said Abdoul, eagerly.

"Surely I must desire thou shouldst," said Amador, "if it were possible thou couldst be in the same army."

Abdalla looked at the cavalier with a bewildered and confused countenance, as if not understanding him.

"I must acquaint thee, good Sidi," said Amador, "with one fact, of which thou seemest ignorant, and which may wholly change thy desires in this matter. Thy destination is to this town of Zempoala, and mine to the very far city of Tenochtitlan; thy fate is to submit thee into the hands of the General Narvaez, as thou hast heard, to serve him as a cannonier, while mine is to betake myself to the General Cortes, his sworn and most indomitable enemy. Thou mayest therefore inquire of thyself, if thy boy go with me, whether thou wilt ever again look upon him—a question I cannot myself answer in a satisfactory manner. Make thy election, therefore, whether thou wilt keep him at thy side, or intrust him to my guardianship; being assured, that if the latter be thy desire, I will bid thee call him, and straightway take him into my keeping."

"It cannot be," said Abdallah, vehemently; "I cannot trust him from my sight: it cannot be! God is just; and justice may come with misery!"

Thus lamenting, Abdoul al Sidi retired from the side of the cavalier; and Amador, whose pity was not a little touched, suffered his image to be crowded from his mind by the new and strange spectacles which were now opening upon him.

CHAPTER IX.

While he still talked with the Morisco, Don Amador was able to cast his eyes about him, and to perceive on either side a great multitude of low houses of wickered cane, which seemed to him more to resemble gigantic baskets than the habitations of men; but which, even in these latter days, are found sufficient to protect the humble aborigines from the vicissitudes of that benignant clime. Each stood by itself in an enclosure of shrubs and flowers, and where it happened that the inmates were within, with torches or fires burning, the blaze, streaming through the wattled walls, illuminated every thing around, and disclosed the figures of the habitants moving about like shadows in the flame. Other buildings, equally humble in size, were constructed of less remarkable but not less romantic materials; and where the moonbeams fell over their earthen walls and palmy roofs, both were often concealed by such a drapery of vines and creeping flowers, perhaps the odoriferous vanilla and the beautiful convolvulus, as might have satisfied the longings of a wood-nymph. As he approached nearer to the centre of the town, these lowly and lovely cottages were exchanged for fabrics of stone, many of them of considerable size, and several with walls covered with the bright and silvery plaster which ornamented the temples. Each of these, the dwellings of the Tlatoani, or, as the Spaniards called them, in the language of Santo Domingo, the caciques of the city—stood alone in its garden of flowers, with vines trailing, and palm trees bending over its roof, commonly in darkness, though sometimes the myrtle taper of a fair Totonac, (for such was the name of this provincial people of the coast,) or the oily cresset of a Spanish captain who had made his quarters wherever was a house to his fancy, might be seen gleaming from behind the curtains of cotton stuff, which were hung at the doors and windows. These sights had been seen by Amador, while yet engaged in conversation with Abdalla; but when the Morisco dropped sorrowfully away, he found himself on the great square of the city, immediately fronting the sanctuaries, and gazing upon a scene of peculiarly wild and novel character. The centre of the square was occupied by a broad, and indeed a vast platform of earth, raised to a height of eight or ten feet, ascended from all sides by half as many steps—having the appearance of a low truncated pyramid, serving as a base to the three towers which crowned it. Upon its summit or terrace, immediately in advance of the towers, was kindled a great fire, the blaze of which, besides illuminating the temple itself and all the buildings which surrounded the square, fell upon sundry groups of Indian tumblers, engaged in feats of activity, as well as upon a host of cavaliers who surveyed them close at hand, and many throngs of common soldiers and natives who looked on at a distance from the square.

Here the detachment was halted; the burthens of the Tlaméme were deposited on the earth; the horses were freed from their packs; and Amador, at the suggestion of Salvatierra, dismounted, and leaving Fogoso to the care of his attendants, and these again to the disposition of the captain, ascended the pyramid, followed by the secretary,

He was somewhat surprised, when this worthy commander, whom he looked for to conduct him to the general, resuming much of the stately dignity he had found it inconvenient to support on the march, made him a low bow, and informed him with much gravity he would find the commander-in-chief either on the terrace among his officers, or at his head-quarters in the middle tower. The feeling of indignation which for a moment beset him, would have been expressed, had not Salvatierra with another bow retired, and had he not perceived, at the same moment, the young Fabueno draw from his girdle the letter which was doubtless to secure him the good-will of Narvaez. Checking, therefore, his anger, he straightway ascended the platform. Arrived at its summit, he now beheld the scene which he had imperfectly witnessed from below. The great fire, crackling and roaring, added the ruddy glare of a volcano to the pallid illumination of the moon; and in the combined light, the operations of the gymnasts and dancers, the athletes and jugglers, were as visible as if performed in the glitter of noonday. For a moment Amador thought, as had been thought by all other Spaniards, when looking for the first time on the sports of these barbarous races, that he had got among a group of devils, or, at least, of devilish musicians; and he crossed himself with an instinctive horror, when he beheld, so to speak, three piles of men, each composed of three individuals, half-naked, standing one upon the head or shoulders of another, whirling about in a circle, and each, as he whirled, dancing on the head or shoulders of his supporter, and tossing abroad his *penacho*, or long plume of feathers, as if diverting himself on the solid earth. This spectacle entirely distracted his attention from others scarcely less worthy of observation—as was indeed that, where two men see-sawed on a pole, in the air, and, as might be said, without support, except that which was occasionally rendered by the feet of a sinewy Pagan, who lay on his back, and ever and anon as the flying phantoms descended, spurned them again into the air. Such also was that magical dance of the cords, brought from the unknown tribes of the south, wherein a score of men, each holding to a rope of some brilliant colour, and each decorated with the feathers of the parrot and the flamingo, whirled in fleet gyrations round a garlanded post, till their cords were twisted together in a net of incomprehensible complexity, but which, before the observer had leisure to digest his amazement, were again unravelled in the rapid and mysterious evolutions of the dance. A thousand other such exhibitions, similar in novelty but different in character, were displayed at the same moment; but the eyes of the neophyte were lost to all but that which had first astounded him; and it was not till the voice of the secretary roused him from his bewitchment, that he collected his senses, and observed an officer of the household of the general standing before him, and doing him such reverence as was evidently the right of his dignity. It was then that Don Amador looked from the dancers to the cavaliers whom they were diverting. The fire flashed over the walls of the square and lofty towers up to the shelving thatch of palm-leaves, under which they were grouped, making, with the glitter of their half-armed persons, a suitable addition to the romance of the scene. In the centre of that group which lounged before the middle and loftiest tower, in a chair, or indeed, as it might be called, a throne, of such barbaric beauty as was known only to the magnificos of this singular people, sat a cavalier, tall and somewhat majestic of stature, with a ruddy beard, and yellow locks falling over an agreeable countenance; in whom, not so much from the character of his deportment and the quality of his decorations, as from the evident homage rendered him by the officers around, Don Amador did not doubt he beheld the Biscayan general. At the very moment when his eyes fell upon this smiling dignitary, he was himself perceived by the general; and Narvaez started up with a sort of confusion, as if ashamed to be discovered in such trivial enjoyment by so gallant a cavalier. In fact, the glittering casque of steel had supplanted the velvet cap on the head of the novice; and as he approached in full armour, clad also in the dignity with which he was wont to approach his fellows in rank, Don Amador presented a figure, to say the least, equally noble with that of the commander—and, what was no slight advantage in those days, with the additional manifestation of high blood, such as was certainly less questionable in him than in Narvaez. It seemed for a moment as if the general would have retreated into the temple, doubtless with the view of assuming a more stately character for the interview; but, perceiving that Don Amador had already recognised him, and was advancing, he changed his purpose, and making a step forward to do honour to his visitor, he stood still to receive him. The eyes of all those gallant adventurers were turned from the dancers to the new comer; but Don Amador, not much moved by such a circumstance, as indifferent to their curiosity as their admiration, approached with a stately gravity, and, making a courteous reverence to the general, said—" I have no doubt it is my felicity at this present moment to offer my devoirs to the noble and very respected senor, the General Don Panfilo de Narvaez; on the presumption of which, I, Amador de Leste, of Cuenza, a novice of the holy hospital of St. John of Jerusalem, do not hesitate to claim the hospitalities, which, as an hidalgo of Spain, and kinsman of the noble senor, the Admiral Cavallero, your excellency's confederate, I hold myself entitled to expect.

" The very noble and valiant Senor Don Amador de Leste shall not claim those hospitalities in vain," said the general, with a voice whose natural and voluminous harshness did not conceal an attempt at amenity; " and I hope he will not anticipate in them too little of the roughness of a soldier, by reason that he has seen us unbending a little from the toils of war to the foolish diversions of these ingenious barbarians."

" I will not take upon me to judge either of the tactics or the recreations of your excellency," said Amador, very coolly. " I will only demand of your favour to accept, at this present moment, such protestations of respect as become me in my function of suitor; and, in especial, to accredit my companion, the Secretary Fabueno, the messenger of the admiral, who is charged with certain letters to your excellency, of which, I believe, I am myself, in part, the subject."

" I receive them with respect, and I welcome the very distinguished Don Amador with much joy," said Narvaez; " in token of which I must beg him to allow himself to be considered, at least so long as he honours my command with his presence, as my own peculiar guest: and that I may the sooner know in what it may be my happiness to do him service, I must entreat him to enter with me into my poor quarters."

With such superb expressions of etiquette, the common compliments of an over-chivalrous age and people, Don Amador was ushered into the interior of the temple. A curtain of a certain strong and checkered matting, that served the purpose of a door, was pushed aside, and, entering with the general and two or three of his most favoured officers, he found himself in the heathen sanctuary. A table covered with brilliant drapery of cotton—a product of the country—and strewed over with pieces of armour, as well as with divers vessels wherein glowed some of the rich wines ripened by the breath of the Solano, contained also a great silver cresset filled with oil tempered with liquid amber, which, besides pervading the whole atmosphere with a delicious odour, shed abroad such a light as enabled Don Amador to survey the apartment. It was of good height, and spacious: the walls were hung with arras of a sombre-hued cotton, and the floor covered with thick matting. In one corner was a ladder, leading to the upper chambers. Two sides of it were occupied by a low platform, on which lay several mattresses stuffed with the down of the ceiba; over one of which, on a small altar of wood, illuminated by tapers of the myrtle wax, was a little image of the Virgin. In this chamber, the chief adoratory of the temple, where now flashed the weapons of the iconoclasts, stood once the altar of an idol, whose fiendish lips had been often dyed with the blood of human sacrifices. There were rude chairs about the table; and Amador, at the invitation of the general, did not hesitate to seat himself, and cast an eye of observation on his companions, while Narvaez, with the assistance of the secretary, proceeded to decipher the advices of the admiral.

The individuals with whom Amador found himself in contact, were of a genteel and manly presence: and though evidently burning with desire to make the acquaintance of the novice of Rhodes, and certainly also with curiosity to know what strange event had cast him among themselves, had yet sufficient breeding to conceal their anxieties,—excepting one, who, although of riper years than the rest, and even of more gravity of deportment, was nevertheless twice or thrice guilty of a very inquisitive stare. This Don Amador did himself at last perceive, and felt greatly moved to discover the cause of so remarkable a scrutiny. Nevertheless, before he had resolved in what manner to commence the investigation, and before the general had well looked into the advices of the admiral, they were both interrupted in their purpose by the abrupt intrusion of an officer, who, approaching Narvaez, said something to him in a low voice, of which all that Amador could distinguish were the words, twice or thrice repeated, of *nigromante* and *astrologo*. The officer received a direction equally obscure with his information; and Amador observed that as Narvaez gave it, his face flushed over with some sudden excitement. The speculations of the neophyte were soon terminated. Before the curtain had yet closed upon the retreating officer, the cavalier, whose curious looks had attracted his own attention, rose and addressed the general. "Senor general and go-

vernor," he cried, "I doubt whether this knavish impostor be worthy your attention. He is accounted both a liar and traitor, and he can tell us nothing that will not be spoken to deceive us."

"The Senor Don Andres de Duero cannot be better persuaded of the man's character than myself," said the general; "and he will not assure me that a good general can refuse to listen to any intelligence of his enemy, though it be brought by a traitor. The noble Don Amador de Leste will pardon me, if I make so free with him, as in his presence to introduce and examine a prisoner, or deserter, I know not which, on matters which it concerns me as a commander to know. And moreover," continued the Biscayan, with a laugh, "I know not what better diversion I can give my guest, than to make him acquainted with a man who pretends to read the mysteries of the stars by night, and to have a devil who gives him knowledge of men's destinies by daylight."

Before Amador could reply to this appeal, the Senor Duero spoke again. "Surely he can bring us no information of Cortes which we have not received at better hands; and as for his magical art, I think your excellency holds that in too much doubt and contempt to set much store by its crazy revelations."

"What may be my doubt, and what my contempt for his art," said the general, "is more than I have yet resolved: only there is one thing of which I am quite certain, and that is, that, with the blessing of Our Holy and Immaculate Lady, I defy the devil and all his imps, whether they come at the bidding of a heathenish magician or a Christian enchanter; and, moreover, that if there be any knowledge to be gained of the devil, without jeopardy of soul, one is a fool not to receive it. Senor," continued Narvaez, addressing himself again to Amador, "I may as well tell you, that the magician Botello, whom you will presently behold, is a favourite soldier and chief enchanter to that infidel rebel, Cortes (whom God confound, with all his mutinous friends and upholders, high and low, strong and feeble, Amen!) I say, senor, his chief magician," continued the general, speaking so rapidly and impetuously as utterly to prevent Don Amador from making the amendment he meditated to the curse, and insisting that Narvaez should revoke it, as far at least as it concerned his kinsman, the knight,—"his chief magician, by whose aid, it is supposed, the runagate desperado has been enabled to imprison the Indian emperor. And, knave or not, Don Amador, it cannot be denied, that when struck down, after surrendering himself, this morning, by the currish soldier, Caboban, he cursed the smiter with 'a short life and a long death;' which curse was fulfilled upon him on the instant; for striking Botello with his spear again, his horse plunged, threw him violently, and, falling, he was instantly spitted on the spear of a footman. He has been dying ever since; and some time, doubtless, his agony will be over; but he is as good as a dead man now."

"I am by no means certain," said Don Amador, 'that there was any connexion between the curse of the magician and the calamity of the soldier: though, as it appears to me, Heaven could not visit with judgment any one more righteously than the dastard who strikes an enemy after he has rendered himself a captive. Nevertheless, and though I am somewhat impatient your excellency should determine upon my own affairs, I have such respect for the superior claims of your duties, that I will willingly defer my anxiety until your excellency has examined the prisoner."

There were several very meaning glances exchanged among the cavaliers at this speech, which seemed to imply a feeling of neglect and resentment on the part of the speaker; but Narvaez did not notice it, or if he did, the impression was immediately driven from his mind by the entrance of the enchanter, conducted by several soldiers and officers, among whom was the Captain Salvatierra.

CHAPTER X.

Amador surveyed the prisoner, though somewhat indifferently. He was, in figure and age, very much such a man as Baltasar, but in other respects very dissimilar. His face was wan, and even cadaverous; but this might have been the effect of the blows he had received from the dying soldier, as was made probable by the presence of several spots of blood encrusted over his visage. His cheeks were broad, and the bones prominent; his eyes very hollow, and expressive of a wild solemnity, mingled with cunning; his beard long and bushy, and only slightly grizzled, and a rugged mustache hung over his lips so as almost to conceal them. His apparel of black cloth,—none of the freshest, the principal garment of which was a long loose doublet, under which was buckled an iron breast-plate—his only armour; for, instead of a morion, he wore a cloth hat of capacious brim, stuck round with the feathers of divers birds, as well as several medals of the saints, rudely executed in silver. Besides these fantastic decorations, he had suspended to his neck several instruments of the Cabala—a pentacle of silver, and charms and talismans written over with mystical characters, as well as a little leathern pouch filled with various dried herbs and roots. This mystagogue, an agent of no little importance among many of the scenes of the Conquest, was led into the presence of the general, and approached him without betraying any signs of fear or embarrassment; nor, on the other hand, did ne manifest any thing like audacity or presumption; but, lifting his eyes to the visage of the Biscayan, he gazed upon him with a silent and grave earnestness, that seemed somewhat to disconcert the leader.

"Sirrah sorcerer," said he, "since the devil has deserted you at last, call up what spirits you can muster, and find me why I shall not hang you for a spy, early in the morning."

"*Tetragrammaton Adonai!*" muttered the warrior-magician in the holy gibberish of his art, with a voice of sepulchral hollowness, and with a countenance gleaming with indignation and enthusiasm. "In the name of God, Amen. I defy the devil, and am the servant of his enemy; and in the land of devils, of Apollyon in the air, Beelzebub on the earth, and Satan in men's hearts, I forswear and defy, contemn and denounce them; and I pray for, and foresee, the day when they shall tumble from the high places!"

"All this thou mayst do, and all this thou mayst foresee," said the general; "but nevertheless thy wisdom will be more apparent to employ itself a little in the investigation of thine own fate, which, I promise thee, is approaching to a crisis."

"I have read it in the stars, I have seen it in the smoke of waters, and of blessed herbs, and I have heard it from the lips of dead men and the tongues of dreams," cried the professor of the occult sciences, with much emphasis. "But what is the fate of Botello, the swordsman, to that of the leaders of men, the conquerors of kings and great nations? I have read mine own destinies; but why shouldst thou trifle the time to know them, when I can show thee the higher mysteries of thine own?"

"Can'st thou do it? By my faith then, I will have thee speak them very soon," said Narvaez. "But first let me know what wert thou doing when thou wert found prowling this morning so near to my camp?"

"Gathering the herbs for the suffumigation which shall tell me in what part of the world thou shalt lay thy bones," said the magician, solemnly. "The moon, in the house Alchil, showed me many things, but not all; a thick smoke came over the crystal, and I saw not what I wanted; I slept under the cross, with a skull on my bosom, but it breathed nothing but clouds. Wherefore I knew, it should be only when the wolf spoke to the vulture, and the vulture to the red star, that Camael the angel should unlock the lips of destiny, and lead me whither I longed to follow."

"I am ever bound to thee," said the general, with a manner in which an attempt at mockery was mingled with a natural touch of superstition, "for the extreme interest thou seemest to cherish in my fate; and again I say to thee, I will immediately converse with thee on that subject. But at present, senor nigromante, I warn thee, it will be but wisdom to confine thy rhapsodies within the limits of answers to such interrogatories as I shall propose thee. Where lies thy master, the outcast and arch-rebel, my enemy?"

"My master is in heaven!" said Botello, with a devout and lofty earnestness, "and there is no outcast and rebel but he that dwelleth in the pit, under the foot of Michael; and he is the enemy."

"Sirrah! I speak to thee of the knave Cortes," cried the general, angrily. "When wert thou last at his side? and where?"

"At midnight, on the river of Canoes, where he has rested, as thou knowest, for a night and a day."

"Ah!" said the Biscayan, fiercely; "within a league of my head-quarters, whither my clemency has suffered him to come."

"Whither God and his good star have drawn him," said the magician.

"And whence I will drive him to the rocks of the mountains, or the mangroves of the beach, ere thou art cured of thy wounds!"

"Lo! my wounds are healed!" said Botello, "the hand that inflicted them is stiff and cold, and Hernan Cortes yet lies by the river. Ay, the holy unguent, blessed of the fat of a Pagan's heart, hath dried the blood and glued the skin; and yet my captain, whose fate I have seen and spoken, even from the glory of noon to the long and sorrowful shadows of the evening, marshals his band within the sound of thy matin bell; and woe be to his foeman, when he is nearer or further."

"Prattling fool," said the commander, "if thou hadst looked to the bright moon to-night, thou wouldst have seen how soon the cotton-trees of the river should be strung with thy leader and companions, and with thyself, as a liar and an imposter, in their midst!"

"I looked," said the veteran, tranquilly, "and saw what will be seen, but not by all. There was thunder in the temple, and peace by the river and more wailing than comes from the lips of the Penitent Knight."

The angry impetuosity with which Narvaez was about to continue the conference, was interrupted by the impatience of the novice. He had listened with much disgust both to the mystic jargon of the soldier and the idle demands and bravados of the general. The interest with which he discovered how short a distance separated him from his kinsman, was increased by an irresistible excitement, when he heard the title with which, as the admiral had told him, the knight was distinguished among the invaders on the lips of Botello. Rising, therefore, abruptly, he said, " Senor Narvaez, I have to beg your pardon, if, in my own impatience to be satisfied in a matter which I have much at heart, I am somewhat blind to the importance of this present controversy. If your excellency will do me the favour to examine the letters of the admiral, you will discover that it is not so much my purpose to lay claim to your hospitable entertainment, the proffer of which I acknowledge with much gratitude, as to request your permission to pass through the lines of your army, to join my kinsman, the Knight Calavar. Understanding, therefore, from the words of this lunatic, or enchanter, whichever he may be, that I am within the short distance of a league from my good knight, to whom all my allegiance is due, I see not wherefore I should not proceed to join him forthwith, instead of wasting the night in slumber. I must, therefore, crave of your excellency to grant me, to the camp of the Senor Cortes, a guide, to whom I will, with my life and honour, guarantee a safe return—or such instructions concerning my route as will enable me to proceed alone—that is to say, with my attendants."

The effect of this interruption and unexpected demand, on the countenances of all, was remarkable enough. The cavaliers present stared at the novice with amazement, and even a sort of dismay; and the Secretary Fabueno, looking by chance at the Captain Salvatierra, observed the visage of this worthy suddenly illuminated by a grin of delight. As for the general himself, nothing could be more unfeigned than his surprise; nothing more unquestionable than the displeasure which instantly began to darken his visage. He rose, thrust his hand into his belt, as if to give his fingers something to gripe, and drawing himself to his full height, said, haughtily and severely—" When I invited the Cavalier de Leste to share the shelter of this temple, I did not think I received a friend of the traitor Cortes or any of his people; nor did I dream an adherent of this outlaw would dare to beard me at my head-quarters with so rash and audacious a request."

" The Senor Narvaez has then to learn," said Amador, with a degree of moderation that could only be produced by a remembrance of his engagement to the admiral, and his promise to the secretary not causelessly to provoke the anger of the general—but nevertheless with unchanging decision, " that if I boast not to be the friend of Cortes, whom you call a traitor, I avouch myself to be very much the creature of mine own will; and that if I cannot be termed the adherent of an outlaw, I am at least a Spanish hidalgo, bent on the prosecution of my designs, and making requests more as the ceremonies of courtesy, than the tribute of humility. I will claim nothing more of your excellency than your excellency is, without claim, inclined to grant; and allowing therefore that you invited me to your lodgings under a mistaken apprehension of my character, I will straightway release you from the obligation, only previously desiring of your excellency to reconsider your expressions, wherein, as I think, was an inuendo highly unjust and offensive."

" Now, by Heaven!" exclaimed the Biscayan, with all the irascibility of his race, and the arrogant pride of his station, " I have happened upon a strange day, when a vagabond esquire, wandering through my jurisdiction, asks my permission to throw himself into the arms of my enemy; and when I admonish him a little of his rashness, rebukes me with insult and defiance."

" A very strange day indeed!" muttered a voice among the cavaliers, in which Amador, had he not been too much occupied with other considerations, might have recognised the tones of Salvatierra.

" Biscayan," said he, with an eye of fire, " I have given you all the respect, which, as a governor's governor, and a captain's captain, you had a right to demand; I have also done you the homage of a guest to his host, and of a gentleman to a reputed hidalgo; but neither as a governor nor commander, neither as a host nor a nobleman, have you the privilege to offend with impunity, or to insult without being called to a reckoning."

" Is this another madman of the stock of Calavar, that the silly admiral hath sent me?" cried the infuriated leader, snatching up a sword from the table, and advancing upon the novice.

" Senor Panfilo," cried Amador, confronting the general, and waving his hand with dignity, " unless thou force me by thine own violence, I cannot draw my sword upon thee on thine own floor, not even although thou add to thy wrongs a sarcasm on my knight and kinsman. Nevertheless I fling this glove at thy feet, in token that if thou art as valiant as thou art ill-bred, as ready to repair as inflict an injury, I will claim of thee, as soon as may suit thy convenience, to meet me with weapons, and to answer thy manifold indignities."

" Dios santisimo!" cried the commander, foaming with rage and stamping furiously on the floor. " What ho! swords and pikemen! shall I strike this galofero braggart with my own hands? Arrest him."

" The blood of him that stays me be on his own head!" said Amador, drawing his sword and striding to the entrance. I will remember thee, uncourteous cavalier, when I see thee in a fitter place.

The arm of the governor had been arrested by Duero; and in the confusion of the moment, though the door of the tower was instantly beset by a dozen gaping attendants, Don Amador would doubtless have passed through them without detention, notwithstanding the furious commands of Narvaez. But at the moment when, as he waved his sword menacingly, the hesitating satellites seemed parting before him, Salvatierra stepped nimbly behind, and suddenly seizing his outstretched arm, and calling to the guards at the same time, in an instant Don Amador was disarmed and a prisoner. His rage was for a moment unspeakable; but it did not render him incapable of observing the faithful boldness of the secretary.

" Senor General!" cried Lorenzo, though with a stammering voice, " if your excellency will read this letter to the end, your excellency will find my master recommends Don Amador as of a most noble and lofty family, and, at this moment, raised above arrest and detention, by being charged with authority from the Grand Master of Rhodes."

The only answer of the general was a scowl and a wave of the hand, which instantly left

Fabueno in the predicament of the cavalier. He was seized, and before he could follow the example of his patron, and draw his sabre, it was snatched from his inexperienced hand.

All this passed in a moment; and before the neophyte could give utterance to the indignation which choked him, he was dragged, with Fabueno, from the sanctuary.

CHAPTER XI.

The dancers had fled from the terrace; the fire had smouldered away; but in the light of the moon, which shed a far lovelier radiance, Don Amador, as he was hurried to the steps, saw, in place of the gay cavaliers, a few sentries striding in front of the towers, and among the artillery which frowned on either edge of the platform. Nevertheless, if his rage had left him inquisitive, he was not allowed time to indulge his observations. He was hurried down the steps, carried a few paces further, and instantly immured in the stone dwelling of some native chief, which, by the substitution of a door of plank for the cotton curtain, and other simple contrivances, had been easily converted into a prison.

In the mean while, the rage of the governor burned with a fury that was not much lessened by the remonstrances of his officers; and to the counsel of Duero—the personal secretary of Don Diego Velasquez, accompanying the expedition less as an adviser than as a spy over the general, and therefore necessarily held in some respect—he answered only with heat and sarcasm. " I have ever found the Senor Don Andres," he cried, without regarding the presence of Botello, " to be more friendly with the friends of Cortes than may seem fitting in the honourable and confidential secretary of Velasquez !"

" I will not deny that such is my temper," said Duero; " nor will I conceal from you that such leniency springs less from affection than interest. Sure am I, that had your excellency, from the first, held out the arms of conciliation, instead of the banners of vengeance, at this moment, instead of being arrayed against you in desperate hostility, the forces of Cortes would have been found enrolled under your own standard, and Cortes himself among the humblest and faithfulest of your captains."

" While I doubt that effect," said the general, sharply, " I cannot but be assured of the strength of Don Andres's interest, while I listen to the whispers of his enemies."

Duero coloured, but replied calmly—" It is not unknown to me, that certain ill-advised persons have charged me with being under the influence of a secret compact with Cortes, formed before his appointment to the command of the first army of invasion, whereby I was to share a full third of the profits of his enterprise. Without pretending to show the improbability of such an agreement, I will, for an instant, allow your excellency to take it for granted, in order that your excellency may give me credit for my present disinterestedness, in doing all I can to ruin my colleague; in which I reckon, as no slight matter, taking every opportunity to decoy away his followers."

" If thou wilt show me in what manner sub-

mission to the whims and insults of this insolent boy could have detached any of the mutineers from Cortes, I will confess myself in error, and liberate him forthwith," said the general.

" The insult has been passed, the blow has been struck," said Duero, gravely; " and unless your excellency chooses to measure swords with him immediately after his liberation, nothing can be gained by such a step. I should rather counsel your excellency to have the prison watched with a double guard. But, in arresting him, you have, besides giving deep offence to your colleague, the admiral, for ever won the hate and hostility of the Knight of Rhodes; and when this is told him in the camp of Cortes, it will harden the hearts of all against us."

" When it is told in the camp of Cortes," said Narvaez, with a bitter smile, " it shall be with mine own lips; and if I hang not upon a tree afterwards the Knight Calavar himself, it will be more out of regard to his madness than to the dignity of his knighthood. I will attack the rebel to-morrow !"

" Your excellency is heated by anger," said Duero, temperately, " or you would observe you have a follower of the rebel for a listener."

" Ay, Botello !" cried the general, with a laugh of scorn. " He will carry my counsels to Cortes when the cony carries food to the serpent, and the sick ox to the carrion crow. Hark, sirrah—thou hast read the fate of thy master : will I attack him to-morrow ?"

" Thou wilt not," said Botello, with an unmoved countenance.

" Hah !" cried Narvaez; " art thou so sure of this that thou wilt pledge thy head on the prophecy ? Thou shalt live to be hanged at sunset, with thy old comrades for spectators."

" Heaven has written another history for to-morrow," said Botello, gravely; " and I have read that as closely as the page of to-day; but what is for myself, is, and no man may know it. The fate in store for the vain pride and the quick anger, may, in part, be spoken "

" Sirrah," said Narvaez, remember, that though the vain pride might overlook one so contemptible as thyself, the quick anger is not yet allayed; and if thou wilt not have me beat thee in the morning, proceed forthwith to discourse of our destinies."

" Blows shall be struck," said the magician, earnestly: " but whether upon my own head or another's, whether in this temple or another place, whether in the morning or the evening, I am not permitted to divulge. Repent of thy sins; call in a confessor, and pray; for wrath cometh, and sorrow is behind! By the spirits that live in the stars, by the elves that dwell in stones and shrubs, by the virtues that are caged in matter where the ignorant man findeth naught but ignorance, have I been made acquainted with many things appertaining to thy fate, but not all. If thou wilt, I will speak thee the things I am permitted."

" Speak then," cried the general; " for whether thy knowledge be truth or lies, whether it come from the revelations of angels, or the diabolical instructions of fiends, I will listen without fear."

" *Adonai Melech !* under the heaven, and above the abyss—with my hand on the cross, and the rosary in my bosom—in Rome, near to the footsteps of his holiness, and with one who was his favourite astrologer, studied I mine art; and there is nothing in it that is not blessed," said Botello, with a solemn enthusiasm, that made a deep impression upon all. "Give me a staff, that I may draw the curtain from this loop," he continued.

The sword of a younger officer was instantly extended, the curtain removed, and the moon, climbing the blue hills of paradise, looked down into the apartment. The cavaliers stared at the astrologer and magician, for Botello was both, some with an unconcealed awe, and others, the general among the rest, with an endeavour at looks of contempt not in good character with the interest they betrayed in all his proceedings. He raised his eyes to the beautiful luminary, enough to create by her mystic splendour the elements of superstition in the bosom of a rhapsodist—crossed himself devoutly twice or thrice, mumbled certain inexplicable words, and then said aloud, with a mournful emphasis—"Woe to him that sits in the high place, when the moon shines from the house Allatha! But the time has not come: and I dare not speak the hour of its visitation."

"And what shall it advantage me to know my peril, if I have not such knowledge as may enable me to prevent it?" demanded Narvaez, with a frown.

"And what would it benefit thee to know the time of thy peril," said the astrologer, "when God has not given thee the power to avert it? What is written must be fulfilled; what is declared must be accomplished. Listen—the queen of night is in the eighteenth mansion, and under that influence discord is sown in the hearts of men, sedition comes to the earth, and conspiracy hatches under the green leaf."

The general turned quickly upon his officers, and surveyed them with an eye of suspicion. They looked blankly one upon another, until Duero, laughing in a forced and unnatural manner, cried—"Why should we listen to this madman, if we are so affected by his ravings? Senor General, you will straightway look upon us all as traitors!"

"There have been villains about us before," muttered the general. "but I will not take the moon's word for it; and the more especially that I must receive it through this man's interpretation."

"It is the influence, too, that is good for the friendless captive," continued the magician; "and many a heart that beats under bonds to-night, will leap in freedom to morrow."

"Every way this is bad for us," said Duero, banteringly. "I would advise your excellency to clap chains on the legs of De Leste and the scribe, who are, I think, saving the few rogues of Cortes who have craved to enter into our service, the only prisoners in our possession."

"And dost thou think this gibberish will move me to any such precaution?" cried Narvaez, with a compelled smile. "Thou canst not believe I listen to it for aught but diversion?"

"Surely not, if your excellency says so. But still may we guard the prisoners, without fear of being laughed at for our superstition—as long as we have faith in the discretion of all present."

"Guard them thyself if thou wilt," said the general; "I am not moved enough for such condescension. Continue thy mummeries, Botello," he went on, "and when thou art done with the moon, of which I am heartily tired, I will look for thee to introduce me to some essence that speaks a clearer language."

"What wouldst thou have?" cried the astrologer; "what plainer language wouldst thou have spoken? In the house Allatha is written the defection of friends, the dethronement of princes, the fall of citadels in a siege."

"Villain and caitiff! dost thou dare to insinuate that this citadel of Zempoala is in a state of siege?" cried the Biscayan, with a ferocious frown.

"I speak of the things that are to come," said Botello. "What more than this wilt thou have?"

"It will, doubtless, be well," interrupted Duero, significantly, "to evacuate this city in the morning. By encamping in the fields we can certainly avoid the danger of a besieged citadel."

"Dost thou gibe me, Don Andres?" said Narvaez, with a brow on which jealousy struggled with rage.

The secretary of Velasquez laid his hand on his heart with a gesture of respectful deprecation.

"Ay! I see thou art stirred by these phantasms!" cried the governor, with a harsh laugh, looking from Duero to the other cavaliers. "What means this, my masters? Do ye all stare as if ye had got among you a dead Samuel, telling ye of your deaths on the morrow? Cheer up—for, by'r lady, I intend, if this old fellow's command of the black art runs so far, to divert you with a more horrible companion. What sayest thou, Botello? It is whispered thou canst raise devils, and force them to speak with thee!"

"Ay!" said Botello, with a ghastly grin, staring the general in the face, until the latter faltered before him. "Wilt thou adventure then so far? Canst thou, whose eyes tremble at the gaze of a living creature, think to look upon the face of a fallen angel? Hast thou confessed to-day and been absolved?—hast thou been free, since the sunrise, of thoughts of treachery and feelings of wrath? The pentacle and the circle, the consecrated sword and the crucifix, the sign of the cross and the muttered paternoster will not protect the unshriven sinner from the claws of a raised demon."

"If thou canst raise him," said Narvaez, stoutly, "do so, and quickly. I fortify myself in the name of God and the holy ones, against all spirits and devils. It will be much satisfaction to my curiosity to look upon one of the accursed."

"They are about us in the air—they are at our elbows and ears," said Botello; "and it needs but a spell to be spoken to bring them before us. But woe to him that hath thought a sin to-day, when the evil-one looks on him!"

"Senor Narvaez," cried Duero, with a most expressive and contagious alarm, "if it be your inclination to raise the devil, you must indulge it alone. For my part, I confess there have been, this day, certain sinful thoughts about my bosom, which have unfitted me for such an interview; and—I care not who knows it—my valour has in it so little of the fire of faith, I would sooner, at any moment, speak with ten men than one devil. God be with you, senor—I wish you a good evening."

"Tarry, Duero; stay, cavaliers!" cried Narvaez, losing much of his own dread in the contemplation of the apprehension of others. "Why, you are such a knot of sinners as I dreamed not I had about me! Faith, I am ashamed of you, and of you in particular Duero; for I thought thy shrewdness would have seen, in this knave's attempt to frighten us from the exhibition, an excellent evidence of his inability to make it."

"I could show thee more than thou couldst see," said Botello, "and I know more things will come to thee than thou shalt see. I know, with all thy vaunting, thou wouldst perish in the gaze of an angel of hell: for thy heart would be the heart of a boy, and it flutters already, even at the thought of the spectacle. I will show thee an essence thou mayest look upon without alarm."

"Do so," said Narvaez, sternly; "and remember, while saying what may be necessary by way of explanation, that thou speakest to the chief and governor of these lands, who will whip thy head from thy neck in spite of all the devils, if thou discoursest not with more becoming reverence."

"My fate is written!" cried Botello, with neither indignation nor alarm; and drawing calmly from his bosom an implement of his art, he advanced to the light, and displayed it freely to the cavaliers. It was, or seemed to be, an antique jewel of rock-crystal, not bigger than a pigeon's head, set in the centre of the triangular disk of gold, on which last were engraved many unknown characters and figures. Crossing himself twice or thrice, the enchanter swung it, by a little silver chain to which it was pendant, in the full blaze of the lamp; so that either of the persons present might have handled it, had any been so disposed. But, in truth, the superstition of an age for which no marvel was too gross, no miracle too wonderful, was more or less shared by all; and they merely surveyed it at a distance with curiosity and fear.

"This," said the magician—"a gem more precious to the wise than the adamant of the East, but in the hands of the unfaithful, more pernicious than the tooth of a viper—is the prison-house of an essence that was once powerful among the spirits of night. The great Agrippa wedged him in this stone; and from Agrippa, when I rested at his feet in the holy city, did I receive the inestimable gift. Kalidon-Sadabath! the night is thy season, the midnight thy time of power! The lord of men calls thee from thy prison-house, the armed man calls thee with the sword! Lo! he wakes from his slumber, and will image out the destiny of the seeker."

The cavaliers, starting, gazed behind them with fear, as if expecting to behold some mighty fiend rising shadowy from the floor; but no intelligence more lofty or more ignoble than themselves was visible in the sanctuary. They bent their eyes upon the crystal, and beheld, some with surprise and others with deep awe, a little drop as of some black liquid, glittering in the very centre of the jewel.

The haughty soldiers who would have rushed with cries of joy upon an army of infidels, shrank away with murmurs of hesitation, when Botello extended the talisman towards them. But they mistook the gesture of the magician; his arm was outstretched more to display the wonder than to part with it. He surveyed it himself a moment with much satisfaction; then turning to Narvaez, he said—"Lay thy hand upon the cross of thy sword, say a paternoster over in thy heart, and thou shalt be protected from the mischief of this inquisition, while I tell thee what I behold in the face of Kalidon-Sadabath."

"With your favour," cried Narvaez, suddenly and boldly snatching the enchanted crystal from the hands of Botello, "I will choose rather to see his visage myself, than trust to your interpretations; and as for the protection, I can con over a paternoster while I am looking: though, why it needs to bestow so much piety upon this juggler's gewgaw, is more than I can understand."

"Say at least the prayer," cried Botello, earnestly, "for neither enchanted crystal nor consecrated gold can hold the strong spirit from the wicked and self-sufficient."

"I have much trust in the saints and in myself," said the governor, coolly, greatly assured and inspirited by the harmless appearance of the little mystery. Nevertheless, I will follow your counsel, in the matter of the prayer,—the more readily that it will keep my mind from wandering to more important affairs; and because, in part, I am somewhat burdened with the sin of neglecting such duties, when there is more occasion for them."

He drew the lamp to him, grasped the crystal firmly in his hand, and bending over it so closely that his warm breath sullied its lustre, regarded it with a fixed attention. The cavaliers noted the proceeding with interest; they gazed now at the jewel almost concealed in his grasp, and now at the general, as his lips muttered over the inaudible prayer. Suddenly, and before he had half accomplished the task, they observed his brows knit, and his lip fall; his eye dilated with a stare of terror, a deadly paleness came over his visage, and starting up, and loosing the talisman from his grasp, he exclaimed wildly—"By Heaven, there is a living creature in the stone!"

The sorcerer caught the magical implement as it fell from the hands of Narvaez; and throwing himself upon his knees, while the cavaliers looked on in mute astonishment, exclaimed—"Forget not the prayer, and be content to hear what is revealed by the imp of the crystal. Kalidon-Sadabath! He flingeth abroad his arms, and is in wrath and trouble!"

"It is true," said Narvaez, looking to his officers in perturbation. "While I looked into the shining stone, the black drop increased in size, and grew into the similitude of a being, whose arms were tossed out as if in agony, while spots of fire gathered round his visage."

"Say the prayer, if thou wilt not die miserably before the time that is otherwise ordained!" cried Botello with a stern voice, that was remarkable enough, to be addressed by one of his station to the proud and powerful commander. "Once, twice—Ay! is there no more to be reckoned by thee, Sadabath? Once, twice—Yea, as the star sayeth, so sayest thou—Once, twice."

"What sayest thou?" said Narvaez, ceasing the prayer he had resumed, to question the oraculous adept.

"To thy prayer! Listen, and ask not.—Ay! thou speakest in mystery. I turn thee to the north, which thou knewest not, and the south, where thou hadst thy dwelling,—to the east, which thou abhorrest, and to the west, where was thy dark chamber; to the heaven, whose light thou lovest not,—to the pit under the earth, where thou wast a wanderer,—and to man's heart, which was pleasanter to thee than the bonds of the crystal. In the name of the Seven that are of power under the earth, and of the Seven that are mighty above, I call to thee Kalidon-Sadabath, the bright star that is quenched. In shadows, in fire and smoke—in thunder and with spears—with blows and with bloodshed, thou speakest, and I hear thee!"

"I hear nothing save thy accursed croaking, worse than that of the crows of Biscay," cried Narvaez, hotly. "If thy devil have no more intelligible gabble, cast him out, and call another."

"He speaks not, but by images and phantasms pictured on the crystal. Now listen, for thy story cometh. I see a great house on fire—"

"Ay, I shall perish then in a conflagration!" said the governor, hastily. "I have ever had a horror of burning houses."

"The smoke eddies, the flame roars, and one sitteth blindfold under the eaves, with the flakes and cinders falling about him, which he sees not."

"If thou meanest, that I shall rest, in that stupid state, under such peril, thy devil Sadabath is a liar, and I defy him!"

"And he that takes thee by the hand," cried Botello, without regarding the interruptions—"thy friend?"

"Ay, answer me that question," said the governor; "for if I am to be led out of the fire by a foeman, I will straightway forswear my friends, and give my heart to the magnanimous."

"Thou doest him obeisance!" cried the magician, with extraordinary emphasis.

"Villain!" exclaimed the general.

"Thou placest thy neck upon the earth, and he tramples it!"

"Liar and traitor!" roared the Biscayan, spurning the magician with his foot, and, in his fury, snatching up a weapon to dispatch him.

"Why shouldst thou stain thy hand with the blood of the dotard?" cried Duero, interposing for a second time between the intemperate commander and the object of his anger. "He is a madman, incapable of understanding what he says; and were he even sane, and speaking the truth, your commands to have him entertain you with his mummeries, should have ensured him against your anger.

"Very true," said Narvaez, with a scowl; "I was a fool to strike him. Trample on my neck! Thou grizzly and cheating villain!—Go! begone!—Thy devil, though he cannot tell thee what awaits thee in the morning, may show thee what thou deservest."

"I deserved not to be spurned," said Botello, tranquilly, after having gathered up his enchanted crystal, and raised himself to his feet; "and the dishonour will fall not on the side that was bruised, but on the limb that was raised against it. Once already, to-day, have I cursed the man that struck me in my captivity, and he lies a corpse on his couch."

"It is true," said a young cavalier, shuddering. "I inquired after Caboban, when I came from the prison with Botello—he was dead!"

"I will curse no more to-day," said the magician, sorrowfully; "for it is a sin upon the soul to kill with maledictions; and, moreover, thou, that has done me this wrong, wilt suffer enough, without a new retribution."

The general waved his hand angrily and impatiently, and Botello was led away, followed by most of the cavaliers.

CHAPTER XII.

When Don Amador found himself alone in the prison with Fabueno, with no other prospect before him than that of remaining therein till it might please the stars to throw open the doors, the rage that was too philosophic to quarrel with stone walls, gradually subsided into a tranquil indignation. Nay, so much command of himself did he regain, that hearing his companion bewailing his fate in a manner somewhat immoderate, as if regarding his incarceration as the prelude to a more dismal destiny, he opened his lips to give him comfort.

"I must counsel thee, friend Lorenzo," he said, "to give over this vain and very boyish lamentation, as being entirely unworthy the spirit I beheld thee display in presence of that Biscayan boor. The insult and shame of our present imprisonment are what thou dost not share; and therefore thou shouldst not be grieved on that account. And, doubtless, as thou wert arrested less because thou wert in fault, than because the foolish governor was in a passion, he will liberate thee, when he cools in the morning."

"I have no such hope," said Fabueno, piteously. "Don Panfilo is a most bitter and unforgiving man, sudden in his wrath, inexorable in his vengeance; and he has already indulged fury at the expense o men so much more elevated and powerful than myself, that I am in great fear he will give me to some heavy punishment, for daring to oppose his humours."

"Know, Lorenzo," said the novice, "that, in that opposition, thou didst show thyself possessed of a spirit which has won my respect; and unless thou dost already repent thy boldness, I will confess I am grateful to thee, that thou didst grasp thy sword in my cause. For which reason, when we are again free, I will beseech the admiral to grant thee thy wish, and immediately receive thee into my service, as a pupil in war."

"And how is your worship to be freed?" said Lorenzo, disconsolately. "Sure am I, Don Panfilo will no more regard your worship's honour and dignity than he did the privileges of the licentiate Vasques de Ayllon, the agent of the holy monks of San Geronimo, and, what is more, an *oidor* of the king himself; whom, notwithstanding all these titles, he imprisoned and banished, for thwarting him in a small matter."

"I have, in my own present situation, a sufficient and never-to-be-forgotten proof of his violence and injustice," said Amador. "Nevertheless, I entertain hopes of being soon at freedom; for if some lucky opportunity do not enable me myself to break my bonds, I am assured, the news of this most causeless and tyrannical outrage, will, in some way, be carried to the ears of my kinsman, the Knight Calavar, after which I shall be very confident of liberation, and, after liberation, as I may add, of satisfaction on the body of my wronger. But before we give ourselves to despondence, let us see in what manner we may be able to help ourselves. We should at least look a little to the various entrances that seem to lead into this dungeon."

The apartment was spacious but low; a narrow casement opened on one side, at the distance of six feet from the floor, and admitted the moonbeams, by which the captives were enabled to conduct their examination. The door through which they had entered was strongly barricaded on the outside. A passage leading to the interior was similarly secured, and equally impassable. The neophyte, with a sigh, turned to the casement A thick grating defended it, and shut out all hopes of escape.

"We can do nothing unless assisted from without," said Amador. "I would to heaven I had kept my knaves at my side. With such a wary servant as Baltasar at my back, and so faithful a desperado as Lazaro at my side, I should have made another sort of departure from that abhorred tower. The varlets are, perhaps, sleeping in security, without a thought of their master. Nay, by my faith, it is not probable they should give themselves to rest, without being made acquainted with my instructions for the night. Perhaps they may be lurking in the neighbourhood, ready to hear my call, and obey it. At all events, senor secretary, I would thou couldst mount to those iron stanchions, and take note of what is passing on the outside."

"Iron!" cried the secretary, quickly: "by San Iago of Compostella! a thought strikes me. I know well, senor, that in these lands, iron has almost the value of gold, and is too scarce to be wasted on the defences of a temporary dungeon, where it might be stolen too, at the first opportunity, by the Indians."

"Dost thou mean to say that these bars are of wood?" demanded Amador.

"Indeed I think so, senor; and if I had but a knife or a dagger, and the means of climbing into the window, I would warrant to be at liberty before morning."

"Here is a poniard, of which the villains forgot to divest me," said Amador. "Strike it against the stanchions—if they be of wood, we have much hope of freeing ourselves."

The secretary did as he was directed. He raised himself on tiptoe, and the sharp weapon buried itself in the flimsy barrier.

"If I had but something to stand on," he cried, eagerly, "how soon might we not be free."

"There is neither stool nor chair in this vile den," said Don Amador; "but I will not shame to give thee the support of my shoulder, and the more readily, that I think thy slight frame would be incapable of supporting my own greater weight. Pause not," he continued, observing that Fabueno hesitated: "if thy foot be near my neck, I shall know it is not the foot of an enemy. I will kneel to take thee on my back, as the Saracen camel does to his master. Stretch thyself to thy full height, so as to cut through the top of the bars; after which, without further carving, thou canst easily wrench them from their places."

Fabueno submitted to the will of the novice, and Amador rising without much effort under his weight, he was soon in a position to operate to advantage.

"Why dost thou falter?" demanded the novice, as Lorenzo, after making one or two gashes in the wood, suddenly ceased his labour.

"Senor," replied the secretary, in a low voice, "there is a guard at a little distance, sitting under the shadow of the pyramid. A cavalier stands in advance, watching—it is the Captain Salvatierra."

"May Heaven strike me with pains and death," cried Amador, with an abrupt ardour, that nearly tumbled the secretary from his station, "if I do not covet the blood of that false and cowardly traitor, who, after hiding his wrath under the cloak of magnanimity and religion, was the first to seize upon me, and that from behind."

"What is to be done, senor?" demanded Fabueno, in a whisper. "He will discover me; and even if I can remove the grating, there will be no possibility to descend without observation."

"Cut through the wood as silently as thou canst," said Amador; "and then when the window is open, I will myself spring to the earth, and so occupy the dastard's notice, that thou shalt escape without peril. Cut on, and fear not.

The secretary obeyed, but had not yet divided a single stake, when suddenly a noise was heard as of the clattering of armour, as well as the voice of Salvatierra, exclaiming furiously, "To your bows, ye vagabonds! Quick and hotly! Drive your shafts through and through!—Shoot."

"Descend," said Amador.

But before the secretary could follow his counsel, there came four crossbow shafts rattling violently into the window: and Fabueno, with a loud cry, sprang, or rather fell, to the floor.

"Have the knaves struck thee?" demanded Amador, as he raised the groaning youth in his arms.

"Ay, senor," replied the youth, faintly, "I shall never see the golden kings of Mexico."

"Be of better heart," said Amador, leading him to where the moonlight shone brightest on the floor. "Art thou struck in the body? If thou diest, be certain I will revenge thee. Where art thou hurt?"

"I know not," replied Lorenzo, piteously; "but I know I shall die. Oh Heaven! this is a pang more bitter than death! Must I die?"

"Be comforted," said the novice, cheeringly; "the arrow has only pierced thy arm. I will snap it asunder, and withdraw it. Fear not; there is no peril in such hurt; and I will bear witness thou hast won it most honourably."

"Will I not die then?" cried Fabueno, with joy. "Pho, it was the first time I was ever hurt, and I judged of the wound only by the agony. Pho, indeed, 'tis but a scratch."

"Thou bearest it valiantly," said Amador, binding his scarf round the wound; "and I have no doubt thou wilt make a worthy soldier. But what is now to be done? If thou thinkest thou hast strength to support me for a minute or two, I will clamber to the window myself, and remove the bars, without fear the arrows of these varlets can do me much harm through my armour."

"They are not above three-score yards distant," said Fabueno, "and, senor, I feel a little faint I know not, moreover, how I could escape, even if your honour should be so lucky as to reach the ground."

"I should not have forsaken thee, Lorenzo," said the cavalier, giving over, with a sigh, all hope of escape. "There is nothing more to be done. The foul fiend seize the knave that struck thee, and the dastard that commanded the shot! I would to Heaven I had beaten him soundly. How feelest thou now? If thou canst sleep, it will be well."

"I have no more pain," said the secretary, "but I feel a sort of exhaustion, which will doubtless be relieved by rest."

"Sleep, then," said Amador, "and have a care that thy wounded member be not oppressed by the weight of thy body. I will myself presently follow thy example. If aught should occur to disturb thee, even though it should be but the pain of thy hurt, scruple not to arouse me."

The neophyte watched till persuaded the secretary was asleep; then devoutly repeating a prayer, he stretched himself on his hard mat, with much tranquillity as if reposing on a goodly bed in his own mountain-castle, and was soon lost to his troubles.

CHAPTER XIII.

The cavalier was roused from his slumbers by a cause at first incomprehensible. The moonlight had vanished from the prison, and deep obscurity had succeeded; but in the little light remaining, he saw, as he started up, the figures of several men, one of whom had been tugging at his shoulder, and now whispered to him, as he instinctively grasped at his dagger—"Peace, cavalier! I am a friend and I give you liberty."

"I will thank thee for the gift, when I am sure I enjoy it," said the neophyte, already on his feet; "I remember thy voice—thou art one of the followers of the knave Narvaez?"

"I am one who laments, without extenuating, the folly of the general," said the voice of Duero. "But tarry not to question. Hasten—thy horse is ready."

"Where is the youth Fabueno? It is not in my power to desert the secretary."

"Here, senor," whispered Lorenzo. "I am ready."

"Ah, friend Fabueno! I am glad to hear thee speak so cheerily; it assures me thy wound does not afflict thee.—And my varlets, senor?"

"They wait for thee, Don Amador. Delay not: the door is open. The magician will guide thee to thy kinsman. Commend me to Cortes; and if thou art at any time found fighting on the pyramid of Zempoala, remember that Duero is not thine enemy."

"By Heaven! I should think I dream!" said Amador. "Stay, senor, I would thank thee for thy honourable and most noble benevolence; and, in addition, would tax thy charity in favour of a certain Moor—"

"*Tetragrammaton!* thou pratest as if thou wert among thy friends in Christendom, and of infidels too, as if there were no Christians to be thought of," said a voice in which Amador instantly recognised the tones of the enchanter. "I said, the captive should be freed; but never a jot that he should not be reduced to bonds again by his own folly. Be silent, and follow me."

The neophyte had collected his scattered senses, and instantly assuming the prudence, which, he now understood, was necessary to his safety, he issued from the prison. The moon was sinking behind the vast and majestic peaks of the interior. A deep shadow lay over the great square, on one side of which stood the dungeon; and only on the top of the principal tower trembled a lingering ray. A silence, still deeper than the darkness, invested the Indian city; and Amador could distinctly hear the foot-fall of a sentinel as he strode to and fro over the terrace of the pyramid. He looked to that quarter, whence, as he judged, had come the shafts which had so nearly robbed him of his fellow-prisoner. The crossbow-men slept on their post, in the mild and quiet air at the base of the temple.

"Give me thy hand, Fabueno," said Amador, drawing his poniard again from the sheath. "I will shield thee from the dogs this time. And now that I snuff the breath of freedom, I think it will need a craftier knave's trick than that of Salvatierra to deprive me of it a second time."

Following the magician, as he stole cautiously along, the brothers in misfortune crept on with a stealthy pace under the shadows of buildings and trees; till, exchanging the more exposed openness of the square for the safer gloom of a street, they advanced with greater assurance and rapidity. The stone dwellings of the Tlatoani gave place to the earthen and wicker cabins of the suburbs. The grey glimpses of morning had not yet visited the east when they reached the extreme edge of the town, and betook themselves to the covert of a clump of trees, under which, in the figures that were there visible, Don Amador recognised with joy his war-house and his followers.

"Rejoice in silence," said Botello, interrupting his raptures; "for there is an ear at no great distance very ready to hear thee. Mount and be ready.—Senor secretary, thy sorrel is tied to the mimosa. You can look to your equipments a little, while I see if Heaven will not confirm the fate of visions; for I dreamed I should ride back to Cortes on a good roan charger to-day."

The magician disappeared, and Amador, scarcely suppressing his ardour, when he found that not only his attendants and horses, but even the well-fleshed sword wrested from him in the evening, was in readiness to be restored to him, grasped it with exultation, and sprang into the saddle. Then passing towards Fabueno, and finding that his arm caused him much pain in the act of mounting, he assisted him to ascend with his own hand—a condescension that went to the heart of the secretary. From Fabueno also he learned, in a few words, somewhat of the secret of their liberation. Less than an hour after Amador had fallen asleep, and while Lorenzo was still kept awake by the pain of his wound, the door of the prison was opened, and Botello thrust in who comforted the secretary with a mystic, but still an unequivocal assurance of freedom before sunrise; and commanded him not to wake the novice, but to follow his example—he would need invigoration from slumber to support the toils of the coming day. What previous understanding might have existed between the enchanter and the Senor Duero he knew not; but certain he was, Botello had predicted a speedy deliverance for all, and all were now delivered.

"I have often considered," said the novice, thoughtfully, "that the existence of magical powers, either for the purposes of prediction or enchantment, was incompatible with the known goodness and wisdom of God; for surely if the power to foresee would have added any thing to the happiness of man, God would not have denied it to men generally. And as for the powers of enchantment, as they can only be used for good or bad purposes, it seems to me that to employ them for the first, would be to accuse the Divinity of an insufficient benevolence; while to exercise them for the last, would imply a supposition that Heaven had not all men equally under its protection. This, therefore, is my opinion; though I must confess that, sometimes, when governed more by passion or imagination than by reason, I have had my misgivings on the subject. Nevertheless, good Fabueno, in this particular case of Botello, I must advise thee not too much to abuse thy credulity; for, I think, all circumstances go to show, he grounded his prophecy of our deliverance more on a knowledge of the resolutions of the good Senor Duero than on the revelations of stars or spirits. Yet must I confess," continued Amador "that this very goodness of Duero, implying, as it truly does, a state of opposition and rebellion to the will of the uncivil Narvaez, his general, is so very miraculous, as almost itself to look like magic."

Before the secretary could reply, the sound of hoofs was heard approaching; and Botello, as they discovered by his voice, rode up to the trees. "The dream was true; the imp that speaks to slumber was not a liar!" he cried, exultingly. "We leave the jailer afoot; and Kalidon-Sadabath shall swing on a galloping horse. God is over all, by night and by day, afoot and on horse, in battle and in flight, Amen! Now ride, and Santiago for Spain!" He shouted this sudden cry with a voice that amazed Amador, after his often-repeated injunctions for silence—"Santiago for Spain! San Pedro for the invaders! and San Pablo for flying prisoners! Whip and spur, guide and cheer! and rocks and thorns spread over the path of pursuers!"

As Don Amador anticipated, the shout of the lunatic, for such he began to esteem Botello, was carried even to the head-quarters of the Biscayan. An arquebuse was discharged from the pyramid, and, as the fugitives began their flight, the flourish of a trumpet in one quarter of the town, and the roll of a drum in another, convinced them that the alarm had been given, and was spreading from post to post in a manner that might prove exceedingly inconvenient. The cavalier pressed to the side of Botello—an achievement of some little difficulty, for he perceived his guide was well mounted. "Senor Magico," he cried, as he galloped in company with him, "dost thou know thou couldst not have fallen upon a better plan to oppose our flight, and perhaps reduce us again to bonds, than by the indulgence of this same untimely and obstreperous shouting?"

"Trust in God, and fear not!" replied the magician. "This day shalt thou look upon the face of Cortes; and though the enemy follow us, yet shall his pursuit be vain and unlucky."

"I will allow that such may be the termination," said Amador; "yet, notwithstanding, can I perceive no advantage in being pursued, but much that is to be deprecated, inasmuch as we shall exhaust that strength of our horses in our hurry, which might have been reserved for a more honourable contingency."

"Your valour will by and by perceive there is more wisdom than looks to the moment," said Botello, coolly, without slacking his pace; "and, provided you can keep your followers from swerving from the path, and that inexperienced youth from falling out of his saddle, I will, with my head, answer for your safety."

Amador dropped behind a little; Lazaro and Baltasar required no instructions to keep them in the neighbourhood of their master; and the secretary, though complaining that he rode in pain, professed himself able to keep up with the party. From his henchmen, as he rode, Don Amador obtained but little to unravel the mystery of his escape. The two attendants had been quartered alone in a deserted building, in the garden of which they were instructed to provide for their steeds. They had been roused by a cavalier, who commanded them to follow him to their master, in token of whose authority he showed them the well-known blade of the novice. He had conducted them to the grove, and left him, with charges to remain, as they had done, in tranquillity, until the appearance of Don Amador.

At the dawn of day, the neophyte became convinced he had ridden more than the distance which,

he supposed, separated the camps of the rival generals; and wondering at the absence of all signs of life in the forest through which he was passing, he again betook himself to Botello.

The magician had halted on the brow of an eminence, where, though the dense wood, as well as the obscurity of the hour, greatly contracted the sphere of vision, he looked back as if striving to detect the figures of pursuers among the thick shadows. The shouts of men were heard far behind; but this circumstance, instead of filling the mind of Botello with alarm, gave, on the contrary, to his countenance an expression of great satisfaction.

"We are pursued, enchanter; and yet, I perceive neither tent nor outpost of thy friends, to give us refuge from our enemies," said Don Amador.

"Let them come," cried Botello, tranquilly; "it is worse for the stag, when the pack is scattered; but better for the kite, when the pheasants have broke the covey."

"There may be much wisdom in thy tropes, as well as in thine actions," said the novice; "yet am I slow to discover it in either. Whether we are to be considered the stag or the hounds, the hawk or the pheasants, entirely passes my comprehension; but sure am I that, in either case, our safety may be considered quite as metaphorical as thy speech. I understood from thee, last night, and I remember it very well, because it was that communication which exasperated me into a quarrel with the governor,—that the river whereon Cortes was encamped was but a league from Zempoala; yet am I persuaded we have galloped twice that distance."

"He travels no straight road who creeps through the country of a feoman," said Botello, resuming his journey, though at a more moderate gait than before; "and Don Amador should be content, if he can avoid the many scouts and vedettes that infest the path, by riding thrice the two leagues he has compassed already."

"Fogoso is strong, and, it seems to me, his spirit revives at every new step he takes through these forests," said the cavalier; "yet even for his sake, were there no other reason, would I be fain to pick the shortest road that leads to the camp of Cortes. I am greatly concerned about my young friend, the secretary, who, as thou hast doubtless learned, was last night shot through the arm with an arrow, by those knaves who kept watch at the window of the prison; and therefore, for his sake, am I desirous to find a resting-place as soon as possible. If I should give thee my counsel, (a thing I am loath to do, as thou seemest experienced in all the intricacies of this woody wilderness, in which I am a stranger), it would be, to forsake all these crooked and endless by-ways without delay, and strike upon the shortest path, without consideration of any small party of scouts we might meet. For, even excluding the wounded Fabueno, we are here together four strong men, armed, and well mounted, who, fighting our way to freedom, would doubtless be an overmatch for twice the number of enemies."

"The youth must learn the science of a soldier," said Botello, "and suffering is the first letter of its alphabet. Happy will he be, if, in the life he covets, he encounter no more agony than he shall endure to day. When we have time to rest, I will anoint his arm with a salve more powerful than the unguents of a physician. What I do, senor, and whither I guide, are best, as you will acknowledge when the journey is over. Why should your honour desire to enchange blows with poor scouts? I shall win better thanks of the Knight Calavar, when I conduct you to him unharmed. Faster senor—the pursuers are gaining on us."

The neophyte gave the rein to Fogoso, and, greatly inflamed by the mention of his kinsman's name, rode by the side of Botello, to demand of him such intelligence of the knight as it might be in his power to impart. Little more, however, had the astrologer to communicate than Amador had already acquired. The Knight Calavar was in the camp of Cortes, among the most honoured of his followers, if such he could be called, who divided the perils, without claiming to share the profits of the campaign, and fought less when he was commanded or entreated, than when moved by his own wayward impulses. That he was in good bodily health was also another point on which Botello was able to satisfy curiosity; and as he made no mention of another subject, on which Don Amador scrupled to speak, he was glad to believe the distractions of the new world had given some relief to the mental maladies of his kinsman.

A very little circumstance served, however, almost at the same moment to reveal one of his own infirmities. As the morning dawned and objects were seen more distinctly, he began to bend an eye of observation on the horse which Botello rode—a spirited beast, as he had already determined, by many evidences of fleetness and mettle. When he came to regard it more closely, he perceived, by signs not to be mistaken, that it was no other than the animal which had the day before caracoled under the weight of Salvatierra. Botello grinned, when an exclamation made him acquainted with the thoughts of the cavalier. To the demand where and how he had obtained possession of the charger, the answer was brief and significant. The Captain Salvatierra, like many other officers of Narvaez, preferred rather to waste the moonlight nights with the olive-cheeked Dalilahs of the suburbs, than with enemies and prisoners, even though they might be men of such merit and distinction as Don Amador. This was a peculiarity with which (he did not say whether by the instrumentality of his art, or the intervention of human agents,) Botello had contrived to become acquainted; and being also apprised of Salvatierra's favourite retreat, which was at no great distance from the grove wherein Don Amador had found his followers, he did not hesitate to deprive him of so superfluous an appendage as his charger.

"By St. John!" cried the neophyte, in a heat, "I would have bestowed upon thee more cruzadoes than thou canst gain by a month's exercise of thine art, hadst thou but made me acquainted with his hiding-place. I now know, the man who could strike a boy, and attack one he hated from behind, is a most execrable caitiff, more worthy of misprision than revenge; but despite all this, I should have begun this day's labours with more tranquillity and self-approval, had I but enjoyed two moments of conference with him previously."

"Your worship may have a day for acquitting scores with him more conveniently than you could have done this morning," said Botello.

"Harkee, Botello," cried Amador, eagerly—"It is thy absolute opinion we are at this moment pursued —is it not?"

"I do not doubt it—I hear shouts behind, ever and anon."

"I will tell thee what I will do," continued the neophyte: "I will tarry here with Lazaro and Baltasar: thou, if thou thinkest fit, canst advance with the secretary—I should be loath to bring him into combat before his wound is healed, and before Lazaro has given him some instructions in the management of his arms."

"All this thou wilt do then," said Botello, interrupting him, "on the presumption that Salvatierra is among the pursuers? Your worship may satisfy yourself, the vigilant cavalier is, at this moment, either abiding the reproof of Narvaez for his negligence, or biting his thumbs with disgust, as, among mounted captains, he walks through the streets of Zempoala. Horses are not in this land so plentiful as rabbits; and I thank the blessed influences, which have given me so good a friend this day," he went on, patting the neck of the steed—"so very good, that, until there comes a new fleet from Cuba, the Captain Salvatierra will be scarce able to follow after his charger. This may satisfy your honour on one point. As to another, I beg to assure you, Don Amador, that I am no lying juggler, selling my revelations for money. I tell what is told me, when I am moved by the spirit that is given to dwell within me; and neither real silver nor doubloon of gold can otherwise buy me to open my lips!"

CHAPTER XIV.

To the surprise, and much also to the dissatisfaction of Don Amador, the noon-day sun still found him struggling, with his companions, among the rocks and forests. It seemed to him, from a review of his journey, that he had been doubling and turning, for the whole morning, like a boy at blindman's-buff, within a circle of a few leagues; and though he could not, upon the closest inspection, detect a single tree or brook which he remembered to have passed before, he shrewdly suspected it was Botello's intention to make him well acquainted with the forest, before dismissing him from its depths. It was, however, vain to wonder, and equally fruitless to complain. For the whole morning, at different intervals, he was assured, sometimes from hearing their shouts in the thicket, and sometimes from beholding them from a hill-top crossing an opposing eminence, that his pursuers were close at his heels: of which fact, and the necessity it presented to move with becoming caution, the enchanter took advantage in the construction of his answers to every remonstrance. At length, perhaps two hours after noon, the travellers approached a hill, whence, as Botello assured them, they might look down upon the River of Canoes. This was the more agreeable intelligence, since the day was intolerably hot, and they almost longed for the bursting of a tempest which had been brooding in the welkin for the last half-hour, the drenching of which, as they thought, would be far more sufferable than the combustion of sunshine. They reached the hill, and from its bushy and stony side, looked down upon the valley, where the river, or, more properly speaking, the rivulet, went foaming and fretting over its rugged channel. On the hither side of the stream, the vale was bare and sandy, and on the other, though doubtless partaking of the same character, the trees which bordered upon the water, making divers agreeable groves, entirely shut out the view, so that Don Amador saw not, as he had fondly anticipated, the encampment of the invader of Mexico, and the resting-place of his kinsman. But if he beheld not what he so much desired to see, he surveyed another spectacle, which caused him no little wonder.

At a short distance, and almost at the bottom of the hill, he was struck with the unexpected apparition of the army of Narvaez, drawn out in order of battle, as if awaiting the approach of a foe, and commanding the passage of the river. He rubbed his eyes with astonishment; but there was no delusion in the view.

"Senor," said Botello, in a low voice, as if reading his thoughts, "you marvel to see this army, which we left sleeping at the temple, arrived at the river before us; but you forget Zempoala lies only a league from the river."

"Let us descend, and cross to the other side," said Amador, impatiently. "I see the very spot where sits the knave Narvaez on his horse; and if the valiant Cortes have it in intention, as I do not doubt, to give him battle, I should sharply regret to watch the conflict from this hill-side."

"I told Narvaez himself," said the magician, with a sort of triumph, "he should not join battle with Cortes to-day; and he shall not! When the time comes, Don Amador may join in the combat, if he will. Be content, senor: we cannot stir from this hill without being observed, and captured or slain. The thunder roars, the bolt glitters in the heaven; the storm that levels the tall ceibas will open us a path presently, even through that angry army."

Almost while Botello spoke, and before the cavalier could add words to the disinclination with which he regarded so untimely a delay, there burst such a thunderbolt over his head, as made Fogoso, in common with every other horse in the party, cower to the earth, as if stricken by its violence. This was immediately followed by a succession of separate explosions and of multisonous volleys, less resembling the furious roar of the ordnance of a great army than of the artillery of volcanoes; and it became immediately necessary for each man to dismount, and allay, as he could, the frantic terrors of his charger. In the midst of this sublime prelude, the rushing of a mighty wind was added to the orchestre of the elements; and, in an instant, the face of day, the black vapours above and the varied valley below, were hidden in a cloud of dust, sand, and leaves, stripped in a moment from the plains and the forest; and in an instant also, the army of Narvaez was snatched from the eyes of the cavalier. Presently, also, came another sound, heard even above the peal of the thunder and the rush of the wind; the roar of a great rain, booming along like a moving cataract, was mingled with the harsh music of nature; and Don Amador looked anxiously round for some place of shelter. Happily, though no cavern welcomed them into its gloomy security, there was a spot hard by, where certain tall and massive rocks lay so jammed and wedged together, as to present most of the characteristics of a chamber, except that there was wanting the fourth side, as well as the roof, unless indeed the outstretched branches of the great trees that grew among these fragments, might have been considered a suitable canopy. A spring bubbled up from among these mossy ruins, giving nourishment to a thick growth of brambles and weeds, which added their own tangled covert to the stouter shelter of the rocks and trunks. Into this nook the party, guided by Botello, to whom it seemed not unfamiliar, penetrated forthwith; and here they found themselves, in a great measure, sheltered from the rain. Here also, taking advantage of a period of inactivity, and at the instigation of Don Amador, who perceived with solicitude the visage of the secretary covered not only with languour, but flushed with fatigue and fever, the enchanter set about relieving the distresses of the youth. He removed the bandage and garment, and examined the wound, bathed the inflamed member in the cool waters of the fountain; and having thus commenced proceedings with so reasonable a preliminary, he drew a little silver vessel from his wallet, containing the unguent, 'blessed,' as he had before said, "of the fat of a Pagan's heart," and which, as may be repeated to those who might doubt the efficacy of so remarkable a compound, was not only much used, but highly commended by the Christian soldiers of that day in America. The magician commanded Fabueno to repeat a paternoster as slowly and devoutly as possible (for none of Botello's conjurations were conducted without the appearance of deep devotion), and mumbling himself another, or perhaps repeating some superstitious invocation, he applied the ointment, previously spread over green leaves, to the wound: and when it was again bound up, the secretary declared its anguish was much mitigated, as well as his whole body refreshed.

Don Amador regarded the youth for a moment with much grave kindness; and then said—"I owe this man so much gratitude for the good he seems to have, and doubtless has, done thee, whom I now, Fabueno—at least until I can receive instructions from my kinsman, the admiral—must esteem as being my ward and follower, that I am unwilling to offend him by seeming to throw any discredit on his remedy. Nevertheless I am not less bound to instruct thee with counsel, than to repay him with thanks; for which reason I must charge thee to remember, that, when any miracle of a very unusual or unnecessary character is wrought upon thyself, much more of it may possibly be the product of thine own imagination, than of that agent which seems to thee to be the only cause."

"Faith will work miracles, but fancy will not!" said Botello, gravely.

"If I were a better philosopher, good Botello," said Don Amador, "I would attempt to show thee how that which thou callest faith, is, in such a case as this, nothing but imagination in very fervent action, differing as much from that calm assurance which constitutes true faith, as doth a potter's pitcher gilded to resemble true gold, from a golden pitcher; which difference, in the latter case, may be instantly detected, by ringing them. And here I may tell thee, Botello, by way of continuing the figure, that, as the earthen vessel will really tinkle more pleasantly than the vessel of gold, so also will the excited imagination give forth a sound so much more captivating than the tranquil utterance of belief, that, in attempting to distinguish between them, men are often seduced into error. Nevertheless, I will not quarrel with thee on this subject, for I perceive thou art religious; and what thy religion does not blame in thee, I have no right to censure."

This was a degree of liberality doubtless produced rather by the amiable feeling of gratitude than by any natural tolerance of disposition or education; for the neophyte was in all respects a representative of the nobler spirits of his age, in whom the good qualities inherited from nature were dashed, and sometimes marred, by the tenets of a bad philosophy.

CHAPTER XV.

This discourse of the novice, together with the magical unction of the wound, occupied so much time, that when it was finished, the storm had in a great measure passed away; and Botello, either feeling his inability to reply to it with an allegory of equal beauty, or despairing to overcome the scepticism of the cavalier, instead of answering, rose from his seat, and led the way to the post on the hill-side, which they had lately deserted.

Drops of rain still occasionally fell from the heavens, or were whirled by the passing gusts from the boughs; the clouds still careered menacingly in the atmosphere: and though the sunbeams ever and anon burst through their rent sides, and glimmered with splendour on the shivered tops and lacerated roots of many a fallen tree, it was still doubtful at what moment the capricious elements might resume their conflict. The river, that was before a brook, now rolled along a turbid torrent, and seemed, every moment, to augment in volume and fury, as its short-lived tributaries poured down their foaming treasures from the hills.

"The boy to his bed, and the fool to his fireside!" cried the enchanter, with a sudden exultation, as, pointing down the hill, he disclosed to the cavalier the valley deprived of its late visitors. The armed men of Cadmus had not risen from the soil with a more magical celerity than had the soldiers of Narvaez vanished: the valley was silent and solitary. "I said the tempest should open for us a path!" continued Botello: "and lo! the spirit which was given to me does not lie!"

"I must confess," quoth Don Amador, with surprise, "you have in this instance, as in several others, verified your prediction. What juggler's trick is this? Where is the hound Narvaez?"

"Galloping back to Zempoala, to amuse himself with the dancers on the pyramid," said Botello, with a grin of saturnine delight. "He came out against Cortes, and his heart failed him in the tempest: he loves better, and so do his people, the comfort of the temple, than the strife of these tropical elements. Woe be to him who would contend with a strong man, when he hides his head from the shower! He shall vapour in the morning, but tremble when the enemy comes to him in dreams!"

"And I am to understand, then," said Amador, with a voice of high scorn and displeasure, "that these effeminate hinds, after drawing out their forces in the face of an enemy, have taken to their heels, like village girls in a summer festival, at the dashing of rain?"

"It is even so," said Botello: "they are now hiding themselves in their quarters; while those veterans who awaited them beyond the river, stand yet to their arms, and blush even to look for the shelter of a tree."

"Let us descend, then," said the cavalier, "and join them without delay? for I believe those men of Cortes are true soldiers, and I long to make their acquaintance."

"It is needful we do so, and that quickly," said the astrologer; "for this river, though by midnight it shall again be shrunk to a fairy brook, will, in an hour, be impassable."

It required not many moments to convey the party to the banks of the stream; but when they had reached it, it was apparent it could not be forded without peril. Its channel was wild and rocky; fallen and shivered trees fringed its borders with a bristling net-work, over and among which the current raved with a noisy turbulence. The cavalier regarded it with solicitude; but perceiving that the magician was urging his horse into it without hesitation, he prepared forthwith to follow his example. He saw, however, that the secretary faltered; and feeling as much pity for his inexperience, as commiseration for the helplessness to which, as he supposed, the arrow-hurt had reduced him, he rode up to him with words of comfort and encouragement.

"Thou perceivest," he said, "that Botello goes into the water without fear. Thou shalt pass, Lorenzo, without danger; for besides Lazaro on one side of thee, I will myself take station on the other. If thou shouldst, by any mischance, find thyself out of depth, all that thou canst do, will be to trust the matter to thy horse, who is doubtless too sagacious to thrust himself into any superfluous jeopardy. Be of good heart; this is a small matter: thou wilt one day, perhaps, if thou continuest to desire the life and fame of a soldier, have to pass a more raging torrent than this, and that, too, in the teeth of an enemy."

The secretary blushed at his fears, and willing to retrieve his character, dashed into the flood with an alacrity that carried him beyond his patron. For a moment he advanced steadily and securely, at the heels of Botello; but becoming alarmed at the sight of a tree surging down towards him, he veered a little from the direction, and instantly found his horse swimming under him. Before Lazaro or the cavalier could approach to his aid, his discomposure got so much the better of his discretion, that he began to jerk and pull at the reins, in such a manner as to infuse some of his own disorder into the steed. Don Amador beheld the sorrel nag not only plunging and rearing in the water, but turning his head down the stream, and swimming with the current. "Give thy horse the reins, and perplex him not, Lorenzo!" he cried, urging the dauntless Fogoso to his rescue; "jerk not, pull not, or thou wilt be in great danger."

But before the secretary could obey the voice of Don Amador, and before the latter could reach him, the hand of Lazaro had grasped the bridle, and turned the animal's head to the bank. "Suppose thou wert in the midst of a company of fighting spearmen, instead of this spluttering gutter," said the man-at-arms, in his ear, "wouldst thou distract thy beast in this school-boy fashion?"

The contemptuous composure of the soldier did more to restore the spirits of Fabueno, than the counsels of the cavalier; and yielding up the guidance of himself as well as his animal to Lazaro, he was soon out of danger.

In the meanwhile, Don Amador, in his hurry to give the secretary relief, had taken so little note of his own situation, that when he beheld his ward in safety, he discovered that he was himself even more disagreeably situated. A few yards below him was a cluster of rocks, against which, as he discerned at a glance, it would be fatal to be dashed, but which he saw not how he could avoid, inasmuch as the bank above them was so pali-

saded by the sharp and jutting boughs of a prostrate tree, that it seemed impossible he could
effect a landing there. While balancing in doubt,
at a time when doubt, as he well knew, was
jeopardy, he heard a voice suddenly crying to him
from the bank—"What, ho, senor! holla! 'ware
the rocks, and spur on: your hope is in the tree top."

While Don Amador instinctively obeyed this
command, and urged his steed full towards the
threatening branches, he raised his head and perceived a cavalier on a dun horse riding into the
water, above the rocks hard by the tree, as if to
convince him of the practicability of the passage,
and the shallowness of the water. This unknown
auxiliary stretched forth his hand, and doing to
Amador the service rendered by Lazaro to the
secretary, the neophyte instantly found himself in
safety, and ascending the bank of the river. Not
till his charge was on dry land, did the stranger
relax his hand, and then perhaps the sooner, that
Don Amador seized it with a most cordial gripe,
and while he held it, said, fervently, " I swear to
thee, cavalier ! I believe thou hast saved me from
a great danger, if thou hast not absolutely preserved
my life; for which good deed, besides giving thee
my most unfeigned present thanks, I avow myself,
till the day of my death, enslaved under the
necessity to requite thee with any honourable risk
thou canst hereafter impose."

While Don Amador spoke, he perused the
countenance and surveyed the figure of his deliverer. He was a man in the prime and midway
of life, tall and long-limbed, but with a breadth
of shoulders and development of muscle that
proved him, as did the grasp with which he
assisted the war-horse from the flood, to possess
great bodily strength. His face was handsome
and manly, though with rather delicate features,
and a very lofty and capacious forehead shone
among thin black locks, and under a velvet cap
worn in a negligent manner, with a medal of a
saint draggling loosely from it. His beard was
black and thin like his hair, and Amador plainly
perceived through it the scar of a sword-cut
between the chin and mouth. His garments were
of a fine and dark cloth, without much ornament;
but his fanfarrona, as it was called in the language
of the cavaliers, was a gold chain of at least thrice
the weight and bigness of the neophyte's, linked
round his neck and supporting a pendant of Christ
and the Virgin; and in addition Don Amador saw
on a finger of the hand he grasped, a diamond ring
of goodly size and lustre. Such was the valiant
gentleman, who won the friendship of the neophyte not less by his ready good will than by his
excellent appearance; although this last qualifi-
cation was not perhaps displayed to advantage,
inasmuch as his whole attire and equipments, as
well as the skin and armour of his horse, were
dripping with wet, as if both had been lately plunged into the river, or exposed to all the rigour of the
storm. He replied to Don Amador's courtesies
with a frank and open countenance, and a laugh of
good humour, as if entirely unconscious of any
discomfort from his reeking condition, or any merit
in the service he had rendered.

"I accept thy offers of friendship," he said,
"and very heartily, senor. But I vow to thee,
when I helped thee out of the stream, I thought I
should have had to give thee battle the next moment, as a sworn friend of Don Panfilo, the Biscayan."

"How little justice there was in that suspicion,"
said Amador, "you will know when I tell you,
that, at this moment, next to the satisfaction of
finding some opportunity to requite your true service, I know of no greater pleasure the saints
could send me, than a fair opportunity to cross
swords with this ill-mannered general, in serious
and mortal arbitrement. Know, senor, I am at
this moment a captive escaped out of the hands of
that most dishonourable and unworthy person,
seeking my way, with my followers, under guidance of a certain conjurer called Botello, to the
camp of the valiant Senor Don Hernan Cortes: and
I rejoice in this rencounter the more, because I am
persuaded you are yourself a true friend of that
much-respected commander."

" Ay, by my conscience, you may say so !" cried
the blithe cavalier; "and I would to Heaven
Cortes had many more friends that love him so
well as myself. But come, senor; you are hard
by his head-quarters. Yet, under favour, let us,
before seeking them, say a word to Botello, who,
with your people, I perceive, has crossed the
river."

A few steps of their horses brought the two
cavaliers into contact with the travellers, with
whom Don Amador beheld some half-a-dozen
strangers, all of hidalgo appearance, on horseback,
and dripping with wet like his new friend, but,
unlike him, armed to the teeth with helm, mail, and
buckler.

"How now, Botello, *mi querido ?*" he cried, as
he rode in among the party; "what news from
my brother Narvaez? and what conjuration wert
thou enacting, while he was scampering away
before the bad weather ?"

" Nothing but good, senor !" said Botello,
baring his head, and bending it to the saddle.

The neophyte was surprised to see this mark of
homage in the enchanter, whom he had found,
though neither rude nor presumptuous, not over-
burthened with servility. Looking round to the
other hidalgos, he discovered that they all kept
their eyes upon his companion with looks of the
deepest respect. At the same moment, and as the
truth entered his mind, he caught the eye of his
deliverer, and perceived at once, in this stately
though unarmed cavalier, the person of the renowned Cortes himself. For a moment, it seemed
as if the general were disposed to meet the disclosure with a grave and lofty deportment suitable
to his rank; but as Don Amador raised his hand
to his casque with a gesture of reverence, a smile
crept over his visage, which was instantly succeeded by a good-humoured and familiar laugh.

"Thou seest, senor !" he cried, "we will be
masking at times, even without much regard
either for our enemies or the weather. But trust
me, caballero, you are welcome; and doubtless
not only to myself, but to these worthier gentlemen, my friends." And here the general pronounced the names of Sandoval, De Morla, De
Leon, De Olid, and others,—all, as was afterwards
proved, men of great note among the invaders of
Mexico. The neophyte saluted them with courtesy,
and then, turning to the general, said—"I am
myself called Amador de Leste, a poor hidalgo of
Cuenza, a novice of the order of St. John of the
Holy Hospital, and kinsman of the Knight Gines
Gabriel de Calavar, to seek whom am I come to
this land of Mexico, and to the tents of your excellency."

All bowed with great respect to this annunciation; and Cortes himself, half raising his drooping cap, said—"I doubly welcome the Cavalier De Leste; and whether he come to honour me with the aid of his good sword, or to rob me of the true friendship of the Knight Calavar, still am I most glad to see him; and glad am I that Heaven has sent us a kinsman to watch by the side of the good knight. Senor," continued the general, anticipating the questions of the neophyte, "if you will moderate your patience a little, until I fulfil my duties with my mad friend here, the astrologer, I will be rejoiced in person to conduct you to your kinsman."

The courteous manners of Hernan Cortes did more to mollify the ardour of the novice than could any degree of stateliness. He smothered his impatience, though it was burning with a stronger and an increasing flame; while the general proceeded to confer with the magician.—"How is it, Magico mio?" he cried. "I had a deserter this morning, who told me thou hadst been entrapped, that my brother Narvaez had cudgelled thee with his own hands, and had some thoughts of hanging thee."

"Such is, in part, the truth," said Botello, tranquilly. "He was incensed at the stars, and struck me with his foot, because the Spirit of the Crystal gave not an answer to his liking."

"Ah, indeed!" cried Cortes, curiously; "and Kalidon hath been speaking to him! What said Kalidon-Sadabath of Narvaez?"

"He said that to-night," replied Botello, with his most solemn emphasis, "the foot of Cortes should be on the pyramid, and that to-morrow the Biscayan should do homage to his rival."

"Ay! and Kalidon told him all this?" said Cortes, quickly, and, as Amador thought, angrily.

"He told only that which it was fitting the Biscayan should know," said Botello, significantly; "he told him that which brought his forces into the field to-day, so that they shall sleep more soundly for their labours to-night; and yet he told him, no blow should be struck in the field. He showed him many such things; but he told him not, in manner as it was written in the heaven and figured in the stone, that to-night should his enemy creep upon him as he slept blind and besotted, and while his best friends guided the assailant to his bedside."

"Ay, by my conscience!" cried Cortes, turning with meaning looks to his companions; "this Kalidon reads men's thoughts; for it was but an half hour since, when I beheld these delicate warriors turning their backs to the gust, that I vowed in my heart I would, to-night, give them a lesson for their folly. What thinkest thou, son Sandoval? Will thy sun-burnt, lazy fellows of the Rich City march to Zempoala by night?"

"Ay, by night or by day, whenever they are bidden," said the sententious stripling, who, at this early period of the campaign and of his life, was not only the favourite of the general, but his second in fame. As Don Amador listened to his rough voice, and surveyed his bold and frank countenance, adorned with a curly beard and hair, both of amber hue, he bethought him of the story of the heralds summoning him to surrender his post into their hands, and receiving an answer which they digested in the nets of the Tlamémé, on the road to Tenochtitlan.

"And thou Juan Velasquez de Leon," said the general, turning to a young and powerfully-framed cavalier, with a red beard and fierce countenance, who, besides being clad in a heavier coat of mail than any other present, was more bountifully-bedecked with golden chains, and who set on a noble grey mare—"What sayest thou? Wilt thou play me a bout with Narvaez, the captain of thy kinsman, the Governor Velasquez?"

"Ay, by my beard, I will!" replied De Leon, with a thick ferocious voice, suiting the action to the word, and wringing the rain-drops from the beard he had invoked; "for, though I love the governor, I love not his dog; and if this godly enchanter will assure me the stars are favourable to the enterprise, I will be the last man to say, our two hundred and fifty men are no match for the thousand curs that bark at the heels of the Biscayan."

"It is written that, if we attack to-night, we shall prevail," said Botello.

"If I am permitted to say any thing in a matter of such importance," said the neophyte, "I can aver, that if the people of Narvaez design to revel away this night, as they did the last, their commanders trifling with jugglers and ropedancers, their guards sleeping on their posts, or straying away into the suburbs, as we discovered them when we escaped at dawn, it is an opinion which I formed on the spot, that some ten or fifteen score of resolute men may take them by surprise, and utterly vanquish them."

"I respect the opinion of Don Amador," said Cortes, "as well as the counsels of Kalidon-Sadabath and the stars, which have never yet told me a falsehood. But how comes it, Botello? Hast thou been flying since dawn? I cannot understand the necessity thou wert under to lead my worthy friend, Don Amador, so long a ramble; and moreover I perceive that, though yester thou wert constrained to trudge upon foot, thou art, to-day, master of a steed that may almost compare with Motacila, the wag-tail, of my son Sandoval."

"I stole the beast from the captain of the watch, Salvatierra, while he kept guard over us at some distance in the fields," said the magician, while all the cavaliers laughed heartily at the explanation; "and as for the long day's travel—when I found myself upon a good horse, I thought I could do no better than give the alarm, and draw a party in pursuit, and so entangle them among the woods, or wear them out with fatigue, that they should make little opposition when we came to attack their comrades at midnight."

"A shrewd and most laudable device!" cried Cortes, with unconcealed delight: "I have ever found thee as good a soldier as astrologer; and if the fates be as favourable to thee as I am myself, Botello, I can promise thee many an acre of maize fields or gold mountains, to recompense thy services."

"It must be as it is written," said Botello gravely. "Many a peril shall encompass me, but know that, in the worst, as it has been revealed to me, I shall be rescued out of it on the wings of eagles!"

"Amen!" cried Cortes, "for the day of miracles is not over. If the Senor de Leste" he continued, "claim to discharge his just anger for his imprisonment on my brother Narvaez, I will invite him to such a post of honour as shall be most likely to gratify his longings. And after that, if my very noble friend be inclined to exercise some of that skill in naval warfare which he has doubtless acquired among the knights of Rhodes, I will rejoice to intrust to him the attack upon the fleet of Cavallero."

" Senor," said Amador, " though I burn to assist you in the attack on Narvaez, I must first receive the command of my knight, Don Gabriel. I am not so eager to draw sword upon the admiral; for know, valiant Don Hernan, I have discovered in Cavallero a kinsman of my mother. And, senor," continued the neophyte, " I am now reminded of a message which he charged me to deliver to your excellency, wherein he begs to assure you, that, though fate has arrayed him as your enemy, he cannot forget the friendship of his former life."

" Ay!" cried Cortes, briskly, " does the excellent admiral say me that?"

" He bade me also avow to you, that, though it became him not, as an officer of Velasquez, to hold any communications with you, except those of simple form and courtesy, he should be well rejoiced when Heaven has removed the obstruction, and left him at liberty to meet you with former friendship and confidence."

" By my conscience," cried the general, turning to his officers, and exchanging meaning and joyous glances with them, " though these betidings which Kalidon hath not revealed, yet are they of such pleasant import, that I shall ever thank Don Amador for being the bearer of them. Eh, my masters!" he exclaimed; " did I not tell you, when we left Tenochtitlan in gloom, we should return to it in merriment? that when we sank our rotten fleet among the surges of Villa Rica, Heaven should send us another and a better? Let us move on, and spread this good news through the camp."

The neophyte perceived, by the exultation of the general, that he had been in a manner cajoled by Cavallero; but he was not sorry to think his kinsman should rather prefer to command his fleet as the ally of Cortes than as the friend of Narvaez.

CHAPTER XVI.

The sun was declining fast, when the travellers made their way to the camp of Cortes. The River of Canoes ran through a fertile valley; but this was of no great extent, and towards its upper termination, the scene of the events of the day, it was arid and broken with rocks. Immediately beyond the river, in a place made strong by rocks and bushes, impenetrable to cavalry, and affording the safest covert to his arquebusiers and crossbowmen, the wary rival of Narvaez had pitched his quarters. Temporary huts of boughs and fresh-woven mats were seen withering among the green shadows, and from these ascended the smoke of fires, at which the soldiers were dressing their evening meal. But in advance of this primitive encampment, dripping with rain like their commanders, yet standing to their arms with a patient and grave constancy, as if still in readiness for an enemy, Don Amador beheld the forces of Cortes. They had a weather-beaten and veteran appearance; most of them were apparelled in the escaupil, cut in separate pieces, resembling cumbrous plate armour, and occasionally

so hacked by the weapons of the natives, that the white lining gaped out somewhat ludicrously from its darker covering. Those arrayed in a better investment, had their morions and breastplates commonly covered with rust, as if kept too much occupied with perils by night and day to allow leisure for burnishing them. Nevertheless, they looked like disciplined and experienced soldiers. Amador observed that few of them had fire-arms: the crossbow, the sword, and the great lance of Chinantla, with its long double head of bright copper, were almost their only arms; but they handled them as if well acquainted with their value. Behind this advanced guard, under the shelter of the rocks and bushes, he remarked several officers, a few of them mounted, as well as divers groups of Indian menials; and, as his ear caught a low exclamation from the general, he turned his eyes and beheld the object of his long and painful search.

Under the shadow of a tall tree, remote from the rest, and attended only by a single armed follower—on a coal-black horse, heavily harnessed, which stood under his weight with a tranquillity as marble-like as his own, sat the Knight of Calavar. He was in full armour, but the iron plates were rusted on his body, and in many places shattered. The plumes were broken and disordered on his helmet; the spear lay at the feet of his steed; his buckler was in the hands of his attendant; and instead of the red tabard which was worn in a season of war by the brothers of his order, the black mantle of peace, with its great white cross, hung or drooped heavily from his shoulders. His beaver was up, and his countenance, wan and even ghastly, was fully revealed. The ravages of an untimely age were imprinted upon his aspect; yet notwithstanding the hollow cheeks and grizzled beard, the brow furrowed with a thousand wrinkles, the lips colourless and contracted into an expression of deep pain, he presented the appearance of a ruin majestic in its decay. His hands were clasped, and lay on the pommel of the saddle, and, together with his whole attitude and air, indicated a state of the most profound and sorrowful abstraction. In truth, he seemed the prey of thoughts, many and deep, and it scarcely needed the simple and touching legend, *Miserere mei, Deus!* which usurped the place of a scutcheon or other device on his shield, to know that if fame sat on his saddle, sorrow rested under his bosom.

No sooner had the neophyte beheld this gloomy apparition, than, with a loud cry, he threw himself from his horse; and, rushing forward, he seized the relaxed hand of the figure, and pressed it to his lips with reverence and affection. But the knight, not yet roused from his reverie, or struggling vainly with imperfect recollections, looked only in his face with wistful stare.

" Patron and cousin! my friend and my father!" cried the novice, passionately, " do you not know me? I am Amador!"

" Amador!" muttered the knight, with a troubled look and tone of perplexity. " Very well—to-morrow—to-morrow!"

" He will not understand you now," said the general. " He is often in these trances."

" Mi padre! mi amigo!" cried the youth, vehemently, without regarding the interruption of the commander, " will you not know me? I am Amador! Look—here is Baltasar, old Baltasar! your servant and favourite, that has been at your side ever from the days of the Alpuja——— to the fall of Rhodes."

" The Alpujarras!" echoed the knight, with a deep sigh. "Woe is me!—miserere mei, Deus!"

"He will recollect us now," said Baltasar, who had also descended, and who testified his fidelity by a tear that glittered in his ancient eye. "I never knew that word fail to call him out of his mood, though I have often known it fling him into one. Master! I am Baltasar; and here is your honour's kinsman, Don Amador!"

"Ay! is it so indeed? I thought I was dreaming," said the knight. "Art thou here indeed, my son Amador? Give me thy brows, for I am rejoiced to find thee in the world again." And stooping and flinging his arms round his neck, he kissed the forehead of the neophyte, with a parental affection.

"This, my master," said Cortes in an under voice, "is not a spectacle for us. Let us pass on, and arrange proceedings for the attack." And with his suite he instantly departed.

"And how dost thou prosper at Almeria?" continued Calavar, mildly, and without any incoherence of manner, though it was evident his thoughts were far away. "Hast thou found me any brave hearts, who will march with me against the infidels of Barbary?"

"Dear knight and patron," said Amador, "we are not now in Spain, but in the heathen lands of Mexico."

"Ay! Dios mio, I had forgotten that!" said Don Gabriel, with a bewildered air.

"Whither I have come," said the novice, "to beg your pardon for my negligence and desertion, and never more to part from your side.'

" I remember me now," said the knight, slowly and sadly. "Woe is me! a sore infirmity is on my brain; and sometimes I am not master of my own acts. But I remember thee, my friend: I remember that, in an evil hour of forgetfulness, I forsook thee, to come to this unknown land. But I beg thy pardon, my son; the dark mood took me from thee, and in truth I knew it not."

The tears came into the eyes of Amador, as he listened to the self-accusation of his kinsman, and remembered how much the blame should rest on his own momentary defection.

"It is I that must bear the reproach, and I that must look for forgiveness," he cried. "But I will never need to be rebuked or forgiven again; for I swear, dear kinsman, I will follow thee truly now, until my death."

"And thou hast left the fair hills of Spain, thy true friends, and thy lady-love," said Calavar, with a mournful voice, "to follow me over the wide seas and the hostile deserts? I welcome thee with gratitude, for thy love is great, and thy task will be bitter. I welcome thee well, Amador, but surely it is with sorrow; for I heard thou hadst won the love of a noble and virtuous lady: Heaven forbid I should not lament to sever thee, in thy youth, from the enjoyment of thy affection."

A flush of shame and pain mantled the countenance of the devoted novice, as he replied—"I confess I have much need of thy forbearance, dear knight; but they did me wrong, who said I could forget thee for the love of woman. I acknowledge no duty that is not to thee, and no passion but that of serving thee with constancy and truth. But I am sent to thee, not more by the impulses of my own love, than by the commands of his most eminent highness, the grand master, who leaves it to thyself, as a well-beloved and much-trusted follower of the holy order, whether thou wilt remain fighting the infidels of this new world, or return at thy pleasure to the island of Malta, which his majesty, the king and emperor, Don Carlos of Spain and Austria, hath promised to bestow upon the good knights, the defenders of Christendom."

"Among the infidels of the new world, then," said Calavar, casting his eyes meekly to heaven; "for I know, that what poor service I may yet render the faith, must be rendered soon; and if God uphold me, I will render it truly and well. But thou, Amador, my son, my faithful and my beloved! I adjure thee that, when my task is finished, thou returnest to the land of thy birth, and give thyself to a life of virtue, and, if possible, of peace. Watch well the creatures that are in thy breast, for among them are devils, which, if thou dost not chain them, will rend thee. Check thy wrath, fetter thy fury!" continued the knight, vehemently; "and when thou drawest thy sword, call on God, that it may not fall unjustly; for when blood is shed, that should not have been shed, it lives on the soul for ever! Ay de mi! Miserere mei, Deus!"

Don Amador feared, as he listened with a superstitious reverence to the adjurations of the knight, that he was about to relapse into his gloomy stupor; but he was deceived.

The lips of Calavar muttered on for a moment, as if continuing to repeat the solemn and impassioned appeal of the psalmist: and then, making the sign of the cross on his breast, he turned again to the novice with a kind of dismal cheer, and said —"I welcome thee again to this land, Amador. And Baltasar—What now, Baltasar? is it possible I should forget thee? I am glad to look upon thy loyal countenance; thine old friend Marco will rejoice to fight again at thy side. If I do not err, this is thy henchman, Lazaro: I greet thee well, Lazaro: be very true to thy master, and forget not thy religion. And this youth, that rests behind thee—if he be thy follower, my son, he shall share thy welcome."

"I recommend the youth Fabueno to thy kindness," said Amador, well pleased to perceive his kinsman so collected. "He is the secretary of the Admiral Cavallero, who claims to be related to your honour, and sends you the assurance of his love. I have been constrained, without yet knowing the pleasure of his excellency, to receive the youth into my protection; and this I did the more cheerfully, that he was my fellow-sufferer in the camp of Narvaez, and did, for my sake, very courageously expose himself to the painful shot of a crossbow, which now maims his right arm."

"If he have suffered for thee, my friend, I will not forget him," said the knight: "and I am rejoiced for his sake, that now, in this season of peace, we may cure his wound before we call upon him to endure another."

The countenance of Don Amador fell; he thought the knight's dream of peace denoted that he was sinking again into abstraction.

"Call this not the season of peace," he cried. "The Commander Cortes is resolute to fall upon his enemy, Narvaez, the enemy of honour; and it needs we should burnish up our arms, to give him help."

Calavar looked seriously at the youth, and touching his black mantle with an expressive gesture, said —"It is the time of peace, my son—the time of peace for those that follow the good St. John. I remember me now, that Cortes came down from the mountains, to fight the man Narvaez and his host; but these are not infidels, but Christians."

"Cousin," said the cavalier, warmly, "though

this man have the name, yet do I very much doubt if he possess any of the religion of a Christian; and I have to assure you, I have endured such causeless indignities at his hands, such as direct insult, violent seizure, and shameful imprisonment, as can only be washed away with his blood."

"Woe's me! woe's me!" cried the knight: "the blood that is poured in anger will not flow like water; it will not dry like water; nor will water, though blessed by the holy priest in the church, wash its crust from the hand! Thou seest," he cried, extending his gauntleted member, and gazing piteously into the face of his heated kinsman—"thou seest, that though, for thrice five years, I have washed it in brook and font, in the river that flows from the land of the Cross, and in the brine of the sea, it oozes still from between the scales, like a well that must trickle for ever, and will not be hidden. Thou art very wroth with me, Heaven!—Miserere mei, Domine!"

Don Amador was greatly shocked and grieved, that his imprudent obstinacy had so nearly recalled the distraction of his kinsman. But it needed not many expressions of gentleness and submission, to divert the current of his thoughts. The appearance of the young and devoted follower had come to the spirit of the penitent knight, like a cool breeze over the temples of a fevered man; and having once been roused from his gloom, he could not be long insensible to the excitement of his presence. He cast an eye of kindness and affection on the youth, and obeying, as one who had been long accustomed to such control, the humble suggestion of Marco, he turned to the tents of the encampment.

CHAPTER XVII.

The sun had not yet set, when the ray, stealing through the vapours that gathered among the distant peaks, beheld the Senor Cortes and his little army crossing the River of Canoes. A quarter-league above his encampment was the very ford which had given him passage, when, with a force short of five hundred men, and a few score of wild Totonacs, taken with him less as warlike auxiliaries than as beasts of burden and hostages for the fidelity of their tribe, he set out to cross mountains of snow and fire, rocky deserts and foaming rivers, in the invasion of an empire, whose limits, as well as its resources and power, were utterly unknown. Here the stream was more shallow than at that spot where it had been the fate of Don Amador to ford it; the flood had also in a measure subsided; and while the mounted individuals passed it with ease, the waters came not above the breasts of the footmen. Don Amador rode at the side of his knight, and though chafing with discontent at the thought that he should share no part in the brave deeds of the coming night, and be but a looker-on, while strangers were robbing him of his vengeance, yet did he conceal his troubles, lest the exhibition of them should give new pain to his unhappy kinsman. The three attendants were behind, and Fabueno, though evidently regarding the Knight Calavar with a deep and superstitious awe, rode not far from his patron.

The rivulet was crossed, and the hardy desperadoes who were now marching with spears to attack a foe of five times their own number fortified with cannon on an eminence, gathered about their leader as he sat on his horse on the bank, as if expecting his final instructions and encouragement. He surveyed them not only with gravity but with complacency, and smiling as if in derision of their weakness—for they did not number much over two hundred and fifty men—he said, with inimitable dryness—"My good friends and companions, you are now about to fight a battle, the issue of which will very much depend on your own conduct; and I have to inform you that if, as seems reasonable enough, you are vanquished, there is not a man of you that shall not hang at some corner of Zempoala to-morrow."

A murmur running through the whole crew, marked the disgust of all at this unsavoury exordium.

"The reasons for this opinion," continued the leader, gravely, "both as to the probable fate of the battle and of yourselves in the event of your being beaten, I shall have no trouble in speaking, only that, like one who knows how to use the butt as well as the blade of his lance, I shall discourse first of the hinder part of my argument; that is to say, of the very great certainty with which a gibbet shall reward every man who, this night, handles his weapon too tenderly. Know, then, my good brothers, that at this moment, though you very loyally and truly avow yourselves the soldiers of his majesty, our king and master, it hath somehow entered into the head of the General Narvaez, the lieutenant of his majesty's governor, to consider you as villain rebels and traitors—an imputation so exceedingly preposterous and eccentric, that, were we in a Christian land, you should not be required to deny it; but, standing as you do, with no better present judge than your accuser, it is certain your innocence could not be made apparent to his majesty, until after the gallinazas had picked the last morsel from your bones; at which time, as I think you will agree with me, a declaration of your true loyalty would not be a matter of much consequence to any of you."

Again a murmur, accompanied by sundry ferocious looks and savage interjections, testified the discontent of the adventurers.

"What I say is the truth," continued Cortes, adopting the scowl which darkened the visages of all, extending his drawn sabre above his head, and speaking with a fierce and resolute indignation; "in the face of that Heaven, which has seen us, for its honour and glory, devote ourselves to pain and peril, landing friendless and unaided, save by its own divine countenance, on the shores of bitter and murderous barbarians, overthrowing their bloody idols, and even in the chief sanctuaries of their diabolic superstition, on the palaces of their emperors and the pyramids of their gods, erecting the standard of the crucified Saviour—I say, even in the face of that Heaven that has seen us do these things, that will immortalise us on earth and glorify us in Heaven, the man Narvaez has dared to call us traitors to our king and faith, has denounced us more as infidel Moors than as Christian Spaniards, and declaring war upon us with sword, fire, and free rope, has sworn to give us to the death of caitiffs and felons.'

The answer to this passionate appeal was loud and furious. The cavaliers clashed their swords upon their bucklers, the footmen drove their spears into the soil, and, foaming with rage, swore they would thus answer the calumny in the heart of their enemy.

"Does it need I should give you more proof of the

lloody and insolent Narvaez?" said the general. "He hath set a price upon my head, and on the head of my loyal friend Sandoval, as though we were vile bandits and assassins."

"What needs more words?" cried the young captain, thus referred to. "He shall have my head for three thousand crowns, if he can take it."

"How it happens he has not thought any other head in this company worth buying," said the commander, with an adroit bitterness, "is an insult he must himself explain."

There was not a cavalier present that did not swear, in his heart, he would revenge such forbearance with the full swing of his weapon.

"It must be now manifest," continued Cortes, with composure, "that defeat will be the warrant and assurance of a gallows-death to all that may render themselves prisoners. And having convinced you of this, I may now betake me to the first article of my discourse, as one that concerns the possibility of your defeat. It is quite probable," he went on to say, with an irony more effectual than the most encouraging argument of hope, "that being but two hundred and fifty strong, and enfeebled by your divers battles with the Tlascalans, and the knavish herds of Cholula, you will be easily beaten by a thousand men, who, besides being fond of the valiant diversions of Indian dancers, and the martial delights of house shelter and soft beds, have hardened their bodies and perfected their knowledge of arms among the plantain patches of Cuba; and who, in addition, are of so magnanimous a turn, that they would, the half of them, at this moment, rather join your ranks than draw a sword against you. But why do I talk thus? A live dog is better than a dead lion—and a score of waking men better than a hundred sleepers. Know, then, ye grumbling and incensed companions, if ye will conquer this man that comes with a rope, ye may. Botello hath shown me how the stars are propitious, and how the Spirit of the Crystal hath promised us success. Heaven fights on our side, for we fight for Heaven—St. Paul be with us, for we contend for the privilege of converting the heathen—and Santiago will not forget us, for with every thrust of our spears we shall strike a brave blow for Spain."

"Let us on!" cried all, with a shout of exultation—"we will conquer."

"Nay," cried the general, with a mock discretion, "rush not too eagerly on danger. Let us wait a day for those two thousand brown varlets of Chinantla, whom the loitering Barrientos conduct hitherward; for though it be somewhat dishonourable to share a triumph with Indian soldiers, yet will they doubtless make that triumph the more certain."

"We will win it ourselves," cried the excited desperadoes.

"Ye will have hotter work than ye think," said Cortes; "and surely I believe ye will take to your heels, like the old Arrowauks of Cuba, leaving me to die at the pyramid, for I swear you, if ye force me to conduct you to Zempoala, I will not come from it alive, unless as its master."

"Let it be proclaimed death to any one that turns his back," cried an hundred voices.

"Ay, then, ye mad, valiant rogues, ye shall have your wish," cried Cortes, yielding to an excitement he had not easily suppressed, rising in his stirrups, and looking round him with that fiery and fanatical enthusiasm which was the true secret of his greatness, and which left him not for a moment even in the darkest and most perilous hour of his enterprise. "We will march to Zempoala, with God in our hearts, and the name of the Holy Spirit on our lips; and remembering that, under such influence, we scattered the tens of thousands that beset us on the plains of Tlascala, we will show this dog of a Biscayan what it is to oppose the arms of Heaven—Amen."

And Amen was uttered fiercely and frantically by the adventurers, as they prepared to follow their leader. But a wave of his hand checked their ardour for a moment; a few words explained the order of attack, and the duties of the several leaders, of whom the young Sandoval was appointed to the most honourable and dangerous task—to seize the artillery by a *coup-de-main*, and thus give passage for De Leon in the assault of the towers, while Cortes himself should stand by with a chosen body of reserve, to witness the valour of his captains, and give assistance where it was needed. Again, when the announcement of these orders seemed to have taken the restraint from the ardour of his followers, the general checked them. A huge and rugged cross of cotton-wood raised its mouldering bulk before them on their path—a holy landmark, raised by the piety of the invader, nine months before, while on his march to Tenochtitlan.

"Under the cross we will commend ourselves to God, and prepare ourselves for battle," said the leader, riding forward, and dismounting. His example was followed by all the cavaliers who, together with the footmen, knelt upon the dank grass and, baring their heads, prepared for the rites of penitence and absolution. None knelt with more devout submission than the Knight of Calavar; none exposed with more humility their youthful heads to the evening breeze than did he his silver-touched locks and withered temples; and none, as the holy chaplain dictated the act of general confession and contrition, echoed his words with a more fervent sincerity. Under the rude crucifix in the desert, knelt those men who were about to imbrue their hands in blood, and that the blood of their countrymen.

The words of penitence were said, the rite of absolution pronounced, and the followers of Cortes rose to their feet, with their hearts full of conquest. But before the helm was buckled and the horse mounted, there came on the twilight air, from the towers of Zempoala, the sound of the vesper-bell of Narvaez.

"It is long since we have worshipped at the sound of a Christian bell," said Cortes, again flinging himself on his knees. "God speaks to us in the omen. We have not forgotten, among infidel savages, that we are Christians."

As if those tones were rung in the chapel of a brother, instead of the barracks of an enemy, and as if to join that enemy in one act of piety, before springing upon him, sword in hand, all again knelt down; and the ave-marias of the two hostile armies, on the brink of engagement, went up to Heaven together.

CHAPTER XVIII.

Hard by the town of Zempoala ran a little brook, coursing through agreeable meadows, and here and there skirted by green forests. In a wood that overshadowed this current, but at the distance of a quarter league from it, lay concealed the forces of Hernan Cortes, waiting patiently for the time when the squadrons of Narvaez, satiated with the sports of their tawny neighbours, should additionally recomsense the exploits of the day with the oblivion of slumber. They had watched with contempt, and with joy (for they perceived in such spectacle a symptom of the infatuated security of their enemies), the great fire that lighted the diversions of the evening, blazing on the pyramid, until it began to die away, as did many of the sounds of revelry, that, in the still hour of the night, were borne to their ears. But it was not until their spies brought word that the last brand was flinging its decaying lustre over the eaves of the towers that they were bidden to arise, cross the stream, and array for battle.

In deep silence—for they knew there were sentinels on the path—they reached and forded the rivulet: trooper and footman passed over, and were ranked under their several leaders, and all seemed in readiness for the assault.

Still, however, the Knight of Calavar sat motionless on his sable steed, as if all unaware of the tempest of war that was brewing; and Don Amador beheld, with a pang of unutterable grief and vexation, the departure of those bold spirits to the scene of strife and honour, in which he was to have no share. As he sat fuming and frowning, now on the point of urging his kinsman for permission to follow, now reproaching himself in bitter reprehension, as if the unuttered wish might recall some of those thoughts of misery which so often perplexed the brain of the crazed knight, he heard the foot-fall of a horse, and perceived a cavalier riding towards him. To his grief was superadded a pang of shame, as he saw in this individual the person of Cortes himself, and conceived the object of his return.

"I am loath to see that the noble Calavar still abides by the black mantle," he said, as if content to waste no arguments on the knight; "but if the very valiant Don Amador de Leste be desirous to repay upon Narvaez the injuries done to his honour, or if he be minded to bestow upon me that great favour whereof he spoke on the River of Canoes, there can never come a better opportunity than this present; and for the services he may render me personally, as well as a most loyal cause, this night, by leading his followers with me to the pyramid, I shall ever remain in thankful remembrance."

The words stuck in the throat of the novice, as he replied—"I am the slave of my kinsman; I burn to follow you—but my knight must command."

He turned to Calavar, with a look of despair; but the night which concealed it from the eye, could not preserve the reproach from the ear.

"Stay thou by my side, Amador, my son," said Calavar, sorrowfully; "and let no man that follows thee or me, think to draw his sword this night; for we are the followers of St. John, and may not contend with a Christian, except in self-preservation."

"God shield thee, Sir Knight!" cried the general, anxiously; "every man who strikes with us to-night, strikes for his own life: victory preserves us, and defeat conducts us to the scaffold; and I am free to confess to thee, what I dared not speak to my companions, that unless every man does his duty, and God looks kindly upon all, I know not how soon we may be under the foot of our enemy."

"I have not refused thee my sword," said the knight, calmly, "when an infidel stood in thy path; nor will I, when such opposition is again made."

"But thy noble and valiant kinsman, and thy people," said the general, hastily; "they long to divide the honour of this combat, and they have no vows to restrain them. Every sword to-night is as valuable as a Cid's right arm."

"Tempt them not, delude them not into the commission of a great sin, that will fill their future days with remorse," said Calavar, earnestly. But before he could add any thing further, the report of an arquebuse from the front filled the forest with its roar, and Cortes, plunging the spur into his charger, was instantly borne out of sight.

"For God's sake!" cried Amador, with despairing entreaty, "let us cross the brook, and follow these brave men a little, though we join not in the battle."

"I will not refuse thee so much as that," said the knight, with some little animation, which was perhaps caused by the martial associations of the explosion. "It is not forbidden us, at least, to look on; and by so doing, Heaven may perchance allow us the happiness to save some wretched life."

In a moment the little party had crossed the brook, and spurring their horses hard, followed, as they thought, in the path of their late companion. But though the moon frequently displayed her resplendent visage through loop-holes in the scudding clouds, the many clumps of trees that dotted over the meadows in the environs of Zempoala, so confounded the vision, that they had reached the very suburbs, without yet obtaining a view of the adventurers. Indeed it had so happened, that not being provided with a guide acquainted with the various approaches to the town, they fell upon one entirely different from that trodden by the assailants. Not doubting however that they were following closely upon their rear, they pushed boldly on through a deserted street, echoing loudly to the clatter of their steps; nor did they discover their error until, to their great surprise, they found themselves issuing upon the great square, in full view of the temple.

They paused an instant in confusion. No tumult of shouts or fire-arms came from the sanctuaries; a deep silence brooded over the city as with wings; in fact, no sound broke the solemn tranquillity of midnight, save one which was the evidence and representative of peace. The faint twanging of a lute, mingling with the sweet tones of a youthful voice, came from the chief tower; to hear which the sentinels had doubtless stolen from their posts among the cannon, which were now seen frowning in solitude on the verge of the platform.

Before Don Amador could take time to ponder on the infatuated recklessness of the Biscayan General, or bethink him much of the young Moor of Fez, whose voice it was, he did not doubt, that sounded so plaintively from the tower, and which, by some inexplicable principle of association, instantly wafted his spirit to Granada, and wrung it with a sharp and sudden anguish—the clattering of a horseman riding furiously up a neighbouring street, roused him from the imperfect reverie; and his heart waxed hot and fierce, as the loud cry—"Arma! Arma! A las Armas!" burst from the lips of the flying sentry. In a moment of time this faithful watchman was seen dashing across the square; and as he flung himself from his steed, and rushed up the steps of the pyramid, still shouting the alarm at the top of his voice, there was heard another sound following at his heels, in which the practised ear of the neophyte detected the tramp of footmen, pursuing with the speed of death. In a moment also, ceased the lute and the voice of the singer torches flashed suddenly from the doors of the towers and as their light shot over the open square, there was seen a hurried mass of men running in confusion over the area of the pyramid. But the same flash that revealed this spectacle, disclosed also the wild figures and hostile visages of the men of Cortes, rushing to the assault, and sending forth a shout, that made the whole town ring and tremble to its foundations.

It was not in the nature of man to see these sights and hear these sounds with composure; and accordingly Don Amador had no sooner dismounted and flung the reins of Fogoso into the hands of Lazaro, than he perceived the Knight Calavar, on foot, at his side. He turned an inflamed, and perhaps a rebellious eye on his kinsman; but the countenance of Calavar was bent on his own, with a ghastly placidity; and as the hand of the knight was laid on his shoulder, as if to restrain his fury, the youth groaned in bitterness and anger. "By Heaven!" he cried, "I see the very face of Sandoval, as he darts at the steps! Oh, my friend! my father!"

"Shed no blood!" said the knight, with a hollow, but stern and vehement voice. "The avenger will follow thee by night and by day, at prayers and in battle—Shed no blood!"

"We are alone, too!" cried Amador, with ungovernable fire, as he found that Marco, Lazaro, and Baltasar, after flinging the reins of their horses round the shrubs that grew at the corner, had vanished from his side. "Even the varlets may strike at the knave who has wronged me; yet may I not raise my hand!"

"Shed no blood!" reiterated Don Gabriel, in a sort of frenzy: "forget thy rage, forswear thy fury; slay thyself; but strike not in vengeance! Miserere mei, Deus!"

All these wild words, though they take moments to record, were the utterance of an instant; and while the piteous plaint of the Knight Calavar still winged its way to heaven, and before Amador could reply a single word, the shouts of the assailants, as they rushed up the steps, were met by the roar of a cannon discharged by a skilful hand, illumining tree and tower with a hideous glare, and flinging death and havoc among their ranks. But the foot of desperation was on the earth of the temple; and before another piece of artillery could answer to the hollow thunder of the hills, the spear of Chinantla was drinking the blood of the cannoniers. At this moment, and while even the young Fabueno grasped the sword in his feeble hands, and turned his pale face to the battle—while Amador gnashed his teeth with rage—there rose from the platform, above the shouts and yells of the combatants, a shriek as though of a woman struck by the spear of some ferocious dastard. If the blow of an enemy had fallen upon his cheek, the young cavalier could not have started from the grasp of his kinsman, and drawn his sword, with a more irresistible impulse. But, in truth, the same cry that inflamed his own brain, went also to the heart of Calavar; when he dashed up the pyramid with furious haste, as if to the rescue of a sworn friend, the knight of Rhodes, drawing his weapon, followed fiercely after.

The scene that awaited the neophyte on the platform, though composed of men writhing together in thick affray, did not dwell an instant on his eye. It had caught, as if by providential direction, in the very chaos of combat, the figure that had sent forth the cry of affliction; and as he bestrid the body of Abdalla, and caught up the childish minstrel from his person, he shivered with a single stroke of his sabre, the spear that, in a moment, would have pinned to the earth both father and son.

"Dog of a conjuror!" he cried, as he discovered the person of Botello in the discomfited slayer, and prepared, while the stripling clung convulsively to his body, to shield him from the weapons of others; "dog of a conjurer! thy cruelty cancels thy services, and I will cleave thee for a viper!"

"What is written is written—God be thanked! I knew not 'twas a boy." And in an instant Botello vanished among the combatants.

"I thought thee a woman, thou scared varlet. Cheer up, Abdalla! they shall not harm thee. Father! my knight and my father! wilt thou protect my boy, that I have saved, and his sire, the Christian Moor?" cried Amador, as he perceived the knight stand staring wildly at his side. "I leave them to thee. Surely there may be other lives to save!" And thus concealing his excitement in what seemed an excuse for his disobedience, and without waiting for an answer, he rushed instantly into the thickest of the combat.

CHAPTER XIX.

When Don Amador fled from the side of Calavar, the instinct of his vengeance carried him to the spot where it seemed most likely to be gratified. The chief tower, as well as the two others, was invested; but in the crowd of musketeers and crossbowmen who stood valiantly at its door, repelling the assailants, he not only heard the voice, but very plainly perceived the tall figure of his enemy, Don Panfilo. Infuriated at the sight, he rushed forwards, and calling out with an indiscreet vigour that drew both the attention of that general and the thickest shots of his companions, he quickly found himself in a situation of great jeopardy. Though bullet and crossbow shaft fell harmless from his mail of proof, the thrust of some half a score partisans aimed at his shining and exposed breast, beat down the insufficient defence of his buckler, and hurled him instantly to the ground. But the voice with which he had challenged the Biscayan had been heard by friends as well as enemies; and as his faithful Lazaro dashed aside the most threatening weapon, the shield of another friend was extended over his body, and he found himself raised by the hand of Cortes.

"I knew my valiant friend would not desert me this night!" cried the commander. "But risk thyself no further. We will sack these towers, without the loss of so invaluable a life. What ho! yield thee, Narvaez!" he exclaimed, with a voice heard above the din; "yield thee up a prisoner, or thine own cannon shall bury thee under the temple!"

El Espiritu Santo, and on!" cried fifty eager men, as they rushed by their leader, and drove the followers of Narvaez into the sanctuary. They vanished; but the pikes and muskets bristling through the curtain, checked the audacity of the besiegers at the door; and the voice of Sandoval was heard exclaiming from behind—"Clear for the cannon, and stand aside!" when suddenly a firebrand, dashed by some unseen hand to the roof, lodged among the palm-leaves, and in a moment the whole superstructure was in flames.

"Spare your powder, and stand by for the rats!" cried Lazaro, for it was he who had achieved this cunning and well-timed exploit. "Basta! So we catch rabbits in La Mancha!"

"An hundred crowns to the knave of the firebrand!" cried Cortes, exultingly: "and three thousand paid in gold to him who lays the first hand on Narvaez!—Burn, fire! smother, smoke! the night is ours!"

"Ay, Don Panfilo! I await thee!" exclaimed Amador, as the rushing descent of beams and embers drove the besieged from the temple, and again discovered the person of his wronger. He sprang towards the commander, who, however hot and foolish of temper, now bore himself like a courageous soldier, and struck fast and fiercely at his foes, while shouting good cheer to his friends. But before Don Amador could well reach him, he saw the unfortunate man struck down, and in the act of being transfixed by many spears. Magnanimity—for the fury of a brave man cannot live without opposition—took the place of wrath; and no sooner did he hear Don Panfilo exclaim, with a piteous voice—"*Dios mio!* I am slain, and mine eye is struck out for ever!" than he rushed to his assistance, and seemed resolved to perform in his service the same act of valour with which he had befriended Abdalla. Again, too, as he caught an out-stretched arm, did he find himself confronted with Botello: but this time the magician's arm was extended in the office of mercy; and as he raised the vanquished general, and displayed his countenance, covered with blood oozing from his right eye, he exclaimed with a triumphal solemnity—"I saw him blindfold; and lo, his eye is blinded with blood!—Victory! victory! A Dios, à Cristo, y al Espiritu Santo, gracias! gloria y gracias! Amen!—Victory!"

Loud was the shout with which the besiegers responded to the cry of the magician; and the disordered and unavailing shots from the other towers were lost in the uproar of voices exclaiming—"Viva Cortes, el soldado verdadero! Viva Don Carlos, el rey! Viva el Espiritu Santo! el Espiritu Santo santisimo!"

"Away with him!" cried Cortes. "Guard thy prisoner, magico mio—thou hast won the prize. Leave shouting, ye rebel hounds, and bring up the cannon! What ho, ye rogues of the towers! will ye have quarter and friendship, or flames and cannon-balls? Point the ordnance against the flank towers! Bury me the knaves that resist us longer. In the name of God and the emperor, fire!"

But this measure was unnecessary. The shout of triumph with which the assailants proclaimed the capture of the Biscayan, was carried to every ear in the adoratories; and it was at this instant that the besieged, as much bewildered by the surprise as discomfited by the fury of the attack, disheartened, too, by the misadventure of their general, looked from the loops of their strong-holds, and made that famous blunder of converting the host of *cucujos*, or fire-flies, into a multitude of match-locks; whereby their hearts were turned to water, and their assurance of victory humbled to the hope of capitulation.

At the very moment that Don Amador, foiled in the gratification of his passions in one quarter, turned to indulge them in another, and rushed, with increasing animation, to that tower around which he heard many voices echoing the name of Salvatierra, he beheld that worthy captain issue from the door, fling his weapon to the earth, and stretch out his arms as if beseeching for quarter.

"Oh thou thing of a white liver!" cried the young cavalier, with extreme disgust, "hast thou not the spirit to strike me one blow? I would I had brought the boy Jacinto, to inflame thy valour a little. Thou wilt fight me a boy!"

As the neophyte thus gave vent to his indignation, he felt his arm touched, and, turning round, he beheld the secretary, holding a sword ornamented with drops of blood, and otherwise looking as though he had commenced his pupilage in a manner that would not shame his instructor.

"Well done, Fabueno!" he exclaimed, encouraging: "thou lookest like a soldier a ready. I am glad thine arm is so strong."

"I struck but one blow, senor, and I believe I have killed a man! God forgive me!" he cried, in more affright than elation—"I am not sure I did right; for the very moment I struck the blow, my arm twinged with a most horrible pang, which was perhaps a judgment on me, for striking a man who had done me no wrong."

"These things must not be thought of too much," said Don Amador, hastily; "in battle, we must look upon all opponents as our sworn enemies, at least, so long as they keep to their feet. But the battle is over—I will have thy wound looked to by some better surgeon than this crazy conjurer."

"Senor," said Fabueno, "I sought you out, not to trouble you with my pains, but to recall you to the knight, your kinsman, who is in some difficulty with certain men, about the Moor, that may end in blows, and never a henchman but old Marco by the good Don Gabriel."

Amador followed the secretary instantly, and found his kinsman—not unprotected, however, for both Marco and Baltasar were at his side—surrounded by several men speaking with loud and fierce voices, among which he quickly detected the tones of the master of the Incarnation.

"I say, and I aver," cried this man, as the neophyte approached, "the two knaves, both father and son, are my slaves, as can be proved by these runagate men, my sailors; and no man shall have them from me, without payment of my price."

"Ay! we can bear witness to that," said his companions. "These are true Pagan slaves, captured in a fight at sea, out of a Barbary pirate; very honest, lawful slaves; and though we have deserted our captain, to fight these other pagans, we will not see him robbed of his property."

To the great joy of Don Amador, he observed that his kinsman was calm and collected, and though he spoke with his usual voice of affliction, his answer was still full of dignity and gravity.

"The Moor that is a Christian cannot be enslaved; neither can he be bought and sold—and these claim to be both *Gazics*, Christian Moriscos. I guard them at the desire of their protector, who can assuredly support their claims; in which event thou must cease thy importunity, and think of them no more."

"They are my slaves, and I will have them!" said the master, ferociously. "I meet nothing but robbers in these lands; but robber peasant, or robber knight, neither shall wrong me for naught."

"Thou base and covetous cur!" said Amador, advancing before the sailor, "if thou usest no better language, I will strike thy head from thy shoulders! Dost thou remember me, sirrah? Did not the admiral satisfy thee in this matter? and dost thou follow me still, like a blood-hound, after the prey that is not thine?"

"Calm thy rage, son Amador," said the knight. "Thou hast done a good act to-night, in saving the lives of this poor child and his father, and thou shalt not want my aid to preserve their freedom. But let us not quarrel: enough Christian blood has already been shed, and a woful sight will the sun see, when he presently rises. Let us go before Cortes: he shall judge between this man, and these creatures whom thou hast rescued from destruction."

"I ask nothing but justice and my right," grumbled the master, somewhat pacified by the angry bearing of the neophyte—for this was a more commanding argument than the mildness of Calavar.

He fell back, and without further contention,

though with a lowering look, followed the two cavaliers and the Moriscos in search of Don Hernan.

CHAPTER XX.

The morn, which by this time was breaking over the sea, was ushered in with a thousand sounds of triumph; and the drums of the vanquished rolled in concert with the trumpets of the victors. In truth, saving to the wounded and broken-spirited Biscayan, and some few cavaliers who had remained faithful to him and to his employer, the change of others from rivalry to subjection, was a circumstance more of gratulation than regret; as was proved by the ready alacrity with which they betook themselves to the audience of their conqueror.

In the gilded and feather-broidered chair in which he had first seen the person of the unlucky Narvaez, Don Amador de Leste now perceived the figure of the conqueror, a rich mantle of an orange hue thrown over his shoulders, his head bare, but his heel resting on a certain footstool or ball of variegated feathers, and altogether preserving an appearance of singular but superb state. His valiant and well-beloved officers stood ranked on either side, and on either side, also, his resolute followers were displayed, as if performing the duties of a body-guard. In this situation of pride, he prepared to receive the congratulations or the griefs of his enemies; and, as if to add still further to the imposing magnificence of the ceremony, at that moment, as a wild roar of conchs and drums mingling with the wilder shouts of human beings, burst over the city, a great multitude of native warriors from the province of Chinantla, marching in regular and alternate files of spearmen and archers, and glittering with feathers and brilliant garments, strode upon the square, and dividing upon either side of the pyramid, halted only when they had surrounded it with their warlike and most romantic array. The spectacle was no more surprising to the people of Narvaez than to those friends of Cortes, who had not before looked upon an Indian army, among whom Don Amador was one. He regarded the picturesque barbarians with much admiration; though his eye soon wandered from them to dwell upon the leader, and the ceremonious part he was then enacting. He sat in his chair like a monarch, and though, at times, when some conquered cavalier more honoured, or better beloved, than others, approached, he arose, and even extended his arms with a friendly embrace, in the greater number of instances he was content to pronounce some simple words of compliment, and present his hand to be kissed—a mark of homage reverentially rendered by all.

It did not become Don Amador, though he surveyed these proceedings with some little contempt, as indicating on the one side too much arrogance, and on the other too much humility, to interrupt them; in which persuasion he stood patiently aside with his company, watching until such moment when he might approach with propriety. Being thus a witness of the degree of friendliness which characterised the receptions, as well as the many petitions which the comers made to be accredited and enrolled among the general's true friends and followers, he began to lose somewhat of the wonder with which he had regarded the suddenness and facility of the victory. It was apparent that most of the officers of Narvaez had long made up their minds to devote themselves to the service of his enemy; and when they had paid their compliments to Don Hernan, they dropped among his officers, as if joining old friends and comrades.

It gave the neophyte some pain when, at the conclusion of these ceremonies, he beheld the Biscayan led forward in chains (for he was heavily ironed), to salute his rival. His casque was off; a bandage covered his eye; his face was very pale; and he strode forward with an uncertain gait, as if feeble from the loss of blood, or agitated by shame and despair. Nevertheless, he spoke with a firm and manly voice, when he found himself confronted with his vanquisher.

"Thou mayest congratulate thyself, Cortes," said the fallen chief. "Thy star has the ascendant, thy fate is superior; and so much do I admire my own misfortune, that I could compliment thee upon it, did I not know it was wrought less by the valour of my enemies than the perfidy of my friends."

"Thou doest thyself, as well as all others, a great wrong to say so, brother Narvaez," said the victor, gravely; "and it would better become thee magnanimously to confess thou art beaten by thine own fault, rather than to follow the example of little-minded men, and lay the blame upon others."

"I confess that I am beaten," said the captive; "and that the shame of my defeat will last longer than my grave. But I aver to God, and I maintain in thy teeth, though I am but a captive in thy hands, that this victory is altogether so miraculous, it could not have happened unless by the corruption of my people."

"To Heaven and my good soldiers it is all owing," said Cortes, composedly: "and so little miraculous, my brother, do I myself esteem it, after having twice or thrice beaten thirty thousand Tlascalans at a time, all valiant men, that I vow to thee on my conscience, I cannot do other than consider this triumph as altogether the least of my achievements in Mexico."

"It must be so, since you say it," responded Narvaez, his breast heaving under the sarcasm, with a bitter and suffocating pang; "yet it matters not. Let the glory be ever so little, the shame is not the less notorious; and though thou scornest thy reward of fame, I will not fly from mine own recompence of contempt. What more is expected of me? Dios mio! I cannot, like the rest, kiss thy hand, and take upon me the oaths of service. I am thy prisoner."

"Had I been thine," said Cortes, gravely, "thou wouldst have fulfilled thy word, and hanged me, wouldst thou not?"

"What matters it?" replied the unfortunate man, with a firm voice. "Doubtless if the passion that beset me at the time of the proclamation had lasted after a victory, I should have been as good as my word: for which reason I will anticipate thy excuses, and assure thee, out of mine own mouth, thou wilt but retaliate fairly, to dismiss me to the same fate."

"Thou canst not understand the moderation thou hast not practised," said Cortes, rising, and speaking with dignity. "The foolish rage that provoked thee to set a price upon my head I remember not; the madness that proclaimed these true and most loyal men for rebels and traitors, must be passed by as other hallucinations: but as in doing this thou hast greatly injured and jeoparded the interests of thy master the king, thou art worthy to suffer the death of a rebellious subject, for such thou hast acted. Nevertheless, I will do thee a grace thou wouldst not accord to me; I will conceive that, however traitor was have been thy actions, thou mayest have been faithful at heart—mistaken, but not disloyal: in which thought I give thee thy life, and will recommend thee into the hands of his majesty for judgment and mercy."

The conqueror waved his hand, and Narvaez was led away—to terminate, in after years, a life of mischance by a death of misery, among those ruder tribes of the north who are but now vanishing from the borders of the Mississippi, and to add his melancholy tale to the gloomy histories of De Leon and De Soto."

" What will my noble and thrice honoured friend, Don Amador de Leste?" cried Cortes, as he perceived the neophyte approaching him. " We should be good friends, senor ; for I owe thee much, and we have been in peril together."

" Twice, I thank your excellency," said Amador, "you have done me the office of a true cavalier; for which I will not trifle the time to thank you, inasmuch as my arm is henceforth unshackled, and I can write my gratitude better with it than with my tongue. What I have now to require is, that your excellency will judge between me and this fellow, the master of a ship, in the matter of a Moor called Abdalla, otherwise Esclavo de la Cruz, and his son Jacinto ; both of whom being Christian Moors, though captured in a Barbary vessel, this man doth claim to be his slaves ; I, on the other hand, as their vowed protector and champion, upholding them to be free, and in the condition of wards to his majesty the king."

" They are my slaves," said the master—but a frown from the general instantly closed his lips.

" It is well for the Moor," said Cortes, as, at his command Abdalla approached, followed by Jacinto: " it is well for the Moor that he has so powerful a protector as Don Amador ; for otherwise, having discovered it was his accursed hand shot off the falcon which destroyed me four brave men, and maimed as many more, I had resolved to hang him like a hound this very morning."

" There is no better cannonier in all your excellency's train," said the master, who, however likely to be robbed of his property, could not check the impulse to praise it.

" I fired the cannon with the fear of death in my eyes, if I refused," said Abdalla, humbly ; " and my lord should as well be wroth with the linstock as with myself."

" Say not a word, sirrah Moor," said Cortes, " for the favour of Don Amador having saved thy life, I have nothing further to do but to judge thy claims to liberty ; the which if thou establish, I will not scruple to employ thee in mine own service."

" The freedom of these twain," said Amador, " was recognised by his excellency the Admiral Cavallero ; and I thought he had satisfied this ship-master."

" His excellency, the admiral, protested he would represent the matter to the Governor Velasquez." said the surly captain ; " and I was content to abide his decision. But my sailors, hearing there was more gold to be gathered among these hills than on the sea, deserted me ; and not having the means to carry my ship to Cuba, I was fain to follow after them ; hoping the excellent cavaliers would do me justice, and pay me for my captives."

" Sirrah," said the general, " wert thou with Narvaez, or with me, in this battle ?"

" With neither," said the sailor. " I arrived at nightfall ; and not being able to make my way to Narvaez, I slept off my fatigue in a hut below, till roused by the din of this siege ; coming forth to behold which, I discovered my slaves, and straightway claimed them : and my sailors yonder will witness I won them in fair fight."

" The Moriscos are Christians, and therefore thy property," said the commander ; " and if they were, being taken out of the camp of an enemy, they should be reckoned spoils of war, and for that reason, my possessions, and not thine. Cease therefore thy demands : follow thy sailors, if thou wilt—for on the lakes of Mexico, I shall have employment for thy best skill ; and if, in time, I discover thee faithful, and this Moor as dexterous as thou representest, I will, without allowing thee any right to the same, give thee very good guerdon for his services."

The master, concealing his dissatisfaction, retired.

" I hoped," said Amador, " your excellency might be persuaded to send Abdalla and the boy to Spain."

" I am loath to say to Don Amador, that may not be," replied Cortes. " As a good Christian, Abdalla will doubtless rejoice to fight the infidel ; and as for his boy, if ther be no other cavalier willing to advance him to the honours of a page, I will myself receive him. I hear he is a good musician ; and I want a playmate for my little Orteguilla, whom I left dancing boleros before the emperor Montezuma."

The fame of Jacinto as a lutist and singer, had already spread among the cavaliers ; and his appearance was at the same time so prepossessing, that many of them stepped forward, and avowed themselves ready to receive him into service. Don Amador himself, now for the first time perusing his countenance at leisure, and moved as much by its beauty as by its air of grief and destitution, added himself to the number ; and it seemed as if the claims of the various applicants might lead to heat and misunderstanding. The cap of Jacinto had fallen from his head, and long ringlets, such as greatly stirred the envy of the younger cavaliers, fell over his fair brow and exceedingly beautiful countenance. His delicately chiseled lips, parted in alarm and anxiety, moved and played with an ever-varying expressiveness ; while his large black eyes, in which brilliancy was mingled with a pensive gentleness, rolled from general to cavalier, from Amador to his father, with a wild solicitude.

The difficulty was terminated at last by Don Hernan. " I vow by my conscience," said he, " I like the boy's face well ; but I will not oppose my wishes to those of worthier gentlemen here present. In my opinion, no man hath so fair a claim to the boy as Don Amador de Leste, who first befriended him ; and not doubting that, herein, the boy will agree with me, I propose the election of a master to be left to himself, or, what is the same thing, to his father, as a measure equally agreeable to all. Choose, therefore, Abdalla, between these cavaliers and thy benefactor ; for it is not possible the stripling can remain with thyself."

Abdalla bent his troubled eyes around the assembly ; and Amador, not doubting his choice, regarded him with a benignant encouragement. Long did the Almogavar survey him, now with eagerness, as if about to throw himself at his feet and beseech his protection, and now faltering with hesitation and doubt. Amador, mistaking the cause of his embarrassment, prepared to reassure him ; when the eyes of the Moor, wandering away from himself, fell upon the figure of Don Gabriel standing hard by. The same hesitation that disturbed him before, again beset him ; but it lasted not long. Amid the clouds of dejection and distraction that characterised the countenance of the Knight of Rhodes, there shone a ray of benevolence as if the emanation of a fixed and constant principle; and Abdoul al Sidi, as he remarked it, forgot that Calavar was the slayer of his people.

"If my lord, my very noble lord," he said, bending to the earth, "will hear the prayer of his servant, and waste his charity on so great a wretch as Abdoul, there is no one of all this noble assembly to whose benevolent protection Abdoul would sooner confide his helpless and sinless child."

The cavaliers stared; yet Abdalla had not erred, when he reckoned on the humanity of Calavar.

The knight received the hand of Jacinto from his father, and regarding him with a paternal kindness, said—"For the sake of Him who did not scorn to protect little children, I will receive this boy into my arms, and protect him with my best strength, both from sorrow, and the sin that is the parent of sorrow."

"And I may see him sometimes!" said the Moor, lingering, though the general had motioned him away.

"Surely I keep him from harm, not from the love of his father."

"I commend thee to Heaven, my child," said the Almogavar, embracing him. "Confide in thy master, remember thy father, and pray often.—Farewell."

But the boy, with a cry that drew the commiseration of all present, threw himself into Abdalla's arms, and clasping him as if for ever, wept on his bosom.

"Thy master waits thee, my child," said Abdalla, disengaging his hands, and again leading him to Calavar. "Be wise and faithful, and remember, if not always in thy presence, I shall not often be far from thy side."

The stripling once more kissed the lips of the Morisco, and then checking his lamentations, as his father left him, wrapped his cloak round his head, as if to hide his tears, and stood by the knight in silence.

While this incident was passing, the attention of Cortes was attracted by two Indians differing much in equipment from the warriors of Chinantla, but still of a soldier-like bearing, who, in company with two or three of his chief cavaliers, hastily approached him, and conferred with him through the medium of an interpreter.

A cloud came over his countenance; he arose, and smote his hands together with fury. "What, ho, cavaliers!" he cried; "We must think of other matters than crying babes and jingling pages. I thank God for this victory, for never came one more opportunely; and ye, true friends, who have this moment protested your allegiance, prepare now to make it more manifest. Sharpen your swords, saddle your horses; for to-day we must march to Tenochtitlan!"

A murmur of surprise ran through the multitude that thronged the pyramid; and Amador forgot both the boy and the touch of indignation with which he had seen him transferred to another, though his kinsman, as he pressed towards the excited general.

"Know ye, friends and brothers," continued Cortes, "that the devil has, at last, waked up in the infidel city; blood has been shed—the blood of Spaniards as well as of Pagan Mexicans—and, at this moment, Alvarado is besieged in the palace by the whole hordes of the valley; and he swears to me, by these Tlascalan messengers, that unless I

render him speedy assistance, he must die of starvation, or perish under the sword of the barbarians. So God speed us to the Venice of the New World! the Babylon of the mountains! The gold shall not be snatched out of our hands, nor the fame blotted from our histories: we have this good day numbers enough to chase the imps from the islands, and to tumble the gods from their temples; and so will we, in the name of God and St. Peter! Amen!—God speed us to Tenochtitlan."

The shout that answered this pious and valiant rhapsody, from the pyramid and the square, gave note of the zeal with which his followers, both old and new, were prepared to second the resolution of their leader.

CHAPTER XXI.

A history of modern epidemics, drawn up by a philosophic pen, would add much to our knowledge of the mysteries of human character and human power, as well as of the probable contingencies of human destiny. In the prosecution of such a subject, besides tracing the development of those little causes which, in former days, have spread their effects from man to man, until whole communities have laboured under a disease resulting in revolutions of the most stupendous nature, we should, doubtless, perceive many of those points of susceptibility and chains of impulsion, which render men the creatures of change; and which, being definitely understood and wisely influenced, might at once put it in the power of philanthropists to govern the operations of reform in such manner as to avoid the evils of ill-considered innovation. Religion and liberty have both come to us as diseases; and the propaga them throughout the lands of the heathen and the slave, is yet a measure of pain and peril, because we have not considered, or not yet learned, how to address ourselves to infirmity. What man will not say, that the enthusiasm which cumbered the sands of Syria with the blood of the Crusaders, might not, if properly directed, have brought light and happiness to all Europe? or that the fever, which has left the revolution of France a horror on the page of history, might not, under the guidance of a less speculative philosophy, have covered her valleys and filled her cities with security and peace? Enthusiasm comes and goes; and because we know not enough of its weak and governable qualities to direct it in the paths of justice and virtue, it is allowed yet to fill the world with wrong and misery; and, misapplied to the purposes of glory, avarice, and fanaticism, the engine which God has given us to advance our civilisation, is still the preserver of barbarism.

In the facility with which the aboriginal empires of America were subverted by a handful of hot-headed Spaniards, mankind has been willing to find a proof of the savage imperfection of their institutions. In the case of Mexico, at least, this testimony is deceptive. If we remember that the tribes of Anahuac, like the other races of America, were struggling against obstacles which did not impede the advancement of other nations, we shall be surprised at the point of civilisation they had reached. Heaven had denied all the useful domestic animals to America. The bison, which is perhaps not altogether untameable, roamed only over the prairies and the forest lands of the north, among tribes that were yet in the bottom class of humanity. The horse and the ass added not their strength to the labours of man; and the little llamo, bearing the burden of its master over the icy Cordilleras of the south, was but a poor substitute for the camel of the desert, to which it has been compared. Accident, or the knowledge of a thousand years, can alone teach men the use of that metal which will bring him civilisation, when gold will not buy it; but the discovery even of the properties of iron will soon follow the invention of an alphabet, however rude or hieroglyphic. The Mexicans could already record and perpetuate their discoveries. Without the aid of iron and domestic animals, they were advancing in refinement. Civilisation had dawned, and was shedding a light, constantly augmenting, over their valleys; and, apart from these deficiencies, saving only, perhaps, additionally, in the article of religion, which was not yet purged of its abominations, (and which, perhaps, flung more annual victims on the altars than did, in after days, even the superstition of their conquerors, in Spain,) the Mexican empire was not far behind some of the monarchies of Europe in that method, purpose, and stability of institutions, both political and domestic, which are esteemed the evidences of civilisation.

A moral epidemic nerved the arm of the invaders; another paralyzed the strength of the invaded. Superstition covered the Spaniard with armour stronger than his iron mail, and left the Mexican naked and defenceless: and, in addition, the disease of disaffection, creeping from the extremities to the centre of the empire, added its weight to the lethargy of religious fear. When Hernan Cortes set out on his march, the second time, against Tenochtitlan, believing that God had chosen him to be a scourge to the misbeliever, he knew well that thousands and tens of thousands of malecontents were burning to join his standard. Mexico was the Rome of the New World—a compound of hostile elements, an union of tribes and states subdued and conjoined by the ambition of a single city, but not yet so closely cemented as to defy the shocks of a Gothic irruption. What might have been the condition of the empire of Montezuma, if the divine ray which conducted the Genoese pilot over the Atlantic had been reserved for an adventurer of the present day, it is impossible to determine; but it is quite clear, its condition as such at the time of the invasion, that, had not the indecision of its monarch, founded on such a conjuncture of coincidences as might have confounded a more enlightened prince, entirely repressed its powers of resistance, no armies, raised by the Spanish colonists, or even by their European master, could have penetrated beyond the shores; and the destiny of Cortes would have been written in letters as few and as obscure as those which have recorded the fate of Valdivia among the less refined, but better united Araucanians of Chili.

The heart of the leader was bold, the spirits of his confederates full of resolution and hope; and notwithstanding the evil intelligence that their victims were awakening to a knowledge of their strength, and confirming their audacity in the blood they had already shed, the united followers of Narvaez and Hernan Cortes began their march over the mountains with alacrity and joy.

The novelties and wonders that were each day disclosed, were remarked by no one with more satisfaction than by Don Amador de Leste. He rejoiced when, ascending among the mountains, the fens and sandhills of the coast were exchanged for picturesque lakes and romantic crags; when the oak woods and pine forests began to stretch their verdant carpets over the hill-sides; when, standing among the colossal ruins of some shivered peak, he cast his eye over glen and valley, glittering with verdure and fertility, far away to the majestic ridges over whose hazy sides tumbled the foamy fall, or crept the lazy cloud, while among their gorges glistened the distant cones of snow. Now he admired the ferns, lifting their arborescent heads, like palms, among other strange trees; now, as he exchanged the luxuriant slopes for those valcanic deserts which strew the base of Perote with lava and cinders, he beheld the broad nopal, and the gigantic maguey, rearing their massive leaves over the fissures, while a scorched forest withered and rotted above. Sometimes, while pursuing his weary way over these mountain *paramos*, or deserts, he advanced bewildered, as what seemed a fair and spacious lake, withdrew its vapoury waters from before him, and revealed a parched and barren expanse of sand. The journey was an alternation of mountain and valley, forest and plain, with sometimes a pleasant little Indian village, and, twice or thrice, a town of no mean magnitude and splendour, rising in pleasant nooks among the horrors of the waste.

Over this rugged region it was not possible to drag the ordnance and heavy stores, with which Cortes was now abundantly provided, without much labour and delay; and it was not until about the time of the summer solstice, more than a month after the fall of Zempoala, that, at the close of a pleasant day, the new invaders laid their eyes, for the first time, on Tlascala—the capital of that warlike republic, which, for the singular object, as certain historians have conjectured, of preserving an enemy to exercise their armies, as well as to furnish victims for their gods, the Mexican monarchs permitted to subsist in the heart of their empire.

The slowness of their march was productive of many advantages to those particular individuals, whose adventures it is the object of this history to record. It gave to Don Amador an opportunity to make the acquaintance of many of his new companions, among whom were some not unworthy his friendship. The services of the Senor Duero were remembered not without gratitude; and although he reflected, at times, with some unreasonable disgust, that these denoted as much treachery to a friend as humanity to a stranger, the attentions of that cavalier were so sedulously continued, that he could not well refuse him his regard. The taciturn but ever-resolute Sandoval,—the lofty and savage, but not the less courteous De Leon,— the fiery De Olid,—the daring de Ordaz, who, thirsting to accomplish exploits not dreamed of by his confederates, had clambered among the snowy pinnacles and burning caverns of the great Volcan, and had thereby won the right, confirmed to him afterwards by the Spanish king, to carry a fire-mountain for his arms;—these, as well as divers others of no mean renown, so recommended themselves to the esteem of the neophyte, that he dismissed much of his preconceived contempt, and began to consider himself among honourable and estimable cavaliers. But to none of them did his spirit turn with so much confidence and affection as to Don Francisco de Morla, a young hidalgo of his own native town, greatly beloved throughout the army, as a man of honour and tried courage. In this cavalier, a modest carriage was united to great gaiety of disposition, and a warm heart, governed by gentleness of temper. A milder enthusiasm than that which beset his comrades, softened him to the barbarians, in whose land he was more desirous to consider himself a guest than an enemy ; and without lacking any sincerity of devotion to his own faith, he seemed to regard the ferocious superstitions of the natives with less abhorrence than pity. He had followed at the side of Cortes from Tobasco to Zempoala ; and, being as observant as brave, was not only able to acquaint Don Amador with the marvellous events of the invasion,—its perils, sufferings, and triumphs, but could also instruct him in many of the remarkable characteristics of the land and the people.

The effects of this delay on the Knight of Rhodes were equally beneficial, though differently wrought. The paroxysms of lethargy, as well as the fits of distraction, which, as Don Amador learned from the faithful Marco, had been many and ungovernable, whenever the excitement of battle was over, began to vanish under the interest of the society, and the influence of the careful government of the neophyte, who, from long acquaintance with his kinsman's eccentricities, had acquired a power to soothe them. But if such was the influence of Don Amador, the power of the little Moorish page over his moody moments was still more remarkable. The sorrows of Jacinto vanished with the capriciousness of childhood ; and perceiving that, in the long and toilsome march, he was never so far separated from his father that he might not look to see him at nightfall, he quickly recovered his spirits. Then, as if to express his gratitude to the good knight who protected him, he studied, with wonderful diligence and address, how best to please and divert him. With a thousand pretty stories, chosen with such discretion and prattled with such eloquence, as often surprised the neophyte ;—with countless songs, which no one could sing with more sweetness, or accompany with more skill on the lute,—he would seduce the knight from his gloom, and cheat him out of his melancholy. No dagger shone so brightly as that polished by the hand of Jacinto ; no plume of feathers waved with more grace than that set by the young Moor on the casque of Don Gabriel. If a tiger-flower glittered on the path, if a chirimoya put forth its fruit by the way-side, before the knight could turn his eyes upon them, they were in his hand ; and Jacinto smiled with delight, as he received the thanks of his patron. The benevolence of Don Gabriel soon changed to affection ; he almost smiled—not so much with joy as with love—when, sometimes, the boy sat at his feet at evening, and sang with fervour a hymn to the Virgin ; he was troubled, if by chance, Jacinto strayed from his sight ; and Don Amador sometimes found himself beset by a sort of jealousy, when he perceived, or thought he perceived, this stripling robbing him of the heart of his kinsman. But, to do Don Amador justice, it needed not many suggestions of his honour or pride to rid him of such envious emotions. The zeal of the boy in the service of Calavar, as he confessed, deserved much of his own gratitude ; to which should be added many acknowledgments of the satisfaction with which he himself listened to his

instrument and voice. If the boy sang with alacrity at the wish of Calavar, he was not less ready to obey the command of the neophyte. Nevertheless, Don Amador fancied this obedience was rendered less from love than duty : he thought the stripling looked on him with fear, sometimes with dislike ; and he was persuaded that (though on occasions of difficulty—when a thunder-storm met them on a hill, or a torrent roared over the path—Jacinto chose rather to fly to him for protection, than to remain by the side of the knight) he was oftener disposed to shrink from his kindness. This troubled Don Amador, for he loved the boy well ; and often he said to himself—" I have saved this urchin from a beating, and, as I may add, from the imminent danger of being speared like a frog ; I have given him gentle words, as also praises for his singing, which is indeed very excellent ; I have helped him over divers rivers, and a thousand times offered him a seat on Fogoso's crupper, which it was his own fault, or his own cowardice, he did not accept ; in short, I have helped him out of countless troubles, and was, besides, the first to befriend him in these lands— without reckoning what protection I have given to his father, Sidi Abdalla ; and yet the lad loves me not. It is a pity he was not born of Christian parents ; ingratitude runs in Moorish blood !"

So thought Don Amador a thousand times ; but a thousand times, as his displeasure waxed hot at the unthankfulness of the lad, it was dissipated by some little circumstance or another. Once, when he was in a talkative mood, and desirous to have Jacinto at his side, he was so displeased at his evident wish to escape, as to vent his displeasure in a reprimand. The boy ran to his side, kissed his hand, and raised his eyes, suffused with tears, to the countenance of his preserver. The cavalier never rebuked him again. On two or three occasions, also, greatly to his surprise, he caught the stripling weeping ; which was the more wonderful, since he seemed not only reconciled, but greatly pleased with his state of easy servitude. On all such occasions, he excused himself with such persuasive simplicity, as not only to remove all suspicions of discontent, but greatly to increase the affection of the neophyte. He was a favourite as well with the men-at-arms, as with their masters ; and Don Amador often reflected with wonder, how quickly he had wound himself into the hearts of all. " If I could persuade myself into a belief of magic," he pondered, " I should think him a truer conjurer than Botello. What Botello prophesied concerning Narvaez, is very remarkable ; yet, when a man is prognosticating all his life, it is hard if he do not sometimes blunder upon the truth. Truly he blundered wrong about Lorenzo's arm, which is not yet well healed ; and I vow to St. John, I thought, one time, it would have gangrened. But as to Jacinto, he has enchanted my knight's heart. I have ever thought he abhorred the Moors, and surely he slew great numbers in the war of the Alpujarras. As for myself, I was born with a natural detestation of the Moorish race ; and I never before knew but one that I did not hate at first sight." Here he sighed dolefully. But this boy I love ; yet loves he not me. I have heard of philters and love medicines ; and surely, as many drugs attack the stomach, brain, and other parts, there is no reason some should not be found to affect the heart."

But while the neophyte thus marvelled and reasoned, Jacinto stole still deeper into his favour; and at the end of a days march, Don Amador was oftener found sitting at the door of some Indian cabin, or under the shade of its flower-garden, listening with Calavar to the lays of the young musician, than sharing the martial sports of his companions, or even superintending the warlike exercises of his ward, Fabueno.

CHAPTER XXII.

To those invaders who had not yet witnessed with their own eyes the peculiar wonders of the interior, the approach to Tlascala was full of surprise and interest. As the sun sank, the four hills on which lay the republican city, and the pyramids and towers that crowned them, sent their long shadows over the plain to the feet of the cavaliers, and in the gloom, they beheld a vast multitude—the armies of the four tribes which composed the nation, under their several banners, glittering with feathers, and marching in regular divisions to the sound of wild music, as well as a host of women and children waving knots of flowers, and uttering cries of welcome—advancing to do them honour. Don Amador forgot the valiant appearance of the warriors of Chinantla, while gazing on the superior splendour of the armed Tlascalans. These warlike people, in imitation of their Christian confederates, had learned to divide their confused throngs into squadrons and companies, ranked under separate leaders, and now approached in what seemed well-ordered columns. Bunches of red and white feathers waved among their long locks, and ornamented their wickered shields; the short tunic of *nequen*, a coarse white cloth of the maguey, left their muscular and well-sculptured limbs free for action; and as they strode along, brandishing their swords of obsidian (the *maqua-huitl*—a heavy bludgeon, armed on either side with blades of volcanic glass,) or whirling in their slings those missiles of hardened copper armed with sharp horns, which were capable of piercing the toughest armour—and ever and anon mingling their fierce cries with the savage sound of drum and flute, they made a show not more remarkable than glorious. At the head of each division, under his peculiar standard (the image of some bird of prey, or wild beast, very gorgeously decorated), marched each chieftain, with the great plume of distinction, or *penacho*, as it was called, rising full two feet above his head, and nodding with a more than barbarous magnificence. Thus apparelled and thus displayed, they advanced to the head of the Christian army, and dividing on either side, so as to surround the Spanish host with a guard of honour, each individual, from the naked slinger to the feather-crowned chief, did homage to the Christian general, by touching the earth with his hand, and then kissing the humbled member; while at the same moment, a number of priests with black robes, and hair trailing almost to the ground, waved certain pots of incense before him, as if to a demigod—a mark of distinction which they afterwards extended to the cavaliers that surrounded him. The religious ire of Don Amador de Leste was inflamed, when it became his turn to receive this fragrant compliment; and looking down fiercely upon the innocent censer-bearer, and somewhat forgetting that Castilian was not the language of the realm, he cried—"What dost thou mean, thou Pagan dog! to smoke me in this idolatrous manner, who am neither a god nor a saint?"

"Senor," said De Morla, who sat at his side, "be not offended at this mark of reverence, which the customs of the country cause to be rendered to every man of dignity; and which is a harmless compliment, and no idolatrous homage, as was first thought among us. Thou wilt presently see them smoke their own generals and senatorial law-givers, the last of whom thou mayest see yonder approaching us in a group—those old men with the feather fans in their hands."

As De Morla predicted, the priests were no sooner done smoking their Christian visitors, than they turned to do similar reverence to their own dignitaries; and Don Amador's concern was soon changed to admiration, to behold with what lofty state these noble savages received the tribute due to their rank.

"This fellow with the red plume, and the sword that seems heavy enough for a giant's battle-axe," he cried—"the knave over whom they hold a great white bird like an ostrich—he must needs be a king! He bends to Cortes, like an emperor doing courtesy to some brother monarch."

"That," said De Morla, is Xicotencal, of the tribe of the White-Bird, the most famous general of the Tlascalans, and, in fact, the captain-in-chief of all their armies. He is not less valiant than famous, and not less arrogant than valiant; and at this moment, beshrew me, I think he would rather be knocking his bludgeon over our heads, out of pure love of war, than kissing his fingers in friendship. This is the man who commanded the armies which fought us on our first approach; and truly I may say, he fought us so well, that had he not been commanded by the senators, who are the civil rulers of Tlascala, to make peace with us, there is much suspicion we should have seen heaven sooner than the vale of Mexico. For, senor, after having supplied us with food, as scorning to be assisted in his victory by famine, which was somewhat pressing with us, he fell upon us to win it in person; and I must confess, as will be recorded in history, he quite broke and confounded, and would have utterly destroyed us, had it not been for a providential mutiny in his camp in the very midst of his triumph; whereby we had time to rally, and take advantage of his distresses. The same good fortune might have been his, another time, without so inconvenient an interruption. But it seems the senators of Tlascala only made war on us, to prove whether or not we were valiant men, and worthy to be received as their allies, according to our wish; which being now proved to their satisfaction, they ordered the war to be ended, and welcomed us as friends. There never were more valiant men than these soldiers of Tlascala."

"Of a surety," said Don Amador, "I begin to thing the Captain Gomez of the caravel was somewhat mistaken as to the courage of these barbarians."

"Thou seest the second chief—he of the green penacho, with whom Cortes confers so very courteously! That is Talmeccahua, chief of the tribe Tizatlan, a very young warrior, but second in fame only to Xicotencal; and being more docile and friendly, he is much a favourite with our general, and doubtless will be selected to accompany us to the great city. Of those reverend old senators I could also give you an account; but we who are soldiers, care not for lawgivers. It is enough to assure you, that they are the rulers of Tlascala; and that though these proud people, the commoners, call themselves free republicans, they are to all intents and purposes the servants of many masters—a sort of freedom somewhat more questionable than that of a nation governed by one king. Thou seest, they kiss their hands to us, as we enter their city. For my part, I think them rogues to love us, their truest enemies, better than their domestic rivals, the people of Tenochtitlan. Woe betide them who help us to conquer their foes, when their foes are conquered!"

As De Morla spoke, Don Amador found himself entering the city of Tlascala. Twilight had darkened over the hills, and in the obscurity (for the moon had not yet risen) he perceived long masses of houses, not very lofty, but strong, on the terraced roofs of which stood many human beings, chiefly women and children, who waved a multitude of torches, and, as they sung what De Morla told him were songs of welcome, threw flowers down upon their guests. Flambeaux were also carried before them in the streets; and with this sort of pomp, they were ushered to a great building with extensive courts, sufficient to lodge the whole army, which was assigned them for their quarters.

While the cannoniers were arranging the artillery, the officers of the guard choosing their watchmen, and preparations were made to hold a conference with the chiefs of the republic, the neophyte was invited by De Morla to accompany him to a pyramid on one of the four hills, whence, he assured him, was a noble prospect of those huge mountains which separated them from the valley of Tenochtitlan. Don Amador looked about him for his kinsman. He had retired with the chaplain of the army, in some sudden disorder of spirit, for prayer or confession; and Don Amador sighed, as he bethought him that yearly, about the time of midsummer, the knight's disease seemed to reach its intensest point. "If thou couldst but sing to him that holy song of the Virgin, written many years back by the priest of Hita —'Quiero seguir a ti, Flor de las flores!' said Don Amador to the Moorish page (for it was Jacinto who gave him this information), "I have no doubt thou wouldst do him more good than the reverend father Olmedo; for, though I know not why it should be so, he ever seems to me more troubled than relieved by confession."

"It was a song chanted the evening before that had thrown the knight's spirit into disorder; and Baltasar had commanded him never to sing again;" so said Jacinto.

"Baltasar is an ass! though very zealous for his master," said the neophyte, in a heat, "and thinks there is nothing comforts my kinsman's heart, save the clanging of swords and bucklers; whereas, I know very well, thy ditties are true medicine to him; and, with Heaven's blessing, thou shalt sing him very many more."

"Let the boy follow with us," said De Morla: 'I like his piping well; and methinks, if he have not forgotten that tender love song about the Christian knight who adored a Pagan Morisca, I can listen to it again with much good will, as I look towards the mountains of Montezuma."

"I am loath to have him away, for perhaps my good knight may call for him when the confession is over; and there is something raw in this night air, that may be prejudicial to the youth."

"Yo seguire a mi senor, I will follow my master,' said Jacinto, with simplicity. "My lord the knight bade me this night remain by the side of my lord, lest some evil should happen to me among the infidels."

"Take up thy instrument then," said the neophyte, "for thou seemest to-night to remain by me in good will; and I am ever glad to have thy foolish company, when such is the case. If thou wilt carry a torch also, 'tis very well: 'twill be some half hour yet ere moonrise."

The two cavaliers, followed by the page bearing a torch, as well as his lute, strode through the streets, which were still thronged with their savage allies, as in a gala-day, singing and shouting; many of whom, from affection or curiosity, seemed disposed to add themselves to the little party. Nevertheless, such inquisitive individuals were easily repelled by De Morla pointing in the direction he was pursuing, and pronouncing a few words in their language, the effect of which, as Don Amador observed, was always to check their ardour, and cover their visages, when these could be seen, with sadness and awe.

"I tell them," said De Morla, in answer to the inquiries of the neophyte, "that we are going to the hill to look upon the fire-mountain, Popocatepetl; and why they are so stricken with superstition at the name, I will explain to thee when we reach the temple."

The temple was soon reached. The city—a congregation of cabins and rude stone dwellings, of vast size—lying on the prolonged base of a great mountain, reared its principal sanctuaries on the spurs of this elevation, on the highest of which stood that consecrated to the god of the air. This was an earthen pyramid, huge and lofty, surmounted by towers such as Don Amador had seen at Zempoala. As the friends approached this, the deep silence that surrounded it was broken by the voices of men, speaking vehemently in a strange tongue; and as they advanced, they beheld two or three figures glide behind the pyramid, as if to escape observation.

This would not perhaps have attracted the notice of the neophyte, had not his companion exclaimed, "Sidi, the cannonier, again! plotting his knaveries with the two Moorish slaves of Cortes! There is some villany in the wind: I have twice or thrice seen Abdalla in close conference with these two varlets, and he is often seen talking with his other countrymen that we have in the army. I will represent this matter to the general; for there can no good come of such secret proceedings. I have all along distrusted that infidel cannonier to have some mischief in him."

"Please, my lord, my father is no infidel," said Jacinto, trembling; perhaps as much at his presumption in contradicting a noble hidalgo, as at the presumed danger of his parent; "no infidel, but a Christian Moor; as the good padre Olmedo will witness to my lord."

"Young page," said De Morla, pleasantly, "I should not have said so grievous a thing of thy father, but that I forgot thou wert in hearing. I will grant thee Abdalla to be a good Christian, if the padre say so! but if thou art as much of a wit as a singer, tell me, how is it thy father is found so often skulking about by night, in company with the Moorish slaves, who are yet unbelievers, instead of resting with Christian soldiers?"

"Though the Moors be slaves and Mahometans," said the page, with much of the submissiveness of his father, though recovering from his trepidation, "they were born in the same land with my father, and are his countrymen. As for the Christian soldiers, they will not forget, that though a Christian, he was born of poor Moriscos : and, my lord knows, it is hard to rest with those who hate us."

"I should give thee a ducat for thy argument," said De Morla, good-humouredly, "but that I know thou art so unsophisticated as to prefer sweet praise to gold; and I intend soon to bestow some of that upon thee. Thy oration has utterly persuaded me I have wronged Abdalla; in token of my penitence for which, I will relieve thee of the burden of the torch, whilst thou art climbing up these steps, which are none of the smoothest nor shortest."

"Take thou my hand, Jacinto," said the novice, benevolently; "for, as my friend says, these steps are indeed very rugged; and I am willing to show thee, that though thou art of Moorish blood, I myself do by no means either hate or despise thee."

The page humbly and hesitatingly placed his hand in the grasp of Don Amador, and ascending at his side, soon stood on the summit of the pyramid.

Here, besides two towers of stone, that reared their lofty bulk over head, the novice perceived, in advance of them, two great urns of rude workmanship, each apparently carved out of a solid block of stone, and each glowing with the remains of a fire not yet extinguished—though no priests stood by, to guard and replenish them. They had forsaken their altars, to join the festivities of the evening.

"Let us break these idolatrous censers!" said Don Amador, "for my blood boils to look upon them."

"Nay," said the moderate De Morla, "let us wait for Heaven's own time, as is strenuously advised by our wise and holy chaplain, who must know better than ourselves how to attack the impieties of the land. We have ever found these heathens more easily converted by gentle persuasions than by violent assaults on their prejudices; and father Olmedo has shown us how persecution strengthens, instead of overturning, an absurd superstition. He has also proved to the satisfaction of most of us, that it is our bounden duty to subdue the arms of the Pagans, and leave their faith to be conquered by the good priests who will follow in our path. Turn, senor, from these pigmy vases to the great censers, which God has himself raised to his majesty!"

As De Morla spoke, he turned from the altars, and Don Amador, following with his eyes the direction in which he pointed, beheld a spectacle which instantly drove from his mind the thought of the idolatrous urns. Far away in the southwest, at the distance of eight or ten leagues, among a mass of hills that upheld their brows in gloomy obscurity, a colossal cone elevated its majestic bulk to heaven, while the snows which invested its resplendent sides, glittered in the fires that crowned its summit. A pillar of smoke, of awful hue and volume, rose to an enormous alti-

tu le above its head, and then parting and spreading on either side through the serene heaven, lay still and solemn, like a funeral canopy, over its radiant pedestal. From the crater, out of which issued this portentous column, arose also, time by time, great flames, with a sort of lambent playfulness, in strange and obvious contrast with their measureless mass and power; while ever and anon globes of fire, rushing up through the pillar of vapour, as through a transparent cylinder, burst at the top, and spangled the grim canopy with stars. No shock creeping through the earth, no heavy roar stealing along the atmosphere, attested the vigour of this sublime furnace; but all in silence and solemn tranquillity, the spectacle went on,—now darkling, now waxing temporarily into an oppressive splendour, as if for the amusement of those shadowy phantoms who seemed to sit in watch upon the neighbouring peaks.

"This is indeed," said Don Amador, reverently, "if God should require an altar of fire, such a high place as might be meeter for his worship than any shrine raised by the hands of man. God is very great and powerful. The sight of such a spectacle doth humble me in mine own thoughts : for what is man, though full of vanity and arrogance, in the sight of Him who builds the fire-mountains?"

"Padre Olmedo," said his companion, "will ask you, what is this fire-mountain, though to the eye so majestic, and to appearance so eternal, to the creeping thing whose spark of immortality will burn on, when the flames of yonder volcano are quenched for ever?"

"It is very true," said the neophyte; "the mountains burn away, the sea wastes itself into air, but the soul that God has given us consumes not. The life of the body passes away like these flames; the vitality that is in the spirit, is a gift that Heaven has not extended to the stars!"

"My friend," said De Morla, willing to pass to more interesting discussions, "will now perceive for what reason it was that the Tlascalans were dismayed and sorrowful when I pronounced the name of Popocatepetl. The name signifies the Mountain of Smoke; for this great chimney, though ever pouring forth dark vapours, has not often been known to kindle into flames. The present eruption, beginning about the time of our descent upon the coast, has ever since continued; and was considered to have heralded our appearance. The Tlascalans, though as securely fettered under the sway of their senators, as are the people of Anahuac under their kings, are, as I told thee, very intolerant of such chiefs as carry the open names of masters. Nay, so bitterly do they detest all tyrants, that they have constructed a fable, which they now believe as a truth—namely, that the souls of such persons are concocted and elaborated among the flames of yonder awful crater; whence, at the times of eruptions, they are sent forth, in the shape of meteors and fire-balls, to afflict and desolate the world. The globes that fall back into the cavity, they think, are despots recalled by their relenting gods; whereas, those that fall beyond the brim and roll down the sides of the mountain, are tyrants let loose upon them without restraint. This being their belief, it may seem strange to you, they have conceived so preposterous an affection for ourselves, who are much liker to prove their tyrants than any of the lords of Anahuac; but yet, so savage is their detestation of these native kings, that, though nightly terrified with the spectacle of so many fiery tyrants flying through the air, they seem quite to have lost sight of the danger of intrusting their liberties to our care."

"I hope," said Don Amador, "we have come to rid them of the bondage of idolatry, not to reduce them to a new slavery."

"We will see that by and by," said De Morla. "We broke the chains of superstition in the islands, but we followed them with more galling fetters; and what better fate awaits the good Montezuma, is more than I can tell."

"Dost thou call that savage emperor the good Montezuma?" demanded the novice.

"I cannot do otherwise," said De Morla, mildly. "A thousand times might he have swept us from the face of the earth; for his armies are numberless. A grain of sand from the hand of each of his warriors, would have covered us with a mountain. But age has come to him with a disgust of blood; and all his actions have proved him rather a humane host than a barbarous destroyer. I must confess, we have repaid his gentleness and beneficence both with perfidy and cruelty; yet, notwithstanding all this, and notwithstanding that he is sorely afflicted by our harshness, such is the goodness of his heart, that he will not permit his people to do us any injury, nor, by any violence, rescue him out of our hands."

"I have heard another story from Don Hernan," said Amador; "and, truly, I thought these ferocious assaults upon the garrison left with the Senor Alvarado in the city, were proof enough of his deceitful malice."

"I will not take upon me to contradict what is averred by Don Hernan," said De Morla. "But, senor, we have had other representations of these tumults, by envoys from Montezuma himself, which, if Cortes had not refused to hear them, would have entirely changed the nature of our belief. I have myself spoken with these ambassadors," continued the young cavalier, earnestly, "some of whom were sent to us at Zempoala, and others have met us at divers places since, though without being hearkened to—and having no inducements to remain in a rage, like Cortes himself, I was very easily persuaded, to my shame, that the fault lay all on the side of the garrison. Senor, for the sake of lucre, we have done many unjust things! We were received with all hospitality by Montezuma, the great lord of Tenochtitlan; he gave us a palace to live in, supplied us with food and raiment, and enriched us with many costly presents. We repaid all this kindness, by seizing him, in a moment of confidence, and conveying him to our dwelling, where we have kept him ever since a prisoner, forcing him, by the fear of death, to submit to many indignities unworthy his high rank and benevolent character; and once even forcing him to sit in chains and witness the cruel execution of some of his own officers, for a certain crime in which he could have had no part. He forgave us this, as well as other insults, and, while we were absent against Zempoala, preserved his promise sacred, to remain in ward of Alvarado until our return. Now, senor, you shall hear the truth of the assault, of which so much is said by Cortes, as fully proving the iniquitous duplicity of the captive emperor. While we were gone, there occurred the anniversary of the great festival of Mexitli, the war-god, in which it is customary for all the nobles, arrayed in their richest attire, to dance on the terrace of the great pyramid, before the emperor. Alvarado, dreading lest such an assemblage of chiefs, heated, as we well knew them to be, on account of the imprisonment of their king, might encourage them to rescue him from his thrall, refused to let the Mitotes (for so they call this ceremony) be danced on the temple; and, at his invitation, the Tlatoani assembled in the court-yard of the palace which Montezuma gave us for our quarters; and here the rite began. Now, senor," continued De Morla, speaking indignantly, "you will blush to hear that our Christian garrison were so inflamed with cupidity at the sight of the rich and precious jewels, with which their guests were decorated, that they resolved to possess them, though at the cost of blood-guiltiness; and falling upon these poor unsuspicious and unarmed revellers, when wearied with the dance, and calling out 'Treason,' as if to justify themselves, though there was no treason, except that in their own hearts, they butchered all that could not leap the high walls, and rifled the corses, even in the sight of the emperor. This, as you may well believe, excited the people to fury, and drove them to vengeance. They assaulted the palace, killed many of the perfidious garrison, and would have destroyed all, but that Montezuma, whom they call the traitor and murderer, moved by the entreaties and excuses of Alvarado, commanded them to retire, and such is their love and subjection to this monarch, that they instantly obeyed him, and have remained in peace ever since, waiting the return and the judgment of Don Hernan. And Don Hernan will doubtless command us to give them justice, by slaying as many as shall dare to demand it."

"By Heaven!" said Don Amador, "if this be the truth, there are more barbarians than those who worship Pagan idols; and I vow to God, if I find thy narrative well confirmed, I will draw no sword, not even at the bidding of my Knight Calavar, on the people of Tenochtitlan. Were I even sworn, like a vowed Knight of Rhodes, to keep no peace with the infidel, I could not fight in an unjust cause."

"I am glad to hear you say so," said De Morla frankly; "for I have often, ever since I have been assured of the friendly and docile character of the Mexicans, been persuaded it would be wiser, as well as juster, to teach them than to destroy. Your favour will find the nobles very civilised; and surely their daughters, if converted to the true faith, would make more honourable wives for Spanish hidalgos, than the Moorish ladies of our own land."

A sigh came from the lips of Jacinto as he heard this narrative, to which he had listened with boyish interest, terminated with a slur so degrading to his people. But his mortification was appeased by Don Amador exclaiming, with great emphasis—"That these Mexican princesses may make very good wives, when true Christians, I can well believe; but I have my doubts whether they have any such superiority over the Moorish ladies of Granada, who possess the religion of Christ. I have, once or twice, known very noble Moriscas, honoured among the wives of Granada as much as those who boasted the pure blood of Castile; and for myself, without pretending to say I shall ever condescend to such a marriage,

may aver, that I have seen at least one fair maiden,
and she of no very royal descent, whom—that is,
if I had loved her—I should not have scorned to
wed. But these things go by fate: a Christian
Moor is perhaps as much regarded by Heaven as a
Christian Spaniard; and surely there are some of
them very lovely to look on, and with most angelic
eyes!"

The gentle cavalier smiled in his own conceits,
as he listened to the argument of his friend; but,
without answering it, he said—"While we have
the authority of the Cid Ramon of Leon before
our eyes, I am much disposed to agree with Don
Amador; for the cid adored an infidel, and why
should not we love proselytes? Come, now, my
pretty page: of all thy ballads, I like best that
which treats of the loves of Cid Ramon; and if
thou hast not forgotten it, I shall rejoice to hear
thee chant it once more, while we sit under the
tower and gaze on the fire-mountain, that looks
down on Mexico."

The boy agreed with unusual alacrity, and sitting
down at the feet of the cavaliers, on the flags that
surrounded the sanctuary, with the torch stuck in
the earth near him, he tuned his instrument with
a willing hand.

CHAPTER XXIII.

Lighted not more by the torch at his feet than
by the flames that crested the distant mountain,
the Moorish boy struck the lute with a skilful
touch, whispered, rather than wailed, the little
burthen that kept alive the memory of the Alhambra, and then sang the following Romance—a
ballad that evidently relates to the fate of Mohammed Almosstadir, king of Seville, dethroned by the
famous Yussef ben Taxfin, emir of Morocco. In
the wars of the Moorish kings of Spain with
Alfonso VI. of Leon, about the year 1090, the
Christian monarch prevailing, his infidel enemies
invited Yussef to their assistance. The emir obeyed
the call; but having fought one or two battles
with Alfonso, contented himself with turning his
arms on his confederates, and dethroning them—
Mohammed Almosstadir among the number. It
is recorded, that his chivalrous enemy, the King
Alfonso, moved by the distresses of Mohammed,
sent an army of twenty thousand men to assist
him against Yussef: but in the obscurity of the
historic legends of that day, nothing can be discovered in relation to the devout condition of
" kissing the cross," nor, indeed, of the name
or fate of the leader of the Spanish army. We
should know nothing of the good cid, but for the
ballad, which was doubtless of very antique origin;
though the simple burthen, *Me acuerdo de ti,
Granada!* commemorative of the fall of the Moorish
city, must have been added four hundred years
after, perhaps by the singer from whom Jacinto
had learned it.

ROMANCE OF CID RAMON.

I remember thee, Granada!
Cid Ramon spurr'd his good steed fast,
His thousand score were near;
And from Sevilla's walls aghast,
The watchmen fled with fear;

For Afric's emir lay around,
The town was leaguer'd sore,
And King Mohammed wept with shame
To be a king no more.
I remember thee, Granada!

The emir's powers were round and nigh,
Like locusts on the sward;
And when Cid Ramon spurr'd his steed,
They struck him fast and hard.
" But," quoth the cid, " a knight am I,
With crucifix and spear;
And for Mohammed ride I on,
And for his daughter dear."—
I remember thee, Granada!

" Cheer up, dark king, and wail no more,
Let tears no longer flow;
Of Christian men a thousand score
Have I to smite thy foe.
The King Alfonso greets thee well·
Kiss thou the cross, and pray;
And ere thou say'st the Ave o'er,
The emir I will slay."
I remember thee, Granada!

" Or let the African be slain,
Or let the emir slay,
I will not kiss the cross of Christ,
Nor to his Mother pray.
A camel-driver will I live,
With Yussef for my lord,
Or ere I kiss the Christian's cross,
To win the Christian's sword."
I remember thee, Granada!

" Mohammed, now thou griev'st me much—
Alfonso is my king:
But let Suleya kiss the cross,
And let her wear the ring.
The crucifix the bride shall bear,
Her lord shall couch the spear:
And still I'll smite thy foe for thee,
And for thy daughter dear."
I remember thee, Granada!

Then up Suleya rose, and spoke—
" I love Cid Ramon well;
But not to win his heart or sword,
Will I my faith compel.
With Yussef, cruel though he be,
A bond-maid will I rove,
Or ere I kiss the Christian's cross,
To win the Christian's love."
I remember thee, Granada!

" Suleya! now thou griev'st me much—
A thousand score have I:
But, saving for a Christian's life,
They dare not strike or die.
Alfonso is my king, and thus
Commands my king to me·
But, for that Christian, all shall strike,
If my true love she be."
I remember thee, Granada!

" Ill loves the love, who, ere he loves·
Demands a sacrifice;
Who serves myself, must serve my sire
And serve without a price

Let Yussel come with sword and spear,
  To fetter and to read;
I choose me yet a Moorish foe
  Before a Christian friend!'—
    I remember thee, Granada!

" Ill loves the love, who pins his love
  Upon a point of creed;
And balances in selfish doubt,
  At such a time of need.
His heart is uosed, his hands untied,
  And he shall yet be free
To wear the cross, and break the ring,
  Who will not die for me!"
    I remember thee, Granada!

The emir's cry went up to heaven:
  Cid Ramon rode away—
" Ye may not fight, my thousand score,
  For Christian friend to-day.
But tell the king, I bide his hest
  Albeit my heart be sore;
Of all his troops, I give but one
  To perish for the Moor."
    I remember thee, Granada!

The emir's cry went up to heaven;
  His howling hosts came on;
Down fell Sevilla's tottering walls—
  The thousand score were gone.
And at the palace-gate, in blood,
  The Arab emir raves;
He sat upon Mohammed's throne,
  And look'd upon his slaves.
    I remember thee, Granada!

The lives of all that faithful be,
  This good day, will I spare;
But woe betide or kings or boors,
  That currish Christians are!"—
Up rode Cid Ramon bleeding fast;
  The princess wept to see;
" No cross was kiss'd, no prayer was said
  But still I die for thee!"
    I remember thee, Granada!

The Moorish maid she kiss'd the cross,
  She knelt upon her knee;
" I kiss the cross, I say the prayer,
  Because thou diest for me.
To buy thy thousand score of swords,
  I would not give my faith;
But now I take the good cross up,
  To follow thee in death."
    I remember thee, Granada!

" Holy Maria! Come to us,
  And take us to the blest;
In the true blood of love and faith,
  Receive us to thy rest!"
The emir struck in bitter wrath,
  Sharp fell the Arab blade;
And Mary took the cid to heaven,
  And bless'd the Christian maid.
    I remember thee, Granada!

" I like that ballad well," said De Morla, with a pensive sigh, when the singer had finished; "and, to my thought, no handsome maiden, though such always makes the best ballad-singer, could have trolled it with a more tender and loving accent than Jacinto. 'The Moorish maid,' " he continued, humming the words in a sentimental manner—

" ' The Moorish maid she kissed the cross,
  She knelt upon her knee—'

To my mind, it would read better, if we could say, ' The Mexican maid—'

' The Mexican maid she kiss'd the cross—'

But, pho upon it! that spoils the metre. Is it not thy opinion, senor, the princess Suleya would have shown more true love, as well as wisdom, to have kissed the cross before the cid came to his death-gasp?"

" By my faith, I cannot doubt it," said Don Amador; "yet, considering that she avowed herself a proselyte, when the sword of that accursed emir was suspended over her head, and so provoked and endured the death of a martyr for Don Ramon's sake, it must be acknowledged she acted as became a loving and truly devout lady. But what I chiefly esteem in this ditty, is the magnanimous art with which the Cid Ramon both preserved his faith to his king, and devoted himself to death for his mistress—a reconciliation of duties which some might have considered impracticable, or, at least, highly objectionable."

" Amigo querido mio," cried De Morla, grasping the neophyte's hand, and speaking with a voice half comical, half serious, " if thou livest a hundred years longer than myself, thou wilt hear some such mournful madrigal as this sung in memory of my foolish self; only that, in place of a Moorish Infanta, thou wilt hear the name of a Mexican princess; and Minnapotzin will doubtless be immortalised along with De Morla."

" Minnapotzin!" exclaimed Don Amador, with a stare rendered visible enough by the distant flashings of the volcano. " I swear to thee, my brother, I understand not a word thou art saying!"

" To make the matter clear to thee then," said De Morla, with forced gaiety, " conceive me for a moment to be the cid of whom we have been singing; and imagine my Suleya to be wandering by the lake side in the figure of a certain Minnapotzin, received to our holy faith under the name of Doena Benita—a princess among these poor barbarians."

" Dost thou indeed love one of these strange maidens, then—and is she baptised in our holy faith?" demanded Don Amador, with much interest. " If she be worthy of thee, Francisco, I pray Heaven to make thee happy with her."

" Now, may I die," cried De Morla, grasping Don Amador's hand warmly, " if I did not fear thou wouldst either censure or laugh at me—or perhaps turn thy ridicule upon Benita—a wrong I never could have forgiven thee; for I protest to thee, there is no such gentle and divine being in all the world beside. I make thee my confidant, hermano mio, because I shall have much need of thy friendship and counsel; for though I come not, like Cid Ramon, with a ' thousand score' to rescue her Pagan father, sure am I, I cannot love the princess, and yet be blind to the miseries of the king."

" Assuredly," said Don Amador, " I will aid thee, and for thy sake, both the fair princess and her unconverted sire, wherever, in so doing, I may not oppose my allegiance and religion."

"I will not claim any sacrifice," said De Morla "unless so much as will rob thee of thy prejudices against this deluded people. In fact, I desire thee more as a confidant than as an abettor; for there is nothing to oppose my happiness, saving the present uncertainty of the relations betwixt ourselves and the Mexicans. Minnapotzin is a Christian; I dare be sworn the cid was not better beloved than myself; and Cortes hath himself promised to ask the consent of our Christian king to the marriage, as soon as Montezuma has properly confirmed his vassalage. No, there is nothing to oppose me," continued De Morla, with a sudden sadness, "saving only this uncertainty I have spoken of, and the darkness that hangs over my own destiny."

"I vow to thee, I am as much in the dark as before," said Don Amador.

"In good faith, my friend," said the young cavalier, with a faint smile, "it is promised me, I shall die very much like Don Ramon. Did I never tell thee what Botello hath prophesied?"

"Not a jot," said the neophyte. "But I trust thou puttest no faith in that worthy madman?"

"How can I help it?" said De Morla, seriously. "He has foretold nothing that has not been accomplished, from the quarrel of Cortes with the Adelantado Velasquez, even to the fall of Zempoala"

"I have reflected on this prediction with regard to Zempoala, as well as all others whereof I have heard," said the neophyte, with a sagacious nod, "and I have settled in mine own mind that there is nothing in them beyond the operation of a certain cunning, mingled with a boldness which will hazard any thing in prognostic. Much credit is given to Botello for having, as I am informed, predicted, even before the embarkation of Cortes, the rupture between him and his governor that afterwards ensued. Now, any man, acquainted with the unreasonable rashness and hot jealousy of the governor, might have foretold a quarrel; and I see not how it could have been otherwise. So also, as I may say, I did myself, in a manner, foretel the disaster of Narvaez, as soon as I perceived his foolish negligence, in choosing rather to divert his soldiers with legerdemain dances than to set them about his city as sentinels. The victory comes not to the indiscreet general."

"All this might have been conjectured, but not with so many surprising particulars," said the cavalier. "How could Botello have predicted, that, though Narvaez should sally out against us, no blow should be struck by daylight?"

"Marry, I know not; unless upon a conviction that Cortes was too wise to meet his enemy on the plain; and from a personal assurance, that the rocks wherein the general had pitched his camp were utterly unassailable."

"How could he have guessed that flames should drive the Biscayan from the tower?"

"Did he guess that, indeed?" said the neophyte, staring. "He could not have known that; for the brand was thrown by mine own rogue Lazaro, who, I know, was not his confederate."

"How could he have averred that Narvaez should lose his eye, and come blindfold to his conqueror?"

"Is it very certain Botello foretold that?" demanded Don Amador, his incredulity shaking.

"The Senor Duero was present, as well as several other honourable cavaliers, and all confirm the story," said De Morla. "Nay, I could give thee a thousand instances of the marvellous truths he has spoken; and so well is Cortes convinced of his singular faculty, that he will do no deed of importance, without first consulting the magician."

"When my head is very cool," said Amador, "I find no difficulty to persuade myself that the existence of the faculty of soothsaying is incredible, because subversive of many of the wise provisions of nature; yet I will not take upon me to contradict what I do not know. And surely, also, I may confess I have heard of certain wonderful predictions made by astrologers, which are very difficult to be explained, unless by admission of their powers."

"What Botello has said to me," said De Morla, with a hurried voice, "has been in part fulfilled though spoken in obscure figures. He told me, long since, that I should be reduced to bondage—'at such time as I behold a Christian cross hanging under a Pagan crown.' This I esteemed a matter for mirth; 'for how,' said I, shall I find a Pagan wearing a crucifix? and how shall I submit to be a captive among strange and cruel idolators, when I have the power to die fighting?' But I have seen the cross on the bosom of one who wears the gold coronet of a king's daughter; and now I know that my heart is in slavery!"

Don Amador pondered over this annunciation; but while he deliberated, his friend continued— "When Botello told me this, he added other things,—not many but dark,—to wit, as I understood it, 'that I should perish miserably with my enslaver,' and, what is still more remarkable, with an infidel priest to say mass over my body! Senor, these things are uncomfortable to think on; but I vow to heaven, if I am to die in the arms of Minnapotzin, I shall perish full as happily as did Cid Ramon in the embraces of Suleya!"

De Morla concluded his singular story with a degree of excitement and wildness that greatly confounded Don Amador; and before the neophyte could summon up arguments enough to reply, a voice from the bottom of the pyramid was heard pronouncing certain words, in a tongue entirely unknown to him, but among which he thought he recognised the name of Minnapotzin. He was not mistaken. De Morla started, saying, hastily —"I am called, senor. This is the voice of one of the envoys of Montezuma, with whom I have certain things to say concerning Donna Benita. I will return to thee in an instant." And so saying, he descended the stairs of the mound, and was straightway out of sight.

CHAPTER XXIV.

The moon had now risen, and was mingling her lustre with the blaze of the volcano. The shouts of revelry came less frequently from the city, and, one by one, the torches vanished from the housetops and the streets. A pleasant quiet surrounded the deserted temple; a few embers, only glowed in the sacred urns; but the combined light of the luminary and the mountain covered the terrace with radiance, and fully revealed the few objects which gave it the interest of life. In this light, as Don Amador turned to his youthful companion, he beheld the eyes of the page suffused with tears. "How is it, Jacinto?—what ails thee?" he cried. "I vow to heaven, I am as much concerned at thy silly griefs, as though thou wert mine own little brother Rosario, who is now saying his prayers at Cuenza. Art thou weary? I will immediately conduct thee to our quarters. Is there any thing that troubles thee? Thou shouldst make me thy confidant; for surely I love thee well."

"Senor mio! I am not weary, and I am not grieved," said the stripling, with simplicity, as the good-natured cavalier took him by the hand, to give him comfort. "I wept for pity of the good Don Francisco and the poor Minnapotzin; for surely it is a pity if they must die!"

"Thou art a silly youth to lament for evils that have not yet happened," said Amador.

"But besides, senor," said the page, "when Don Francisco made me sad, I looked at the moon, and I thought how it was rising on my country!"

"It is now in the very noon of night, both in thy land and mine," said the neophyte, touched by the simple expression, and leading the boy where the planet could be seen without obstruction;—"it is now midnight over Fez, as well as Castile: and, perhaps, some of our friends, in both lands, are regarding this luminary, at this moment, and thinking of us."

The page sighed deeply and painfully:—"I have no friends—no, neither in Fez nor in Spain," he said; "and save my father, my master, and my good lord, none here. There is none of my people left, but my father; and we are alone together!"

"Say not alone," said Amador, with still more kindness—for as Jacinto made this confession of his destitute condition, the tears fell fast and bitterly from his eyes. "Say not, alone; for, I repeat to thee, I have come, I know not by what fascination, to love thee as well as if thou wert my own little brother; and there shall no wrong come to thee, or thy father, while I love to be thy friend."

Jacinto kissed the hand of the cavalier, and said—"I did not cry for sorrow, but only for thinking of my country."

"Thou shouldst think no more of Fez; for its people are infidels, and thou a Christian."

"I thought of Granada—for that is the land of Christians; and I long to be among the mountains where my mother was born."

"Thou shalt live there yet, if God be merciful to us," said the cavalier: "for when there is peace in this barbarous clime, I will take thee thither for a playmate to Rosario. But now that we are here alone, let us sit by the tower, and while I grow melancholy, bethinking me of that same land of Granada, which I very much love, I will have thee sing me some other pretty ballad of the love of a Moorish lady;—or I care not if thou repeatest the romance of the cid: I like it well—'Me acuerdo de ti'—" And the neophyte seemed, while he murmured over the burthen, as if about to imitate the pensiveness of De Morla.

"If my lord choose," said the page, "I would

rather tell him a story of Granada, which is about a Christian cavalier, very noble and brave, and a Christian Morisca, that loved him."

"A Christian Morisca!" said Amador; "and she loved the cavalier?—I will hear that story. And it happened in Granada too?"

"In one of the Moorish towns, but not in the royal city. It was in the town Almeria."

"In the town Almeria!" echoed Amador eagerly. "Thou canst tell me nothing of Almeria that will not give me both pain and pleasure, for therein—but pho! a word doth fill the brain with memories!—Is it an ancient story?"

"Not very ancient, please my lord: it happened since the fall of Granada."

"It is strange that I never heard it then; for I dwelt full two months in this same town; and 'tis not yet forty years since the siege."

"Perhaps it is not true," said the stripling, innocently; "and, at the best, 'tis not remarkable enough to have many repeaters. 'Tis a very foolish story."

"Nevertheless, I am impatient to hear it."

"There lived in that town," said Jacinto, "a Moorish orphan—"

"A girl?" demanded the neophyte.

"A Moorish maiden, of so obscure a birth, that she knew not even the name that had been borne by her parents; but nevertheless, senor, her parents, as was afterwards found out, were of the noblest blood of Granada. She was protected and reared in the family of a benevolent lady, who, being descended of a Moorish parent, looked with pity on the poor orphan of the race of her mother. When this maiden was yet in her very early youth, there came a noble cavalier of Castile—"

"A Castilian?" demanded Don Amador, with extraordinary vivacity—"art thou a conjurer?— What was his name?"

"I know not," said Jacinto.

"Thou learnest thy stories, then, only by the half," said the neophyte, with a degree of displeasure that amazed the youth. "And, doubtless, thou wert forgetful, also, to acquire the name o the Moorish orphan?"

"Senor," said the page, discomposed at the heated manner of his patron, "the Moorish maiden was called Leila."

"Leila!" cried the neophyte, starting to his feet, and seizing Jacinto by the arm, "Canst thou tell me aught of Leila?"

"Senor!" murmured Jacinto, in affright.

"Leila, the Morisca, in the house of the Senora Donna Maria de Montefuerte!" exclaimed Don Amador, wildly. "Dost thou know of her fate? Did she sleep under the surges of the bay? Was she ravished away by those exile dogs of the mountains? Now, by Heaven, if thou canst tell me any thing of that Moorish maid, I will make thee richer than the richest Moor of Granada!"

At this moment, while Jacinto, speechless with terror, gazed on his patron as doubting if his senses had not deserted him, a step rung on the earth of the terrace, and De Morla stood at his side.

The voice of his friend recalled the bewildered wits of the neophyte; he stared at Jacinto, and at De Morla; a deep hue of shame and confusion flushed over his brow, and perceiving that his violence had again thrown the page into tears he kissed him benevolently on the forehead, and said

as tranquilly as he could—"A word will make
fools of the wisest! I think I was dreaming while
thou wert at thy story. Be not affrighted Jacinto:
I meant not to scold thee—I was disturbed. Next
—next," he added, with a grievous shudder, " I
shall be as mad as my kinsman !"

"My brother! I am surprised to see thee in this
emotion," said De Morla.

"It is nothing," responded Amador, hastily and
gloomily; " I fear there is a natural infirmity in
the brains of all my family. I was moved by an
idle story of Jacinto into the recollection of a certain sorrowful event which, one day, perhaps, I
will relate to thee. But let us return to our quarters. The air comes down chilly from the mountains—it is time we were sleeping."

The friends retired from the temple, leaving the
torch sticking in the platform; for the moon was
now so high as to afford a better illumination.
They parted at the quarters; but Don Amador,
after satisfying himself that the knight of Rhodes
was slumbering on his pallet, drew Jacinto aside
to question him further of the orphan of Almeria.
His solicitude was, however, doomed to a disappointment; the page was evidently impressed with
the fear that Don Amador was not without some of
the weakness of Calavar; and adroitly, though
with great embarrassment, avoided exciting him
further.

"It is a foolish story, and I am sorry it displeased my lord," said he, when commanded to
continue the narrative.

"It displeased me not—I knew a Moorish maid
of that name in Almeria, who was also protected
by a Christian lady; and, what was most remarkable, this Christian lady was of Moorish descent
like her of whom thou wert speaking; and, like
the Leila of thy story, the Leila of my own memory vanished away from the town before——"

"Senor," cried Jacinto, "I did not say she
vanished away from Almeria : that did not belong
to the story."

"Ay, indeed! is it so? Heaven guard my wits!
what made me think it? And thy Leila lived in
Almeria very recently?"

"Perhaps ten or fifteen years ago."

"Pho!—Into what folly may not an ungoverned
fancy lead us? Ten or fifteen years ago! And
thou never heardst of the Leila that dwelt in that
town within a twelvemonth?"

"I, senor?" cried Jacinto, with surprise.

"True—how is it possible thou couldst?—Thou
hast, this night, stirred me as by magic. I know
not by what sorcery thou couldst hit upon that
name !"

"It was the name of the lady," said Jacinto,
innocently.

"Ay, to be sure! There is one Mary in heaven,
and a thousand on earth—why should there not
be many Leilas? Did I speak harshly to thee,
Jacinto? Thou shouldst not kiss my hand if I
did; for no impatience or grief could excuse wrath
to one so gentle and unoffending. Good night—
get thee to thy bed, and forget not to say thy
prayers."

So saying, and in such disorder of spirits as the
page had never before witnessed in him, Don
Amador retired.

Jacinto was left standing in a narrow passage,
or corridor, on which opened a long row of chambers with curtained doors, wherein slept the soldiers, crowded thickly together. In the gallery,

also, at a distance lay several dusky lumps which,
by the gleaming of armour about them, were seen
to be the bodies of soldiers stretched fast asleep.
As the boy turned to retire in the direction of the
open portal, it was darkened by the figure of a
man entering with a cautious and most stealthy
step. He approached, and by his voice (for there
was not light enough yielded by the few flambeaux
stuck against the wall to distinguish features),
Jacinto recognised his father. "I sought thee, my
child!" he whispered, "and saw thee returning
with the hidalgos. The watchmen sleep as well
as the cannoniers. It is as I told thee—art
thou ready?"

"Dear father!" stammered the page.

"Speak not above thy breath! The curs, that
are hungering after the blood of the betrayed
Mexicans, would not scorn to blunt their appetites on the flesh of the Moor. Have thyself in
readiness at a moment's warning. Our destinies are written—God will not always frown
upon us !"

"Dear father," muttered Jacinto, "we are of
the Spaniards' faith, and we will go back to our
country."

"It cannot be!—never can it be !" said Abdalla, in tones that were not the less impressive
for being uttered in a whisper. "The hills of thy
childhood, the rivers of thy love—they are passed
away from thee ;—think of them no more ;—never
more shalt thou see them! In the land of barbarians, Heaven has willed that we should live and
die; and be thou reconciled to thy fate, for it
shall be glorious! We live not for ourselves;
God brings us hither, and for great ends! To-
night, did I—Hah !"—(One of the sleepers stirred
in the passage.)—"Seek some occasion to speak
with me, to-morrow, on the march," whispered
Abdalla in the page's ear; and then, with a gesture for silence, he immediately retired.

"_Fuego! Quien pasea alli?_" grumbled the voice
of Lazaro, as he raised his head from the floor.
"_Fu! el muchacho!_—I am ever dreaming of that
cursed Turk, that was at my weasand, when Baltasar brained him with the boll of his crossbow.
Laus tibi, Christe!—I have a throat left for snor-
ing." And comforting himself with this assurance,
before Jacinto had yet vanished from the passage,
the man-at-arms again slumbered on his mat.

CHAPTER XXV.

In the prosecution of his purpose, our historian,
the worthy Don Cristobal Ixtlilxochitl, though
ever adhering to his " neglected cavaliers" with
a generous constancy, is sometimes seduced into
the description of events and scenes of a more
general character, not very necessarily connected
with his main object, and which those very authors
whom he censures, have made the themes of much
prolix writing. The difficulties that beset an historian are ever very great; nor is the least of them
found in the necessity of determinating how much,
or how little, he is called upon to record; for
though it seems but reasonable he should take it
for granted that his readers are entirely unac-
quainted with the matters he is narrating, and
therefore that he should say all that can be said,
this is a point in which all readers will not entirely

agree with him. Those who have acquired a smattering of his subject, will be offended if he presume to re-instruct them. For our own part, not recognising the right of the ignorant to be gratified at the expense of the more learned, we have studied as much as is possible, so to curtail the exuberances of our original as to present his readers chiefly with what they cannot know; for which reason, it will be found, we have eschewed many of the memorable incidents of this famous campaign, in which none of the neglected conquerors bore a considerable part; as well as all those minute descriptions which retard the progress of the history. We therefore dispatch in a word the glories of the morning that dawned over Tlascala, the gathering together of the Spaniards, who, upon review, were found to muster full thirteen hundred men, and their savage allies two thousand in number, commanded, as had been anticipated, by Talmeccahua, of the tribe Tizatlan.

Amid the roar of trumpets and drums, and the shouts of a vast people, the glittering and feathered army departed from Tlascala, and pursuing its way through those rich savannas covered with the smiling corn and the juicy aloe, which had gained for this valley its name of the Land of Bread, proceeded onwards towards the holy city, Cholula.

What rocky plains were crossed, and what rough sierras surmounted, it needs not to detail: before nightfall, the whole army moved over the meadows that environ Cholula; and there, where now the traveller sees nought but a few wretched natives squatting among their earthen cabins, the adventurers beheld a city of great size, with more than four hundred lofty white towers shining over its spacious dwellings. The magnificent mountains that surrounded it—the sublime Popocatepetl, still breathing forth its lurid vapours—the forbidding Iztaccihuatl, or the White Woman, looking like the shattered ruins of some fallen planet, vainly concealing their deformities under a vestment of snow—the sharp and serrated Malinche —and last (and seen with not the less interest that it intercepted the view towards home,) the kingly Orizaba, looking peaceful and grand in the east—made up such a wall of beauty and splendour as does not often confine the valleys of men. But there is one mountain in that singular scene, which human beings will regard with even more interest than those peaks which soar so many weary fathoms above it: the stupendous Teocalli —the *Monte hecho a manos* (for it was piled up by the hands of human beings.)—reared its huge bulk over the plain; and while looking on the stately cypresses that shadowed its gloomy summit, men dreamed, as they dream yet, of the nations who raised so astonishing an evidence of their power, without leaving any revealment of their fate. Whence came they? whither went they? From the shadows—back to the shadows. The farce of ambition, the tragedy of war, so many thousand times repeated in the three great theatres that divided the whole world, were performed with the same ceremonies of guilt and misery, with the same glory and the same shame, in a fourth of which knowledge had not dreamed. The same superstitions which heaped up the pyramids and the Parthenon, were at work on the Teocallis of America; and the same pride which built a Babylon to defy the assaults of time, gave to his mouldering grasp the tombs and the palaces of Palenque. The people of Tenochtitlan and Choluia worshipped their ancient gods among the ruined altars of an older superstition.

Great crowds issued from this city—the Mecca of Anahuac—to witness the approach of the Spaniards; but although they bore the same features, and the same decorations, though perhaps of a better material, with the Tlascalans, it was observed by Don Amador, that they displayed none of the joy and triumph with which his countrymen had been ushered into Tlascala. In place of these, their countenances expressed a dull curiosity; and though they kissed the earth and flung the incense, as usual, in their manner of salutation, they seemed impelled to these ceremonies more by fear than affection. He remarked also, with some surprise, that when they came to extend their compliments to the allies—the Tlascalans, from their chief down to the meanest warrior, requited them only with frowns.

All these peculiarities were explained to him by De Morla:—" In ancient days," said the cavalier, " the Cholulans were a nation of republicans, like the Tlascalans, and united with them in a fraternal league against their common enemies, the Mexicans. In the course of time, however, the people of the holy city were gained over by the bribes or promises of the foe; and entering into a secret treaty, they obeyed its provisions so well, as to throw off the mask on the occasion of a great battle, wherein they perfidiously turned against their friends, and, aided by the perfidious Mexicans, defeated them with great slaughter. From that day they have remained the true vassals of Mexico; and, from that day, the Tlascalans have not ceased to regard them with the most deadly and unrelenting hatred."

" The hatred is just; and I marvel they do not fall upon these base knaves forthwith!" said Amador.

" It is the command of Don Hernan, that Tlascala shall now preserve her wrath for Tenochtitlan; and such is his influence, that, though he cannot allay the heart-burnings, yet can he, with a word, restrain the hands of his allies. Concerning the gloomy indifference of these people," continued De Morla, " as now manifested, it needs only to inform you how we discovered, or, rather (for I will not afflict you with the details,) how we punished a similar treachery, wherein they meditated our own destruction, more than half a year ago, when we entered their town, on our march to Mexico. Having discovered their plot to destroy us, we met them with a perfidious craft which might have been rendered excusable by their own, had we, like them been demi-barbarians; but which, as we are really civilised and Christian men, I cannot help esteeming both dishonest and atrocious. We assembled their nobles and priests in the court of the building we occupied; and having closed the gates, and charged them once or twice with their guilt, we fell upon them; and some of them having escaped and roused the citizens, we carried the war into the streets, and up to the temples: and so well did we prosper that day, and the day that followed (for we fought them during two entire days), that, with the assistance of our Tlascalans, of whom we had an army with us, we slaughtered full six thousand of them, and that without losing the life of a single Spaniard."

" Dios mio!" cried Don Amador, " we had not

so many killed in all the siege of Rhodes! Six thousand men! I am not certain that even treachery could excuse the destruction of so many lives."

"It was a bloody and most awful spectacle," said De Morla, with feeling. "We drove the naked wretches (I say naked, senor, for we gave them no time to arm) to the pyramids, especially to that which holds the altar of their chief god—the god of the air; and here, senor, it was melancholy to see the miserable desperation with which they died; for, having at first refused them quarter, they declined to receive it, when pity moved us afterwards to grant it. About the court of this pyramid there were many wooden buildings, as well as tabernacles of the like materials among the towers, on the top. These we fired; and thus attacked them with arms and flames. What ruin the fire failed to inflict on the temple, they accomplished with their own hands; for, senor, having a superstitious belief, that the moment a sacrilegious hand should tear away the foundations of their great temple, floods should burst out from the earth to whelm the impious violator, they began to raze it with their own hands, willing, in their madness, to perish by the wrath of their god, so that their enemies should perish with them. I cannot express to you the horrible howls with which they beheld the fragments fall from the walls of the pyramid, without calling up the watery earthquake: then, indeed, with these howls they ran to the summit, and crazily pitched themselves into the burning towers, or flung themselves from the dizzy top—as if, in their despair, thinking that even their gods had deserted them!"

"It was an awful chastisement, and, I fear me, more awful than just," said Amador. "After this, it is not wonderful the men of Cholula should not receive us with joy."

Many evidences of the horrors of that dreadful day were yet revealed as Don Amador entered into the city. The marks of fire were left on various houses of stone, and here and there were vacuities, covered with blackened wrecks, where, doubtless, had stood more humble and combustible fabrics.

The countenance of Cortes was observed to be darkened by a frown, as he rode through this well-remembered scene of his cruelty; but perhaps he thought less of remorse and penitence, than of the spirit of hatred and desperation evinced by his victims, as if, in truth, the late occurrences at Mexico had persuaded him that a similar spirit was waking and awaiting him there. It was in his angry moment, and just as he halted at the portals of a large court-yard, wherein stood the palace he had chosen for his quarters, that two Indians, of an appearance superior to any Don Amador had yet seen, and followed by a train of attendants bearing heavy burdens, suddenly passed from the crowd of Cholulans, and approached the general.

"Senor," said De Morla, in a low voice, to his friend, "observe these new ambassadors, they are of the noblest blood of the city: the elder, he that hath the gold grains hanging to his nostrils, in token that he belongs to the order of Teuctli, or Princes by Merit, is one of the lords of the four quarters of Mexico—the quarter Tiatelolco, wherein is our garrison. His name, Itzquauhtzin, will be to you unpronounceable. The youth that bears himself so loftily, is no less than a nephew of the king himself; and the scarlet fillet around his hair, denotes that he has arrived at the dignity of what we should call a chief commander—a military rank that not even the king can claim, without having performed great actions in the field. 'Tis a sore day for Montezuma, when he sends us such princely ambassadors. I will press forward, and do the office of interpreter; for destiny, love, and my mother wit, together, have given me more of the Mexican jargon than any of my companions."

As the ambassadors approached, Don Amador had leisure to observe them. Both were of good stature and countenance; their loins were girt with tunics of white cotton cloth, studded and bordered with bunches of feathers, and hanging as low as the knee; and over the shoulders of both were hung large mantles of many brilliant colours, curiously interwoven, their ends so knotted together in front, as to fall down in graceful folds, half concealing the swarthy chest. Their sandals were secured with scarlet thongs, crossed and gartered to the calf. Their raven locks, which were of great length, were knotted together, in a most fantastic manner, with ribands, from the points of which, on the head of the elder, depended many little ornaments, that seemed jewels of gold and precious stones; while from the fillets, that braided the hair of the younger, besides an abundance of the same ornaments, there were many tufts of crimson cotton-down, swinging to and fro in the wind. In addition to these badges of military distinction, (for every tuft thus worn was the reward and evidence of some valiant exploit,) this young prince—he seemed not above twenty-five years old—wore, as he had been noticed by De Morla, the red fillet of the House of Darts—an order not so much of nobility as of knighthood, entitling its possessor to the command of an army. His bearing was, indeed, lofty, but not disdainful; and though, when making his obeisance, he neither stooped so low, nor kissed his hand with so much humility as his companion, this seemed to proceed more from a consciousness of his own rank, than from any disrespect to the Christian leader.

"What will these dogs with me now?" cried Cortes, at whose feet (for he had dismounted,) the attendants had thrown their burthens, and were proceeding to display their contents. "Doth Montezuma think to appease me for the blood of my brothers, and pay for Spanish lives with robes of cotton and trinkets of gold? What say the hounds?"

"They say," responded De Morla to his angry general, "that the king welcomes you back again to his dominions, to give him reparation for the slaughter of his people."

"Hah!" exclaimed the leader, fiercely. "Doth he beard me with complaint, when I look for penitence and supplication?"

"In token of his love, and of his assured persuasion that you now return to punish the murderers of his subjects, and then to withdraw your followers from his city for ever," said De Morla, giving his attention less to Cortes than to the lord of Tlatelolco, "he sends you these garments, to protect the bodies of your new friends from the snows of Ithualco, as well as —"

"The slave!" cried Don Hernan, spurning the pack that lay at his foot, and scattering its gaudy textures over the earth: "if he give me no man to protect my friends from the knives of his assassins, I will trample even upon his false heart, as I do upon his worthless tribute!"

"Shall I translate your excellency's answer word for word?" said De Morla tranquilly. "If it be left to myself, I should much prefer veiling it in such palatable language as my limited knowledge will afford."

But the scowling general had already turned away, as if to humble the ambassadors with the strongest evidence of contempt, and to prove the extremity of his displeasure; and it needed no interpretation of words, to convince the noble savages of the futileness of their ministry. The Lord of Tlatelolco bowed again to the earth, and again kissed his hand, as if in humble resignation, while the retreating figure of Don Hernan vanished under the low door of his dwelling; but the younger envoy, instead of imitating him, drew himself proudly up, and looked after the general, with a composure that changed, as Don Amador thought, to a smile. But if such a mark of satisfaction—for it bore more the character of elation than contempt—did illuminate the bronzed visage of the prince, it remained not there for an instant. He cast a quiet and grave eye upon the curious cavaliers who surrounded him, and then beckoning his attendants from their packs, he strode, with his companion, composedly away.

"In my mind," said the neophyte, following him with his eye, and rather soliloquising than addressing himself to any of the neighbouring cavaliers, "there was more of dignity and contempt in the smile of that heathen prince, than in all the rage of my friend Don Hernan."

"Truly he is a very proper-looking and well-demeanoured knave," said the voice of Duero. "But the general has some deep policy at the bottom of all this anger."

"By my faith, I think so, now for the first time!" exclaimed the neophyte: "for although unable to see the drift of such a stratagem, I cannot believe that the Senor Cortes would adopt a course, that seems to savour so much of injustice, without a very discreet and politic object."

Here the discourse of the cavaliers was cut short by the sudden appearance of Fabueno, the secretary.

"What wilt thou, Lorenzo?" said his patron. "Has Lazaro again refused to tilt with thee? I very much commend the zeal with which thou pursuest thine exercises; but thou shouldst remember, that Lazaro may, sometimes, be weary after a day's march."

"Senor, 'tis not that," said the secretary. "But just now, as Baltasar told me, he saw the page Jacinto very rudely haled away by one of Cortes's grooms; and I thought your favour might be glad to know, for the boy seemed frightened."

"I will straightway see that no wrong be done him, even by the general," said Amador, quickly, moving toward the door into which he had seen Cortes enter. "I marvel very much that my good knight did not protect him."

"Senor," said Fabuena, "the knight is in greater disorder to-day than yesterday. He took no note of any body, when we came to this palace: but instantly concealed himself in some distant chamber, where, a soldier told me, he was scourging himself."

"Thou shouldst not talk with the soldiers of Calavar," said Amador, with a sigh. "Get thee to Marco. If my kinsman need me, I will presently be with him."

Thus saying, he discharged the secretary at the door; and those servants who guarded it, not presuming to deny admittance to a man of such rank, he was immediately ushered into the presence of Cortes.

CHAPTER XXVI.

In a low but spacious apartment, the walls and floor of which were both covered with mats, the neophyte found Don Hernan, attended by Sandoval and one or two other cavaliers, busy, to all appearance, in the examination of the page and a Moorish slave of Cortes's own household, whom he seemed to confront with the other. It needed no more than the tears which Amador discovered on the cheeks of the youth, to rouse him to a feeling very like anger.

"Senor," said he, stepping forward to the side of Jacinto, and looking gravely on his judge, "I have exercised the privilege of a master—or rather, as I should say, of a servant—for this boy is in the ward of Don Gabriel, whom I myself follow—to enter into your presence, without the ceremony of a previous request; for which liberty, if it offend you, I ask your pardon. But I was told the boy Jacinto was dragged away by one of your excellency's menials; and I claim, as asking in the stead of his master, to know for what offence?"

"By my conscience, for none at all!" said Cortes, courteously; "at least, for none of his own commission. And had he truly been guilty, both of treason and desertion, I should have pardoned him, for the precocious shrewdness of his answers. Senor," continued the general, "it was my intention to beseech your presence at this examination; and nothing but the suddenness of it, as well as the present defection among my servants, could have caused me to defer the invitation for a moment. By my conscience, you have a treasure of wisdom in this boy!"

This was an assurance Don Amador did by no means deny; for, in addition to the singular address with which he adapted himself to the humours of the knight, he had seen in Jacinto many other evidences of a discretion so much in advance of his years, as to cause him no little wonder; added to which, the incident of the past night, in which the page had stumbled upon a name, and indeed (for the after explanations had not removed the first impression) a story, which he did not remember to have breathed to any living creature, had attached to the youth a sort of respect that bordered almost on superstition. But Don Hernan gave the cavalier no time for reflections.

"Senor Don Amador," said he, "the fault, if there be any, which we are now striving to investigate, lies, not in the page, but in his father, Sidi Abdalla, the cannonier, who is charged by my varlet here, this unconverted heathen, to the meditating, if not now engaged in the accomplishment of a very heinous, and yet, let me add, for your satisfaction, a very improbable conspiracy. This is charged to be nothing less than desertion from our standard, with a design to throw himself into the arms of the enemy; and what makes the matter worse, allowing it for a moment to be credible, is, that he plots to carry away with him all his countrymen who are slaves with us, in number, I think, somewhat above half a score."

"This is, assuredly," said Don Amador, "a very vile offence; for which, if guilty, I must needs allow the Sidi deserves to suffer. Yet I agree with your excellency, the design seems quite as incredible as its accomplishment must be impossible."

"No one," said Cortes, "could have shown

this with better argument than this same weeping boy; for, 'First,' said he, ''tis wrong to receive the accusation of an unconverted man against a Christian;' and such an infidel hound is Yacub, whom I will, at some future day, give over to be burned for his idolatry; but, at present, I cannot spare so precious a servant, for he is an excellent cook, and a good maker of arrow-heads for the crossbowmen. In addition to this argument, senor," continued the general, "the boy advances me another of still more force: 'For how,' says he, shrewdly, 'would my father leave his Christian masters and protectors, to go over to savages, whose language he cannot understand, and who would sacrifice him as a victim to their detestable gods?' which gods may Heaven sink into the pit, whence they came! and I say, Amen. Now, though one part of this argument is answered by the subtle art of Yacub; for whether he have Yacub, or any other Moor who hath picked up something of the tongue, to interpret for him, or whether he have no interpreter at all, it is not the less certain, that the moment he intrusts himself into the power of the barbarians, that moment will he be clapped into a cage like a wild beast, and devoured what time he is fat enough for the maws of their diabolical divinities; I say, nevertheless, for that very reason, it is not probable Abdalla should be so besotted a fool."

"Please your highness," said Yacub, with the obstinacy of one who presumed on his master's indulgence, or on the strength of his cause, "he urged me, last night, at the pyramid of Tlascala; and this noble gentleman, as well as this boy, saw me in his company."

Don Amador started, as he perceived the eyes of Yacub fastened on him, as well as those of every other individual in the chamber. The look that Jacinto gave him was one of terror and be-seeching earnestness; "Senor," said he, hesitating a little, "though what I have to say may, in part, confirm the charge of this fellow, I cannot scruple to speak it: and though I may not aver, on mine own knowledge, that I beheld, last night, either this man Yacub, or his countryman, Abdalla, yet must I admit that I saw, stealing by the basis of that heathen temple, three men, whom my friend De Morla, who accompanied me, pronounced to be the cannonier and two of your excellency's servants." Jacinto wrung his hands. "But what passed between them," the cavalier went on, "whether they were hatching a plot, or discours-ing together of their hard fate, as would seem reasonable for men like them, that have neither friends nor country, I cannot take upon me to pronounce; though, from what I know of Abdalla, as a courageous and honest man, I am fain to think their communication could not have been of an evil nature."

"He said," muttered the treacherous Moor, "that, provided he had but some one to interpret for him, he had no fear of the Mexicans; but could promise us much favour and wealth from their kings, by virtue of certain arts possessed by his son; and thereby he hinted the boy was an enchanter."

All started at this sudden announcement, and none more than Don Amador de Leste; for though, as he had said himself, he was, in his cooler moments, very sceptical in affairs of magic, this in-credulity was no consequence either of nature or education; and besides the shock that had been

given to his doubts by the disclosures of De Morla, the story of Jacinto, so unaccountably begun, and so abruptly terminated, had made a deeper im-pression on his mind than such a trifle should. Its importance had been imputed by his own feel-ings; but either he did not remember, or he knew not that. He stared at Jacinto, who stood pale as death and trembling, now rolling his eyes wildly on Don Hernan, and now on his patron. Before the latter could summon composure to answer, he was relieved by the general saying, humorously—"I cannot doubt that this little caitiff is an enchanter, because he has the faculty of exciting both admiration and pity in an emi-nent degree; and, though I doubt the power of such a charm over the ears of barbarians that delight in the thunder of wooden drums, and the yelling uproar of sea-shell trumpets, yet I can believe, for it has been told me by good judges, that the art with which he touches his lute is as magical as it is marvellous."

The boy clasped his hands in delight, and seemed as if he would have thrown himself at the feet of his judge.

"Wherefore, my most worthy and honoured friend," continued Cortes, "have no fear that I will rob thee of so serviceable a henchman. I could not burn so pretty a log in the fire that was kindled for one who had sold his soul; and I cannot, by allowing the claims of a rival to lawful magic, kill my astrologer Botello with envy."

"He has a talisman round his neck, wherein is a devil, that I have overheard him talking to," said the resolute Yacub.

"Thou art an ass," said Cortes, laughing at the trepidation of Jacinto; for he again turned pale, and lifted his hands to his neck, as if both to confess and guard his treasure. "'Tis some gewgaw, given him by his mother, or, perhaps, by some sweetheart wench; for these Moorish boys are in love when a Chris-tian urchin is yet in his grammar. Senor," (he addressed himself to the neophyte) "you may perceive that the very grossness of Yacub's credulity has destroyed the force of his testimony; for he who can believe such a junior as this to be a conjurer will give credit to any other ridiculous imagination. I will now confess to you, that, beside these charges, which are already answered, there is only one more circumstance against Abdalla; and that is, that at the very moment of our halt, and while engaged in audience with those ambassadors (whom I treated somewhat harshly, but for a cunning purpose, which you will soon understand), he vanished away, in company with another dog of my household called Ayub, and hath not been since seen. Nevertheless, I attach no more importance to this matter than to the others; but, I swear to Heaven, if he be caught stealing turkeys, or any such trumpery things from these villains of Cholula, I will give him to the bas-tinado."

"Senor," said Amador, earnestly, "the Sidi is of too magnanimous a nature to steal turkeys."

"I will take Don Amador's word for it, then. But I see the page is still in some mortal fright, as dreading, if he remain longer in our presence, lest some new accusation should be brought against him."

"If Jacinto be absolved from censure, and is no longer desired by your excellency, I will withdraw him from your presence; and, thanking you, senor, for the mildness with which you have questioned him, I will beg your permission to take my own leave."

Don Hernan bowed low, as the neophyte withdrew with Jacinto; he waved his hand to Yacub, and the Moor immediately retired.

"What think ye now, my masters?" he cried, as soon as these were out of hearing. "Is it possible this stupid cannonier hath either the wit or the spirit to hatch me a brood of treason, to help the kites of Mexico?"

"If he have," said Sandoval, "he should hang."

"Very true, son Gonzalo," said the general; "for, in our condition, to be suspected, should be a crime worthy death, especially in so contemptible a creature as a Moor. Didst thou observe what mortal consternation beset our worthy and very precise friend, Don Amador, when Yacub called his boy a conjurer."

"I think that should be examined into," said Sandoval; "for if he be, 'twill be well to give him to Botello, as a pupil; lest Botello should be, some day, knocked on the head, as is not improbable, from his ever thrusting it into jeopardy, and we be left without a diviner."

"By my conscience, 'tis well thought on," said Cortes, laughing, "for this boy, if he had but as good a reputation, is much superior in docility, as well as shrewder in apprehension; whereas Botello hath such a thick-headed enthusiasm for his art, as to be somewhat unmanageable; and, every now and then, he prophesies me all wrong, as was the case when he anointed the wound of De Leste's secretary, and stupidly told him 'twould be well in a few hours; and yet all the camp knew the lad was near losing his arm."

"Botello excuses himself there," said Sandoval, "by protesting that his injunctions were disobeyed, especially that wherein he charged the youth not to touch his weapon for twenty-four hours; whereas he killed a man, that very night, on the pyramid, very courageously, as I witnessed—though the man was hurt before; for I had charged him with my own partisan——"

"Amigo mio," said Cortes, abruptly, "in the matter of these Moors, I must have thine aidance. I know not how it may have entered into the brain of such a boor, to suppose he could make himself useful to the frowning infidels in Tenochtitlan; but I would sooner give them a dead lion than a living dog. If thou hast any very cunning and discreet rogues among thy fighting men, send them, in numbers of two and three, secretly about the city; and especially charge some that they watch at the gate that opens to Mexico."

"I will do so," said Sandoval, "and I will myself hunt about the town till I find the rascal. Shall I kill him?"

"If it appear to thee he is deserting, let him be slain in the act. As for Ayub, if he be found in the cannonier's company, bring me him alive: I will hang him for an example; for in his death shall no intercessor be offended. I have no doubt, that, for the boy's sake, both Don Amador and Calavar would beg for Abdalla, if he were brought a prisoner; and it would grieve me to deny them. Kill him, then, my son, if thou findest him, and art persuaded he is a deserter."

With this charge, very emphatically pronounced, and very composedly received, the friends separated.

CHAPTER XXVII.

During the whole time of the march from Tlascalato Cholula, an unusual gloom lay upon the spirits of Calavar; and so great was his abstraction, that though pursuing his way with a sort of instinct, he remained as insensible to the presence of his kinsman as to the attentions of his followers. He rode at a distance from the rear of the army; and such was the immobility of his limbs and features, saving when, stung by some secret thought, he raised his ghastly eyes to heaven, that a stranger, passing him on the path, might have deemed that his grave charger moved along under the weight of a stiffened corse, not yet disrobed of its arms, rather than that of a living cavalier. When the army halted at noon to take food, he retired with his attendants to the shadow of a tree; where, without dismounting, or receiving the fruits which Jacinto had gathered to tempt him to eat, he sat in the same heavy stupor until the march was resumed. Neither food nor water crossed his lips during the entire day; nor did the neophyte suffer any to be proffered him, when he came to reflect that this day was an anniversary, which the knight was ever accustomed to observe with the most ascetic abstinence and humiliation. For this reason, also, though lamenting the necessity of such an observance, he neither presumed himself to vex his kinsman with attentions, nor suffered any others to intrude upon his privacy, excepting, indeed, the Moorish page, whose gentle arts were so wont to dispel the gathering clouds. But this day, even Jacinto failed to attract his notice: and, despairing of the power of any thing but time, to terminate the paroxysm, he ceased his efforts and contented himself with keeping a distant watch on all Don Gabriel's movements, lest some disaster might happen to him on the journey. No sooner, as had been hinted by Fabueno, had the army arrived at its quarters in the sacred city than the knight betook him to the solitude of a chamber in the very spacious building; where, after a time, he so far shook off his lethargy as to desire the presence of the chaplain, with whom he had remained ever since engaged in his devotions. Hither, guided by Marco, came now Don Amador, conducting Jacinto. The interview with Cortes had swallowed up more than an hour, and when the neophyte stood before the curtained door of his kinsman a light, flashing through the irregular folds, dispelled the darkness of the chamber. As he paused for an instant, he heard the low voice of the priest saying—" Sin no more with doubt *Spera in Deo:* grace is in Heaven, and mercy knoweth no bounds. *Misereatur tui omnipotens Deus.*"

A few other murmurs came to his ear; and then the chaplain, pushing aside the curtain, issued from the apartment. "Heaven be with thee, my son," he said to Amador, "thy kinsman is greatly disordered, but not so much now as before."

"Is it fitting I should enter, father?"

"Thy presence may be grateful to him; but surely," he continued, in an under voice, "it were better for the unhappy knight if he were among the priests and physicians of his own land. A sore madness afflicts him: he thinks himself beset with spectres. I would thou hadst him in Spain."

"If Heaven grant us that grace," said Amador, sorrowfully. "But he believes that God will call him to his rest among the heathen. Tarry thou at the door, Jacinto," he went on, when the father had departed; "have thyself in readiness, with thy lute, for perhaps he may be prevailed upon to hear thee sing; in which case I have much hope the evil spirit will depart from him."

He passed into the chamber: the knight was on his knees before a little crucifix, which he had placed on a massive Indian chair; but though he beat his bosom with a heavy hand, no sound of prayer came from his lips. Don Amador placed himself at his side, and stood in reverential silence, until his kinsman, heaving a deep sigh, rose up, and turning his haggard countenance towards him, said—"Neither penance nor prayer, neither the remorse of the heart nor the benediction of the priest, can wipe away the sorrow that comes from sin. God alone is the forgiver; but God will not always forgive."

"Say not so, my father," cried Amador, earnestly; "for it is a deep crime to think that Heaven is not ever merciful."

"Keep thyself free from the stain of blood-guiltiness," said Don Gabriel, with a manner so mild, that the neophyte had good hope the fit had indeed left him, "and mercy will not be denied thee. Have I not afflicted thee, my friend?" he continued, faintly. "Thou wilt have much to forgive me; but not long. I will remember in my death hour that thou hast not forsaken me."

"Never will I again leave thee," said Amador, fervently. "I forgot thee once; and besides the pang of contrition for that act, Heaven punished me with a grief that I should not have known had I remained by thy side. But now, my father, wilt thou not eat and drink, and suffer Jacinto to sing to thee?"

"I may neither eat nor drink this night," said Calavar; "but methinks I can hear the innocent orphan chant the praises of the Virgin; for to such she will listen."

Amador strode to the door, but Jacinto had vanished. He had stolen away the moment that his patron entered.

"Perhaps he has gone to fetch his instrument. Run thou in search of him, Marco, and bid him hasten."

Before the novice could again address himself to his kinsman Marco returned. The page was not to be found; the sentinel at the door had seen him pass into the court-yard, but whether he had re-entered or not he knew not; he had not noted.

"Is it possible," thought Don Amador, "that the boy could so wilfully disobey me? Perhaps the general hath sent for him again; for, notwithstanding all his protestations of satisfaction, it seemed to me that, while he spoke, there was still a something lurking in his eye, which boded no good to Abdalla. I will look for the boy myself."

He charged Marco to remain by his lord, sought an audience with the general, whom he found engaged in earnest debate with Duero, De Leon, and other high officers. Don Hernan satisfied him that he had not sent for Jacinto—that he had not thought of Abdalla; and, with an apology for his intrusion, the novice withdrew.

"The story is true," said Cortes, with a frown, "and that pestilent young cub of heathenism has fled to give the traitor warning. But he that passes, unquestioned, at the gate where Sandoval stands the watchman, must have the devil for his leader, or at least his companion. I hope he will not murder the boy; for he is a favourite with Calavar, a subtle knave, a good twangler; and it is natural he should play me even a knave's trick for his father."

In the mean while after hunting in vain about the different quarters of the building, as well as the court-yard, for the vanished Jacinto, the novice returned to the chamber of his kinsman. But Calavar also had disappeared—not indeed in disorder, but in great apparent tranquillity; and he had commanded Marco not to follow him.

"He has gone to the fields," muttered Amador; "such is his practice at this season: but there is no good can come of solitude. I know not what to think of that boy; but assuredly, this time, it will be my duty to censure him." And so saying, Don Amador also passed into the open air.

CHAPTER XXVIII.

It was late in the night; a horizontal moon flung the long shadows of the houses over the wide streets of Cholula, when the Knight Calavar, wrapped in his black mantle, strode along through the deserted city. With no definite object before him, unless to fly, or perhaps to give way in solitude to the bitter thoughts that oppressed him, he suffered himself to be guided as much by accident as by his wayward impulses; and as he passed on, some mutation of his fancies, or some trivial incident on the way, conspired to recall his disorder. Now, as a bat flitted by, or an owl flew, hooting from its perch among some of those ruins, which yet raised their broken and blackened walls in memory of the cruelty of his countrymen, the knight stared aghast, and a mortal fear came over him; for, in these sounds and sights, his disturbed senses discovered the signs of the furies that persecuted him; and even the night-breeze, wailing round some lonely corner, or whispering among the shrubbery of a devastated garden, seemed to him the cries of haunting spirits.

"Miserere mei, Deus!" muttered Don Gabriel, as a tree, bowing away from the wind, let down a moonbeam through a fissure on his path; "the white visage will not leave me. Heavy was the sin, heavy is the punishment; for even mine own fancies are become my chastisers."

Thus, at times conscious, in part, of his infirmity, and yet yielding ever, with the feebleness of a child, to the influence of unreal horrors, he wandered about, sometimes driven from his path by what seemed a gaunt spectre flitting before him, sometimes impelled onwards by a terror that followed behind: thus he roved about, he knew not whither, until he found himself, by chance, in the neighbourhood of the great temple, the scene of the chief atrocities enacted on that day which has been called, by a just metonymy, the Massacre of Cholula. Here it was, as had been mentioned by De Morla, that the miserable natives, huddled together in despair, had made their last cry to their gods, and perished under the steel and flames of the Christians; and the memorials of their fate were as plainly written as if the tragedy had been the work of the previous day. No carcasses, indeed, lay crowded among the ruins, no embers smouldered on the square; weeds had grown upon the place of murder, as if fattening on the blood that had besprinkled their roots; life had utterly vanished from the spot; and it presented the appearance of a desert in the bosom of a populous city.

A great wall running round the temple had enclosed it in a large court, once covered with the houses of priests and devotees. The wall was shattered and fallen, the dwellings burned and demolished; and the pyramid itself, crumbling into ruins, lay like the body of some huge monster among its severed and decaying members. The flags of stone, tumbled by the victims in their fury from its sides and terraces, though they had not called up the subterraneous rivers, had exposed the perishable earth, that composed the body of the mound, to the vicissitudes of the weather; and, under the heavy tropical rains, it was washing rapidly away. The sanctuaries yet stood on the summit, but with their walls mutilated, and their roofs burnt; and they served only to make the horror picturesque. A wooden cross of colossal dimensions, raised by the conquerors, in impious attestation that God had aided them in the labour of slaughter, flung high its rugged arms, towering above the broken turrets, and gave the finish of superstition to the monument of wrath. It was a place of ruins, dark, lugubrious, and forbidding; and as Don Gabriel strode among the massive fragments, he found himself in a theatre congenial with his gloomy and wrecking spirit.

It was not without many feelings of dismay that he plunged among the ruins; for his imagination converted each shattered block into a living phantasm. But still he moved on, as if urged by some irresistible impulse, entangling himself in the labyrinth of decay, until he scarcely knew whither to direct his steps. Whether it was reality, or some coinage of his brain, that presented the spectacle, he knew not; but he was arrested in his toilsome progress by the apparition of several figures rising suddenly among the ruins, and as suddenly vanishing.

"Heaven pity me!" he cried; "they come feathered like the fiends of the infidel. But I care not, so they bring no more the white face that is so ghastly. And yet, this is her day—this is her day."

Perhaps it was his imagination that decked out the spectres with such ornaments; but a less heated spectator might have discovered in them only the figures of strolling savages. With his spirits strongly agitated, his brain excited for the reception of any chimera, he followed the direction in which these figures seemed to have vanished; and this bringing him round a corner of the pyramid into the moonshine, he instantly found himself confronted with a spectacle that froze his blood with horror. In a spot where the ruins had given space for the growth of weeds and grass, and where the vision could not be so easily confounded—illuminated by the moonbeams as if by the lustre of the day—he beheld a figure, seemingly of a woman, clad in robes of white, of an oriental habit, full before him, and turning upon him a countenance as wan as death.

"Miserere mei, Deus!" cried the knight, dropping on his knees, and bowing his forehead to the earth. "If thou comest to persecute me yet, I am here and I have not forgot thee."

The murmur, as of a voice, fell on his ear, but it brought with it no intelligence. He raised his eyes—dark shadows flitted before him; yet he saw nothing, save the apparition in white: it stood yet in his view; and still the pallid visage dazzled him with its unnatural radiance and beauty.

"Miserere mei! miserere mei!" he cried, rising to his feet and tottering forwards. "I live but to lament thee, and I breathe but to repent. Speak to me, daughter of the Alpujarras; speak to me, and let me die."

As he spoke, the vision moved gently and slowly away. He rushed forwards, but with knees smiting together; and, as the white visage turned upon him again, with its melancholy loveliness, and with a gesture as of warning or terror, his brain spun round, his sight failed him, and he fell to the earth in a deep swoon.

CHAPTER XXIX.

Motion is the life of the sea: the surge dashes along in its course, while the watery particles that gave it bulk and form, remain in their place, to renew and continue the coming billows, heaving to each successive oscillation; but not departing with it. Thus the mind—an ocean more vast and unfathomable than that which washes our planet—fluctuates under the impulses of its stormy nature, and passes not away, until the last agitation, like that which shall swallow up the sea, or convert its elements into a new matter, lifts it from its continent, and introduces it to a new existence. Emotion is its life, each surge of which seems to bear it leagues from its resting-place; and yet it remains passively to abide and figure forth the influence of new commotions. Thus passed the billow through the spirit of Calavar; and when it had vanished, the spirit ceased from its tumult, subsided, and lay in tranquillity to await other shocks—for others were coming. When he awoke from his lethargy, his head was supported on the knee of a human being, who chafed his temple and hands, and bowed his body, as well as his feeble strength allowed, to recall the knight to life. Don Gabriel raised his eyes to this benignant and ministering creature; and in the disturbed visage that hung over his own, thought—for his mind was yet wandering—he beheld the pallid features of the vision.

"I know thee, and I am ready," cried Don Gabriel. "Pity me and forgive me—for I die at thy feet, as thou didst at mine."

"Senor mio, I am Jacinto," exclaimed the page (for it was he), frightened at the distraction of the knight—"thy page,—thy poor page, Jacinto."

"Is it so, indeed?" said Calavar, surveying him wildly. "And the spectre did now but smite me to the earth;—hath she left me?"

"Dear master, there is no spectre with us," said the Moorish boy. "We are alone among the ruins."

"God be thanked!" said the knight, vehemently, "for if I should look on it more, I should die. Yet would that I could—would that I could, for in death there is peace—in the grave there is forgetfulness. This time, was it no delusion either of the senses or the brain: mine eyesight was clear, mine head sane, and I saw it, as I see mine own despair. Pray for me, boy!" he continued, falling on his knees, and dragging the page down beside him; "pray for me," he cried, gazing piteously at the youth; "God will listen to thy prayers, for thou art innocent, and I am miserable. Pray that God may forgive me, and suffer me to die; for this is the day of my sin."

"Dear master," said the page, trembling, "let us return to our friends."

"Thou wilt not pray, thou wilt not beseech God for me?" said Calavar, mournfully. "Thou wilt be merciful, when thou knowest my misery. Heaven sends thee for mine intercessor. I confess to thee, as to Heaven, for thou art without sin. Manhood brings guile and impurity, evil deeds and malign thoughts; but a child is pure in the eyes of God; and the prayers of his lips will be as incense, when wrath turns from the beseeching of men. Hear thou my sin; and then, if Heaven bid thee not to curse, then pray for me, boy—then pray for me."

In great perturbation, for he knew not how to check the knight's distraction, and fearing its increasing violence, Jacinto knelt, staring at him, his hands fettered in the grasp of his master; who, returning his gaze with such looks of woe and contrition as a penitent may give to heaven, said wildly, yet not incoherently—"Deeply dyed with sin am I, and sharply scourged with retribution. Age comes upon me before its time, but brings me nothing but memory—nothing but memory. Grey hairs and wrinkles, disease and feebleness, are the portions of my manhood; for my youth was sinful, and guilt has made me old. Oh that I might see the days when I was like to thee—when I was like to thee, Jacinto—when I knew innocence, and offended not God. But the virtues of childhood weigh not in the balance against the crimes of after years: as the child dieth, heaven opens to him; as the man sinneth, so doth he perish. Miserere mei, Deus! and forgive me my day in the Alpujarras."

As Don Gabriel pronounced the name of those mountains, wherein Jacinto knew his father had drawn the first breath of life, and around which was shed, for every Moor, such interest as belongs to those places where our fathers have fought and bled, the page began to listen with curiosity, although his alarm had not altogether subsided.

"Long years have passed; many days of peril and disaster have come and gone; and yet I have not forgotten the Alpujarras," cried Calavar, shivering as he uttered the word, "for there did joy smile, and hope sicken, and fury give me to clouds and darkness for ever. Those hills were the haunts of thy forefathers, Jacinto; and there, after the royal city had fallen, and Granada was ruled by the monarchs of Spain, they fled for refuge, all those noble Moriscos, who were resolute to die in their own mistaken faith, as well—in after years—as many others, who had truly embraced the religion of Christ, but were suspected by the bigotted of our people, and persecuted with rigour. How many wars were declared against those unhappy fugitives—now to break down the last stronghold of the infidel, and now to punish the suspected Christian—thou must know if thy sire be a true Moor of Granada. In mine early youth, and in one of the later crusades that were proclaimed against those misguided mountaineers, went I, to win the name and the laurels of a cavalier. Would that I had never won them, or that they had come to me dead on the battle-field. Know then, Jacinto, that my nineteenth summer had not yet fled from me, when I first drew my sword in conflict with men; but if I won my reputation, at that green age, it was because Heaven was minded to show me, that shame and sorrow could come as early. In those days, the royal and noble blood of Granada had not been drawn from every vein; many of the princely descendants of the Abencerrages, the Aliatars, the Ganzuls, and the Zegris, still dwelt among the mountains; and, forgetting their hereditary feuds, united together in common resistance against the Spaniards. With such men for enemies, respected alike for their birth and their valour, the war was not always a history of rapine and barbarity; and sometimes there happened such passages of courtesy and magnanimity between the Christian and Moorish cavaliers, as recalled the memory of the days of chivalry and honour. Among others who made experience of the heroic greatness of mind of the infidel princes was I myself; for, in a battle wherein the Moors prevailed against

us, I was left wounded and unhorsed on the field to perish, or to remain a prisoner in their hands. In that melancholy condition, while I commended my soul to God, as not thinking I could escape from death, a Moorish warrior of majestic appearance and a soul still more lofty approached, and had pity on my helplessness, instead of slaying me outright, as I truly expected. 'Thou art noble,' said he, 'for I have seen thy deeds; and though this day thou hast shed the blood of a Zegri, thou shalt not perish like a dog. Mount my horse and fly, lest the approaching squadrons destroy thee; and, in memory of this deed, be thou sometimes merciful to the people of Alharef.' Then knew I that this was Alharef-ben-Ismail, the most noble of the Zegris—a youth famous, even among the Spaniards, for his courage and humanity; and in gratitude and love, for he was a Christian proselyte, I pledged him my faith, and swore with him the vows of a true friendship. How I have kept mine oath, Alharef," he cried, lifting his eyes to the spangled heaven, "thou knowest—for sometimes thou art with my punisher."

The knight paused an instant in sorrowful emotion, while Jacinto, borne by curiosity beyond the bounds of fear, bent his head to listen; then making the sign of the cross, and repeating his brief prayer the cavalier resumed his narrative.

"As my ingratitude was greater than that of other men, so is my sin; for another act of benevolence shall weigh against me for ever. Why did I not die with my people, when the smiles of perfidy conducted us to the hills, and the sword was drawn upon us sleeping? That night there was but one escaped the cruel and bloody stratagem; and I again owed my life to the virtues of a Moor. Pity me, Heaven! for thou didst send me an angel and I repaid thy mercy with the thankfulness of a fiend. Know, then, Jacinto, that in the village wherein was devised and accomplished the murder of my unsuspecting companions, dwelt one that now liveth in heaven. Miserere mei! Miserere mei! for she was noble and fair, and wept at the baseness of her kindred. She covered the bleeding cavalier with her mantle, concealed him from the fury that was unrelenting and, when she had healed his wounds, guided him in secret, from the den of devils, and dismissed him in safety near to the camp of his countrymen. Know thou now, boy, that this maiden was Zayda, the flower of all those hills, and the star that made them dearer to me than the heaven that was above them; and more thought I of those green peaks and shady valleys that encompassed my love, than the castle of my sire, or the church wherein rested the bones of my mother. Miserere mei! Miserere mei! for the faith that was pledged was broken: my lady slept in the arms of Alharef, and my heart was turned to blackness. Now thou shalt hear me, and pray for me," continued Don Gabriel, with a look of the wildest and most intense despair, "for my sin is greater than I can bear. Now shalt thou hear how I cursed those whom I had sworn to love; how I sharpened my sword, and with vengeance and fury went against the village of my betrayers. Oh God! how thou didst harden our hearts, when we gave their houses to the flames, and their old men and children to swords and spears; when we looked not at misery, and listened not to supplication, but slew! slew! slew! as though we struck at beasts, and not at human creatures. 'Thou sworest an oath!' cried Alharef. I laughed; for I knew I should drink his blood. 'Be merciful to my people!' he cried—and I struck him with my sabre. Oho!" continued the knight, springing to his feet, wringing his page's hands, and glaring at him with the countenance of a demon, "when he fled from me, bleeding, my heart was full of joy, and I followed him with yells of transport. This is the day, I tell thee! this is the day, and the hour! for night could not hide him. And Zayda! ay, Zayda! Zayda!—when she shielded him with her bosom, when she threw herself before him—Miserere mei, Deus! Miserere mei, Deus!"

"And Zayda?" cried the page, meeting his gaze with looks scarcely less expressive of wilderness.

"Curse me, or pray for me," said the knight, "for I slew her!"

The boy recoiled: Don Gabriel fell on his knees, and, with a voice husky and feeble as a child's, cried—"I know, now, that thou cursest me, for thou lookest on me with horror! The innocent will not pray for the guilty! the pure and holy have no pity for devils. Curse me then, for her kindred vanished from the earth, and she with them!—curse me, for I left not a drop of her blood flowing in human veins, and none in hers!—curse me, for I am her murderer, and I have not forgot it!—curse me, for God has forsaken me, and nightly her pale face glitters on me with reproach! —curse me, for I am miserable!"

While Don Gabriel still grovelled on the earth, and while the page stood yet regarding him with terror, suddenly there came to the ears of both, the shouts of soldiers, mingled with the roar of firelocks; and, as three or four crossbow shafts rattled against the sides of the pyramid, there were visible in the moonlight as many figures of men running among the ruins, now leaping over, now darting around the fragments, as if flying for their lives from a party of armed men, who were seen rushing after them on the square. The knight rose, bewildered, and, as if in the instinct of protection, again grasped the hand of the page. But now the emotions which had agitated the master, seemed transferred to his followers; and Jacinto, trembling and struggling, cried—"Senor mio, let me loose! For the sake of Heaven, for the sake of the Zayda whom you slew, let me go!— for they are murdering my father!"

But Don Gabriel, in the confusion of his mind, still retained his grasp, and very providentially, as it appeared; for at that very moment a voice was heard exclaiming—"Hold! shoot not there; 'tis the Penitent Knight!—Aim at the fliers. Follow and shoot!—follow and shoot!"

Immediately the party of pursuers rushed up to the pair, one of whom paused, while the others, in obedience to his command, continued the chase, ever and anon sending a bolt after the fugitives.

"On, and spare not, ye knaves!" cried Sandoval, for it was this cavalier who now stood at the side of the knight of Rhodes. "On, and shoot! on and shoot! and see that ye bring me the head of the Moor! Oho, my merry little page!" he cried, regarding Jacinto; "you have been playing Sir Quimichin, Sir Rat, and Sir Spy? A cunning little brat, faith; but we'll catch thy villain father, notwithstanding!"

The page bowed his head and sobbed, but was silent; and Don Gabriel, rallying his confused spirits a little, said—"I know not what you mean, senor. We are no spies, but very miserable penitents."

"Oh, sir knight, I crave your pardon," said Sandoval without noticing the eccentric portion of his confession, "I meant not to intrude upon your secrecy, but to catch Abdalla, the deserter; of whom, and of whose rogueries, not doubting that this boy has full knowledge, I must beg your permission to conduct him to the general."

"Surely," said Calavar, mildly, "if Jacinto have offended, I will not strive to screen him from examination, but only from punishment. I consent you shall lead him to Cortes; and I will myself accompany you."

"It is enough, noble knight, if thou wilt thyself condescend to conduct him," said the cavalier; "whereby I shall be left in freedom to follow a more urgent duty. God save you, sir knight; I leave the boy in your charge." So saying, Sandoval pursued hastily after his companions; and Calavar, leading the page, now no longer unwilling (for the Almogavar, with his companions, was long since out of sight), pursued his melancholy way to the quarters.

CHAPTER XXX.

While these occurrences were transpiring, Don Amador de Leste, in search of the knight, had rambled through the streets, and following, very naturally, the only path with which he was acquainted, soon found himself issuing from that gate by which he had entered from Tlascala. The domination of the Spaniards had interrupted many of the civil, as well as the religious, regulations of the Cholulans; and, with their freedom, departed that necessity and habit of vigilance, which had formerly thronged their portals with watchmen. No Indian guards, therefore, were found at the gate; and the precautions of the general had not carried his sentinels to this neglected and seemingly secure quarter. The neophyte passed into the fields, and though hopeless, in their solitudes, of discovering the retreat of the penitent, was seduced to prolong his walk by the beauty of the night, and by the many pensive thoughts to which it gave birth. How many times his reflections carried him back to the land of his nativity, to the surges that washed the Holy Land, to the trenches of Rhodes, to the shores of Granada, need not be here related; nor, if he gave many sighs to the strange sorrow and stranger destiny of his kinsman, is it fitting such emotions should be recorded. He wandered about, lost in his musings, until made sensible, by the elevation of the moon, that he had trespassed upon the hour of midnight. Roused by this discovery from his reveries, he returned upon his path, and had arrived within view of the gate, when he was arrested by the sudden appearance of four men, running towards him at a rapid rate, and presenting to his vision the figures of Indian warriors. No sooner had these fugitives approached near enough to perceive an armed cavalier intercepting the road, than they paused, uttering many quick and, to him, incomprehensible exclamations. But though he understood not their language, he was admonished by their actions, of the necessity of drawing his sword and defending himself from attack; for the foremost, hesitating no longer than to give instructions to his followers, instantly advanced upon him, flourishing a heavy axe of obsidian.

Somewhat surprised at the audacity of this

naked barbarian, but in nowise daunted at the number of his supporters, the cavalier lifted up his trusty Bilboa, fully resolved to teach him such a lesson as would cause him to remember his temerity for ever; but, almost at the same moment his wrath vanished, for he perceived, in this assailant, the young ambassador of the preceding evening; and, remembering the words of De Morla, he felt reluctant to injure one of the princes of the unhappy house of Montezuma.—
"Prince!" said he, elevating his voice, but forgetting his want of an interpreter, "drop thy sword, and pass by in peace; for I have not yet declared war against thy people, and I am loath to strike thee."

But the valiant youth, misconceiving or disregarding both words and gestures, only approached with the more determination, and swung his bulky weapon over his head, as if in the act of smiting, when one of his followers exclaiming eagerly—"Ho, Quauhtemotzin! forbear!" sprang before him, and revealed to Don Amador the countenance of the Moor Abdalla.

"Thou art safe, senor!" cried the Almogavar, "and Heaven be thanked for this chance, that shows thee I have not forgotten thy benefits!"

The assurance of Abdalla was presently confirmed; for the young prince, seeing the action of the Moor, lowered his weapon, and merely surveying the cavalier with an earnest look, passed by him on his course, and was followed by the two others. Meanwhile Don Amador, regarding the Almogavar, said—"I know not, good Sidi—notwithstanding this present service, for which I thank thee—not so much because thou hast stepped between me and danger (for, it must be apparent to thee, I could, with great ease, have defended myself from such feeble assailants), but because thou hast freed me from the necessity of hurting this poor prince;—I say, notwithstanding all this, Abdalla, I know not whether I should not now be bound to detain thee, and compel thee to return to the general; for it is not unknown to me, that thou art, at this moment, a deserter and traitor."

"Senor!" said the Moor, withdrawing a step, as if fearing lest the cavalier would be as good as his word, "my treason is against my misfortunes, and I desert only from injustice; and if my noble lord knows thus much, he knows also, that to detain me, would be to give me to the gallows."

"I am not certain," said Don Amador, "that my intercession would not save thy life, unless thou hast been guilty of more crimes than I have heard."

"Guilty of nothing but misfortune!" said the Moor, earnestly; "guilty of nothing but the crimes of others, and of griefs, which are reckoned against me for sins!"

"Guilty," said the cavalier, gravely, "of treating in secret with these barbarians, who are esteemed the enemies of thy Christian friends; and guilty of seducing into the same crime thy countrymen, the Moriscos; one of whom, I am persuaded, did but now pass me with the Indians, and one of whom, also, hath charged thee with tempting him."

"Senor," said Abdalla, hurriedly, "I cannot now defend myself from these charges, for I hear my enemies in pursuit."

"And guilty," added Don Amador, with severity, "as I think, of deserting thine own flesh

and blood—thy poor and friendless boy, Abdalla!"

The Almogavar flung himself at the feet of the cavalier, saying, wildly—"My flesh and blood! and friendless indeed! unless thou wilt continue to protect him. Senor, for the love of Heaven—for the sake of the mother who bore you, be kind and true to my boy! Swear thou wilt protect him from malice and wrong; for it was his humanity to thy kinsman, the knight, that has robbed him of his father."

"Dost thou confess thou wert about to steal him from his protector? Now, by heavens, Moor, this is but an infidel's gratitude!"

"Senor!" said Abdalla, "you reproached me for forsaking him; and now you censure me for striving not to forsake him! But the sin is mine, not Jacinto's. I commanded him to follow me, senor; and he would have obeyed me, had he not found thy Knight Calavar swooning among the ruins. He tarried to give him succour, and thus was lost; for the soldiers came upon him."

"Is this so, indeed? My kinsman left swooning! Thou wert but a knave, not to tell me this before."

"The knight is safe—he has robbed me of my child," said Abdalla, throwing himself before the neophyte. "Go not, senor, till thou hast promised to requite his humanity with the truest protection."

"Surely he shall have that, without claiming it."

"Ay, but promise me, swear it to me!" cried the Moor, eagerly. "Don Hernan will be awroth with him. The cavaliers will call him mine accomplice."

"They will do the boy no wrong," said Amador; "and I know not why thou shouldst ask me the superfluity of an oath."

"Senor, I am a father, and my child is in a danger of which thou knowest not! For the love of God, give me thy vows thou wilt not suffer my child to be wronged!"

"I promise thee this; but acquaint me with this new and unknown peril. If it be the danger of an accusation of witchcraft, I can resolve thee, that that is not regarded by the general."

"Senor, my pursuers are nigh at hand," cried Abdalla, "and I must fly! A great danger besets Jacinto, and thou canst preserve him. Swear to me, thou wilt not wrong him, and suffer me to depart."

"Wrong him!" said the cavalier. "Thou art beside thyself. Yet, as it does appear to me, that the soldiers are approaching us, I will give thee this very unreasonable solace. I swear to thee very devoutly, that, while Heaven leaves me my sword and arm, and the power to protect, no one shall, in any way, or by any injustice, harm or wrong the boy Jacinto."

"I will remember thy promise, and thee!" cried the Almogavar, seizing his hand and kissing it.

"Tarry, Abdalla. Reflect: thou rushest on many dangers. Return, and I will intercede for thy pardon."

But the Moor, running with great speed after his companions, was almost already out of sight; and Don Amador, musing, again turned his face towards Cholula.

"If I meet these soldiers," he soliloquised, "I

must, in honour, acquaint them with the path of the Moor; whereby Abdalla may be captured, and put to death on the spot. I am resolute, I cannot, by utterly concealing my knowledge of this event, maintain the character of a just and honest gentleman; yet it appears to me, my duty only compels me to carry my information to the general. This will I do, and by avoiding the pursuers, preserve the obligations of humanity to the fugitive, without any forfeit of mine honour."

Thus pondering, and walking a little from the path, until the pursuers had passed him, he returned to the quarters.

CHAPTER XXXI.

The day that followed after the flight of Abdoul-al-Sidi, beheld the army of Cortes crossing that ridge which extends, like a mighty curtain, between the great volcano and the rugged Iztaccihuatl; and many a hardy veteran shivered with cold and discontent, as sharp gusts, whirling rain and snow from the inhospitable summits, prepared him for the contrast of peace and beauty which is unfolded to the traveller, when he looks down from the mountains to the verdant valley of Mexico. Even at the present day, when the axe has destroyed the forest—when the gardens of flowers, the cultivation of which, with a degree of passionate affection that distinguished the Mexicans from other races, seemed to impart a tinge of poetry to their character, and mellow their rougher traits with the hues of romance, when these flower gardens have vanished from the earth; when the lakes have receded and diminished, and with them the fair cities that once rose from their waters, leaving behind them stagnant pools and saline deserts; even now, under all these disadvantages, the prospect of this valley is of such peculiar and astonishing beauty, as, perhaps, can be no where else equalled among the haunts of men. The providence of the Spanish viceroys in constructing a road more direct and easy of passage, to the north of the great mountains, has robbed travellers of the more spirit-stirring impressions which introduced them to the spectacle, when pursuing the ancient highway of the Mexicans. It ascends among gloomy defiles, at the entrance of which stand, on either hand, like stupendous towers guarding the gate of some Titan stronghold, the two grandest pinnacles of the interior. It conducts you among crags and ravines, among clouds and tempests, now sheltering you under a forest of oaks and pines, now exposing you to the furious blasts that howl along the ridges. A few dilapidated hamlets of Indians, if they occasionally break the solitude, destroy neither the grandeur nor solemnity of the path. You remember, on this deserted highway, that you are treading in the steps of Cortes.

As the army proceeded, Don Amador, alive to every novelty, took notice that, regularly, at short distances from each other, not excepting even in the wildest and loneliest places, there were certain low and rude but strong cabins of stone built by the way-side, but without inhabitants. These, he was told, were the houses that were always constructed by the Mexican kings on such friendless routes, to shelter the exposed traveller.

He thought such benignant provision betokened some of the humaner characteristics of civilisation, and longed eagerly to make acquaintance with those nobler institutions which might be presented below. This desire was not the less urgent, that the frozen winds, penetrating his mailed armour, made him shiver like a coward on the back of his war-horse. He felt also much concern for his kinsman, who rode at his side with a visage even wanner and more woe-begone than ordinary. But in the deep and death-like abstraction that invested his spirits, Don Gabriel was as insensible to the assaults of the blast, as to the solicitude of his friend. The page Jacinto, moreover, caused him no little thought; for the flight of his father, though this had exposed him neither to the anger nor inquiries of Don Hernan (who affected to treat the desertion of the Moors as an affair of little consequence, save to themselves), had left the boy so dejected and spiritless, that, as he trudged along between the two cavaliers, he seemed to follow more by the instinct of a jaded house-dog, than with the alacrity of a faithful servant. To the pity of his young master he returned but a forced gratitude, and to his benevolent counsel that he should ride behind Lazaro, he rendered the oft-repeated excuse—" Senor mio I am afraid of horses; and 'tis better to waltk han ride over these cold hills."

"There is much wisdom in what thou sayest, as I begin now to perceive," said Amador, dismounting and giving his steed to Lazaro: "'tis better to be over-warm with marching on foot, than turned into an icicle on horseback. My father!" he said, gently and affectionately, to Calavar, "wilt thou not descend, and warm thyself a little with exercise?" But the knight only replied with a melancholy and bewildered stare, which convinced the novice that entreaty and argument upon the subject, as, at present, upon all others, would be alike unavailing. Sighing, therefore, and, with a gesture, directing Baltasar to assume his station at the side of Don Gabriel, he took the page by the hand, and removing to a little distance from the group, as well as from all other persons, he walked on, entering into discourse with Jacinto.

"I do not marvel at thee, Jacinto," he said, "nor can I altogether censure thee for grieving thus at the flight of thy father. Nor will I, as was, last night, my resolve, reprimand thee for leaving me, contrary to my bidding, at the chamber of my good knight; for, besides finding thee in grief enough at present, I perceive thou wert instigated to this disobedience by anxiety for thy parent, which would have excused in thee a greater fault. But let me ask thee, not so much as a master as a friend, two or three questions. First, Jacinto," he continued, "art thou dissatisfied with thy service, or with thy master, who loves thee as well as myself?"

"Service—master!—senor!" said the boy, confused.

"I demand of thee, art thou discontented with thy duties, or grieved by any unkindness which has been manifested to thee by thy master, or by any of us, who are his followers?"

"I cannot be discontented with my duties," said the boy, a little cheerfully, for it was not possible long to withstand the benevolence of his patron; "I cannot be discontented with my duties; for, in truth, it seems to me, there are none imposed upon me, except such as are prompted by my own fancies. I am very skilless in the customs of service, never having been in service before; yet, senor, I like it so well, that with such masters, methinks, I could remain a contented servant to the end of my days. That is—that is"—But here the page interrupted himself abruptly. "As for any unkindness, I own with gratitude, I have never received from my lord, from my master, nor from his people, any thing but great favour, as well as forgiveness for all my faults."

"Thou answerest well," said the novice, gravely. "I did not apprehend any body could treat thee rudely, except Lazaro, who is a rough fellow in his ways, and being in some sort a wit, is oft betrayed into saying sharp things, in order that people may laugh at them. Nevertheless, Lazaro has a good heart; for which reason I pardon many of his freedoms: but, I vow to thee, though he is a brave soldier, and albeit is opposed to all my feelings and principles to degrade a serving-man by blows, nevertheless, had I found him venting his wit upon thee, I should have been tempted to strike him, even with the hardest end of my lance."

"I never had a better friend than Lazaro," said the page, with a faint smile; "and I love him well, for he affects my singing, and praises me more than any body else. Then, as for Marco and Baltasar, though they delight more in cleaning armour than listening to a lute; and as for the secretary, Senor Lorenzo, who cares for nothing but tilting with any one who will take the trouble to unhorse him; they are all good-natured to me, and they never scold me."

"This, then, being the case," said Amador, and allowing thy first and most natural obedience to be to thy father, rather than to a master, how dost thou excuse to thyself the intention of deserting the service of thy friends, without demanding permission, or at least acquainting us with thy desires."

"Senor!" exclaimed Jacinto, surprised and embarrassed.

"It is known to me, that such was thy resolutions," said the cavalier, with gravity; "for it was so confessed to me, last night, by thy father. But, indeed, though I cannot avoid expressing my displeasure at such intention, which seems to me both treacherous and ungrateful, I led thee aside less to scold thee, than to give thee intelligence of Abdalla, I myself being, as I think, the last Christian that beheld him."

"Oh, senor! and he escaped unharmed?" cried the boy.

"Verily without either bruise or wound, save that which was made on his soul, when I reproached him for deserting thee?"

"I am deserted by all?" exclaimed Jacinto, clasping his hands.

"For the thousandth time I tell thee, no!" said his patron; "and thy father made it apparent to me he abandoned thee unwillingly; nor would he leave me though the pursuers were approaching fast, until he had exacted of me the very superfluous vow, that I would give thee a double protection from all wrong and injustice. Dry thy tears: I have already obtained of Cortes a promise of full pardon for Abdalla, when he returns to us, as doubtless he will, at Tenochtitlan."

"I hope so! I pray he may!" said Jacinto, hurriedly "or what, oh! what shall become of us!"

"I will have him sought out, and by and by take thee and him along, to Cuenza. 'Tis hard by to Granada."

The boy remained silent, and Amador continued —"Thy father also showed me, that it was thy faithful love, in remaining by my kinsman during a swoon, which prevented thee from escaping with him. This, though it does not remove the fault of thy design, entirely forces me to pardon it; and, indeed, Abdalla did as much as acknowledge thou wert averse to the plan."

"Senor, I was: for though our degradation was great, I knew not how much greater it might be among the Pagans."

"Degradation! dost thou talk of degradation? In good faith, thou surprisest me!"

"Senor," said the boy, proudly, "though you will deride such vanity in poor barbarians of the desert, yet did we ever think ourselves, who had always been free and unenslaved, debased by servitude. At least, my father thought so; and I myself, though speedily solaced by the kindness which was shown to me, could not but sometimes think it had been better to have perished with my father in the sea, along with our unhappy people, than to remain as I was—and as I am—a servant in the house of my master!"

"A silly boy art thou, Jacinto," said Amador, surveying him with surprise: "for, first, thy office, as the page of a most noble and renowned knight, is such a one as would be coveted by any grandee's son, however, noble, who aspired to the glory of arms and knighthood: and I admonish thee, that, had not his infirmity driven Don Gabriel from Spain entirely without the knowledge of his servants, thou shouldst have seen the son of a very proud and lofty nobleman attending him in the very quality which thou thinkest so degrading. I did myself, though very nearly related to him, and though sprung of such blood as acknowledges none superior, not even in the king that sits on the throne, enter first into his service in the same quality of page; and, trust me, I esteemed it great honour. In the second place, I marvel at thee, having already confessed that thy service is both light and pleasant."

"It is even so, senor," said the boy, meekly, "and I am not often so foolish as to repent me. It was not because I thought so yesternight, but because my father bade me, that I strove to escape from it; for he was in danger, or feared he was, and it was my duty to follow him without repining."

"I come now to ask thee another question," said the neophyte. "By what good fortune was it, that thou stumbledst upon my kinsman, among the ruins of that profane pyramid?"

"It was there, senor, that the princes met us."

"Hah! Oh, then, thou wert plotting with my bold prince, hah! Faith, a very gallant Pagan! and in nowise resembling the varlets of Cuba. If thou knowest aught of these men that may concern our leader to know, it will be thy duty to report the same to him, Jacinto, and that without delay."

"Nothing, senor," said the page, hastily. "I discovered that my father was to fly with the ambassadors; that he was to seek them at the pyramid; and it was there we found my master swooning."

"Didst thou see aught there that was remarkable, or in any way inexplicable?"

"I saw my lord fainting, my father and the

princes flying, and the soldiers pursuing and shooting both with crossbow and musket."

" 'Tis already," said the cavalier, turning his eye askaunt to Don Gabriel, " yet I know not by what revealment, whispered through the army, that my kinsman saw a spectre—some devilish fiend, that, in the moment of his doubt, struck him to the earth!"

"Ah!" said Jacinto, turning towards the knight, and eyeing him with a look of horror; " he thought 'twas Zayda, whom he slew so barbarously among the Alpujarras!"

The cavalier laid his hand upon Jacinto's shoulder, sternly—"What art thou saying?—what art thou thinking?—Hast thou caught some of the silly fabrications of the soldiers? I warn thee to be guarded, when thou speakest of thy master."

"He confessed it to me!" said the page, trembling, but not at the anger of his patron. "He killed her with his own hands, when she screened from his cruel rage her husband Alharef, his vowed and true friend!"

"Peace!—thou art mad!—'Twas the raving of his delirium. There is no such being as Zayda."

"There is not, but there was," said Jacinto, mournfully.

"And how knowest thou that?" demanded Amador, quickly. "Thou speakest as if she had been thy kinswoman. Art thou indeed a conjurer? There is no dark and hidden story with which thou dost not seem acquainted!"

"She was of my tribe," said Jacinto, mildly, though tremulously, returning the steadfast gaze of his patron: " I have heard my father speak of her, for she was famous among the mountains. Often has he repeated to me her story—how she drew upon herself the anger of her tribe, by preserving their foe, and how their foe repaid her by—oh Heaven! by murdering her! Often have I heard of Zayda; but I knew not 'twas Calavar who killed her!"

"Can this be true?" said Amador, looking blankly towards his unconscious kinsman. "Is it possible my father can have stained his soul with so foul, so deadly, so fearful a crime! And he confessed it to thee—to thee, a boy so foolish and indiscreet that thou hast already babbled it to another?"

"I could not help speaking at this time," said Jacinto, humbled at the reproach; " but if my lord will forgive me, I will never speak it more."

"I do forgive thee, Jacinto, as I hope Heaven will my father. This then is the sin unabsolved, the action of wrath, the memory of sorrow, that has slain the peace of my kinsman? May Heaven have pity on him, for it has punished him with a life of misery! I forgive thee, Jacinto: speak of this no more; think of it no more; let it be forgotten—now and for ever—Amen!—I have but one more question to ask thee; and this I am, in part, driven to by thy admission of the most wondrous fact, that Don Gabriel confessed to thee his secret. Many of thine actions have filled me with wonder; thy knowledge is, for thy years, inexplicable; and thou minglest with thy boyish simplicity the shrewdness of years. Dost thou truly obtain thy knowledge by the practice of those arts, which so many allow to be possessed by Botello?"

"Senor," exclaimed the boy, " startled by the abruptness of the question.

"Art thou, indeed, an enchanter, as Yacub charged thee to be? Give me to understand, for it is fitting I should know."

The exceeding and earnest gravity with which the cavalier, repeated the question, dispelled as well the grief as the fears of the page. He cast his eyes to the earth, but this action did not conceal the humour that sparkled in them, while he replied—"If I were older, and had as much acquaintance with the people as Botello, I think I could prophecy as well as he; especially if my lord Don Hernan would now and then give me a hint or two concerning his designs and expectations, such as, it has been whispered, he sometimes vouchsafes to Botello. I have no crystal imp like him indeed, but I possess one consecrated gem that can call me up, at any time, a thousand visions. It seems to me, too, that I can recall the dead; for once or twice I have done it, though very much to my own marvelling."

"Thou art an enigma," said Amador. "What thou sayest of Botello, assures me the more of thy subtle and penetrating observation; what thou sayest of thyself, seems to me a jest; and yet it hath a singular accordance, as well with my own foolish fancies and the charges of that Moorish menial, as with the events of the two last nights. Either there is, indeed, something very supernatural in thy knowledge, or the delirium of my kinsman is a disease of the blood, which is beginning to assail my own brain. God preserve me from madness! Hearken in thine ear (and fear not to answer me):—Hadst thou any thing to do with the raising of the phantom thou callest Zayda? or is it the confusion of my senses, that causes me to suspect thee of the agency?"

"Senor!" said the boy, in alarm, " you cannot think I was serious?"

"What didst thou mean, then, by acknowledging the possession of that consecrated and vision-raising jewel?"

"I meant," responded the youth, sadly, " that, being a gift associated with all the joys of my happiest days, I never look at it, or pray over it, without being beset by recollections, which may well be called visions; for they are representations of things that have passed away."

"And the story of Leila?—Pho—'tis an absurdity!—I have heard that the cold which freezes men to death, begins by setting them to sleep. Sleep brings dreams; and dreams are often most vivid and fantastical, before we have yet been wholly lost in slumber. Perhaps 'tis this most biting and benumbring blast, that brings me such phantoms. Art thou not very cold?"

"Not very, senor: methinks we are descending; and now the winds are not so frigid as before."

"I would to Heaven, for the sake of us all, that we were descended yet lower; for night approaches, and still we are stumbling among these clouds, that seem to separate us from the earth, without yet advancing us nearer to heaven."

While the cavalier was yet speaking, there came from the van of the army, very far in the distance, a shout of joy, that was caught up by those who toiled in his neighbourhood, and continued by the squadrons that brought up the rear, until finally lost among the echoes of remote cliffs. He pressed forward with the animation shared by his companions, and, still leading Jacinto, arrived at last at a place where the mountain dipped downwards so sudden and precipitous a declivity, as to interpose no obstacle to the vision. The mists were rolling away from his feet in huge wreaths, which gradually, as they became thinner, received and transmitted the rays of an evening sun, and were lighted up with a golden and crimson radiance, glorious to behold, and increasing every moment in splendour. As this superb curtain was parted from before him as if by cords that went up to heaven, and surged voluminously aside, he looked over the heads of those that thronged the side of the mountain beneath, and saw, stretching away like a picture touched by the hands of angels, the fair valley embosomed among those romantic hills, whose shadows were stealing visibly over its western slopes, but leaving all the eastern portion dyed with the tints of sunset. The green plains studded with yet greener woodlands ; the little mountains raising their fairy-like crests ; the lovely lakes, now gleaming like floods of molten silver, where they stretched into the sunshine, and now vanishing away, in a shadowy expanse, under the gloom of the growing twilight; the structures that rose, vaguely and obscurely, here from their verdant margins, and there from their very bosom, as if floating on their placid waters, seeming at one time to present the image of a city crowned with towers and pinnacles, and then again broken by some agitation of the element, or confused by some vapour swimming through the atmosphere, into the mere fragments and phantasms of edifices—these, seen in that uncertain and fading light, and at that misty and enchanting distance, unfolded such a spectacle of beauty and peace as plunged the neophyte into a reverie of rapture. The trembling of the page's hand, a deep sigh that breathed from his lips, recalled him to consciousness, without however dispelling his delight. " By the cross which I worship !" he cried, " it fills me with amazement, to think that this cursed and malefactious earth doth contain a spot that is so much like to Paradise! Now do I remember me of the words of the Senor Gomez, that ' no man could conceive of heaven, till he had looked upon the valley of Mexico;' an expression which, at that time, I considered very absurd, and somewhat profane ; yet, if am not now mistaken, I shall henceforth, doubtless, when figuring to my imagination the seats of bliss, begin by thinking of this very prospect."

" It is truly a fairer sight than any we saw in Florida, most noble senor," said a voice hard by.

The cavalier turned, and with not less satisfaction than surprise (for the delight of the moment had greatly warmed his heart), beheld in the person of the speaker, the master of the caravel. " Oho! senor capitan !" cried Don Amador, stretching out his hand to the bowing commander. " I vow I am as much rejoiced to see thee, as if we had been companions together in war. What brings thee hither to look on these inimitable landscapes ? Art thou come to disprove thy accounts of the people of Tenochtitlan ? I promise thee, I have heard certain stories, and seen certain sights, which greatly shake my faith in thy representations. What news dost thou bring of my kinsman, the admiral ?"

" Senor," said the master, " the stars have a greater influence over our destinies, than have our desires. It seems to me that that very astonishing victory of the most noble and right valiant Senor Don Hernan, at Zempoala, did utterly turn the brains of all the sailors in the fleet : and his excellency the admiral having declared himself a friend to the conqueror, they were all straightway seized with such an ambition to exchange the handspike for the halbert, and mine own thirteen vagabonds among them, that, in an hour's time after the news, my good caravel was as well freed of men as ever I had known her cleared of rats after a smoking of brimstone. So, perceiving the folly of remaining in her alone, and receiving the assurance from my knaves that, if I went with them, I should be their captain, and his excellency consenting to the same, I forthwith armed myself with these rusty plates (wherein you may see some of the dints battered by the red devils of Florida), and was converted into a soldier—the captain of the

smallest company in this goodly army, and perhaps the most cowardly ; for never did I before hear men grumble with such profane discontent, as did these same knaves this very day, at the cold air of the mountains. If they will fight, well ; if they will not, and any body else will, may I die the death of a mule, if I will not make them ; for one hath a better and stronger command in an army than in a ship. Last night I came to that great town they call Cholula, and was confirmed in my command by the general. His excellency the admiral bade me commend his love to your worship ; and hearing you have enlisted his secretary into your service, sends by me a better suit of armour for the youth, and prays your favour will have him in such keeping, that he shall be cured of his fit of valour, without the absolute loss of life, or his right hand, which last would entirely unfit him for returning to his ancient duties—as, by my faith! so would the former. But, by'r lady, my thoughts run somewhat a wool-gathering at this prospect ; for I see very clearly, 'tis a rich land here, that hath such admirable cities ; and, I am told we shall have blows enow, by and by, with the varlets in the valley. Nevertheless, I am ready to wager my soul against a cotton neck-piece, that if these infidels have half the spirit of the savages of Florida, we shall be beaten, and sent to heaven, Amen !—that is, for the matter of heaven and not the beating !"

" I applaud thy resolution, mine ancient friend," said the cavalier, " and methinks thou art more vigorous, both of body and mind, on land than thou wert at sea. I will, by and by, send the secretary to receive the armour, and will not forget his excellency's bidding, as far as is possible. But let us not, by conversation, distract our thoughts from this most lovely spectacle ; for I perceive it will be soon enveloped in darkness ; and how know we, we shall ever look upon it again."

Thus terminating the interview, the neophyte, as he descended, watched the unchanging yet ever-beautiful picture, till the sun buried himself among the mountains, and the shadows of night curtained it in obscurity.

CHAPTER XXXII.

Passing the night in a little hamlet on the mountain side, the army was prepared, at the dawn of the following day, to resume its march. But the events of this march being varied by nothing but the change of prospect, and the wonder of those by whom the valley was seen for the first time, we will not imitate the prolixity of our authority, the worthy Don Cristobal, but dispatch, in a word, the increasing delight and astonishment with which Don Amador de Leste, after having satiated his appetite with views of lake and garden, surveyed the countless villages and towns of hewn stone that rose, almost at every moment, among them. A neck of land now separates the lakes of Chalco and Xochimilco; and the retreat of the waters has left their banks deformed with fens and morasses, wherein the wild-duck screams among waving reeds and bulrushes. Originally, these basins were united in one long and lovely sheet of water, divided, indeed, yet only by a causeway built by the hands of man, which is now lost in the before-mentioned neck, together with its sluices and bridges, as well as a beautiful little city, that lay midway between the two shores called by the

Spaniards Venezuela (because rising, like its aristocratic godmother, from among the waters), until they discovered that this was a peculiarity presented by dozens of other cities in the valley. Here was enjoyed the spectacle of innumerable canoes, paddled, with corn and merchandize, from distant towns, or parting with a freight of flowers from the *chinampas*, or floating gardens. But this was a spectacle disclosed by other cities of greater magnitude and beauty; and when, from the streets of the royal city Iztapalapan, the army issued at once upon the broad and straight dike that stretched for more than two leagues in length, a noble highway, through the salt floods of Tezcuco; when the neophyte beheld islands rocking like anchored ships in the water, the face of the lake thronged with little piraguas, and the air alive with snowy gulls; when he perceived the banks of this great sheet, as far as they could be seen, lined with villages and towns; and especially when he traced, far away in the distance, in the line of the causeway, such a multitude of high towers and shadowy pyramids looming over the waters, as denoted the presence of a vast city—he was seized with a species of awe at the thought of the marvellous ways of God, who had raised up that mighty empire, all unknown to the men of his own hemisphere, and now revealed it, for the accomplishment of a destiny which he trembled to imagine. He rode at the head of the army, in a post of distinction, by the side of Cortes, and felt moved to express some of the strange ideas which haunted him; but looking on the general attentively, he perceived about his whole countenance and figure an expression of singular gloom, mingled with such unusual haughtiness, as quickly indisposed him to conversation.

The feelings that struggled in the bosom of the conqueror were, at this instant, akin to those of the destroyer, as he sat upon "the Assyrian mount,' overlooking the walls of Paradise, almost lamenting, and yet excusing to himself, the ruin he was about to bring upon that heavenly scene. Perhaps ' horror and doubt' for a moment distracted his thoughts; for no one knew better than he the uncertain chances and tremendous perils of the enterprise, or mused with .more fear upon the probable and most sanguinary resistance of his victims, as foreboded by the tumults that followed after the late massacre. But when he cast his eye backward on the causeway, and beheld the long train of foot and horse following at his beck; the many cannons, which, as they were dragged along, opened their brazen throats towards the city; and rows of spears and arquebuses bristling, and the banners flapping, over the heads of his people, and behind them the feathered tufts of his Tlascalans; and heard the music of his trumpets swell from the dike to the lake, from the lake to the shores, and die away, with pleasant echoes, among the hills; when he surveyed and listened to these things, and contrasted with them the imperfect weapons and naked bodies of his adversaries—the weakness of their institutions—the feebleness of their princes—the general disorganisation of the people—and counted the guerdon of wealth and immortal renown that should wait upon success, he stifled at once his apprehensions and his remorse, ceased to remember that those, whose destruction he meditated, were, to him, 'harmless innocence,' and satisfied himself, almost with the arguments of the fiend, that—

Public reason just,
Honour and empire, with revenge, enlarged,
By conquering this new world, compels me now
To do what else, though damn'd, I should abhor.

Triumph and regret were at once dividing his bosom; he knew he was a destroyer, but felt he should be a conqueror.

There were many things in Don Hernan, which, notwithstanding the gratitude and the desires of the neophyte, prevented the latter from bestowing upon him so much affection as he gave to one or two of his followers. The spirit of the leader was wholly, and, for his station, necessarily, crafty; and this very quality raised up a wall between him and one who was of so honourable a nature that he knew no concealment. The whole schemes and aims of the general were based upon such a foundation of fraud and injustice, that, he well knew, he could not, without expecting constant and vexatious opposition, give his full confidence to any truly noble spirit; and the same wisdom that estranged him from the lofty, taught him to keep aloof from the base. While artful enough to make use of the good qualities of the one, and the bad principles of the other class, he was satisfied with their respect; he cared not for their friendship. It was enough to him, that he had zealous and obedient followers: his situation allowed him no friends; and he had none. Of all the valiant cavaliers who shared with him the perils and the rewards of the invasion, there was not one who, after peace had severed the bonds of companionship, did not, at the first frown of fortune, or the first invitation of self-interest, array himself in arms against his leader.

While the general gave himself up to his proud and gloomy imaginings, the novice of Rhodes again cast his eyes over the lake. It seemed to him, that notwithstanding the triumphant blasts of the trumpet, the neighing of horses, and the multitudinous tread of the foot-soldiers, as well as the presence of so many canoes on the water, there was an air of sadness and solitude pervading the whole spectacle. The new soldiers were perhaps impressed with an awe like his own at the strange prospect; the veterans were, doubtless, revolving in their minds some of the darker contingencies over which their commander was brooding. Their steps rang heavily on the stone mole; and as the breeze curled up the surface of the lake into light billows, and tossed them against the causeway, Don Amador fancied they approached and dashed at his feet, with a certain sullen and hostile voice of warning. He thought it remarkable, also, that, among the throngs of canoes, there rose no shouts of welcome: the little vessels, forming a fleet on either side of the dike, were paddled along, at the distance of two or three hundred yards, so as to keep pace with the army; and the motion of the rowers, and the gleaming of their white garments, might have given animation, as well as picturesqueness, to the scene, but for the death-like silence that was preserved among them. The novelty of every thing about the cavalier, gave vigour to his imagination — he thought these paddling hordes resembled the flight of ravens that track the steps of a wounded beast in the desert—or a shoal of those ravenous monsters that scent a pestilence on the deep, and swim by the side of the floating hospital, waiting for their prey.

"What they mean, I know not," mused the cavalier. "After what De Morla has told me, I shall be loath to slay any of them; but if they desire to make a dinner of me, I swear to St. John I will carve their brown bodies into all sorts of dishes, before I submit my limbs to the imprisonment of their most damnable maws! And yet, poor infidels! methinks they have some cause, after that affair of the festival, to look upon us with fear, if not with wrath; for if a garrison of an hundred men could be prompted to do them such a foul and murderous wrong, there is much reason to apprehend this well-appointed thousand might be, with a slittle provocation and warning, incited to work thema still more deadly injury. I would, however, that they might shout a little, were it only to make me feel more like a man awake; for, at present, it seems to me, that I am dreaming all these things which I am look-ing at"

The wish of the cavalier was not obeyed; and many a suspicious glance was cast, both by soldier and officer, to the dumb myriads paddling on their flanks; for it could not be denied, though no one dared to give utterance to such a suggestion, that were these countless barbarians provided with arms, as was perhaps the case, and could they but conceive the simple expedient of landing both in front and rear, and thus cut off their invaders from the city and the shore, and attack them at the same time, with good heart, in this insulated and very disadvantageous position, there was no know-ing how obscure a conjecture the historian might hazard for the story of their fate. But this sus-picion was also proved to be groundless; no sort of annoyance was practised, none indeed was meditated. The thousands that burthened the canoes, had issued from their canals to indulge a stupid curiosity, or, perhaps, under an impulse which they did not understand, to display to their enemies the long banquet of slaughter which fate was preparing for them.

The army reached, at last, a point where another causeway, of equal breadth, and seemingly of equal length, coming from the south-west, from the city Cojohuacan, ruled by a king (the brother and feudatory of Montezuma), terminated in the dike of Iztapulapan. At the point of junction was a sort of military work, consisting of a bastion, a strong wall, and two towers, guarding the ap-proach to the imperial city. It was known by the name of Xoloc (or, as it should be written in our tongue, Holoc), and was in after times made famous by becoming the head-quarters of Cortes, during the time of the siege. It stood at the distance of only half a league from the city; and from hence could be plainly seen, not only the huge pyramids, with their remarkable towers rising aloft, but the low stone fabrics whereon, among the flowers (for every roof was a terrace, and every terrace a garden) stood the gloomy citizens, watching the approach of the Christian army.

At this point of Xoloc, at a signal of the general, every drum was struck with a lusty hand, every trumpet filled with a furious blast, and the Chris-tians and Tlascalans, shouting together, while two or three falconets were at the same time dis-charged, there rose such a sudden and mighty din as startled the infidels in their canoes, and con-veyed to the remotest quarters of Tenochtitlan, the intelligence of the advance of its masters.

Scarcely had the echoes of this uproar died away on the lake, when there came, faintly indeed, but full of joyous animation, the response of the Christian garrison; and as the army resumed its march, they repeated their shouts loudly and blithely, for they now perceived, by the waving of banners and the glittering of spears, that their friends, rescued, as they all understood, by their presence, from the fear of a miserable death, were ——ing forth to meet them. Two or three

mounted cavaliers were seen to separate them-selves from this little and distant band, and gallop forwards, while the causeway rung to the sound of their hoofs. Don Amador, being in advance, was able, as they rushed forwards with loud and merry halloos, to observe their persons, as well as the reception they obtained from Don Hernan. His eye was attracted to him who seemed to be their leader, and who, he already knew, was Don Pedro de Alvarado, a cavalier that had no rival (the gal-lant Sandoval excepted) in fame and in the favour of Lis general. He was in the prime of life, of a noble stature, and of a countenance so engaging and animated, that this, in addition to the constant splendour of his apparel, whether the gilded mail of a warrior, or the costly vestments of a courtier —had won him from the Mexicans themselves the flattering title of *Tonatiuh*, or the Sun—a compli-ment which his friends did not scruple to perpe-tuate, nor he to encourage. He rode immediately up to Cortes, and stretching out his hand, said gaily, and, indeed, affectionately—" Long life to thee, Cortes! I welcome thee as my saint. God be praised for thy coming—Amen! Thou hast snatched me from a most ignoble and hound-like death; for Sir Copilli, the emperor, has been starving me."

Don Hernan took the hand of the cavalier, and eyeing him steadfastly and sternly, while his old companions gathered around, said, with a most pointed asperity—" My friend Alvarado! thou hast done me, as well as these noble cavaliers, thy friends, and also thy lord and king, a most grievous wrong; for, by the indulgence of thy hot wrath and indiscretion, thou hast, as I may say, dashed the possession of this empire out of our hands: and much blood shall be shed, and many Chris-tian lives sacrificed, in a war that might have been spared us, before we can remedy the consequences of thy rashness."

A deep gloom, that darkened to a scowl, in-stantly gathered over the handsome visage of Don Pedro; and snatching his hand roughly away, he drew himself up, and prepared to reply to the general with wrath, and perhaps with defiance. But it was no part of the policy of Cortes to carry his anger further than might operate warningly on the officer and on those around; for which reason offering his hand again, as if not noticing the discontent of his lieutenant, he said, with an artful appearance of sincerity—" I have often thought how thou mightest have been spared the necessity of slaying these perfidious and plotting hounds; and it seems to me, even now, if thou couldst, by shutting thyself in thy quarters and avoiding a contest, have submitted to the foolish imputations some might have cast on thee, of acting from fear rather than from prudence, this killing of the nobles might have been avoided. I say, some, indeed, might have accused thee of being in fear, hadst thou not killed the knaves that were scheming thine own destruction; but this is an aspersion which thou couldst have borne with as little injury as any other brave cavalier in this army, being second to none in a high and well-deserved reputation: and so well am I per-suaded that none could have better than thyself withstood the uncommon dangers of thy command in this treasonable city, that I should have excused any precaution of peace, that might have seemed cowardly to others. Nevertheless, I must own, thou wert forced to do as thou hast done; for no brave man can submit to be thought capable of fear; and, I know, 'twas this thought alone that drove thee out to kill the nobles."

No cloud in these tropical skies could have vanished more suddenly in the sunbeam, than did the frown of Alvarado at these complimentary words of his general. He caught the hand that was still proffered, shook it heartily, kissed it, and said—his whole countenance beaming with delight and pride—"I thank your excellency for this just consideration of my actions, and this expression of a true excuse for what seems, and what perhaps may have been, a great indiscretion. Your excellency, and these noble senors, my friends, would have esteemed me a coward, had I sat securely and quietly in the palace, watching, without attempting to forestall, the conspiracy of the lords of Mexico; and I have great hopes, when I have permission to explain all these things to your excellency, though I do not much plume myself on wisdom, but rather on fighting (which is the only thing I have studied with diligence), that you will say I acted as wisely as, in such case, was possible."

"I have no doubt of it," said Cortes, smiling, as he rode onwards. "But nevertheless, there is more wisdom in thy knocks than in thy noddle," he muttered to himself. The shame of the reproof, though dispelled by the flattery of the rebuker, did not wholly disappear from the bosom of Alvarado. A word of sarcasm will live longer than the memory of a benefit. Alvarado was, in after days, a traitor to his general.

But without now giving himself leisure for consideration, the cavalier addressed himself to his old companions; and even (for his joy at being so rescued out of peril, warmed his heart to all) made up with much satisfaction to the Knight Calavar. But since the confession of Cholula, the distemper of Don Gabriel had visibly increased; and his fits of abstraction were becoming, every hour, so frequent and so profound, as to cause the greatest alarm and anxiety to his kinsman. He neither heard nor saw the salutations of Don Pedro; nor indeed did he seem at all sensible to any part of the strange scene that surrounded him. Foiled in this attempt, the courteous and vivacious soldier turned himself to Don Amador, as presenting the appearance of a noble and gallant hidalgo, and would speedily have been on the footing of the most perfect friendship with him, had it not been that the neophyte still freshly remembered the story of the massacre, and met his advances with a frigid haughtiness.

"By'r lady!" said the offended cavalier, "it seems to me that the devil, or the cold mountain, has got into the bosoms of all; for here am I, with my heart at this moment as warm as a pepperpod, or a black cloak in the sunshine, and ready to love every body, old and young, vile and virtuous, base and gentle; and yet every body, notwithstanding, meets me with a most frosty unconcern. I swear to thee, valiant cavalier, whosoever thou art, my breast is open to thee, and I crave thy affection; for, besides perceiving that thou art assuredly an hidalgo, I see thou hast a Moorish page at thy side, with a lute at his back; and if his pipe be half so good as his face, I cannot live without being thy friend, for I love music."

Jacinto shrunk away from his admirer, alarmed as much at the suddenness of his praise, as at the many evolutions of the lance, which, by way of gesticulation, he flourished about him in a very vigorous manner. But Don Amador, greatly amused at the freedom, and, in spite of himself, gained by the frankness of Don Pedro, replied with good humour—"Senor," said he, "I am Amador de Leste, of the Castle del Alcornoque, near to Cuenza; and having heard certain charges against you, in the matter of the Mexican nobles, I replied to you, perhaps, with prejudice. Nevertheless, what the general has said, does, in some sort, seem to lessen the force of the charge; and if you will, at your leisure, condescend to satisfy my doubts, as I begin to be assured you can, I will not hesitate to receive your friendship, and to tender you my own in return. Only, previous to which, I must beg of you to turn your lance-point another way, so that the boy Jacinto, who is somewhat afraid of its antics, may be enabled to walk again at my side."

"Senor Don Amador de Leste," said the soldier, taking this speech in good part, "I avow myself satisfied with your explanation, and so determined to pursue your friendship (inasmuch as I have not heard any good singing since the little Orteguilla, the page of the Indian emperor, or, what is the same thing, of Cortes, lost his voice in a quinsy), that I will give you the whole history of the nobles, their atrocious conspiracy and their just punishment, as soon as we have leisure in our quarters. And now, if you will have the goodness to ride with me a little in advance, I will have much satisfaction, as I perceive you are a stranger, to introduce you to this great and wonderful city, Tenochtitlan, of which I have been, as I may say, in some sort, the king, for two long and tumultuous months; and I swear to you, no king ever clutched upon a crown with more good will and joy than do I, this moment, abdicate my authority."

Thus invited by his courteous and jocund friend, the neophyte rode onwards so as to reach the heels of Cortes, just as the garrison, inspired by the sight of their leader, broke their ranks, and rushed forwards to salute him.

CHAPTER XXXIII.

The soldiers of Alvarado differed in nowise from those veterans whom Don Amador had found standing to their arms on the banks of the River of Canoes; only that they presented, notwithstanding their loudly vented delight, a care-worn and somewhat emaciated appearance—the consequence of long watches, perpetual fears, and in part, of famine. They broke their ranks, as has been said, as soon as they beheld their general, and surrounded him with every expression of affection; and, while stretching forth their hands with cries of gratitude and joy, invoked many execrations on their imperial prisoner, the helpless Montezuma, as the cause of all their sufferings. Among them Don Amador took notice of one man, who, though armed and habited as a Spaniard, seemed in most other respects an Indian, and of a more savage race than any he had yet seen; for his face, hands and neck were tattooed with the most fantastic figures, and his motions were those of a barbarian. This was Geronimo de Aguilar a companion of Balboa, who being wrecked on the coast of Yucatan had been preserved as a slave, and finally, adopted as a warrior among the hordes of that distant land; from which he was rescued by Don Hernan—happily to serve as the means of communication, through the medium of another and more remarkable interpreter, with the races of Mexico. This other interpreter, who approached the general with the dignified gravity of an Indian princess, and was received with suitable respect, was no less a person than that maid of Painalla, sold by an unfeeling parent a slave to one of the chieftains of Tobasco, presented by him to Cortes, and baptized in the faith under the distinguished title of the Senora Donna Marina; who, by interpreting to Aguilar, in the language of Yucatan, the communications that were made in her native tongue, thus gave to Cortes the means of conferring with her countrymen, until her speedy acquisition of the Castilian language removed the necessity of such tedious intervention. But at this period many Spaniards had acquired a smattering of her tongue, and could play the part of interpreters: and for this reason, Donna Marina will make no great figure in this history. Other annalists have sufficiently immortalised her beauty, her wisdom, and her fidelity: and it has been her good fortune, continued even to this day, to be distinguished with such honours as have fallen to the lot of none of her masters. Her Christian denomination, Marina, converted by her countrymen into Malintzin (a title that was afterwards scornfully applied by them to Cortes himself), and this again in modern days corrupted by the Creoles into Malinche, has had the singular fate to give name both to a mountain and a divinity; the sierra of Tlascala is now called the mountain of Malinche; and the descendants of Montezuma pay their adorations to the Virgin, under the title of Malintzin.

Don Amador de Leste, attended by De Morla, as well as his new acquaintance, Alvarado, was able to understand, as well as admire, many of the wonders of the city, as he now, for the first time, planted his foot on its imperial streets.

The retreat of the salt waters of Tezcuco has left the present republican city of Mexico a full league west of the lake. In the days of Montezuma, it stood upon an island, two miles removed from the western shore, with which it communicated by the dike or calzada of Tlacopan—now called Tacuba. The causeway of Iztapalapan, coming from the south, seven miles in length, passed over the island and through the city, and was continued in a line three miles further to the northern shore, and to the city Tepejacac, where now stands the church and the miraculous picture of Our Lady of Guadalupe. Besides these three great causeways, constructed with inconceivable labour, there were two others—that of Cojohuacan, which, as we have mentioned, terminated in the greater one of Iztapalapan, at the military point Xoloc, a half league from the city; and that, a little southward of the dike of Tacuba, which conveyed, in aqueducts of earthenware, the pure waters of Chapoltepec to the temples and squares of the imperial city. The island was circular, saving that a broad angle or peninsula ran out from the north-west, and a similar one from the opposite point of the compass: it was a league in diameter; but the necessities of the people, after covering this ample space with their dwellings,

extended them far into the lake; and perhaps as many edifices stood on piles, in the water, as on the land. The causeways of Iztapalapan and Tacuba, intersecting each other in the heart of the island, divided the city into four convenient quarters, to which a fifth was added, some few generations before, when the little kingdom of Tlateloeco, occupying the north-western peninsula, was added to Tenochtitlan. On this peninsula, and in this quarter, Tlateloeco, stood the palace of an ancient king, which the munificence of Montezuma had presented to Cortes for a dwelling, and which the invader, six days after the gift, by an act of as much treachery as daring, converted into the prison of his benefactor.

The appearance of this vast and remarkable city so occupied the mind of the neophyte, that, as he rode staring along, he gave but few thoughts, and fewer words, either to his kinsman or the page. It was sunset, and in the increasing obscurity he gazed, as if on a scene of magic, on streets often having canals in the midst, covered alike with bridges and empty canoes; on stone houses, low indeed, but of a strong and imposing structure, over the terraces of which waved shrubs and flowers; and on high turrets, which, at every vista, disclosed their distant pinnacles. But he remarked also, and it was mentioned by the cavaliers at his side as a bad omen, that neither the streets, the canals, nor the house-tops, presented the appearance of citizens coming forth to gaze upon them. A few Indians were now and then seen skulking at a distance in the streets, raising their heads from a half-concealed canoe, or peering from a terrace among the shrubs. He would have thought the city uninhabited, but that he knew it contained as many living creatures, hidden among its retreats, as some of the proudest capitals of Christendom. Even the great square, the centre of life and of devotion, was deserted; and the principal pyramid, a huge and mountainous mass, consecrated to the most sanguinary of deities, though its sanctuaries were lighted by the ever-blazing urns, and though the town of temples circumscribed by the great Coatepantli, or Wall of Serpents, which surrounded this Mexican Olympus, sent up the glare of many a devotional torch, yet did it seem, nevertheless, to be inhabited by beings as inanimate as those monstrous reptiles which writhed in stone along the internal wall. In this light, and in that which still played in the west, Don Amador marvelled at the structure of the pyramid, and cursed it as he marvelled. It consisted of five enormous platforms, faced with hewn stone, and mounted by steps so singularly planned, that, upon climbing the first story, it was necessary to walk entirely round the mass, before arriving at the staircase which conducted to the second. The reader may conceive of the vast size of this Pagan temple, by being apprised, that, to ascend it, the votaries were compelled, in their perambulations, to walk a distance of full ten furlongs, as well as to climb a hundred and fourteen different steps. He may also comprehend the manner in which the stairways were contrived by knowing that the first, ascending latterly from the corner, was just as broad as the first platform was wider than the second; leaving thus a sheer and continuous wall from the ground to the top of the second terrace, from the bottom of the second to the top of the third, and so on, in like manner, to the top.

But the pyramid, crowned with altars and censers, the innumerable temples erected in honour of nameless deities at its foot, and the strange and most hideous Coatepantli, were not the only objects which excited the abhorrence of the cavalier. Without the wall, and a few paces in advance of the great gate which it covered as a curtain, rose a rampart of earth or stone, oblong and pyramidal, but truncated, twenty-five fathoms in length at the base, and perhaps thirty feet in height. At either end of this tumulus, was a tower of goodly altitude, built, as it seemed at a distance, and in the dim light, of some singularly rude and uncouth material; and between them, occupying the whole remaining space of the terrace, was a sort of framework or cage, of slender poles, on all of which were strung thickly together, certain little globes, the character of which Don Amador could not penetrate, until fully abreast of them. Then, indeed, he perceived, with horror, that these globes were the skulls of human beings, the trophies of ages of superstition; and beheld in like manner, that the towers which crowned the Golgotha (or Huitzompan, as it was called in the Mexican tongue), were constructed of the same dreadful materials, cemented together with lime. The malediction which he invoked upon the builders of the ghastly temple was unheard; for the spectacle froze his blood and paralysed his tongue.

It was not yet dark, when, having left these haunts of idolatry, Don Amador found himself entering into the court-yard of a vast, and yet not of a very lofty, building—the palace of Axajacatl; wherein, with drums beating, and trumpets answering joyously to the salute of their friends, stood those individuals of the garrison who had remained to watch over their prisoners and treasures. The weary and the curious, thronging together impatiently at the gate, mingling with the garrison and some two thousand faithful Tlascalans, who had been left by Cortes as their allies, and who now rushed forward to salute the viceroy of their gods, as some had denominated Don Hernan, made such a scene of confusion, that, for a moment, the neophyte was unable to ride into the yard. In that moment, and while struggling both to appease the unquiet of Fogoso, and to drive away the feathered herd that obstructed him, his arm was touched, and looking down, he beheld Jacinto at his side, greatly agitated, and seemingly striving to disengage himself from the throng.

"Give me thy hand," cried Don Amador, "and I will pull thee out of this rabble to the back of Fogoso."

But the page, though he seized upon the hand of his patron, and covered it with kisses, held back, greatly to the surprise of Don Amador, who was made sensible that hot tears were falling with the kisses.

"I swear to thee, my boy, that I will discover thy father for thee, if it be possible for man to find him," said the cavalier, diving at once, as he thought, to the cause of this emotion.

But before he had well done speaking, the press thickening around him, drew the boy from his side; and when he had, a moment after, disengaged himself, Jacinto was no longer to be seen. Not doubting, however, that he was entangled in the mass, and would immediately appear, he called out to him to follow; and riding slowly up to Cortes, he had his whole attention immediately absorbed by the spectacle of the Indian emperor.

Issuing from the door of the palace, surrounded as well by Spanish cavaliers as by the nobles, both male and female, of his own household, who stood by him—the latter, at least—with countenances of the deepest veneration—he advanced a step to do honour to the dismounting general.

In the light of many torches, held by the people about him, Don Amador, as he flung himself from his horse, could plainly perceive the person and habiliments of the Pagan king. He was of good stature, clad in white robes, over which was a huge mantle of crimson, studded with emeralds and drops of gold, knotted on his breast, or rather on his shoulder, so as to fall, when he raised his arm, in careless but very graceful folds: his legs were buskined with gilded leather; his head covered with the copilli, or crown (a sort of mitre of plate-gold, graved and chased with certain idolatrous devices), from beneath which fell to his shoulders long and thick locks of the blackest hair. He did not yet seem to have passed beyond the autumn of life. His countenance, though of the darkest hue known among his people, was good, somewhat long and hollow, but the features well sculptured; and a gentle melancholy, a characteristic expression of his race, deepened, perhaps, in gloom, by a sense of his degradation, gave it a something that interested the beholder.

In the abruptness with which he was introduced to the regal barbarian, Don Amador had no leisure to take notice of his attendants, all princely in rank, and two or three of them the kings of neighbouring cities: he only observed that their decorations were far from being costly and ostentatious—a circumstance which, he did not then know, marked the greatness of their respect. In the absurd grandeur which attached to the person of their monarch, no distinction of inferior ranks was allowed to be traced, during the time of an audience; and in his majestic presence, a vassal king wore the coarse garments of a slave. So important was esteemed the observance of this courtly etiquette, that, at the first visit made him, in his palace, by the Spaniards, the renowned Cortes and his proud officers did not refuse to throw off their shoes, and cover their armour with such humble apparel as was offered them. But those days were passed; the king of kings was himself the vassal of a king's vassal. Yet notwithstanding this, it had been, up to this time, the policy of Don Hernan to soften the captivity and engage the affections of the monarch, by such marks of reverence as might still allow him to dream he possessed the grandeur, along with the state, of a king. Before this day, Cortes had never been known to pass his prisoner, without removing his cap or helmet; and indeed such had been so long the habit of his cavaliers, that all, as they now dismounted, fell to doffing their casques without delay, until the action of their leader taught them a new and unexpected mode of salutation.

The weak spirit of Montezuma had yielded to the arts of the Spaniard; and forgetting the insults of past days, the loss of his empire, and the shame of his imprisonment, he had already conceived a species of affection for his wronger. Cortes had no sooner, therefore, leaped from his horse, than the emperor, with outstretched arms, and with his sadness yielding to a smile, advanced to meet him.

"Dog of a king!" said the invader, with a ferocious frown, "dost thou starve and murder my people, and then offer me the hand of friendship? Away with thee! I defy thee, and thou shalt see that I can punish!" Thus saying, and thrusting the king rudely aside, he stepped into the palace.

A wild cry of lamentation, at this insult (it needed no interpretation) to their king, burst from the lips of all the Mexicans; and the Spaniards themselves were not less panic-struck. The gentle manners of Montezuma, and his munificence (for he was in the daily habit of enriching them with costly presents), had endeared him to most of his enemies; and even the soldiers of the garrison, who had so lately accused him of endeavouring to famish them, had no belief in the justice of their charges. Many of them, therefore, both soldiers and hidalgos, indignant and grieved at the wanton insult, had their sympathies strongly excited, when they beheld the monarch roll his eyes upon them with a haggard smile, in which pride was struggling vainly with a bitter sense of humiliation. De Morla and several others rushed forwards to atone, by caresses, for the crime of their general. But it was too late; the king threw his mantle over his head, and without the utterance of any complaint, passed, with his attendants, into his apartments. His countenance was never more, from that day, seen to wear a smile.

Don Amador de Leste was greatly amazed and shocked by this rudeness; and it was one of many other circumstances, which, by lessening his respect for the general, contributed to weaken his friendship, and undermine his gratitude. But he had no time to indulge his indignation. He was startled by a loud cry, or rather a shriek, from the lips of the Knight Calavar; and running to the gate, beheld, in the midst of a confused mass of men, rushing to and fro, and calling out as if to secure an assassin, his kinsman lying, to all appearance dead, in the arms of his attendants.

CHAPTER XXXIV.

The first thought of the young cavalier was, that Don Gabriel had been basely and murderously struck by some felon hand; an apprehension of which he was, in part, immediately relieved by the protestations of Baltasar, but which was not entirely removed until he had assisted to carry the knight into a chamber of the palace, and beheld him open his eyes, and roll them wildly round him, like one awaking from a dream of night-mare.

"I say," muttered Baltasar, as he raised the head of the distracted man, and beckoned to clear the room of many idle personages who had thrust themselves in, "he was hurt by no mortal man, for I stood close at his side, and there is not a drop of blood on his body. 'Twas one of the accursed ghosts, whom may St. John sink down to hell; for they are ever persecuting us."

"Mortal man, or immortal fiend," whispered Lazaro, knitting his brows, but looking greatly frightened, "I saw him running away, the moment the knight screeched; and I will take my oath, he had such a damnable appearance, as belongs to nothing but the devil, or one of these Pagan gods, who are all devils. Had he been a man, I should have slain him, for I struck at him with my spear."

"Miserere mei!" groaned the knight, rising to his feet, they are all unearthed—Zayda at the temple, and he in the palace!"

Don Amador trembled, when he heard his kinsman pronounce the name of Zayda, for he remembered the words of Jacinto. Nevertheless he said—"Be not disturbed, my father; for we are none here but thy servants."

"Ay!" said the knight, looking gloomily but sanely to his friend: "I afflict thee with my folly; but I know now that it will end. Let the boy Jacinto sing to me the song of the Virgin; I will pray and sleep.'

Don Amador looked round, and Jacinto not being present, began to remember that the page had been separated from him in the crowd, and that he had not seen him since the moment of separation. None of the attendants had noticed him enter the court-yard; and a superstitious fear was mingled with his anxiety, when Don Gabriel, casting his eyes to heaven, said, with a deep groan —"The time beginneth, the flower is broken, and now I see how each branch shall fall, and the trunk that is blasted shall be left, naked, to perish! Seek no more for the boy," he went on to Amador, with a grave placidity, which, coupled with the extravagance of his words, gave the youth reason to fear that his mind, wavering under a thousand shocks, had at last settled down for ever in the calm of insanity—"seek for the good child no more, for he is now in heaven. And lament not thou, my son Amador, that thou shalt speedily follow him; for thy heart is yet pure, thy soul unstained, and grace shall not be denied thee!"

"Jacinto is not dead, my father," said the neophyte, earnestly; "and if thou wilt suffer Baltasar to remove thy corslet, and make thee a couch under yonder canopy, I will fetch him to thee presently, and he shall sing thee to sleep."

"Remove the armour indeed," muttered Don Gabriel, submitting passively, "for now there is no more need of aught but the crucifix, prayers, and the grave. Poor children! that shall die before the day of cauker, what matters it? I lament ye not—ye shall sleep in peace!"

Thus murmuring out his distractions, in which his servants perceived nothing but the influence of some supernatural warning that boded them calamity, the knight allowed himself to be disarmed and laid upon a couch, on a raised platform, at the side of the chamber, over which the voluminous arras that covered the walls were festooned into a sort of not inelegant tester.

Meanwhile, the neophyte, beckoning Lazaro with him, and charging him to make good search throughout the palace for the page, began to address himself to the same duty. And first, attracted by the lights and by the sounds of many voices coming from a neighbouring apartment, he advanced to the door, where he was suddenly arrested by the appearance of a Mexican, of very majestic stature, though clad in the same humble robes which had covered the attendants of Montezuma, issuing from the chamber, followed by a throng of cavaliers, among whom was the general himself. At the side of Cortes stood a boy, in stature resembling Jacinto; and in whom, for a moment, Don Amador thought he had discovered the object of his desires. But this agreeable delusion was instantly put to flight, when he heard Don Hernan address him by the name of Orteguilla, and saw that he exercised the unctions of an interpreter.

"Tell me this knave, my merry muchacho," said the general—"tell me this knave (that is to say, this royal prince), Cuitlahuatzin, that I discharge him from captivity, under the assurance that he shall, very faithfully, and without delay, command his runagate people to bring me corn to the market; of which it is not fitting we should be kept in want longer than to-morrow. And give him to understand, that I hold, as the hostage of his good faith and compliance, the dog Montezuma (translate that, the king, his brother); who shall be made to suffer the penalty of any neglect, on his part, to furnish me with the afore-mentioned necessary provision.'

The little Orteguilla, in part acquainted with the Mexican tongue, did as he was directed; and the prince Cuitlahuatzin (or, as it should be pronounced in English speech, Quitlawatzin), receiving and understanding the direction, bowed his head to Cortes with stately humility, and immediately withdrew.

Not discovering or hearing aught of Jacinto in this throng, Don Amador continued his search in other parts of the palace, the court-yard, and even the neighbouring street; but with such indifferent success, that, when stumbling upon Lazaro, and made acquainted that he had been equally unfortunate, he began to entertain the most serious fears for the fate of the boy.

"Perhaps he was carried off by the spectre," muttered Lazaro, superstitiously, "as his worship, Don Gabriel, as much as hinted."

"Or perhaps," said the neophyte, with a thrill of horror, "by some of those bloody cannibals, to be devoured! And I remember now, that there were many savages about me at the time, though I thought them Tlascalans. I would to Heaven I had speared the knaves that came between us; but I swear to St. John of the Desert, if they have truly robbed me of the boy, and for that diabolical purpose, I will pursue their whole race with a most unrelenting vengeance."

At this moment, the cavalier was startled by a sudden "Hark!" from Lazaro, and heard, at a distance in the street, though objects were lost in the darkness, a great tumult as of men in affray, and plainly distinguished a voice crying aloud, "Arma! arma! and Christian men, for the love of God, to the rescue of Christians beset by infidels!"

"Draw thy sword, Lazaro, and follow!" cried the cavalier, "for these are other victims; and, with God's favour, we will rescue them!"

Thus exclaiming, and without a moment thinking of the unknown perils among which he was rushing, he ran rapidly in the direction of the cries, and straightway beheld, a little in advance of a great crowd of people, a group, consisting of four or five persons, several of them women, in strange attire, who, shrieking with terror, while at their feet rolled three or four on the ground in close and murderous combat. The cries of one of these prostrate figures bespoke him a Spaniard; and while one sinewy Pagan seemed to hold him upon the earth, another stood with his uplifted weapon, in the very act of dispatching him. At this moment Don Amador rushed forwards, and shouting his war-cry, Dios, y buena esperanza! (that is, 'God and good cheer!') struck the menacing savage a blow that sent him yelling away, and seized upon the other by the shoulder to stab him; when suddenly the Spaniard rose to his feet, with a leap that tumbled the infidel to the earth, and showed him to be already dead, crying aloud, in the well-remembered voice of the magician—"Tetragrammaton! thou wert a good shield, though a bloody one, sir carcass!—Save the princesses, and fly, or we are all dead men!—Arma! arma! to the rescue!"

Thus shouting, and seizing upon one of the women, while Don Amador snatched the arm of the other (for he perceived they were like to be cut off by the approaching crowd), the sorcerer, with his rescuers, ran towards the palace. His cries had reached the quarters; and presently they were surrounded by a hundred soldiers and cavaliers bearing lights, in the glare of which Don Amador had scarce time to note the countenance of his new ward, before she was locked in the arms of De Morla.

"Minnapotzin! Benita!" cried the joyous cavalier. "Amigo mio! thou hast saved my princess!"

"Stop not to prate and be happy, for the storm comes!" exclaimed Botello. "To the palace, all of ye! and to the cannon! for were you five hundred men, there are wolves enow at your heels to devour you?"

Thus admonished, and perceiving, in fact, that a vast though silent multitude was approaching, all were fain to fly, and in an instant they were crowding into the gates of the court-yard.

"This comes of insulting the king!" cried a voice from the melée, as Cortes, shouting out to clear the gates, was seen himself assisting to draw a piece of artillery to the opening.

"I see nought—I hear nothing," cried the general, affecting not to remark this reproach (which was indeed just, for it was this over-refinement of policy, spread with wonderful celerity throughout the city, which dashed the last scale from the eyes of the Mexicans, convinced them that their monarch was indeed a slave, and let loose the long-imprisoned current of fury), "I see nought—I hear nought: and my brave Rolands have been flying from shadows!"

"Say not so; the town is alive," cried the magician. "The hounds set on me, as I was bringing, at your excellency's command, these princesses from Tacuba; and it was only through the mercy of God, my good star, an Indian that I killed for a buckler, and the help of this true cavalier (whose fate, out of gratitude, I will reveal to him to-morrow), that we were not all killed by the way:—for small reverence did the false traitors show to the maidens."

"Clear the way, then. Discharge me the piece, Catalan, true cannouier!" said Cortes; "and we will see what our foes look like, so near to midnight."

The match was applied—the palace shook to the roar—and the blaze, illumining the street to a great distance, disclosed it, to the surprise of all, entirely deserted.

"I will aver upon mine oath," said Don Amador, "that the street was but now full of people; but where they have hidden, or whither they have fled, wholly passes my comprehension."

"Hidden, surely, in their beds," cried the general, loudly and cheerfully, for he perceived the crowds about him were panic-struck. "They set on Botello, doubtless, because they thought he was haling away the princesses with violence; and convinced of their error, they have now gone to their rest—a mark of wisdom in which I would advise all here to follow their example.'

Thus cheered by their leader, the soldiers began to disperse, and Amador, musing painfully on the mysterious fate of the page, was accosted by Cortes, who, drawing him aside, said—"It has been told me, senor, that your Moorish boy has made his escape."

"His escape!" echoed the novice, in surprise. "He did indeed vanish away from me, and I know not how, though much do I fear, in a manner that it shocks me to think on. I was about to ask of your excellency, as the boy is a true Christian, as well as a most faithful servant, for such counsel and assistance as might enable me, this night, to rescue him out of the hands of the cannibals; for it would be a sin on the souls of us all, should we suffer him to come to harm."

"And are you so well persuaded of his faith, as to believe him incapable of treachery?" demanded Don Hernan, earnestly: "thou forgettest, he has a father concealed among these infidels."

"Ay! by my faith!" cried Amador, joyously; "I thought not of that before. And yet, and yet—" Here his countenance fell. "How should he be so mad, as to leave us in this strange and huge city, without any hope of discovering Abdalla?"

"I can resolve thee that," said Cortes; "for it is avouched to me by Yacub, that he saw this wretch (whom may Heaven return to me for punishment, for he is a most subtle, daring, and dangerous traitor), this very knave Abdalla, at thy horse's heels; but he could not believe 'twas he, until made acquainted with the flight of the page."

"Ay! now I see it," said Amador; "and I remember that he wept, as he held my hand, as if grieving to desert me. But, methinks 'twill be well to seek him out, and reclaim him. Will your excellency allow me the services of any score or two of men, who, for love or gold, may be induced to follow me in the search?"

"I will answer thee in thine own words," said Cortes: "where wouldst thou look in this strange and huge city, with any hope of discovering him? Be content, senor; the boy is with the fox, his father. That should convince thee he is in present safety. And, senor, I will tell thee, what I conceal from my people (for thou art a soldier, and, therefore, as discreet as fearless), that I would not, this night, dispatch an hundred men a mile from the palace, without looking to have half of them slain outright by the rebels that are around us."

"And dost thou think," said Amador, "that these besotted, naked madmen, would dare to assail so many?"

"You will see, by my conscience!" cried the general, with a grim and anxious smile. "Sleep with thine armour at thy side; and forget not thy buckler, for I have known a Tlascalan arrow pierce through a good Biscayan gorget; and they say, the Mexicans can shoot as well. Let not any else arouse thee, unless it be that of a trumpet. I would have thee sleep well, my friend; for I know not how soon I may need thy strong arm and encouraging countenance."

Thus darkly and imperfectly apprising the novice his fears (for now, indeed, a demon had roused a thousand apprehensions in his breast), the general parted; and Don Amador disconsolately pursued his way to the chamber of the Knight of Rhodes.

CHAPTER XXXV.

When Don Amador returned to the chamber, he was rejoiced to find his kinsman asleep, and not offended that the faithful Marco and Baltasar were both nodding, as they sat at his side. He threw himself softly on a cot of mats, covered with robes of fine cotton, over which was a little canopy—such being the beds of the better orders of Mexico. The crowded state of the palace (for it is recorded, that the number of Totonac and Tlascalan allies, who remained in the garrison with Alvarado, now swelled the army of Cortes to nearly nine thousand men,) left him no other choice; and he felt, that his presence was perhaps necessary, in the unhappy condition of his knight. He was mindful to obey the counsels of Don Hernan, and lie with his weapons ready to be grasped at the first alarm; and he remembered also, the hint that had been given him, not to be surprised at such tumults, when he heard a sound, continued throughout the greater part of the night, as of heavy instruments knocking against the court-yard wall, convincing him as well of the military vigilance and preparations, as of the fears of his general. In addition to this disturbance, he was often startled by moans and wild expressions, coming from the lips of the sleeping knight, showing him that even slumber brought no repose to his distempered spirit. But, above all (and this made manifest the hold that the Moorish boy had got upon his affections), he was troubled with thoughts of Jacinto; and often, as the angel of sleep began to flutter over his eyelids, she was driven away, by some sudden and painfully intense conception of the great peril which must surround the friendless lad, now that the events of the evening proved him to be in the midst, and doubtless in the power, of an enraged multitude, to whom every stranger was an enemy. Often, too, as he was sinking into slumber, the first voice of dreams would cry to him in the tones of Jacinto, or the silent enchanter would bring before his eyes the spectacle of the boy, confined in the cage of victims, or dragged away by the hands of ferocious priests, to the place of sacrifice. These distractions kept him tossing about in great restlessness, for a long time; and it was not until the sounds of the workmen in the yard were no longer heard, and until a deep silence pervaded the palace, that he was able to drown his torments in sleep.

He was roused from slumber by a painful dream, and fancying it must be now approaching the time of dawn, he stole softly to the bed-side of Calavar, without disturbing the attendants. A taper of myrtle-wax, burning on a little pedestal hard by, disclosed to him the countenance of the knight, contracted with pain, and flushed as if with fever, but still chained in repose. He stepped noiselessly away, and gathering his sword and a few pieces of armour in his hands, left the apartment.

From the door of the palace, he could see, dimly —for it was not yet morning—that vast numbers of Tlascalans were lying asleep in the court-yard among the horses, while many sentinels were stalking about in silent watchfulness. He was now able, likewise, to understand the cause of the heavy knocking, which had annoyed him. The gates were closed; but in three rude embrasures, which had been broken in the wall by the workmen, frowned as many pieces of ordnance, commanding the street by which he had approached the palace.

Entering this again, and attracted by the distant murmur of voices, he discovered a staircase at the end of a passage, ascending which, he immediately found himself on the terraced roof of the building. And now he could perceive the exposed condition of the royal citadel, as well as the preparations made to sustain it, in the event of a siege.

The palace itself extended over a great piece of ground, in the form of a square, the walled sides of which were continuous, but the centre divided by rows of structures, that crossed each other, into many little courts. The buildings were all low, consisting, indeed, of but one floor, except that, in the centre, were several chambers on the roofs of others, that might be called turrets or observatories. The terraces were so covered with flowers and shrubs, that they seemed a garden. This mass of houses was surrounded on all sides by a spacious court, confined by a wall, six or eight feet high, running entirely round the whole. The palace, with its outer court, did not yet occupy all of the great square upon which it stood. It was a short bowshot from the battlements to the houses, which lined the four sides of the square. Opposite to each side or front of the fabric was a great street, along which the eye, in full day-light, could traverse, till arrested by the surrounding lake. Directly opposite, likewise, to each of these streets, as Don Amador soon discovered, the careful general had caused to be broken as many embrasures as he had seen on the quarter of the principal entrance; and now there were no less than twelve pieces of artillery (with those who served them sleeping in cloaks hard by), looking with formidable preparation down the yawning and silent approaches.

The neophyte had not yet given a moment to these observations, when he perceived on the top of one of the turrets, a group of cavaliers, who, being relieved against the only streak of dawn that tinged the eastern skies, were plainly seen, gesticulating with great earnestness, as if engaged in important debate. He approached this turret, and mounting the ladder that ascended it, was assisted to the roof by the hand of Cortes.

"I give you good cheer, and much praise for your early rising, Don Amador," cried the general, with an easy courtesy and pleasant voice, which did not, however, conceal from the novice that he was really affected by anxiety and even alarm: "for this, besides convincing me that no one is more ready than thyself for a valiant bout with an enemy, will give thee an opportunity to note in what way these Pagan Mexicans advance to assault —a matter of which I am myself ignorant, though assured by my friend Alvarado, that nothing can be more warlike to look upon."

"I vow to God, and to Saint Peter, who cut off a knave's ear," said Don Pedro, "that there are no such besotted, mad, dare-devils in all the world beside, as you shall quickly see; and I swear to you, in addition, my friends, I did sometimes think, of a morning, the very devils that dwell in the pit were let loose upon me. But fear not: with my poor five-score, and the seven thousand Indians, who should not be counted against more than one hundred Christians, I felt no prick of dismay, except when I thought of starvation; and with the force that now aids us, 'twill be but a boy's pastime to kill ten thousand of the bold lunatics, each day, before breakfast."

To this valiant speech, which was characteristic of Alvarado—as notorious for boasting as for bravery—Don Amador replied, complacently—"To my mind, nothing could be stronger than this citadel against such enemies as we may have, especially since the placing of those cannon opposite to the great streets—a precaution which should be commended. Nevertheless, noble cavaliers, it does not appear to me that we are in any immediate peril of assault: the infidels are not yet arisen."

"Cast thine eye down yonder street!" said Cortes, with a low voice; "keep it fixed intently, for two or three moments, on the shadows, and tell me what thou seest among them. And, while thou art so doing, do not shame to hold thy buckler a little over thy face; for, now and then, methinks, I have seen on yonder house-tops something unlike to rose-buds, glancing among the bushes."

"By my faith," said Don Amador, hastily, "it does seem to me, that there are men stirring afar in the street—nay, a great body of them, and doubtless clad in white—ay, I perceive them now! But I thought 'twas a dim mist, creeping up from the lake."

"If thou wilt look to the other three streets," said Cortes, knitting his brows and scowling around him, "thou wilt see other such vapours gathering about us. Thus do they surround stags, in the sierras of Salamanca! but sometimes hunters have found more wolves than deer among their quarry; and by my conscience, so will the dogs of Mexico find their prey, this day, when they come a-hunting against Castilians!—Hah! did I not warn thee well?" cried the general, as an arrow, shot from a distant terrace, and by some unseen hand, struck against the guarding shield with such violence as to shiver its tone head into a thousand fragments. "'Ware such Cupids; for, when they miss the heart, they are content to rankle among the ribs. What say ye now, my masters? The knaves are coming nearer! Such big rain-drops do not long fall one by one, but show how soon the flood will follow. Cover yourselves! for by my conscience, that was another, though it fell short. I see the house it comes from; and I will reward the messenger shortly with such a cannon-shot as shall leave him houseless. How now, mi trompetero? art thou nodding? Wake me thy bugle, and let the sleepers look on the white clouds!"

A trumpeter, who stood ready at the base of the turret, instantly wound a loud blast on his instrument. It was answered immediately by others from every part of the court and building; and, as if by magic, the dead silence of the palace was straightway exchanged for the loud din and confusion of a thousand rising and springing to their arms. During this tumult, Cortes descended from the turret.

Don Amador, fascinated by the spectacle (for now, the light of dawn, increasing every moment, fully convinced the most sceptical, that countless barbarians were thronging in the streets, and advancing against the palace), remained for a time on the terrace in company with others, surveying their approach, and kindling into ardour. The four streets were blocked up with their dusky bodies, for they seemed nearly naked; and answering the drums and bugles of the Spaniards with the hollow sound of their huge tabours, and the roaring yells of great conches, and adding to these the uproar of their voices, and, what greatly amazed the neophyte, the shrill and piercing din of loud whistling, they pressed onwards, not fast indeed, but fearlessly, until they began to pour like a flood upon the open square. Nevertheless, and notwithstanding their very menacing appearance, not a bow was yet bent, nor a stone or dart discharged against the Christians; and they were arraying, or rather grouping themselves (for they seemed to preserve no peculiar order), about the square, as if rather to support some peaceable demand with a show of strength, than to make an absolute attack, when the neophyte beheld Don Hernan, clad in complete armour, spring upon a cannon, and thence to the top of the wall, and wave his hand towards them with an air of imposing dignity. The vast herds stilled their cries, and immediately Malintzin, guarded by two soldiers who held shields before her, was seen to ascend and stand by the side of her master.

"Ask me these hounds," cried the general, with a voice that seemed meant by its loudness to strike the infidels with awe, "wherefore they leave their beds, and come, like howling wolves, to disturb me in my dwelling? What is their desire? and wherefore have they not come with baskets of corn, rather than with slings and arrows?"

The clear voice of Donna Marina was instantly heard addressing the multitude; and was followed by a shout such as may come from thrice a thousand score men, wherein, and among other inexplicable sounds, Don Amador heard the word *Tlatoani! Tlatoani!* repeated with accents in which entreaty seemed mingled with fury. He could not discover the meaning of these cries from the imperfect Castilian, and the low voice with which Malintzin interpreted them. But he could conjecture their signification by the reply of Cortes. "Tell the traitorous dogs," he exclaimed, sternly, "that their princes have avowed themselves the vassals of my master, the great monarch of Spain; that their lord and king, Montezuma, is my friend and contented guest, and will therefore remain in my dwelling. Tell them also, he charges them to disperse, throw by their arms, and return laden wih corn and meat. And add, moreover, that if they do not immediately obey this command, the thunders which God has given me to punish them, shall be let loose upon them, and scatter their corses and their city into the air. Tell we them this, and plainly; and, hark'ee, cannoniers! stand fast to your linstocks!"

No sooner was this haughty and threatening answer made known to the barbarians, than they uttered a yell so loud and universal that the palace and the earth under it seemed to shake with the din; and immediately every quarter of the edifice was covered with arrows, stones, and other missiles, shot off with extraordinary violence and fury.

Don Amador prepared to descend, but paused an instant to observe the effect of artillery, for he heard the strong tones of the general shouting. "Now, cannoniers! to your duty, and show yourselves men!"

The very island trembled, when twelve cannon, discharged nearly at the same moment, opened their fiery throats, and, aimed full among the multitude, poured innumerable death into their ranks. The island trembled, but not so the naked barbarians of Tenochtitlan. If the screams of a thousand wretches, mangled by that explosion, rose on the morning air, they were speedily drowned by the war-cries of survivors; and before the smoke had cleared away, the bloody gaps were filled, and the infuriated multitudes were rushing with savage intrepidity full upon the mouths of the artillery.

Don Amador hesitated no longer. He ran down the staircase, paused a moment at the side of Calavar, whom he found raving in a low delirium, for he was burned by fever—paused only long enough to charge Marco not to leave him, no, not even for a moment—and snatching up and rapidly donning the remaining pieces of his armour, immediately found himself in the court yard, among the combatants.

CHAPTER XXXVI.

The neophyte had been informed by his friend De Morla, as a proof of the degree of civilisation reached by the Mexicans, that their armies were formed with method, and as regularly divided and commanded as those of Christendom—each tribe displaying under a peculiar banner, representing the arms, or, as we should say of our northern bands, the *totem*, of the race, each tribe separated into squadrons and companies, led by subalterns of precisely ascertained rank and power. He perceived none of these marks of discipline among the assailants; and, while properly appreciating their devoted courage, was obliged to consider them no better than a furious and confused mob. He was right: the warriors of Mexico had not yet appeared, and these wild creatures, who came ungeneralled and unadvised to the attack, were no more than the common citizens, fired by the distresses of their king, and rushing to his aid, without any bond of connexion or government, save the unanimity of their fury. The violence with which they leaped to the attack, carried them to the gates of the court, and to the mouths of the artillery, where they fell under the spears of the Spaniards, or were scattered like chaff at each murderous discharge of the cannon. Added to this, the Tlascalans, animated by their ancient hatred, and the presence of him whom they esteemed almost a god, clambered upon the wall, and with their clubs and lances did bloody execution on the multitudes below. The Tlascalans were, indeed, almost the only persons of the garrison who suffered much loss; for the Spaniards, cased in iron and escaupil, and fenced behind the wall, or the battlements of the terrace, discharged their crossbows and muskets, and handled their long spears, in comparative safety.

The din of yells and screams, mingled with the crash of arquebuses and the sharp clang of steel crossbows, was in itself infernal; while the peals of artillery, served with such skill and constancy, that every half-minute there was one or other discharged from some quarter of the palace, leaving at each discharge a long avenue of death among the crowds, averted what might have seemed a scene of elysium into a spectacle of hell. No man could reckon, no man could imagine, the slaughter made by the besieged army, among their foes, in the short space of half an hour. But the sun rose, and still found the infatuated barbarians rushing—now with shouts of defiance, and now with mournful cries, as if calling upon their imprisoned king—to add yet another and another layer to the bloody ridges growing in the paths of the cannon-shot.

All this time the captive monarch, unseen by his people, though quickly detected by the sharp eye of Cortes, sat in one of the turrets, witnessing the devoted love of his people, and feeling, with sharp pangs, that he had not deserved it. And now too (for the suddenness of the punishment had convinced him of the impolicy of the fault,) did Don Hernan himself feel a touch of compunction for the wanton injury he had done his prisoner; and, fearing lest the work of this day should be but the prelude of a storm it might not be in his power to allay, he sent to him De Morla, a cavalier whom more than others he seemed to favour, to persuade him, if indeed he might be persuaded, to exercise his authority, and by commanding his people to disperse, preserve them from that destruction which, the general avowed, he was loath to bring upon them.

No smile lit the countenance of Montezuma, at the appearance of his favourite; and to the demand of Don Hernan, he replied with dignity, yet with a bitter sorrow—" The *Teuctli*," (so they called Don Hernan, not because they esteemed him a divinity, but a great prince, this being the title of one of the classes of nobility) " has made me a slave; my subjects are his. Let the king govern his people."

So saying, and immediately descending from the roof, he shut himself in his apartments, and resolutely refused to admit another messenger to his presence.

" And the dog denies me, then !" cried Cortes, when this answer was repeated to him. " He says the truth: he is my slave; his people are mine : and I will straightway convince them of their subjection. To horse, to horse, brave cavaliers !" he shouted aloud. " Let it not be said we wasted powder on miserable naked Indians, when we have swords to strike them on the neck, and horses' hoofs to tread them to the earth !"

No one was more ready to obey this call than Don Amador de Leste. He had stood upon the wall, occasionally striking down some furious assailant with his spear, but oftener cheering others with his voice, and yet remaining more as a spectator than a combatant, disdaining to strike, except when personally attacked, until his blood was heated by the spectacle.

" Mount now, my knave Lazaro ! and perhaps we shall find my poor Jacinto among these outrageous infidels. Get thee to horse, Fabueno; for to-day thou shalt see what it is to be a soldier !"

Fogoso stood, in his mail, like the steed of a true knight, champing the bit, and whinnying, for he longed to be in the midst of the combat; and loud was the sound of his neighing, when he felt the weight of his master, and turned his fierce eyes towards the gate.

. Before the cavaliers, forming three abreast (as many as could at once pass through the gates),

loosed their sabres in the scabbards, and couching their spears, had yet received the signal to dash upon the opposing herds, there came from the great pyramid, which was seen rearing its mountainous mass above the houses of the square, the sound as of a horn, sad and solemn, but of so mighty a tone, that it swelled distinctly over all the din of the battle, and sent a boding fear to the heart of Christians. They knew, or they thought it the sacred bugle of Mexitli, sounded only during the festivals of that ferocious deity, or on the occasion of a great battle, when, it was supposed, that Mexitli himself spoke to his children, and bade them die bravely. There was not a Spaniard present, who had not heard that the effect of this consecrated trumpet, so sparingly used, was to nerve even the vanquished with new spirit, and those fighting with additional rage; and that the meanest Mexican, however overpowered, thought not of retreat, when thus cheered by his god. The surprise of all was therefore great, when, at the first blast, the Mexicans ceased their cries, and stood as if turned into statues; and they were still more amazed, when, as the brazed instrument again poured its lugubrious roar over the city, the barbarians, responding with a mournful shriek, turned their backs upon the besieged, and instantly began to fly. A third blast was sounded, and nothing was seen upon the great square, or the four streets, save heaps of carcasses, and piles of human beings, writhing in the death-agony.

" Here is diabolical magic !" cried Cortes, joyfully. " There are more signals made by that accursed horn than we have heard of; and it seems to me, Huitzilopochtli may be sometimes a coward ! Nevertheless, we will look a little into the mystery; for I perceive shining cloaks, as well as the priestly gowns, on the temple which we will make claim to: for doubtless the traitor Cuitlahuatzin is under one of them. Take thou thy party, Sandoval, and scour me the streets that lie eastward. We meet at the temple ! For ourselves, my master ! we are fifty horse, and three hundred foot, all good Christian men; for in this work we shall need no Tlascalans. Let us go, in the name of God, and God will be with us. Only, 'tis my counsel and command, that we keep together, with our eyes wide open, lest we should have company not so much to our liking."

The cavaliers cheered, as they rode from the gates—and, with a savage delight, urged their horses over the piles of dead, or smote some dying struggler with the spear—an amusement in which they were occasionally imitated by the foot soldiers, who followed at their heels.

CHAPTER XXXVII.

The same solitude which had covered the city the preceding evening, now seemed again to invest it. Corses were here and there strown in the street, as of fugitives dying in their flight; and once a wounded man was seen staggering blindly along, as if wholly insensible to the approach of his foes. The sight of this solitary wretch did more to disarm the fury of Don Amador, than did the spectacle of thousands lying dead on the square; and certain grievous reflections, such as sometimes assailed him after a battle, were beginning to intrude upon his mind, when a cavalier, darting forward with a loud cry, and couching his lance, as if at a worthier enemy, thrust the wounded barbarian through the body, and killed him on the spot. A few hidalgos, and most of the footmen, rewarded this feat of dexterity with a loud cheer; but there were many, who, like the neophyte, met the triumphant looks of the champion, Alvarado, with glances of infinite disgust and frowning disdain.

As the party approached the neighbourhood of the great temple, they began to perceive in the streets groups of men, who, being altogether unarmed, commonly fled at the first sight of the Christians; though sometimes they stood aside, with submissive and dejected countenances, as if awaiting any punishment the Teuctli might choose to inflict upon them. But Cortes, reading in this humility the proofs of penitence, or willing to suppose that these men had not shared in the hostilities of the day, commanded his followers not to attack them; and thus restrained, they rode slowly and cautiously onwards, their fury gradually abating, and the fears which had been excited by the late assault, giving place to hope, that it indicated no general spirit, and no deep-laid plan, of insurrection.

The groups of Mexicans increased, both in numbers and frequency, as the Christians proceeded, but still they betrayed no disposition to make use of the arms, which were sometimes seen in their hands; and the Spaniards, regulating their own conduct by that of the barbarians, rode onwards with so pacific an air, that a stranger, arriving at that moment in the city, might have deemed them associated together on the most friendly terms, and proceeding in company, to take part in some general festivity. Nevertheless, the same stranger would have quickly observed, that these friends, besides keeping as far separated as the streets would allow, and even, where that was possible, removing from each other's presence entirely, eyed each other, at times, with looks of jealousy, which became more marked as the Mexicans grew more numerous. In truth, the feelings which had so quickly passed from rage to tranquillity, were now in danger of another revulsion; and many an eye was rivetted on the countenance of the general, as if to read a confirmation of the common anxiety, as, ever and anon, it turned from the prospect of multitudes in front, to the spectacle of crowds gathering at a distance on the rear.

"All that is needful," whispered, rather than spoke, Don Hernan, though his words were caught by every ear, "is to trust in God and our sharp spears. There is, doubtless, some idolatrous rite about to be enacted in the temple, which draws these varlets thitherward; and the gratitude with which they remember our exploits of this morning, will account for their present hang-dog looks. If they mean any treachery, such as a decoy and ambuscado, why, by my conscience, we must e'en allow them their humour, and punish them when 'tis made manifest. I counsel my friends to be of good heart, for I think the dogs have had fighting enough to-day. Nevertheless, I will not quarrel with any man, who keeps his hands in readiness, and puts his eyes and ears to their proper uses."

As if to set them an example, Don Hernan now began to look about him with redoubled vigilance; and it was remarked that he passed no house, without eyeing its terrace keenly and steadfastly, as if dreading more to discover an enemy in such places than in the street. This was in fact, a situation from which an enemy might annoy the Spaniards with the greatest advantage, and at the least risk.

The houses of this quarter were evidently inhabited by the rich, perhaps by the nobles of Mexico. They were of solid stone, spacious, and frequently of two floors, lofty, and their terraces crowned with battlements and turrets. Each stood separated from its neighbour by a little garden or alley, and sometimes by a narrow canal, which crossed the great street, and was furnished with a strong wooden bridge, of such width that five horsemen could pass it at a time. Often, too, the dwelling of some man in power stood so far back, as to allow the canal to be carried quite round it, without infringing upon the streets; but more frequently it was fronted only with a little bed of flowers. The stones of which such structures were composed, were often sculptured into rude reliefs, representing huge serpents, which twined in a fantastic and frightful manner about the windows and doors, as if to protect them from the invasion of robbers. Indeed, these were almost the only defences; for the green bulrush lying across the threshold, could deter none but a Mexican from entering; and perhaps none but a barbarian would have seen, in the string of cacao-berries, or of little vessels of earthenware, hanging at the door, the bell to announce his visitation. A curtain commonly hung flapping at the entrance; but neither plank nor bar gave security to the sanctity of the interior.

Notwithstanding the fears of the general, he beheld no Mexicans lurking among the terraces, or peering from the windows, but his anxiety was not the less goading for that reason; for having now drawn nigh to the great square, it seemed to him that he had, at last, thrust himself into that part of the city, where all the multitudes of Tenochtitlan were assembled to meet him—and whether for purposes of pacification or vengeance, he dared not inquire.

The appearance of things, as the party issued upon the square, and faced the House of Skulls, was indeed menacing. That enormous pyramid, which Don Amador had surveyed with awe, in the gloom of evening, was now concealed under a more impressive veil—it was invested and darkened by a cloud of human beings, which surged over its vast summit, and rolled along its huge sides like a living storm. The great court that surrounded it was also filled with barbarians; for though the Coatepantli, or Wall of Serpents, with its monstrous battlements and gloomy towers, concealed them from the eye, there came such a hum of voices from behind, as could not have been produced alone, even by the myriads that covered the temple. In addition to these, the great square itself was alive with Mexicans, and the sudden sight of them brought a thrill of alarm into the heart of the bravest cavalier.

The people of Tenochtitlan, thus, as it were, hunted by their invaders, even to their sanctuaries, turned upon them with frowns, yet parted away from before them in deep silence. Nevertheless, at this spectacle the Christians came to an immediate stand, in doubt whether to entangle themselves further, or to take counsel of their fears, and retreat, without delay, to their quarters. While they stood yet hesitating, and in some confusion, suddenly, and with a tone that pierced to their inmost souls, there came a horrid shriek from the top of the pyramid, and fifty Castilian voices exclaimed—"A sacrifice! a human sacrifice! and under the cross of Christ that we raised on the temple!"

"The place of God is defiled by the rites of Hell!" cried Cortes, furiously, his apprehensions vanishing at once before his fanaticism. "Set on, and avenge! Couch your lances, draw your swords, and if any resist, call on God, and slay!" So saying, he drew his sword, spurred his dun steed, and rushed towards the temple.

The halk-naked herds fled, yelling, away from the infuriated Christian, opening him a free path to the walls: and had that fearful cry been repeated, there is no doubt he would have led his followers even within the Coatepantli, though at the risk of irretrievable and universal destruction. Before, however, he had yet reached the wall, he had time for reflection; and, though greatly excited, he could no longer conceal from himself the consequences of provoking the Pagans at their very temple, and during the worship of their god. He was, at this moment, well befriended, and numerously, indeed; but at a distance from the garrison, without musketry, surrounded by enemies whom the eye could not number, and who had not feared to assail him, even when fortified in a situation almost impregnable, and assisted by three times his present force, as well as several thousand bold Tlascalans: and in addition to all these disadvantages, there came neither sound of trumpet nor such distant commotion among the Indians as might admonish him of the approach of Sandoval.

He checked his horse, and waving to his followers to halt, again cast his eyes around on the multitude, as if to determine in what manner to begin his retreat, for he felt that this measure could be no longer delayed. The Mexicans gazed upon him with angry visages, but still in silence. Not an arm was yet raised; and they seemed prepared to give him passage which ever way he might choose to direct his course.

While hesitating an instant, Don Hernan perceived a stir among the crowds, close under the Wall of Serpents, accompanied by a low but general murmur of voices; and immediately the eyes of the Pagans were turned from him towards the Coatepantli, as if to catch a view of some sight still more attractive and important. His first thought was, that these movements indicated the sudden presence of Sandoval and his party—a conceit that was, however immediately put to flight by the events which ensued.

The murmurs of the multitude were soon stilled, and the Pagans that covered the pyramid were seen to cast their eyes earnestly down to the square, as the sound of many flutes, and other soft wind instruments, rose on the air, and crept, not unmusically, along the Wall of Serpents, and thence to the ears of the Spaniards. Before these had yet time to express their wonder at the presence of such peaceful music amidst a scene of war and sacrifice, the crowds slowly parted asunder, and they plainly beheld (for the Mexicans had opened a wide vista to the principal gate) a procession seemingly of little children, clad in white garments, waving pots of incense, conducted by priests, in gowns of black and flame colour, and headed by musicians and men bearing little flags, issue from the throng, and bend their steps towards the savage portal. In the centre of the train, on a sort of litter, very rich and gorgeous, borne on men's shoulders, and sheltered by a royal canopy of green and crimson feathers, stood a figure, which might have been some maiden princess arrayed for the festival, or, as she seemed to one or two of the more superstitious Castilians, some fiendish goddess, conjured up by the diabolical arts of the priests, to add the inspiration of her presence to the wild fury of her adorers. She stood erect, her body concealed in long flowing vestments of white, on which were embroidered serpents, of some green material; in her hand she held a rod, imitative of the same reptile; and on her forehead was a coronet of feathers, surrounding what seemed a knot of little snakes writhing round a star, or sun, of burnished gold.

As this fair apparition was carried through their ranks, between the great wall and the House of Skulls, the Mexicans were seen to throw themselves reverently on the earth, as if to a divinity; and those that stood most remote, no sooner beheld her, than they bowed their heads with the deepest humility.

Meanwhile the Spaniards gazed on with both admiration and wonder, until the train had reached the open portal; at which place, and just as she was about to be concealed from them for ever, the divinity, priestess, or princess, whichever she was, turned her body slowly round, and revealed to them a face of a paler hue than any they had yet seen in the new world, and, as they afterwards affirmed, of the most incomparable and ravishing beauty. At this sight all uttered exclamations of surprise, which were carried to the ears of the vision: but Don Amador de Leste, fetching a cry that thrilled through the hearts of all, broke from the ranks, as if beset by some sudden demon, and dashed madly towards the apparition.

Before the Spaniards could recover from their astonishment, the members of the procession—deity, priests, censer-bearers, and musicians—with loud screams vanished under the portals; and the infidels, starting up in a rage that could be suppressed no longer, rushed upon the novice, to avenge, in his blood, the insult he had offered to their deity.

"Quick, a-God's name! and rescue!" cried Cortes, "for the young man is mad."

There seemed grounds for this imputation; but, besides the inexplicable folly of his first act, Don Amador appeared now, for a moment, to be lost in such a maze that the blows of the heavy maquahuitl were raised upon his stout armour, and several furious hands had clutched not only upon his spear, but upon himself, to drag him from the saddle, before he bethought him to draw his sword and defend his life. But his sword was at last drawn, his fit dispelled; and before his countrymen had yet reached him, he was dealing such blows around him, and so urging his courageous steed upon the assailants, as quickly to put himself out of the danger of immediate death.

The passions of the multitude, restrained for a moment by their superstition or their rulers, were now fully and unappeasably roused; and with veils that came at once from the pyramid, from the temple yard, from the great square, and the neighbouring streets, they rushed upon the Christians, surrounding them, and displaying such ferocious determinations, as left them but small hopes of escape.

"God and Spain! honour and fame!" cried Alvarado, spearing a barbarian at each word, "what do you think of my Mexicans now, true friends?"

His cheer was lost in the roar of screams; and nothing but the voice of Don Hernan, well known to be as clear and powerful in battle as the trumpet which he invoked, was heard pealing above the din.

"Now show yourselves Spaniards and soldiers, and strike for the love of Christ. Ho, trumpeter, thy flourish, and find me where lags my lazy Gonzalo?"

As he spoke he fought; for so violent had been the attack of the infidels, that they were mingled among and fighting hand to hand with the Christians—a confused and sanguinary chaos. Scarcely, indeed, had the trumpeter time to wind his instrument before it was struck out of his hand by a brawny savage; and the same blow which robbed him of it, left the arm that held it a shattered and useless member. The blast, however, had sounded; and, almost instantaneously, it was answered by a bugle, afar indeed, and blown hurriedly, as if the musician were in as much jeopardy as his fellow, but still full of joy and good cheer to the Christian combatants.

"Close and turn! Footmen to your square!" cried Cortes; "and, valiant cavaliers, charge me now as though ye fought against devils, with angels for your lookers-on."

"To the temple! to the temple!" cried Amador, with a voice rivalling the general's in loudness, and turning in a frenzy towards the pyramid, down whose sides the infidels were seen rushing with frantic speed.

But the head of Fogoso was seized by two friendly followers, and while Don Amador glared fiercely at the pale but not affrighted secretary, he heard, on the other side, the tranquil voice of Lazaro.

"Master," said the faithful servant," if we separate from our friends, we are dead men; and Don Gabriel is left without a kinsman in this land of demoniacs."

"Close and turn, I bid ye!" cried Cortes, furiously. "Heed not the wolves that are fast to your sides. Charge on the herds! charge on the herds! and overthrow with the weight of your hoofs. Charge, I bid ye; and care not though ye should find your lances striking against the breast of Sandoval. Charge on the herds! charge on the herds!"

So saying, Don Hernan set an example, followed by the cavaliers; and as the fifty horsemen spurred violently upon the mob, shouting and cheering, the naked multitude quailed before them, though only to gather again on their flanks with renewed desperation.

"Will ye desert us that are a-foot?" cried voices from behind, with dolorous cries.

"Ho, Sandoval! art thou sleeping?"

"Santiago! and God be thanked!—'tis the voice of the general!" cried Sandoval, in the distance. His voice came from the surge of battle,

ike the cheer of a sailor who recks not for the tempest. It filled the cavaliers with joy.

"Good heart now, brave hearts," shouted Cortes; "for my son, Sandoval, answers me. Rein me round, and charge me back the infantry."

Backwards galloped the fifty cavaliers, strewing the earth with trampled Pagans; and the footmen shouted with delight, as they again beheld their leader. But the relief and the joy were only momentary.

"Fight ye, my dogs, and slay your own sheep. Be firm; wall yourselves with spears, and presently ye shall be lookers-on. Sweep the square again, brave cavaliers. Goad flanks! couch spears! and this time let me see the red face of my lieutenant."

Turning and shouting with a louder cheer (for the experience of the two first charges had warned the Mexicans of their destructive efficacy, and they now recoiled with a more visible alarm), the cavaliers again rushed through their foes with a whirlwind; and brushing them aside, as the meteor brushes the fogs of evening, they dashed onwards, until their shouts were loudly re-echoed, and they found themselves confronted with Don Gonzalo and his party.

The greetings of the friends were brief and few, for the same myriads, attacking with the same frenzied desperation, invested them with a danger that did not seem to diminish.

"Bring thy foot in front," cried Cortes, "and, while they follow me, charge thou behind them. Be quick and be brave. March fast, ye idle spearmen; and stare not, for these are not devils, but men. God and Spain! Santiago, and at them again, peerless cavaliers. We fight for Christ and immortal honour."

The valiant band of cavaliers again turned at the voice of their leader, and again they swept the corse-encumbered square, rushing to the relief of their own infantry. Following the counsel he had given to Sandoval, the wary general passed by his foot-soldiers, and bidding them march boldly forwards, and join themselves with the infantry of Don Gonzalo, he charged the infidels from their rear with a fury they could not resist; and then rushing backwards with equal resolution, discovered the foot-soldiers in the position in which it had been his aim to place them. The united infantry, full seven hundred in number, were now protected, both in front and rear, by a band of cavalry; their flanks looking, on one side, to the temple, and, on the other, to a great street that opened opposite. Arranging them, at a word, in two lines, standing back to back, and seconding himself the manœuvre which he dictated to Sandoval, the general swept instantly to that flank which bordered on the Wall of Serpents, while Gonzalo rode to the other. Thus arranged, the little army presented the figure of a hollow square, or rather a paralellogram, the chief sides of which were made by double rows of spearmen, and the smaller by bands of horsemen. Thus arranged, too, the Christians fought with greater resolution and success; for, parting at once from a centre, the infantry drove the assailants from before them on two sides, while the cavalry carried death and horror to the others; until, at a given signal, all again fell back to their position, and presented a wall altogether inexpugnable to the weak though untiring savages.

It was the persuasion of Don Hernan, that, in

this advantageous position, he could, in a short time, so punish his enemies, as to teach them the folly of contending with Christian men, and perhaps end the war in a day. But, for a full hour, he repeated his charges, now pinning his foes against the wall, or the steps of the House of Skulls, now falling back to breathe; and, at each charge, adding to the number of the dead, until their corses literally obstructed his path, and left it nearly impassable. At every charge, too, his cavaliers waxed more weary, and struck more faintly, while the horses obeyed the spur and voice with diminishing vigour; and it seemed that they must soon be left unable, from sheer fatigue, to continue the work of slaughter. The Pagans perished in crowds at each charge, and at each volley of bow-shots; but neither their spirit nor their numbers seemed to decrease. Their yells were as loud, their countenances as bold, their assaults as violent, as at first; and the Spaniards beheld the sun rising high in the heavens without any termination to their labours, or their sufferings. Twenty Christians already lay dead on the square, or had been dragged, perhaps, while yet breathing, to be sacrificed on the pyramid. This was a suspicion that shocked the souls of many; for, twice or thrice they heard, among the crowds who still stood on the lofty terrace, shooting arrows down on the square, such shouts of triumphant delight as, they thought, could be caused by nothing but the immolation of a victim.

Grief and rage lay heavily on the heart of Cortes; but though the apprehension, that if much longer overworn by combat, his followers might be left unable even to fly, added its sting to the others, shame deterred him, for a time, from giving the mortifying order. Harassed, and even wounded (for a defective link in his mail had yielded to an arrow-head, and the stone was buried in his shoulder), he nevertheless preserved a good countenance; cheered his people with the assurance of victory; fought on, exposing himself like the meanest of his soldiers; and several times, at the imminent risk of his life, rescued certain foot-soldiers from the consequences of their fool-hardiness.

There was among the infantry, a man of great courage and strength, by the name of Lezcano, whose only weapon was a huge two-handed sword, the valiant use of which had gained him among his companions the title of *Dos Manos*, or Two-hands. No spearman of his company advanced to the charge with more readiness than did this fellow with his gigantic weapon, and none retreated with more constant reluctance. Indeed, he commonly fell back so leisurely as to draw three or four foes upon him at once; and it seemed to be his pleasure, to meet these in such a way as should call for the praises of his companions. His daring, that day, would have left him with the additional name of the bravest of the brave, had it been tempered with a little discretion. But inflamed by the encomiums of his comrades, not less by the complimentary rebukes of his captain, his rashness knew no bounds; and twice or thrice he thrust himself into situations of peril, from which he was rescued with great difficulty. He had been saved once by Don Hernan. It was his fate, a second time, to draw the notice of the general; who, falling back on the infantry, beheld him beset by a dozen foes, surrounded, and using his great scimitar furiously, yet, as it seemed, in vain; for he was unhelmed.

"What ho Don Amador!" cried Cortes to the cavalier, who was at his side, "let us rescue *Dos Manos*, the mad!"

In an instant of time, the two hidalgos had reached the group, and raised their voices in encouragement, while each struck down a savage. At that moment, and while Lezcano elevated his scimitar, to ward off the blow of a maquahuitl, the massive blade, shivered as if by a thunder-bolt, fell to the earth; but, before it reached it, the sharp glass of the Indian sword had entered his brain. The cavaliers struck fast and hard, on either hand; the barbarians fled; but Lezcano, the Two-handed, lay rolling his eyes to heaven, his head cloven to the mouth.

"If we slay a thousand foes for every Christian man that dies, yet shall we be vanquished!" said Cortes, turning an eye of despair on his companion, and speaking the feelings he had concealed from all others. Indeed, he seemed to rejoice that destiny had given him one follower, to whom he might unbosom himself, without the apprehension of creating alarm—he hesitated not to relieve himself of his grief to Don Amador; for he knew him to be inaccessible to fear. "Be of good heart, my friend. I have drawn thee into a den of devils. We must retreat, or die."

"I will advance or retreat, as thou wilt," said Amador, with a visage in which Don Hernan now, for the first time, beheld an expression so wild and ghastly, that he was reminded of Calavar. "It matters nothing—here or at the palace! But it is my duty to assure thee of mine own persuasion: retreat may bring us relief—there is no victory for us to-day."

"God help thee! art thou wounded?" cried Cortes.

"A little hurt by the skilless hand of Fabueno," said the novice, tranquilly, "who, not yet being perfected in the use of the spear, thrust this weapon into my back, while aiming at the throat of a cacique. But that is not it. I have, this day, seen a sight which convinces me we are among magicians and devils; and persuades me, along with certain other recent occurrences, that the time of some of us is reckoned. Therefore I say to thee, I will advance with thee or retreat, as thou thinkest best. To me it matters not; but my counsel is, to fly. We may save others."

"It is needful," replied Don Hernan, mournfully. He gave his orders to certain officers; and the retreat was commenced in the order in which they had fought—that is to say, the infantry, drawing their lines closer together, and facing to the flank, began to march down the street, preceded by Sandoval, charging the opponents from the front, while Cortes and his band, at intervals, rushing back upon the pursuers, kept the triumphant barbarians from the rear.

CHAPTER XXXVIII.

The distance between the great temple and the palace of Axajacatl was by no means great; though Cortes, for the purpose of prying into many streets, had led his followers against it by a long and circuitous course—a plan which had been followed by Don Gonzalo, though in another direction. Indeed they were not so far separated, but that a strong bowman or a good slinger might, from the top of the pyramid, drive his missile upon the roof of the garrison, to the great injury of the besieged, as was afterwards fully made manifest. The distance, therefore, to be won by the retreating Spaniards was small; but it took them hours to accomplish it. It seemed as if the infidels, fearing lest their foes might escape out of their hands, if they slackened their efforts for a moment, were resolved to effect their destruction at any cost, while they were still at a distance from succour. They pressed ferociously and rapidly on the fugitives; they gained their front; and thus encompassed them with a compact mass of human beings, against which the cavaliers charged, as against a stone wall; slaying and trampling, indeed, but without penetrating it for more than a few yards. Each step gained by the van was literally carved by the cavalry, as out of a rock; while the utmost exertions of Don Hernan could do nothing more than preserve his rear band in the attitude of a dike, slowly moving before the shocks of a flood, which it could not repel.

In addition to these alarming circumstances, there were others now developed, of a not less serious aspect. The canals that, in two or three places, intersected the street, were swarming with canoes, from which the savages discharged their arrows with fatal aim, or sprang, at once, upon the footmen, striking with spear and maquahuitl, and were driven back only by the most strenuous efforts. They had destroyed the bridges, and the canals could only be passed by renewing them with such planks as the infantry could tear from the adjoining houses, and hastily throw over the water, a work of no less suffering than time and labour. Besides all this, the annoyance which Don Hernan had first dreaded, was now practised by the crafty barbarians. The terraces were covered with armed men, who, besides discharging their darts and arrows down upon the exposed soldiers, tore away, with levers, the stones from the battlements, and hurled them full upon the heads of their enemies.

The sound of drums and conches, the fierce yells, the whistling, the dying screams, the loud and hurried prayers, the neighing of horses—and now and then the shriek of some beast mangled by a rough spear—the rattling of arrow-heads, the clang of clubs upon iron bucklers, the heavy fall of a huge stone crushing a footman to the earth, the plunging of some wounded wretch strangling in a ditch, and the roar of cannon at the palace, showing that the battle was universal—these together now made up such a chorus of hellish sounds, as Don Amador confessed to himself he had never heard before, not even among the horrors of Rhodes, when sacked by other infidels, then esteemed the most valiant in the world. But to these dismal tumults others were speedily added, when Cortes, raging with a fury that increased with his despair, commanded the footman to fire every house, whose top afforded footing to the ferocious foes—a command that was obeyed with good will, and with dreadful effect; for though from the nature of its materials, and the isolated condition of each structure, it was not possible to produce a general conflagration, yet the great quantity of cotton robes, of dry mats, and of resinous woods about each house, left it so combustible, that the application of a torch to the door curtains, or the casting of a firebrand into the interior, instantly enveloped it in flames. Among these, when they burst through the roofs of light rafters, and the thatching of dried reeds, the Pagan warriors perished miserably; or flinging themselves desperately down, were either dashed to pieces, or transfixed by the lances of the Spaniards.

But the same agent which so dreadfully paralysed the efforts of the Mexican, brought suffering scarcely less disastrous to the Christian ranks. They were stifled with smoke, they were scorched by the flames of the burning houses; and, ever and anon, some frantic barbarian, perishing among the fires of his dwelling, and seeking to inflict a horrid vengeance, grasped, even in his death-gasp, a flaming rafter in his arms, and sprang down with it upon his foes, maiming and scorching where he did not kill.

Thus fighting, and thus resisted, weary and despairing, their bodies covered with blood, their garments sometimes burning, the Spaniards at last gained the square that surrounded the palace; and fighting their way through the herds that invested it (for, almost at the same moment that they had been attacked at the temple, the quarters were again assailed), and shouting to the cannoniers, lest they should fire on them, they placed their feet in the court-yard, and thanked God for this respite to their sufferings.

It was a respite from death, for behind the stone wall they were comparatively secure; but not a respite from labour. The Mexicans abated not a jot of their ardour. The same herds that covered the square at dawn, were again yelling at the gates, and with the same unconquerable fury; and the soldiers, already fainting with fatigue, with famine, and thirst (for they had taken no refreshment since the preceding evening), were fain to purchase, painfully, a temporary safety, by standing to the walls, and keeping the savages at bay, as they could.

The artillery thundered, the crossbows twanged, the arquebuses added their destructive volleys to the other warlike noises; but the Mexicans, disregarding these sounds, as well as the havoc made among their ranks, rushed, in repeated assaults, against the walls, and sometimes, with such violence, that they drove the besieged from the gate, and entered pell-mell with them into the court-yard. Then, indeed, ensued a scene of murder; for the Christians, flying again to the portal, cut off the retreat of such desperadoes, and slew them within the walls, without loss, and almost at their leisure.

On such occasions, no one showed more spirit in attacking, or more fury in slaying, than the young secretary. The suit of goodly armour sent him by the admiral, and his rapid proficiency in the practice of arms, had inflamed his vanity; and he burned to approve himself worthy the companionship of cavaliers. The native conscientiousness which filled him with horror at the sight of the first blood shed, the first life destroyed, by his hand, had vanished as a dream: for it is the excellence of war, that, while developing our true nature, and remaining itself as the link which binds man to his original state of barbarism, it preserves him the delights of a savage, without entirely depriving him of the pleasures of civilisation. The right of shedding blood mankind enjoy in common with brutes; and doubtless, a conformable philosophy will not frown on the privilege, so long as the loss of it would contract our circle of enjoyments. There is something poetical in the diabolism of a fiend, and as much that is splendid in the ferocity of a tiger; and though these two qualities be the chief elements of heroism, they bring with them such accompaniments of splendour and sentiment, that he would rob the world of half its glory, as well as much of its poetry, who should destroy the race of the great, and leave mankind to the dull innocence of peace. There are more millions of human beings, the victims of war, rotting under the earth, than now move on its surface.

The pain of wounds had also produced a new effect in the bosom of Lorenzo; for, instead of cooling his courage, it now inflamed his rage, and helped to make him valiant. The mild and feeling boy was quite transformed into a heartless ruffian; and so great had become his love of slaughter, and so unscrupulous his manner of gratifying it, that, once or twice, Don Amador noticed him, and would have censured him sharply, but that his attention was immediately absorbed by the necessity of self-defence. The cavaliers had dismounted, and the neophyte fought at the gates on foot. In the midst of an assault, in which the defenders had been driven back, but which disgrace they were now repairing, he beheld his ward struggling with a wounded savage, who grasped his knees and hands, but in entreaty, not hostility; and greatly was Don Amador shocked, when he beheld the secretary disengage his arm, and, with a shout of triumph, plunge his steel into the throat of the supplicating barbarian.

"Art thou a devil, Lorenzo" cried the cavalier, indignantly. "That was a knave's and a coward's blow! Thou shalt follow me no longer."

While he spoke, and left himself unguarded, a gigantic Pagan, taking advantage of his indiscretion, leaped suddenly upon him, and struck him such a blow with a maquahuitl, as, but for the strength of his casque, would have killed him outright. As it was, the shock so stunned him, as to leave him for a moment incapable of defence. In that moment the savage, uttering a loud yell, sprang forward to repeat the blow, or to drag him off a prisoner; when Fabueno, perceiving the extremity of his patron, and fired with the opportunity of proving his valour, rushed between them, and with a lucky blow on the naked neck of the Mexican, instantly dispatched him.

"A valiant stroke, Lorenzo!" said the neophyte, losing somewhat of his heat, as he recovered his wits. "But it does not entirely wipe out the shame of the other. Moderate thy wrath, curb thy fury, and remember that cruelty is the mark of a dastard. Strike me no more foes that cry for mercy!"

As his anger had been changed into approbation, so now were his censures abruptly ended by exclamations of surprise. For at that instant, Fabueno, grasping his arm with one hand, and with the other pointing a little to one side, turned upon him a countenance full of alarm. He looked around, and beheld with amazement his kinsman, Don Gabriel, entirely unarmed, except with sword and buckler, mingled with the combatants, shouting a feeble war-cry, striking faintly, and, indeed, preserved less by his courage than by his appearance, from the bludgeons of the infidels. His grizzly locks (for he was entirely bareheaded) fell over his hollow and bloodless cheeks, whereon glittered, black and hideous, a single gout of gore. His face was like the face of the dead; and the savages recoiled from before him, as if from a spirit rousing from Mictlan, the world of gloom, to call them down to his dark dwelling.

In a moment the neophyte, followed by Fabueno and Lazaro, who answered to his call, and Marco, who seemed to have been separated by the melée from his master, was at the side of Calavar. The mind of the knight was wholly gone; and he seemed as if, at the point of death, raised from his couch by the clamours of the contest, and urged into it by the instinct of long habit, or by the goadings of madness.

He submitted patiently, and without words, to the gentle violence of his kinsman, and was straightway carried to his apartment.

CHAPTER XXXIX.

After much search and persuasion, a surgeon was found, and induced to visit the knight. He dispatched his questions almost in a word, for he was a fighting Bachelor, and burned with impatience to return to the contest. He mingled hastily a draught, which he affirmed to be of wondrous efficacy in composing disordered minds to sleep, gave a few simple directions, and excusing his haste in the urgency of his other occupations, both military and chirurgical, he immediately departed.

"Marco!" said the neophyte, when the draught was administered, and Don Gabriel laid on the couch, "thou deservest the heaviest punishment for leaving thy master an instant, though, as thou sayest, while fast asleep. Remain by him now, and be more faithful. As for thee, Lorenzo," he continued, to the secretary, who stood panting at his side, "there is good reason thou shouldst share the task of Marco, were it only to repose thee a little; but more need is it, that thou suffer thy blood to cool, and reflect, with shame, that thou hast this day cancelled all thy good deeds, by killing a prostrate and beseeching foe. Remain, therefore, to assist Marco: and by and by I will come to thee, and declare whether or not thou shalt draw thy sword again to-day."

And thus leaving his kinsman to the care of the two followers, and beckoning Lazaro along, Don Amador returned to the court-yard and the conflict.

The history of the remainder of the day (it was now noon) is a weary tale of blood. Wounds could not check, nor slaughter subdue, the animosity of the besiegers; and the Spaniards, tired even of killing, hoped no longer for victory over men who seemed to fight with no object but to die, and who rushed up as readily to the mouth of a cannon, whose vent was already blazing under the linstock, as to the spears that bristled with fatal opposition at the gates.

But night came at last, and with it a hope to end the sufferings that were already intolerable. The hope was vain. The barbarians, apparently incapable of fatigue, or perhaps yielding their places to fresh combatants, continued the assault even with increasing vigour and boldness. They rushed against the court-wall with heavy beams—rude battering-rams—with which they thought to shake it to its foundations, and thus deprive the Christians of their greatest safeguard. In certain spots they succeeded; and the soldiers cursed the day of their birth, as the ruins fell crashing to the ground, and then saw themselves reduced to the alternative of filling the breaches with their bodies, or remaining to perish where they stood. It is true, that in this kind of defence, as well as under other urgent difficulties, they received good and manly aid from their numerous allies, the Tlascalans, who fought, during the whole day, with a spirit and cheerfulness that put many a repining Castilian to shame. But these, though battling equally for their lives, were incapable of withstanding long the unexampled violence of the assaults; and it was soon found that the naked bodies of the Tlascalans offered but slight impediment to the frenzied Mexicans.

The Spaniards, in the expedient used to drive the citizens from their house-tops, had taught them a mode of warfare which they were not slow to adopt. The palace was of a solid structure, and seemed to bid defiance to flames. But the same cedars that finished the interior of meaner houses, formed its floors and ceilings; every chamber was covered with mats, and most of them were hung with the most inflammable kind of tapestry. In addition to this, the five thousand Tlascalans, who had been left with Alvarado, and who slept in the court-yard, besides strewing the earth with rushes—their humble couches—had constructed along the walls of the palace itself, many rude arbours, or rather kennels, of reeds from the lake, to shelter them from the vicissitudes of the rainy season, which had already in part set in. And, to crown all, the cavaliers, whose horses, as they well knew, were each worth a thousand Tlascalans, had caused stalls to be constructed for them, wherein they were better protected from the weather than their fellow-animals, the allies. With these arrangements, the Mexicans were well acquainted.

No sooner, therefore, had they succeeded in beating down several breaches in the wall, and found that they could sometimes drive the besieged from them, than they made trial of the expedient. They rushed together against the walls in a general assault, waving firebrands and torches, which those who forced their way through the breaches applied to the stalls and harbours, or scattered over the beds of the Tlascalans. The dying incendiary, pierced with a dozen spears, ended his life with a laugh of joy, as he beheld the flames burst ruddily up to his brand.

The misery of the Spaniards was now complete. They were parched with thirst. The sweet fountains of Chapoltepec gushed only over the square of the temple. A well, dug by Alvarado, in his extremity, furnished a meagre supply of water, and that so brackish, that even the brutes turned from it in disgust, till forced to drink by pangs that would allow them to be fastidious no longer. The nearest canal, conducting the briny waters of Tezcuco, was shut out by ramparts of savages. The Spaniards, with one universal voice, sent up a cry of despair, as they beheld the flames run over the court, the stalls, the kennels, and up the palace walls, and knew not how to extinguish them. The cry was answered from without with such yells of exultation as froze their blood; and in the glare of the sudden conflagration, they saw the barbarians rushing again to the attack, darting through the breaches, and leaping over the walls.

In this strait, beset at once by two foes, equally irresistible, equally pitiless, they struck about them blindly and despairingly, cursing their fate, their folly, and the leader who had seduced them from their island homes, to die a death so ignoble and so dreadful.

For a moment, the spirit of the general sunk, and turning to Don Amador, whose fate it was again to be at his side, he said, with a ghastly countenance, rendered hideous by the infernal glare—"We die the death of foxes in a hole, very noble friend! Commend thy soul to God, and choose thy death; for we have no water to quench this hell!"

"God help my kinsman and father, and all is one!" said Amador, with a desperate calmness. "The flames are hot, but the grave is cold."

"The grave is cold!" shouted Cortes, with the voice of a madman. "Live in my heart for ever! Cold grave, moist earth! and Santiago, who strikes for a true Christian, speaks in thy words! What ho, mad Spaniards!" he continued, shouting aloud, and running as he spoke round the palace; "earth quenches flames, like water! Swords and hands to the task; and he works best who delves as at the grave of his foeman!"

If there was obscurity in the words of the general, it was dispelled by his actions; for, dashing the rushes aside, he loosened the damp soil with his sabre, and flung the clods lustily on the nearest flames. Loud and joyous were the shouts of his people, as hope dawned upon them with the happy idea; and, in a moment, the hands of many thousand men were tearing up the earth of the court, and casting it on the flames, while the savages, confidently expecting the result of their stratagem, intermitted their efforts for a while, leaving the gates and breaches nearly unguarded.

It is probable, that even this poor resource, in the hands of so great a multitude of men, toiling with the zeal of desperation, might have sufficed to quell the flames. But, as if Heaven had at last taken pity on their sufferings, and vouchsafed a miracle for their relief, there came, almost at the same moment, the pattering of rain-drops, which were quickly followed by a heavenly deluge; and, as the flames vanished under it, the Christians fell upon their knees, and, with devout ardour, offered up thanks to the Providence that had so marvellously preserved them.

They sprang from their knees, with bolder hearts, as the Mexicans again advanced to the assault. But this was the last attack. As if satisfied with the toils of the day, or commanded by some unknown ruler, the barbarians, uttering a mournful scream, suddenly departed. They were heard during the night; and in the morning, when the waning moon shone dimly through the rack, were seen stirring about the square, but in no great numbers; and as they did not attempt any annoyance, but seemed engaged in dragging away the dead, Don Hernan forbade his sentinels to molest them.

The guards were set, and the over-worn soldiers retired, at last, to throw their wounded bodies on their pallets. But throughout the whole night the noises of men repairing the breaches, and constructing certain military engines, assured those who were too sore or too fearful to sleep, that the leader they had cursed was sacrificing a second night to the duties of his station.

CHAPTER XL.

Don Amador sought out the apartment of his kinsman with a troubled heart. A deep dejection, in part the effect of extreme fatigue, but caused more by the strange and melancholy events of the last twenty-four hours, weighed upon his spirits, and had increased, ever since the spectacle of the divinity, notwithstanding the bustle and excitement of the conflicts which ensued.

In the passage, before he had yet reached the chamber, he stumbled upon Fabueno. The secretary looked confused and abashed, as if caught in a dereliction of duty; but before the cavalier could upbraid him, he commenced his excuses. "The opiate was strong; the knight was in a deep slumber," he said; "and, as Marco was sitting at his side, he thought he might leave him for a moment, to discover where the soldiers had ceased fighting. He hoped his noble patron would pardon him: he would presently return."

"Seek thy pleasure now, Lorenzo," said the novice, with a heavy sigh. "Return when thou wilt—or not at all, if thou preferest to rest with thy companions of last night. I will now, myself, watch by Don Gabriel."

His head sunk upon his breast as he went on, for his heart was full of painful reflections. Near the door of the chamber, he was roused by a step, and looking up, he beheld the padre Olmedo approaching.

"Holy father, it rejoices me to see thee," he said. "I had, indeed, thoughts to seek thee out, and claim thy benevolent counsels and aidance, but that I deemed me there were many among the wounded, and perchance the dying, who had stronger claims on thy good offices."

"Thou art not hurt, my son?"

"I have a scratch, made by the unlucky spear of a friend, but no harm from the enemy," said the cavalier. "I had indeed a blow also on the head, that made my brain ring; but both I had quite forgotten. I am well enough in body, reverend father; and perhaps may be relieved in mind, if thou wilt vouchsafe me thy ghostly counsels."

The good Bartolome, making a gesture of assent, followed the youth into the chamber.

The knight was, as Fabueno had declared, lost in a deep and, his kinsman was pleased to see, a placid slumber: but Marco, instead of watching, lay sleeping full as soundly, hard by. This circumstance seemed to embarrass the cavalier.

"Father," said he, "I thought no less than to find the serving-man awake; and it was my intent to discharge him a moment from the chamber, not fearing that what I may say to thee, would disturb my afflicted friend. But I have not the heart to break the rest of this old man—a very faithful servant—who closes not his eyes, except when to keep them open would no longer be of service to Don Gabriel."

"He sleeps as soundly as his master," murmured the priest. "A good conscience lies under his rough breast, or it would not heave so gently."

"My father breathes gently, too," said Amador, mournfully.

"May Heaven restore him," said the padre. "His guilt lies deeper in his imagination than in his soul."

"Dost thou think so indeed, father?" said Amador, warmly, though in a low voice.

The father started—"The history of thy kinsman is not unknown to thee?"

"What I know is but very little, save that my friend is the unhappiest of men," said the novice. "But Heaven forbid I should seek to fathom the secrets of the confessional. I was rejoiced to hear thee say, my kinsman was not so miserable as he deems himself: for indeed I have begun to think there is something in the blood that courses in both our veins, so inclined to distemperature, that a small sin may bring us the pains of deep guilt, and a light sorrow pave the way to madness."

The knight and the man-at-arms lay in a slumber not to be broken by the whispers of confession. The father retired to the remotest corner of the apartment, and Don Amador knelt humbly and penitentially at his feet. A little taper shed a flickering ray over his blanched and troubled forehead, as he bent forward to kiss the crucifix extended by the confessor.

"Buen padre," said he, "the sins I have to confess I know thou wilt absolve, for they are sins of a hot blood, and not a malicious heart. I have been awroth with those who wronged me, and thirsted to shed their blood. For this I repent me. But the sins of pride and vanity are deep in my heart. I look about me for those acts of darkness, which should have caused the grief wherewith I am afflicted; but in my self-conceit I cannot find them.

And yet they must exist; for I am beset with devils, or bewitched."

The father gazed uneasily from the penitent to the sleeping knight; but the look of suspicion was unnoticed.

"We are all, as I may say, my son, beset by devils in this infidel land. They are worshipped on the altars of the false gods, and they live in the hearts of the idolaters; but if thou hast no heavy sin on thy soul, these are such devils as thou canst better exorcise with the sword, than I, perhaps, with prayers. I think, indeed, thou hast no such guilt; and, therefore, no cause for persecution."

"Holy father, I thought so myself, till late. But cast thine eyes on Don Gabriel. Thou seest him, once the noblest of his species, yet, now, the shadow and vapour of a man—a wreck of reason—a living death—for his mind hath left him. This I say to thee with much anguish. I could strike another who said it; but it is true—he is a lunatic! It is I that have robbed him of reason. This is my sin; and I feel that it is heavy."

"Thou ravest, good youth. Thy love and devotion are well known; and he hath, out of his own mouth, assured me, that thy affection surpasses the love of man. Rest thee content. A deeper cause than this, and one wherein thou hast no part, has afflicted him. An accident of war, tortured, by a moody imagination, into wilful guilt, hath turned him into this ruin."

"It was an accident, then, and no murder!" said the cavalier, joyously, though still in a whisper. "I thank God that my father is unstained with the blood of a woman."

"I may not repeat to thee secrets revealed only to God," said the confessor; "but this much may I say, to allay thy fears, that the blow which destroyed a friend, was meant for a foe; for rage veiled his eyes, and the steel was in the hands of a madman. This will assure thee, that thou hast had no agency in his affliction, but hast ever proved his truest comfort."

"This indeed is the truth," murmured the novice, "and this convinces me, that by robbing him of his comfort, I gave him up to the persecution of those thoughts and memories which have destroyed him. When I fought by his side at Rhodes, when I followed at his back through Spain his malady was gentle. It brought him often fits of gloom, sometimes moments of delirium; he was unhappy, father, but not mad. I had acquired the art to keep the evil spirit from him; and, while I remained by him, he was well. I left him, at his command, indeed, but he did not command me to forget him. The servant slept, and the sick man perished. While I was gone, his infirmity returned; and the madness that brought him to this infidel world, though I follow him, I am not able to remove. I found him changed; and by my neglect, he is left incurable."

"I think, indeed, as thou sayest," replied the confessor, mildly, "there is something in thy blood, as well as in Calavar's, which inclines to convert what is a light fault into a weighty sin. Thou wrongest thyself: this present misery is but the natural course of disease, and thou hast no reason to upbraid thyself with producing it."

"Father, so thought I, myself, till lately," said the cavalier, solemnly; "for we have ever in our hearts some lying spirit, that glosses over our faults with excuses, and deludes us from remorse. But it has been made manifest to me by strange revealments and coincidences, by griefs of my own as well as of others, that my neglect was a grievous sin, not yet forgiven. And verily, now I do believe, that had I remained true to my knight, much sorrow would have been spared to both him and me."

"I cannot believe that thy unfaithfulness was a wrong of design," said the father. "If it be, make me acquainted with it, and despair not of pardon. Thou wert parted from the knight at his own command?"

"To gather him followers for the crusade meditated against the infidels of Barbary," said the novice; "a brave and pious enterprise, from which the emperor was quickly diverted by other projects. This change being proclaimed, there remained nothing for me to do, but, like a faithful friend and servant, to return to my kinsman. Had I done so, what present affliction and disturbing memories might not have been prevented! Know, father, for I tell thee truth, that it was my fortune, or rather my unhappiness, to discover, at the seaport in which I sojourned, a Moorish maiden, of so obscure, and, doubtless, so base, a birth, that even the noble lady who gave her protection knew not the condition of her parents. Yet, notwithstanding this baseness of origin, and the great pride of my own heart (for truly I am come of the noblest blood in the land), I was so gained upon by the beauty and excellent worth of this maiden (for I swear to thee, her superior lives not in the world), that I forgot even that she was the daughter of an idolater, and loved her."

"A Moorish infidel!" said the confessor. "It is not possible thou couldst pledge thy faith to an unbeliever?"

"Holy father," said Don Amador, "this sin was at least spared me. The maiden was a Christian, tenderly nurtured in all the doctrines of our faith, and almost ignorant that the race from which she drew her blood knew any other; and, father, I thought, until this day, that the soul of Leila dwelt among the seraphs. Moreover, if the plighting of troth be sinful, I am again innocent; for before I had spoken of love, she was snatched away from me."

"She is dead, then?" demanded the padre.

"Surely, I think so," said the cavalier, mournfully; "yet I know not the living creature that wots of her fate. Father! the sin of deserting my kinsman was first visited to me through her; and because I was a sinner, Leila perished. How, father, I cannot tell thee. She vanished away by night—carried off, as some averred, by certain Moorish exiles, who, that night, set sail for Barbary; or, as others dreamed, murdered by some villain, and cast into the sea; for the veil she wore was found the day after, dashed ashore by the surf. But, whether she be dead, or yet living, again I say, I know not; though I affirm on the cross which I hold in my hand, I beheld her this day, or some fiend in her likeness, under the similitude of a priestess, or a divinity, I know not which, carried on the shoulders of the infidels, and by them worshipped!"

The confessor started back in alarm, surveying the excited feature of the penitent, and again cast his eyes towards Don Gabriel. Then laying his hand on the head of the cavalier, he said, gently, warningly—"Cast such thoughts from thee, lest thou become like to thy kinsman!"

"Ay!" cried the cavalier, clasping his hands, and turning an eye of horror on the father— "thou speakest confirmation of mine own fears; for I have said to myself, this is a frenzy, and therefore I have come at last to be like my kinsman! The thing that I have seen is not; and the reason that made me a man has fled from me!"

"Nay, I meant not that," said the padre, endeavouring to soothe the agitation he had in part caused. "I desired only to have thee guard thyself against the effects of thy fancy, which is, at present, greatly over-excited. I believe that thou didst indeed see some Pagan maiden, strongly resembling the Moorish Leila—a circumstance greatly aided by the similarity of hue between the two races."

"And dost thou think," said the cavalier, his indignation rising in spite of his grief, "that the adored and most angelic Leila could, in any wise, resemble the coarse maids of this copper-tinted, barbarous people? I swear to thee, she was fairer than the Spanish girls of Almeria, and a thousand times more beautiful!"

"In this I will not contend with thee," said the father, benignantly, well satisfied that anger should take the place of a more perilous passion. "But I may assure thee, that, among the princesses of the royal household, whom, I think, thou hast not yet seen, there are many wondrous lovely to look upon; and, to show thee that even a barbarian may resemble a Christian, it is only needful to mention that when, at our first coming to these shores, the portrait of Cortes, done by an Indian painter, was carried to Montezuma, he sent to us, by the next messengers, with rich presents, a noble of his court so strongly resembling Don Hernan, both in figure and visage, that we were all filled with amazement."

"Well, indeed, thou speakest to me words of comfort," said Don Amador, more composedly, though still very sadly; "but I would to Heaven I might look again on this woman, or this fiend, for I know not if she may not be a devil! In truth, I thought I beheld a spectre, when she turned her eyes upon me; and, oh father! you may judge my grief, when thus thinking, and beholding her a spirit worshipped by idolaters, I knew she must be of the accursed!"

"I have heard of this woman from others who beheld her," said the father, "and, I doubt not, she is a mortal woman, esteemed holy, because a priestess, and therefore received by the people with those marks of respect, which thou didst mistake for adoration. It was reported to me, that she was of marvellous great beauty."

"Marvellous, indeed!" said the youth. "But, father, here is another circumstance that greatly troubled me; and, in good sooth, it troubles me yet. It is known to thee that my kinsman had until yester night, a little page—a Moorish boy, greatly beloved by us both. As for myself, I loved him because he was of the race of Leila; and I protest to thee, unnatural as it may seem, I bore not for my young brother a greater affection than for this most unlucky urchin. A foolish fellow charged him to be an enchanter; and sometimes I bethink me of the accusation, and suppose he has given me magical love-potions. Last night he was snatched away, I cannot say how; but what is very wonderful, my kinsman and two of his people saw, almost at the same moment, a terrific phantom. Father, you smile! If it were not for my sorrow, I could smile too, and at myself: for greatly am I changed, since I set foot on this heathen land. A month since, I held a belief in ghosts and witchcraft to be absurd, and even irreligious. At this moment, there is no menial in this place more given over to doubts and fears, and more superstitious. Is not this the first breathing of that horrible malady?"

'It is the first perplexity of a scene of novelty and excitement. Fatigue doth itself produce a temporary distraction, as is very evident when we come to fling our over-worn bodies on our couches to sleep. This is the land of devils, because of idolaters; and I may not deny, that the fiends have here greater power to haunt us with supernatural apparitions, than in the lands of our true religion. Yet it is not well to yield too ready a belief to such revelations; for Heaven will not permit them, without a purpose. Rather think that the infirmity of thy kinsman, and the ignorance of his people, were deluded by an accidental deception, which a cooler observer might have penetrated, than by any real vision. But what wert thou saying of the Moorish page?"

"Father," said Amador, earnestly, "at the moment when the train that surrounded that wonderful priestess, alarmed to see me rush towards them (for that supernatural resemblance did greatly move me,) fled into the temple, I heard the voice of Jacinto screaming aloud among the infidels, as if, that moment, offered by them a victim to their accursed divinities."

"God be with his soul, if it be so!" said the confessor, "for barbarous and bloody in their fanaticism are the reprobates of Tenochtitlan. Yet I would have thee, even in this matter, to be of good heart; for it is believed among us, that Abdalla, his father, has been received into the service of Mexican nobles, to teach them how to resist our arts, and how to compass our destruction; and it must be evident, that for the traitor's sake, they will spare his boy, stolen away from us, as it appears to me to be proven, by the knave Abdalla himself. But think thou no more of the boy. He was born to inherit the perfidy of his race; deception and ingratitude have rendered him unworthy of thy care; and if, some day, the nobles should yield him to the priests for a victim, it will be but a just punishment for his baseness. Give thy mind to other thoughts, and refresh thy body with sleep; for much need have we of all the assistance thou canst now render us. Sleep, and prepare for other combats; for this day is but the prologue of a tragedy, whose end may be more bloody and dreadful than we have yet imagined. Thy soul is without stain, and Heaven absolves thee of sin. Brood over no more gloomy thoughts; believe that Providence overshadows thee; sleep in tranquillity—and be prepared for the morning."

The good father concluded the rite of absolution with a blessing parental and holy, and stole away from the chamber. Don Amador sighed heavily, but with a relieved mind, as he rose from his knees. He gazed upon the marble features of the sleeping knight, smoothed the covering softly and tenderly about his emaciated frame, and then crept to his own couch. His thoughts were many and wild, but exhaustion brought slumber to his eyelids; and starting, ever and anon, at some elfin representation of the captive page, or the lost maid of Almeria, bending over him with eyes of woe, he fell, at last, into a sleep so profound, that it was no longer disturbed by visions.

CHAPTER. XLI.

At the earliest dawn, Don Amador arose from his couch, refreshed, but not reanimated, by slumber. An oppressive gloom lay at his heart, with the feeling of physical weight; and without yet yielding to any definite apprehension, he was conscious of some presentiment, or vague foreboding of sorrow. The taper had expired on the pedestal, but an obscure light, the first beam of morning, guided him to the bed-side of his kinsman. The form of Baltasar was added to that of Marco on the floor; and the serving-men slept as soundly as their master. He bent a moment over Don Gabriel, and though unable to perceive his countenance in the gloom, he judged, by the calmness of his breathing, that the fever had abated. "Heaven grant that the delirium may have departed with it!" he muttered to himself, "and that my poor friend may look upon me rationally once more! If we are to perish under the knives of these unwearying barbarians, as now seems to me somewhat more than possible, better will it be for my kinsman's soul, that he die with the name of God on his lips, instead of those of the spirits which torment him."

While the cavalier gave way to such thoughts, he heard very distinctly, though at a great distance, such sounds as convinced him that "the unwearying barbarians" were indeed rousing again for another day of battle. He armed himself with more haste, that he heard also, in the passage, the sound of feet, as if the garrison had been already summoned, and were hurrying to the walls.

As he passed from the apartment, he found himself suddenly in the midst of a group of cavaliers, one of whom grasped his hand, and pressing it warmly, whispered in his ear—"I will not forget that I owe thee the life of Benita! Come with me, my friend, and thou shalt see how pride is punished with shame, and injustice with humiliation."

"I thought," said Don Amador, "that we were about to be attacked, and that my friends were running to the defence."

"Such is the case," said De Morla. "The millions are again advancing against the palace, and we go to oppose them, though not to the walls. We have raised devils, and we run to him that we have most wronged, and most despised, to lay them. In an instant, you will hear the shrieks of the combatants. If we find no other way to conquer them than with our arms, woe betide us all!—for we are worn and feeble, and we know our fate."

Several of the cavaliers had lights in their hands; but the chamber into which Don Amador followed them, was lit with a multitude of torches, chiefly of the knots of resinous wood, burning with a smoky glare, and scattering around a rich odour. The scene disclosed to the neophyte was imposing and singular. The apartment was very spacious, and indeed lofty, and filled with human beings, most of them Mexican nobles of the highest rank, and of both sexes, who stood around their monarch, as in a solemn audience, leaving a space in front, which was occupied by the most distinguished of the Spaniards, among whom was Don Hernan himself. A little platform, entirely concealed under cushions of the richest feathers, supported the chair (it might have been called the throne), on which sat the royal captive, closely invested by those members of his family who shared his imprisonment. A king of Cojohuacan, his brother, stood at his back, and at either side were two of his children, two sons and two daughters, all young, and one of them—a princess —scarce budding into womanhood. Their attire, in obedience to the laws of the court, was plain, and yet richer than the garments of the nobles. But it was their position near the king, the general resemblance of their features, and the anxious eyes which they kept ever bent on the royal countenance, which pointed them out as the offspring of Montezuma.

As for Montezuma himself, though he sat on his chair like an emperor, it was more like a monarch of statuary than of flesh and blood. The Christian general stood before him, dictating to the interpreter Marina, the expressions which he desired to enter the ear of his prisoner; but though speaking with as much respect as earnestness, the Indian ruler seemed neither to hear nor to see him. His eye was indeed fixed on Don Hernan, but yet fixed as on vacancy: and the lip, fallen in a ghastly contortion, the rigid features, the abstracted stare, the right hand pressed upon his knee, while the left lay powerless and dead over the cushions of his chair, as he bent a little forward, as if wholly unconscious of the presence of his people and his foes, made it manifest to all, that his thoughts were absorbed in the contemplation of his own abasement.

The neophyte heard the words of Don Hernan.

" Tell his royal majesty, the king," said the general, with an accent no longer resembling that which had fixed the barb in the bosom of his prey, " that it mislikes me to destroy his people, like so many dumb beasts; and yet to this end am I enforced by their madness and his supineness. Bid him direct his subjects to lay down their arms, and assail me no further; otherwise shall I be constrained to employ those weapons which God has given me, until this beauteous island is converted into a charnel-house and hell, and the broad lake of Tezcuco into the grave of his whole race"

The mild and musical voice of Marina repeated the wish in the language of Anahuac; and all eyes were bent on the monarch as she spoke. But not a muscle moved in the frame or the visage of Montezuma

" Is the knave turned to stone that he hears not?" muttered the chief. " Speak thou, my little Orteguilla. Repeat what thou hast heard, and see if thine antics will not arouse the sleeper."

The youthful page stepped up to the king, seized his hand, which he strove to raise to his lips, and looking up in his face, with an innocent air, endeavoured to engage his attention. This boy had, from the first days of his imprisonment, been a favourite with Montezuma; and being very arch and cunning, Don Hernan did not scruple to place him as a spy about the king, under colour of presenting him as a servant. In common Montezuma was greatly diverted with his boyish tricks, and especially with his blundering

efforts to catch the tongue of Mexico. But there was no longer left in the bosom of the degraded prince a chord to vibrate to merriment. Habit, however, had not yet lost its hold; and as the boyish voice stammered out the accustomed tones, he gradually turned his eyes from the person of the general and fixed them on the visage of Orteguilla. But as he gazed, his brows contracted into a gloomier frown, he laid his hand on the prattler's shoulder, and no sooner had the urchin ceased speaking, than he thrust him sternly though not violently, away. Then drawing himself erect he folded his arms on his bosom, and without uttering a word, fixed his eyes on the face of Cortes, and there calmly and sorrowfully maintained them,

" This is, doubtless, a lethargy," said the general; " but it suits not our present occasions to indulge it. Where is my friend, De Morla? He was wont to have much influence with this humorous man."

" I am here," said De Morla, stepping forward; " and if you demand it, I will speak to the king, though with no hopes of persuading him to show us any kindness."

As De Morla spoke, Don Amador, who had followed him to the side of Cortes, observed one of the princesses turn from her sire, and look eagerly towards his friend. In this maiden, he doubted not, he perceived the fair Minnapotzin; and he ceased to wonder at the passion of his countryman, when he discovered with his own eyes how little her beauty had been overrated. Though of but small stature, her figure, as far as it could be perceived through the folds of peculiar vestments, was exceedingly graceful. The cymar was knotted round her bosom with a modest girdle, and left bare two arms prettily moulded, on which shone bracelets of gold, fantastically wrought. Her hair was long, and fell, braided with strings of the same metal, on her shoulders, on which also was a necklace of little emeralds alternating with crystals, and suspending a silver crucifix of Spanish workmanship. These were her only decorations. Her skin was rather dark than tawny, and the tinge of beautifying blood was as visible on her cheeks as on those of the maids of Andalusia. Her features were very regular; and two large eyes, in which a native timidity struggled with affection at the sight of her Christian lover, rendered her countenance as engaging as it was lovely. She hung upon De Morla's accents with an air of the deepest interest, as he expressed, in imperfect language, the desires of his general.

As he spoke, the infidel king surveyed him with a frown—a notice that he now extended to all the Christians present, but without deigning to reply. It was evident that he understood the desires of his jailer, and equally plain that he had resolved to disregard them. The angry spot darkened on the brow of Cortes; and he was about to degrade the captive with still more violent marks of his displeasure, when, at this moment, the roar of his artillery, mingled with the shouts of the besiegers, suddenly shook the palace to its foundations, and drowned his voice in the shrieks of the women.

Montezuma started to his feet, and cast a look upon Cortes, in which horror did not wholly conceal a touch of ferocious satisfaction. His people were, indeed, falling under those terrific explosions like leaves before the mountain gust; but well he read in the dismayed visages of the Spaniards, that fate was at last avenging his injuries on the oppressors.

"Speak thou to thy father, my Benita!" cried De Morla, in her own language, to the terrified princess, "and let him stay the work of blood; for none but he has the power. Tell him, we desire peace, repent the wrongs we have done him, and will redress them. If he will regain his liberty and his empire—if he will save his people, his children, and himself, from one common and fearful destruction, let him forget that we have done him wrong and pronounce the words of peace."

The Indian maiden threw herself at the feet of the king, and bathing his hands with tears, repeated the charge of the cavalier.

Montezuma gazed upon her with sorrow, and upon his other children; then looking coldly to Don Hernan, he said, with a tranquil voice, while Donna Marina rapidly interpreted his expressions. "What will the Teuctli have? He commands a captive to shield him from the darts of free warriors: Montezuma is a prisoner. He calls upon me to quiet a raging people: Montezuma has no people. He commands me to regain my liberty: the Mexican that hath once been a slave, can be a freeman no more. He bids me save my children: I have none! they are servants in the house of a stranger. He that is in bonds, hath no offspring!"

While he spoke, the din increased, as if the yelling assailants were pressing up to the very walls of the palace; and many cavaliers, incapable of remaining inactive, and despairing of his assistance, rushed from the apartment to join in the combat.

'Why does he waste time in words?" cried Cortes. "At every moment there are slain a thousand of his subjects!"

"If there were twenty thousand," said the captive, assuming, at last, the dignity that became his name, and speaking with a stately anger, "and if but one Christian lay dead among them, Montezuma should not mourn the loss. Happier would he be, left with the few and mangled remnants, with his throne on the grave of the strangers, than, this moment, were he restored to his millions, with the children of the East abiding by him in friendship. Thou callest upon me to appease my people. Thou knowest that they are thine. Why should they not listen to thee?"

"Ay, why should they not?" said Don Hernan, speaking rather to himself than to Montezuma, and flinging sarcasms on his own head. "By my conscience, I know not; for though I was somewhat conceited to grasp at the sceptre so early, I think I may hold it with as much dignity as any infidel, were he a Turkish sultan. Hearken, Montezuma; thou art deceived: thy people are not mine, but thine, and through thee, as his sworn vassal, the subjects of my master, the king of Spain. Confirm thy vassalage to him by tribute, be true to thy allegiance, and remain on thy throne for ever; and, if such be thy desire, I will straightway withdraw my army from the empire, so that thou mayest reign according to thine own barbarous fancies."

"I trust thee not," said the king, "for already hast thou deceived me! I revoke my vows of vassalage; for he that has no kingdom, cannot be a king's deputy. Do thy worst," continued the monarch, with increasing boldness, no longer regarding the furious looks of Don Hernan, and learning, at last, to deserve the respect of his foes—"Do thy worst: thou hast degraded me with chains and

with words of insult; nothing more canst thou do, but kill! Kill me, then, if thou wilt; and in Mictlan will I rejoice, for I know that my betrayers shall follow me! Yes!" he added, with wild energy, "I know that, at this moment, your heart is frozen with fear and your blood turned to water, seeing that revenge has reached you, and that your doom is death! The wronger of the lords of Tenochtitlan has learned to tremble before its basest herds; and let him tremble—for the basest of them shall trample upon his body!"

"Am I menaced by this traitor to his allegiance?" cried Cortes.

"Senor," said De Morla, "let us trifle the time with no more deception. There is no one of our people who does not perceive that we can maintain our post in this city no longer, and that we cannot even escape from it, without the permission of our foes. This knows Montezuma, as well as ourselves. Why incense him, why strive to cajole him further? Let us tell him the truth, and buy safety by restoring, at once, what we cannot keep; and what otherwise we must yield up with our lives."

"Ay, faith—it cannot be denied: we are even caught in a net of our own twisting. Tell the knave what thou wilt. We will leave his accursed island. But how soon we may return, to claim the possessions of our master, thou needst not acquaint him. But, by my conscience, return we will, and that right briefly!"

A thousand different expressions agitated the visage of Montezuma, while listening to the words of De Morla. Now a flash of joy lit his dusky feature; now doubt covered them with double gloom; and now he frowned with a dark resolution, as if conceiving the fate of the Christians, if left to themselves, still caged in their bloody prison. The memory of all he had suffered, mingled with the imagination of all the vengeance he might enjoy, covered his countenance with a mingled rage and exultation. While he hesitated, his eye fell upon his children, for all had thrown themselves at his feet; and he beheld them, in fancy, paying the penalty of his ferocity. The stern eye of Cortes was upon him; and he thought he read, in its meaning lustre, the punishment which awaited his refusal.

"Will the Teuctli depart from me," he cried, eagerly, "if I open a path for him through my incensed people."

"I will depart from him," replied Don Hernan, "if his people throw down their arms and disperse."

"They will listen to me no more!" exclaimed Montezuma, suddenly clasping his hands, with a look and accent of despair, "for I am no longer their monarch. The gods of Anahuac have rejected the king that has submitted to bonds; a great prophetess has risen from Mictlan, bearing the will of the deities: and, by the bloody pool Ezapan, that washes the wounds of the penitent, the people have heard her words, and sworn faith to a new ruler, beloved by Heaven, and reverenced by themselves. They have seen the degradation of Montezuma, and Cuitlahuatzin is now the king of Mexico!"

"He speaks of the strange priestess we saw at the temple," said De Morla. "It is, indeed, said, among all the Mexicans (but how they have heard of her, I know not), that she has been sent by the gods, to dethrone our prisoner, and destroy the Christians."

"Thou art deceived," said Cortes, to the monarch, without regarding this explanation; "there is no king, but thyself, acknowledged by thy people; and at this moment, they are fighting to rescue thee from what they falsely consider bondage—falsely, I say, for thou knowest thou art my guest, and not my prisoner—free to depart whenever thou wilt—that is, whenever thou wilt exert thy authority to appease the insurrection. It is their mad love for thee that reduces us to extremity."

"And thou swearest then," cried Montezuma, catching eagerly at the suggestion and the hope, "thou swearest, that thou wilt depart from my empire, if I appease this bloody tumult?"

"I swear that I will depart from thy city," said the crafty Spaniard; "and I swear, that I hope to depart from thy empire—one day, at least, when I am its master." He muttered the last words to himself.

"Give me my robes—I will speak to my people!"

No sooner was this speech interpreted, than the Spaniards present uttered exclamations of pleasure; and some of them running out with the news to their companions, the court-yard soon rung with their shouts. Despair at once gave place to joy; and even to many of those who had been most sick of battle, the relief came, with such revulsions of feeling, that they seemed loath to lose the opportunity of slaying.

"Quick to your pieces! charge, and have at the yelling imps!" cried divers voices, "for presently we shall have no more fighting!"

CHAPTER XLII.

The cannoniers, moved by this new feeling, discharged their last volley with good will, and, at the same moment, the crossbowmen and musketeers shot off their pieces from the wall and the terraces. The four sides of the palace were thus, at the same instant, sheeted with flame; and the effect of the combined discharge was incalculably great and fatal among the dense bodies of besiegers. As they staggered, and fell back a little, to recover from their confusion, the mounted men, who had placed themselves in readiness for the final charge, rushed at once, spear in hand, on the disordered multitude, dealing death at every thrust and almost at every tramp of their charges.

It was precisely at this moment, that the Indian emperor, arrayed in the pompous and jewelled robes in which he was wont to preside at the greater festivals of the gods, with the *Copilli* on his head, and the golden buskins on his feet, preceded by a noble bearing the three rods of authority and attended by half a dozen cavaliers (of whom the neophyte was one), holding their bucklers in readiness to protect him from any ill-directed missile, stepped upon the terrace, and advanced towards the battlements. The spectacle that presented itself in the dawning light, was, to him at least, grievous and horrid. The earth of the square, and the dwellings that surrounded it, were torn by the cannon-shots, and many of the houses had tumbled into ruins. From this height also could be seen the blackened wrecks, which marked the path of the army, returning, the previous day, from the temple. But a more sorrowful sight was presented to the unfortunate monarch, in the prospect of his people, great numbers already lying dead on the furrowed square, while the survivors were falling fast under the lances of the horsemen.

Don Hernan enjoyed for a moment, with malicious satisfaction, the exclamations of grief with which his prisoner beheld this sight; for it was his pleasure to believe, that Montezuma was himself the planner of the insurrection. Then, giving a sign to a trumpeter, who was with the party, to wind a retreat, the horsemen instantly reined round their steeds, and galloped back to the court-yard. With a loud yell of triumph, the Mexicans, thinking their pursuers fled from fear, prepared to follow them, and poisoned their weapons as a prelude to the assault. At that critical period, the cavaliers moved aside from their prisoner, and he stood confronted with the people. The great cry with which the barbarians beheld their monarch, had something in it that was touching, for it expressed childish joy; but there was something still more affecting in the result, to those whose hearts were not utterly steeled, when they beheld the universal multitude, as with one accord, fling themselves upon their knees, and, dropping their weapons and pronouncing the name of the king, extend their hands towards him, as to a father.

"Is it possible then," muttered, or rather thought, Don Amador de Leste, smothering a sudden pang of remorse, "that these blood-thirsty barbarians are only seeking our lives, to liberate their king? Surely, we do a great sin, to slay them for their love. I would that my knight, my people, and myself, were fighting the Turks again."

The sudden change from the furious tumult of war to such stillness as belongs to midnight, was impressive, and even awful; and solemn looks, both from his subjects and his foes, from those who fought in the court-yard, and those who manned the roof and the turrets, were bent on the royal captive, as he stepped upon the battlement, and addressed himself to his people.—"My children!" said Montezuma, for so his words were rapidly interpreted by De Morla—"if ye are shedding your blood to convince me of your affection, know that I feel its constancy, without approving its rashness. Though I be a prisoner—" He paused, for the word stuck in his throat, and groans and lamentations showed how unpalatable it was to his subjects. "Though I be a prisoner with the Teuctli, yet have you to know, it is, in a great measure, with mine own consent; and, at this moment, I remain not by enforcement, but by choice."

The unhappy monarch, by so expressing his address as to steer clear of offence to the Spaniards (for well he knew they dreaded lest his confessions should still more inflame the citizens), committed the more fatal error of displeasing his people. A murmur of indignation ran through the mass, when Montezuma, with his own lips, confirmed his abasement. Several rose, frowning, to their feet, and a young man, parting quickly from the crowd, advanced so near to the palace that his features could be plainly distinguished. He was of noble stature, countenance, and mien, evidently of the highest order of nobility, and enjoyed the distinction of a principality in the House of Darts, as was shown by the red fillet in his hair, suspending the tufts of honour. His trunk and shoulders were invested in a coat of armour, either of scales of copper or of leather, richly gilt, bordered at the bottom with lambrequens of green and red feathers. His limbs were naked, saving only the bright sandals on his feet, and the glittering bracelet on his arms. His left arm supported a light buckler doubtless of wicker-work, though painted with many bright and fantastic colours; and, from the bottom of it, waved a broad penacho, as well as a bulky maquahuitl, which he held in his left hand, while balancing a copper javelin in his right. A tall plume of the most splendid hues nodded majestically on his head.

As this bold and noble-looking youth stepped up to the very mouths of the cannon, and raised his fiery eyes to the king, Don Amador de Leste thought that he recognised in him the princely ambassador of Cholula—the young fugitive, who had been so ready to dispute the path with him, under the walls of the holy city. "Dost thou say this, thou that wert once their lord, to the people of Mexitli?" said the young prince (for, as has been recorded by other historians. it was the valiant Quauhtimotzin, the nephew of the king, who now so sharply rebuked him). "Dost thou indeed confess, son of Axajacatl! that thou art, by thine own consent, the friend of a perfidious stranger—by thine own choice, oh conqueror of many nations, the serf and slave of him who is the brother of Tlascala? Then art thou, indeed, what we have called thee—the slayer of thy people—for this blood has flown at thy bidding; a traitor to thy throne—for thou hast surrendered it to a master; an apostate to thy gods—for thou hast shut thine ears, when they called upon thee for vengeance. Miserable king—and yet a king no more! When thy people wept to see thee degraded, thou gavest them up to slaughter; and while they come to restore thee to thy rights, thou confessest, that thou lovest these less than the shame of captivity. Know then, that, for thy baseness, the gods have pronounced thee unworthy to be their viceroy, and thy people have confirmed the degree. We break the rods of authority; we trample upon the robes of state: and Montezuma is no longer a king in Tenochtitlan!"

The unhappy monarch trembled, while he listened to this insulting denunciation, for he felt that he had deserved it. But his people still lay prostrate on the earth; and, hoping that they shared not the indignation of his kinsman, he elevated his voice again, and spoke sternly—"Why doth Quauhtimotzin forget that he is the son of my brother, and my slave? Is the young man that smiles in jewels, wiser than he that hath grey hairs? and the people that delve in canals and build up the temples, have they more cunning than the king who councils with the spirits at the altar? Know that, what has been done, has been done wisely, for it was according to the will of Heaven; and Heaven, which has tried our fidelity, is about to reward it with happiness and peace. The strangers have promised to depart from us: throw down your arms, and let them be gone."

"And wilt thou," said the prince, elevating his voice to a still angrier pitch, "who hast been so many times deluded, counsel us to listen to their lies? Oh, fallen Montezuma! thou leaguest with them against us. Wilt thou suffer them to escape, when we have them enclosed in nets, as the birds that sing in thy gardens? Oh, degraded chief! thou hast not the courage to desire the blood of them that have dethroned thee! Thou art not he that was Montezuma; thy words are the words of a Christian; thou speakest with the lips of a slave, and the heart of a woman; thou art a Spaniard, and thy fate shall be the fate of a Spaniard! Cuitlahuatzin is our king; and we strike thee as a foeman!"

As the prince concluded his indignant oration, he swung round his head the javelin, which, all this time, he had balanced in his hand, and launched it, with all his force, full at the breast of Montezuma. The shield of the novice, quickly interposed before the body of the king, arrested the sharp weapon, and it fell, innocuous, on the terrace. At the same moment, the Mexicans all sprang to their feet, with loud cries, as if giving way to repressed fury, and brandished their arms. The bucklers of the cavaliers were instantly extended before the monarch, to protect him from the dreaded missiles. But, as if desperation had robbed him of his fears, and restored to him, for the last hour, some share of that native spirit which had elevated him to the throne, he pushed them immediately aside, and raising himself to his full height, and spreading forth his arms, gazed majestically though with a ghastly countenance, on his people. The words of mingled entreaty and command were already on his lips, but they were lost even to the Spaniards who stood by, in the thunder of shouts coming from twenty thousand voices; and the warning cry of Cortes was equally unheard, bidding the Spaniards to "Save the king!" The shields were interposed, however, without command, and caught many of the missiles—stones, arrows, and darts—which fell like a shower on the group—but not all. An arrow pierced the right arm, a stone maimed the right leg, and another, striking upon the left temple of the abandoned monarch, crushed the bone in upon the brain; and he fell into the arms of the cavaliers, like a dead man.

The cannoniers, at that moment, seeing the returning rage of the barbarians, shot off their pieces. But the battle was done. No sooner had the Mexicans beheld their monarch fall under the blows of their own weapons, than they changed their cries of fury to lamentations; and throwing down their arms, as if seized with a panic, they fled from the square, leaving it to the Christians and the dead.

CHAPTER XLIII·

In great grief and consternation of mind, the cavaliers carried the king to his apartments, and added their own sharp regrets to the tears of his children, when the surgeon pronounced his wounds mortal. Even the Senor Cortes did not disdain to heave a sigh over the mangled form of his prisoner; for in his death, he perceived his innocence, and remembered his benefactions; and, in addition, he felt, that, in the loss of Montezuma, he was deprived of the strongest bulwark against the animosity of his people.

"I have done this poor infidel king a great wrong," he said, with a remorse that might have been real, and yet, perhaps, was assumed, to effect a purpose on his followers; "for now, indeed, it is plain, he could not have been unfaithful to us, or he would not thus have perished. I call God to witness, that I had no hand in his death; and I aver to yourselves, noble cavaliers, that, when I have seemed to treat him with harshness and injustice, I have done so for the good of my companions, and the advantage of our king; for barbarians, being, in some sort, children, are to be governed by that severity which is wholesome to infancy. Nevertheless, I do not wholly despair of his life; for there are some score or two lusty fellows in the garrison, who have had their skulls cracked, and are none the worse for the affliction. I trust much in thy skill, Senor Boticario," he continued, addressing the surgeon; "and I promise thee, if thou restore Montezuma to his life and wits, I will, on mine own part, bestow upon thee this golden chain and crucifix, valued at ninety pesos, besides recommending thee likewise to the gratitude of my brother captains, and the favourable notice of his majesty, our king—whom God preserve ever from the wrath and impiety of such traitorous subjects as have laid our Montezuma low. I leave him in thy charge. As for ourselves, valiant and true friends, it being now apparent to you, that we have none but ourselves to look to for safety, and even food (the want of which latter would, doubtless, create many loud murmurs, were it not for the jeopardy of the former), I must recommend you to betake you to your horses, and accompany me in a sally which it is needful now to make, both for the sake of reconnoitring the dikes and gathering food. What now, Botello!" he cried, observing the enchanter passing through the throng, " what dost thou here? Thou never madest me a prophecy of this great mishap!

" I never cast the horoscope, nor called upon Kalidon-Sadabath, to discover the fate of any but a Christian man," said Botello, gravely ; " for what matters it what is the fate of a soul predoomed to flames, whether it part with violence or in peace? I have sought out the destiny of his people, because I thought, some day, they should be baptised in the faith; but I never cast me a spell for the king."

" Wilt thou adventure thine art in his behalf, and tell me whether he shall now live or die."

" It needs no conjuration to discover that," said the magician, pointing significantly to the broken temple. " The king will die, and that before we are released from our thraldom. But hearken, senor," he continued, solemnly, " I have sought out the fate that concerns us more nearly. Last night, while others buried their weariness in sleep, and their sorrows in the dreams of home, I watched in solitude, with prayers and fasting, working many secret and godly spells, and conversing with the spirits that came to the circle."

The wounded monarch was forgotten, for an instant, by the cavaliers, in their eagerness to gather the revelations of the conjurer ; for scepticism, like pride, was yielding before the increasing difficulties of their situation, and they grasped at hope and encouragement, coming from what quarter soever

" And what have the spirits told thee, then ?" demanded the general, meaningly. " Doubtless, that, although there be a cloud about us now, there shall sunshine soon burst from it ; and that, if we depart from this city, it will only be like the antique battering ram, pulled back from a wall, that it may presently return against it with tenfold violence."

" I have not questioned so far," replied Botello, earnestly. " I know that we must fly. What is to come after, is in the hands of God, and has not been revealed. Death lies in store for many, but safety for some. The celestial aspects are unfavourable, the conjunctions speak of suffering and blood ; dreams are dark, Kalidon is moody, and the fiends prattle in riddles. Day after day, the gloom shall be thicker, the frowns of fate more menacing, retreat more hopeless. Never before found I so many black days clustered over the earth! In all this period, there is but one shining hour ; and if we seize not that, Heaven receive us! for. beyond that, there is nothing but death. On the fifth day from this, at midnight, a path will be opened to us on the causeway ; for then, from the house Alpharg, doth the moon break the walls of prisons, and light fugitives to the desert. But after that, I say to thee again, very noble senor,

all is hopelessness, all is woe! starvation in the palace, and shrieking sacrifices on the temple!"

" On the fifth night, then," said Cortes, gravely, " if the fates so will it, we must take our departure—provided we die not of famine on the fourth. I would the devils that thou hast in command had revealed thee some earlier hour, or some good means of coming at meat and drink. Get thee to thy horoscopes again, thy prayers and thy suffumigations; and see if thou hast not, by any mischance, overlooked some favourable moment for to-morrow, or the day after."

" It cannot be," said Botello; " my art has disclosed me no hope ; but, without art, I see that, to-morrow, the news of Montezuma's death (for surely he is now dying) will fill the causeways with mountaineers, and cover the lake with navigators, all coming to avenge it."

" I like thy magic better than thy mother wit," said Don Hernan, with a frown. " Give me what diabolical comfort thou canst to the soldiers ; but croak no common sense alarms into their ears."

" I have nothing to do with the magic that is diabolic," said the offended enchanter. " God is my stay, and the fiends I curse! If I have fears, I speak them not, save to those who may handle them for wise purposes. This, which I have said, will surely be the fate of to-morrow ; and the besiegers will come, in double numbers, to the walls. What I have to speak of to-day, may be of as much moment, though revealed to me neither by star nor spirit. The Mexicans are struck with horror, having slain their king ; they hide them in their houses, or they run, mourning, to the temples ; the soldiers are fresh, and the streets are empty. What hinders that we do not gird on our packs, and, aiming for the near and short dike of Tacuba, which I so lately traversed, with the king's daughters, make good our retreat this moment!"

" By Santiago!" cried Cortes, quickly, " this is a soldier's thought, and honoured shalt thou be for conceiving it. What ho, Sandoval, my friend! get the troops in readiness. Prepare thy litters for the sick and wounded—have all ready at a moment's warning. In the mean while, I will scour the western streets, and if all promise well, will return to conduct the retreat in person."

" We can carry with us," said Botello, " the wounded king, and his sons and daughters ; and if it chance we should be followed, we will do as the tiger-hunter does with the cubs, when the dam pursues him—fling a prisoner, ever and anon, on the path, to check the fury of our persecutors. The king will be better than a purse of gold."

" Ay! now thou art my sage soldier again !" said the general. " Get thee to the men, and comfort them. Apothecary, look to the emperor, and see that he have the best litter. Forget not thy drugs and potions. And now, Christian cavaliers, and brothers, be of good heart. Let us mount horse, and look at the dike of Tacuba."

The officers, greatly encouraged at the prospect of so speedy a release from their sufferings, followed the general from the apartment. Their elation was not shared by Don Amador de Leste. He rejoiced, for his kinsman's sake, that he was about to bear him from the din and privation of a besieged citadel; but he remembered that the Moorish boy must be left behind to perish ; and it seemed to him, in addition, that certain mystic ties, the result of a day's adventure, which began to bind his thoughts to the Pagan city, were, by the retreat, to be severed at once, and for ever.

But if his gloom was increased by such reflections, it was, in part, dispelled, when he reached the chamber of his kinsman. The delirium had vanished, and the knight sat on his couch, feeble, indeed, and greatly dejected, but quite in his senses. He turned an eye of affection on the youth, and with his trembling hand grasped Don Amador's.

"I have been as one that slept, dreaming my dreams," he said, "while thou hast been fighting the infidel. Strange visions have beset me; but thanks to Heaven. they have passed away; and, by and by, I will be able to mount and go forth with thee; and we will fight, side by side, as we have done before. among the Mussulmans."

"Think not of that, my father," said the novice, ' for thou art very feeble. I would, indeed, thou hadst but the strength, this day, to sit on the saddle; for we are about to retreat from Tenochtitlan. Nevertheless, Baltasar shall have thy couch placed on a litter, which we can secure between two horses."

"Speakest thou of retreating?" exclaimed Don Gabriel.

"It is even so, my friend. The numbers, the fury, and the unabating exertion of the Mexicans, are greater than we looked for. We have lost many men, are reduced to great extremities for food, altogether dispirited, and now left so helpless, by the disaster of the king, that we have no hope but in flight."

"Is the king hurt?—and by a Spaniard?"·

"Wounded by the stones and arrows of his own people, and now dying. And, it is thought, we can depart to best advantage, while the Mexicans are repenting the impiety that slew him."

"And we must retreat?"

"If we can—a matter which we, who are mounted, are about to determine, by riding to the nearest causeway. This, dear father, will give Marco and Baltasar time to prepare thee. I will leave Lazaro and the secretary to assist them. Presently we will return; and when we march, be it unopposed, or yet through files of the enemy, I swear to thee I will ride ever at thy side."

"And my boy—my loving little page, Jacinto?" exclaimed the knight, anxiously: "hath he returned to us? I have a recollection that he was stolen away. 'Twill be a new sin to me, if he come to harm through my neglect."

"Let us think no more of Jacinto," said the novice, with a sigh. "If he be living, he is now in the hands of Abdalla, his father, who has deserted from us, and is supposed to be harboured by the Mexicans. God is over all—we can do him no good—God will protect him!"

Don Gabriel eyed his kinsman sorrowfully, saying—"Evil follows in my path, and overtakes those who follow after me. Every day open I mine eyes upon a new grief. I loved this child very well; and, for my punishment, he is taken from me. I love thee, also, Amador, whom I may call my son; for faithful and unwearying art thou; and, belike, the last blow will fall, when thou art snatched away. Guard well thy life, for it is the last pillar of my own!"

A few moments of affection, a few words of condolence, were bestowed upon Don Gabriel; and then the novice left him, to accompany the cavaliers to the causeway.

As he was stepping from the palace door into the court-yard, his arm was caught by the magician, who, looking into his face with exceeding great solemnity, said—"Ride not thou with the cavaliers to-day, noble gentleman. Thou art unlucky."

A faint smile lit the countenance of the youth. It was soon followed by a sigh.

"This is, indeed, a truth, which no magic could make more manifest than has the history of much of my life. I am unfortunate; yet not in affairs of war—being now, as you see, almost the only man in this garrison who is not, in part, disabled by severe wounds. Yet why should I not ride with my friends?"

"Because thou wilt bring them trouble, and thyself misery. I cannot say, senor," added Botello, with grave earnestness, "that thou didst absolutely save my life, when thou broughtest me succour in the street, seeing that this is under the influence of a destiny, well known to me, which man cannot alter. It was not possible those savages could slav me. Nevertheless, my gratitude is as strong, for thy good will was as great. I promised to read thee thy fortune; but in the troubles which beset me, I could not perfect thy horoscope. All I have learned is, that a heavy storm hangs over thee; and that, if thou art not discreet, thy last hour is nigh, and will be miserable. The very night of thy good and noble service, I dreamed that we were surrounded by all the assembled Mexicans, making with them a contract of peace; to which they were about swearing, when they laid their eyes upon thee, and straightway were incensed, at this sight, as at the call of a trumpet, to attack us. Thou knowest, that it was thy rash attack on the accursed prophetess, which brought the knaves upon us. Thrice was this vision repeated to me: twice has it been confirmed—once at the temple, and, but a moment since, on the roof. Hadst thou not stood before the king with thy shield, the rage of the Mexicans would not have destroyed him Therefore, go not out now; for he that brings mischief twice to his friends, will, the third time, be involved in their ruin."

The neophyte stared at Botello, who pronounced these fantastic adjurations with the most solemn emphasis. His heart was heavy, or their folly would have amused him. "Be not alarmed, Botello," he said, good-humouredly, "I will be very discreet. My conscience absolves me of all agency in the king's hurts; and if I did, indeed draw on the attack at the pyramid, as I am by no means certain, I only put match to the cannon, which, otherwise, might have been aimed at us more fatally. I promise thee to be rash no more —no, not even though I should again behold the marvellous prophetess, who, as Montezuma told us, has risen from his Pagan hell."

The enchanter would have remonstrated further; but, at this moment the trumpet gave signal that the cavaliers were departing, and Don Amador stayed neither to argue nor console. He commanded the secretary, whom he found among the throng, to return to Don Gabriel; and Lorenzo reluctantly obeyed. Lazaro was already with the knight.

Thus, without personal attendants, Don Amador mounted, this day, among the cavaliers, prepared to disprove the enchanter's predictions, or to consummate his destiny. ··

CHAPTER XLIV.

The sufferings of the Spaniards in the streets, when returning from the pyramid, had admonished the general of the necessity of devising some plan of protection against those citizens, who fought from the house-tops, whenever constrained to attempt a second sortie. Accordingly, the artisans, in obedience to his commands, had spent the preceding night in the construction of certain wooden turrets, sufficiently lofty to overlook the commoner houses, and strong enough to bid defiance to the darts of the enemy. They were framed of timbers and planks, torn from different parts of the palace. Each was two stories in height, and, in addition, was furnished with a guard, or battlement over the roof, breast-high, behind which, some half a score musketeers might ensconce themselves to advantage, while nearly as many crossbowmen could be concealed in either chamber, discharging their weapons from narrow loop-holes. A little falconet was also placed in the upper chamber. They were mounted on gun-carriages, and meant to be drawn by the Indian allies. They were called at first *mantas*, or blankets; but afterwards were nicknamed *burros*—either because they were such silly protections as might have been devised by the most stupid of animals, which is one signification of the word, or, because the cannon-wheels, revolving under their mass, reminded the soldiers of the great wheel of a mill, which is another meaning. One of these machines had been completed, and was now ordered to be taken out, not from any apprehension that it might be needed, but because it appeared to the sagacious general, that, if fate should imprison him longer in Tenochtitlan, the present was the best opportunity to instruct his soldiers in the management of it.

It was already lumbering slowly and clumsily over the broken square, drawn by some two hundred Tlascalans, and well manned with soldiers, when Don Amador passed from the gates. As the cavaliers rode by, its little garrison, vastly delighted with their safe and lazy quarters, greeted them with a merry cheer, the gayest and most sonorous strain of which was sounded by those who defended the roof. As Don Amador looked curiously up, he was hailed by a voice not yet forgotten, and beheld, perched among others, whom he seemed to command, on the very top of the manta, the master of the caravel.

"I give you a good day, noble Don Amador," said this commander, with a grin. "I am not now aboard of such a bark as the little Sangre de Cristo; but, for navigating through a beleagured city, especially among such cut-throats as we have here in Tenochtitlan, perhaps a better ship could not be invented."

"Thou art then resolved," said the cavalier, with a smile, "that this people is not far behind the race of Florida?"

"Ay! I cannot but believe it; and I ask their pardon, for having so greatly belied them," said the captain; "for more ferocious devils than these never saw I; they dwell not among the lagoons of the north."

"And dost thou remember thy wager?" said Don Amador, losing the little gaiety that was on his visage, at the recollection."

"Concerning my soul (which Heaven have in keeping), and the cotton neckpiece?" cried the sailor, with a grim look. "Ay, by my faith, I do. If we fly this day, the first part of the venture is accomplished; for true valour must acknowledge a defeat, as well as boast a victory. And if we do not, I am even ready to wager over again for the second, touching Heaven. Three more such days as yesterday, and God bless us all! But it is a good death to die, fighting the heathen. At the worst, I have cheated the devil; for the padre Olmedo absolved me this morning."

Don Amador rode forward, relapsing into gloom.

The streets were, for a time, deserted and silent, as if the inhabitants had fled from the island; and when, now and then, the cavaliers halted, to deliberate on their course, to list for the cries of human voices, or to watch the progress of the tottering manta, already far behind, the sound of shrubs rustling together on the terraces came to their ears with the melancholy cadences of a desert. Sometimes, indeed, in these pauses, they heard from the recesses of a dwelling, which otherwise seemed forsaken, faint groans, as of a wounded foeman dying without succour; and, occasionally, to these were added the low sobs of women, lamenting a sire or brother. But they had approached the limits of the island, and almost within view of the causeway, without yet beholding an enemy, when a warning gesture from the hands of Don Hernan at the front, brought them to a halt; and, as they stood in silence, they heard, coming faintly on the breeze, and as it seemed, from a street which crossed their path, a little in advance, such sounds of flutes and tabours as had, the day before, conducted the mysterious priestess to the pyramid.

Don Amador's heart beat with a strange agitation as he listened; and he burned again to look on the countenance of this divine representative of a Pagan divinity. Whether it was the dejection of his spirits, which gave its own character to the music, or whether indeed this was now breathed from the lips of mourners, he thought not to inquire; but others were struck with the wild sadness of the strain, and gazed inquisitively upon one another, as if to gather its meaning. While they thus exchanged looks, and awaited the issue of the event, the sounds approached, growing louder, but losing none of their melancholy; and a train of priests, in long black robes, and with downcast eyes, followed by boys with smoking censers, at last stole on their view, slowly crossing the street on which they had halted. At this moment, and just as the prophetess (for it was she who stood, as before, under the feathered canopy carried by the devotees), came into sight, the roar of a cannon, bellowed afar from the palace, startled the cavaliers from their tranquillity; and, in the assurance of new conflicts, destroyed at once their hope of peaceful escape. This explosion, as was afterwards discovered, was rather the cause than the consequence of hostilities; for the Mexicans, after the sortie of Cortes, approaching the citadel in great numbers, to beseech the body of their king, not doubting that he was slain, the Spaniards had mistaken their grief for renewing rage, and immediately fired upon them

A furious scowl darkened the visage of Don Hernan, as this distant discharge swept away his hopes; and rising on his stirrups, he cried to his companions—"Let us seize the person of this accursed priestess—demon, or women—who profanes the holiness of Our Lady, and incenses the hearts of the rabble! On, and be quick; for 'tis an easy prize, and may replace the emperor!"

Until this moment, the train, casting their eyes neither to the right nor left, and raising them not even at the roar of the cannon, had been ignorant of the presence of the Spaniards. But when the harsh voice of the Christian drowned the breathings of the flutes, they paused, looking towards him in affright and again, for an instant, the lustrous eyes of the prophetess fell upon the visage of Don Amador. His heart heaved with a sickening sensation; and the impulse which had before driven to flight his better judgment, assailed him anew with violence. His voice shouted with the rest, but it uttered the name of Leila; and, as if, indeed, he beheld the lost maid of Almeria, or her phantom, he spurred towards the prophetess, full as madly as when she vanished, before, under the Wall of Serpents. But the train, scattering at once, fled in horror from the Spaniards, escaping into the neighbouring houses. The object of the outrage, nevertheless, seemed in the power of the cavaliers; for though the bearers deserted her not, they fled but slowly under their burden.

But there were protectors nigh, of whom the Spaniards had not dreamed; and even Cortes himself reined back his horse with dismay, when, suddenly, there sprang from the intersecting street a multitude of armed nobles, interposing their bodies between him and his victim; and his eye running an instant down the street, beheld them followed by a myriad of Pagans without end.

"Back to the manta!" cried the general, hastily; "for these dogs are armed, and the men of the turret have no aid!—Hark! hear ye not the howls? Rein round, and back! They are slaying my Tlascalans!"

Before the neophyte could recover from his confusion of mind, he found himself turned round and borne along with the mass of galloping horsemen. The Mexicans uttered a cry, as with one impulse, and followed furiously after.

In the crowd of thought that distracted him, Don Amador remembered the words of Botello, and believed that he was, indeed, labouring under some enchantment, which made him a misfortune to his friends. But not long had he leisure for such meditations. The loud yells of combatants, and the sounds of arquebuses in front, increased at each step; and, quickly turning an angle in the street, he found himself in the midst of conflict.

An immense herd of men had surrounded the manta, and were engaged hand to hand with the Tlascalans who drew it; while the Spaniards on its top defended themselves, at a disadvantage, from many Mexicans, stationed on the terrace of a lofty house, the dwelling of some superb Tlatoani. So near indeed was the turret to the walls of this edifice, and so high above it was the latter, that the huge stones tumbled from the battlements, fell with great certainty on its roof, crushing the men of the caravel, and beating down both the wooden parapet and the platform. At the same time, certain savages, with long poles, struck at the defenders, and thrusting the points of their weapons into its breaches, endeavoured to topple it to the ground. As it rocked thus to and fro, the violent motion entirely prevented the little garrison from making use of their arms; and with wild cries to their friends, to seize the ropes, dropped by the Tlascalans, and drag the manta from the palace, they were seen holding by its sides as well as they could, receiving, without returning, the blows of their adversaries. The necessity of obeying their prayer was seen more plainly than the means; for the crowd of mingled Tlascalans and Mexicans that surrounded the crazy machine was impenetrable; and had it been so, the appearance of the manta, threatening each moment to fall, would have deterred the boldest from approaching its dangerous vicinity.

As it was, the cavaliers gave what aid they could. They thrust their spears into the mass of Indians, shouting to the Tlascalans to disengage themselves from the enemy. But these shouts, if the allies did not indeed receive them rather as encouragement to fight the more fiercely, dissolved not the bloody melée into its components of friend and foe; and many a Tlascalan died that day, pierced through the heart by spears, which their bearers thought were thrust through the breasts of Mexicans.

In the mean while, the heavy burro was shaken still more violently; and Don Amador looking up, beheld the master of the caravel alone on the top (for his sailors were already slain,) grasping despairingly at a fragment of the parapet; while stones and darts were showered upon him from the adjoining terrace, and a heavy pole, aimed by a lusty barbarian, struck him with merciless severity. His countenance was pale, his eye haggard, and his honourable scars, now livid and almost black, were relieved, like fresh wounds, on his ghastly brow. His helmet had fallen to the ground; and the sight of his grey hairs shaking over his scarred front, as he was tossed up and down, like one bound hand and foot on the back of a wild animal, inflamed the neophyte with both rage and pity.

"Loose thy hold! drop upon the Indians, and take thy chance among them!" he cried, at the top of his voice. "What ho! friend Gomez! wilt thou lie there and perish?"

It seemed as if the voice of the cavalier had not passed unheard, for the wretched man was seen to raise himself on his knees, and look down to the fighting men below, as if meditating a leap; when suddenly a great stone fell on the platform with a crashing noise, and, at the same moment, the manta, lurching like an ill-ballasted ship before a hurricane, staggered over its balance, and fell with a tremendous shock to the ground. The neophyte thought not of the miserable combatants, crushed in its fall. He beheld the voyager, at the instant, of its destruction, hurled from the ruin, as if from some mighty balista of ancient days, clear over the heads of the Indians, and dashed, a mangled and hideous corse, almost at his feet.

"God pity thee!" he cried, with a shudder; "thy words are made good, thy wager is won—and the saints that died for the faith, take thee to paradise!"

"Do ye hear? Ho! to your lances, and back upon the wolves that are behind us!" cried the trumpet voice of Don Hernan. The neophyte turned, and clapping spurs to Fogoso, charged, with the cavaliers, upon those squadrons which had pursued them; but, like his companions, he checked his horse with surprise, and no little consternation, when he beheld in what manner the infidels were prepared to receive them. The street was packed with their bodies, as far as the eye could see; and darts and swords of obsidian were seen flashing above the heads of the most distant multitude; but he perceived that those combatants who stood in front, stretching from wall to wall, were armed with long spears, mostly, indeed, with wooden points, sharpened and fire-hardened, though some few were seen with copper blades, full a yard in length, which they handled with singular and menacing address. Thus, no sooner did the cavaliers approach them, than those of the first rank, dropping, like trained soldiers, to their knees, planted the butts of their weapons on the ground, while those held by others behind, were thrust over the shoulders of the kneelers, and presented, together, such a wall of bristling spines, as caused the bravest to hesitate.

"Have we Ottomies of the hills here!" cried Don Hernan, aghast. "Or are these weapons, and this mode of using them the teaching of the traitor Moor?"

A loud shout, mingled with laughs of fierce derision, testified the triumph of the barbarians; and Cortes, stung with fury, though hesitating to attack, called for his musketeers, to break the line of opponents.

"Our musketeers are in heaven! carried up in the fiend of a burro!" cried Alvarado, waving his sword, and eyeing the vaunting herd. "Before the days of saltpetre, true men were wont to shoot their foes without it. All that is to be done, is to conceive we are hunting foxes, and leaping over a farmer's wall. Soho! Saladin, mouse! And all that are brave gentlemen, follow me! Hah!—"

As he concluded, the madcap soldier spurred his steed, Saladin, and, uttering a war-cry, dashed fearlessly on the spearmen. Before he had yet parted from his companions, Don Amador de Leste, fired, in spite of his melancholy, by the boldness of the exploit, and unwilling to be outdone by a cavalier of the islands, brushed up to his side, and spurring Fogoso at the same moment, the two hidalgos straightway vaulted among the barbarians.

The show of resolution maintained by the exulting spearmen, while the Christians stood yet at a distance, vanished when they beheld those animals, which they always regarded with a superstitious awe, rushing upon them with eyes of fury, and feet of thunder. To this faltering, perhaps, it was owing that the two dons were not instantly slain; for, though the heavy armour that guarded the chests and loins of the steeds, could repel the thrust of a wooden spear as well as the corslets of their riders, no such protection sheathed their bellies; and had they been there pierced, their masters must instantly have perished. As it was, however, the front rank recoiled, and when it closed again, the cavaliers were seen wielding their swords (for in such a melée their spears were useless,) and striking valiantly about them, but entirely surrounded.

"Shall we thus be shamed, my masters?" cried Don Hernan, sharply. "Methinks there are two more such cavaliers in this company? Santiago, and at them!"

Thus saying, and, with a word, inflaming their pride, he leaped against the foe, followed by all the horsemen.

The two leaders in this desperate assault had vanished—swallowed up, as it were, in the vortex of contention; and it was not until his friends heard the voice of Alvarado exclaiming, wildly, as

if in extremity—"Help me, De Leste, true friend. for I am unhorsed! Help me, or the hell-hounds will have me to the temple!"—that they were convinced the young men were living.

"Be of good heart!" cried Don Amador (for he was at his side,) drawing his sabre, with a dexterous sleight, over the sinewy arms that clutched his companion, and releasing, without doing him harm. "If thou art disarmed, draw my dagger from the sheath and use it; and fear not that I will leave thee, till rescued by others."

"Who gets my sword, takes the arm along with it!" cried Alvarado, grasping again his chained weapon, and dealing fierce blows, as he spoke. "I will remember the act—Ho! false friends! forsworn soldiers! condemned Christians! why leave ye us unsupported?"

"Courage, and strike well! we are near," answered Don Hernan. "Press on, friends; trample the curs to death! Join we our true cavaliers; and then sweep back for victory!"

"Where goest thou now, mad Amador?" they heard the voice of Alvarado exclaiming—"Return: thy horse is shoed with piraguas; but mine sticks fast in this bog of flesh. Return; for by Heaven, I can follow thee no further!"

"Come on, as thou art a true man; for I am sore beset, and wounded!" These words, from the lips of the neophyte, came yet through the din of yells; but it seemed to those who listened, that there was feebleness in the voice that uttered them.

"Onward!" cried Cortes, with a voice of thunder, and urging his dun steed furiously over the trampled barbarians; "the young man shall not perish!"

A wolf-hound, weary and spent with the chase, suddenly surrounded by a whole pack of the destroyers he has been tracking, and falling under the fangs of his quarry, may figure the condition of Don Amador de Leste, surrounded and seized upon by the enemy. Nothing but the vigour of powerful and fiery-spirited steeds could have carried the two cavaliers so far into a crowd of warriors almost compacted. While the neophyte gave assistance to his friend, a dozen blows of the maquahuitl were rained upon his body; and so closely was he invested immediately after (when, as Alvarado reined in his steed to await the rest, the two cavaliers were separated,) that he thought no longer of warding off blows; but giving himself up to smiting, he trusted to the strength of his mail for protection. But the heavy bludgeons bruised where they could not wound; and his armour being, at last, broken by the fury of the blows, the sharp glass penetrated to his flesh, and he began to bleed. He cast his eye over his shoulder, for his strength was failing; but the plume of Don Pedro waved at a distance behind, and the shouts of Cortes seemed to come from afar. He turned his horse's head, to retreat; but half a dozen savages, emboldened by this symptom of defeat, clutched upon the bridle; and the hand he raised to smite at them, was seized by as many others. It was at this moment he called out to his companion, in the words we have recorded; but the answer, if answer were made, was drowned in the savage yells of exultation with which his foes beheld him in their power. He collected all his energies, struggled violently, and striking the rowels deep, and animating Fogoso with his voice, hoped, by one bound, to spring clear of his capturers. The gallant steed vaulted on high, but fell again to the earth, under the weight of the many that clung to him: and a dozen new hands were added to those that already throttled the rider.

"Rescue me, if ye be men!" he cried, with a voice that prevailed over the uproar. The cry was echoed by twenty Christian voices hard by, and a gleam of hope entered into his heart. Another furious struggle, another plunge of Fogoso, and he thought that the hands of his enemies were at last unclenching. A bright weapon flashed before his eyes—it was steel, and therefore the falchion of a friend!—It fell upon his helmet with irresistible weight; his brain spun, his eyes darkened, and he fell, or rather was dragged, like a dead man, from his horse. But ere his eyes had yet closed, their last glance was fixed on the visage of the striker; and the sting of benefits forgotten was added to the bitterness of death, when, in this, he perceived the features of Abdalla the Moor.

In an instant more the barbarians parted in terror before the great Teuctli. "Where art thou, De Leste?" he cried. "We are here, to rescue thee!"

As he spoke, there sprang, with a fierce bound, from among the Mexicans, the well-known bay, Fogoso, his foamy sides streaked with gore, the stirrups rattling against his armed flanks, the reins flying in the air—but no rider on the saddle.

"By Heaven! false friends! craven gentlemen! you have lost the bravest of your supporters!" cried Don Hernan. "On! for he may yet live: on! for we will avenge him!"

The band, resolute now in their wrath, plunged fiercely through the mob. They struck down many enemies—they trampled upon many corses; but among them they found not the body of De Leste.

CHAPTER XLV.

Whether it was that this attack was caused by an ebullition of popular fury, which yielded to some mysterious and religious revulsion of feeling, or whether, indeed, the leaders of the barbarians, persuaded of the madness of fighting the Christians hand to hand, and resolved to conquer them rather by famine than arms, had called off their forces—was a secret the Spaniards could never penetrate. No sacred horn was sounded on the pyramid; but, in the very midst of what seemed their triumph, when the cavaliers were nearly exhausted and despairing, it became manifest that the Mexicans were giving way, and vanishing, not one by one, but in great clusters, from the field.

The Christians had no longer the spirit to pursue. They found the street open; and dashing through the few foemen that lingered on the field, they made their way good to the palace. Before they reached t, they were joined by a powerful detachment, sent out to their assistance. They returned together. At the gate of the court-yard stood Baltasar, Lazaro, and the secretary, looking eagerly for the appearance of Don Amador. His horse was led by a cavalier, whose countenance was more dejected than the rest. It was De Morla; and as he flung the bridle to Lazaro, he said—"Hadst thou been with thy master this thing had not happened; for,

though a serving-man, thou wouldst have remained behind him, when a cavalier deserted."

"Dost thou accuse me of deserting the noble youth?" said Alvarado, fiercely. "God forbid I should shed Christian blood! but, with my sword's point, I will prove upon thy body that thou liest!"

"And upon thine," said De Morla, with calm indignation, "I will make good the charge I have uttered, that thou didst abandon, in extremity, when he called upon thee for aid, the man who had just preserved thine own life."

"Are there not deaths enow among the infidels," cried Cortes, angrily, "that ye must lust after one another's blood?—Peace! and be ye friends, lamenting our valiant companion together; for, De Morla, thou doest a wrong to Alvarado; and, Don Pedro, thou art a fool to quarrel with the peevishness of a mourning friend."

The secretary listened to the cavaliers with a face of horror; not a word said Lazaro, but as he wiped the foam from his steed, and, with it, the blood of his master, he eyed Don Pedro with a dark and vindictive scowl. As for Baltasar, his rugged features quivered, and he did not hesitate to stand in the way of the Tonatiuh, saying—"If any cavalier have, indeed, been false to my young lord, I, who am but a serving-man, will make bold to say, he has played false to a gentleman who would have perilled his life for any Christian in need! and the act, though it be answered to man, God will not forgive. Who will tell this to my master, Don Gabriel?"

Alvarado, extremely enraged, had raised his spear to strike the old soldier; but he dropped his arm at the last words, and said with great mildness—"Thou art a fool to say this. I lament thy lord; I loved him, and I did not desert him."

For the remainder of that day the garrison were left in peace. No foes appeared on the square; but, twice or thrice, when parties were sent out to reconnoitre, they were met, at a distance from the palace, by herds of Mexicans, and driven back to their quarters.

The desperate situation of the army was now evident to the dullest comprehension. The barbarians had removed from the reach of the artillery, and drawn, with their bodies, a line of circumvallation round their victims, patiently waiting for the moment when famine should bring them a secure vengeance. All day there were seen, on the top of the pyramid, priests and nobles, now engaged in some rite of devotion, and now looking down on the besieged, like vultures on their prey; but without attempting any annoyance.

The murmurs of the garrison, exasperated by despair and want of food, were loud and stern; but Don Hernan received them only with biting sarcasms. He bade those who were most mutinous to depart if they would; and laughed scornfully at their confessions of inability. To those who cried for food, he answered by pointing grimly to the stone walls, and the carcasses that lay on the square; or he counselled them to seek it among their foes. In truth, the general knew their helplessness, and in the bitterness of his heart at being thus foiled and jeoparded, he did not scruple to punish their discontent, by disclosing the full misery of their situation. They were dependent upon him for life and hope, and he suffered this dependence to be made apparent. He revealed to them no scheme of relief or escape; for, in fact, he had framed none. He was, himself, as desperate as the rest, seeing nothing befor him but destruction, and not knowing how to avoid it ; and what measures he did take, during these sorrowful hours, were rather expedients to divert his thoughts than plans to diminish the general distress

Notwithstanding the memorable fate of the burro, and the disinclination of the soldiers to die the death of its garrison, he obstinately commanded those which were unfinished to be completed, with some additional contrivances to increase their strength and mobility. He sent out parties to ransack the deserted houses in the vicinity, for provisions, though hopeless of obtaining any ; and he set the idlers to mending their armour of escaupil, and the smiths to making arrow-heads, as if still determined rather to fight than fly. He held no councils with his officers, for he knew they had no projects to advise ; and the desperate resort over which he pondered, of sallying out with his whole force, and cutting his way through the opposing foe, was two full of horror to be yet spoken. Moreover, while Montezuma yet lived, he could not think his situation entirely hopeless. The surgeon, upon a re-examination of the king's wounds, had formed a more favourable prognostic ; and this was strengthened, when Montezuma at last awoke from stupor, and recovered the possession of his intellects. It was told him, indeed, that the royal Indian, as if resuming his wits only to cast them away again, had no sooner become sensible of his condition, and remembered that his wounds had been inflicted by his people, than he fell into a frenzy of grief and despair, tearing away the bandages from his body, and calling upon his gods to receive him into Tlacocan, the place of caverns and rivers, where wandered those who died the death of the miserable. Don Hernan imagined that these transports would soon rave themselves away, and persuaded himself that his captive, yielding at last to the natural love of life, would yet remain in his hands, the hostage of safety, and perhaps the instrument of authority.

Sorrow dwelt in the palace of Axajacatl ; but her presence was more deeply acknowledged in the chamber of Calavar. From the lips of Baltasar— and the rude veteran wept, when he narrated the fall of the young cavalier, whom he had himself first taught the knowledge of arms—Don Gabriel learned the fate of his kinsman. But he neither wept like Baltasar, nor joined in the loud lamentations of Marco. His eyes dilated with wild expression, his lip fell, he drooped his head on his breast, and clasping his hands over his heart, muttered an unintelligible prayer—perhaps the ejaculation which so often and so piteously expressed his desolation. Then falling down upon his couch, and turning his face to the wall, he remained for the whole day and night without speaking a word.

CHAPTER XLVI.

The fate of Don Amador de Leste, though so darkly written in the hearts of his companions, was not yet brought to a close. Some of his late friends deemed only that he had been overpowered and slain ; but others, better acquainted with the customs of the foe, shuddered over the assurance of a death yet more awful. They knew that the pride of the Mexican warrior was, not to slay, but to

capture ; as if, indeed, these demi-barbarians made war less for the glory of taking life, than for the honour of offering it in sacrifice to the gods. Such, in truth, was the case ; and to this circumstance was it owing that the Christians were not utterly destroyed in any one encounter in the streets of Tenochtitlan. The fury of their foes was such as may be imagined in a people goaded to desperation by atrocious tyranny and insult, and fighting with foreign oppressors at their very firesides ; yet, notwithstanding the deadly feeling of vengeance at their hearts, they never forgot their duties to their faith ; and they forbore to kill, in the effort to take prisoner. Twice or thrice, at least, in the course of the war that followed after these events, the life of Cortes himself was in their hands ; and the thrust of a javelin, or the stroke of a bludgeon, would have freed them from the destroyer. But they neither struck nor thrust ; they strove to bear him off alive, as the most acceptable offering they could carry to the temple ; thus always giving his followers an opportunity to rescue him out of their grasp. Every captive thus seized and retained, died a death too terrible for description ; and high or low—the base boor and the noble hidalgo alike —expiated, on the stone of sacrifice, the wrongs done to the religion of Mexitli.

Knowing so much of the customs of Anahuac, and not having discovered his body, the more experienced cavaliers were convinced that Don Amador de Leste had not yet enjoyed the happiness of death they persuaded themselves that he had been taken alive, and was preserved for sacrifice. Many a Castilian eye, that afternoon, was cast upon the pyramid, watching the steps, and eagerly examining the persons of all who ascended. But no victim was seen borne upon their shoulders.

When the cavalier of Cuenza opened his eyes, after the stunning effects of the blow were over, it was in a confusion of mind, which the objects about him, or, perhaps, the accession of a hot fever—the result of many severe wounds and contusions—soon converted into delirium. He lay—his armour removed—on a couch, in a spacious apartment, but so darkened, that he could not distinguish the countenances of two or three dusky figures, which seemed to bend over him. His thoughts were still in the battle : and in these persons he perceived nothing less than Mexican warriors still clutching at his body. He started up, and calling out—" Ho, Fogoso , one leap more for thy master," caught fiercely at the nearest of the individuals. But he had overrated his strength ; and almost before a hand was laid upon him, he fell back, fainting, on the bed.

" Dost thou strike me, too, false villain ?" he again exclaimed, as his distempered eyes pictured, in one silent visage, the features of Abdalla. " Be thou accursed for thy ingratitude, and live in hell for ever."

A murmur of voices, followed by the sound of retreating steps, was heard ; and in the silence which ensued, his fancy became more disordered, presenting him phantasms still more peculiar—" Is this death?" he muttered, " and be I now in the world of shadows ? God be merciful to me a sinner ! Pity and pardon me, oh, Christ, for I have fought for thy faith ! Take me from this place of blackness, and let me look on the light of bliss !"

A gentle hand was laid upon his forehead, a low sigh breathed on his cheek ; and suddenly a light, flashing up as from some expiring cresset, revealed to his wondering eyes the face and figure of the mysterious prophetess. "Oh, God! art thou indeed a fiend? and dost thou lead me, from the land of infidels, to the prison-house of devils?" he cried, again starting up, clasping his hands and gazing wildly on the vision. "Speak to me, thou that livest not; for I know thou art Leila!"

As he uttered these incoherent words, the figure, bending a little away, and fastening upon his own, eyes of strange meaning, in which pity struggled with terror, seemed gradually to fade into the air; until, as suddenly as it flashed into brightness, the light vanished, and all was left in darkness.

From this moment, the thoughts of the cavalier wandered with tenfold wildness; and he fell into a delirium, which presented, as long as it lasted, a succession of exciting images. Now he struggled in the hall of his own castle of Alcornoque, or the Cork-tree, with the false Abdalla, the knee of the Almogavar on his breast, and the Arab poniard at his throat—while all the time, the perfidious Jacinto stood by, exhorting his father to strike; now he stood among burning sands, fighting with enraged fiends, over the dead body of his knight, Calavar, to protect the beloved corse from their fiery fingers; now the vanished Leila sat weeping by his side, dropping upon his fevered lips the juice of pleasant fruits, or now she came to him in the likeness of the Pagan Sibyl, beckoning him away, with melancholy smiles, to a distant bay; while ever, when he strove to rise and follow, the page Jacinto, converted into a giant, and brandishing a huge dagger, held him back with a lion's strength and ferocity

With such chimeras, and a thousand others, equally extravagant, disturbing his brain, he passed through many hours; and then as a torpor like that of death gradually stole over him, benumbing his deranged faculties, the same gentle hand, the same low suspiration, which had soothed him before, but without the countenance which had maddened, returned to him, and made pleasant the path to annihilation.

CHAPTER XLVII.

From a deep slumber, that seemed, indeed, death, for it was dreamless, the cavalier at last awoke, somewhat confused, but no longer delirious; and, though greatly enfeebled, entirely free from fever. A yellow sunbeam—the first or the last glimmering of day, he knew not which—played through a narrow casement, faintly illuminating the apartment, and falling especially upon a low table at his side, whereon, among painted and gilded vessels of strange form, he perceived his helmet and other pieces of armour, as well as a lute, of not less remembered workmanship. He raised his eyes to the attendant, who sat musing hard by, and with a thrill and exclamation of joy, beheld the Moorish page, Jacinto.

"Is it thou, indeed, my dear knave Jacinto! whom I thought in the maws of infidels?" he cried, starting up. "And how art thou? and how is thy lord, Don Gabriel, to-day? Tell me, where hast thou been these two troubled days? and how didst thou return? By my faith, this last bout was somewhat hard, and I have slept long!"

"Leave not thy couch, and speak not too loud, noble master," said the page, kneeling and kissing his hand—"for thou art sick and wounded, and here only art thou safe."

"Ay, now indeed!" said Don Amador, with a sudden and painful consciousness of his situation

"I remember me. I was struck down and made a prisoner. What good angel brought me into thy company? Thanks be to Heaven! for my hurts are not much; and I will rescue thee from captivity."

"I am not a captive, senor," said the boy, gently.

"Are we then in the palace? Where are our friends? Am I not a prisoner?"

"Senor, we are far from the palace of Axajacatl. But grieve not; for here thou art with thy servants."

"Thou speakest to me in riddles," said the novice, with a disturbed and bewildered countenance. "Have I been dreaming? Am I enchanted? Am I living, and in my senses?"

"The saints be praised, thou art indeed," said the page, fervently; "though, both nights and all day, till the blessed potion set thee asleep, I had no hopes thou wouldst recover."

"Both nights!" echoed Don Amador, fixing his eyes inquiringly on the boy; "has a night—have two nights passed over me, and wert thou, then, with me, during it all?—Ha! Was it thine acts of sorcery which brought me those strange and melancholy visions? Didst thou conjure up to me the image of Leila? That priestess, that very supernatural prophetess. By Heaven! as I see thee, so saw I her standing at my bed-side, in some magical light, which straightway turned to darkness. Didst thou not see her? Tell me, boy, art thou indeed an enchanter? Prepare me thy spells again—reveal me her fate, and let me look on the face of Leila!"

As the cavalier spoke, he strove in his eagerness to rise from the couch.

"Senor," said the page, a little pleasantly, "if thou wilt have me satisfy thy questions, thou must learn to acknowledge me as thy physician and jailer, and give me such obedience as thou wouldst formerly have claimed of me. Rise not up, speak not aloud, and give not way to the fancies of fever: for here are no priestesses, and no Leilas. I will sing to thee, that will content thee with bondage. But now thou must remain in quiet, and be healed of thy wounds."

"I tell thee, my boy Jacinto," went on the cavalier, "wounds or no wounds, jailed or not jailed, I am in a perplexity of mind, which, if thou art able, I must command, or, what is the same thing, beseech thee to remove. First, therefore, what house is this? and where is it? (whether on the isle Mexico, the lake side, the new world, or the old, or, indeed, in any part of the earth at all?) Secondly, how got'st thou into it? Thirdly, how came I hither myself?—and especially, what good Christian did snatch my body out of the paws of those roaring lions, the Mexicans, when I was hit that foul and assassin-like blow by—by—"

"Senor," said the page, not doubting but that his patron had paused for want of breath, "to answer all these questions is more than I am allowed. All that I can say is, that if prudent and obedient (I say obedient, noble and dear master," continued the boy, archly, "for now you are my prisoner), you are safer in this dungeon than are your Spanish friends in their fortress—reduced to captivity, indeed, but preserved from destruction—"

"By the false, traitorous, and most ungrateful knave Abdalla, thy father!" exclaimed the neophyte, with a loud and stern voice; for just as he had hesitated to wound the ears of the boy, he beheld, slowly stalking into the apartment, and eyeing him over Jacinto's shoulder, the Almogavar himself; and the epithets of indignation burst at once from his lips. Jacinto started back, alarmed; but Abdalla approached and regarding the wounded cavalier with an unmoved countenance, motioned the boy to retire. In an instant the Moor of Barbary and the Spaniard of Castile were left alone together.

"Shall I repeat my words, thou base and cut-throat infidel?" cried Don Amador, rising so far as to place his feet on the floor, though still sitting on the platform which supported his mattress, and speaking with the most cutting anger. "Was it not enough, that thou wert a renegade to the rest, but thou must raise thy Judas hand against thy benefactor?"

"My benefactor indeed!" said Abdoul calmly, and with the most musical utterance of his voice. "Though I wear the livery of the Pagans," (he had on an armed tunic, somewhat similar to that of Quauhtimotzin, though without a plume to his head, and looked not unlike to a Mexican warrior of high degree,) "and though I am, by birth, the natural enemy of thee and thine, yet have I not forgot that thou art my benefactor! I remember, that, when a brutal soldier struck me with his lance, thy hand was raised to protect me from the shame; I remember, when a thousand weapons were darting at my prostrate body on the pyramid of Zempoala, that thou didst not disdain to preserve me; I remember, that, when I fled from the anger of Don Hernan, thou offeredest me thine intercession. Senor, I have forgotten none of this; nor have I forgotten," he went on, with earnest gratitude, "that, to these favours, thou didst add the greater ones, of shielding my feeble child from stripes, from ruin, and perhaps from death. This have I not forgotten, this can I never forget! The name of Spaniard is a curse on my ears; I hate thy people, and when God gives me help, I will slay even to the last man! but I remember, that thou art my benefactor, and the benefactor of my child."

"And dost thou think," said the neophyte, "that these oily words will blind me to thy baseness? or that they can deceive me into belief, when the actions have so foully belied them? Cursed art thou, misbelieving Moor! an ingrate and apostate; and had I no cause, in mine own person, to know thy perfidy, it should be enough to blazon thy villany, that thou hast, on thine own confession, deserted the standard of Christ, and the arms of Spain, to enlist in the ranks of their Pagan foes!"

"The standard of Christ," said the Moor, with emphasis, "waves not over the heads of the Spaniards, but the banner of a fiend, bloody, unjust, and accursed, whom they call by his Holy name, and who bids them to defile and destroy; while the Redeemer proclaimeth only good-will and peace to all men. Have thy good heart and strong mind been so deluded? Canst thou, in truth, believe, that these oppressors of a harmless people, these slayers, who raise the cross of Heaven on the place of blood, and call to God for approval, when their hands are smoking with the blood of his creatures, are the followers of Christ the peaceful, Christ the just, Christ the holy? These friends whom thou hast followed, are not Christians; and God, whom they traduce and belie in all their actions, has given them over to the punishment of hypocrites and blasphemers, to sufferings miserable and unparalleled, to deaths dreadful and memorable! May it be accomplished—Amen!"

"Dost thou speak this to me, vile Almogavar! of my friends and countrymen? Dost thou curse them thus in my presence, most unworthy apostate?"

"Sorrowful be their doom, and quickly may it come upon them!" cried Abdalla, with ferocious fervour, "for what are they, that it should not be just? and what am I, that I should not pray that it

be accomplished? I remember the days of Granada! I remember the sack of the Alhambra! I remember the slaughter of the Alpujarras! and I have not forgotten the mourning exiles, driven from those green hills, to die among the sands of Africa, the clime of their fathers, but to them a land of strangers! I remember me how the lowly were given to the scourge, and the princely to the fires of Inquisitors—our children to spears, our wives to ravishers and murderers! Cursed be they that did these things, even to the last generation!"

The cavalier was amazed and confounded at the vehement and lofty indignation of the Morisco; and as the form of Abdoul-al-Sidi swelled with wrath, and his countenance darkened under the gloomy recollection, he seemed to Don Amador rather like one of those mountain princes, who had defied the conquerors, to the last, among the Alpujarras, than a poor herdsman of Fez, deriving his knowledge and his fury only from the incitations of exiles. His embarrassment was also increased by a secret consciousness, that the Moor had cause for his hate and his denunciations. He answered him, however, with a severe voice—"In these ills and sufferings thou hadst no part, unless thou hast lied to me; having been a child of the desert, afar from the sufferers of Granada."

"I lied to thee, then," said Abdalla, elevating his figure, and regarding the cavalier with proud tranquillity. "From the beginning to the end, was I a chief among the mourners and rebels—the first to strike, as I am now the last to curse the oppressor—a child of the desert, only when I had no more to suffer among the Alpujarras; and thou mayst know, now, that my fury is as deep as it is just—for the poor Abdalla is no Almogavar of Barbary, but a Zegri of Granada!"

"A Zegri of Granada!" cried Don Amador, with surprise.

"A Zegri of Granada, and a prince among Zegris!" said the Moor with a more stately look, though with a voice of the deepest sorrow; "one whose fathers have given kings to the Alhambra, but who hath lived to see his child a menial in the house of his foe, and both child and father leagued with and lost among the infidels of a strange land, in a world unknown!"

"I thought, by Heaven!" said the cavalier, eyeing the apostate with a look almost of respect, "that that courage of thine in the pirate rover did argue thee to be somewhat above the stamp of a common boor; and therefore, but more especially in regard of thy boy, did I give thee consideration myself, and enforce it, as well as I could, to be yielded by others. But, by the faith which thou professest, Sir Zegri, be thou ignoble or regal in thy condition, I have not forgotten that, by the blow which has made me (as it seems to me I am) thy prisoner, thou hast shown thyself unworthy of nobility; and I tell thee again, with disgust and indignation, that thou hast done the act of a base and most villanous caitiff."

"Dost thou still say so?" replied the Zegri, mildly. "I have acknowledged that no gratitude can repay thy benefactions; this do I still confess; and yet have I done all to requite thee. Thou lookest on me with amazement. What is my crime noble benefactor?"

"What is thy crime? Art thou bewitched, too? Slave of an ingrate, didst thou not, when I was already overpowered, smite me down with thine own weapon?"

"I did—Heaven be thanked!" said the Moor, devoutly

"Dost thou acknowledge it, and thank Heaven too?" said the incensed cavalier.

"I acknowledge it, and I thank Heaven!" said Abdalla, firmly. "Thou saidst thou wert already overpowered. Wert thou not in the hands of the Mexicans, beyond all hope of rescue?

"Doubtless I was," replied the neophyte; "for Cortes was afar, and Alvarado full three spears' length behind. Nevertheless, I did not despair of maintaining the fight until my friends came up to my relief."

"Thou wert a captive!" cried the Zegri, impetuously—"a living captive in the hands of Mexicans! Dost thou know the fate of a prisoner in such hands?"

"By my faith," said Don Amador, "I have heard that they put their prisoners to the torture.'

"They sacrifice them to the gods," cried the Moor. "And the death," he continued, his swarthy visage whitening with horror, " the death is of such torment and terror as thou canst not conceive; but I can, for I have seen it. Now hear me; I saw my benefactor a captive, and I knew his life would end on the stone of sacrifice, offered up, like that of a beast, to false and fiendish gods. I say I saw thee thus; I knew this would be thy doom; and I did all that my gratitude taught me to save thee. I struck thee down, knowing that if I slew thee, the blow would be that of a true friend, and that thou shouldst die like a soldier, not like a fatted sheep. Heaven, however, gave me all that I had dared to hope: I harmed thee not; and yet the Mexicans believed that death had robbed them of a victim. I harmed thee not; and the heathens suffered me to drag away what seemed a corse, but which lived, and was my benefactor—the saviour of myself and the protector of my child."

As Abdalla concluded these words, spoken with much emphasis and feeling, a tear glistened in his eye, and the neophyte, starting up and eagerly grasping his hand, exclaimed—"Now, by Heaven! I see all the wisdom and truth of thy friendship; and I beg thy pardon for whatever insulting words my folly has caused me to speak. And now that I know the blow was struck for such a purpose, I confess to thee, as thou saidst thyself, it would have been true gratitude and love though it had killed me outright."

"I have done thee even more service than this," said the Zegri, calmly: "but before I speak it I must demand of thee, as a Christian and honourable soldier, to confess thyself my just and true captive."

"Thy captive!" cried Don Amador. "Dost thou hold me then as a prisoner, and not as a guest and friend? Dost thou check my thankfulness in the bud, and cancel thy services, by making me thy thrall?"

"I will not answer thy demands," said Abdalla." "I call upon thee, as a noble and knightly soldier, fairly captured in open war by my hands, to acknowledge thyself my captive; and, as such, in all things, justly at my disposition."

"If thou dost exact it of me," said the cavalier, regarding him with much surprise and sorrow, "I must, as a man of honour, so acknowledge myself. But I began to think better of thee, Abdalla.'

"And, as a prisoner, to whose honour is confided the charge of his own keeping, thou engagest to remain in captivity, without abusing the confidence which allows such license, by any efforts to escape?"

"Dost thou demand this much of me?" said Don Amador, with mortified and dejected looks. "If thou art thyself resolved to remain in the indulgence of thy treason thou surely wilt not think to keep

me from my friends in their difficulties, and especially from my poor kinsman, who is now greatly disordered, and chiefly, I think, because thou hast robbed him of Jacinto '

"This I am not called upon to answer," said Abdalla, gravely. "I only demand of thee, what thou knowest thou canst not honourably refuse—thy knightly gage, to observe the rules of captivity, until such time as I may think proper to absolve and free thee."

"Sir Almogavar, or Sir Zegri, or whatsoever thou art," said the cavalier, folding his arms, and surveying his jailer sternly, "use the powers which thou hast—thy chains and thy magical arts, for I believe thou dealest with the devil—get me ready thy fetters and thy dungeon. Thou hast the right so to use me, and I consent to the same; but I will gage thee no word to keep in bonds, inglorious and at ease, while my friends are in peril. However great the service thou hast done to me, I perceive thou art a traitor. I command thee, therefore, that thou have me chained and immured forthwith; for, with God's will and help, I will escape from thee as soon as possible, and especially whensoever my friends come to assist me."

"I grant thee this privilege, when thy friends come near to us," said Abdalla, coolly, "whether thou art chained or not. It is not possible thou canst escape, otherwise, at all. Thou art far from the palace, ignorant of the way, and, besides, divided from it by a wall of Mexicans, who cannot be numbered. What I ask thee is for thy good, and for the good of myself and Jacinto. If thou leave this house thou wilt be immediately seized, and carried to the stone of sacrifice.'

Don Amador shuddered, but said—"I trust in God! and the thought of this fate shall not deter me."

"Go, then, if thou wilt," said the Zegri, haughtily. "The service I have done thee has not yet released me from thy debt; and thou canst yet command me. Begone, if thou art resolute: the door is open; I oppose thee not. Preserve thy life, if thou canst; and, when thou art safe at the garrison, remember that Abdoul-al-Sidi and the boy Jacinto have taken thy place on the altar of victims."

"What dost thou mean? I understand thee not. What meanest thou?"

"Even that thou canst not escape without the same being made known to the Mexicans; and that it cannot be made known to this vindictive people that I have robbed them of their prey without the penalty of my own life, and that of Jacinto, being immediately executed. When thou fliest the father and the son perish.'

"Dost thou speak me this in good faith?" said the cavalier, greatly troubled. "God forbid I should bring harm to thee, and especially to the boy. If I give thee my gage thou wilt not hold me bound to refrain from joining my friends, should I be so fortunate as to see them pass by, and am persuaded the Mexicans will not discover thou hast harboured me?"

"If they pass by, I will myself open the doors," said Abdalla; "for I protest to thee, I keep thee here only to ensure thy security."

"Hark'ee, Sir Moor—Don Hernan is about to retreat. Dost thou intend I shall remain in captivity—a single victim among the barbarians—while my countrymen are flying afar, perhaps returning to Christendom?"

"I swear to thee, senor," said the Zegri, earnestly "that when the Spaniards fly from this city thou shalt be free to fly with them. I repeat, I make thee a prisoner to prevent thy becoming a victim."

"And what hinders that we do not fly together to the palace? Thy knowledge may conduct us through the streets by night; and, with my head, I will engage thee a free pardon and friendly reception."

"God hath commissioned me to the work, and it shall go on," said the Moor, with solemn emphasis. "I know that thou couldst not save me from the fury of Don Hernan: he would grant thee my life at midnight, and, on the morrow, thou wouldst find me dead in the court-yard. Fly if thou wilt, and leave me to perish by the hands of Mexicans: Spaniards shall drink my blood no more."

"I give thee my gage, said the cavalier, "with this understanding, then, that I am free to fly, whenever I may do so without perilling thy life and the life of Jacinto."

"And thou wilt hold to this pledge, like a true cavalier?" demanded Abdalla, quickly.

"Surely I cannot break my plighted word."

"God be thanked!" cried the Zegri, grasping the hand of the cavalier, "for, by this promise, thou hast saved thy life. Remain here; Jacinto shall be thy jailer, thy companion, thy servant. Be content with thy lot, and thank God: for thou art the only brand plucked out of the burning, while all the rest shall perish. God be praised! I save my benefactor."

With these exclamations of satisfaction, Abdalla departed from the chamber.

CHAPTER XLVIII.

The cavalier pondered in perplexity over the words of Abdalla; and, the longer he reflected, the more he began to lament his captivity, and doubt the wisdom of his gage. "It is apparent to me," he soliloquised, "that my countrymen are in greater jeopardy than I before apprehended, and that it has been the plot of this subtle Moor (whom I confess, however, to have something elevated and noble in his way of thinking, and much gratitude of heart, though of a mistaken character), to keep me out of harm's way, while the Mexicans are murdering my companions. Heaven forgive me my rash parole, if this be true; for such safety becomes dishonour and ignominy. I will talk with him further on the subject; and if I find he hath thus schemed to preserve me at such a price of degradation, I will straightway revoke my engagement, as being wrung from me by deceit, and quite impossible to be fulfilled. I marvel where loiters the boy Jacinto? Methinks I could eat something now, for I know not how long it is since I have tasted food—an orange or a bunch of grapes were not amiss. But Heaven save me! I have heard oranges do not grow in this land; and perhaps these poor Moriscos are no better off than my friends at the palace. God help them! for the Mexicans fight like Turks; and once or twice that evening of the conflagration, I thought I had got me again into the trenches of Rhodes; and as for those knaves that wounded me, never did I see more valiant devils. I am glad I left my knight so possessed of his wits. That Botello doth seem very clearly to have apprehended my fate, though the mishap be not so miserable as death. Truly, there did, a third time, war come out of peace; and yet, I assure myself, that this time it was brought about by Don Hernan rushing against that supernatural creature, that looks on me in the street, and eyes me even by my bed-side."

The cavalier was startled from his reverie by a light step, and as the curtain was drawn aside from the door, he almost thought, for an instant, that he beheld the visage of the priestess peering through its folds. A second glance, however, showed him the features of the Moorish page, who came in, bearing a little basket of fruits and Indian confections, as if anticipating his wants. These Jacinto placed before him, and then sat down at his feet.

For a few moments Don Amador, in the satisfaction of the boy's presence, forgot many of his perplexities; but observing, at last, that Jacinto's smiles were ever alternating with looks of distress and alarm, and that, sometimes, he surveyed his imprisoned master with eyes of great wildness, the cavalier began again to recur to his condition, to the mysteries which surrounded him, and especially to the suspicions which so often attributed to the page the possession of magical arts.

"Thou saidst, Jacinto," he abruptly exclaimed, after thrusting aside the almost untasted food, and regarding the boy with a penetrating look, "that thou wert for the two last nights at my bed-side? God be good to me! for 'tis an evil thing to be benighted so long."

"Senor, I was."

"And, during all that time, I was entirely dispossessed of my wits?"

"Senor mio, yes. But now, Heaven be thanked, your honour will recover."

"And thou art sure I did not labour more under enchantment than fever?"

The page smiled, but very faintly, and without replying

"To me it seems no longer possible to doubt," said the cavalier, "that I have been divers times, of late, entirely bewitched; and that thou hast had some agency in my delusions."

Jacinto smiled more pleasantly, and seemed to forget the secret thoughts which had agitated him.

"Dost thou," demanded the cavalier, "know aught of a certain supernatural priestess, that goes about the streets of this town, in Pagan processions, followed by countless herds of nobles and warriors?"

The page hesitated while replying—"I have indeed heard of such a creature, and—I may say—I have seen her."

"Thou hast seen her! Is she mortal?"

"Surely I think so, noble senor," replied Jacinto, with increasing embarrassment.

"For my part," said the novice, with a deep sigh and a troubled aspect, "I am almost quite convinced that she is a spectre, and an inhabitant of hell, sent forth upon earth to punish me with much affliction, and, perhaps, with madness. For I think she is the spirit of Leila; and her appearance in the guise of a Pagan goddess or a Pagan priestess—the one or the other, shows me that she whom I loved dwells not with angels but with devils. This is a thought," continued the cavalier, mournfully, "that burns my heart as with a coal; and if God spare my life, and return me to mine own land, I will devote my estates to buy masses for her soul; for surely she cannot have fallen from sin into irreparable woe, but only into a punishment for some heresy, the fault of bad instruction, which may be expiated."

Jacinto regarded the distressed visage of his patron with concern and with indecision, as if impelled, and yet afraid, to speak what might remove his anguish. Then, at last, moved by affection, and looking up with arch confidence to Don Amador, he said—

"Senor, I can relieve you of this unhappiness. This is no spirit, but a woman, as I know full well, for I am in the secret. I am not sure that it will not offend my father, to divulge such a secret to any Spaniard: yet can its revealmen tprejudice none. Know, senor, and use not this confession to my father's injury, that all this interlude of the prophetess, devised by the Mexican nobles and priests, with my father's counsel and aid, is a scheme to inflame the people with fresh devotion and fury against the Spaniards, your countrymen. For, being very superstitious and credulous, the common people are easily persuaded that their gods have sent them a messenger, to encourage and observe their valour; as, it is fabled, they have done in former days. The prophetess is but a puppet in their hands."

The cavalier eyed the young speaker steadfastly, until Jacinto cast his looks to the earth. "Set this woman before me; let me look upon her," he said, gravely, and yet with earnestness.

The page returned his gaze with one of confusion, and even affright.

"Thou wilt not think to deceive me," continued his patron, "after confiding to me so much? Know thou, that it will rejoice me, relieving my mind of many pangs, to find that thy words are true, and to look upon this most beauteous, and, to my eyes, most supernatural barbarian. If she be a living creature, thou hast it in thy power to produce her, for she dwells in this house. I say this, Jacinto, on strong persuasion of the fact, for last night I beheld her, and did almost touch her."

"Senor," said the boy, briskly, "that was one of the fancies of thy delirium. It was my poor self thou wert looking on. Twenty times or more didst thou call to me, as being the prophetess; and as often didst thou see in me some other strange creature. Now, I was my lord, Don Gabriel, your worship's kinsman; now, some lady that your honour loved; now, an angel, bringing you succour in battle; now, my lord's little brother; now, his enemy; and, twice or thrice, I was my own poor self, only that I was killing my lord with a dagger—as if I could do any wrong to my master."

"Is this the truth, indeed?" said the cavalier, dolorously. "I could have sworn that I saw that woman, and that I was very sane when I saw her. As for the after-visions, I can well believe that they were the phantasms of fever, being very extravagant, and but vaguely remembered. Thou deniest, then, that thou hast the power of casting spells?"

The page smiled merrily, for he perceived his patron was relieved of one irrational distress, and banteringly replied—"I will not say that—I can do many things my lord would not think—and I know many he would not dream."

The cavalier was too sad and too simple-minded to jest.

"I believe thee," he said, seriously; "for, in every thing thou art a miracle and mystery. Why is it that thou hast obtained such a command over my affections? Why is it that I have come to regard thee, not as a boy, young and foolish, but as one ripe in years and wisdom? It must needs be, because thou derivest thy power and thy knowledge from those astral and magical arts, which I once esteemed so vain; for I remember me, that at thy years I was myself not half so much advanced in intelligence and art, but was, on the contrary, quite a dull and foolish boy."

"It all comes of my music," said the page: "for that is a talent which matures faster than any other, and drags others along with it; besides giving one

great skill in touching hearts. Your worship remembers how soon young David gained the love of the Jewish king, and how he would have cured him of his melancholy, but that Saul had a bad heart. Now, my lord seems to me to have, like this king, an evil spirit troubling him; and perhaps, if he will let me, I can sing it away with the ballad of the Knight and the Page; for my lord's heart is good."

"The Knight and the Page? I have never heard thee sing that," said Don Amador, somewhat indifferently. "What is it about?"

"It is about a brave cavalier, that loved a noble lady, who loved him; but being made to believe her false to her vows, he went to the wars to die, followed by a little page, whom he thought the only true friend he had left in the world."

"By my faith," said Don Amador, regarding the boy kindly, "in this respect methinks I am, at present, somewhat like that knight; for thou that art, likewise, a little page, seemest to be the only friend I have left in the world—that is in this city—that is to say, in this part of it; for I have much confidence in the love several at the palace, notwithstanding that I think some others were a little backward in supporting me, when beset that evil day by the barbarians. Was he a Spanish knight? and of what parts?"

"Of the Sierra Morena, at some place where the Jucar washes its foot."

"In good truth," cried the cavalier, "that is the very river that rolls by Cuenza; and herein again is there another parallel. But I should inform thee, that when the mountain reaches so far up as the Jucar, and runs up along its course, it is then called the Sierra of Cuenza, and not Morena. But this is a small matter. I shall be as glad to hear of the Knight of Jucar as of one of my ancestors."

"He resembled my lord still more," said the page, "for he had fallen, fighting the infidel, very grievously wounded; and his little page remained at his side to share his fate."

"That I have in a manner fallen, and, as I may say, fighting the infidel, is true; but by no means can it be said that I am grievously wounded. These cuts that I have on my body are but scratches as one might make with a thorn; and, were it not for my head, which doth ever and anon ring like to a bell, and ache somewhat immoderately, I should think myself well able to go out fighting again; not at all regarding my feebleness, which is not much, and my stiff joints, which a little exercise would greatly reduce into suppleness."

"It was the resemblance of my lord's situation to the Knight of Jucar's that reminded me of the roundelay," said Jacinto, taking up his lute, and stringing it into accord; "and now your worship shall represent the wounded knight, and I the young page that followed him. But your worship should suppose me, instead of being a boy, to be a woman in disguise."

"A woman in disguise!" said the cavalier: "is the page, then, the false mistress? There should be very good cause to put a woman in disguise; for, besides that it robs her, to appearance, if not absolutely, of the natural delicacy of her sex, it forces her to be a hypocrite. A deceitful woman is still more odious than a double-faced man."

"But this lady had great cause," said Jacinto, "seeing that love and sorrow together forced her into the henchman's habit, as my lord will presently see."

So saying, with a pleasant smile, the minstrel struck the lute and sang the following little

ROMANCE OF THE KNIGHT AND THE PAGE.

A Christian knight in the Paynim land,
　Lay bleeding on the plain;
The fight was done, and the field was won,
　But not by the Christian train:
The cross had vail'd to the crescent,
　The Moorish shouts rose high—
'Lelilee! Lelilee!'—but the Christian knight
　Sent up a sadder cry.
"My castle lies on Morena's top,
　Jucar is far away:—
My lady will rue for her vows untrue,
　But God be good for aye!—
Young page! thou followest well;
　These dog-howls heed not thou."—
'Lelilee! Lelilee!'—
"Get thee hence to my lady now.
Tell her this blood, that pours a flood,
　My heart's true faith doth prove—
My corse to earth, my sighs to thee—
　My heart to my lady love."

The page he knelt at the Christian's side,
　And sorely sobb'd he then.
"The faithless love can truer prove
　Than hosts of faithful men.
The cross has vail'd to the crescent,
　The Moorish shouts are high"—
'Lelilee! Lelilee!'—"but the love untrue
　Hath yet another cry.
Thy castle lies on Morena's top,
　Jucar is far away;
But dies the bride at her true lord's side—
　Now God be good for aye!
The page that followeth well,
　Repeats the unbroken vow'—
'Lelilee! Lelilee!'
"Oh, look on thy lady now!
For now this blood, that pours a flood,
　Doth show her true love's plight.
My soul to God, my blood to thine—
　My life for my dying knight."

"Is that all?" said the cavalier, when Jacinto had warbled out the last line. "There should have been another stanza, to explain what was the cause of separation, as well as how it happened that the lady came to follow the knight as a servant; neither of which circumstances is very manifest."

"Senor," said Jacinto, "if all the story had been told, it would have made a book. It is clear, that an evil destiny separated the pair, and that love sent the lady after her lord."

"Be thou a conjurer or not," said Don Amador, musingly, "thou hast the knack ever to hit upon subjects, as well in thy songs as in thy stories, which both provoke my curiosity and revive my melancholy. My castle, as I may say, doth 'lie on Morena's top,' that is to say, on the ridge of Cuenza; and Jucar is, indeed, 'far away;' but Heaven hath left me no lady-love, either to die with me among the infidels, by whom I am made to bleed, or to lament me at home. An evil destiny (how evil I know not, and yet do I dread, more dark than that which prevails with a jealous heart), hath separated me from one whom I loved, and, doubtless, separated me for ever." The cavalier sighed deeply, bent his eyes for a moment on the ground, and then raising them, with a solemn look on the page, said, abruptly, "I have come to

be persuaded, altogether beyond the contradiction of my reason, that thou hast somehow, and, perhaps, by magical arts, obtained a knowledge of the history of my past life. If thou knowest aught of the fate of Leila, the lamented maid of Almeria, I adjure thee to reveal thy knowledge, and without delay. Thou shakest thy head. Wherefore didst thou refuse to finish the story of her who bore her name, and who dwelt in the same city?"

"My lord will be angry with me," said the page, rising in some perturbation; "I have deceived him."

"I am sorry to know thou couldst be, in any way, guilty of deceit, though I do readily forgive thee; charging thee, however, at all times, to remember, that any deceitfulness is but a form of mendacity, and therefore as mean and degrading as it is sinful. In what hast thou deceived me?"

"When I told my lord the story of Leila, and perceived how it disturbed him," said Jacinto, with a faltering voice, "I repented me, and told him a thing that was not true, to appease him. The Leila of whom I spoke had dwelt in Almeria within a year past; and, perhaps, she was the maid that my lord remembered."

As the page made his confession, Don Amador sprang eagerly to his feet, and, as he seized the speaker's arm, cried, with much agitation—"Dost thou tell me the truth? and does she live? God be praised for ever! doth the maiden live?"

"She lived, when my father brought me from Barbary."

"Heaven be thanked! I will ransom her from the infidels, though I give myself up to captivity as the price!"

"Senor," said the page, sorrowfully, "you forget that you are now a prisoner in another world."

The cavalier smote his breast, crying—"It is true! and the revealment comes too late! Silly boy!" he continued, reproachfully, "why didst thou delay telling me this, until this time, when it can only add to my griefs? Why didst thou not speak it at Tlascala, that I might have departed forthwith from the land, to her rescue?"

"My lord would not have deserted his kinsman, Don Gabriel?"

"True again!" exclaimed Don Amador, with a pang. "I could not have left my knight, even at the call of Leila. But now will I go to Don Gabriel, and, confessing to him my sorrow, will prevail upon him straightway to depart with me; for here, it must be plain to him, as it is to me, that God is not with us."

"Alas! senor," said the page, "it is not possible that you should go to Don Gabriel, nor that you should ever more leave this heathen land."

"Dost thou confess, then," demanded the novice, "that Abdalla has deceived me, and that I am held to perpetual captivity?"

"Senor," said the boy, clasping his hands, and weeping bitterly, "we shall never more see Spain, nor any land but this. The fate of Don Hernan, and of all his men, is written; they are in a net from which they cannot escape; and we who are spared obtain our lives only at the price of expatriation. My father remembered his protector—my lord is saved; but he shares our exile!"

At this confirmation of his worst suspicions, the countenance of Don Amador darkened with despair and horror.

"And Abdalla, thy father, has plotted this foul, traitorous, and most bloody catastrophe? And he thinks that, for my life's sake, I will divide with him the dishonour and guilt of my preservation?"

"My lord knows not the wrongs of my father," said Jacinto, mournfully, "or he would not speak of him so harshly."

"Thy father is a most traitor-like and backsliding villain," said Don Amador, "and this baseness in him should entirely cancel in thee the bonds of affection and duty; for thou art not of his nature. Hark thee, then, boy: it is my purpose straightway to depart from this house, and this durance. I desire to save thee from the fate of a Pagan's slave. Better will it be for thee, if thou shouldst die with me, in the attempt to reach the palace (and I swear to thee, I will protect thee to the last moment of my life), than remain in Tenochtitlan, after thy Christian friends have left it, or after they are slain. It is my hope, and, indeed, my belief, that when the valiant general, Don Hernan, comes to be persuaded of his true condition, he will immediately, and at any cost, cut his way out of this most accursed city. In this manner will we escape, and thou shalt find in me a father who will love thee not less truly, and more in fashion of a Christian, than the apostate Zegri."

"If my lord could but protect my father from the anger of Don Hernan, and prevail upon him to return with my lord!" said Jacinto, eagerly.

"I have already proposed this to him, and, in his fury, he denies me."

"Heaven help us then!" cried Jacinto, "for there is no other hope; and we must dwell with the barbarians!"

"Dost thou think that I will rest here, when they are murdering Don Gabriel? Hark thee! what knave has stolen away my sword? Know, that I will straightway make my escape, and carry thee along with me; for God would not forgive me, did I leave thee abandoned to barbarians, to the eternal loss and perdition of thy soul. I say to thee again, thou shalt accompany me."

"I will remain with my father!" said the boy, stepping back, and assuming some of that dignity and decision, which the neophyte had so lately witnessed in Abdalla; "and so will my lord likewise; for my lord has given him a pledge, which he cannot forfeit."

"Miserable wretch that I am!" said the cavalier;—"in either case, I am overwhelmed with dishonour. My gage was sinful, and the infraction of it will be shame. Bring me hither Abdalla; I will revoke my promise to him in person; and, after that, I can depart without disgrace."

"Thou canst not escape, without shedding blood, at least," said the boy, with a pale and yet determined countenance, "for, first, thou must slay my father, who saved thee from the death of sacrifice. If thou goest in his absence, then must my lord strike down the son; for with what strength I have, I will prevent him!"

The amazement with which the war-like cavalier heard these words, and beheld the stripling throw himself manfully before the door of the apartment, entirely disconcerted him for a moment. Before he could find words to express his anger, or perhaps derision, the page, with a sudden revulsion of feeling, ran from the door, and flinging himself at his patron's feet, embraced his knees, weeping and exclaiming, with much passion—"Oh, my dear master! be not incensed with me;

for I am but weak and silly, and I have no friends but my father and thee! If thou takest me from my father, then shall he be left childless, to live and to die alone; if thou goest without us, we shall be deserted to perish without a friend; for no one has smiled on us but my lord; and if thou goest while my father is absent, he will curse me, and I will curse myself—for thou must needs die in the streets!"

The novice was touched, not so much by the last and undeniable assurance, as by the pathetic appeal of the Morisco.

"Be comforted, Jacinto," he cried; "for now, indeed, it appears to me, that, whether I had passed my gage or not, I could not take advantage of the weakness of such a jailer, and fly, without the greatest shame. And, in addition, it seems to me inhuman and unjust, that I should think of escaping, without doing my best to snatch thee and thy father also (whose sinfulness does, in this case, at least, spring from affection), out of thraldom. Be thou therefore content: I will remain thy patient prisoner, until such time as Abdalla returns; hoping that I can, then, advance such remonstrance and argument as shall convert him from his purpose, and cause him to repent what wrongs he has already done Don Hernan, and to accept his mercy, which I do again avow myself ready to secure with my life, and even with my honour. But I warn thee, that I can by no means remain captive, while my friends are given up to destruction."

"Senor," said Jacinto, rising, "there is a hope they will be spared, if the king should recover; for greatly have the Mexicans mourned the rage which wounded their monarch. If he live, and again command peace, there will be peace; and all of us may yet be happy."

"God grant that this may be so!" said the cavalier, catching at the hope. "I will therefore remain with thee a little; for if my friends be not starved outright, I have no fear but they can easily maintain themselves a week in the palace."

"And beside, senor," said the page, returning to his playful manner, "if you were to leave me, how should you hear more of the maid of Almeria?"

"Of Leila?" cried the cavalier, forgetting at once his honour and his friends; "now do I remember me, that you have not yet told me how you acquired your most blessed and blissful knowledge. Heaven forgive me! I did not think it possible—but, I believe, I had entirely forgotten her! How comest thou to know aught of her? Answer me quickly, and be still more quick to tell me all you know."

"Will not my lord be satisfied with my knowledge, without seeking after the means of acquiring it?" demanded the page hesitatingly.

"If, indeed," said Don Amador, solemnly, "thou hast obtained it by the practice of that kind of magic which is forbidden, though my curiosity will not permit me to eschew its revelations, yet must I caution thee, from this time henceforth, to employ it no more; for herein dost thou peril thy soul. But, if it be by those arts which are not in themselves sinful, thou shouldst not be ashamed to confess them; for the habit of concealment is the first step in the path of deception; and I have already assured thee, that a deceiver is, as one may say, a life in the face of his Maker. But of this I will instruct thee more fully hereafter: at present, I burn with an unconquerable desire to hear thee speak of Leila."

"But how know I," said the page, again hesitating, "that she of whom I speak is the Leila after whom it pleases my lord to inquire? And why indeed, now that I think of it, should my lord inquire at all after one of a persecuted and despised race?"

"Wilt thou still torment me? Have I not told thee that I forgot her origin, and loved her?"

"And did she love my lord back again?"

"Thou askest what I cannot with certainty answer," replied the cavalier, "for she was snatched away from me, before I had yet overcome the natural scruples of my pride, to discourse of love to one who seemed so much beneath the dignity of my birth and fortunes."

"And my lord gave her no cause to think she had obtained favour in his eyes?"

"In this thou dost not err; for, saving some gifts, which were, indeed, more the boons of a patron than the tribute of a lover, I did nothing to address me to her affection. In all things, as I may say, I did rather assume the character of one who would befriend and protect her from wrong, than of a man seeking after her love."

"But if she accepted my lord's gifts, she must have loved him," said Jacinto.

"They were very trifles," rejoined the cavalier, "saving only one indeed, which, as she must have perceived, could not have been more properly bestowed than upon one so innocent and friendless as herself. This was a very antique and blessed jewel—a cross of rubies—fetched by mine ancestor, Don Rodrigo of Arragon, more than three hundred years ago, from the Holy Land, after having been consecrated upon the sepulchre itself. It was thought to be a talisman of such heavenly efficacy in the hands of an unspotted virgin, that no harm could ever come to her who wore it upon her neck. For mine own part, though I could tell thee divers stories of its virtue, recorded in our house, yet was I ever inclined to think, that a natural purity of heart was, in all cases, a much better protection of innocence than even a holy talisman. Nevertheless, when I beheld this orphan Moor, I bethought me of the imputed virtues of those rubies; and I put them upon her neck, as thinking her friendless condition gave her the strongest claim to all such blessed protection."

"A cross of rubies!" cried the page: "it is she!"

"And thou canst tell me of her resting-place? and of her present condition?" cried the overjoyed cavalier. "I remember that, at the temple of Tlascala, thou didst aver, that, notwithstanding the apparent baseness of her origin, it had been discovered that she was descended of very noble parentage!"

"What I can tell thee, and what I will," said Jacinto, gravely, "will depend upon thine own actions. If thou leavest this place without my father's consent, hope not that thou shalt know any thing more than has been spoken. If thou art content to remain a little time in captivity, and to yield me the obedience which I demand, thou shalt find that a child of a contemned race may possess wisdom unknown to men of happier degrees. Thou hast acknowledged thyself the captive of my father; wilt thou promise obedience to me?"

Don Amador surveyed the boy with a bewildered stare—"Is it possible," said he, "that I am yet dreaming? for it seemeth to me very absurd, that thou, who art a boy, and wert but yesterday a servant, shouldst make such a demand of subjection to a man and a cavalier, and, as I may say, also thy master."

"My lord will not think I would have him become a servant," said Jacinto. "The subjection I require is for the purpose of securing him that gratification of his curiosity, which he has sought—and thus only can he obtain it. In all other respects, I remain myself the slave of my lord."

"Provided thou wilt demand me nothing dishonourable nor irreligious (and now that I know, from thy father's confession, that thou art of noble descent, I can scarcely apprehend in thee any meanness), I will make thee such a promise," said Don Amador. "But I must beseech thee not to torment me with delay."

"My lord shall not repent his goodness," said the page, with a happy countenance; "for when he thinks not of it, his wishes shall be gratified. But, at the present let him be at peace, and sleep; for the time has not yet come. I claim, now, the first proof of my lord's obedience. Let him eat of this medicinal confection, and, by a little rest, dispel the heats of fever, which are again returning to him."

"I declare to thee," said Don Amador, "I am very well; and this fever is caused by suspense, and not disease."

"Thou must obey," said the page. "While thou art sleeping, I will inquire for thee the fate of Leila; for it is yet wrapped in darkness, and it cannot be discovered but by great efforts."

The cavalier obeyed the injunctions of his young jailer, ate of the confection, and, Jacinto leaving the apartment, he yielded to exhaustion and drowsiness, and notwithstanding his eager and tormenting curiosity, soon fell fast asleep.

CHAPTER XLIX.

Gloom and fear still beset the garrison at the palace of Axajacatl; and the mutiny of soldiers, and fierce feuds among the cavaliers, were added to other circumstances of distress. Those ancient veterans, who had followed Don Hernan from the first day of invasion, and who had shared with him so many privations and perils, were, in general, still true to their oaths of obedience, and preserved, through all trials, an apparent, if not a firm reliance on the wisdom of their leader. But the followers of Narvaez, uninured to combat, and but lately acquainted with suffering—their sanguine expectations of conquest without danger, and of wealth without labour, changed to a mere hope of disgraceful escape, and that hope, as they all felt, founded, not in reason, but imagination—turned their murmurs into the most bitter execrations, and these again into menaces. The officers, too, rendered peevish by discontent, and reckoning each the discomfiture of his neighbour as the evidence of feebleness or fear, spoke to one another with sarcasms, and even sometimes to Don Hernan himself with disrespect. The self-command of the general, however, never deserted him; he rebuked insult with tranquil indignation and so far prevailed over his fiery subordinates as to compose most of their quarrels, without suffering them to be submitted to the ordeal of honour. One feud had arisen, nevertheless, which his skill could not allay; and all that he could effect by remonstrance, and even supplication, was an agreement of the parties to postpone its final arbitrement, until such time as the providence of Heaven should conduct them afar from Tenochtitlan. The wrath engendered in the bosom of the Tonatiuh, by the angry reproaches of De Morla, after their return from the battle of the Manta, had been inflamed by a new circumstance, which, though of a trivial nature, the pride of Alvarado and the resentment of his opponent had converted into an affair of importance.

There was among the many kinswomen of Montezuma, who shared his captivity (for the policy of the general had reduced nearly all the royal blood to bonds), a certain young maiden, a daughter of the lord of Colhuacan, and therefore a niece of the king; who, in the general partition which the nobler of the cavaliers had, in prospective, made of the Indian princesses, had fallen to the lot of Alvarado. In those days of legitimacy, there was some degree of divinity allowed to hedge the person of even a barbaric monarch; and happy was the hidalgo, who, by obtaining a royal maid for his wife, could rank himself, in imaginary dignity, with the princes of Christendom. At the present moment, the companions of Cortes had rather made their selections, than endeavoured to commend themselves to the favour of their mistresses;—dropping thereby so much of their reverence for royalty, as not to suppose the existence of any will, or opposition, in the objects of their desire. The Donna Engracia (her native title has entirely escaped the historians) was therefore beloved by Don Pedro; but not having been made acquainted with the hidalgo's flame, she stooped, at the first promptings of affection, to a destiny less brilliant and lofty. Her heart melted at the handsome visage of the young Fabueno; and the secretary, flattered by the love of so noble a maiden, and emboldened by his success in arms, did not scruple to become the rival of the Tonatiuh. The rage of Don Pedro would have chastised, in blood, the presumption of such a competitor; but De Morla, remembering the novice, did not hesitate, for his sake, to befriend his servant; and, when he avowed himself the champion of Lorenzo, he dreamed that he was about to avenge the fall of his brother-in-arms.

The result of this opposition to the humours of Alvarado, was a quarrel, so fierce and unappeasable, that, as had been said, all which the general could effect was a postponement of conflict; and when Don Pedro surrendered the princess to her plebeian lover, it was with the assurance, that, as soon as the army had left the city and lake, he should reckon her ransom out of the life-blood of his companion.

The discovery of the unfaithfulness of his betrothed (for, in this light did the cavaliers regard the captive princesses) had been made the preceding evening; and the angry contest of the cavaliers, and the arrangements of combat, occurred at the moment while Don Amador was lamenting the backwardness of his friends to support him, when he became a captive.

To allay the heart-burnings of his officers, who had arrayed themselves, according to their friendships, on either side, the general caused his trumpets to sound, and bade them all to prepare for an expedition of peril. He had, all along, eyed the great pyramid, frowning over his fortress, with peculiar anxiety. This was caused, in part, by the consciousness of the advantage it would give his enemies, as soon as they should dare to profane its sanctity, by making it the theatre of conflict. This very morning it was made apparent, by the presence of many barbarians thronging up its sides, and by an occasional arrow or stone discharged from its top, that the Mexicans were aware of its usefulness. In addition to this cause for attempting to gain possession of it, the leader was moved by a vague hope, that, once master of the holiest of temples, he might obtain the same advantages, through the superstition of his foes, which he had lately possessed, in the person of Montezuma, through their reverence for the king. He meditated an assault, and resolved to attempt it, before the pyramid should be covered with Mexicans.

The strength of the army, both horse and foot, was straightway displayed upon the square; and the war-worn Christians once more marched against the triumphing infidel.

The Knight of Calavar, sitting on his sable steed, with an air of more life than was ordinary, appeared in this band; and the three serving-men, with the secretary followed at his back.

CHAPTER L.

In his sleep, the wounded cavalier was no longer a captive. Memory and imagination, acting together, bore him to the shores of the Mediterranean; and as he trod the smooth beach, his eye wandered with transport to the blue Alpujarras, stretching dimly in the interior. But not long did he gaze on those mountains, which intercepted the view of his distant castle. He stepped joyously along over the sands, obeying the voices and gestures of his conductors; for it seemed to him, that his hands were grasped, the one by the page Jacinto, the other by the priestess of Mexico, both of whom urged him on with smiles, while pointing to a group of palm-trees, under which reclined the long-lost maid of Almeria. The cross of rubies shone upon her breast, and her downcast eyes regarded it with a gaze of sadness; but, ever and anon, as the cavalier vainly strove to approach, and called to her with his voice, they were raised upon him in tears; and the hand of Leila was uplifted, with a melancholy gesture, towards Heaven. With such a vision, repeated many times in his brain, varied only by changes of place, (for now the scene was transferred to the deserts of Barbary, now the fair vales of Rhodes, and now the verdant borders of Tezcuco), he struggled through many hours of torture; and, at last, awoke as a peal of thunder, bursting on the scene, drove, terrified away, as well his guides, as the maid of his memory.

As he started from his couch, confused and bewildered, the thunders seemed still to roll, with distant murmurs, over the city. His practised ear detected, in these peals, the explosions of artillery, mingled with volleys of musketry; but for a while, in his disorder, he was unable to account for them, and in a few moments they ceased. Night had succeeded to day; no taper burned on the table, and scarcely enough light shone through the narrow casement into the apartment, to show him that he occupied it alone.

His lips were parched with thirst: he strode to the table, and finding nothing thereon to allay the burnings of fever, he called faintly on Jacinto. No answer was made to the call; he seemed to be the only tenant of the house; and yet he fancied that the deep silence which succeeded his exclamation, was broken by distant and feeble lamentations. He listened attentively; the sounds were repeated, but yet with so low a tone, that they would have escaped him entirely, had not his senses been sharpened by fever.

Obeying his instincts of benevolence, rather than his reason, for this had not yet recovered from the disorder of slumber, he stepped from the chamber; and, following not so much the sounds, which had become nearly inaudible, as a light that gleamed at a little distance, he found himself soon at the door of an apartment, through the curtain of which streamed the radiance.

The image of Leila, surveying the cross of rubies, had not yet departed from his imagination, when he pushed aside the flimsy arras, and stood in the room; and his feelings of amazement and rapture, of mingled joy and terror, may be imagined, when he beheld at the first glance, what seemed the incarnation of his vision. Before a little stool, which supported a taper of some vegetable substance, burning with odours and smoke, there knelt, or seemed to kneel, a maiden of exquisite beauty, whose Moorish character might have been imagined in her face, but not detected in her garments, for these were of Spanish fashion. The light of the taper streamed full upon her visage, from which it was not two feet removed, and showed it to be bathed in tears. Her eyes were fixed upon some jewel held in her hands, close to the light, which was attached by a chain of gold to her neck; and the same look which revealed to Don Amador the features of the maid of Almeria, showed him, in this jewel, the well-known and never-to-be-forgotten cross of rubies. The cavalier stood petrified; a smothered ejaculation burst from his lips, and his gaze was fixed upon the vision as on a basilisk.

At his sudden exclamation, the maiden raised her eyes, gazed at him an instant, as he stood trembling with awe and delight; and the next moment, whether it was that she struck the light out with her hand, or whether the taper and the figure were alike spectral, and snatched away by the same enchantment which had brought them into existence—the chamber was left in darkness, and the pageant of loveliness and sorrow had vanished entirely away.

No sooner had this un.ooked-for termination been presented, than Don Amador recovered his strength, and, with a cry of grief, rushed towards the spot so lately occupied by the vision. The stool still stood on the floor, but no maiden knelt by it. A faint gleam of dusky light shone suddenly on the opposite wall, and then as suddenly disappeared. It had not been lost to the cavalier; he approached it; his outstretched hands struck upon a curtain hung before another door, which admitted him into a passage, where a pleasant breeze, burdened with many perfumes, as from a garden, puffed on his cheeks. The sound of steps echoing at the end of the gallery, and the

gleaming of a light, struck at once upon his ears and eyes; he rushed onwards with a loud cry, gained the door, which, he doubted not, would again reveal to him the blessed vision, and the next moment found himself arrested by the Zegri.

Behind Abdalla stood the slave Ayub, bearing a torch, whose light shone equally on the indignant visage of the renegade Moor, and the troubled aspect of his captive.

"Hath the senor forgot that he made me a vow?" cried Abdalla, sternly; "and that, in this effort to escape, he covers himself with dishonour?"

To this reproach, Don Amador replied only by turning a bewildered and stupified stare on his host; and the Zegri, reading in this the evidence of returning delirium, relaxed the severity of his countenance, and spoke with a gentler voice.

"My lord does not well," he said, "to leave his chamber, while the fever still burns him."

He took the cavalier by the arm, and Don Amador suffered himself to be led to his apartment. There, seating himself on the couch, he surveyed the Moor with a steadfast and yet disturbed look, not at all regarding the words of sympathy pronounced by his jailer. At last, rousing himself, and muttering a sort of prayer, he said—"Are ye all enchanters? or am I mad? for either this thing is the fabrication of lunacy, or the illusion of unearthly art!"

"Of what does my lord speak?" said the Moor, mildly, and soothingly. "He should not think of dreams."

"Dost thou say dreams?" cried the cavalier, with a laugh. "Surely mine eyes are open, and I see thee. Dost thou not profess thyself flesh and blood?"

The Moor regarded his captive with uneasiness, thinking that his wits had fled.

"My noble patron does not ask me of his countrymen and friends," he said, willing to divert his prisoner's thoughts. "This day did I behold his followers, and, in addition, his kinsman, the Knight of Calavar."

At this name, the neophyte became more composed. He eyed the speaker more attentively, and now remarked, that, besides the leathern mail which he wore in the manner of the Mexicans, his chest was defended by an iron corslet, which, as well as the plumes of his tunic, was spotted with blood. As the Moor spoke, Don Amador perceived him to lay upon the table, along with the torch, which he had taken from Ayub, a sword dyed with the same gory ornament; and he started to his feet, with a feeling of fierce wrath, which entirely dispelled his stupefaction, when he recognised in this his own vanquished weapon.

"Knave of Zegri!" he cried, "hast thou used my glave on Spaniards, my friends and brothers?"

"When I struck thee the blow which saved thy life," said Abdalla, calmly, "I was left without a weapon; for the steel shivered upon thy casque. I borrowed the sword, which, to thee, was useless, and I returned it, not dishonoured, for it has drunk the blood of those who are, in the eyes of Heaven, idolaters and assassins. I give it back to thee, and will not again use it, even in a just and righteous combat: for, thanks be to God! it has been the means of providing me a store, which I hope to increase into an armoury."

"Thou avowest this to me? and with exultation?" said the cavalier, passing at once, in the excitement of anger, from the effects, and even the remembrance, of the vision.

"If my lord will listen," replied Abdalla, not unrejoiced at the change, and willing to confirm the sanity of the prisoner, "he shall hear what good blows this rich and very excellent weapon hath this day struck. A better never smote infidel or Christian."

"I will hear what thou hast to say," said the novice, with a stern accent; "and, wondering what direful calamity shall befall thee, for having thus profaned and befouled the sword of a Christian soldier, I hope thou wilt tell me of such things as will prove to me that God has punished the same, if not upon thy head, yet, at least, upon the heads of divers of thy godless companions."

"There are many of the godless, both heathen and Christian, who have slept the sleep of death this day," said Abdalla, knitting his brows with the ardour of a soldier; "many shall die to-morrow, some the next day, but few on the last—for who shall remain to perish? Every day do I look down from the pyramid, and hearken to the groans of those who destroyed Granada: and every day, though the lamentings be wilder and louder, yet are they fewer. Heaven be thanked! a few days more, and not a bone shall be left to whiten on the square, that does not speak of vengeance for the Alpujarras!"

"Moor!" said the frowning Spaniard, "have a care that thy ferocious and very unnatural triumph do not cause me to forget that I am thy prisoner. It was, perhaps, proper, that thou shouldst fly from Don Hernan, seeing that the slanders of very base caitiffs had prejudiced thee, and left thy life in jeopardy; perhaps, also, the necessity to gain the favour of Mexicans for thyself and Jacinto, by fighting with them against their foes, may, in part, extenuate the sin of such impiety; but I warn thee, thou leapest wantonly into superfluous crime, when instead of mourning thy cruel fate, thou rejoicest over the blood thou art shedding."

"Whose fault is it? and who shall account for my crime?" said the Zegri, with energy. "I came to these shores against my will; when I landed upon the sands of Ulua, my heart was in the peace of sorrow. I besought those who held me in unjust bondage, to discharge me with my boy: had they done so, then had I left them, and no Spaniard should have mourned for his oppression; the wrongs of Granada had not been repaid in Mexico. My prayers were met with mockery; the Zegri that hath set in the seat of kings, was doomed to be the bearer of a match-stick; and the boy, whose blood runs redder and purer than that in the veins of the proudest cavalier of all, was degraded into the service of a menial, in the house of the bitterest enemy of his people! What was left for me? To choose between slavery and exile, contempt and revenge. The senor thinks that the base Yacub belied me: Yacub spoke the truth. From the moment when I perceived I could not escape from the land, then did I know that God had commissioned me to the work of revenge; and I resolved it should be mighty. I meditated the flight I have accomplished, the treason I have committed, the revenge I have obtained. I saw that I should remain in woe, with benighted barbarians; but I saw also that I should be afar from Spaniards. God be thanked! It was bitter to be parted, for

ever, from the land of my birth, and the people of my love; but it is goodly and pleasant, to see the Castilian perish in misery, and remember Granada!"

Throughout the whole of this harangue, Don Amador de Leste preserved a countenance of inflexible gravity. "Sir Zegri," said he, with a sigh, when it was concluded, "I perceive that Heaven hath erected a wall between us, to keep us for ever asunder. Whether thy bitter hatred of Spaniards be just or not, whether thy appetite for revenge be allowable or accursed, still is it apparent, that, while thou indulgest the one, and seekest to gratify the other, it is impossible I should remain with thee on any terms, except those of enmity and defiance; for those whom thou hatest, and dost so bloodily destroy, they are my countrymen. I love thy boy, but thee I detest. And now, having discovered that thou art of very noble blood, and being impelled to punish on thee the very grievous and unpardonable wrongs which thou art doing to my country, I beg thou wilt release me from my parole, and fetch hither one of those swords which thou hast rifled from Spanish corses, I arming myself with my own weapon, here befouled with Spanish blood. We will discharge upon each other the obligations we are under, thou to hate and slay Spaniards, and I to punish the haters and slayers of the same; for it is quite impossible I can live longer in peace, suffering thee to destroy my friends. Fetch hither, therefore, a sword, and let us end this quarrel with the life of one or the other; and, to ease thee of any anxiety thou mayest have, in regard to Jacinto, I solemnly assure thee, that, if thou fall, I will myself take thy place, and remain a father to him to the end of my days."

As the cavalier made this extraordinary proposal, Abdalla surveyed him, first with surprise, then with a gloomy regret; and when he had finished, with a glistening eye. Before Don Amador had yet done speaking, the Zegri unbuckled his corslet, and, flinging it on the floor, at the last word, said, with mild and reproachful dignity—"Behold! thy sword is within reach, and my breast is naked. What hinders that thou shouldst not strike me at once? Thou speakest of Jacinto—it is enough that thy hand saved him from the blow of thy countryman: at that moment, I said, in my heart, though I spoke it not, 'Thou hast bought my life.' If thou wilt have it, it is thine. If thou hadst killed my father, I could not aim at thine!"

"Of a truth," said the cavalier, moodily, "I should not slay thee out of mere anger, but duty: yet I would that thou mightest be prevailed upon to assault me, so as to enforce me into rage; for, I say to thee again, so long as thy hostile acts continue, I must very violently abhor thee."

"They will not continue long," said Abdalla. "After a few days, there will remain in my bosom no feeling but gratitude; and then, my lord shall see, that the fury which has slain all others, has been his own security."

"Of this," said Don Amador, "I will have a word to speak to thee anon. At present, I am desirous that thou shouldst relate to me the fate of this day's battle, which I am the more anxious to know, since thou hast spoken the name of Calavar."

"I am loath to obey thee," said the Zegri, struggling with the fierce satisfaction that beset him at the thought, "for it may again excite thee to anger.

"Nevertheless I will listen to thy story, with such composure as I can, as to a thing it may be needful for me to know; after which, I have myself a matter of which it is quite essential I should acquaint thee."

Thus commanded, the Moor obeyed; and his eyes sparkled, as he conned over in his mind the events of a day so dreadful to the Spaniards.

CHAPTER LI.

"Yesterday, when thou wert sleeping," said the Zegri, "or lay as one that slept—"

"That day, then," muttered Amador, "is a blank in my existence! and very grievous it is, to think that so great a space of so short a period as life should be lost in a stony lethargy. It seems to me, that that blow thou gavest me was somewhat rounder than was needful. Nevertheless, I am not angry, but grateful."

"Yesterday was a day of comparative peace," continued the Zegri. "The Spaniards shut themselves in their citadel, preparing for the greater exploit of to-day. It was evident to the dullest of the nobles, that Don Hernan had cast an evil eye on the temple."

"Did he so?" cried the cavalier. "It was the thought of a good Christian: and, methinks, my countrymen had not been judged with so many of these present torments, if they had sooner torn down that stronghold of the devil, which is detestable in the eye of Heaven."

"To-day they marched against it," said Abdalla, "with all their force, both of Spaniards and Tlascalans; and I will say for them, that they marched well, fought boldly, and revenged their own heavy losses, in the blood of many barbarians, as well on the pyramid as in the temple-yard and the streets. They came against us, with four such turrets, moving on wheels—"

"Is it possible," cried Amador, "that the general was not sufficiently warned of the inefficacy of those engines, by the doleful fate of the manta, that day, when it was my mishap to be vanquished? I shall remember the death of the ship-master, Gomez, to the end of my life. Twice or thrice did I long to be with him, among the fire-worshippers, who must be a very strange people. But the Mexicans are very valiant."

"Of a truth they are," said the Zegri. "I will not detain my lord with the account of the battle in the streets, wherein the mantas were again, in great part, destroyed; nor will I relate with what suffering the Castilians won their way to the Wall of Serpents, and the temple-yard. It was here that I beheld my lord's kinsman, the Knight of Calavar, unhorsed, and in the hands of the infidel—"

"Accursed assassin!" cried the neophyte, springing to his feet, "and hast thou kept me in the bonds, that my knight should perish thus without succour?"

"The foe of Granada did not perish, and he was not without succour," said the Zegri, loftily. "When his steed, slipping on the polished stones with which that yard is paved, fell to the earth, and many savage hands were fastened on his body, there was a friend hard by, who raised both the knight and charger, and preserved them from destruction."

"Give me the name of that most noble friend," cried Don Amador, ardently, "for I swear I will reckon this act to him, in my gratitude, as the salvation of my own life. Tell me, what true Christian was he?"

"One," said Abdalla, calmly, "who hated him as the slayer of his people, but remembered that he repented his evil acts with misery and distraction—one who abhorred him for these deeds of sin and yet loved him, because he was, like his kinsman, the protector of childhood and feebleness."

"I doubt not that thou wert the man," said the cavalier, faltering; "and therefore I return thee my thanks. But I would have thee know, that, whatever blood was improperly shed by my kinsman, was shed by accident and not design; for no man is more incapable of cruelty than the noble knight, Don Gabriel. But this shows me, that thou art really of lofty blood; for none but a magnanimous soul can render justice to a hated enemy."

"Why should I dwell upon the conflict in the yard?" continued the Moor, hastily. "Through the flames of the many chapels that filled it—with shouts and the roar of muskets—the Christians, ever victorious, and yet ever conquered even by victory, rushed against the steps of the pyramid, disregarding the stones tumbled on them from the terraces, the darts flung down from the little barbicans or niches in the wall, and the flaming logs shot down endwise from the steps. Terrace after terrace, stair after stair, were won; and the Christians stood at last on the summit, fighting hand to hand with the four thousand nobles who defended it. My lord cannot think that even these numbers of naked men could long withstand a thousand Christians, robed in iron, and infuriated by desperation. Score after score were slain, and tumbled from the top; the flames burst from the altar of Mexitli — the priest died in the sanctuary—the Tlatoani at the downfallen urns; and in an hour's time the Spaniards were masters of the pyramid."

"Thanks be to Heaven which fought with them!" cried Amador, devoutly: "and thus may the infidel fall!"

"Does not my lord pity the wretches who die for their country?" said the Zegri, reproachfully. "This is not a war of heaven against hell, but of tyranny against freedom. I did see some sights this day upon the pyramid, which caused me to remember those noble Roman generals, who, in ancient times, were wont to devote themselves to death for the good of the state. At the very moment when the condition of the Mexicans was most dreadful, when, despairing of the usefulness of longer resistance, they rushed frantically upon the Spanish spears, transfixing themselves by their own act, or flung themselves from the pyramid to be dashed to pieces below—at this moment I beheld, with mine own eyes, two very young and noble Tlatoani, to whom I had myself just shown a means of escape, rush upon Don Hernan, who fought very valiantly throughout the day. They cast away their arms, flung themselves at his feet, as if to supplicate for mercy; and having thus thrown the general off his guard, they seized him, on a sudden, in their arms, and hurried him to the edge of the terrace. From that dizzy brink they strove to drag him, willing themselves to die dreadfully, so that the great enemy of Tenochtitlan should fall with them. But the strength of boys yielded to the iron grasp of the Christian; and flinging them from him like drops of water, or gouts of blood from his wounded hand, he beheld them fall miserably to the earth—dead, but not yet avenged."

"Thanks be to God again!" cried the cavalier, warming with excitement; "for though these youths met their death very bravely, they were guilty of a most vile treachery, for which death was but a just punishment. And so, my true and excellent friends did win this battle? By Heaven! it galls me to the marrow, to think that I lie here idle, while such things are doing around me!"

"They won the temple top," said Abdalla, with a laugh of scorn, "that they might look down from that height, and behold themselves surrounded by an hundred thousand men, who were busy slaying their Tlascalan slaves, and waiting for the masters. Very plainly did I hear their cries of despair at that sight; and these were goodly music. For myself, I escaped, as did some few others, by dropping from terrace to terrace, upon the dead bodies, which, being tumbled in great numbers from the top, lay, in some places, in such heaps along the galleries, as greatly to lessen the dangers of a fall. Well were the Mexicans revenged for this slaughter," continued the Moor, his eyes glittering with ferocious transport, "when the Spaniards descended, to cut their way to the quarters, encumbered with captive priests, and such provisions as they had gathered in the chapels. How many fell in the squares and streets, how many were suffocated in the canals, how few were able to pierce through the myriads that invested the palace (for all this time had there been thousands assailing the weak garrison, and tearing down the court-yard wall), why should I speak of these?" It is enough, that the gain of the pyramid—lost as soon as gained, cost them irreparable woe; and that the wounded fugitives (for the Mexican glass drank of the blood of all), now lie in their desolate house, their court-walls prostrate, the buttresses of their palace cracked by fire, their steeds unfed and starving, their ammunition expended—hopeless and helpless, calling to the leaders who cannot relieve, the saints who will not hear, and waiting only for death. Death then! for it cometh; death! for it is inevitable; death! for it is just; and death, for it repays the wrongs of Granada!"

As the triumphing Moor concluded his fiery oration, the cavalier, whose excitement was raised to the last pitch, and whose indignation and remorse were alike kindled by a full knowledge of the condition of his countrymen, cried aloud—"Hark thee, Sir Moor! with these friends, thus reduced to extremity and despairing, it is needful I should straightway join myself, to endure what they endure, to suffer as they suffer, to die as they die. I refuse to save my life, when the forfeit of it to an honourable purpose may relieve them of their distresses. I repent me of the gage which I gave thee, I revoke my promise of captivity, and am, therefore, free to make my escape, which I hereby attempt—peacefully if I can—but warning thee, if thou oppose, it shall be at the peril of thy life!"

So saying, the cavalier snatched up the sword from the table, and sprang towards the door. So quickly, indeed, did he act, and so much did he take his jailer by surprise, that he had nearly arrived at the curtain before Abdalla had time to intercept him. His brain was in a ferment of passion, and the various excitements of the evening had inflamed him again into fever; so that, in the fury of the moment, when the Zegri leaped before him, endeavouring to catch him in his arms, he forgot every thing but his purpose, and the necessity of escaping. He caught the Moor by the throat, and struggling violently, raised the crimson steel to strike. The life of Abdalla seemed not to have a moment's purchase—the weapon was already descending on his naked head, when—at that very instant—the curtain was drawn from the door, and dimly, but yet beyond all shadow of doubt, in the light of the torch, the cavalier beheld the pale visage of the maid of Almeria, shining over the shoulders of the Moor.

The sword fell from his hand, and his whole frame shook, as, with wild eyes, he returned the gaze of the vision. The Zegri, amazed, yet not doubting that this sudden change was the mere revolution of delirium, took instant advantage of it, snatched the leathern strap from the lute of Jacinto; and when the curtain, falling again, had concealed the spectral countenance, the arms of the cavalier were bound tightly behind him. This was a superfluous caution. His strength had been supplied by fury, and the instant that this had subsided, the exhaustion of two days illness returned; and had not his spirits been otherwise unmanned, he would now have been as a boy in the hands of Abdalla.

The Moor conducted him to the couch, on which he suffered himself to be placed without opposition, and without speaking a word. His whole faculties seemed lost in a sudden and profound stupor; and Abdalla began to fear that, in his prisoner, he had found, in more respects than one, a true representative of his kinsman, Don Gabriel.

CHAPTER LII.

A certain degree of monotony prevails among all the vicissitudes of life, and even the most exciting events fail, after a time, to interest. A paucity of incidents will not much sooner disgust us with the pages of history, than the most abundant stores of plots and battles, triumphs and defeats, if too liberally dispensed;—for these are composed of the same elements, and have, on the whole, the same wearisome identity of character. For this reason, though the many battles fought in the streets of Mexico, during the seven days which intervened betwixt the second coming and the second departure of Cortes, have something in them both of interest and novelty, we have not dared to recount them in full, nor, indeed, to mention all of them; being satisfied to touch only such, and, in truth, only such parts of such as, in themselves, have each some peculiar variety of characteristic. We pass by, with a word, the increased sufferings of the Christians—their murmurs and lamentations—their despair and frenzy.

The day that followed after the fatal victory of the pyramid, brought its battle like others. That day it became apparent that the last fibre which bound hope to the palace wall, was about snapping—it was known to all, that the Indian monarch was expiring. The prediction of Botello had made all acquainted with the day on which a retreat might be accomplished. That day was drawing nigh; but the impatience of the soldiers, and the anxiety of the officers to prepare, or, at least, to reconnoitre the path of retreat, again drove them from their quarters. A weak, but well chosen and trusty garrison, was left in charge of the palace; while Don Hernan, with all the forces that could be spared of his reduced army, sallied from the court-yard, and fought his way to the dike of Iztapalapan.

In this exploit, new difficulties were to be overcome, and new proofs were exhibited of the sagacity and determination of the barbarians. Besides the obstacles offered by the ditches, robbed of their bridges, the Mexicans had heaped together across the streets, the fragments of their demolished houses, thus forming barriers, which were not passed without the greatest labour and suffering. Nevertheless, the Spaniards persevered, and not only gained the causeway, but approached nigh to Iztapalapan, before a Tlascalan messenger, creeping in disguise through the crowds of enemies, recalled them to the palace, which was furiously assailed, and in imminent danger of being carried by storm.

It is not to be supposed, that this attempt on the great dike, and the return, were effected without the most bloody opposition. The lake suddenly swarmed with canoes full of fighting men, and when Don Hernan again turned his face towards Tenochtitlan, he beheld the causeway covered with warriors, who, besides disputing his passage with unappeasable rage, broke, as well as they could, the bridges over the sluices, seven in number, wherein were mingled the floods of Chalco and Tezcuco. His valour, however, or his good fortune, prevailed; and by nightfall he reached the square of Axajacatl, and fell with renewed fury upon the savages who still struggled with the garrison. When he had carved his way through them, and had directed the exertions of his united forces against the besiegers, who still raved like wolves around him, he gave some thought to those companions, whose fate it had been to lay their bodies on the causeway, or to take their rest, with such exequies as could be rendered in the lamentatious of men expecting each instant to share their fate, under the salt bosom of Tezcuco.

It became known, that, among these unhappy victims, was the Knight of Calavar—but how slain, or where entombed, no one could relate. From the day of the loss of his kinsman, he had been reckoned by all entirely insane. He held communion with none, not even his attendants; but casting aside his abstraction, and resuming his armour, he was present in every conflict which ensued, fighting with an ardour, fury, recklessness, as astonishing as they were maniacal. All that was remembered of his fate, this day, was that, when at the farthest part of the causeway the trumpets were ordered to sound a retreat, he was seen, without attendants, for they were wedged fast in the melée, dashing onwards amid the 'usky crowds that came rushing upon the front from the suburbs of Iztapalapan. Cortes had himself called to the knight to return, and not doubting that he would extricate himself without aid, had then given all his attention to the Mexicans attacking on the rear. This was known; it was known also that Don Gabriel had not returned: beyond this, all was mystery and gloom.

CHAPTER LIII

Two hours after nightfall, and while the Spaniards were still engaged in close battle with the besiegers, who this night seemed as if their rage was never to be appeased, the cavalier, Don Amador de Leste, rested in his chamber (the Moorish boy sitting dejected at his feet), now starting up with cries of grief and impatience, as the continued explosions of artillery admonished him of the straits of his friends, and now, as these seemed to die away and be followed by silence, giving his mind to other not less exciting thoughts, and questioning the page of the events of the past day.

"Not now, not now—ask me not now!" replied the page, with great emotion, to one of his demands, "for now can I think of nought but my father. It is not his custom to leave me so long by night, even when the battle continues. Heaven protect him! for at any moment he may die; and what then am I, in this land, and among this people? Would to Heaven we had perished in Spain—nay, in Barbary —in the sea, along with our friends; for then might we have died together!"

"Give not way to this passion," said the cavalier, with an attempt at consolation, which drove not the gloom from his own countenance; "for thou knowest that whatever evil may happen to Abdalla, I will myself befriend thee."

"My father is slain!" cried Jacinto, wringing his hands, "or long since would he have been with us."

"If this be the case," said Amador, with grave benevolence, "and I will not deny that Abdalla doth keep his life in constant jeopardy, it plainly shows that I am bound to make a father's effort to protect thee, and thou to follow my counsels. Hark!" he exclaimed, as a furious cannonade, seemingly of all the pieces shot off together, brought its roar and its tremor to his prison-house; "dost thou not hear how ferocious is the combat at this moment? Know, Jacinto, that every explosion seems like a petard fastened to and bursting upon mine own bosom—so very great are the shock and pang of mind with which, at such time, I bethink me of the condition of my countrymen. Much longer I cannot endure my captivity; I have resolved that it shall end, even if that be needful, by the breach of my solemn vow; for I am persuaded, the dishonour and compunction which must follow upon that will be but light, compared with the great ignominy of my present inactivity, and the unspeakable remorse which rends my vitals, while submitting to it. But I can by no means escape, while thou art left alone to be my jailer; if I escape by force of arms, it shall be when thy father is here to oppose me. I counsel thee, however, as thinking with thee that Abdalla may be dead—"

Here Jacinto burst into the most bitter lamentations.

"Be not thus afflicted; for I speak to thee only of a possibility which may be feared, and not of a certainty to be mourned. What I mean is, that this possibility should be enough to release thee, as well as myself, from this house; for if Abdalla be really deceased, it must be evident to thee, nothing could be more foolish, and even dangerous, than to remain in it alone; seeing that, if we be not found out and murdered by the Mexicans, we must surely expect to be starved. Guided by the sounds of battle, we can easily find our way to the palace; and perhaps, by wrapping ourselves in some of these cotton curtains, we may make our way through the herds of Mexicans, without notice, as being mistaken for some of their fellow-combatants. Once arrived within ear-shot of the palace, I have no fear but that we shall be very safe; and I pledge my vow to thee, that I will so faithfully guard thee on the way, that no weapon shall strike thee that has not first pierced my own bosom."

The page clasped his hands, and regarded his master with looks in which affection struggled with despair.

"But if my father should live—oh, if my father should live, and returning to this desolate house, should find that his child has deserted him!"

"If he live," said the cavalier, "then shall he know thou hast taken the only step to preserve him from destruction, both temporal and eternal. I will not rest till I have procured for him a free pardon; I will hold thee as a hostage, which, in addition to the assurance of forgiveness, will speedily bring him into the garrison: for knowing his love to thee, I know he cannot live without thee. Besides, I will obtain, for I will demand it, permission for him to return with thee to Spain; and if my knight consent, we will depart together; for now I am convinced that Heaven doth fight against us, even to upholding the godless heathen. Let us therefore depart, making our trust in God, who will cover us this night, as with shields, to protect our weakness."

"Alas, alas!" cried the boy, faltering with grief and fear; "my lord is sick and wounded, feeble and helpless."

"That I have not all the vigour which a few days since was mine," said the cavalier, snatching up his sword, and brandishing it once or twice in the air, as if to make trial of his strength, "I cannot deny. Nevertheless, I am stronger than yesterday, and besides, while placing great reliance on the protection of Heaven, I shall trust less to my weapon than to such disguises as it may be in our power to adopt. With these figured curtains wrapped about us, and, if here be any feathers about the house, a bunch or two tied to our heads, I have no doubt we can delude the Mexican fighting men, and, in the tumult of battle, pass through their ranks entirely unmolested."

While the page hesitated and wept, visibly struggling between his wishes and his fears, there occurred a sudden interruption in the cannonade; and, in the dead silence that followed, both heard the sound of rapid footsteps approaching the door accompanied by smothered groans.

The page started: in an instant the steps were heard in the passage, followed by a heavy sound, as of a man falling upon the floor.

"Oh God! my father! my poor father!" cried Jacinto, springing to the door

He was arrested by the arm of the neophyte, who plainly distinguished, along with the groans that came from the passage, a noise as if the sufferer were struggling to his feet: and in a moment after, as he pushed aside the curtain to go out himself, the slave Ayub, covered with blood, rushed by him into the apartment, and again fell prostrate.

"My father, Ayub! my father!" cried the page, kneeling at his side.

"Allah il Allah! praised be God, for now I am safe!" said the Morisco, rising on his arm, and, though his whole frame shook as in the ague of death, regarding the pair with the greatest exultation. "I thought they had shot me through the liver with a bullet; but Allah be praised, 'twas naught but an arrow. Help me up, noble senor—Eh? ay? Trim the taper a little, and give me a morsel of drink.

"Thou sayest naught of my father, Ayub?" said Jacinto, eagerly, and yet with mortal fear; for he knew by the gesture of Don Amador, as he ceased

his unavailing attempt to lift the wounded man, but more by the countenance of Ayub himself, that he was a dying man.

"How can I speak without light?" cried the Moor, with a sort of chuckle. "Trim the torch, trim the torch, and let me see where these boltheads be rankling. Praise be to Allah, for I thought myself a dead man."

"Wilt thou not speak to me of my father!" exclaimed Jacinto, in agony.

"A brave night, a brave night!" muttered Ayub, fumbling at his garments. "Valiant unbelievers! Praised be God, the Wali—"

"Ay, the Wali! the Wali, thy master!" cried Jacinto, his voice dwindling to a hoarse and terrified whisper;—"my father, thy master, Ayub?"

"The Wali—Hah!" exclaimed the unbeliever, roused by the distant explosions. "At it yet, brave Pagans? Roar, cannon! Shout, infidel! shout and whistle—shout, whistle, and kill! Save me the Wali, save me the Wali!"

Oh Heaven, Ayub!—thou sayest nothing of him, of my father!"

"They took him a prisoner—but we'll have him again!—Lelilee! Lelilee!—Strike fast Pagan!—A brave day for Granada!"

At these words, Jacinto seemed not less like to die than the fugitive. But as he neither fell to the floor nor screamed, Don Amador still held fast to Ayub, who was now struggling in the most fearful convulsions, and yet, strange to hear, still uttering broken expressions of joy.

"A prisoner, a prisoner!—A little drink, for the sake of Allah!" he cried, incoherently. "Ha, ha! one runs not so far with a bullet in the liver!—Now they are at it! now they are killing the great senores! now, they murder 'em!—Great joy! a great night for a Moor! great—great—great revenge!—Many days agone—Great—great revenge! says the Wali. They killed my mother—Great revenge—great—great—Oho! great revenge for Granada!"

With these accents on his lips, mingled with sounds of laughter, and horrid contortions of countenance, the infidel Moor (for such was Ayub,) sprang suddenly to his knees; and flinging abroad his arms, and uttering a yell of agony, fell back instantly upon the floor, quivered a moment, and then lay a disfigured corse.

"Dost thou see, Jacinto," said Don Amador, taking the shivering boy by the arm. "Ayub is dead, and thy father a prisoner. If thou wilt save the life of Abdalla, the Wali, (I never before knew that Abdalla, though noble, was of this dignity—but this shall help me to plead for him,) get thyself instantly in readiness, and let us be gone."

The page turned a tearless countenance on his patron, and replied, with a tranquillity that seemed to come from desperation—"I will go with my lord, for I have no friend now but him—I will go with my lord to look upon my father's dead body, for I know the Spaniards will not spare his life a moment—I will go with my lord—and would that I had gone sooner, for now it is too late."

As Jacinto pronounced these words, he began to weep anew, though hearkening passively to the instructions of the cavalier.

"If thou canst find me any plumes," said Amador, "fetch them to me straight; and if thou hast about the house any Mexican garment which thou canst wear, hast thou to don it. As for myself, I will first arm, and then robe me in the tunic of this poor dead misbeliever. Be of good heart, I charge thee—God will protect us."

"There are robes enough, both for my lord and me," said the sobbing boy—"and shrouds too—It is too late. But I can die with my lord."

"Why, that is spoken with more valour than I thought thou hadst," said the cavalier. "But bring me the robes, without thinking of thy shrouds; and be very quick, for I must have thee to buckle some of these straps of my jambeux."

The page took up a little taper that lay near the flambeau, and, shuddering as he passed by the body, instantly departed on his errand.

CHAPTER LIV.

When the boy returned, bearing a bundle of garments, and two or three such crests as were worn by the nobler Mexicans, in time of war, the cavalier had more than half armed himself. He sighed, as he flung the habergeon over his shoulders, to find the many rents made among the Flemish links by the Mexican glass; but he sighed more, when he discovered how greatly his bodily powers were enfeebled by feeling, almost for the first time in his life, the oppressive weight of the mail Nevertheless, the cannon still roared at the palace, every moment was expediting the doom of Abdalla, perhaps also that of his friends and kinsman; and he seized upon cuish and greave, gauntlet and helm, with activity and eagerness.

"What is that huge mantle thou placest upon the table?" he demanded of the page, without relaxing in his efforts.

"A tilmatli, or Indian cloak, large enough to hide my lord's armour," replied Jacinto, hurriedly. "If the Mexicans should see the gleaming of but a single link, death on the spot, or, still more horrid, on the pyramid, will be the fate of my lord."

"Now that I know that such would be the consequence of captivity," said the cavalier, fiercely, "I swear to God and St. John, I will die fighting—that is, if it please Heaven that I shall be struck no more blows that overpower without killing."

"And this great penacho," said the boy, "I will tie to my lord's crest, so that it shall entirely veil the helmet. I have fastened some of the red tufts among the feathers, whereby the Pagans may think my lord is a war-chief, and noble, if they should see them.'

"Of all boys that I have ever yet seen, thou art by far the shrewdest and wisest," said Don Amador, with complacency, but without ceasing a moment to do on his armour. "What disguise hast thou provided for thyself?"

"A garment," said Jacinto, "which being flung about my body and hooded over my head, will cause the Mexicans to think me a woman devoted to the service of one of the gods."

"A most damnable delusion," said the novice; "and I would thou hadst fallen upon some other device. But perhaps thou hadst no choice; and now that I think of it, thy small stature, and very smooth and handsome visage, will perhaps suit this disguise better than another. If there be any sin in assuming it, Heaven will allow the necessity, and forgive the commission. Quick, and don it—for I would have thee tighten these greave-straps before I pull on my boots."

"It will but encumber me; I will fling it over me in the passage," said Jacinto, kneeling, and endeavouring with an unsteady hand to perform the office required of him.

"Be of good heart, I charge thee, and tremble not. Thou art unused to this service; but think not, though thou beest the son of a Moorish Wali of the noblest blood, that this duty can dishonour thee. I have performed it myself, times without number, to my good knight, Don Gabriel. I would thou wert somewhat stronger though. Fear not to pull with all thy strength. I have shrunk somewhat with the fever—greatly to the disparagement of my leg—and the strap is of the stiffest."

"It is stiffened with my lord's blood!" said the page, trembling more, but succeeding at last in securing it. Then rising, and knotting a broad and shadowy plume over his patron's helmet, so as in a great measure to conceal the gleaming iron, he assisted to fasten it. There remained nothing then for the cavalier but to arrange the tilmatli about his person—a feat in which, with the aid of the page, he succeeded so well, as quite to hide his martial equipments, without yet depriving him of the power, in case of necessity, of using the sword, which he held naked in his hand.

"Thy woman's weeds! Why dost thou hesitate, Jacinto?" he cried, prepared, and now eager to make his departure. "Thou thinkest of thy lute? By my faith, I shall be loath thou shouldst lose it, for much good has it done, and yet may do, to Don Gabriel. I will bear it under my arm.'

"Think not of the lute," said Jacinto, sorrowfully. "What need have we now of music? It will overburden my lord, whose hands should be free; and in mine it would only serve to expose the deception of my apparel.'

"Cast it aside then; and now, in God's name, let us depart!"

Jacinto stepped, faltering, up to the body of Ayub, lying stiff and cold, the countenance, illuminated by the slanting torch-light, still mingling a grin of exultation with the contortion of the death-agony. A tear dropped upon the swarthy cheek, and a deep sob burst from the bosom of Jacinto, when he gazed his last upon the dead Morisco.

"Why dost thou tarry to weep?" said Amador, impatient; "Ayub was an infidel."

"My lord does not know how those who have not many friends, can value the few," said the page.

"This man was faithful to my father, and therefore do I lament him, as one whose loss is a sore misfortune; and, infidel though he were, yet was he of the faith of my ancestors."

"Remember, however, that while thou weepest over a dead friend of Abdalla, thou deprivest him of the services of a living one."

Thus rebuked, Jacinto moved rapidly into the passage, and flinging, as he went, the garment he held about his person, stepped with the cavalier into the street.

A thick scud, threatening rain, careered over the heaven, and the smoke of cannon, mingling with the mists of the lake, covered the city with a gloom so deep, that Don Amador could not easily distinguish the peculiar habiliments of his companion. Nevertheless, he could well believe that his appearance was that of an Indian maiden. He bade Jacinto to take him by the hand, adding an injunction, under all circumstances that might arise, to maintain his grasp. To this Jacinto answered, "Let it not be so—at least not until we are so environed as to be in danger of separating. My lord must now consent to be guided by me." (He spoke with singular coolness, as if restored, by the urgency of the occasion, to all that self-command and discretion, which had so often excited the wonder of his patron.) "I will walk a little before; and if the people should approach, let my lord take no notice, but follow calmly in my steps, as though he were a great noble, disdaining to look upon his inferiors. Be not amazed at what may happen, and, especially, do not speak a word until close by the Spaniards."

"Dost thou mean," said the cavalier, suddenly struck with the memory of the vision, not yet accounted for by the page—"dost thou mean to practise any arts of magic? for if so——"

"I beseech my lord not to speak," said the boy with a hurried voice: "for, if a word be heard, neither valour nor magic can save us from destruction. By and by my lord shall see the wisdom of this counsel; and all that is strange in its consequences shall be explained to him."

Thus speaking, Jacinto strode forwards, and Don Amador, wondering, yet yielding to his instructions, followed in silence. The cannon still roared at the palace, and the shouts of the infuriated combatants were plainly heard in the intervals of the discharges: so that, as the cavalier had hinted, there could be no difficulty in determining their path. Nevertheless, it appeared to him that Jacinto walked forwards with the boldness and certainty of one familiar with the streets he was treading.

For a time, their course lay through a street entirely deserted; but by and by, passing into one of greater magnitude, they beheld shadowy masses, now of single figures, now of groups darting about, many of them with lights, as if flying, some from the scene of combat, and others, like themselves, approaching it. It was apparent that this street was one of the four great avenues leading to the square of Axajacatl; for no sooner had the two Christians stepped upon it, than the sounds of conflict came to them with tenfold loudness; and they could behold, ever and anon, as the deadly discharges burst from the artillery, the flames flashing luridly up through the mists, like the jets of a distant volcano.

With the consciousness that he now trod a principal street, Don Amador became aware that he was, of a certainty, advancing full upon the mouth of at least one piece of ordnance; and as Jacinto paused suddenly, as if dismayed at his peril (for at that moment a ruddy flame shot out of the mist, and a falconet bellowed down the street), he approached the boy, and said—"For thy sake, Jacinto (it does not become me to say for my own, though I confess some repugnance to advance thus on the cannon of my friends), I should wish thou couldst find some other path, not so much exposed to be raked as this."

"Speak not—we have no choice," muttered the boy, "But God be thanked, the bullet that strikes my lord will first pass through my own body."

This little expression of devotion was pronounced with an earnestness that touched the heart of the cavalier; and he was about to utter his satisfaction, when a gesture of Jacinto, who immediately began to resume his pace, warned him into silence. The usefulness of the caution was soon made manifest; for two or three Mexicans suddenly brushed by, though without seeming to notice them. An instant after there passed several groups, bearing wounded men in their arms; and by and by, while every moment seemed to surround them yet more with isolated individuals, there came a party in some numbers, uttering lamentations, as if over the body of a great noble. Several of these bore torches in their hands, wherewith they were enabled to descry the pair; and Don Amador's heart beat quick, as he saw three or four detach themselves from the group and run forwards, as if to make sure of a prey. He grasped at his weapon, invoked his saint, and moved quickly up to Jacinto, to give him what protection he could: but at the very moment when he feared the worst, he was amazed to behold the barbarians come to a dead halt, and, at the waving of Jacinto's hand, part from before him, with countenances of reverence and fear. The same remarkable change was observed in those who composed the party bearing the corse, with the addition of new marks of homage; for leaving the body in the hands of a few, they seemed about to follow the page in a tumultuous procession, until he turned round, waving his hand again, at which gesture nearly all immediately fell on their knees, and so remained until he passed. All this time, the wondering cavalier was conscious that he was himself unregarded.

Little by little, while the screams and cannon-shots grew louder at each step, Don Amador perceived that the groups began to grow into crowds, and then into dense masses, every moment; while every moment also, it became still more apparent that his guide exercised some powerful, though to him inscrutable, influence over the mob; for no sooner did their torches reveal his figure, than all were straightway seized with admiration, falling upon their knees or returning on their path, and following him towards the battle.

The gestures of Jacinto served no longer to repel them; and in a few moments there were hundreds of men, their numbers increasing at each step, who pressed after him eagerly though reverentially—uttering at first low murmurs, and then, at last, shouts of joy and triumph. These reaching the ears and drawing the attention of others in front, they in turn added their respect to the homage of the rest.

However surprising, and, indeed, confounding, this notice, and these salutations to Don Amador, they were far from agreeable; for the train followed so close upon his heels, that he dreaded every moment lest some derangement of his mantle or plumes might expose to their gaze the hidden ensigns of a Christian. Greatly was he rejoiced, therefore, when the steady and persevering advance of the page had carried him so deeply into the crowd, that it was scarcely practicable for more than one or two individuals at a time to look upon him, and quite impossible that the noisy train should follow. He ceased, therefore, to lament his proximity to the cannon-mouths, which still at intervals flung death among the besiegers; for he thought that in that alone there was safety. His desire in this particular was soon gratified; for he was, at last, wedged with the page among a mass of men so dense and so disordered, that he no longer feared a scrutiny. He was in sight of the palace, his foot planted upon the square, and but a few paces separated from his friends and his knight.

In the flash of the arquebuses, but more particularly in the fiendish glare of the cannon, when disemboguing their contents upon the barbarians, he beheld the terraces covered with his countrymen, resisting as they could, and with every shot from the musket, every bolt from the arbalist, adding a life to the reckoning of their revenge, and yet fainting with fatigue over a slaughter which had no end. The square was filled with men, as with a sea, and when the fiery flashes of the ordnance lit it up as with a momentary conflagration, the commotion following upon each, made him think of those surges of fire which roll in the crater of a volcano, and of the billows of blood that dash upon the shores of hell. A more infernal spectacle could not, indeed, have been imagined; and when the harsh yells of the Pagan myriads were added, the tophet was complete, and man appeared—as he yet appears—the destroyer and the demoniac.

This spectacle, however horrible it might have been to one accustomed to look upon man as the image of his Maker, and the blow struck at the life of man as a stroke aimed at the face of God, had the effect to stir the blood of Don Amador de Leste to such a degree, that, had he not been checked by the cold hand and the deadly pale visage of his companion, he would have followed the impulse of his valour, uncovered his weapon, and shouting a war-cry, dashed at once upon the throat of the nearest infidel. The look of Jaciuto recalled him to his senses; he made him a signal to clutch upon his mantle and follow, and then plunged again into the gory crowd.

The tempest, both physical and mental, which beset all that rout of Pagans, reduced the intelligence of each to but two objects of thought—his enemy and himself. Not one turned to wonder or observe, when the strong shoulders—strong from excitement —of the cavalier thrust him aside, or the hard touch of an iron-cased elbow crushed into his bosom; nor, perhaps, was a look cast upon the effeminate figure, that seemed a girl, at the back of this impetuous stranger. Thus, then, unresisted and disregarded, the cavalier made his way, step by step, taking advantage of every moment when the barbarians gave way before an explosion of artillery or a charge of the garrison—hoping, at each effort, to issue upon the open space betwixt the besiegers and the besieged, and at each arrested by a denser crowd— speaking words of encouragement to the horror-struck page, for well he knew he might speak without fear in such a din—and feeling at each moment his strength melting away, like burning wax, under the prolonged exertion. He toiled for his life, for the life of the boy, perhaps for the life of Don Gabriel; but human nature could not sustain the struggle much longer. Despair came to his heart, for he knew not how far he stood from the palace wall, and felt that he could labour no more. His eye darkened, as he looked back to Jacinto—the boy was swooning where he stood.

"God be merciful to us both! But, at least, thou shalt die in my arms, poor boy!" he muttered, making one more effort, and raising the page from the earth; "God be merciful to us—but especially to this child, for he is sinless, and, I fear me, fatherless."

At this moment a dreadful scream burst from the lips of all around the novice, and immediately he felt himself borne back by barbarians, as they recoiled, seemingly, from a charge of cavalry. The thought was hope, and hope again renewed his strength. He planted his feet firmly on the earth, and with his elbow and shoulder dashed aside the fleeting Pagans, pressed the senseless boy to his heart, raised his voice in a shout, and the next moment stood free from the herd, ten feet from the muzzle of a cannon, from which the Mexicans had been recoiling. His eye travelled along the tube;—the magician Botello stood on the broken wall at its side, and the linstock he held in his hand was descending to the vent.

"For the love of God, hold!" shouted the cavalier, "or you will kill Christian men!"

The match fell to the earth, and the cavalier sprang forward. But if his voice had reached the ears of friends, it had not escaped the organs of foes. A dozen savages, forgetful of their fears, sprang instantly towards him, endeavouring to lay hold upon him. A back-handed blow of his weapon loosed the grasp of the most daring, and the hands of others parted along with the flimsy disguise of Jacinto. He left this in their grasp, tottered forward, and the next moment, as the cannon belched forth its death upon the pursuing herds, stood in the court-yard of the palace.

CHAPTER LV.

As the cavalier sprang among his countrymen, almost fainting with exhaustion, he loosened, with as much discretion as dexterity, the knot of the tilmatli, and dropped it to the earth, so that he might not be mistaken for a foe. The sudden gleam of his armour, and the sight of his wan visage, struck all those who had rushed against him with horror. Among the foremost of all was the man-at-arms, Lazaro, who no sooner perceived that he had raised his trusty espada against what he doubted not was the spectre of the novice, than he fell upon his knees, yelling aloud, "Jesu Maria! my master! my master's ghost!" with other such exclamations of terror.

At this moment, the page revived in the arms of his patron, but only to add to the cry of Lazaro a shriek so wild and heart-piercing, that it drove all other sounds from the ears of Don Amador. The cavalier observed the cause of this cry, and again his eye lighted up with fires of passion. A group of soldiers, agitated by some tumult, which had no part in the conflict around, stood against the palace wall, under a casement, from which was projected a bundle of partisans. Round this extempore gibbet was fixed a rope, one end of which being pulled at by those below, the cavalier beheld, shooting up above the heads of the mass, a human being, to all appearance bound hand and foot; and in the blackened and horribly-convulsed countenance of the sufferer, he perceived the features of Abdalla, the Wali.

With a bound, that carried him at once into their midst, and with a rapidity that prevented opposition, he rushed up to the wall, and before the Morisco was elevated above his reach, struck the halter with his weapon. The Zegri fell to the earth;—the executioners looked upon the visage of his bold preserver, and being persuaded, like Lazaro, that the very ghastly apparition before them was nothing less than the ghost of an hidalgo, universally reckoned dead, they recoiled in affright. Before they had recovered from their confusion, the culprit rose to his feet, glared a moment on the cavalier, and then springing away, was instantly lost among the combatants. A wild and exulting cry of "Moro! Moro! Tlatoani Moro!" rose among the barbarians; and the Spaniards knew that their prey was beyond pursuit.

"Santos santisimos! Holy Mother of Heaven! grace upon all, and amen! If thou beest a living creature, speak, or I will smite thee for a devil!"

These words came from the lips of Alvarado, who had himself commanded the body of hangmen, and who now, though his teeth chattered with terror, advanced his rapier towards the bosom of his late companion. As he gazed and menaced, Don Amador, yielding at last to the consequences of labours altogether above his enfeebled powers, sunk swooning to the earth: and Jacinto, rushing from

'Viva! praise God, and let the cry go round; for we have saved the noble De Leste!" shouted Don Pedro, with a voice of joy, raising the senseless cavalier. "Now shall ye hear from his own mouth, ye caitiffs that have belied me, that I played not the foul companion. Viva! I swear it rejoices me to behold thee! Why, thou little rascal traitor, art thou here too? It was God's will thy vagabond father should purchase me my brother; for which reason, I am not incensed he has escaped me. One day is as good as another for hanging. How now, my noble friend! art thou hurt beyond speaking? God's lid! but I would hug thee, if thou didst not look so dismal!"

All this time the neophyte surveyed the astonished visages around him with a bewildered eye; and doubtless his obtuse senses could not at that moment of clamour detect the accents of Don Pedro.

"Tetragrammaton! did I not tell thee the truth?" cried the harsh voice of Botello.

"Master! dear master!" exclaimed Lazaro, as he embraced the knees of the novice.

"Thanks be to God! the noble senor has escaped," shouted the secretary.

"God be praised! but would it had been yesterday; for then might it have been better for Don Gabriel."

The name of his kinsman, spoken by the well-known voice of Baltasar, dispelled at once the dreamy trance of the cavalier.

"How fares my noble kinsman?" he cried.

The head of Baltasar fell on his breast, and a loud groan came from his fellow-servitor. Don Amador looked to the Tonatiuh, and witnessed the change from blithe joy to gloomy hesitation, which instantly marked his handsome aspect; the face of Fabueno darkened; and the magician strode away.

"Clear for me, if ye will not speak," said the cavalier, with sudden sternness; "for there is no sight of woe I cannot now look upon."

He grasped the arm of Jacinto, and pushing into the palace, made his way toward the chamber of the knight. The hand of devastation had been upon the walls of the passage; beams and planks had been torn away to supply the materials for the mantas and other martial engines; and Don Amador no longer knew the apartment of his kinsman. A dim light and a low sound of wailing came from a curtained door. Before the secretary and the other attendants who followed could intercept him, he stooped into the room.

The sight that awaited him instantly fastened his attention. He was in the chamber of Montezuma, and the captive monarch lay on the bed of death. Around the low couch knelt his children, and behind were the princes of the empire, gazing with looks of awe on the king. In front were several Spanish cavaliers, unhelmed and silent; and Cortes himself, bare-headed and kneeling, gazed with a countenance of remorse on his victim, while Olmedo stood hard by, vainly offering, through the medium of Donna Marina and the cavalier De Morla, the consolations of religion.

The king struggled in a kind of low delirium, in the arms of a man of most singular and most barbarous appearance. This was a Mexican of gigantic stature, robed in a hooded mantle of black; but the cowl had fallen from his head, and his hair, many feet in length, plaited and twisted with thick cords, fell like cables over his person and that of the dying king. This was the high-priest of Mexico, taken prisoner at the battle of the temple.

The countenance of Montezuma was changed by suffering and the death-throe; and yet, from their hollow depths, his eyes shot forth beams of extraordinary lustre. As he struggled he muttered, and his broken exclamations being interpreted, were found to be the lamentations of a crushed spirit and a broken heart.

"Bid the Teuctli depart," were some of the words which Don Amador caught, as rendered by the lips of Marina: "before he came I was a king in Mexico. But the son of the gods," he went on, with a hoarse and rattling laugh, "shall find that there are gods in Mexico who shall devour the betrayer. They roar in the heavens, they thunder among the mountains"—(the continued peals of artillery, shaking the fabric of the palace, mingled with his dreams and gave a colour to them)—"they speak under the earth, and it trembles at their shouting. Ometeuctli, that dwelleth in the city of heaven, Tlaloc, that swimmeth on the great dark waters, Tonatricli and Meztli, the kings of day and night, and Mictlanteuctli, the ruler of hell—all of them speak to their people; they look upon the strangers that destroy in their lands, and they say to me, 'Thou art the king, and they shall perish.' Woe! woe! woe!" he continued, with an abrupt transition to abasement and grief; "they look upon me and laugh, for I have no people. In the face of all I was made a slave; and, when they had spit upon me, they struck me as they strike the slave—so struck my people. Come, then, thou that dwellest among the rivers of night: for among the rivers with those who die the death of shame shall I inhabit. Did not Mexico strike me, and shout for joy? Woe! woe! for my people have deserted me; and in their eyes the king is a slave."

"Put thy lips to this emblem of salvation," said the Spanish priest, extending his crucifix, eagerly; "curse thy false gods, which are devils; acknowledge Christ to be thy master; and part—not to dwell among the rivers of hell, which are of fire, but in the seats of bliss, the heaven of the just and happy."

"I spit upon thy accursed image," said the monarch, rousing with indignation, into temporary sanity, and endeavouring to suit the action to the word; "I spit upon thy cross, for it is the god of liars and deceivers—of robbers and murderers—of betrayers and enslavers. I curse thy god, and I spit upon him."

All the Spaniards present recoiled with horror at the impiety, which was too manifest in the act to need interpretation; and some, in the moment, half drew their swords, as if to punish it by dispatching the dying man at once. But they looked again on the king, and knew that this sin was the sin of madness.

As they started back the person of De Leste, whom, in their fixed attention to Montezuma, none of them had yet perceived, was brought into the view of the monarch. His glittering eye fell upon the penacho, which the cavalier had not yet thought to remove from his helmet, and which yet drooped with its badges of rank over his forehead. A laugh, that had in it much of the simple exultation of childhood, burst from the king's lips; and, raising himself on the couch, he pointed at the ruddy symbols of distinction. The cavaliers following the gesture with their eyes, beheld, with great agitation, their liberated companion; and even Cortes himself started to his feet, with an invocation to his saint, when his eye fell upon the apparition

The words of Amador—"Fear me not, for I live though not lost were unanswered; for, notwithstanding that many of the cavaliers immediately seized upon his hands to express their joy, they instantly cast their regards upon Montezuma, as not having the power to withdraw them for a moment from him.

'Say what they will," muttered the king, still eyeing the penacho with delight; "I also am of the House of Darts; and in Tlascala and Michoacan, among the Otomies of the hills, have I won me the tassals of renown. Before I was a king I was a soldier: so will I gather on me the armour of a general, and drive the Teuctli from my kingdom. Ho, then, what ho! Cuitlahuatzin! and thou son of my brother, Quauhtimotzin, that are greater in war than the sons of my body, get ye forth your armies, and sound the horns of battle. Call upon the gods and smite! on Mexitli the terrible, on Painalton the swift! call them, that they may see ye strike and behold your valour. Call them, for Montezuma will fight at your side and they shall know that he is valiant."

The struggles of the king, as he poured forth these wild exclamations, were like convulsions. But suddenly, and while the Spaniards thought he was about to expire in his fury, the contortions passed from his countenance, his lips fell, his eyes grew dim, and his voice was turned to a whisper of lamentation.

"I sold my people for the smile of the Teuctli; I bartered my crown for the favour of the Christian; I gave up my fame for the bonds of a stranger; and now what am I? I betrayed my children—and what are they? Let it not be written in the books of history—blot out the name of Montezuma from the list of kings; let it not be taught to them that are to follow. Tlaloc, I come! Let it be forgotten."

Suddenly, as he concluded, and as if the fiend of the world of waters he had invoked had clutched upon him, he was seized with a dreadful convulsion, and as his limbs writhed about in the agony, his eyes, dilating with each struggle, were fixed with a stony and basilisk glare upon those of Cortes; and thus—his gaze fixed to the last on his destroyer—he expired.

When the neophyte beheld the last quiver cease in the body, and knew by the loud wail of the Mexicans that Montezuma was no more, he looked round for Don Hernan; but the general had stolen from the apartment. The visage of Cortes revealed not the workings of his mind; but his heart spoke to his conscience, and his soul recorded the confession: "I have wronged thee, Pagan king; but thy vengeance cometh."

Don Amador's arm was touched by his friend De Morla.

"In the chamber of death," said the cavalier, sadly, "thou mightest best hear of death; but I cannot discourse to thee, while Minnapotzin is mourning. Let us depart, brother."

Don Amador motioned to the page, and followed his friend out of the apartment.

CHAPTER LVI

On the following morning, it was known to all the garrison that they were, at night, to depart from Tenochtitlan. The joy, however, that might have followed the announcement was brief; for, at the same moment that the exhausted Christians were roused from slumber and bidden to prepare, the warders sent word down from the turrets, that their enemies were again approaching. The shrewdest of all could perceive no other mode of retreat than by

cutting their way through the besiegers; and it require but little consideration in the dullest to disclose the manifold dangers of such an expedient. They manned the walls and the court-yard, therefore, with but little alacrity, and awaited the Mexicans in sullen despair.

But Don Hernan, quick to perceive, and resolute to employ the subtle devices of another, had not forgotten the words of Botello, when that worthy counselled him to make such use of Montezuma and his children as had been made of the golden apples, by Hippomenes, when contending in the race with the daughter of Schœneus.

The Mexicans advanced, as usual, with whistling and shouts, filling the square with uproar; and, as usual, the cannoniers stood to their pieces, and the Tlascalans to their spears; but before a dart had been yet discharged, those who looked down from the battlements beheld a funeral procession issue from the court-yard.

A bier, constructed rudely of the handles of partisans, but its rudeness in a measure concealed by the rich robes of state flung over it, was borne on the shoulders of six native nobles, all of them of high degree in Tenochtillan. It supported the body of the emperor, which was covered only by the tilmatli, leaving the countenance exposed to view. The royal sandals were on his feet, and the copilli, with the three sceptres, lay upon his breast. The Pagan priest in his sable garment, his face covered by the cowl, and his head bending so low, that his hideous locks swept the earth, stepped upon the square, chanting a low and mournful requiem; and the bearers, stalking slowly and sorrowfully under their burden, followed after

The murmurs were hushed in the palace; and the square, so lately filled with the savage shouts of the enemy, became suddenly as silent as the grave. The monotonous accents of the priest were alone heard, conveying to the Mexicans, in the hymn that ushered a spirit into the presence of the deities, the knowledge of the death of their king.

For a while the barbarians stood in stupid awe but at last, as the train approached them, and they perceived, with their own eyes, the swarthy features of their monarch fixed in death, they uttered a cry of grief, low indeed, and rather a moan than a lament; but which being caught and continued by the voices of many thousand men, was heard in the remotest parts of the city. They parted before the corse of one, to whom, before the days of his degradation, they had been accustomed to look as to an incarnate divinity. They fell upon their knees, and bowed their faces to the earth, as he was carried through them; and again the Spaniards beheld the impressive spectacle of a great multitude prostrate in the dust, as if in the act of adoration.

When the bearers and the body were alike concealed from their view, the Mexicans rose, and turning towards the palace, brandished their weapons with fierce gestures and many exclamations of hatred against the destroyers of their king. For a moment Cortes doubted if his expedient had not served rather to increase than to divert the fury of his opponents; and he beckoned from his stand on the terrace to the cannoniers to prepare their matches. But an instant after he revoked the command: the Mexicans were retiring—a great army was suddenly converted into a funeral train, and thus they departed from the square after the body of their ruler, without striking a blow at the invader.

This circumstance re-assured the garrison; and the prospect of speedy release from intolerable suffering and from destruction, wrought such a change over all, that visages, emaciated by famine, and haggard from despair, were lit up with smiles; and songs and laughter re-echoed through chambers, which, but the night before, had resounded with prayers, groans, and curses. Nothing was now thought of but the bread and fruits of Tlascala,—the mines and fandangos of Cuba; and many a sedate and sullen veteran clapped his hands with a sudden joy, as he bethought him of the urchins sporting in the limpid Estero, or climbing the palm that grew at his cabin-door. Escape from the miseries which had environed them, and the privilege to discourse for life of the marvels of Tenochtitlan—of the beauty of its valleys, the magnificence of its cities, the wealth of its rulers, the ferocious valour of its citizens—to wondering listeners, were the only offsets thought of to the many labours, sufferings, and risks of the campaign. The little property amassed by each—the share of Montezuma's presents, and the spoils stripped from the dead, were stored, along with such trifles as might add the interest of locality to legends of battle, in the sacks of the soldiers. All made their preparations, and all made them in hope.

The only melancholy men in the palace, that day, were Cortes and Don Amador de Leste. The latter remembered his knight, falling ingloriously and alone on the causeway; and the general pondered over the griefs of defeated ambition

But whatever were the pangs of Don Hernan, he forgot not the duties of a general. Besides other precautions, he caused his carpenters to construct a portable bridge of sufficient strength to support the weight of his heaviest artillery, and yet not so ponderous but that it might be carried on the shoulders of some half a hundred strong men. This he provided, fearing lest the barbarians had destroyed the bridges, not only of the great dike of Iztapalapan, but that of Tacuba, on which it was his determination to attempt his flight, and which, running westward from the island, was, as has been intimated, but two miles in length.

In accordance with the advice of the necromancer, the hour of departing was put off until midnight—a period of time which had the double advantage of being recommended by Botello, and of ensuring the least molestation. Each individual, therefore, made his preparations, and looked forward to that hour.

The melancholy hour that oppressed the spirits of the neophyte was so great, that he betrayed little curiosity either to acquaint himself with the events which had occurred during his captivity, or even to inquire further into the mysterious knowledge and acts of the page. But, however indisposed to conversation, he could not resist the attentions of De Morla. From him he learned the imputation he had cast on the valour and gratitude of Alvarado—a charge which the novice removed, by magnanimously confessing that his own indiscretion had carried him beyond the reach of Don Pedro, who should be in nowise held accountable for his misfortune. He heard with more interest, and even smiled with good-natured approbation, at the story of Fabueno's fortune; but a frown darkened on his visage, when De Morla pictured the anger and domineering fury of the Tonatiuh; and this was not diminished, when his friend confessed himself the champion of the secretary, announced that Cortes had sanctioned the quarrel, and claimed of him the offices of a friend.

"If blood must be shed in this quarrel," he said,

"it must be apparent to you, my very noble and generous friend (for surely your kindness to Lorenzo merits this distinction)—it must be apparent, I say, that I am he who is called upon to shed it. The youth is my own follower; for which reason I am bound to give him protection, and support him in all his just rights, whereof one, I think, is to love any woman who may think fit to give him her affections, whether she be princess or peasant. I must, therefore, after repeating to thee my thanks for thy very distinguished generosity, require thee to yield up thy right to do battle with Don Pedro, if battle must indeed be done, though I have hopes that his good sense will enforce him to surrender the maid without the necessity of bloodshed."

"I cannot yield to thee, hermano mio," said De Morla, quickly; "for there is deadly feud betwixt the Tonatiuh and myself, and were he to fight thee a dozen times over, still should he, of a necessity, measure weapons with me."

"It doth not appear how this difference can call for more than one combat; and, as I have told thee, I think it can be composed, provided thou allowest me to resume thy place entirely without conflict."

"Know thou, my friend," said De Morla, "that I have already in the matter of thy fall and capture at the fight of the manta, charged Alvarado with many terms of opprobrium and insult, for which reason a duello has become very inevitable."

"Having already heard from myself," said Don Amador, with gravity, "that Don Pedro cannot justly incur reproach for my mishap, thou canst do nothing else as a true cavalier, but instantly withdraw thy charges, and make him the reparation of apology; after which there will remain no need of enmity."

"Thou speakest the truth," said De Morla, impetuously, "and I am but a knave to have said, or even thought, except at the moment when I was grieved and imbittered by thy supposed death, that Don Pedro could demean himself in any battle like a craven. I freely avow, and will justly bear witness, that he is a most unexceptionable cavalier. So far I am impelled to pronounce by simple veracity. But yet is there mortal, though concealed, feud betwixt us."

The neophyte looked on his friend with surprise, seeing which, De Morla took him by the arm, and said, with great heat—"I have come to hear, by an accident, that Don Pedro did once ('tis now many months ago), in the wantonness of his merriment, fling certain aspersions upon the innocence of Benita—a crime that I could not have forgiven even in thee, amigo querido, hadst thou been capable of such baseness. I now confess to thee, without having divulged the same to any one else, that this circumstance did greatly inflame my anger, and that, from that moment, I have sought out some means to quarrel with Alvarado, and so slay him without involving the fame of Minnapotzin; for it is clear to me, as it must be to any lover who doth truly reverence his mistress, that to associate her name with a quarrel, would be at once to darken it with the shadow of suspicion. I should say to Alvarado, 'Thou hast maligned my mistress, thou cur, and therefore I will fight thee;' then should he, for the credit of his honour, aver that he spoke the truth, and whether he lived or died, the maiden should still be the sufferer. I have, therefore, resolved, that my cause of vengeance shall be concealed; and thou wilt see that the present pretext is the honourable cloak I have been so long seeking.

This I confess to thee; but I adjure thee to keep my counsel."

There was a degree of lofty delicacy and disinterestedness in this revealment, which chimed so harmoniously with the refined honour of Don Amador, that he grasped De Morla's hand, and, instead of opposing further remonstrance, assured him both of his approval and his determination to aid him, as a true brother in arms, in the conflict.

"But how comes it, my friend," he demanded, with a faint smile, "thou darest look so far into futurity for such employment? Hast thou forgot the prophecy of Botello? Methinks, to be fulfilled at all, the consummation should come shortly for with this night we finish the war in Mexico."

"For a time, senor mio," said De Morla. "Though the griefs of Montezuma be over (Heaven rest his soul, for he was the father of Minnapotzin,) the pangs of his race are not yet all written. I will abide with Don Hernan; and if Botello do not lie, thou shalt yet see me sleep on the pyramid."

"Heaven forbid!" cried Amador. "I would rather thou wouldst follow mine own resolutions, and, for once, show Botello that he hath cast a wrong figure."

"Dost thou mean to desert us?"

"My kinsman sleeps in the lake," said the novice, sadly; "the tie that bound me to this fair new world is therefore broken. In mine own heart I have no desire to fight longer with these infidels, who cannot injure the faith of Christ, nor invade the churches of Christendom. The Turks are a better enemy for a true believer; and, if I put not up my sword altogether, it shall be drawn hereafter on them. The little page whom I have by a miracle recovered, I will convey with me to Cuenza, after having, in like manner, recovered his father (a very noble Morisco), or been otherwise assured of his death. I would greatly persuade thee, having made the princess thy wife, to follow with me to thy native land. 'My castle lies on Moreno's top,'" continued the cavalier, insensibly falling upon the melody of the Knight and the Page, and beginning to muse on the singer, and to mutter. "Surely Jacinto is the most wonderful of boys."

"My patrimony is worn out," said De Morla, without regarding the sudden reverie of his friend; "and I give it to my younger brothers. By peace or war, somehow or other, this land of Mexico will be one day conquered, and then a principality in Anahuac will count full as nobly as a sheep-hill in Castile. I abide by Don Hernan. But let us be gone to the treasury—I hear the ingots chinking, and thou hast not yet looked upon our spoils."

The exchequer thus alluded to, and to which De Morla speedily conducted his friend, was the sleeping apartment of the general. Of the wealth that was there displayed—the stores of golden vessels and of precious stones, as well as of ingots melted from the tribute-dust long since wrung from the unhappy Montezuma—it needs not to speak. The whole treasury of an avaricious king,—a predecessor of the late captive,—walled up in former days, and discovered by a happy chance, was there displayed among the meaner gleanings of conquest. An hundred men, as Don Amador entered, were grasping at the glittering heaps, while the voice of Don Hernan was heard gravely saying—"The king's fifth here partitioned and committed to the trust of his true officers, we must defend with our lives; but while granting to all Christian men in this army free permission to help themselves here as they like, I solemnly warn them of the consequences, should we, as mayhap my fear may prove true, be attacked this night, while making our way through the city. The richest man shall thereby purchase the quickest death. The wise soldier will leave these baubles till we come back again to reclaim them. This night I will insure the life of none who carries too rich a freight in his pockets."

He spoke with a serious emphasis, and some of the older veterans, raising their heads, and eyeing his countenance steadfastly for a moment, flung down the riches they had grasped and silently retired from the apartment. But many others bore about their persons a prince's ransom.

CHAPTER LVII.

At midnight the Mexican spy, looking over the broken wall, beheld, in the court-yard which it environed, a scene of singular devotion, or rather he caught with his ears—for the grave was not blacker than that midnight—the smothered accents of supplication. The Christians were upon their knees listening, with a silence, broken only by the fretful champing of steeds and the suppressed moans of wounded men, to a prayer, pronounced in a whispering voice, wherein the father Olmedo implored of Heaven to regard them in pity, to stupify the senses of their enemies, and surround his servants with the shields of mercy, so that this night they might walk out of the city which was their prison-house, and from the island which had been their charnel, oppressed no more by the weight of His anger

The prostrate soldiers, to that moment, full of confident hope, and not anticipating the danger of any opposition, hearkened with solicitude to the humble and earnest supplication; and when the padre besought the Deity to endow their arms with strength and their hearts with courage—to sustain the toils, and perhaps the perils, of retreat, they were struck with a vague but racking fear. The petition, which was meant to embolden, deprived them of hope, and they rose from their vain devotions in unexpected horror

The gloom that invested the ruinous palace prevailed equally over the Pagan city. No torch shone from the casements or house-tops,—no taper flickered in the streets, and the urns of fire on the neighbouring pyramid—the only light visible—save, now and then, a ghastly gleam of lightning bursting up from the south—burned with a dull and sickened glare, as if neglected by their watchers. A silence, in character with the obscurity, reigned over the slumbering city; and when at last the steps of those who bore the ponderous bridge, and the creaking of artillery-wheels were heard ringing and rolling over the square, the sounds smote on the hearts of all like the tolling of distant funeral bells.

The plan of retreat determined, after anxious deliberation, and carefully made known to all, was adopted with readiness, as these footsteps and this rolling sound of wheels—the only signals made—were heard; each man knew his place, and without delay assumed it. In little more than half an hour the whole train of invaders, Christian principals and Tlascalan abettors, was in motion, creeping, with the low and stealthy pace of malefactors, over the street that led to the dike of Tacuba. Few glances were sent back to the palace, as those dim sheets of lightning flashing up over the path they were pursuing, revealed obscurely ever and anon its broken and deserted turrets. Its gloomy pile associated nothing but the memory of disaster and grief. Fearful looks, however, were cast upon the dusky fabrics on either side of the street, as if the fugitives apprehended that each creak of a wheel—each clattering of horses' hoofs, or the rattling of armour, might draw the infidel from his slumbers; and many an ear was directed anxiously towards the van in fear, lest the trumpet should at last be sounded, with the signal of enemies already drawn up, a thousand deep, on the path they were treading. But no sounds were heard, save those which denoted the continued progress of their own bands; no wakeful barbarian was seen lurking in the streets, and hope again slowly returned to the bosoms of the tremblers.

Before they had yet reached the borders of the island the night became still more dark than at the outset; for the lightning grew fainter at each flash, and finally sank beneath the horizon, to continue its lurid gambols among the depths of the South Sea. This was witnessed with secret satisfaction, for with these treacherous scintillations departed the dread that many felt, lest they should betray the march of the army.

It has been mentioned, that the people of Tenochtitlan had not only covered the surface of the island with their dwellings, but had extended them, on foundations of piles, into the lake, wherever the shallowness of the water permitted. This was especially the case in the neighbourhood of the great dikes; in which places, not only single houses, but entire blocks, deserving the name of suburbs, were constructed. Such a suburb jutted out, for some distance, along the causeway of Tacuba.

The van of the army hrd already passed beyond the furthest of these black and silent structures, and yet no just cause existed to suppose the retreat had been discovered: though many men of sharper ears or fainter hearts than their fellows, had averred that they could, at times, distinguish, on the rear, a dull sound, as of men moving behind them in heavy masses. The wiser, however, were satisfied, that no such sounds could prevail even over the subdued noise of their own footsteps: but some of these bent their ears anxiously towards the front, as if afraid of danger in that quarter. The reason of this was not concealed. All day, sounds of lamentation had been heard coming from the dike, upon which they were now marching, or from its neighbourhood. It was rumoured, that the cemetery of the Mexican kings lay on the hill of Chapoltepec, under the huge and melancholy cypresses which overshadow the green promontory; and that there, this day, Montezuma had been laid among his ancestors. A whole people had gone forth to lament him; and how many of the mourners might be now returning by the causeway, was a question which disturbed the reflections of all.

But this apprehension was dispelled, when the front of the army had reached the first of the three ditches which intersected the dike of Tacuba. Its bridge was removed and gone, and the deep water lay tranquilly in the chasm. The foe, relying on this simple precaution, had left the dike to its solitude; and the expedient for continuing the imprisonment of the Spaniards was the warrant of their security.

A little breeze, dashing occasionally drops of rain, began to puff along the lake, as the bridge-bearers deposited their burden over the abyss. This was not the labour of a moment; the heavy artillery, which still preceded the train of discomfited slayers, like a troop of jackals in the paths of other destroyers, required that the ponderous frame should be adjusted with the greatest care. While the carriers, assisted by a body of Tlascalans, who slipped into the ditch and swam to the opposite side, were busy with their work, the long train of fugitives behind halted, and remained silent with expectation. The rumbling of the wood over the flags of the causeway, the suppressed murmurs of the labourers, and now and then the dropping of some stones loosened by their feet, into the ditch—added to the sighs of the breeze, whispering faintly over casque and spear—were the only sounds that broke the dismal quiet of the scene; and there was something in these, as well as in the occurrence itself, which caused many to think of the characteristics of a funeral—the mute and solemn expectation of the lookers-on—the smothered expressions of the few—and the occasional rattle of clods, dropping, by accident, upon the coffin.

The bridge was at last fixed, and the loud clang of hoofs was heard, as Cortes himself mad e trial of its strength. The breath of those behind came more freely, when those sounds reached their ears; and they waited impatiently till the advance of those who preceded them should give motion to their own ranks.

The post of Don Amador de Leste had been assigned, at his own demand, in the vanguard—which was a force consisting of twenty horsemen, two hundred foot, and tent imes that number of Tlascalan warriors, commanded by Sandoval the valiant; and, up to this moment, he had ridden at that leader's side, without much thought of unhealed wounds and feebleness, willing, and fully prepared to divide the danger and the honour of any difficulty which might be presented. But being now convinced, by waiting we have mentioned—that is to say t;ie removal of the original bridge—that no enemies lay in wait on the causeway, he descended from the back of Fogoso, giving the rein to Lazaro, and commanding him to proceed onward with the party. In this he was, perhaps, not so much governed by a desire to escape the tedium of riding in company, with the ever-taciturn Sandoval, as to be nearer to the forlorn boy Jacinto, who had, until this moment, trudged along at his side. Some little curiosity to witness the passage of the route of fugitives, had also its influence; for, taking the page by the hand, he led him to the edge of the bridge, where he could observe every thing without inconvenience, and without obstructing the course of others.

The dike of Tacuba was, like that of Iztapalapan, of stone, and so broad that ten horsemen could easily ride on it abreast. Its base was broad, shelving, and rugged, and the summit was, perhaps, six feet above the surface of the water.

The thunder of the twenty horsemen, as they rode over the bridge, interrupted the consolation which the neophyte was about to give to Jacinto, who, hanging closely to his patron's arm, yet looked back towards the city with many sobs for his exiled father. In the gloomy obscurity of the hour, the cavaliers of the van, as they passed, seemed rather like spectres than men; in an instant of time they were hidden from sight among the thick shadows in front. Not less phantom-like appeared the two hundred foot, stealing over the chasm, and vanishing like those who had preceded them. Then came the two thousand Tlascalans, their broken and drooping plumes rustling over their dusky backs, as they strode onward, with steps quickened, but almost noiseless

After these came the cannon—eighteen pieces of different sizes, dragged by rows of Pagans, commanded by the gunners. The bridge groaned under their weight, and a murmur of joy crept over the compacted multitude behind, when they had counted them, one by one, rumbling over the sonorous wood, and knew that the last had crossed in safety.

Much time was necessarily occupied in the passage of these cumbrous instruments; and an interval of several minutes was allowed to intervene betwixt the passage of each, while the cannoniers were looking to the condition of the bridge and the ropes.

It was on these occasions that the greatest quiet prevailed; for then, even breath was hushed in suspense; and it was on these occasions also, that the ears of the neophyte were struck by a sound, which had not, perhaps, at that time, attracted the attention of any other person. The breeze, which occasionally whispered on his cheek, was so light as scarcely to disturb the serenity of the lake; and yet it appeared to him, notwithstanding all this, that in these moments of calm, he could plainly distinguish, upon either hand, and at a little distance, the rippling of water, as if agitated by a moderate wind. He strained his eyes, endeavouring to pierce the gloom, and unravel the cause of this singular commotion—but wholly in vain. The circle of vision was circumscribed into the narrowest bounds; and woe betide the infidel who, fishing in the lake that night, should fall from his canoe in slumber, and be parted from it but twenty feet, in his confusion. The cavalier looked up to the heavens; but the few drops discharged from their stony vault, pattered with a sound almost inaudible upon the water. While he was yet wondering, he heard the voice of one passing him say to a comrade—"Art thou not wroth, Iago, man, to give up yonder rich town to the kites and this fair water to the ducks of Mexico?"

This trivial question gave at once a new colour to his thoughts, for he remembered what millions of wild fowl brooded every night on the lakes; and, almost ashamed that he should have yielded a moment to the suggestions of fear, he turned once more to watch the progress of the army.

The centre division consisted of but an hundred Christian footmen, and half a score cavaliers; but two thousand Tlascalans were added to it, and it was commanded by Cortes in person; who, having ridden across the bridge, as has been said, to prove its strength, now waited for the coming of his party, beyond the breach. Along with this division were conducted the prisoners, and the king's spoil—the latter being carried on the backs of wounded steeds, unfit for other service, as well as on the shoulders of Tlamémé. The prisoners, comprising all the family of Montezuma, whom evil fortune had thrown into the hands of Don Hernan, were environed by the hereditary foes of their race, but protected from any secret stroke of malice, by three or four cavaliers who rode with them.

Among these few horsemen, the neophyte perceived one, across whose saddle-bow there sat what seemed a female, enveloped in thick mantles. In this cavalier he thought, by the murmur of the voice with which he addressed his muffled companion, that he detected his friend, the Senor De Morla.

"Is it thou, Francisco, my brother?" he whispered, inclining towards the cavalier; "and hast thou Benita thus under thy protection?"

"I thank Heaven, yes!" replied De Morla. "But what doest thou on foot, and so far removed from the van? has Fogoso cast thee again? I prythee walk thou by me a little. Dost thou remember thy promise?"

"Surely I do: but speak not of it now; for this moment my heart is very heavy, and I cannot think with pleasure of a contest with Christian man. I will presently follow thee."

"Speak me not what I have told thee to mortal man, for the sake of her whom I hold in my arms, and who already owes thee a life. To-morrow," he continued, exultingly, as he passed—"to-morrow we shall tread upon the lake side; and then, God be with him who strikes for the honour and innocence of woman!"

"Art thou there too, Lorenzo?" said the novice, perceiving the secretary riding at the heels of the young cavalier of Cuenza, and burthened in like manner with the freight of affection. "Guard thy princess well, and have great care of the bridge and the rough edge of the dike; for thy horsemanship is not yet so perfect as De Morla's, nor can thy charger at all compare with the chesnut gelding. Ride on with care, and God be thy speed!"

The centre of the army was, at last, over the bridge. The neophyte cast his eye to the black mass of the rear-guard, which contained the greater part of the troops, both Christian and allied, commanded by Velasquez de Leon and the Tonatiuh; the latter of whom, to show his affection for the island of which he had been, as he said, a king, and to prove his contempt for his late subjects, chose to ride the very last man in the army, while De Leon conducted the front of the division. The latter, stern, decided, and self-willed in all cases, deferred, for a moment, to give the signal to march, in order that the centre might be well cleared of the bridge; but more, perhaps, from a natural love of tyranny, to torture with delay the spirits of his impatient followers.

In this moment of quiet, the sounds which Don Amador had forgotten, were repeated with more distinctness than at first; but still they were of so vague a character, that he could not be certain they were produced by any cause more important than the diving and flapping of water-fowl. Nevertheless, feeling a little uneasiness, he clasped the hand of Jacinto tighter in his own, and strode with him over the bridge. He paused again when he had crossed, and was about to give his whole attention to the mysterious sounds; when, suddenly, he was amazed and startled by the spectre of a man, rising up as from the lake, and springing on the causeway close by his side.

He drew his sword, demanding quickly, but with perturbation—"Who and what art thou, that comest thus from the depths of the waters?"

"Tetragrammaton, peace! Dost thou not hear?'

"Hear what, sir conjurer? Hast thou been listening likewise to the wild fowl? By my troth, I thought thou wert a spirit!"

"Wild fowl!" muttered Botello, with a horse-laugh. "Such wild fowl as eat carrion, and flap the water like crocodiles. Hah! dost thou not hear? Lay thine ear upon the causeway at the water's edge, —but thou hast not time. Get thee to thy horse, and delay not; and if thou seest Cortes, or any other discreet cavalier, bid him draw and be ready. I said, that some should escape, but not all! God be with thee! follow quickly, and sheath not thy sword."

"Surely, this time thou art mad, Botello! Here are no foes."

But the remonstrance of the cavalier was cut short by the instant flight of the magician; and ere the words were out of his mouth, a horseman, crossing the bridge, and riding up to him, said sternly, "Who art thou, Sir Knave and Sir Witless! that babblest thus aloud, in time of peril, contrary to—"

"I am thy very good friend, Senor De Leon " said

the novice, abruptly; "and, waving any difficulty which might spring from the heat of thy words, if duly considered, I think fit to assure thee, that I have just parted from the necromancer, Botello, by whom I am advised to bid thee, as well as all other discreet officers whom I may see, to draw sword, and remain in readiness for a foe; there being certain sounds on the water, which, in his opinion, are ominous of evil. For myself, I bid God guard thee, meaning, in person, to join the van, as soon as possible."

The cavaliers parted, De Leon riding back to his party, without uttering a word; and Don Amador, with the page, stepping forwards fleetly, as soon to find himself among the Tlascalans of the centre. Through these he made his way, ever and anon casting his eye to the lake, and looking for the tokens of a foe, but without perceiving any thing at all unusual. He gained the midst of this band of allies, reached the side of his friend, and laid his hand on De Morla's arm. A low wailing voice came from the folds of the garments, which veiled the countenance of Minnapotzin; and some strong agitation shook the frame of his friend

"Think not of love now, my brother!" cried the neophyte, hurriedly; "but be warned that thou art in danger, and Minnapotzin with thee. It is thought that enemies are at hand."

Having thus spoken, and without waiting for an answer, Don Amador, still urging Jacinto along, endeavoured to make his way through the dense bodies of Tlascalans, which separated him from Don Hernan. He reached their front, he stepped upon the little space left between them and the general, and placed his eyes upon Cortes. But before he had yet spoken, it seemed as if the whole moving mass of the army had been converted into marble on the causeway; for instantly, as if with one consent, the train came to a dead halt, and a cry, low, but breathed from the hearts of men struck with mortal dread, rose from the van to the rear, in one universal groan.

The cavalier turned where all eyes were turned, and beheld a sudden pyramid of fire, like one of the many gushes of flame he had already seen in this volcanic land, save that the blaze was steadier, shoot up, from a vast height in the air, over the distant city, and plunge its sanguine point against the heavens; while, at the same moment, its lurid mass reflected and reversed on the lake, darted over the water to his feet, in a path of blood—as if Mexitli, the Terrible God, had at last roused from slumber and couched his gigantic spear against the slayers of his children. The blaze illumined the lake far round, and shining on the casques of cavaliers and the plumes of Tlascalans, disclosed the whole line of the army, stretched along the calzada. In an instant more, the neophyte, petrified with awe, perceiving that this mighty bale-fire was kindled on the top of the great temple; and in the strong and glaring line, which it struck out upon the water, there was revealed a mass of living objects, floating like birds upon the element, yet specked with the human colours of Mexico. At the same moment, and while his eye yet wavered between the flaming pillar and the moving objects on the water, there came from the pyramid a sound, heard once before, and never more to be forgotten. The horn of the gods was winded; the doleful and dismal note came booming with hideous uproar over the waters; and before the hills had caught up its echoes, the whole lake, right and left, in front, and on the rear, rung, roared, and trembled, under the yells of an hundred thousand infidels.

CHAPTER LVIII.

The situation of the Spaniards at that moment, though sufficiently frightful to every one, was yet known in all its horrors only to the leaders of the van. As hope is ever independent of judgment, ever unreasonable and unreflective, the absence of the bridge, at the first sluice, was not enough to persuade the fugitives, that the passage of the second might be equally interrupted. But, at the moment when the signal-fire was kindled on the temple, Sandoval had already reached this ditch, and perceived that its bridge was also demolished, and, as it seemed, very recently too; for there yet remained a huge timber lying across the chasm—left, as he feared, rather as some decoy and trap, than, as was more probable, deserted suddenly by workmen, scared from their labours by the approach of the Spaniards.

The three ditches divided the dike into four portions, of as many furlongs in extent. On the second of these portions was concentrated the whole retreating army, its front resting upon a sluice of great depth, passable by footmen (for the great beam was soon discovered to be sound), but not by the horse and artillery, without the portable bridge, which yet rested over the first breach. This second obstacle being overcome, it was apparent, that a third would still remain to be surmounted; and the passage of both was to be effected in the presence, and in the midst, of a great enemy.

As we have said, the beacon-light, shooting up from the pyramid, and continuing to burn with intensity, brought light, where all before was darkness; and revealed such innumerable fleets of canoes hovering on both flanks as the novice had not seen, even on that day when he first trode upon a dike of Mexico. But the spirit that then slumbered was now awake, and as the rowers responded with their wild cries to the roar of the sacred trumpet, they struck the water furiously with their paddles until the whole lake seemed to boil up with a spray of fire, and thus they rushed madly against the causeway.

The novice cast his eye upon the general. The ruddy glare of the beacon could not change the deadly pallor that covered his cheeks; but, nevertheless, with this ghastly countenance turned to the foe he cried out cheerily, or at least firmly, to those immediately in advance, "Who ho, cannoniers! your quoins and handspikes! your horns and matches! and show me your throats to the lake-rats!" Then, raising his voice to its trumpet-tones, he continued, as if giving counsel and command to all, "Be bold and fearless, and strike for the honour of God, brave Christians! So ho, De Leon, valiant brother; and thou, Alvarado, matchless cavalier, raise me the bridge, and be quick; for here we need it."

The voices of other officers were heard, faintly mingled with the din, but not long; every moment the shouts of the Mexicans, continued without intermission, became louder, and their canoes were plunging nearer to the causeway.

A pang rent the bosom of Don Amador; "I must get me to my companions," he cried to Jacinto, "and what can I do for thee this night, young page that I love?"

"I will follow thee," said the page, tremulously; "I will die with my lord."

"Would that I had thee but upon the back of Fogoso! for methinks that even De Morla should not strike more truly for Minnapotzin than would I, this night, for thee."

"Where goest thou, De Leste?" cried Cortes, as the novice pushed by. "Pause—thou art best among the cannoniers."

A dreadful yell at that moment drowned the general's voice: but one still more dreadful was heard, when, as the Pagans drew breath to repeat the cry, the Christians in front heard the rear-guard exclaiming with loud and bitter shrieks, "The bridge! the bridge! it is fast and immoveable! The weight of the horses and artillery had sunk it deep into the chasm, and no human strength could stir it from its foundation

These words and sights were all the occurrences of a moment. There was neither time for observation nor lamentation. The infidels on the water rushed to the attack with the same fury which had so often driven them upon the spears of the garrison; and, not less by their cries than their apparent numbers, it was made obvious that the whole strength of the great city was gathered together for this undertaking; for those who had caught a little of their language, could distinguish the different quarters of the island encouraging each other with cries of "Ho, Tlatelolco! shall Majotla strike first at the foe?—Alzacualco! on; for Tecpan is swift and mirthful. On, oh! for Mexitli is speaking; on, for our gods are on the temple, and they hunger for the Teuctli!" The line of the army was full half a mile in length; but, as far as it stretched, and further than the eye could penetrate beyond either extremity, a triple row of canoes, on each side of the causeway, was seen closing upon it with the speed and fury of breakers, dashing against a stranded ship.

"Now, cannoniers!" cried Don Hernan, elevating his voice above the tumult, when the rushing masses were within but a few paces of the causeway; "now to your linstocks, and touch in the name of God."

The damp gunpowder sparkled and hissed on the vents, but did not fail the Christians in their need. The roar of the volley was like the peal of an earthquake; and, right and left, as eighteen horizontal columns of fire darted from the engines, the lake boiled up with a new fury, fragments of canoes and the bodies of men were seen flung up into the air, and yells of agony which chilled the blood, bore witness to the dreadfulness of the slaughter.

"Quick, and again!" cried Don Hernan, eagerly. "Shoot fast, and shoot well; and know that I will shortly be back with ye. Ho; Sandoval! why dost thou loiter? plunge into the ditch, and swim. Rest where thou art, De Leste; for thou art too weak for battle. Give thine aid to the cannoniers."

The confused and huddled Tlascalans, who formed the rear of Sandoval's party, shouted at the cry of the Teuctli, and made way for him. A cavalier, bearing a burthen in his arms, spurred after, with a mad impetuosity, which rendered him regardless of the many naked wretches he trampled to the earth: it was De Morla. The example thus set by the apparent flight of the two hidalgos, was followed by others; and the allies were broken by the hoofs of Christians, while still enduring the arrows, that came like a driving rain from the lake

Meanwhile, it was evident, though the cannon, re-charged and shot off again with extraordinary quickness, served to keep the part of the causeway where they stood free from assailants, that they had effected a landing, perhaps, both in front and rear —certainly on the latter—where they were already engaged hand to hand with the Spaniards. The thunder of the explosions did not conceal from the novice the shrieks of his countrymen. His blood boiled with fury—"Come with me, Jacinto," he cried. "We will reach Fogoso; and then I can do my duty to my friends, and smite these accursed murderers without deserting thee."

He dragged the trembling page after him; he darted among the cannoniers, and passed the artillery. He reached the Tlascalans, who followed the van—but havoc was already among their ranks. As he gained them, he perceived the shelving sides of the causeway lined with canoes, from which were springing up, like locusts, a crowd of Mexicans brandishing their glassy maces, and rushing with the yells of wolves upon their ancient foes. Barbarians were mingled with barbarians in one hideous mass of slaughter, impassable and impenetrable

His heart sunk within him. "I have prejudiced thy life, as well as my own, this night," he said. "Would that I had never left the back of Fogoso."

Before he had yet time to resolve whether to return to the cannoniers, or to make one more effort to pierce the bloody mass, he was descried by the crew of a piragua, which that moment was urged upon the dike with such violence, that it was split in twain by the shock. The eager warriors rushed up the ascent with a shriek of exultation, and brandished their spears. The neophyte retreated; but neither the rapidity of his steps nor the keenness of his blows would, perhaps, have availed against their numbers, enfeebled as he was, and trammelled by the grasp of the affrighted Jacinto, had not a party of Spanish footmen, flying from the rear, come that moment to his aid. These, though they forced the barbarians to give way, were in their turn driven back upon the cannon; and Don Amador was fain to follow them.

The audacity of the foe seemed still to increase rather than diminish, and twice or thrice efforts were made by certain valiant madmen among them, to spring to land immediately in the mouths of the cannon. These were instantly speared by the many desperate Spaniards, who flying from their posts in the rear, which were now known to be in extremity, took refuge among the artillery, as the only place of safety, and there fought with better resolution.

In the meanwhile, the efforts of the enemy still remaining unabated, the prisoners and many of the rear-guard pressing wildly forward, and Don Hernan and most of the officers having fled to the front, from which they had not returned, the gunners were themselves seized with a panic; and, without regarding the death on which they were thus rushing, began to leave their pieces and fly. The representations of Don Amador served to arrest some of them, and other soldiers taking their places at the guns, they yielded passively to his instructions; and he found himself at once in the post of a commander.

The many bitter reflections that harrowed his own bosom he spoke not, and sharply he reprimanded others who were yielding to despair. Whatever might be the difficulty of advancing, he felt that such a measure was become indispensable, as promising the only hope of salvation: for every instant the clamours increased on the rear, as if there the barbarians had attacked in the greatest numbers, and were approaching nearer to the cannon flushed with slaughter and victory. He instructed the gunners in what manner they should rush forwards with their charged pieces, pointed obliquely, so as to sweep the sides of the dike, shoot them off, when arrested by too determined a front of resistance, and loading quickly take advantage of the confusion following each discharge so as to gain as much ground as possible, while still manfully fighting. He hoped thus, besides succouring the Tlascalans in front, and giving room for the rear-guard to follow, to reach the second ditch, where, as he had heard, the beam still gave passage to the footmen, but where his most sanguine wishes could point him out no other hope than to stand by the cannon till relieved, or abandon them and fly, as it seemed to him all had done who had already crossed the breach.

He animated the gunners with his voice, and with his actions; and so great was the effect of the discharges on the Indians landing, that the artillery-men were able to rush forwards perhaps a score yards after each volley; thus convincing all of the wisdom of the measure, and the probability of escape.

Two circumstances, however, greatly diminished the exultation which the cavalier would have otherwise felt at the success of his stratagem. Though the Tlascalans in front ever responded to the shouts of his gunners, and though each discharge seemed to bring him nearer to them, yet ever, when a volley was preceded by the loud "Viva!" meant to encourage the allies, the answer seemed to come from the same distance, and the mass of feathered warriors, lit up by the discharge, disclosed the bodies of none but frowning Mexicans. The other circumstance was still more appalling; the space behind, left vacant by his advance, was no longer occupied by foot or horse, by treasure-bearer or prisoner, by Spanish musketeer or Tlascalan spearman. A few dusky groups could be seen running to and fro, behind; but yet they seemed rather to rush backwards than to follow after.

"God save the rear-guard!" he muttered, "for it is surely surrounded. On, brave cannoniers. Cortes shall not be ignorant of your deeds this night, and Don Carlos, the emperor, shall know of your fame."

"The shout with which the cannoniers again poured forth the deadly volley was repeated with victorious energy, when the Mexicans, scattered by the discharge, or leaping to avoid it into the water, parted away from before them; and they found themselves suddenly upon the brink of the second ditch. The great beam lay in its place; but the dark water in the chasm was filled and agitated by the bodies of men, wounded and suffocating. The white tunic of the Mexican was confounded with the plume of a Christian cavalier; the red arm of an infidel—Tlascalan or foeman—shook by the side of a Castilian spear; the white visages of dead men rolled on the necks of drowning horses; bales of rich cotton stuffs, lances dancing up and down like the leaded bulrushes of children, armour of escaupil, garments, and bodies of dying and dead, were floating together in such horrible confusion, that the water seemed to heave and bubble as with a living corruption.

The sight of the ditch and the beam clear of ene mies, fired the cannoniers with new hopes; and in the frenzy of their joy they would instantly have dropped their fuses and handspikes, and taken to flight, had it not been that Don Amador flung himself upon the beam, and striking the first man dead, commanded them still to stand to their pieces. "Base caitiffs are ye all," he cried "who, thus having the victory and the lives of half the army in your hands, should so desert your posts in the midst of triumph. Wheel round half your pieces, and sweep the causeway sides behind; for I hear the coming of friends. Would ye give up your pieces to infidels? They are your safety".

The reproof of the cavalier, the sight of their dead comrade, and the sword which had punished him, still commanding the narrow pathway, the voices of Christians behind, but, more than all, the manifest truth of the declaration, that their safety depended on their remaining by the artillery, turned the gun-ners at once from their purpose; and their resolution received a new confirmation, when a Christian voice was heard shouting in the front, as if of some cavalier heading a band of returning friends, and when the next moment a Spanish soldier was seen to run towards them, leap on the beam, and then spring from it to the causeway.

"Santiago, and shoot on!" cried the overjoyed gunners; "for Cortes is coming."

"What, ho, knave Lazaro," cried the novice, as the blaze of the discharge showed him in the new comer the countenance of his henchman. "Where goest thou? Wherefore hast thou left the horses? And where is Don Hernan?"

"Master, dear master, is it thou?" cried Lazaro, with such a shout of joy as drowned even the yells of death about him. "Quick, for the love of God! over the beam, with all these varlets—for life! for life! Don Hernan is fled, and all the cavaliers!"

"Peace, thou villain!—Heed not this trembling fool," exclaimed Amador, quickly. "You hear!—the last ditch is bridged and free, and ye can, at any moment, reach the firm land, as the cavaliers have done. Give me another volley or two, for God, for the honour of Spain, and for your friends, who are fast approaching. We will march together with the whole rear, to ensure safety. Quick!—See ye not how yonder fiends are rushing into your muzzles? Viva! A bold shot for St. James, and our people!"

The cavalier turned to Lazaro: he was bleeding, and he cast a look of despair on his master.

"Why art thou idle? thou wert bred to the linstock, sirrah. Show thyself a Christian man and true. Hark! hearest thou not? 'Tis the shout of De Leon! Bravely, bold hearts! the rear-guard is nigh. Hah! halon halon! Don Pedro."

"'Tis the voice of the secretary!" cried Lazaro; "and God help me, but he cries for succour!"

"Ho, Senor, Senor Don Amador! for the love of Christ!"—the wild shout of Fabueno, for the neophyte could no longer doubt it was he, was suddenly interrupted: the shrill shriek of a woman succeeded; and then, every thing was lost in a hurrican of yells, so intermingled that no one could say whether they came from Christians or Pagans.

"Stay—drop thy match—hold me this boy, as thou holdest thy life, and suffer none to pass the beam—"

"For the sake of the cross thou adorest, the maiden thou lovest!" cried the terrified boy, clinging to the cavalier, leave me not, oh, leave me not, in this horror, to die alone. The Mexicans will kill me, for I have no gown of a priestess to protect me."

Notwithstanding the boiling excitement of the novice, these last words filled his brain with strange thoughts, but still so confused that they were more like the momentary phantasms of delirium, than the proper suggestions of reason. But whatever they were, they were instantly driven out of his mind, by another cry from Fabueno, seemingly hard by, but so feeble and wailing, that a less acute ear might have supposed it came from a considerable distance.

He shook the boy off, flung him into the arms of Lazaro, crying—"Answer his safety with thy life!—with thy life!" and immediately darted through the cannoniers, and retraced his steps on the cause-way

By this time, the fire on the pyramid had attained its greatest brilliancy, and the wind having died entirely away, it projected its lofty spire to heaven, and burned with a tranquillity which seemed to leave it motionless; while its reflection on that part of the lake which shared not in the agitations of conflict, produced a spectacle of peace in singular contrast with the horrible scene of carnage, that moment represented on the causeway. The light it shed, though it made objects visible even as far as the second ditch, did not illuminate the furthest part of the dike; and there, whatever deed of death might be presented, was hidden from the eyes of all but the actors themselves.

Raising his voice aloud, and running towards the nearest group, Don Amador sought out the secretary. But this group, before he had yet reached it, started away, and fled, with loud cries, towards the city, or to where the tumult was greatest; and he knew by their shouts of 'Tlatelolco! ho, Tlatelolco!' that they were Mexicans. On the spot they had thus deserted, the novice stumbled over the body of a man, his throat cut from ear to ear, his cotton armour torn to pieces; and from the shreds, as the carcass rolled under his foot, there fell out, rattling and jingling on the stones, divers vessels of gold and jewels, such as had been grasped in the treasury.

Without pausing to survey this victim of covetousness, the cavalier ran on; and, hearing many Christian voices, ringing now with curses, now with prayers, and now with shouts of triumph, he called out at the top of his voice—"On, brothers! on to the artillery! advance! Strike well, and forward! —Ho, Lorenzo! comrade! where art thou? and why answerest thou not?"

A gurgling sound, as of one suffocating in the flood, drew his eye to the lake almost under his feet.

The water rippled, as if lately disturbed by the falling of some heavy body; and just where the circling waves washed sluggishly up the shelving dike, there lay a white mass like a human figure, the head and shoulders buried in the tide. The wash of the ripple stirred the garments, and in part the corse, so that it still seemed to be living; but when the novice had caught it up, he beheld the visage of a very youthful girl, her forehead cloven by a sword of obsidian, and the broken weapon wedged fast in the brain. At the same instant, the water parted hard by, and there rose up a dark object, that seemed the back of a horse, across which lay the body of a man in bright armour, the legs upwards, but the head and breast ingulfed. For an instant, this dreary sight was presented; but, slowly, the steed, whose nostrils were still under water, as if held down by the grasp of the dead rider, rolled over on his side, and the body, slipping off the other way, sunk headlong and silently into the flood, followed presently by the horse; and the next moment the waters were at rest. —"God rest thee, Lorenzo!" cried the novice, laying down the corse of Eugracia. "Thy life and thy hopes, thy ambition and thy love, are ended together —but now can I not lament thee."

He started up, as the causeway suddenly shook with the tramp of hoofs, and a cavalier, without spear or helm, dashed madly by. Almost at the moment of passing, whether it was that the strength of the fugitive had suddenly given out, or whether, as seemed more probable, a flight of arrows had been sent in pursuit, and struck both horse and rider, the steed made a fierce bound in the air; and then pursued his course, masterless. "Follow onwards, ye men of the rear!" cried the novice, struck with a sudden horror for now he became conscious that the artillery had been, for several moments, silent; and when he looked after the flying steed, though he could not, at that distance, perceive any thing, he could hear fierce voices mingled together in strife; and presently the riderless horse, as if driven back by a wall of foes, returned, passing him again with the speed of the wind.

The limbs of the cavalier were nerved with the strength of fury; for he thought he heard the screams of Jacinto, ascending with the harsher cries of the gunners; and scarcely did that frightened charger fly more swiftly from the battle, than he himself now back to it. "Thy duty, knave Lazaro!" he cried. "The boy—save the boy!"

"Don Amador! oh Amador! Don Amador!" came to his ears, in a voice that rent his heart.

"I come, I come," shouted the cavalier, redoubling his exertions, but not his speed, for that was at the highest.

"Oh Heaven, Amador! Amador!—"

In his distraction, the neophyte confounded two voices into one; and while he replied to one, his thoughts flew to another. "I come! Answer me— where art thou? I am here—where art thou?"

As he uttered these words, he sprang through the artillery, which was without servers—among bodies which were lifeless—and stood alone—for there was no living creature there but himself—on the borders of the sluice, the beam over which was broken off in the middle, and the further portion only left standing in its place.

He cast his amazed and affrighted eye from the water, heaving as before with the struggles of dying men, to the corpse on whose bosom he was standing. In the grinning countenance, covered with blood, and horribly mutilated by a blow which had pierced through the mouth, jaws, and throat, to the severed spine, he beheld the features of Lazaro, fixed in death; and looked wildly at his side, to discover the body of the page. No corse of Jacinto was there; but, on the spot where he had charged him to stand, the novice perceived a jewel, catching a ray from the distant fire, glittering red, as with blood, and held by a golden chain to which it was attached in the death-grasp of the henchman. He snatched it from the earth and from the hand of the dead, and looking on it with a stare of horror, beheld the holy and never-to-be-forgotten cross of rubies.

With that night, the scales fell from his eyes, and a million of wild thoughts beset his brain. The magical knowledge of the page, coupled with his childish and effeminate youth—his garments, so fitted to disguise—his scrupulous modesty—his tears, his terrors, his affection, and his power over the mind of the cavalier—the garb of the priestess, so lately acknowledged—the vision in the house of the Wali, Abdalla—the cross of jewels, doubtless snatched from the neck of Jacinto, when barbarians were tearing him from the faithful Lazaro—all these came to the brain of the cavalier with the blaze and shock of a cannon suddenly discharged at his ears. He looked again to the corses about him—they were those of the gunners; to the ditch—it writhed no more; and then, uttering the name of Leila, he sunk, in a stupor to the earth.

CHAPTER LIX.

While these scenes of blood were passing in the centre of the army, and a hideous mystery concealed the fate of the rear, the condition of the advanced guard, though not altogether hopeless, was scarce less terrific. When the forces of Sandoval, comprising many of the followers, both common soldiers and captains, of Narvaez, were made acquainted with fate of the bridge, and beheld the vast number of foes that impelled their canoes towards the further bank of the second ditch, as if to secure the passage, they waited not for directions to cross over, by swimming. They imitated the example of their commander, Sandoval, who, leaping from his horse, and leading him into the water, passed over by the beam, while still holding and guiding the swimming animal. This mode of proceeding being necessarily very slow, and the barbarians rushing, in the meanwhile, against them with unspeakable fury, the impatience of the cavaliers became so great, that many of them spurred their steeds down the sides of the dike, and thus, swimming them along by the beam, passed to the other side. Divers of the footmen, seduced by the example, leaped, in like manner, into the lake ; and the Tlascalans, at all times less formidable opponents than their armed allies, being t the same moment violently assaulted, sprang also .nto the water, so that it became alive with the bodies of man and horse—as if a herd of caymans, such as haunt the lower rivers of that climate, were disporting and battling in the tide. While thus embarrassed and entangled together in the water, the swimmers were set upon by the Mexicans, who, pushing their canoes among them, and handling their heavy paddles, as well as war-clubs, dispatched them, almost without labour, and with roars of exultation.

It was at this instant of confusion, and while those Tlascalans who still remained on the dike contended but feebly with the augmenting assailants, that Don Hernan, followed closely by De Morla, and others, dashed over friend and foe, and reached the ditch. The scene of horror there disclosed, the miserable shrieks of Christian comrades, perishing in the gap and the neighbouring parts of the lake, the increasing yells of infidels behind, touched the stout heart of Cortes with fear. He descended from his steed, sprang upon the beam, and crossed, crying out, at the same time, to those who followed —"Hold cavaliers! Wait ye here for the artillery : leave not this gap to the murderers. Fight ye here well, and ye shall have help from the van."

So saying he sprang again upon his horse. De Morla was at his heels, bearing Minnapotzin in his arms. but on foot the chesnut gelding was left drowning in the sluice, entangled and sinking under the weight of a dozen men, who had seized upon him, in their terror

"God forgive thee cavalier !" cried Cortes, as he caught the eye of Francisco ; "for, for this barbarian puppet, thou playest the coward, and leavest thy friend to perish, without the aid of a blow !"

De Morla answered not, but with a ghastly smile uncovered and pointed at the features of the unconscious princes.

"If she be dead," cried the general, "give her body to the waters of her native lake; if she live, commit her to the care of the Tlascalans ; then call on thy saints, and show that thou art not a craven !"

Then without waiting for an answer, Don Hernan spurred onwards, striking down, almost at every step—for the whole causeway was beset—some luckless savage ; and now and then, in his desperation, smiting at the hands of certain of his own countrymen, who strove to arrest the galloping steed, and spring behind him.

He reached the third and last ditch ; it was bridgeless, like the others, and like the others, a theatre of disorder and massacre. The pillar of fire here revealed its figure but luridly and faintly, through the thick mists and the cannon-smoke, sluggishly driving over the lake; but he thought he could trace, in the distant gloom, in front, the outline of those rugged hills which lie along the western borders of the lake. He turned his face backwards to the city ; a tempest of yells—the Pagan shouts of victory, and the last cries of Spaniards to God—came mingling on a gust, that waved the distant flame to and fro, like a sword of fire in the hands of some colossal fiend. A bolt of ice smote through his bosom ; and when he plunged into the sluice, and rising on the opposite bank, drove the sharp spurs into the flanks of his charger, no man of all the army fled with more craven horror than himself.

An hour afterwards, the moon, diminished to the thinnest crescent, crept, with a sickly and cadaverous visage, to the summit of the eastern hills, and peeped down into the valley, preceding the dawn that was soon to look upon its scenes of death.

At this moment of moonrise, those few Christians who had escaped from the battle were grouped at the end of the dike, deliberating, in unspeakable agitation, upon the course they were to pursue. Many advised that they should instantly resume their flight, and trust to their speed to put them before morning beyond the reach of their merciless enemies ; some insisted upon remaining to give help to such wretches as ever and anon made their way from the causeway, and, with tears of joy and loud thanksgivings, threw themselves among their friends ; a few, more honourable or more insane, among whom were Sandoval and Don Christobal de Olid (a very valiant cavalier, to whom other histories have been juster than this), demanded, with stern reproaches, that their leader should conduct them again to the combat, which was still raging on the lake, and rescue their countrymen out of that fiery furnace, or at once honourably and justly perish with them.

"Is there one here, who, if I refuse this mad counsel, will say I do it from fear ?" demanded the general, with a voice broken by agony and despair. "What I do I do for the good of Heaven, the king, and yourselves. If I suffer you to return, then will ye perish, Spain lose an appanage worthy the firstborn of an emperor, and in that cursed city God be daily grieved by the sight of idolatry and sacrifice. By remaining where we are, we shall save many lives ; and this land of milk and honey, of corn and o gold, though now torn from us for our sins, will be yet the guerdon of our resolution. I aver and protest, that if we return to the hell that is on the lake, we shall be lost to a man. Is there one, then, who says I remain here from fear ?"

Notwithstanding the deep grief and agitation which gave their tone to the words of the general, there was mingled withal a touch of such sternness as forbade even the boldest to reply. Great, therefore, was the surprise of all, when a hollow and broken voice murmured, in answer, from the causeway—"There is one—there are an hundred—there have been (but now they are not) a thousand men, who say that this night Cortes hath proved a craven, a deserter of his friends, a traitor to his king, a betrayer of his God—and therefore a villain."

As these words were uttered, there staggered up the bank on which the party rested, a figure, seemingly of a cavalier, but his armour so rent and demolished as in many places to leave his body naked.

His helmet was gone, and his locks, dripping with water and blood, fell over his breast, leaving their crimson stains on the white mantle muffling the body of some slighter figure, which he bore in his arms.

"I forgive thee, De Morla," cried the general, rushing forwards, and then recoiling, as Don Francisco deposited the burden at his feet, and removing the cloth, reeking with water as with gore, disclosed to the view of all, gently touched by the ray of that wasted and melancholy moon, the countenance of the dead princess. "Who hath struck the daughter of Montezuma? Who hath done this deed?"

"He who hath smitten the hearts of a thousand Christians, by leading them into peril and deserting them in their need," said the cavalier, with a tranquillity that struck all with terror, for it was unnatural. "He who commanded me to fling, while living, this child of a murdered king into the lake, or upon the spears of Tlascalans, and then get me back to the foes, that he might himself fly in safety."

"Thou art mad, Francisco! and thou doest me foul injustice!" said Don Hernan, hurriedly. "I fled not; nor did I bid thee do aught but intrust this hapless maiden to some strong band of allies, thou being thyself on foot, and therefore incompetent to protect her."

'You called me craven, too," said the cavalier, with a hoarse laugh, raising his voice aloud. "Thou liest! I am braver than thou; for my body is covered with wounds—from the crown to the sole there is no part but is mangled; and yet thou hast not a limb but is untouched. You call me craven! God smite you with punishment, for you are all cravens, knaves, and murderers together. You wait on the banks while we are dying, and you call us cravens! God will do us right! God will avenge us! God will hear our prayers! and so God curse you all, and keep your bones for the maws of infidels."

Thus speaking, and concluding with the voice of a madman, the young cavalier cast a look on the dead princess, and uttering a horrid scream ran back distracted to the causeway.

"In the name of God, on!" exclaimed an hundred voices; "we are not cravens and murderers, and Spaniards shall not fall unaided."

Don Hernan himself, stung by the sarcasms of the unhappy and well-beloved cavalier, was the first to clap spurs to his horse; and again the thunder of cavalry, and the quick tread of footmen moving in order, were heard on the dike of Tacuba.

CHAPTER LX.

Thousands of infuriated and exulting savages had, in the meanwhile, landed from their canoes at the second ditch, raised their cries of triumph over the abandoned artillery, and struck, with a rage not to be appeased by death, the Christian corses which lay so thick among them. But while living invaders remained, either in the front or rear, they tarried not long to waste their malice on the dead.

The cavalier Don Amador, when he made the marvellous discovery detailed in a preceding chapter, and perceived that the fair and lamented being of his dreams Heaven had permitted so long to walk by his side in this new and strange world—revealing her to his eyes only at the moment when destined to be snatched from them for ever—felt at that instant

of discovery as if all the ties which bound him to existence were at once dissevered. Rage at his blindness, furious compunctions of remorse for his negligence, and an agony of grief at the supposed dreadful fate of the maiden, were mingled with a sort of wild indignation against the providence which, by veiling his eyes and shutting his ears to the suggestions of his heart (for surely from the moment he looked upon the page his affections were given him), had robbed him of his mistress. It was not, therefore, wonderful, that such a conflict of mind, acting upon a body weakened by previous wounds and sickness, and exhausted by present exertions, should have thrown him across the body of Lazaro, himself, to all appearance, full as lifeless. And thus he lay for half an hour, insensible to the battle, which was now drawing nigh to the ditch, and now leaving it to its charnel solitude.

He was recalled to life, by feeling some one tug forcibly at the sacred jewel, which he retained throughout his lethargy, with the same instinct which had preserved it in the death-grasp of the henchman. More lucky than Lazaro, yet scarce more happy, this violence woke up the sleeping energies of life; and he raised his head, though only to stare about him with a bewildered look of unconsciousness.

"God be thanked!" exclaimed a Christian voice in his ear, as a friendly hand seized him by the shoulder; "lead or gold, glass or precious stone, never was cross of Christ picked up on the wayside, but good fortune followed after it! What ho, senor! up and away! The things that I spoke of have come to pass. Kalidon-Sadabath dances in the Crystal; he loves the smell of blood!—Up! arise and away, for thine hour is not come."

The cavalier arose, and stared at the friendly magician; which Botello seeing, and supposing he was now fully restored to his wits, this lunatic of another sort seized him by the arm, and dragging him towards the water, said—"Fear not; if thou hast not the skill of a crocodile, know that I can bear thee across the channel; and that the more easily, that it is already choked with corses, and no Mexicans nigh to oppose us."

The neophyte broke from his companion, and with wild cries of Leila! Leila! ran towards the cannon.

"God save thee! art thou mad? Dost thou call upon woman or devil? This is no place for girls! and never heard I of imp called Leila."

"Thou knowest not my wretchedness, Botello,' said Don Amador. "Let me look again, if her body be not here. Hah!" he cried, struck with a sudden thought, and turning quickly to the conjurer—"Thou art a magician, and knowest of the dead as well as the living. I have decried thine art, but now I acknowledge thy wisdom. Behold this rubied cross—oh Heaven! that I should hold it in my hand, and know that, but a moment since, it was on the neck of Leila! Look, enchanter; this jewel came from the neck of a woman, whom but now I left standing on this brink. Call her from the dead, if she have perished; or show me what path she hath trodden, if she be living; and I will reward thee, though I give thee the half of my patrimony. A woman, I tell thee! Wilt thou not believe me? Half my estate but to look upon her!"

It was manifest, even to the unhappy novice himself, that Botello regarded him as a madman. But nevertheless he replied earnestly—"Here is no place for conjuration : there be devils enough about us already. Tarry not here; for this will neither benefit thee, nor her of whom thou speakest. Spring into the ditch—rush with me to the main; and then, what thou seekest thou shalt know. Courage, courage! Dost thou not see yonder star, that creeps up by the dim moon, under the rack, dimmer even than the dim moon? Under that star came I into earth; and while it shineth in that conjunction, the dart of a savage cannot wound me—no, not though it strike me upon the naked brow?—Hark! dost thou not hear? The fragments of the rear-guard are approaching. Let us swim this abyss before they reach us, lest we be entangled among them. Hesitate not : we will go together, for I see thou art worn and feeble; and I remember that thou gavest me succour in the streets of Mexico."

The neophyte had yielded, with a sort of captive-like and despairing submission, to the will of Botello; and was descending with him moodily to the water, when suddenly the latter paused, listening to a Christian shout in the distance, as of one approaching them from the shore

" Hark! it is repeated!—Viva! They come from the main; they have beaten the cubs of darkness—Viva! viva! Santiago, and quick, valiant friends!"

The joyous shouts of Botello were re-echoed, though only by a single voice. Yet this was evidently approaching, and with great rapidity.

During the whole time of the resuscitation of Don Amador, and of his dialogue with the enchanter, the causeway in the neighbourhood of the ditch had been free from foes, but only because it was free from Christians; and the lake in the vicinity was equally solitary. But now as they stood listening to the shouts, the two companions could perceive the lake, some distance in front, on both sides of the dike, boiling up in foam under canoes impelled towards them with extraordinary violence, seemingly upon the flank of the party from which proceeded the cry. But whatever was the speed of the canoes, it seemed to be unequal to that of the Christian, whose shouts, wild and loud, and now almost incessantly repeated, grew shriller and nearer every moment.

" On, valiant friends! on!—heed not the Pagans," shouted Botello, as the canoes cut the water within an hundred paces of the ditch.

Thanks be to God! I see them! Hah! good! and here—Hark to his voice! how cheery!—here comes the valorous De Morla!"

As he spoke, the figure of De Morla, outstripping the wind, was seen running towards the ditch, while some of the arrows shot after him by the pursuers, and passing him, fell even at the feet of the expectant pair.

The sight of his friend kindled the ardour of Don Amador. He shouted aloud—" On, valiant brother!—It is I! thy sworn friend of Cuenza!"

To this speech De Morla answered with a yell, that chilled the heart of his townsman; and running without a moment's hesitation, and without slackening his speed, to the end of the broken beam, where it overhung the middle of the sluice, he sprang from it, as if assisted by its elasticity, to so great a height into the air, that it was plain he would clear the chasm in the bound. As he leaped, he waved his sword, and uttered a scream; a cloud of arrows at the same time whistled through the atmosphere; and when he reached the ground, twenty of these deadly missiles were sticking in his body.

The neophyte raised up his head; one arrow was in his brain : it snapped off, as the head rolled on Amador's arm. A thrill and a gasp were the last and only manifestations of suffering. The next instant the body of De Morla rolled down the shelving plane of the ditch, and sunk, with a few bubbles, among a hundred of his countrymen, already sepulchred therein.

CHAPTER LXI.

Meantime the reappearance of the barbarians seemed to cut off the last hope of escape from Amador and his companion; but the magician, answering the cavalier's sullen look of despair with a laugh, and pointing to the little star, which still made its way up the cloudy arch along with the moon, said, dragging him at the same time towards the artillery —" What the spirits say is true! All this said they of De Morla. May he rest with God — Amen! Fear not; be of good heart : while the star shines there is hope —and hope for both; for though I have not yet read thy fate in full, still, while thou art at my side, thou canst be in no great peril. At the worst, and when the worst comes, it is written, that eagles shall come down from heaven, and bear me away on their backs. Hast thou never a flint and dry tinder, to light me a linstock? Here hath some knavish gunner left his piece charged, and the grains of sulphur still heaped up from rimbase to cascable. A good roar now might do marvels. Quick! they are upon us. Fling thee under the wheels, and look but as dead as thou didst erewhile, till the cut-throats be passed. Hah! 'fore God, dost thou hear?" he exclaimed, suddenly leaping up. " Kalidou, soho, brave imp! and thou shalt be a-galloping yet! Hearest thou that shout, like the clang of a bugle on a hilltop? 'Tis Cortes! and he cometh!"

It was even as the magician had said. From the moment that De Morla took the fatal leap, the rowers ceased paddling in their canoes, as if certain of his fate, or unwilling to follow so feeble a prey, and remained huddled together as though they awaited the approach of a more tempting quarry. They had not perceived the two companions. Just as Botello was about to creep under a falconet, around whose wheels the corses lay very thick, the strong voice of Cortes was heard rising over the din, which, at some quarter or other of the causeway, was kept up incessantly during the whole conflict. It echoed again, sustained and strengthened by the voices of a considerable party

" They approach!" said Botello. " They are a-horse too; I hear the trampling. God quicken the rear! Methought there were many who followed me."

" Hark!" cried the cavalier. " The foul knaves desert us; their voices are weaker; they fly again to the land!"

" Here's that which shall fetch them back, if they be men " exclaimed Botello, catching up a port-fuse not yet extinguished, striking it on his arm to shake off the ashes, and whirling it in the air till it glowed and almost blazed. " It will show them there be some living yet; and, with God's blessing, will scatter yon ambushed heathen like plashing water-drops.   Ojala! and all ye fiends of air and water, of earth and of hell, that are waiting for Pagan souls, carry my hail-shot true, and have at your prey!"

So saying, the conjurer applied the match. The roar of the explosion was succeeded not only by the yells of Mexicans, dying in their broken canoes, or paddling away from so dangerous a vicinity, but by Spanish shouts, both on the rear and in front.

"On, brave hearts!" cried Cortes; "there be bold knaves yet at the ordnance!"

The next moment the little band of horse that headed the relief, sprang into the lake, and swimming aside, so as to avoid the sunken bodies, and the bales still floating in the ditch, crossed over to the cannon; while a large body of men, arranged with such order that they blocked up the whole causeway from side to side, came marching up from the rear, fighting as they fled, and still valiantly resisting the multitudes that pursued both on the dike and in the water.

"Thanks be to God!" cried Don Hernan, rejoiced that so many lived, and yet appalled at the numbers and ferocious determination of the foes, who still, like venomous insects following the persecuted herd, pursued whithersoever the Christians fled.   "Art thou alive, De Leon? Praised be St. James, who listened to my prayer! Turn ye now, and let us succour the rest."

"They are in heaven," said De Leon, with a faint voice, for he was severely wounded, as indeed were all his crew.   "Push on, in the name of God, all who can swim.   The others must perish."

"Hold! stay!" exclaimed Cortes.   "Fling the cannon into the sluice.   Think not of the enemy. Heave over my good falconets : they will make a bridge for ye all."

The wounded footmen seized upon the guns with the energy of despair; and flinging over the ropes to that company of their fellow-infantry who had followed Don Hernan, and now stood on the opposite side, the pieces were pushed and dragged into the water, and, together with the mass of corses already deposited in that fatal chasm, made such a footing for the infantry as enabled many to pass in safety. Among these was Don Amador de Leste, his hand grasped by the faithful magician, who perceived that he was sunk into such sluggishness of despair, that he must have perished, if left to himself.

It is not to be supposed that this passage was effected without opposition and loss. On the contrary, the barbarians redoubled their exertions; and while many rested at a distance, shooting whole clouds of arrows, others pushed their canoes boldly up to the gap, and there slew many taken at such disadvantage.

Nevertheless, the passage was at last effected, and the footmen joining themselves to their fellows, and forming, as before, twenty deep, followed the horsemen towards the shore

"Hold!" shouted Botello, when the party was about to start.   "Save your captain, ye knaves of the rear!—Save de Leon! the valiant Velasquez!"

A few, roused by this cry, and heedless of the shafts shot at them, rushed back to the brink, and beheld the wounded and forgotten captain in the

water, struggling in the arms of two brawny barbarians, who strove to drag him into a canoe. While his followers stood hesitating, not knowing how to give him aid, the little vessel, agitated by his struggles, which were tremendous, suddenly overset, and captive and capturers fell together into the water.   The two warriors were presently seen swimming towards a neighbouring canoe; and De Leon, strangling under the flood, heaved not his last groan on the gory block of sacrifice.

The fugitives paused not to lament; they resumed their march, and gained the last ditch.

The events of that march, and of the passage of that ditch, are, like the others, a series of horrors. Enough has been narrated to picture out the dreadful punishment of men who acknowledged no rights but those of power, and preferred to rob a weak and childish race with insult and murder, rather than to subdue them, as could have been done, by the arts of peace.   In the sole incident which remains to be mentioned, we record the fate of an individual whose influence had been felt through most of the events of the invasion, in many cases beneficially, but in this, disastrously enough.   This was the enchanter, Botello—a man just shrewd enough to deceive himself; which is, in other words, to say, that he mingled in his own person so much cunning with so much credulity, that the former was ever the victim of the latter. The devoutness of his own belief in the efficacy of his arts, was enough to secure them the respect and reverence of the common herd, as well as of better men, in an age of superstition.   How much confidence was given to them by Cortes, does not clearly appear in the older historians; but it is plain, he turned them to great advantage, and had the art sometimes to make the stars, as well as Kalidon of the Crystal, furnish revelations of his own hinting; and, it is suspected, not without grounds, that this very nocturnal flight, projected originally under the impression that the barbarians would not go into battle after nightfall, and, when the later events of the siege had disproved this hope, still persisted in from the persuasion that no Mexican would handle a weapon on the day of an emperor's burial, was conceived in the brain of the general before it was counselled by the lips of Botello.

At all events, the enchanter did not this night manifest any doubt in his own powers.   With a strange and yet natural inconsistency, he seemed to rejoice over the slaughter of his countrymen, as over the confirmation of his predictions.   Twice or thrice, at least, he muttered, and once even in the thick of combat, to Don Amador, by whose side he ever walked, at the head of the retreating party—"I said, this night we should retreat—we have retreated : I said, there should be death for many, and safety for some—the many are at rest (God receive their souls, and angels carry them to the seats of bliss!)—and some of us are saved."

"Be not over quick in thy consummations," said Amador.   "We are here now at the third ditch, which is both wide and deep, and no bodies to bridge it; and seest thou not how the yelling curs are paddling in to oppose us?"

"Bodies enow!" cried the enchanter.   "Tomorrow at mid-day, when the sun is hottest, ye shall see corses lying along on both sides of the causeway, like the corks of a fisherman's net; and at the ditches, they will come up like ants out of the earth, when a dead caterpillar falls at their door. Yet say I, we shall be saved, and thou shalt see it; for I remember how thou didst carve the back of that knave that lay on me in the streets of Mexico; and I will carve a dozen for thee in like manner, ere dawn, on this causeway."

"Boast no more: such confidence offends Heaven; for thy life hangs here as loosely as another's."

"The star! the star!" cried Botello, "the dim little star! is it not shining? The morning comes after it, and the eagles are waking on the hills. They will snuff the battle, they will shriek to the vultures, to the crows, and the gallinazas, and down will they come together to the lake-side and the lake. At eventide, ye will see dead men floating about in the wind, and on the breast of each a feeding raven; but devils shall be perched on the corses of the heathen."

"Heaven quit me of thy vile words, for they sound to me unnatural and damnable, as though spoken by one of those same demons thou thinkest of. Speak no more. Look to thy life, for it is in jeopardy."

"Hast thou not seen me in the battle? and, lo you now, I have not a scratch!" said the enthusiast. "I have fought on the dike, when there were twelve men of us, good men, bold and true: eleven were slain, but here am I untouched by flint, unbruised by stone, unhurt by arrow. I fought three screeching infidels in the water, hard by to where two valiant cavaliers were pulled off their horses, and so smothered; and yet strangled I my heathens, without horse or help, or friend to say God speed me. The life that is charmed is invulnerable; the star shines, the eagle leaves her nest, and Kalidon-Sadabath laughs in the crystal —Viva! lo now, how Sandoval, the valiant, will scatter me yon imps in the boats. He spurs into the water; Catalan the Left-handed, Juan of Salamanca, Torpo the Growler, Ferdinand of Bilboa, and De Olid, the Devil's Ketch, they spring after him! There they go. Dance, Kalidon! thy brothers shall have souls, to be fetched up from the mud as one rakes up clams of a fish-day. Crowd hell with damned heathens:—there be more to follow!"

Never before had such life possessed the spirits of Botello. He stood on the edge of the causeway, shouting loud vivas, as the bold cavaliers rushed among the canoes that blocked up the sluice. The novice, though shocked at such untimely exultation, was not able to avoid it; for he was enfeebled, and Botello held him with a fast and determined gripe. Unhand me, conjurer," he cried, "and I will swim the ditch."

"Tarry a little, till the path be made clear: thou wilt be murdered else."

"I shall be murdered, if I remain here; and so wilt thou. Hah! did that shaft hurt thee?"

"Never a jot; how could it? There flies not the arrow this night, there waves not the bludgeon, that can shed my blood."

"Art thou besotted?—God forgive thee!—This is impiety."

The magician held his peace; for about this time the Mexicans, knowing that this band, diminished, disordered, and divided by the ditch into two feeble parties, was the sole remaining fragment of oppression, and determined that no invader should escape alive, rushed upon the causeway on all sides, with such savage violence as seemed irresistible. Those who had not yet crossed, broke

in affright, and flung themselves into the sluice with such speed, that in a few moments Don Amador began to think that he and Botello were the only Christians left. "Why dost thou hold me, madman?" he cried. "Let me free."

"Hark! dost thou hear?—there are Christian men behind us," said Botello. Courage! What if these devils be thicker than the thoughts of sin in man's heart, fiercer than conscience, deadlier than remorse; yet shall we pass them unharmed. Patience! 'Tis the voice of a Spaniard, I tell thee, and behind."

"It is in front:—hark, 'tis don Hernan."

"It is behind, and it is the cry of Alvarado. Let us return, and give him aid. Ho, ye that fly, return! the Tonatiuh is shouting behind us: will ye desert him?—Return, return!"

Before Amador could remonstrate, the lunatic, for at this moment, more than any other, Botello seemed to deserve the name, had dragged him to the top of the dike, where he stood exposed to the view and the shots of the foe. A thousand arrows were aimed at the pair.

"Thou art a dead man!" said Amador.

"Dost thou not see that star?" said the magician, impatiently. "Not a bird hath yet flapped her wing, not an eagle hath fled from her cliff; and my star, my star—"

As he spoke, he let go his hold of the cavalier, to point exultingly at the diminutive luminary. At that very instant an arrow, aimed close at hand, struck the neophyte on the breast, entering the mail at a place rent by blows of a previous day, and without wounding him, forced its way out, through links hitherto uninjured.

"Hah!" said the cavalier, as the arm of Botello fell heavily on his shoulder. "Art thou taught wisdom and humility at last? Let us descend and swim."

As he moved, he became sensible that the shaft was still sticking in his hauberk. He grasped the feathered notch—the head was in the astrologer's heart. The stout wood snapped as Botello fell It struck him in the moment of his greatest hope. He dropped down a dead man.

While Amador stood, confounded and struck with horror, he was seized, he knew not by whom, and suddenly found himself dragged through the water. Before he could well commend his soul to Heaven, for he thought himself in the hands of the enemy, he beheld himself on firm land, while the voice of Cortes shouted in his ear.

"Rouse thee, and die not like a sleeper! Hold me by the hand, and my good horse shall drag thee through the melée. I would sooner that my arm were hacked off, than thou shouldst sleep in the accursed lake! enough of thy blood rests in it, with Don Gabriel."

"Ay," thought the unhappy cavalier, "enough of my blood, and all of my heart. Don Gabriel, De Morla, Lazaro, Lorenzo, and—ay, and Leila. Better that I were with them."

A sudden cry from beyond the ditch interrupted his griefs.

"Pause, pause!" cried the voice. "Leave me not!—I am nigh!—I am Alvarado."

The cavaliers looked back at these words, and beheld a man come flying, as it were, through the air over the ditch, perched on the top of a long Chinantlan spear, the bottom of which was hidden in the water. He fell quite clear of the sluice, after making a leap which even his comrades, who had not individually seen it, held impossible for mortal man, and which even to this day has preserved to the spot the name of the Salto. or leap, of Alvarado

The appearance of the Tonatiuh was hailed with shouts of joy; and the Spaniards receiving it as a good omen, closed their ranks, and slowly, for every inch was contested, fought their way to the shore. When they trode upon the firm ground, the little star had vanished in the grey beams of morning; and a thick mist rising up from the water like a curtain, concealed from the eyes of the fugitives, along with the accursed signal-fire, the fatal towers and temples of Mexico.

Thus closed a night of horror and woe, memorable as the *Noche Triste*, or Melancholy Night, of Mexican history, and paralleled perhaps in modern days, if we consider the loss of the retreating army as compared with its numbers, only by the famous and most lamentable passage of the Berezina. More than four thousand Tlascalans, and five hundred Spaniards, were left dead on the causeway, or in the lake. Of the prisoners, but two or three escaped; two sons and as many daughters of Montezuma, with five tributary kings, as well as many princes and nobles, perished. All the cannon were utterly lost, left to rust and rot in the salt flood that had so often resounded to their roar; and of more than an hundred proud war-steeds that champed the bit so fiercely at midnight, scarce twenty jaded hacks snuffed the breath of morning.

With this broken and lamenting force, with foes still hanging on his rear, and ever flying from his front, Cortes set out to seek a path, by new and unknown mountains, to the distant Tlascala. He turned his eyes but once towards the lake—the Pagan city was hidden among the mists, and the shouts of victorious Mexicans came but faintly to the ear. He beat his breast, and shedding such tears as belong to defeated hopes, and the memory of the dead, resumed his post at the head of the fugitives.

CHAPTER LXII.

We draw a curtain over the events of the first five days of flight, wherein the miserable fugitives, contending at once with fatigue, famine, and unrelenting foes, stole by night, and through darkling by-ways, along the northern borders of the fair valley, from which they were thus ignominiously, and, as seemed, for ever, expelled. Of the twenty mounted men, each, like a Red-Cross Knight, in the ancient days of the order, bore a wounded companion on his crupper; and Don Amador himself, on a jaded beast that had belonged to Marco—for Fogoso had been lost or killed in the melée—thus carried the only remaining servant of himself and his knight—the ancient Baltasar. Other mangled wretches were borne on the backs of Tlascalans, in rudely constructed litters.

In this manner, the ruined and melancholy band pursued its way, by lake-side and hill, over morass and river, ever pursued and insulted by bodies of barbarians, and frequently attacked; till, on the evening of the fifth day, they flung their weary forms to sleep in the city (as it may be called) of Pyramids, among those mouldering and cactus-covered mounds which the idolatry of a forgotten age reared to the divinity of the greater and lesser luminaries of heaven, on the field Micoatl, that is to say, the Plain of Death. The visitor of San Juan de Teotihuacan still perceives these gigantic barriers, rising among the hundreds of smaller mounds—the Houses of the Stars—which strew the consecrated haunts, and, perhaps, conceal the sepulchres, of a holozoic people.

At sunrise, the Spaniards arose, ascended the mountain of Aztaquemacan, at the north-eastern border of the valley, and prepared, with a joyous expectation, which had not been diminished even by the significant and constantly-repeated threats of the pursuers, to descend into the friendly land of the Tlascalans, by way of the vale of Otumba. For the last two days, the name of this valley had been continually on the lips of the Mexicans, following on the rear; and their cries, as interpreted by Marina, who survived the horrors of the Melancholy Night, intimated plainly enough, that the work of revenge, so dreadfully commenced upon the lake, was to be consummated in the gorges of the mountains. Nevertheless, the Spaniards, in the alacrity of spirit which the prospect of soon ending their sufferings in the Land of Bread, produced, forgot these menaces, or regarded them as the idle bravados of impotent fury; and clambered upwards with increasing hope, until they reached the crest of a ridge, and looked down the slope to the wished-for valley. The sight which they beheld will be described in another place. It remains now to return to an individual, whose fate has long been wrapped in mystery

At the moment when the Spaniards approached the highest part of the ravine, by which alone they could pass, in that quarter, from the vale of Tenochtitlan, there lay, in a wild and savage nook of the mountain, which went shelving upwards on the right hand, and at so short a distance, that had a bugle been winded in the army, it must have reached his ears—one who had been a companion in many of their battles and sufferings. A number of huge rocks, fallen ages ago, and rolled from some distant pinnacle, were heaped together on a broad and inclined shelf, and enclosed a space of ground so regular in form, and yet so rudely bounded by those sprawling barriers, that it looked to the imagination not unlike the interior of some stupendous temple, built by a barbaric people, and overwhelmed, many ages before, by some great convulsion. One side was formed by a cliff, in whose shivered side yawned the entrance of a black and dismal cavern, while the broken masses of rock themselves formed the others. Among, and over these, where they lay in contact with the cliff, there rushed a torrent, which, in the times of drought, might have been a meagre and chattering rivulet, making its way, merrily, through gap and hollow, but which, now swollen by the summer rains, came raving and roaring over the rocks, broken by them into a series of foaming cascades; and then, shooting over a corner of the enclosure, and darting through the opposite wall, it went thundering down the mountain. A few stunted trees stretched their withered limbs among these savage masses; and the noontide sun, peeping down into a nook, and lighting up a part of the cliff, fell pleasantly on the mosses and Alpine flowers which ornamented its shelving floor, tinting, with momentary rain bows, the mists that hung over the fall. A sable steed, without bridle or halter, and much the worse for such primitive stabling, but yet, to all appearance, the relic of a once noble war-horse, wandered at liberty through the enclosure, cropping the few plants which bedecked it, or drinking from the little pools at the side of the torrent; while, at the mouth of the cave, at the foot of a wooden crucifix of the rudest description, lay sleeping the figure of his master. A stained and tattered garment of leather, investing his limbs, was not altogether hidden under a black mantle, which partly covered his body. The head of the sleeper lay on his right arm, and this embraced the foot of the cross, so that the grizzly locks which fell from his forehead rested against, and almost twined around, the holy wood.

The sunbeam played, unregarded, on his withered cheeks, and flickered over a heap of rusted armour, both of man and horse, which lay hard by, shining also, with a fierce lustre, upon what appeared a scarlet surcoat, hung, like a banner, on the point of a knightly lance which rested against the side of the cliff.

Disease, as well as age, had furrowed the cheeks and wasted the form of the slumberer; famine seemed to have been at work, as well as all other privations incident to a habitation in the desert; and there was, in his whole appearance, such an air of extreme and utter misery, as would have moved the pity of any beholder. Nevertheless, he slept on, regardless of the roaring fall, and heedless of the fierce sunbeam, in such tranquillity as augured, at least, a momentary suspension of suffering.

As the sun stole up to the meridian, another human creature was suddenly added to the scene. The browsing war-horse pricked his ears, and snorted, as if to do the duty of a faithful sentinel, and convey to his master a note of alarm, as certain dried branches crackled among the rocks of the wall, and a stone, loosened as by a footstep, fell, rattling down their sides, and buried itself in the pool, at the base of the fall. But the anchorite, for such the solitude of his dwelling, the poverty of his raiment, and, more than all, the little rugged cross which he embraced, caused him to appear, heard not these sounds; he slept on, lulled by the accustomed roar of the waterfall; and the steed was left alone, to watch the approach of the stranger.

Presently, he was seen dragging himself up the rocks, by the aid of a drooping bough; and when he had reached their top, he rested for a moment, still clinging to the branch, as if worn out with toil, as was, indeed, made apparent by the youth and feebleness of his appearance. He cast a haggard and uninterested eye on the romantic torrent leaping and foaming at his feet, and seemed to hesitate whether he should descend into the prison-like enclosure, or retrace his steps, and retreat as he had come. But, suddenly, his gaze fell upon the steed, and he started with surprise at a sight so unexpected. The sagacious animal whinnied loudly, as if with recognition; and the youth, devoutly crossing himself, looked, with an agitation that denoted terror, on the red garment, the cross, and the human figure that still lay sleeping or, perhaps, as he thought, dead, under its holy shadow. Then, as if resolved, he hastened to descend from the rugged fragments, and seeking where he might safely cross the brook, over the stones that obstructed its bed, he at last stood at the side of the good steed, which snuffed at him a moment with joy, and then, gambolling about a little, fell to cropping the plants again, satisfied that the comer was a friend.

The youth stole tremblingly to the side of the sleeper, and seemed shocked at his emaciated and neglected appearance. He stooped as if to awake him, and then started back, wringing his hands, in fear and grief. He bent over him again;—a smile passed like a beam over the countenance of the recluse, and a murmur escaped his lips, of which the youth caught only a few broken syllables. "Though I shed thy blood," were the words he distinguished, "yet did I not aim at thee; and, therefore, hast thou forgiven me, for the sin was the sin of frenzy. Thou pardonest me, too, Alharef, for thou art also of the angels. It is good to walk with thee through the seats of bliss."

A tear fell upon the cheek of the Knight Calavar —for it was, indeed, he; but it fell like the spray-drop, or the gentle dew; and it was not until the hand of the youth touched his shoulder, that he awoke, and rose feebly to his feet. "Whoever thou art," said the unfortunate devotee, "thou breakest the only dream of happiness that hath visited my slumbers for long and many years, and callest me from the paradise that filled me with bliss, to the earth which is the wheel whereon I am broken—Miserere mei, Deus!"

"Alas, my lord!"—

"Art thou sent back to bid me prepare?" cried Don Gabriel, starting wildly, at the voice of the intruder. "Lo! I have flung me off the harness of war, and devoted me to penance in the wilderness, giving my body to sleep on the earth and in caves, drinking of the wild floods, and eating of the tough roots with the earthworm; while I sleep, my heart is scourged within me; whilst I wake, I pray—and I pray that I may sleep for ever. Know, therefore, Jacinto, thou that dwellest in paradise, that I am ready, and that I thank Heaven, I am called at last; for weary has been my life, and long my repentance."

"Alas, my lord, I live like thyself; and I call upon thee that thou mayest continue to live. I thought, indeed, that thou wert dead, and so thought, and yet think thy friends—who are now in great peril."

"God snatched me from the hands of the hea then," said the knight, "and brought me to this place, that I might seek for peace. For oh! my heart was but filled with scorpions, that stung me day and night, and my head strewn with coals, ever burning and tormenting, whilst I sat in the infidel city, and remembered how he that hath been my son, was slain by murderers in the streets, because he loved me. All that loved me have perished, and (woe betide the hand that struck, and is not yet withered!) two under mine own steel. Yea, Alharef, thou art remembered; and Zayda, thou art not forgotten. Then came the blow to thee, dear seraph! and thou wert carried off by the angry spirit of Alharef, who defied me at the palace-gate, and in the temple yard, raised me to my feet, and bade me think of Zayda. Verily I remember her, and my heart is black with recollection. Then fell the bolt upon my boy—he that was matchless in honour and love, peerless in war, incomparable in truth. Would that the barb arous knives had struck my bosom, instead of thine

Amador! would that thou wert now upon thy gallant bay, shaking thy lance, and shouting the cry of the Hospital, and I in thy place, mouldering in the streets of Mexico! I lay on my couch, whilst thou wert calling to me for aid; I slept while thou wert dying. Cursed be thy foundations, Pagan city! ruin fall upon thy towers, havoc ride howling through thy palaces, and lamentations come up from thy lakes and gardens! for he that was the last and first, the loving and beloved, rots like a dog upon thy pavement!"

"Noble and dear master," said Jacinto, "in this at least thou art mistaken. My dear lord, thy kinsman perished not that day in the streets; for I myself did watch by his sick couch, and see him after thou hadst departed. return in safety to the palace."

"Dost thou say so?—He died not in the streets? Praised be God, for this his goodness!" cried Don Gabriel, falling on his knees. "My sin then hath not been visited on the guileless and true. My son Amador yet liveth!"

He looked to the page, and now for the first time observed, as far as this could be seen through his thickly-padded garments, that the form of Jacinto was greatly attenuated; his cheeks were hollow and colourless, and his countenance altered, as by some such grief as had been at work in his own bosom. He seemed, too, to be very feeble. But, if such were the appearances of sorrow on his visage, they assumed a yet more striking character of agony and despair, when the knight's words of joy fell on his ear. His face grew paler than death, he trembled like a linden leaf, and his lips scarcely obeyed their function, when he replied, with a faint and fruitless effort at calmness—"I will not deceive my lord; no, Heaven be my stay! I will not deceive my lord. Though my friend—my patron—my protector—the noble Amador—fell not in the streets, but returned to his people, yet is his fate wrapped in mystery—in darkness and in fear. That night, that dreadful night!—Oh Heaven! the causeway covered with men, shrieking and cursing, stabbing and rending! the lake choked with corses, and with dying men still contending and suffocating, each in the grasp of a drowning foe.—But I think not of that, I think not of that. Who lived? who died? We searched for the body of my lord, but found it not: he was not with those they led to the pyramid; his corse floated not among the hundreds, which befouled the lake: yet did they discover his goodly war-horse on the water-side—his surcoat was dragged from a ditch among cannon, under whose heavy bulk lay many bodies, which the Indians strove to push up with poles—but my lord's body rose not among them. And yet, he sleeps in the lake—yes, he sleeps in the lake! for how could he escape that night, and I no more by his side?"

As Jacinto spoke, he wept and sobbed bitterly, giving himself up to despair. But not so the knight: he listened, somewhat bewildered, to the confused narration of an event in which he had shared no part; but catching the idea at last, and mingling it with another, the fruit of his very distempered mind, he said quickly, and almost joyously—"Dry thy tears; for now I perceive that my son is not dead, but liveth; and straightway we will go forth and seek him!" Jacinto regarded the knight with a melancholy look. He noticed the incredulity, and resumed, with much devoted emphasis—"But a moment since, before thou camest into this den, mine eyes were opened upon paradise; it was vouchsafed to me, who must never hope to enjoy such a spectacle again—no, *desdichado de mi!* never again, never again—to look upon the golden city of God; wherein I walked with all those whom, in my life, I had loved, and who were dead. There saw I, among the saints and seraphim, my father, who fell in arms at the sack of Alhama; and my mother, who died in giving me birth; together with all the friends of my childhood, who perished early: there, also, I beheld Alharef and Zayda, the murdered and the blessed—with all others that were truly dead. Now thou wilt see how God opened mine eyes in this trance; for, though I wept thee, dear child, as truly believing thou wert deceased, yet thee I saw not among the blissful, where thou must have been, hadst thou been discarded from earth, as I thought thee. And I remember me, too, and great joy it is to remember, that my son Amador was not among those saints; for which reason, Heaven makes it manifest to us that he lives. Now, therefore, let us go forth from this desert, and seek him. Though mine eyes are sealed among these hills, and my feet stumble upon the rocks, yet will Heaven point us out a path to Mexico!"

"Alas! my lord need not seek so far," said the page. "The Pagans are now alone in the city, having driven out their enemies, with terrible slaughter. Never more will the Spaniards return to it!"

"Ay, now I remember me!" said the knight, catching up some of his battered armour, as he spoke. "This defence, that I had thought for ever rejected, must I again buckle on. I remember me, thou spokest of a night of retreat by the causeway, very dreadful and bloody. Ay! and thou saidst thou wert at Amador's side! How was it, that thou wert taken from him, and didst yet live?"

"My father, Abdalla," said Jacinto, sorrowfully—"my father, by chance, heard me cry at the ditch, when my lord, Don Amador, was gone; and he saved me in his canoe."

"Thy father? thy father, Abdalla? I remember me of Abdalla," said the knight, touching his brow. "There is a strange mystery in Abdalla. I am told—that is, I heard from my poor Marco—that Abdalla, the Moor, did greatly abhor me, even to the seeking of my life."

"He wronged him!" said the page: "whatever was my father's hatred of my lord, he never sought to do him a wrong!"

"Strange!" muttered Don Gabriel; "thou acknowledgedest he hated me then? Wherefore should he, whom I have not injured, hate me? And wherefore, after confiding thyself to my good keeping?"

"Let me not deceive my lord," said Jacinto, sadly, but firmly. "My father intrusted his child to him he hated, because he knew him just and honourable; and my father did receive great wrong, as well as other unhappy Moors, of my lord in the Alpujarras."

The knight dropped the dinted cuishes which he had snatched up, and clasping his hands wildly exclaimed—"Miserere mei, Deus! my sin is inexpiable, and my torment endless; for in the Alpujarras did I slay him whom I had sworn to love, and deface, with a murderous sword, the loveliest of thine images!"

"Dear my lord," said Jacinto, shocked and grieved at his agitation; "forget this, for thy sin is not what thou thinkest, and it has been already forgiven thee. Zayda hath seen from heaven the greatness of thy grief, and she intercedes for thee with our Holy Mother."

"She follows me on earth, she comes to me in visions!" cried Don Gabriel, vehemently. "Rememberest thou not the night Cholula? Then stood she before me, as thou dost; and, with face of snow and finger of wrath, she reminded me of my malefaction."

"My lord is deceived—this was no spectre, but a living woman," said Jacinto, hurriedly.

The knight stared aghast.

"If I make it appear to my lord," continued the page, "that this was, indeed, no phantom sent to reproach, but a living creature, haply resembling her of whom he speaks, and therefore easily mistaken, in the gloom, for one of whom my lord thought, in his delirious moment, will it not satisfy my lord, that he is not persecuted, but forgiven?"

"If thou canst speak aught to remove one atom and grain from this mountain of misery, which weighs upon my heart," said Calavar, earnestly, "I adjure thee that thou speak it. Many times have I thought that she whom I slew stood at my side; but yet had I hopes, and a partial belief, that these were the visions of my disease; for my mind is sometimes very sorely distracted. What I saw at Cholula was beyond such explication—very clearly and vividly represented, and seen by me when my thoughts were not disordered."

"Let my lord be content, and know that this was a living creature, as I have said, and no apparition: let him do on his armour; and by and by all shall be revealed to him."

"Speak to me now," said the knight.

"Not now! not now!" interrupted Jacinto; "for this moment, the myriads of vengeful fiends who seek for the blood of my lord, Don Amador, if he be yet living, are rushing upon the poor fugitives. Doth not my lord hear? Hark!"

"'Tis a trumpet! it blasted for a charge of horse!" cried Calavar, as the distant sound came echoing up the mountain, even over the roar of the fall. The ancient war-horse heard the remembered note, and pricking his ears, neighed loudly and fiercely, running to a gap in the wall, as if to seek the contest, till recalled by the voice of his master.

"The infidels are then at hand, and they do battle with Christians?" exclaimed Don Gabriel, the fire of chivalry again flashing from his eye, and almost driving away the thought of Zayda. "Buckle me these straps, and see that thou art speedy; for this brooks not delay. God hath called me to this mountain, that I should be ready to do battle with the heathen, in defence of the holy cross, which is my sworn vow; and in the fulfilment of the same, I pray God that I may die. Sound again, brave heart! smite me the godless fast and well; for presently I shall be with ye, striking for the faith! Why, how thou loiterest, young knave! Be speedy, for my son Amador is with the Christian host; and this day Heaven wills that I shall bring him succour."

"Alas! my lord," cried the page, "I would

that I could give my life to aid him; but my fingers are skilless and feeble."

"Thou art a godly boy, and well do I love thee. Buckle me as thou canst, and care not to buckle well; for in this fight God will be my armour. Buckle me, therefore, as thou canst; and, while thou art thus engaged, give me to know what good angel brought thee to be my messenger."

"I followed my sire," said the trembling Jacinto, "with the forces of Mexico, that were sent to join the mountain bands, and cut off the fugitives; and being commanded to rest me on the hill till the battle was over, I lost myself; which, with my great grief of heart, caused me to seek some nook wherein I might die. For truly, now, unless my lord Amador be living, I care not myself for life."

"The forces of Mexico! be they many? and these dogs of the hills, are they in numbers?"

"Countless as the drops of spray which the breeze flings over us," said Jacinto, with much perturbation, "so that nothing but the goodness of God can rescue the Spaniards out of their hands, and conduct them forth on the path so blocked up by their bodies. The Mexicans are many thousands in number, and triumphing still in the thought of their horrid victory on the lake. They swear that no Spaniard shall escape them this day."

"I swear, myself," said Calavar, fiercely, "and Heaven will listen to the vow of a Christian, though one sinful and miserable, that, this day, even they themselves, the godless Pagans, shall be scattered as dust under our footsteps! Quick—my war-coat! and now my good lance, that hath drunk the blood of the heathen! *Santa Madre de Dios! Señora beatificada!* the infidel shall fall under the cross, and the true believer rejoice in his slaughter!"

With such exclamations of fervour, the spirit of youthful days returning, at each blast of the trumpet, which was still winded at intervals, the knight ceased doing on his armour, and then, with Jacinto's feeble assistance, caparisoned his impatient steed. When this was done, he bade the page to follow him; and riding through one of the many gaps in the colossal wall, began to descend the mountain.

CHAPTER LXIII.

The midday sun was illuminating the peaks, and darting its beams into the narrowest and darkest ravines of these mountains, when Don Hernan, at the head of his little army, rode to the crest of a hill, and looked down upon the narrow but beautiful valley of Tonan, opening on the fields of Otompan—or, as the name has been more euphonically rendered by Spaniards, Otumba. The level vale itself, as well as the hills on both sides, as far up, at least, as the gentleness of their slope allowed such cultivation, was sprinkled with maize fields, which, being now at their utmost point of luxuriance, covered such places with intense verdure; while the green forests, that here and there overshadowed the upper ridges, with flowery cliffs protruding from their waving tops, added the charm of solitude to the pleasant prospect of human habitation. But there was one sad-

dental beauty at present revealed, which, however disagreeable and even terrible to the leader, he could not but acknowledge in his heart to surpass all the others.

At the cry with which the general beheld this phenomenon, his followers rushed up to his side, and perceived the whole valley, as it seemed —beginning at the bottom of the ridge they now stood upon, and extending not only from hill to hill, but as far as the eye could see—filled, and indeed blocked up, with enemies. The white and scarlet hues of their garments, the plumes of divers colours waving on their heads like a sea of feathers, over whose surging surface there passed, here a bright sunbeam and there the shadow of a cloud—the glittering of copper spears, of volcanic falchions, and of jewels (for this day, the Pagans decorated themselves, as for a triumph, in their richest array), produced a scene which was indeed both glorious and terrific. Through this human flood, Don Hernan knew he must conduct his weary and despairing people; but without daring to hope that the hand which had parted the Sea of the Desert from before the steps of the Israelites would open for him a path through this equally fearful obstruction.

The Christians gathered round their leader in silence. The loud roar of shouts, sounding from below, as if a whole world shrieked at once, shook the mountain under their feet; but they replied not. Every man was, at that moment, commending his soul to his Maker; for each knew there was no path of escape, except through that valley, and felt in addition, that, perhaps, not even the whole army, fresh, well-appointed, full of spirits and resolution, as when, on St. John's Day, it entered the city of the lake, could have made any impression on such a multitude, displayed in such a position. The very extremity of the case was the best counsel to meet it with fortitude; every man considered his life already doomed beyond respite, and, with such consciousness, looked forward to his fate with tranquillity. Their sufferings by famine and fatigue on the road, though the mutinous and lamenting fugitives did not then know it, had better prepared them to encounter such a battle-field, than a series of victories, with spoils of gold and bread; for these torments having already rendered their lives burdensome, they were not greatly frighted at the prospect of ending them. These causes, then, added to the fury of fanaticism, never entirely at rest in the bosom of the invaders, will account for their resolution, and even impatience, to attack an army, rated by many of the conquerors at two hundred thousand men. Had they been happier men, they would not have rushed upon such manifest destruction.

The priest Olmedo stretched forth his arm, holding a crucifix: Christian and Tlascalan knelt down upon the flinty ridge, and mingled together sullen prayers.

As they rose, the ever-composed Sandoval cried out, emphatically—" Now, my merry men all, gentlemen hidalgos and gentlemen commoners, God hath this day given us a great opportunity to signalise our valour;"—which was all the oration it occurred to his imagination to make.

The soldiers looked upon him with a gloomy indifference. Then out spoke the hot-headed Alvarado—" There be, to my reckoning, in yonder plain," he said, with a grin of desperation, " some

five hundred thousand men; we have, of our own body, some four hundred and fifty Christian soldiers, and we may count the two thousand Tlascalans, here at our heels, for fifty more; which just leaves us a thousand dogs apiece, to fight in yonder vale. If we gain the victory over such odds, never believe me, if we be not clapped down in the books by that German enchanter Faust, who hath invented a way of making them in such numbers, and as being more heroical men than either Don Alejandro, the emperor of Egypt, or some other country—or Don Rodrigo himself, who was much greater than any such dog of a heathen king. This much I will say, that never before had starving men such a chance of dying like knights of renown; and as, doubtless, God will send us some fifty or an hundred thousand angels to fight on our side, we may chance stumble on a victory: in hope of which, or in the certainty, on the other hand, of going to heaven, I say, Santiago, and at them! for their bodies are covered with gold and jewels!"

" God will help us!" cried Cortes; " and my friend Alvarado hath very justly said, that there is a rich spoil in that valley for victors. Though there be here, perhaps, fifty thousand men, or more, yet are they infidels, and therefore but as sparrows and gnats before the face of God's soldiers. There are, also, acres of very sweet corn in the valley; and beyond yon yelling herds are the gates of Tlascala. But let it not be thought I will this day compel the sword of any Christian. Yonder are the hill-tops—there are dens enow, wherein one may give his bones to wild-cats, and there be tall cliffs from which they who prefer such end, may throw themselves, and straightway be beyond the reach of battle. For myself, though but one man follow me, yet will I descend to that plain, walk through that multitude, and marshalling an hundred thousand Tlascalans, after I have rested me a little, return, by the same path we are now treading, to the gates of Mexico, to revenge upon such as yonder scum the death of my brothers, who are in heaven, as well as to lay claim to those rich lands and mines of gold, which are our right, and which it is yet our destiny to overmaster. If ye be minded to disperse and starve among the hills, let me be acquainted with your resolution; if ye will fight like soldiers and Christians, speak out your good thoughts, and, in God's name, let us begin!"

" We will fight!" muttered the desperate men.

At this moment, some strong clear voice from the company began to pronounce the words of the chant, *Kyrie Eleison*, and the rest joining in, Cortes gave the signal to descend; and thus they went slowly down towards the host, invoking mercy and singing the praises of God, and waxing in boldness and fanaticism as they sang, until the neighbouring rocks rang with the loud and solemn echoes of devotion.

Whatever was the piety of Don Hernan, it did not, however, prevent his taking all the steps which could be expected of a general in such a situation; and one while joining loudly with others in the chant, and at another, pausing to give deliberate instructions to his officers, he arranged the order and expedients of battle, before the wild anthem was concluded. His instructions were simple, and related but to one point. He counselled no one to be valiant, for he knew the veriest coward in the ranks would be compelled to deeds of heroism that day. He only commanded that the little troop of horse should form five deep, and follow him whithersoever he might lead, and that the footmen should keep their ranks close, and follow after the horse. He knew, as, indeed, did most of his followers, that the orders conveyed to a Mexican army by a Mexican general, instead of being transmitted from division to division by messengers, were directly communicated to all by the general himself, through the medium of the great banner, which he bore in his own hands, and from the lofty litter on which he was carried, kept ever displayed to the eyes of his warriors. A few simple motions of this royal telegraph sufficed to convey all the directions which a barbarous commander was required to bestow upon a barbarous army. Among these, the veiling or dropping the standard was the well-known signal of retreat; and whether it might be lowered by the general himself, or struck from his hands by some fortunate foe, still it was equally certain that, in either case, his followers would immediately, upon seeing it fall, betake themselves to flight. When Cortes eyed this immense multitude, he calculated the chances of victory, not by the probabilities of routing it, but by those of making his way to the great banner.

The imperial standard, which, in the tongue of Mexico, bore the horribly uncouth title of *Tlahuiz matlaxopilli*, was conspicuously visible, even from the mountain Aztaquemacan, which the Spaniards were now descending. In the centre of the Pagan army was a group of warriors, made remarkable by the height and splendour of their penachos, the glittering of their jewelled decorations, and the sheen of their copper lances, the blades of which, like some that had been seen in Mexico, were full a yard in length, and polished so that they shone like gold. These were the guards, a body of young nobles, which surrounded the person of the general, to protect the banner from violence. In the centre of this group, upon a litter of almost imperial gorgeousness, stood the stately barbarian, bearing on a long pikestaff the standard, which was a sort of network, made of chains of gold, and therefore a more significant emblem of the object of conquest, and the fate of subjugation, than any banner of a Christian nation, even at this day. A few white feathers, waving amongst the links, kept it ever conspicuous.

As Don Hernan descended, he explained to the horsemen his design to merge every other object in that of seizing the Mexican standard—a project which met the concurrence of each.

"All that I have now to say to you," he added, when approaching the base of the hill, "is, to charge with me at half-speed, and take no thought of slaying. Those of you who have ever endured the bastinado of a pedagogue, will remember, that Julius Cæsar, or some such knave of a paynim, it matters not who, being opposed in some civil war, to certain cohorts of young gallants and hidalgos of Rome, directed his archers to spare the lives, but to let fly at the faces of these lady-puppets—a counsel of infinite wisdom; for I remember, that in my youth, until I got this gash o' the chin from a gentleman of Saragossa, which somewhat spoils the beauty of my beard, I had a mortal aversion to fight with any man much given to striking at the face. What I have to advise, therefore, is that you will imitate the wisdom of

that same Roman hound, and lance your spears full at the eyes of all who may oppose you. I have given charge to the footmen to finish our work: while they are slaughtering such curs as are not satisfied with scratched faces, we will make free with yon same knave of the gold net. Let it be reckoned—and 'tis worth a king's ransom—the prize of him who overthrows the general. Hark! hear ye how the infidels shout! —Are ye ready? In the name of God, the Virgin, and Santiago, have at them now like men! Amen. *Santiago! Santiago!*"

Thus shouting his war-cry, for now the horsemen had reached the bottom of the hill, Don Hernan couched his spear, with four cavaliers at his side, of whom Don Amador de Leste was one, and followed by all the others, dashed furiously at the first ranks of the Mexicans, who were already rushing against him.

The savages sprang aside, flinging their javelins and swords at the hot Christians, and raining arrows on their armed bodies; but ever, though thus expressing their hostility, yielding rank after rank before the irresistible charge; until it became apparent to the most doubting, that they might succeed, at last, in reaching the banner. They therefore redoubled their exertions, shouted the names of their saints, and aiming continually at the eyes of the foe, made such progress, that they were already almost, as it seemed, within reach of the prize, when a yell of the Indians of more than ordinary loudness, echoed by the infantry with exclamations of alarm, brought them to a sudden stand.

They had penetrated deeply into the mass; but it was as a noble ship ploughs her way through billows, which yield and divide, and only to unite again in her wake, and roar after in pursuit. From their lofty seats, they could overlook the multitude, and behold how quickly the path they had carved was filled up by screaming barbarians, rushing turbulently after them; while others dashed in like numbers, and with equal ferocity, upon the footmen, now left far behind.

As they looked thus over their shoulders, they paused with surprise, and even perturbation; for they perceived, furiously descending the slope of the hill on the left hand, against the infantry which was already sorely beset, what seemed a Christian Cavalier, in black armour, mounted on a noble bay horse, and couching a lance like a trained soldier, only that, behind him, there followed, with savage yells, a band of several thousand Indians, bearing the well-known colours of Tenochtitlan itself.

"God be our stay!" cried the general, looking aghast at this astonishing apparition; have we here an infidel god, in very deed, risen up against us, and riding a horse like a Christian man? Avoid thee, Satan! and all good saints spurn thee again to the pit from which thou comest!"

"'Tis Mexitli himself?" cried one.

"'Tis the devil!" said another.

"Look!" exclaimed Don Pedro; "he rushes down upon the footmen, like a rock, tumbled from the hill-top; and hark! heard ever man such horrible voice? 'Tis Mahound! 'tis Satan! Now all good angels befriend us!"

"For my part," said Don Amador de Leste— But before his words had yet been heard by any of his companions, they were cut short by such loud and thrilling cries of joy from the infantry as equally confounded the cavaliers.

"*Elo! Santiago! elo! nuestro buen amigo, el valoroso Santiago!*" that is to say—"Lo, St. James! behold our good friend, the valiant St. James!" burst from the lips of the footmen, in a frenzy of triumph.

The cavaliers looked again, but to the opposite mountain, and beheld upon that, as upon the other, an armed and mounted cavalier descending with lance in rest, and with the speed of thunder, as if rushing to a tournay with him of the black armour, but without being followed by any one, except a single youth, who staggered far behind.

At this sight, the cavaliers uttered loud cries of joy, not doubting that St. James had indeed come to rescue them from the claws of the accursed Mexitli, as they began to consider the black phantom.

"Our saint fights for us!" cried Cortes. "On! leave the black fiend to him? On, and let him behold our valour! The standard, ho! Santiago is nigh! The standard, the standard!"

The sight of the second apparition seemed to have smitten the Pagans with as much terror as the view of their own champion had infused into the Spaniards. The young nobles who surrounded the banner looked to the vision with awe; and ere they had yet recovered from their confusion, the Christian cavaliers, elated and invigorated, fell upon them with such violence as left the long copper lances useless in their hands.

"On and quick!" shouted Don Hernan, "or the knavish colour-man will spring from his perch, and so rob ye of the gold. On, ho! on! Hah, infidel! art thou not mine own?"

As he uttered these last words, he rose on his stirrups, stretched over his horse's neck, and handling his heavy spear as one would an ordinary javelin, launched it with all his force at the chief. There was never a better mark; for the barbarian, instead of showing, as Cortes had hinted, any desire to desert his litter, advanced to its very verge; and while he balanced the staff and its weighty crest with his left hand, whirled manfully a short dart round his head, looking all the while at the great Teuctli. There never was a better mark—for his breast, covered with a flimsy hauberk of skins, on which were sewed thin plates of gilded copper, was fully exposed; there never was a better aim. Before the dart had left his grasp, the spear of Don Hernan smote him on the chest, and piercing copper and bone alike, hurled him backwards, with the standard, out of the litter.

The cavaliers shouted victory, and trampling down the litter-bearers, and the young nobles, as these began to fly, looked eagerly for the prize.

"Have the knaves robbed us? Hah! mad John of Salamanca, thou pickest my pocket of these crowns, dost thou?"

These words of Don Hernan were addressed to a young hidalgo, who, the moment he had perceived the spear of Cortes take effect, had flung himself from his pied steed, rushed upon the downfallen infidel, and striking his sword into his throat, tore from him the badges of authority.

"He who strikes the quarry," said the elated youth, flinging both plume and golden net over the neck of his general's horse, "has the true claim to the trophy."

"Keep them thyself, for thou hast won them; and if Don Carlos be of mind, brave Juan, thou shalt mount them for thy coat of arms. Soho, De Leste! where art thou? I thought this prize should have been thine!"

"De Leste has gone mad," said Alvarado. "Shall we chase the runagates? See how they scamper."

The words of Alvarado were true. No sooner had the golden banner fallen from its height and been lost among the combatants, than there arose a dismal yell over the whole valley, and the vast multitudes, those near at hand and those afar, alike began to fly, and in the utmost confusion.

"Victory, praise be to God! to God and our noble St. James!" cried Cortes, with a shout that thrilled to the hearts of the flying Pagans. "Follow, not the knaves; leave them to the foot—to the allies and our mighty champion the saint. Soho, De Leste return. Follow not after the knaves."

"'Tis De Olid," cried Don Pedro, "that halloos the hunt's up. I tell thee De Leste is mad."

"Back to our champion," said Cortes. "Hah! what saidst thou of De Leste?"

"That he is gone mad—raving, besottishly, and very blasphemously mad; and that he deserted us the moment he saw thee fling thy spear."

"God forbid the youth should prove to be as was his kinsman before his death-day," said Cortes; "for a more gallant and sufficient soldier, though somewhat self-willed, have I never beheld. Mad, say'st thou?"

"He swore to me, first," said Alvarado, with a devout shrug, "that that paynim god, Mexitli, descending the hill yonder, was mounted on his own good horse Fogoso, which seems to me not unreasonable, for Fogoso was, in some sense, the best charger lost that night (which God punish to the heathen for ever,) and doubtless Huitzlipochtli, if determined to go out a pricking, like a Christian knight-errant, would be wise enough to pick up the best ghost of Christian horse. And secondly," continued Don Pedro, crossing himself, "he swore that his most holy valour, Santiago, who came down from the hill-top to help us, was no more than the ghost of his kinsman the Knight Calavar, who was drowned, horse and all, in the salt lake, near to Iztapalapan. But ho, halon, let us follow the hunt."

"Ha, my masters!" cried Don Hernan; "let us return and fathom this marvel, for it may bode us much to know. But stay—I will not rob ye of pastime. As many of ye as will, spur after the hounds and aid the Tlascalans."

So saying, and the foes now being scattered over the neighbouring hills, the general returned towards the infantry, while the cavaliers, shouting, as if in a boar-chase, urged their steeds up the hills in pursuit of the fugitives.

Thus was fought, and thus won, a battle, in which four hundred and fifty Spaniards, aided by a handful of Tlascalans, contended with a host of such incredible numbers, that, to this day, men remember it with wonder, and would reject it as a fable, were it not that the testimony of a thousand facts has placed it beyond the reach of question.

CHAPTER LXIV.

What Alvarado had reported of Don Amador was true. The neophyte averred, that, dead or alive a spectre or a creature of flesh and blood—the steed, bestridden by the sable phantom, and urged with such fury against the footmen, was neither less nor more than his own good beast Fogoso, and he declared, with even more impetuosity, as Don Pedro had related, that the figure, descending the opposite hill, was the Knight of Calavar on his ancient war-horse—an apparition, perhaps, but no St. James—unless this heavenly patron had condescended to appear in the likeness of a knight so valiant and so pious. Strange fancies beset him, and so great was his impatience to resolve the marvel, that he scarce waited to behold the general balance his good spear, before he turned his horse, and spurred furiously backward.

Meanwhile, the black horseman descended with such violence upon the footman, as threatened their instant destruction, his fierce eyes, as the Christians thought, gleaming with the fires of hell; so that, notwithstanding the sudden relief coming in the person of the supposed saint, they were seized with horror, and gave way before him. At the moment when he rushed among them, uttering what seemed the *Lelilee* of another land, he was encountered by his celestial opponent, whose strong voice shouted out—"God and St. John! and down with thee, paynim demon!"

The shock of two such steeds, both of great weight, each bearing a man cased in thick armour, each urged on by the impetus of the descent from the hills, and meeting midway, in a narrow valley, was tremendous. At the moment of encounter, the sable rider perceived, for the first time, his opponent; he checked his steed suddenly, and flung up his lance, as if to avoid a contest. But the precaution came too late; his rising lance struck the casque of his adversary, tearing it off, and revealing the grim visage and grizzly locks of the Knight of Calavar; while at the same moment the spear of Don Gabriel, aimed with as much skill as determination, smote the enemy on the lower part of the corslet, and piercing it as a buckler of ice, penetrated at once to the bowels and spine. The shock that unseated the riders was shared by the steeds, and horse and man rolled together on the earth.

The loud cry of "Calavar! the Penitent Knight! the valiant Don Gabriel!" set up by the bewildered and awe-struck infantry, reached the ears of the novice. He spurred on with new ardour, and reaching the footmen, just as they divided in pursuit of the flying barbarians, he sprung from his horse, and beheld his kinsman lying senseless, and as it appeared to him, lifeless, in the arms of the wounded Baltasar. "In the name of Heaven, and Amen! what is this? and what do I see?" he cried. "Oh Heaven! is this my knight? and doth he live?"

"He lives," said Baltasar, "and he feels as of flesh and blood; and yet did he die on the lake-side. God forgive us our sins! for neither heaven nor hell will hold the dead."

Just at that moment, the knight opened his eyes, and rolled them on his kinsman—but his kinsman regarded him not. A low moaning voice of one never to be forgotten, fell on the ear of the novice, as he gazed on his friend; and starting up, he beheld, hard by, the page Jacinto, lying on the body of Abdalla, from whose head he had torn the helm, and now strove with feeble fingers, to remove the broken and blood-stained corslet.

"Jacinto!—Leila!" cried Amador, with a voice of rapture, flinging himself at her side (for now, though the garments of escaupil still concealed the figure of the Moorish maid, the disguise could be continued no longer). The joy of the cavalier vanished, for the maiden replied only with lamentations; while the Zegri fixed upon him an eye, in which the stony hardness of death was mingled with the fires of human passion.

"Place my head upon thine arm, cavalier," said Abdalla, faintly, "and let me look upon him who has slain me."

"Oh, my father! my father!" cried the Moorish girl.

"God forbid that thou shouldst die, even for the sake of the maiden I love," exclaimed Amador, eagerly, supporting his head. "Thou art a Wali, a Christian, and the father of her that dwells in my heart. Live therefore; for though thou have neither land nor people, neither home nor friends, neither brother nor champion, yet am I all to thee; for I crave the love of thy daughter."

The maiden sobbed, and heard not the words of the cavalier; but the dying Moor eyed her with a look of joy, and then turning his gaze upon Amador, said—"God be thy judge, as thou dealest truly with her, who, although the offspring of kings, is yet an orphan, landless, homeless, and friendless on the earth."

"I swear to thee," said the novice—"and I protest—"

"Protest me nothing: hearken to my words, for they are few; the angel of death calls to me to come, and my moments fly from me like the blood-drops," said the Zegri. "Until the day, when I dreamed thou wert slumbering in the lake, I knew not of this that hath passed between ye. Had it been known to me, perhaps this death that comes to me might not have come; for what I did, I did for the honour and weal of my child, knowing that in the hand of Spaniards, she was in the power of oppressors and villains. That I have struck for revenge is true; I have shed the blood of Castilians and rejoiced, for therein I reckoned me the vengeance of Granada. Yet, had it been apparent to me, that the feeble maid, who besides myself knew no other protector of innocence in the world, could have claimed the love of an honourable cavalier, and enjoyed it without the shame of disguise and menial occupation, then had I submitted to my fate, and locked up in the darkness of my heart the memory of the Alpujarras."

"Who speaks of the Alpujarras?" cried the Knight of Rhodes, staring wildly around, "who speaks of the Alpujarras?"

"I," said the Moor, with a firm voice, bending his eye on Don Gabriel, and striving, though in vain, for his nether limbs were paralysed, to turn his body likewise; "I, Gabriel of Calavar, I speak of the Alpujarras; and good reason have I to speak, and thou to listen; for I was of the mourning, and thou of the destroyers."

"Pity me, Heaven!" cried the knight, staring on the Moor, in the greatest disorder. "I have seen thee, and yet I know thee not."

"Rememberest thou not the field of Zugar, and the oath sworn on the cross of a blood-stained sword, by the river-side?"

"Hah! cried Don Gabriel, "dost thou speak of mine oath—mine oath to Alharef?"

"And the town of Bucares, among the hills?" continued the Zegri, loudly, and with a frown made still more ghastly by approaching death; "dost thou remember the false and felon blow that smote the friend of Zugar—and that, still falser and fouler, which shed the blood of Zayda, the beloved of the Alpujarras?"

As the Wali spoke, the knight, as if uplifted by some supernatural power, rose to his feet, and approached the speaker, staring at him with eyes of horror. At the name of Zayda, he dropped on his knees, crying—"Miserere mei, Deus! I slew her! and thou that art Alharef, though struck down by the same sword, yet livest thou again to upbraid me."

"Struck down by thy steel, yet not then, but now," exclaimed the Moor. "I live again, but not to upbraid thee—I am Alharef-ben-Ismail, and I forgive thee."

At this name, already made of such painful interest to the novice, his astonishment was so great, that, as he started, he had nearly suffered the dying prince (for such were the Walis of Moorish Spain,) to fall to the earth. He caught him again in his arms, and turned his amazed eye from him to Don Gabriel, who, trembling in every limb, still stared with a distracted countenance on that of his ancient preserver.

"I am Alharef, and, though dying, yet do I live," went on the Zegri, interrupted as much by the wails of his daughter, as by his own increasing agonies. "The sword wounded, but it slew not —it slew not all—Zayda fell, yet live I to tell thee thou art forgiven. Rash man! rash and most unhappy! thine anger was unjust; and therefore didst thou shed the blood of the good, the pure, the loving, and the beautiful, and thereby cover thyself and him that was thy true friend with misery. When thou soughtest the love of Zayda, she was the betrothed of Alharef. Miserable art thou, Gabriel of Calavar, and therefore have I forgiven thee; miserable art thou, for I have watched thee by night, and looked upon thee by day, and seen that the asp was at work in thy bosom, and that the fire did not slumber. Great was thy sin, but greater is thy grief; and therefore doth Zayda, who is in heaven, forgive thee."

"She pardons me not," murmured Don Gabriel, not a moment relaxing the steadfastness of his stare. "At the pyramid of Cholula, on the anniversary of her death, she appeared to me in person, and, oh God! with the beauty of her youth and innocence, yet robed in the blackness of anger."

"And have thine eyes been as dark as the looks of the lover?" cried Alharef. "Stand up, Zayda, the child of Zayda! or turn thy face upon Calavar, that his delusion may leave him."

As he spoke he lifted feebly the arm which embraced his child, removed the cap, and parted the thick clustering locks from her forehead. Still, however, did she look rather the effeminate boy upon whom Calavar had been accustomed to gaze, than a woman; for there is no effort of imagination stronger than that required to transform in the mind the object which preserves an unchanging appearance to the eye. Nevertheless, though such a transformation could not be imagined by Don Gabriel, there came, as he wistfully surveyed the pallid features of the maiden, strange visions and memories which every moment associated a stronger resemblance between the living and the dead. He trembled still more violently, heavy dew-drops started from his brow, and he gazed upon the weeping girl as upon a basilisk.

"Wherefore" continued the Zegri, speaking ra-

pidly, but with broken accents, "when I had resolved to fly to the Pagans, as being men whom I thought God had commissioned me to defend from rapine and slavery, I resolved to take such advantage of their credulity, as might best enable me to defend them—I say, wherefore I resolved this I need not speak. I protected my child by recommending her to their superstition; and, had I fallen dead in the streets, still did I know that reverence and fear would wait upon the steps of one whom I delivered to them as a messenger from Heaven. In this light I revealed her to the princes at the temple, when——"

"It is enough," muttered Don Gabriel, with the deep and agitated tones of sorrow; "I wake from a dream. God forgive me! and thou art of the blood of Zayda? the child of her whom I slew? Alharef forgives me, he says that Zayda forgives me; but thou that art her child, dost thou forgive me?"

"Father! dear father, she doth!" cried Amador, gazing with awe on the altered countenance of Alharef, and listening with grief to the moans of Zayda. "Oh, holy padre!" he exclaimed, perceiving the priest Olmedo rising, at a little distance, from the side of a man, to whom he had been offering the last consolations of religion—"Hither, father, for the love of Heaven, and absolve the soul of a dying Christian!"

"Is there a priest at my side?" said the Zegri, reviving from what seemed the lethargy of approaching dissolution, and looking eagerly into the face of the good Olmedo. Then turning to Amador, he said solemnly, though with broken words, "Thou lovest the orphan Zayda?"

"Heaven be my help as I do!" replied the cavalier.

"And thou, Gabriel, that wert my friend, and standest in the light of this young man's parents—dost thou consent that he shall espouse the daughter of Zayda, saved, while a piteous infant, by Christian men, from out of the house of death?"

The knight bowed his head on his breast, and strove to answer, but in his agitation could not speak a word.

"Quick, father! for Heaven's sake, quick!" cried Alharef, eagerly; "let me, ere I die, know that my child rests on the bosom of a husband. Quick! for the sand runs fast; and there is that in my bosom which tells me of death. Love and honour thy bride; for thou hast the last and noblest relic of Granada. Take her—thou wert her protector from harsh words and the violence of blows. Quick, father, quick! quick, for mine eyes are glazing!"

The strangely-timed and hurried ceremony was hastened by the exclamations of Alharef; and the words of nuptial benediction were at last hurriedly pronounced.

"I see thee not, my child!" muttered the Moor, immediately after. "My blessing to thee, Amador —Gabriel, thou art forgiven. Thine arm round my neck, Zayda; thy lips to mine. Would that I could see thee!—Get thee to Granada, with thy lord—to the tomb of thy mother—I will follow thee—Tarry not in this land of blood—I will be with thee; we have a power yet in the hills—"

"Let the cross rest on thy lips, if thou diest a Christian," said the father.

The novice drew the maiden aside; the Zegri pressed the sacred symbol to his lips, but still they muttered strangely of Granada.

"I am of the faith of Christ, and Mahomet I defy. My people shall be followers of the Cross, but they shall sweep away the false Spaniard, as the wind brushes away the leaves—The emir of Oran is prepared—the king of Morocco will follow. A power in the hills—Ah! We will creep, by night, to Granada—a brave blow!—Africa shall follow—Ha, ha!—Seize the gates! storm the Alhambra! —but spare life—kill no women!—Remember Zayda!—"

With such wild words, accompanied by the faint cries of his daughter, the spirit of the Moor passed away, and Alharef-ben-Ismail lay dead in the land of strangers.

Don Gabriel uttered a deep groan, and fell across the feet of his ancient friend.

At this moment Cortes descended from his horse, and, followed by other cavaliers, stepped up to the lamenting group. "And Calavar, the valiant, has been murdered by this traitor Moor!" he cried.

"Senor Don Hernan," said the novice, sternly, and as he spoke, rising from the earth, and folding the Moorish maiden to his heart, "you speak of him who was Alharef-ben-Ismail, a Wali of Granada, driven by the injustice of our companions, and in part by your own harshness, to take arms against you. As one that am now his representative, and, as I may say, his son, I claim for him the honourable burial of a Christian soldier; and after that will hold myself prepared, with sword and spear, to defend his memory from insult."

CHAPTER LXV.

A few words will finish the first part of the chronicle of Don Cristoval.

The victory so marvellously gained removed the last obstruction from the path of the Spaniards. The ensuing day beheld them entering the territories of their allies; and in four days more the chiefs of Tlascala ushered them, with songs of joy, into the republican city.

Six days after this happy event, the novice of Rhodes sat by the death-bed of his kinsman. From the moment when Calavar roused out of the fit of unconsciousness into which he had fallen on the field of Otumba, his brain wandered with delirium; but it gave his young kinsman, as well as the faithful Baltasar, much relief to perceive that his visions were oftener of a pleasant than a disagreeable character. Thus the re-appearance of Alharef after such long seeming death dwelt in his memory, without the recollection of his subsequent decease; and with this came the conceit that Zayda yet lived with the Alpujarras, restored, like the Wali, to life, and all forgetful of the wrongs he had done her. He prattled of returning now to Spain, and now to Rhodes, and now of making a pilgrimage to the Holy Land. It is true that sometimes dark thoughts crept to his brain, and agitated him with his former griefs; but these were ever chased away by the sight of Leila, whose countenance seemed to him as that of a holy seraph, sent from heaven to bid him be of good cheer.

On the fifth day he recovered his senses, and being sensible of his approaching dissolution, assembled at his bed-side, after having received absolution, the padre Olmedo, and the few friends and followers whom Heaven had spared him in this Pagan land, being the young cavalier of Cuenza, the melancholy Zayda, or Leila, as Amador yet loved to call her, and Baltasar. The spear of Alharef had not harmed him; he was dying, the victim of a long remorse; or rather, as it may be said, he expired when the excitement of this passion no longer supported him. For perhaps the same thing may be said of many mental diseases, which is true of certain physical ones, to which a human constitution has been long accustomed: that is, they may obtain so vital a command over all its functions, as to become in themselves the elements, or at least the bulwarks, of life; so that, when they are arrested by some unskilful leech, death shall almost immediately follow the cure.

"I have now called you, my children," he said, bending an eye of affection upon the pair, and speaking very feebly, "to give you such counsel as may be drawn from the history of my life. Its secrets are revealed to you—its pages all lie open; and as you read your spirits will find their own instruction; for they will discover that the indulgence of passion, especially the passion of anger, doth lodge a barb in the bosom never to be plucked out, save by the hand of death. What I have to say is rather of command than advice; and thou wilt listen to me Amador, my son, for God hath given thee, in the person of this gentle Zayda, an argument of obedience, which will touch thy heart more eloquently than words. Break thy sword, hack off thy spurs, cast thine armour into the sea, and think no more of war, unless to defend thy fire-side, and the altars of thy country from the fury of invaders."

The novice started with alarm.

"Think not that I rave," said the knight. "I speak to thee with the wisdom that comes from the grave. Think no more of war, for war it is that rouses our passions; and passions have made me what I have been, and what I am. I cannot think now (for, at this moment, methinks I stand in the presence of Him who abhorreth contention), that he will pardon the shedding of any blood, except that which the necessity of self-preservation, and the defence of our country, enforce us to lavish. I repent me of that which I have poured, though even from the hearts of Pagans; for Pagans are still the sons of God, though walking in darkness, for which we should pity them, not slay. Thou hast drawn thy sword for glory; but the lives that are taken for fame shall weigh upon the souls of men as murders —for such they are. Thou drawest for religion·— give thy purse to the priest, and bid him convert with the cross; for the wrath of God will rest for ever upon him who maketh proselytes with the sword. Woe is me, that the delusions of glory and Christian zeal have stained me so deeply! Live for happiness, and thou shalt wrong none, neither man nor God, and thus happiness shall be awarded thee; live for honour, and thou shalt know that Heaven acknowledges none but that which is justice; live for peace, which is virtue; and for religion, which is goodness. Get thee to thy castle—to the lands which thou shalt inherit; plant thy vines and olives, relieve the unhappy, succour the distressed; and if thy young brother should pant for the barb and lance, teach him the history of thy kinsman. Be virtuous, be peaceful, be charitable, and be happy. When thou hearest of glory, bethink thee of the poor deluded creatures we have slain in this land; when thou art told of pious crusades, remember the days of the Alpujarras. Would that my days were to pass again!"

He paused with exhaustion.

"The noble knight," said the padre, "hath spoken much good and wholesome truth; nevertheless, in the matter of infidels, what he has counselled is not well. For how is it written——"

"Holy father," murmured Don Gabriel, "there be men enow who will obey thee in this matter, and without exhortation or argument. Defeat not my work; for I rob thee of but one. Let me think that the son of my affection will dwell in peace, and thereby be clean in the eyes of God, and thus happy at his death hour. Would that I might appear before my Maker, without the stain of blood!"

With a few more such precepts of virtue, for grief and the hand of death had made his heart wise, Don Gabriel continued to address the novice. He spoke many words of kindness also to the old and faithful Baltasar, and was about to give his benediction to the child of Zayda, when a film came suddenly over his eyes.

"Give me thy hand," he muttered, faintly and almost inarticulately; "I see thee not, but mine eyes are opened to Zayda. Where art thou, Amador, my son? Heaven is blissful—Alharef—Zayda—all—Miserere mei, Domine!"

Thus he murmured for a moment—his voice dwindling to a whisper; then his lips moved, but without yielding any sound, until at last it was apparent that he had expired, and yet so gently, that not even a spasm of muscle, or change of countenance, indicated the passage of his spirit.

Three days after this, at sunrise, Senor Cortes stood alone with Don Amador de Leste on the terrace of the great dwelling in which he had quartered the remains of his army.

'Thou leavest me, then, De Leste?" he said in a low voice, looking westward to the hills, beyond which lay the valley of the lakes.

"Such is my purpose, very noble senor," said the cavalier mildly, but firmly. "My horses are caparisoned in the court-yard, my little company is in waiting, my friends have been saluted, and nothing remains for me but to thank your excellency for your many manifestations of goodness to me and mine—the living and the dead together—and to pray your excellency wish me God speed."

"And can you look upon yonder blue cliffs, and those snow-capt pinnacles," said Don Hernan, with a smothered voice, "and think of leaving the paradise they encompass, in the hands of the heathen?"

"I know not," said Don Amador, "that it becomes me to intrude any advice upon your excellency. But you have already done deeds, as I am myself a witness, which will give you immortal fame, though you should proceed no farther in the impossible attempt to subjugate this very potent and wonderful empire."

"It shall be mine!" said Cortes, smiting his hands together, and speaking with clenched teeth. "Though there were but an hundred men left with me—nay, were there but ten—I would sooner that they should see me rent under the tusks of the wild mountain hogs, than turning my back for ever against the city of Montezuma. Thou thinkest the case is desperate; yet, with those ten Christians, and the hundreds of thousands disaffected barbarians, whom I will gather together, thou shalt hear, perhaps, ere thou art housed in thy mountain castle of Cuenza, that he whom thou leavest is the lord of Mexico; and the valiant men who remain by him, the barons and counts of the great empire!"

"With mine own hills of olive and cork, have I enough to content me," said the novice, coldly.

"And thou carest not to revenge thy friends massacred so barbarously that fatal night. Flames be on the soul of the enchanter for ever!" exclaimed the general, bursting into fury at the recollection.

"I say, God pardon him!" replied Amador, "and God receive to his rest those friends of whom you speak. I have naught to revenge; I lament their fate, which was dreadful; but I acknowledge that they were slain in honourable combat."

"And thou carest not then to strike for the cause of Christ, and aid in the conversion of countless souls from perdition?

The cavalier regarded his general with a meaning eye. Cortes felt the reproof, and catching his hand, said, hastily—"It is enough! thou hast a young and tender wife—Who would have dreamed that such a creature walked with us throughout that night? It is right thou shouldst desire to bear her from these scenes of tumult, and not unnatural thou shouldst wish to share the peace and happiness to which thou art conducting her. For myself, I sometimes think of my own fair donna in the island and the pleasant sound of the surf, rolling, by night, on the beach under her lattice; but, nevertheless, there are, in this same heathen clime, certain charms, which cause me to forget the fair Catalina, and my merry brats into the bargain."

"For me," said the novice, sadly, "there is nothing in this land but melancholy. Alharef, sire of Zayda, sleeps under a rock at Otumba; and Calavar, whom I may call my father, since such he was to me, now rests in yon grove, on the hill-side. I have buried a faithful servant in the lake and a good youth, whom I loved, an old follower of my knight, and a very dear friend. I shall think of the land with regret, yet must I leave it without a sigh. I have hopes to find me some conveyance to the islands, and there, thank Heaven, it is not so difficult to light upon a trader of Seville bound on the homeward voyage."

"If thou art, indeed, resolute to depart," said Cortes, "I have it in my power not only to wish thee God speed, but to give thee a good ship of my fleet at Ulua, commanded by thy very noble kinsman which he will, doubtless, man to thy liking with choice sailors; and wherein thou canst proceed instantly to Spain, without the tedious necessity of touching at Cuba."

The eyes of the neophyte sparkled. Don Hernan smiled. "Assuredly," said he, "I am rejoiced to pleasure thee so much; and yet thou wilt thyself confer upon me a very ineffable obligation, by sailing in that same good ship, and taking charge of a certain letter I have here written to his majesty, our lord Don Carlos, being the second despatch wherein I have presumed to acquaint him with the success of our arms, fighting in his cause, and in that of the holy church. If it may suit your convenience to bear the same in person to his imperial majesty, I hope you will have no cause to repent doing me so great a favour."

"I will bear it to his majesty in person," said the novice, taking the sealed packet, laying it upon his forehead in token of fealty, and then warmly grasping the general's hand: "I will do this with much satisfaction; and in memory that thou hast, upon three several occasions, done me such personal service, as touch me to answer with a life's thankfulness, if there be any other act wherein I can pleasure thee, I pray thee command me to the same without any reserve; for I will consider that thou dost thereby acquaint me with a way to testify my gratitude."

" I thank you," said Don Hernan: " I have no commission with which I will dare further to trouble you. And yet, and yet—and yet"—He hesitated a moment, and his lip slightly quivered; but instantly resuming an air of indifference, he continued—" If it should suit your good convenience—that is, if you should prefer—to travel rather by the hot mountains of Estremadura, than the barren ridges of La Mancha, while passing to the court at Madrid, I would crave of your goodness to inquire me out a certain village called Medellin, that lieth on the Guadiana, some few leagues above the city of Merida."

" Were it an hundred leagues, and they of the rudest," said Amador, " I should be no less ready to do your bidding. But give me to know, when I am arrived at this same village of Medellin, in what I can pleasure you."

" Inquire me out,' said Cortes, " a certain old man, a poor hidalgo, called Martin Cortes, as also his wife, Catalina By my conscience, senor, they are my father and mother; and they will have some joy to hear you speak of me !"

" Now, I vow to Heaven !" cried Amador, struck by the sudden and impetuous tone of feeling, which Don Hernan strove to hide under a burst of gaiety, " I am sorry they live not as far away as Pampeluna, at once, that I might show you the readiness with which I will be your messenger; for herein do I perceive, I shall be looked on by them as a good angel, sent to them from heaven."

" Be not over-sanguine," said Cortes, affecting a laugh; " for by my conscience, if you tell her not every thing to her liking, my mother hath somewhat of a shrewish way of admonishing you. Nevertheless, it is enough; it hath been some long years since they have heard of my whereabout and my whatabout; since, sooth to say, I one day played them a dog's trick, and a month after was chasing the Indians in Cuba. It will greatly amaze them to hear I have not been absolutely hanged, as my mother oftimes promised me for my sins; and, surely, they will stare at you, when you tell them I have been killing a great emperor, as some idle fellows have charged on me; whereas, you know yourself, having been so forward to shield him, that Montezuma was slain by his own people—a murrain on them !"

" I will bear witness to the truth, and I will say nothing that can give them pain."

" I shall be much beholden to you," said Don Hernan, eagerly; " for my mother is somewhat more righteous than other women, and might be convinced, out of the mouths of some of my friends, that I am given to godless acts on occasions, which is very false and slanderous. I will beseech you to bear them certain curious jewels, and trifles of golden ware, the fabric of my good savages here, more as mementos of my gracelessness than as presents of affection, seeing that they are of no great value. They are such curiosities as will make mine old playmates stare. Ah, the rascals ! they were all better than I at their books, and somewhat less acquainted with the pedagogue's palm. But pho !" he continued, suddenly dropping the tone of bagatelle with which he had spoken, " I do but fool the time: your steed neighs in the court-yard, your lady looks up to the terrace—I will detain you no longer. The king's letter which you bear will authorise you to demand of the admiral the best ship in our small navy, as also to have it sailored and provisioned to your mind; and therein you can voyage, at your good pleasure, to the Guadalquivir. I have presumed to order in waiting, subject to your command, a company of guides, consisting of four Castilian soldiers, ten Tlascalans, and thrice as many Totonacs of the coast, with whom you will take your own will as to speed, though I recommend you to submit to theirs in the matter of the road. Commend me to your kinsman, the admiral, as also very truly to my parents; and if the emperor should see fit to express doubts of the success of this enterprise in which I am engaged, tell him that I, Hernan Cortes, do say, and I gage my head for the fulfilment of the same, that the land shall be his—all that lies between the two seas, and betwixt the narrow neck of Panama to the south, and the huge isle of Florida to the north: this I promise, and this I will fulfil. And now, senor, giving you my thanks for the good deeds you have already done me, as well as those which you meditate, and wishing to your fair and noble wife a green path by land, and a smooth way by sea, I do, very truly and devoutly, and from the bottom of my heart, pray you God speed!—Remember me; for you shall hear of me yet !"

So saying, the two cavaliers descended and parted—Don Amador de Leste to cross the seas; and, discharging the commands of his friend, both to the ancient hidalgo of Medellin and the great Charles of Austria, to seek for happiness in his castle of Alcornoque, in the society of his Moorish bride; and Hernan Cortes to ponder alone upon the fall of Tenochtitlan.

CONCLUSION.

Of the secondary characters of this history, enough has been already narrated. Our respect, however, for the memory of the magician Botello, requires that we should mention two circumstances in relation to his fate, and his chief and most mystical familiar. His unexpected death, instead of destroying his credit among those who survived the Noche Triste, gave him additional claims to respect, even in the grave; for when it was remembered, that the arrows which slew so many Spaniards were adorned with the feathers of eagles, as well as other birds of prey, they perceived, in his fate, only a confirmation of the juggling subtlety of the fiends that ' palter with us in a double sense.' " Truly," said they, " Botello was borne out of danger on the wings of eagles, as he prophesied, albeit he was borne to heaven." In after days, when Mexico had become the prey of the invader, the lake was dragged for the bones of the Christians who had fallen with him in the nocturnal retreat, which were then deposited, with many religious ceremonies, in ground consecrated for the purpose. In the last ditch, at the very spot where Botello had fallen, a fortunate fisherman hooked up the magic Crystal, the prison of Kalidon-Sadabath; who, greatly to the horror of the finder, began instantly, as of old, to dance and curvet, and perform other diabolical antics in his hands. No other conjurer in the army having the skill to interpret the motions of this mysterious imp, his crystal habitation was transmitted, along with divers Mexican rarities, to the shelves of the Escurial, whereit was long viewed with wonder and respect, as an instrument contrived by the hands, and devoted to its unearthly uses by the skill, of the celebrated Cornelius Agrippa. A philosopher, who was thought, as was Feyjoo in later days by his countrymen, to have too little consideration for vulgar prejudices, asserted, after attentive examination, that the marvellous crystal was nothing more than a piece of glass, hollowed by the maker into many singular cavities, wherein was deposited a coloured drop of some volatile liquor, which being at any time expanded by the heat of the breath, or of the hand, would instantly dart about, and assume the most fantastic shapes, according to the sinuous vacuities through which it happened to be impelled. This explanation was received with incredulity; but, nevertheless, Kalidon of the Crystal was treated with neglect, and, in course of time, entirely forgotten. We surmise, however, and the conjecture is not without argument, that the Enchanted Crystal, presented, half a century afterwards, by the angel Uriel to the famous English conjurer, Doctor Dee, was no other than this identical stone, filched by the angelic thief from its dusty repository, and given to him who best knew how to put it to its proper uses.

*   *   *   *   *   *

Late in the autumn of the following year, the Senor Don Amador de Leste sat watching the sunset of a peaceful day, from a little bower on a lawn in front of his Castle Del Alcornoque. A clump of aged oaks flung their branches over a low, square, and mouldering tower—the work of the Moorish masters of Spain many a long year back, and a fragment, as it seemed, of some ancient bath or fountain; for a body of pure water still made its way through the disjointed stones, and fell bubbling into a little basin beneath.

The scene, as beheld from this spot, was one of enchanting beauty and repose. The fountain was, perhaps midway on the slope of a long hill, a few rods in advance of the castle (with which it was, indeed, connected by a somewhat neglected walk of orange trees), whose irregular turrets and frowning battlements rose among groups of cork trees, while a broken forest of these extended behind, up to and over the crest of the hill. In front the little valley, wherein was embosomed the silvery Jucar, was bounded now by sharp cliffs and jutting promontories, and now by green lawns which ran sweeping upwards to the hill-tops on the opposite side. A hazy smoky atmosphere, warmed into lustre by the sinking luminary, while it mellowed all objects into beauty, did not conceal from the eye the flocks of sheep which dotted the distant slopes, the cattle standing at the river-side, and the groups of peasantry, who adding their songs to the lowing of the herds and the cawing of a flight of crows, urged forward the burthened ass from the vine tree. A monastery rose in the forest, a little village glimmered pleasantly on the river bank, under the shadow of a cliff; and over the ridges, which shut in the valley to the south, was seen in the dim outline of those sierras of Morena, from which might be traced the peaks of the Alpujarras.

Over this fair prospect the young cavalier looked with pride, for it was the inheritance handed down to him by a long line of ancestors— not snatched away by violence from vanquished Moors, but reclaimed from them by a bold knight, whose genealogical tree had been rooted in those hills, before Tarik, the Arab, had yet looked upon the Pillars of Hercules. He gazed on it also with joy, for he had learned to love peace; and this seemed the chosen abode of tranquillity

"It doth indeed appear to me now," he muttered, " as if my past life was a foolish dream. There is a rapture in this quiet nook, a happiness in this prospect of loveliness and content, entirely beyond any pleasure which I ever experienced in my days of tumult and fame. What can there be to add a further charm to this paradise?"

Perhaps he muttered this interrogatory in the spirit of an improver and adorner of nature. It was answered by the fall of a gentle footstep. He looked behind him and beheld, standing at his back, pausing a moment with patient and yet dignified affection, the fair figure of a woman, who had no sooner caught his eye, than she smiled, and pointed to a female attendant, who bore in her arms, hard by, a sleeping infant. A cross of rubies glittered on the lady's breast.

"If thou didst apprehend, Lelia,' said the cavalier, with eyes of joy, " that I reckoned this hill-side a paradise, without thinking of thyself and my young Gabriel, thou didst most grievously wrong me; for I protest to thee, I never cease thinking of ye?"

"Never?" murmured the mild voice of the Moorish lady: "Heaven be praised! but sometimes, when thou lookest upon the sports of our little brother Rosario, it seems to me thou dost forget us."

"I vow to thee, my honoured and beloved lady," said the hidalgo, earnestly, " and, if thou wilt believe me the rather for that, I swear by the bright eyes of my young boy, that since I discovered thou wert alive, and especially since thou hast been my own Zayda, I have come to look with new eyes upon those things which were the joys of my youth. Let us sit down upon this mossy stone; and while we gaze a little upon Rosario, who, thou seest, is hacking the woodden Turk's-head on the knoll—thou knowest he did so gash thy young plantation of olive trees, that I was enforced to allow him this block for his recreation—while we thus regard him (for, of a truth, he is a most gallant boy, and of soldierly bearing), I will discourse to thee in such a manner as to convince thee that I have utterly weeded from my bosom the foul plants of ambition, and that I am equally solicitous to cleanse the breast of my brother. Hah! by my faith, what now? Seest thou yonder ill-looking, lurking knave? I doubt me, he has been robbing my vineyard. May I die but the young varlet doth advance his sword against him! Well done, Sir Hector! And he knows not that I am near to give him aidance. What ho! Sirrah Rosario! put up thy sword. This is no robber."

"It is a pilgrim—some poor pilgrim," exclaimed the lady :—" Rosario gives him his hand, and leads him towards us."

It was even as the fair donna had said. The youth Rosario, who had at first advanced valiantly towards the stranger, as if to question his right to walk so near the castle, was now seen to sink his weapon, speak a word or two to the new comer, and then give him his hand, as if to conduct him to the cavalier.

As they approached, Don Amador could perceive that the stranger had robed his figure in a cloak of the humblest texture: he was barefooted; he held a staff in his hand, and his great slouched hat was adorned with scallop shells. He seemed a palmer, who had performed a long and painful pilgrimage; for, though obviously a young man, his frame was wasted, his beard long and haggard, and his cheeks were thin and pale.

"By my faith," said Don Amador, " this palmer hath speedily won the heart of my brother; for thou seest Rosario doth look into his face, as though he had got the hand of some great knight from Judea. I welcome you with peace and good-will, senor pilgrim; and my gates are open to you. Art thou from Compostella or Loretto? Or perhaps thou comest even from the Holy Land?"

While the cavalier spoke, the Moorish lady sur

veyed the features of the pilgrim, with a surprise and agitation which drew the attention of Amador; but before he could speak, the pilgrim replied, "Not from the Holy Land, but from a land accursed—from death and the grave, from the depths of the heathen lake and the maws of the Mexicans——"

At these words, the lady screamed, and Don Amador himself started aghast, as he listened to the voice of the speaker. " In the name of God, amen !" he cried, recoiling a step; " I know thy voice and I saw thee perish !"

"Pardon me, noble patron !" said the pilgrim, hastily—' I spoke but in figures, and therein I spoke not amiss, since I perceived that my noble lord looked upon me as one that was dead. Alas, senor ! I live—I am your honour's poor ward and secretary, Fabueno."

"Fabueno !" cried the cavalier, recovering himself a little · "if thou livest, thou liest; for Lorenzo is dead !"

"Hast thou been lying, then, thou knave ?" cried Rosario, with much indignation. "I will knock the cockles from thy cap; for thou saidst thou hadst fought with the great Cortes, among the Indians !"

"Alas, senor !" cried Lorenzo, " will you still think me dead ? Have sorrow and misery so changed me, that your noble goodness cannot see, in this broken frame and withered visage, your poor follower, Fabueno ?'

"By my troth, I am amazed ! This hand is flesh and blood; this darkened brow and weeping eye. Pho ! look upon him, Zayda ! Thou livest, then ? God be praised ! And thou sheddest tears, too ! Never believe me, but I am rejoiced to see thee; and thou shalt dwell with me till thy dying day—Heaven be thanked ! By what miracle wert thou revived, after being both killed and drowned ? I'faith, thou didst greatly shock my lady. 'Tis wondrous, how soon she knew thee !"

"Knew me ?" exclaimed the secretary, gazing with a bewildered eye upon the lady.

"Why, dost thou forget," cried the cavalier, catching the hand of Leila, over whose brow a faint colour rose at the remembrance—"dost thou forget my dear and beloved page, Jacinto ?"

"Alas, madam,' siad Lorenzo, bending to the earth, " nothing but my confusion could have made me so blind; and this is more wondrous, too, since his excellency Don Hernan had made me acquainted with the happiness of my lord."

"Speakest thou of Don Hernan ?" cried the cavalier. "By my troth, I have an hundred thousand questions to ask thee; and I know not which to demand first. But thine own reappearance is so marvellous, that I must first question thee of that; and afterward thou shalt speak to me of Don Hernan. How wert thou fished up ?"

"Fished up, senor," said Lorenzo, sadly; " I know not well what your favour means. At that moment of distraction and horror," he went on, with a shudder, " when I called to you for succour—

"I heard you," said Amador, "and I ran to your assistance — but, Heaven forgive me ! I cursed the act afterwards, when I discovered that it had lost me my poor Jacinto. Ah, senora mia ! was there ever so dreadful a night ?"

"When I called," continued Fabueno, " I was then beset by the infidels. The princess—the poor princess was slain in my arms, and my horse speared under me, so that we fell to the earth. Senor, I know not well what happened to me then, for my mind fled from me : I only remember that, as they flung me into a canoe, there came a cavalier, the valiant Don Francisco de Saucedo, as I found by his voice, to my assistance, shouting aloud. I think he was slain on the spot ; for I heard a plunging in the water, as if his horse had fallen into the lake."

"It was he, then," said Don Amador, "whom I saw sink so miserably into the flood. Heaven give him rest ! I thought it was thyself."

"Senor," continued the secretary, " I will not weary you now with all the particulars of my sorrow. When Heaven restored me my reason, I found myself lying in a wicker den — a cage of victims—in the temple yard, under thea pyramid ; and I knew that I was saved only to be made a sacrifice."

"Heaven forefend !" cried Amador, while Zayda grew white with horror.

"I tell you the truth, senor," said Fabueno, trembling in every limb. " There were more than thirty such cages around me, and in every one a wounded Spaniard, as I could both hear and see ; and every day there was one dragged out by the priests and immolated. I could hear their yells from the temple top. Senor, these things drove me into a delirium, which must have lasted long ; for when I came again to my wits, I looked out and saw that the cages were empty—all but one. Then I beheld the priests come to mine own dungeon and debate over me. I tried to pray—but in my fear I swooned. When I looked forth again, they were dragging away my fellow-prisoner. I knew that I should die upon the morrow. That night I fell into a frenzy, and with my teeth (for my arms were bound behind me), I gnawed away the wooden bars of my cage. Heaven helped me ! God gave me strength ! and St. James, to whom I cried, sharpened my teeth, as though they were edged with iron. So, by this miracle, I escaped ; and, bound as I was, and beaten to the earth by a tempest which raved over the lake, I made my way, I know not how, up a causeway that lies to the north, until I had reached the shore of the lake. I hid me by day in groves and in marshes, and when the night came, I journeyed onward, though I knew not whither. What sufferings I endured from hunger and thirst, I will not weary you by recounting. Mine arms were still bound behind me ; and when it was my good fortune to find a field of green maize, I could only seize upon the ears, like a beast, with my teeth · I strove, by rolling upon the earth and rubbing against trees, to get rid of the thongs, but all in vain. This maddened me ; and I thought that Heaven had deserted me. But the good St. James showed me one day a place where the Indians had made a fire. I rekindled it with my breath, and when it began to blaze, I prayed and held my arms in the flames, until the green withes wherewith I was bound were burned asunder."

"Good Heaven !" cried Amador, starting from the stone on which he had seated himself, while Zayda bent forward, as if to snatch the poor youth from the flames, which still burned in her imagination, " didst thou suffer all this horrible combustion ? or, perhaps, Heaven vouchsafed thee a miracle, and scorched away the cords without suffering the fire to do thee harm ?"

"Had I been there," said Rosario, doughtily, " I would have cut the thongs with my sword ;

and then I would have killed the bitter Pagans that wronged thee."

"The miracle whereby I escaped from the cage was more than my sins deserved," said the secretary, bending his head upon his bosom, and speaking with an agitated voice. "Heaven took not the pangs from the fire, but it gave me strength to bear them. I am here again, restored to my native land, and among Christian men—but mine arms are withered."

"Were they hacked off at the shoulders," cried Amador, ardently, "ay, and thy legs into the bargain, yet will I so entertain thee here in my castle, that thou shalt cease to lament them."

"Nay," said the youth, looking with gratitude on the cavalier, "'tis not so bad as that, as my lord may see; for though I may never more bear sword, yet I can carry the pilgrim's staff—ay, and I can raise them to my cheek, to brush away my thanks. I have yet strength enough left to wield a pen; and if my noble patron—"

"Speak no more of this, good Lorenzo," said the Moorish lady, quickly and kindly. "My lord hath told thee thou art welcome; and I say to thee also, thou art very welcome."

"By my troth, I say so too," cried Rosario. "But after all thou wilt be but pitiful, if thou hast not strength left to handle a sword. I hoped you should teach me a little; for old Baltasar is grum and crusty."

"Peace, Hector! what art thou talking about?" said Don Amador. "Think no more of thy misfortune, Lorenzo; but give me to know the rest of thy adventures."

"They are spoken in a word," said the secretary. "When mine arms were freed, though so dreadfully scorched, I could travel with more peace of mind. I doubted not, that all the Christians had been slain on the lake; yet, I thought, if I could but reach the sea coast, I might be, some time, snatched out of the hands of the barbarians. Nevertheless, this hope deserted me, when I perceived that the land was covered with people; and one day, finding a cave among the mountains, hard by to a waterfall, with a wooden cross stuck up at the mouth——"

"Surely," said Zayda, "this was the cavern wherein I found my lord, Don Gabriel."

"I doubt it not, noble lady," said Fabueno, "but this I knew not then. I thought it was a retreat provided for me by the good St. James, who willed that there I should pass my life, under the shadow of that little crucifix. So there did I hide me, and feeding upon roots and such living creatures as I could entrap, I remained in my hermitage a full year; until one day, I heard a trumpet sounding at the bottom of the mountain; and running out in wonder, I beheld—thanks be to Heaven! I beheld a company of Spanish soldiers marching up the hill. By these men I was carried to Mexico, which was now fallen—"

"Fallen, say'st thou?" cried Amador. "Is the infidel city fallen?"

"Not the city only, but the empire," replied Fabueno; "and Cortes is now the lord of the great valley."

"Thou shalt tell me of its fate; but first thou must rest and eat. I remember me now of the words of Cortes.'

"His excellency," said Lorenzo, "commanded me to bear to your favour this little jewel, in token that he has made good a certain vaunt which he made you in Tlascala—the same being an emerald from the crown of Quauhtimotzin the king."

"Hah! my valiant ambassador at Tlascala? Hath he been the emperor?"

"And to your noble lady, he craves permission to present this chain of gold, the manufacture of Mexican artists, since Mexico has become a Spanish city."

"It is enough," said the cavalier; "I perceive that his genius is triumphant. I would that I might bear this news to his father, Don Martin, as I did the relation of his disasters; but come, let us retire. Why hast thou on these palmer weeds?"

"I vowed to St. James, on the mountains of Mexico, in my great misery, that if his good favour and protection should ever bless mine eyes with the sight of Christian man, I would make a pilgrimage barefoot to his holy shrine at Compostella. This it has been my good fortune already to accomplish, our ship having been driven by a storm into a port of Gallicia. Not thinking this penance enough for my sins, I resolved to continue my pains, and neither doff my pilgrim's cap, nor do on my shoes, until I had reached your favour's castle of the Cork-tree."

"I welcome thee to it again, and for thy life; and I congratulate thee, that thou art relieved of the love of war; wherein thou wilt find, I have somewhat preceded thee. Enter, and be at peace. When thou art rested a little, I shall desire of thee to speak—for very impatient am I to know—what circumstances of marvel and renown, of romance and chivalry, have distinguished the last days of Tenochtitlan."

www.ingramcontent.com/pod-product-compliance
Lightning Source LLC
Chambersburg PA
CBHW080831250626
47160CB00008B/2894